Elements of Chemistry
(parts 1-3)
ATTRACTION * HEAT * CAPTURE

By PENNY REID

♡ Penny Reid

Caped Publishing

Made in the United States of America

Print Edition: May 2015
Print ISBN: 978-1-942874-10-2

Part 1: ATTRACTION

CHAPTER 1
Atoms, Molecules, and Ions

QUIET, SILENT, MUTED, hushed, stilled, reticent... I moved my mouth, breathed the words—soundlessly—from my hiding place.

This game comforted me, calmed me, settled my nerves. Yes, recalling synonyms while anxious was a bizarre coping strategy, but it worked. And very little usually worked.

The voices from beyond the cabinet grew louder and were accompanied by the click of heels and the dull echo of tennis shoes. I held my breath and strained to decipher how many sets of feet were represented by the approaching shoes. I guessed two, also because only two voices were audible.

"...think that he's going to want to fuck you? After what happened last Friday?" The words were a hiss emanating from an unknown male voice; I tensed at the use of vulgarity.

"I'll get there late. If you do your job then he won't even remember it," came a feminine reply. The female was closest to my hiding spot in the chemistry lab cabinet; her words were, therefore, much clearer.

"Shit," he said. I tried not to huff in disgust at his foul language as he continued. "I don't even know how much to use. I've only used it on bitches."

"I don't know either. Just...double it. Martin is, what? Like, twice the size of the girls you usually dope out?"

I tensed again, my eyes narrowing. The name Martin, in particular, made my heart beat faster. I knew only one Martin.

Martin Sandeke.

Martin Sandeke, the heir to Sandeke Telecom Systems in Palo Alto, California, and smartypants in his own right. I also came from a notable family—my mother was a US senator, my father was the dean of the college of medicine at UCLA, and my maternal grandfather was an astronaut. However, unlike Martin's family, we weren't billionaires. We were scientists, politicians, and scholars.

Martin Sandeke, the six-foot-three modern day physical manifestation of Hercules and captain of our university's rowing team.

Martin Sandeke, unrepentant manwhore extraordinaire and kind of a jerk-faced bully.

Martin Sandeke, my year-long chemistry lab partner and all-around most unobtainable person in the universe—who I never spoke to except to ask for beakers, relay findings, and request modifications to the heat level of my Bunsen burner.

And by Bunsen burner I meant, literally, my Bunsen burner. Not the figurative Bunsen burner in my pants. Because I hoped Martin Sandeke had no idea that he affected the heat levels of my figurative Bunsen burner.

He did affect them. But, obviously—since he was cosmically unobtainable and kind of a bully—I didn't want him to know that.

"He's about two twenty, so...yeah. I guess," the male responded. His tennis shoes made scuffing sounds on the linoleum as he neared my hiding spot.

I rolled my lips between my teeth and stared at the crack in the cabinet doors. I couldn't see his face, but I could now discern he was standing directly in front of the cabinet, next to the unknown girl. Maybe facing her.

"But what's in it for me?" the cuss monster asked, his voice lower than it had been, more intimate.

I heard some rustling then the sloppy sounds of kissing. Instinctively, I stuck my tongue out and mocked gagging. Listening to public displays of affection was unpleasant, especially when lip smacking and groaning was involved, and most especially while trapped in a chemistry lab cabinet that smelled heavily of sulfur.

The next words spoken came from the girl and were a bit whiny. "Money, dummy. Martin's loaded—well, his family is loaded—and they'll buy me off. All you have to do is give him the stuff tonight in his drink. I'll take him upstairs, record the whole thing. Bonus if I get pregnant."

My mouth dropped open, my eyes wide, unable to believe what I'd just heard. The awfulness, rustling, and lip smacking continued.

"You dope him and I'll rope him." The girl's pleasure-filled gasps were audible and rather ridiculous sounding.

"Oh, yeah baby—touch me there." These breathy words were accompanied by the sound of a beaker crashing to the ground and a zipper being undone.

I winced, scowled. Really, people had no manners or sense of decorum.

"No, no, we can't. He'll be here any minute. I need to leave," the girl pleaded. I noted she sounded the perfect mixture of regretful and hurried.

"You need to make sure he stays at the house for the party. I'll be there at eleven, so give him the stuff around ten thirty, okay?"

The zipper came back up, the man backed into the cabinet. I jerked at the resultant bang of the doors. "How do you know where he'll be all the time?"

"We dated, remember?"

"No. He fucked you. You never dated. Martin Sandeke doesn't date."

"Yeah, well, I know his schedule. He comes here on Fridays and does…hell if I know what with his ugly little lab partner."

Ugly?

I twisted my lips to the side, my heart seized in my chest.

I hated the word ugly. It was an ugly word.

Ugly, unsightly, gross, misshapen, repelling…I mentally recited. For some reason, the synonym game didn't help me this time.

"His lab partner? Wait, I've heard about her. Isn't her dad an astronaut, or something?"

"Who cares? She's nobody. Kathy or Kelly or something. Whatever," the girl huffed, the heels of her shoes carrying her farther away. "Forget about her, she's nothing. The point is you need to stay here and make sure he comes tonight, okay? I gotta go before he gets here."

"Bitch, you better not be playing me."

The girl responded but I didn't catch the words. My back itched and while tucked in the cabinet, I couldn't reach the spot. In fact, it would be a difficult spot to reach even if I were standing in an open field. Also, my mind was still reciting synonyms for ugly.

I didn't think I was *ugly*.

I knew my hair was unremarkable. It was long, wavy, and dark brown. I always wore it in a ponytail, bun, or clip. This was because hair, other than warming my head, served no purpose. Mostly, I ignored it.

I rather liked my eyes. They were grey. It was an unusual color I'd been told on more than one occasion. Granted, no one ever said they were pretty, but no one ever said they were *ugly* either. That had to count for something.

I was no supermodel in height or size, at five foot seven and a size ten. But I wasn't Jabba the Hut either.

My teeth were reasonably straight, though I had a noticeable gap between the front top two. I was also pale—the color of paper my best friend, Sam, had once said. My eyebrows were too thick, I knew this.

Sam—short for Samantha—often remarked that I should get them plucked, thinned out.

I ignored this advice, as I didn't care about thick eyebrows so long as they never became a unibrow like my aunt Viki's.

I glanced down at my comfortable clothes—men's wide-leg, navy cargo pants with torn-off cuffs, worn Converse, and an oversized Weezer T-shirt. I might be plain, unremarkable, or even mousy. But it's not like I was a horrible beast who turned people into stone with a single gaze. I was just…low maintenance.

That was okay with me. I didn't need attention, didn't want it. People, especially people my age and especially other girls, made very little sense to me. I didn't see the value in spending hours in front of a mirror when I could be playing video games, or playing the guitar, or reading a book instead.

But sometimes, when I was with Martin and we were calculating particulate levels, I wanted to be beautiful. Really, it was the only time I wished I looked different. Then I remembered he was a jerk-face and everything went back to normal.

I gave myself a mental shake and gritted my teeth. Straining to listen, I pressed my ear against the cabinet door and waited for signs the unknown male was still present.

The itch in the center of my back was spreading and I didn't know how much longer I could stand it. On the itch scale, it was quickly moving from aggravating to brain-exploding torturous.

But then the sound of shuffling footsteps approaching from the hall snagged my attention. They slowed, then stopped.

"Hey man. Whatsup?" said the mystery cussing fiend.

"What are you doing here?" Martin asked. I guessed he was standing at the entrance to the lab because his voice was somewhat muffled. Regardless, it made my stomach erupt in rabid butterflies. I often had a physical response to the sound of Martin's voice.

"Wanted to make sure you're coming to the house party tonight."

I heard more footsteps. They were Martin's. I'd know that nonchalant gait anywhere—because I was pathetic and maybe a little obsessed with all things Martin Sandeke. But the difference between my obsession with Martin and the other girls' obsession with Martin was that I had absolutely no problem admiring his finer features from afar.

Because Martin really was kind of a jerk.

He'd never been a jerk to me, likely because I was an excellent lab partner. We spoke only about chemistry—and he liked acing assignments—but I'd seen him in action. He'd lose his temper and then *BOOM!* he'd go off on whatever poor soul he happened to believe responsible.

If it was a girl, they'd leave crying after coming in contact with his razor wit (and, by razor, I mean cutting and wound inducing). He never called them names, he didn't have to. He'd just tell them the truth.

If it was a guy, he *might* only use words. But sometimes he used fists too. I'd been a witness to this once—Martin beating the crap out of a slightly shorter but also slightly broader jilted boyfriend of one of his one-night stands. At least, that was the rumor that went around after both of them were escorted out of the dining hall by campus police.

Martin was an equal opportunity jerk-face and therefore best avoided outside of the chemistry lab.

No one spoke for a moment; then, I stiffened when I heard Martin ask, "Where's Parker?"

That was me. I'm Parker.

To be more precise, I'm Kaitlyn Parker, Katy for short; but I doubt Martin knows my first name.

"Parker? Who's Parker?"

"My lab partner."

"I thought your lab partner was that girl, the one—"

"She is a girl."

"Her name is Parker?"

I knew Martin was close now because I heard him sigh; his next words were clipped with impatience. "What did you want again?"

"The party tonight—you're still coming, right?"

"I already told you I'd be there."

"Good. Because I'm counting on you to be my wingman." The mystery speaker's voice started to fade. I guessed he was leaving, having secured what he came for.

"Yeah, whatever," was Martin's offhanded response.

"I'll see you tonight, bro. You better come, I'm serious."

Martin didn't respond. I guessed the unknown male finally exited because, after a silent pause, I heard Martin release a very audible huff. It was heavy, exaggerated, and flavored with exasperation; of note, I'd heard him employ this sigh once before with a girl who followed him into our chemistry lab. I never wanted to be on the receiving end of that sigh—so far so good.

Meanwhile, I was still in the chemistry cabinet and the itch of the century had spread to my shoulders and stomach. I was likely going to go crazy if I didn't scratch it within the next ten seconds. It felt like I was being repeatedly stung by a legion of fire ants.

During those ten seconds I debated my options.

I could stay in the cabinet, wait for Martin to leave, go quietly insane, then send him an anonymous note about the conversation I'd overheard.

Or, I could burst forth from my hiding place, scratch my itch, look like the doofus I was, then hope he'd forget as I regaled him with details of the conversation I'd overheard.

In the end it didn't matter, because the cabinet doors were abruptly opened. A whoosh of fresh air followed and I found myself face-to-face with Martin Sandeke.

His eyes were blue and exceptionally beautiful. They reminded me of blue flame. Well, usually they were lovely, at present they were narrowed and sharp, and focused squarely on me. Beginning with my eyes, they moved down then up, ending where they started.

He was truly a magnificent specimen. All broad shoulders and narrow hips, with the thick muscular thighs of a rower. His brown hair was streaked with blond—likely due to all his time on the water and in the sun.

I wasn't used to this—him looking *at* me, standing so close—thus, combined with my normal female palpitations, I couldn't quite draw breath for several seconds.

At length he said, "Parker."

"Sandeke."

"What are you doing?"

"Uh…" I released the breath I'd been holding and unthinkingly arched my back, reaching behind me to scratch my itch.

Maybe it was the effect of his eyes and unavoidable handsomeness, or maybe it was because I'd seen him rip girls to shreds and was therefore a little afraid of a potential non-chemistry related conversation. Or maybe it was the itch between my shoulder blades, because without thinking, I blurted the truth, "I was hiding in the cabinet."

His brow furrowed, but his gaze relaxed slightly, his confusion plain. "Why are you hiding in the cabinet?"

I reached over my shoulder, stretching my arm, and tried to reach the itch with my left hand instead of my right. This didn't work.

"Why does anyone hide in a chemistry cabinet?" I shrugged, mostly because I hoped the movement would help me get to the itch.

He lifted a single eyebrow and grabbed me by my upper arms, pulling and lifting me like I weighed next to nothing. He set me safely on the ground.

Martin's hands on my arms sent a bolt of girly awareness to the pit of my stomach. It was paired with belated embarrassment at being found as a burst of heat spread from my chest to my neck.

He still gripped my arms when he asked, "Do you hide in the cabinet often?"

"Sometimes," I said distractedly, my jaw clenched, willing the mortified blush to recede.

"Is this an everyday thing?"

"No. Only on special occasions, like when strange people arrive to plot your demise." I twisted out of his grip, reached for and failed to find the spot needed to secure relief.

"Plot my demise?" His eyes darted over me again, I could tell he was studying my movements. "What are you doing?"

"Trying to reach an itch between my shoulder blades." My elbow was in the air now, my hand down the neck of my shirt.

Martin's eyes widened then blinked. Without a word he stepped forward into my personal space. Before I could comprehend what was happening, he'd backed me into the lab table and I was trapped. Martin was against me, his arms wrapped around my body, his hands slipped under my T-shirt to the center of my back, and then his fingers itched the unreachable space between my shoulder blades.

At first I tensed because... *MARTIN SANDEKE'S ARMS ARE AROUND ME. HIS HANDS ARE UNDER MY SHIRT. HIS BODY IS PRESSED AGAINST MINE!*

OMG. WTF? BBQ!

But then, my brain's very understandably stunted fan-girl reaction to his movements was quickly eclipsed by the blissful relief of an itch scratched.

I melted in his arms, my forehead resting against his chest, and I moaned my satisfaction.

"Oh, yes, God. That's the spot... Please, don't stop," I murmured, obviously out of my mind. But it felt so good. So very, very good. Like sinking into a hot bubble bath after walking a mile through a nor'easter.

Martin didn't stop.

Well…not precisely.

Rather, over the course of a full minute, he ceased using his nails, and instead began caressing and massaging my back with his fingers and hands. I realized too late that his head had dipped to my neck and his lips were against my ear, his hot breath tickling me and sending delightfully dangerous shivers down my spine, and down the backs of my legs to my toes.

"Did I make it all better?" he whispered, then bit—yes, bit!—my neck, like he was tasting me.

Then he bit me again.

I sucked in a breath and my eyes opened—even as my body instinctively arched toward him. Reality burst through the delightful fog of his ministrations like one of those disturbing and jarring windup jack-in-the-box clowns.

After one and a half semesters of virtually nothing but mundane academic interactions, I was in the chemistry lab with Martin Sandeke and his hands were roaming, liberal, and greedy. His face was tucked in my neck. I was trapped against a lab table. Our bodies were intimately connected.

And I'd just moaned.

What the hiccup was going on?

I raised my palms to his chest and made to push him away. This only caused his hands to still, now on the curve of my waist, and his grip to tighten. He plastered our fronts together more completely.

"Um…" I cleared my throat, found my voice unsteady. "Yeah, yeah—all better," I croaked.

He laughed. Actually, it was more like a lazy chuckle.

One of Martin's hands slipped up my back and under the strap of my bra, where the itch had been, his fingers splayed wide. The other went to the clip on my head and released the spring. My hair fell like a curtain and I felt him wrap his hand around the thick length.

I pushed him again, tilted my head to the side and away, feeling breathless. "I'm all better now. Thanks for the help. Services no longer needed." Everywhere he touched sent ripples of awareness and heat to my core.

My attempt at escape was a failure, because, as soon as I pressed against him in earnest, Martin tugged my hair, encouraging me to tilt my chin upward.

Then he kissed me.

And—damn, damn, damn—he was a good kisser.

More precisely, since I had grossly limited experience in the kissing department, he was what I imagined a good kisser would kiss like. The kind girls fantasize about. The guy who just takes what he wants, like he's hungry and you're on the menu, but somehow makes it epic for both parties involved.

No preamble, prologue, or preface. Just urgent, fervent, worshipful kisses, one right after the other. I had no choice but to wrap my arms around his neck, stand on my tiptoes, and try to kiss him back. Because, honestly, the way he held me, the way he growled when our tongues met, the way his mouth moved over mine—he demanded it.

Also, in the recesses of my mind, I realized that this entire situation was completely preposterous. Likely, he was drunk, or tripping on acid, or was playing some kind of joke.

One day I would persuade my grandchildren to gather 'round while I put in my good dentures—the ones with no space between my two front teeth—and I would tell them for the millionth time about how Hercules had once accidentally kissed me in the chemistry lab at my Ivy League University.

The need for air eventually required our lips to part, though we separated only inches. If I inclined my head forward our noses would touch.

I opened my eyes as wide as they would go and glanced at his, where I found his gaze alternately moving between my lips and my eyes. I also noted I wasn't the only one breathing heavily.

I said and thought in unison, my voice just above a whisper, "What was that?"

His eyes stopped moving over my face and instead settled, held mine captive. They were heated and…hot and…intense. I was starting to understand why the blood of a thousand virgins had been sacrificed at his altar of sexual prowess.

I tried to swallow. I couldn't.

"That was necessary," he finally said. Actually, he growled it.

"Necessary?"

"Yes. That needed to happen."

"It did?"

He nodded once and bent as though he were going to do it again. I stiffened, my hands moved instantly to his chest and I thwarted his advance—because, if he started kissing me, it was surely a sign of

Armageddon. Also, I was so far out of my comfort level, I was in an alternate dimension.

"No-no-no-no." I twisted my head to the side, braced my hands against the imposing wall of his chest. "We're not doing that again. I don't kiss unobtainable boys, it's one of my life rules."

He tugged my hair—I'd forgotten that he'd wrapped his hand around it—and bodily pressed me against the black-topped lab table. His other arm, still under my shirt, wrapped completely around me.

"Yes. We're doing *that* again."

"No. We're not. We're not doing anything unless it involves measuring the composition of trace elements in surface water."

"Parker—" His hand left my hair and slipped under my shirt again, spanning my side and stomach.

"Because we're lab partners and lab partners do not kiss."

"Then we're not lab partners anymore."

"You can't switch lab partners in the middle of the semester."

"I just did."

My fingers moved to catch his wrists because his hands were on their way to second base; I successfully intercepted his northward progress. "Nope. I don't do that."

"Do what?" He nuzzled my neck and whispered against my skin. He must've known that nuzzling was going to cause my insides to melt. I imagined he'd conducted methodical experiments into the fastest way to female self-lubrication.

"I'm not one of your easy girls, or even difficult girls." My voice wavered, so I cleared my throat. "I'm not even really a girl. I'm more like one of the boys. Think of me like a boy."

"Not possible."

"It's true. Do you kiss boys? Because, if not, then I think you must have me confused with someone else."

His movements stilled and a long moment passed. Then his hands fell away, *he* stepped away, and I slumped slightly forward—a weird mixture of feeling bereft and relieved.

"You're a lesbian." He said the words as though they explained a mystery he'd been trying to solve for years.

My eyes shot to his. He was four feet away and I found him watching me with a dawning of… something. If I didn't know any better it looked like disappointment and frustration.

I swallowed, successfully, licked my lips, then shook my head. The irony of his confusion not lost on me.

My first and only boyfriend had been gay. I just didn't know it while we were dating throughout high school.

I was still trying to catch my breath when I responded, "No. I'm not gay. I'm just…not interested in you that way."

This was true—because I'd witnessed his path of devastation with my own eyes.

This was also a lie—because I was most definitely interested in him *that* way, just not the after part where he would say it was meaningless sex, make me cry, and tell me to get over it.

His eyebrows jumped a fraction of a centimeter at my softly spoken declaration.

"Not interested...," he repeated.

I stepped to the side, scaling the length of the table, and reached for my bag. I hefted it to my shoulder, escape now the only thing on my mind. His slightly narrowed eyes followed my movements.

"I know, right?" I tried to sound self-deprecating, which wasn't difficult because I truly meant my next words. "Who am I? I'm nobody."

"You're not nobody," he countered. "Your mother is a senator and your grandfather was an astronaut."

I cringed. I hated it when people brought up my family. "Just because my family is famous, doesn't mean I'm somebody."

He shifted forward and said with a surprising amount of vehemence. "Exactly! That's exactly right."

"I know, right?" I readily agreed. "See, I'm ordinary. And you're you and I'm sure you're used to the deafening sound of underwear hitting the floor every time you enter a room. But I don't do that kind of thing, even for Hercules. Sure, I'll think about the possibility later when I'm safely alone in bed, but I never cross-pollinate fantasy and reality."

"When you're alone in bed?"

I didn't acknowledge his words because…mortification.

Instead, I said, "I'm not a fast and loose girl. I'm a slow and steady girl. Who knows when or if I'll ever cross the finish line?"

He blinked at me, at my deluge of words. I didn't even try to read his expression because I was so focused on walking backward out of the room.

"You're leaving?" he asked.

"Yep." I threw my thumb over my shoulder. "I'm going to go now. And don't worry about the experiment. I'll come in over spring break and finish it up. And when I see you after the break, everything will be back to normal. We can forget this ever happened. We shall never speak of it." My voice cracked on the last word.

"Parker—"

"Have a really great spring break."

"Kaitlyn—" He took two strides forward as though he were going to stop me, but halted at the sound of crunching glass underfoot. He glanced at his feet, noticing for the first time the broken beaker on the floor. "What the hell?"

I seized the opportunity afforded by his split attention and bolted out of the room.

In fact, I ran down the hall like an insane person and slipped into the elevator just before it closed. I even jogged back to my dorm, didn't begin to relax until I crossed the threshold of the keycard access area, climbed the three flights to my room, and locked the door behind me.

I tossed my bag to the corner of the tiny space, threw myself backward on my bed, and rubbed my eyes with the base of my palms. The scene in the lab played over and over behind my closed eyelids—him touching me, kissing me, scratching the impossible itch.

It wasn't until several minutes later that I realized I'd forgotten to tell him about the dastardly plot I'd overheard.

CHAPTER 2
The Atomic Theory of Matter

"I CAN'T BELIEVE you agreed to this."

"Shut it, Sam."

I tucked my long, straightened-with-a-flatiron brown hair behind my ears. Self-consciously, I smoothed the skirt of the little black dress she'd talked me into wearing, annoyed—for the twentieth time—that the hem of the skirt ended mid-thigh.

"You look hot, hooker. Just own it." Sam nudged my elbow with hers and I grimaced.

If someone had asked me twelve hours ago how I'd be spending the first Friday night of spring break, I would have told them I'd be curled up in my bed against fluffy pillows, sipping tea, and eating shortbread while reading.

I would not and could not have fathomed I'd be on my way to a fraternity party dressed in lace-topped thigh highs, a black dress, stiletto heels, with my hair down, *and* wearing makeup.

That's right. Makeup. On my face. With glitter eye shadow.

Also, my eyebrows were plucked. *Plucked!* Gah!

I rolled my eyes and huffed like the disgruntled recluse I was. I would rather shop for a bra than go to a fraternity party, and that was saying a lot.

"Oh, come on, Katy. There was no way we could get into the party wearing band T-shirts and men's pants. This is a skirts-only party."

I'd been educated earlier in the evening that a "skirts-only party" is a fraternity party where all the girls are required to wear short skirts. Upon hearing this news I briefly considered leaving Martin to his fate. In the end, my conscience wouldn't let me.

Jerk conscience. Always making me do things.

"You act like getting dressed up is torture," she continued. "You look hot." Sam, who I suspected had been waiting for a chance like this since our freshman year of high school, didn't sound at all sorry for me.

"I don't look hot. I look ridiculous."

"You're a babe."

"Shut it."

"A hot babe. And guys are going to be wanting some of that." She pointed at me and flicked her wrist, indicating my bosom and backside. "Especially 'dat ass."

I grumbled, but made no other audible response. Inwardly, I cursed myself for the hundredth time that I'd failed to warn Martin about the plot I'd overheard in the chemistry lab earlier. If I'd just kept my wits about me I would be curled up with a book now instead of walking toward a den of inequity dressed like a girl.

Even though we were still two blocks away, I could hear the sounds of the party. My neck felt stiff and my hands were clammy.

The plan was quite simple. I would find Martin, explain about the plot and what I'd overheard, then we would leave. Sam wasn't a frat party kind of girl either. Yes, she liked to get dressed up, but she called sorority girls "sorostitutes" and fraternity guys "fratilos." She labeled them "group thinkers" and claimed they suffered from a herd mentality.

She was kind of judgey that way.

I hadn't given sororities or fraternities much thought because…no point.

"I still don't get why you don't have his cell number. He's your lab partner, right? And he was your lab partner last semester too?" Sam tossed her blonde curls over her shoulder.

Sam was a little shorter than me and was attending the University on a tennis scholarship. She was determined to get into Harvard Law and, therefore like me, she was focused, spent very little of her time looking for ways to sow oats. Her all-business attitude made her an ideal best friend and roommate.

"I just don't. I don't have his number."

"Why not?" she pressed. She'd asked me this question several times as we were dressing—or, rather, as she was dressing me.

"Because," I responded again, wiping my palms on the dress.

"Because why? What if you needed to get in touch with him about a project?"

"I'd leave him a note."

"A note? Where? When? How?"

"In the chemistry lab, in the cabinet."

"You pass each other notes?" Her tone turned teasing.

"No. It's not like that. I'll leave a note if I can't make it on Fridays and he does the same. Or, if I've finished something without waiting for him, that kind of thing."

"But why didn't he want you to have his cell—"

I stopped walking and faced her. "He tried to give it to me, okay? He tried last semester to exchange numbers and I didn't want to. Can you just drop it?"

"You wouldn't take Martin Sandeke's number?" she asked, as though the words I'd just spoken made no sense.

"That's correct."

"But…why the hell not? He's…he's…he's Martin Sandeke!"

"*Because* he's Martin Sandeke. That's why I wouldn't take it." I started walking again, my toes protesting the movement.

"Katy, you've been crushing on Martin Sandeke since the first week of class two years ago when you stalked him outside of physics, before you even knew who he was."

"That's because he's physically beautiful and pleasing to the eye," I mumbled.

"He tries to give you his phone number and you don't take it. Why did you do that? Explain it to me."

"Because, you know me, when I get drunk—even though it's only happened twice—I drunk dial! I called Carter the last time it happened."

Carter was my high school boyfriend who never seemed interested in physical intimacy unless we had an audience. Since he was my only boyfriend, I figured this was normal. We'd parted as friends.

But last year I left him a drunk message asking him why he never tried to sleep with me. When I woke up the next morning, and everything came flooding back, it took me three weeks to return his call.

When I finally did, he informed me that he was, in fact, gay. Additionally, he had appreciated my willingness to be his beard in high school. He also assured me that had he not been gay, he would have tried to get in my pants early and often.

It all sounded like pity.

Worst conversation ever.

Sam stopped me again with a hand on my elbow. "That was last summer and Carter is ancient history."

"Can we just get this over with?" I pleaded, not wanting to talk about Carter or about my stunted romantic history.

Sam released an audible breath. "Katy, you're beautiful and desirable—"

"Oh my God, no more teasing. I'm wearing the dress, aren't I? I even let you put makeup on me."

"I'm not teasing you. I'm trying to get you out of this perpetual funk you're in. You hide yourself behind baggy clothes and eyebrows so thick they could be mustaches. Carter is a lovely person but he shouldn't have used you like that. Now you're all skewed in the head."

"Can we not talk about this?"

"Only if you promise to get Martin's number tonight."

I shook my head, shifted on my feet. "I will not. I don't want to drunk dial Martin Sandeke a few months from now. He won't give me pity, he's vicious. He'll laugh in my face and make me cry."

Sam *tsked,* rolled her eyes, and started walking again. "Fine. Whatever. Go through life repressing your sexuality because one boy—one stupid boy who was confused—used you to hide his own inner turmoil."

"Thank you."

"You're not welcome."

I let her snarky comment slide because we were on the same block as the fraternity house.

It was what one would expect from a fraternity house at an Ivy League school. Large, several stories, classically painted, manicured lawn littered with red solo cups and drunk partygoers. The mass of bodies—standing, sitting, leaning—spilled out the front door, down the sweeping staircase, and onto the grass.

At the entrance to the house stood two very large men. Actually, I got the distinct impression they were bouncer dudes. Both were dressed in fraternity polo shirts and their necks were as thick as my waist. They were chatting up a group of five, tall, sylphlike girls. Their eyes scanned both Sam and me when we mounted the ginormous wraparound porch.

In front of us, two girls in jeans and a guy—also in jeans—began crossing the threshold of the house.

"What do you think you're doing?" One of the big dudes held his hand out and halted their progress.

The shorter of the two jean-clad girls shrugged and faced the big dude. "Goin' to the party."

"Nah-uh, this is a skirts-only party."

The second big dude tipped his chin toward Sam and me. "You can go in, girls."

Sam pushed me gently on my shoulder and we moved around the group stalled at the entrance. Once inside, Sam and I wove through bodies; I had no idea where we were going or how I was going to find Martin.

Looking around, I started to feel a bit better about my dress. It was black cotton, sleeveless, and shorter than I thought appropriate, but it was modest in comparison to some of the dresses and miniskirts we saw as we entered the gigantic entryway.

I did not, however, feel better about the crowd. People, people everywhere; dancing, making out, arguing, drinking, laughing. Even given the mammoth size of the foyer, the crush felt suffocating.

"Excuse me."

I stepped to the side to allow three tall and handsome guys brush past. They looked almost interchangeable—intentionally long brown hair cut in the hipster style, tanned skin; two of them had brown eyes, the other one had blue. They were wearing fraternity polo shirts and all three slowed, their eyes moving over Sam and me with plain interest.

The last of the guys stopped; he grabbed my hips, then issued me a very cute and flirty grin. "Hey, who are you?"

I opened my mouth to respond that I was nobody and that he shouldn't go around touching people without their permission, but Sam tugged on my hand and inserted herself into the conversation. She had to semi-yell in order to be heard over the surrounding music and voices. "We're looking for Martin Sandeke. Is he here?"

The blue-eyed one of the trio huffed a laugh and shook his head. "Get in line, sweetheart."

Sam tipped her head to the side, narrowed her eyes at him. "Listen, we're not staying. This is his lab partner, she needs to speak with him about the class. Do you know where he is?"

The three boys exchanged confused looks; the one with his hands on my hips leaned forward to my ear. "You're Sandeke's lab partner?"

I nodded, finally finding my voice. "Yes. Both semesters. It's really important that I speak to him about, um…a project we're supposed to be doing over the break. Also, I'd really appreciate it if you would remove your hands."

He blinked at me, frowned, then removed his hands and took a step back—or as much of a step back as he could manage in the crush. "You really are his lab partner?"

His eyes seemed to search my face with interest. In fact, all three of them seemed to be looking at me a little funny. I smoothed my hand down my skirt again and was thankful for the dim lights. Under their triple-handsome-perusal, I knew I was blushing uncontrollably.

"She is, she's the astronaut's daughter," the one with blue eyes finally said, as though he'd just realized and therefore, recognized me. He said it as though I were a celebrity.

This was aggravating.

I pressed my lips together before muttering, "He's my grandfather."

"I'm in Professor Gentry's class too." Blue-eyes extended his hand, captured mine; his expression was probing and tinged with respect as it moved over my face. "You look really different outside of class. Did you do something different to…your face?"

I thought about responding that I'd be happy to do something different to his face, like punch it, but Sam spoke first.

"So, can you three amigos take us to Martin?" Sam seemed to dislike this last question about my face just as much as I did, because her tone held moderate aggravation. "We don't have a lot of time."

This was a true statement. It was already 10:10 p.m. and I knew, based on my eavesdropping, that the "drugging" would occur sometime around 10:30 p.m.

Mr. Blue-eyes nodded, still holding my hand. "Sure, sure. Follow me." He tugged me forward.

Mr. Brown-eyes, the one who felt comfortable putting his hands on my body, winked at me as I passed. "Find me later, we'll have some fun."

His companion hit him on the back of the head and I heard him say as we left, "Not likely, dumbass."

"I'm Eric," Blue-eyes tossed at us over his shoulder. "Stroke is this way."

"Stroke?"

"Martin is Stroke." Eric turned briefly to explain. We made a chain, the three of us, as we wove through bodies of scantily dressed females and grabby frat boys. "He's eight seat in the boat. It's called the stroke seat because it sets the stroke rhythm for the rest of the boat. So we call him Stroke."

I gritted my teeth through the jostling, ignored the body parts that pressed against me—or outright palmed my anatomy.

Martin was called *Stroke*. Somehow that nickname fit.

Eric led us to a staircase where another bouncer dude stood. He nodded once to Eric and smirked at Sam and me. I deduced he thought we were on our way to engage in a throupling (a threesome coupling). This, of course, caused my blush to intensify.

Jerk conscience.

I struggled to climb the stairs in the heels, almost asked Eric to stop so I could remove them. I was so busy debating whether or not to take off my shoes that I almost collided with Eric's back when he stopped in front of a pair of overly large double doors.

"He's in here." Eric turned, tilted his head, then let go of my hand to push open the door.

"Thanks." I nodded once and gripped Sam's hand tighter as I moved to enter.

"No. No. She stays out here." Eric shook his head and motioned to Sam.

"What? Why?"

"Only one girl at a time, unless both are invited."

I glanced at Sam and imagined I wore a similarly stunned expression.

"Excuse me?" Sam asked. "What is he? A sultan? Does he have a harem?"

Eric smirked, his eyes moved over Sam with simmering appraisal. "I'll keep you company, cupcake."

"No thanks, dildo," she responded.

This only made his grin widen, though he said, "You're safe with me. I promise the only thing I'll do to you is stare at you."

She glowered. He narrowed his eyes mockingly, though his amusement and enjoyment at the exchange was obvious.

"I'm not worried about me," Sam explained. "I don't trust your boy around my girl, not in this house."

Eric's gaze moved over my dress; his grin waned, softened, like he knew a secret about me.

"Kaitlyn will be safe. But if she's not out in fifteen minutes we'll go rescue her together."

I didn't like what his words inferred or what they implied. I wasn't a damsel. I wasn't going to need rescuing. If anyone was a damsel in this situation it was Martin Sandeke. I was rescuing him, he just didn't know that yet...

I addressed Sam, my voice lowered. "I'll be fine. Martin's not going to do anything. I'll just tell him about the, um, the assignment and then I'll leave."

Sam was teetering, still undecided. After a prolonged moment she blurted, "Oh, all right." Then she shifted her gaze to Eric. "But I'm timing this. I have a watch." She held up her wrist so he could see the evidence of her timepiece.

"Noted," he said with a large smile, then held his hands up as though he surrendered.

Before I lost my nerve, I turned the handle to the door and opened it— only glancing back once at Sam before I stepped in and shut it behind me.

CHAPTER 3
The Periodic Table

I DON'T KNOW what I expected, but it wasn't a pool table.

I hovered at the entrance to the room, just inside the small alcove, and watched as Martin and three other guys good-naturedly knocked the cue ball around with their pool sticks.

No one noticed me at first and this allowed me time to chant my synonyms silently.

Unsteady, uncertain, nervous, anxious, worried, panic…

Then the thought popped in my mind, *Even though you don't feel calm doesn't mean you can't be calm.* This was something my mother had said often when I struggled with childhood angst, frustration, and disappointment. These words were an excellent mantra now.

I wasn't concerned for my safety, but I was concerned. I'd gone through life hiding in cabinets; I was perfectly happy to continue this practice once this task was over. I just had to get it over with first.

Propelled by this determination—to cross this task off my conscience's list and go find a nice, safe cabinet to hide in—I gained a step forward and cleared my throat.

One of the guys was mid-laugh and I wondered at first if they'd heard me. But, eventually, four sets of eyes swung to my position, though I tried to focus only on Martin.

"Uh, hi. Hello." I gave the room a little wave.

Martin, like the rest, looked at me like I was a stranger. However, I felt all pairs of eyes sweep up and down in a way that made me feel like I was a car, or a horse—one they were thinking about riding.

Heated anxiety seized my chest, tightness spread into my stomach. I balled my hands into fists and took another step into the room, further into the light.

"I'm looking for Martin." I kept my eyes on him; at six feet away, he was the closest to my position.

Recognition had not yet registered when he replied sounding both bored and irritated, "What do you want?"

"It's me. Um, it's Parker. Kaitlyn Parker. I was hoping I could speak with you for...a...minute...about chemistry?" I bit my lip, waited for his reaction.

Martin visibly stiffened, blinked, and flinched when I said my name. His eyes—now focused and narrowed—moved over me once more, this time with obvious and renewed interest.

"Parker?" He took a step forward and laid his cue stick on the table; he sounded and looked baffled.

I nodded and hazarded a glance at the others. They were alternately watching me then turning their heads to watch Martin's reaction.

"Yep. I promise I'll just be a minute, it won't take—"

"Everyone out," Martin interrupted, his voice a bit too loud for the space. It was a command.

To my surprise, his three companions set down their pool cues on the table and shuffled out as instructed, and without delay.

One or two of them caught my eye as they left, their expressions plainly curious but none of them spoke. Martin's gaze never left my face; he seemed to recover quickly from the surprise of my arrival. The line of his jaw grew hard, and the muscle at his temple ticked.

I didn't know what to make of the gathering storm in his eyes so I ignored it and attempted to think of a word to use in my synonym game. I also tried not to look at his lips.

I tried and I failed.

I couldn't help it; the memory of his kiss—our kiss—arrived like a tsunami, flooding my body with something heated and tight. I felt overwhelmed by it, surrounded on all sides. I knew what he tasted like, how he sounded when he growled, what his hands felt like on my bare skin.

I tried not to shiver and failed at that too.

The door clicked behind me, but, to me, it sounded like a gunshot—because it signaled that we were alone. I gathered a breath and tucked my hair behind my ears. I needed to focus on reciting the speech I'd practiced in my head for the last five hours.

Then I could leave, my conscience could piss off, and this would all be over.

Ignoring the goosebumps he'd ignited with his scorching glare, I did my best impression of calm and said, "So, the reason I'm here—"

"Let me guess." He crossed his broad arms over his broad chest, his broad shoulders stiff and straight, and leaned his hips, which were narrow and not broad, against the pool table. "Your level of interested has...changed."

I squinted at him. "What?"

"You've changed your mind about me." The way he said the words, deadpan and caustic, led me to the conclusion that he thought I was there to beg for more kisses, entrap him with my feminine wiles.

Little did he know, I possessed no feminine wiles. Only the willies and the heebie jeebies.

I squinted more. I was feeling flustered. He wasn't supposed to talk. He was supposed to listen.

"No. It's not that at all. It's about the cabinet."

He scoffed, like he didn't believe me. "Nice dress."

I glanced down at myself, my hand automatically lifting to my abdomen. "Uh, thanks. It's borrowed."

"Really?" He said *really* like he didn't *really* believe me.

"Yes. It's also a little too short, I think." I tugged at the hem, wishing it longer. "I was told I wouldn't be allowed in without a skirt."

His attention moved to where my hands were now fiddling with the edge of the dress and lingered there. Martin straightened from the pool table and crossed to where I stood—his steps unhurried, his gaze leisurely skating up my body. Again, I felt like a horse being perused for a ride.

"You could always take it off, the dress, if it makes you feel uncomfortable."

A full-on, fire-alarm embarrassed flush rose to my cheeks. He stopped just in front of me. His eyes were shamelessly resting on the swell of my breasts with a suggestiveness that completely crossed the appropriate line.

It was so beyond appropriate it was...

It was...

It was inappropriate.

I gathered a slow breath, hoping to steady myself, and stomped down the rising wave of indescribable sensations plaguing my sensibilities— some pleasant, some not so pleasant.

"Listen," I said through a jaw mostly clenched. "I overheard something when I was in the cabinet, before you arrived, and I thought you should know. That's the only reason I'm here."

His eyes flickered to mine, still hard, disbelieving. He was standing just a foot or so away and I'd tilted my chin upward to meet his glare.

After a pause, during which he studied my face, Martin said, "Go ahead, gorgeous. Enlighten me."

"I heard two people walk into the room. So, I panicked and, yes, I hid in the cabinet. But, in my defense, I was already in there pulling out the reticulation equipment. Anyway, two voices—one female, one male—and they came into the lab together. Whoever the guy was when you walked into the lab, that was the same guy I overheard. The girl wanted the guy to drug you."

Martin's eyebrows bounced upward then pulled low when I said the word *drug*. I didn't want him to interrupt me again so I spoke faster.

"She said she wanted him to drug you. They scheduled it for ten thirty tonight and he is supposed to make sure you stick around at the party. She said she would arrive at eleven then take you, drugged, up to your room and video tape the two of you. Then she said something truly disturbing— not that the rest of it isn't already disturbing—but what she said next kind of blew me away because I didn't know people could be that cold and calculating with no regard for basic decency."

"What did she say?" he asked, his tone impatient. His eyes were still hard, angry, but the severity wasn't focused on me. I didn't appear to be the target—praise Bunsen and his burner!

"She said that if she got pregnant then it would be 'a bonus.'"

Martin's mouth opened then closed and his glare moved from me to the floor. He was visibly stunned. I watched his beautiful face as he processed the information, took the opportunity to examine him in a way I'd never allowed myself to do before.

He was painfully handsome. I kind of knew that before, but I really saw it now.

My chest hurt a little as I studied his features: square jaw, strong nose, perfect shape and size for his face, high cheekbones, like he had Cherokee or Navaho ancestry. Paired with his blue eyes, he was striking. I understood my previous reluctance to gaze at him directly. It was called self-preservation.

I tore my eyes from him and his exceptional form. I tried not to notice his decidedly swoony body—the way his jeans hung on his hips, the way his thighs filled out the jeans—and glanced over his shoulder.

"Well. That was what I needed to tell you. So, I guess I'll be—"

"Why should I trust you?"

My eyes moved back to his and I blinked at this question, because the answer was obvious. "Uh, what?"

"How do I know you're telling me the truth?"

"Why would I lie?"

"What do you expect in exchange?"

"Exchange for what?"

He shifted on his feet just a fraction of an inch closer. However, that fraction brought with it a menacing cloud of suspicion and unpleasantness.

For someone so beautiful, his expression was surprisingly ugly.

"What is it that you want? What are you hoping to gain? Is it money?"

My mouth fell open and my nose wrinkled again, this time in outrage. I looked at him, really looked at him—and this time I wasn't seeing the outer façade of blinding beauty. What I saw was a guy who was bitter, jaded, and maybe a little desperate—for what, I had no idea.

Finally I said, "What is wrong with you?"

His eyebrows shot up. "What's wrong with me?"

"Yes," I countered, my hands coming to my hips. "What is wrong with you? I came here to *help* you, the least you could do is not act like a jerk-face."

"Jerk-face?" he shot back, his eyes growing both hot and cold. "You show up here, looking like that, and you expect me to believe you're not after something?"

"I already told you, jerk-face, it's a skirt party! I wouldn't have made it through the door if I hadn't been wearing this stupid dress, jerk-face. If you don't like how I look, jerk-face, then you can go yell at your stupid sorority brothers."

"You mean fraternity brothers."

"Sorority, sorostitute, fraternity, fratigalo—whatever! It's all the same to me."

"So I'm supposed to believe that you have no ulterior motive? If this is true then why didn't you tell me all of this at the lab?" He gained another half step forward and, since I refused to back down, only inches separated us.

"Because you scratched my itch and then you kissed me—both of which freaked me out because neither of which are in the course syllabus for laboratory experiments this semester. And, furthermore—"

I didn't get to finish because the door opened behind me and a voice I recognized called into the room. "Hey Stroke—dude, why are you up here? I brought you a drink. Some of my special hunch punch."

I'd turned toward the sound of the voice and stumbled a step backward. Martin's arm wrapped around my shoulders, bringing my shoulders to his chest as the owner of the voice leaned halfway in—two red solo cups extended.

The guy, about two inches taller than Martin—therefore, very tall—walked through the door after a short pause. Behind him I could see Eric standing with Sam. They both peered into the room and I noted Eric's face was apologetic as he glanced at Martin.

I tried to step forward but Martin's arm tightened, held me still.

The stranger's clear blue eyes moved from me to Martin, then back again. "Hey—Eric said you had company so I brought one for both of you."

I knew his voice because it was *him*. The cuss monster from the lab.

I felt Martin's chest expand on a slow inhale, his fingers were digging into my arm; it wasn't painful but it was pointed, firm, meant to communicate a message—*don't move*.

"Thanks, Ben," Martin drawled, but the edge in his voice was glacial and he made no move to accept the cups.

Ben gave me a stiff smile, his eyes lingering on where Martin's arm was wrapped around me, then he raised both cups. "You two should have a toast. Come down to the party."

"Leave the drinks and go," Martin said.

Ben frowned, glanced at the two cups and cleared his throat. "You should come downstairs, this is epic—"

"Go," Martin repeated.

This time Ben nodded once and set the cups on a table by the door. "Sure, sure. I'll come back in a bit to see if you need any more." He held his hands up and backed out of the room, his eyes completing another once over of my body before he closed the door.

I exhaled the breath I'd been holding and, just for a moment, allowed myself to lean against Martin.

"That was him. That was the guy—I recognize his voice."

I felt Martin nod, his chin and cheek against the side of my hair. We stood—still, quiet—for a long moment, then he turned me to face him. Both of his hands moved to my waist and he backed me against the pool table.

His eyes, guarded, but also tempered with curiosity, searched mine. I still saw desperation in his features and it still perplexed me. I didn't touch him. Instead I braced my hands on either side of my hips where my body met the pool table.

At length he asked, "What do you want?"

I swallowed then responded, "I'd like to leave."

He shook his head slowly. "That's not what I meant. What do you want from me?"

I shrugged. "It would be great if you could tabulate the findings from last week's assignment, but I'm not going to hold my breath." He never did the tabulations and analyses. It was annoying.

"Parker."

"What?"

His eyes dipped to my mouth and his voice was the softest I'd ever heard it, almost coaxing. "Kaitlyn…"

I stiffened against the feelings associated with my name from his lips, spoken in gentle tones.

I averted my eyes and my voice was a little strained when I said, "Martin, I honestly don't want anything from you. I'd like to leave so I can change into my normal clothes, drink tea, eat cookies, and read a good book in my dorm room."

"Kaitlyn, look at me."

Once again, my neck flushed and my arms broke out in goosebumps.

I tried to ignore both the blush and the goosebumps. "I also want for you to forget any of this happened so that we can go back to being lab partners."

He was quiet for a long time, but I knew—even though I refused to meet his gaze—that he was studying me, examining me like I was something new.

Then he said, "Why do you hide?"

The words startled me so much that my eyes instinctively sought his, and this was a mistake. His gaze—now a lovely blue fire—was taking a survey of my face, as though he were memorizing every detail. It was alarming and my heart quickened.

I tried for a shrug but it likely looked like a poorly executed, convulsive shiver. "Why do you care?"

His gaze met mine then flickered to my lips. "You have fantastic lips."

I half choked, my eyes widening. "You care because I have fantastic lips?"

"And your eyes. They're grey. I noticed them first." His voice was just above a whisper; he sounded as though he was talking to himself.

I cleared my throat, not really sure what to say. But it turned out I didn't need to say anything, because he continued.

"Early last semester you wore a tank top and your hair was down. You kept pulling it off your neck." He lifted his hand and brushed the backs of his fingers against my swell of cleavage, skirting the neckline of the dress, a soft caress. "I tried to get your phone number but you wouldn't give it to me."

"I give out my number as rarely as possible, it's one of my life rules," I said dumbly.

"The red pants, the tight ones that show off your ass. You tortured me, bending over to get supplies out of the cabinet. That isn't very nice."

My voice was unaccountably breathless. "The corduroy ones? I only wear those when all my other laundry is dirty."

"You're better at chemistry than me, you ace all the tests."

"I like chemistry, and you don't study like you should."

"Haven't you ever wondered why I come on Fridays?" His fingers curled around my neck and his thumb traced circles along the line of my collarbone. He encouraged my head to tip backward.

"So that we can get a jump start on the weekly assignment?"

He shook his head. "You."

My eyelashes fluttered. "Me?"

His held me captive with both his heavily lidded gaze and his caressing hands. Martin leaned forward, and he brushed his lips against mine. It wasn't a kiss. It was more like he was using his lips to feel mine, to enjoy my softness.

"You," he whispered again.

My fingers gripped the wood on either side of my hips and I successfully fought a whimper. The tightness in my chest eased and twisted, my stomach fluttered, my breath coming shallow and fast.

My brain wasn't quite working properly because he'd muddled it—with his words, hands, and lips of temptation. Therefore, in a paltry attempt to defend myself from his seduction onslaught, I blurted out one of my greatest fears where he was concerned.

"You'll make me cry."

His eyes widened a little, moved between mine. "I wouldn't."

"You would. I've seen it, I see how you treat girls."

IIis hand at my waist tightened. "I wouldn't do that to you. You're not...I know you're not like that. We wouldn't be that."

"I don't trust you."

He sighed, but not with impatience. "I know." He nodded. "But you will."

He dipped his head again, placed a soft kiss on my lips, just a hint of his tongue. It wasn't enough. My hands lifted on their own and gripped his shirt, staying any retreat he might have planned. I didn't do this on purpose. In fact, I didn't know why I did it.

"Martin, I can't—"

"You can."

"I'm not—"

"You are."

"You don't—"

"I do." He kissed me again and shifted his weight more completely against me. Martin crowded my space so that he filled every inch of it. Four of my senses were overwhelmed by him—the smell of his cologne, his hot and hard body against mine, the taste of his mouth, the low growl in the back of his throat when our tongues met and mated.

Briefly he drew his mouth from mine, and demanded, "Say you'll spend the week with me."

I blinked, started to protest. "Martin, this isn't—"

He kissed me again, placed my arms around his neck, then his hands moved up my ribs and his palm cupped me through the thin material of my dress. His thumb drew tight circles around the center of my breast.

He growled, "Say it. Spend the week with me."

I moaned, because…aroused.

He bit my lip, sucked it between his. I moaned again.

"You're so fucking beautiful, Kaitlyn." He breathed the words suddenly, like he didn't mean to say them out loud, but they burst forth unbidden. "I want you to spend the week with me. Say yes."

He kissed me again, quickly, then trailed wet, hot kisses over my jaw and behind my ear to my shoulder. He bit me—hard—and sucked on my neck in a way that made me squirm and my breath hitch; all the while his large hand massaged my breast and tortured me through the fabric. His other hand had moved to my bottom and pressed my center to his.

"Martin…" was all I could manage, because…*really* aroused. And, not that I was an expert, but judging by the hard length against my stomach, he was also really aroused.

"Please, say yes," he breathed into my ear.

I said, "Yes…"

"Promise me."

"I promise."

To be honest, I said it but I didn't mean it. In that moment, I said yes because he'd asked me to—and he'd used the word *please* and I didn't want all the good feelings to stop—not because I had any intention of spending the week with Martin Sandeke, Hercules, jerk to women, and apparently king of seducing naïve and intimacy-starved virgins.

Regardless, my words seemed to be enough for Martin because he smiled against my skin and stopped talking. He also moved both of his hands from their shockingly effective ministrations and encircled me in his arms. His mouth moved back to mine.

This time the kiss was slow, less urgent, gentle, and sweet. It felt like a prelude, a beginning. When he lifted his head, I opened my eyelids to find him gazing down at me, his eyes alight—blue flames.

"I'll pick you up tomorrow," he said. His voice was different, softer, deeper…content.

"What?" I blinked at him.

"Be ready at eight."

"Eight?"

"You don't need to pack much." He kissed my nose, released me from his arms, threaded his fingers through mine, and tugged me toward the door. "I hope you like private beaches."

CHAPTER 4
Enthalpies of Reaction

"**WHAT ARE YOU** going to do?"

"Nothing."

I heard Sam shift in her seat causing the leather to creak. "What do you mean *nothing*? He's expecting you to go away with him for spring break."

I shrugged, staring out the window of Martin's chauffeured car. That's right. A *chauffeured* car, for a twenty-year-old college student. If I hadn't felt so pensive I might've looked for the Grey Poupon Dijon mustard.

After my lapse in judgment against the pool table, Martin had navigated Sam and me to the back of the fraternity house while calling his driver on the phone. The man was at the back door by the time we arrived.

Martin pulled me in for a quick kiss—which was completely bizarre, provocative, and off-putting—then unceremoniously loaded us in, telling his driver to take us to our dorm.

Sam pumped me for information as soon as the door shut. I related the facts, which gave me an opportunity to recover a measure of sanity. In hindsight, I realized I'd been acting like a crazy person. Proximity to Martin made me lose my sense. I'd been senseless. Without sense. Not any sense. No sense.

Nonsense.

I spoke to the window rather than be faced with Sam's anxious expression. "I mean, I'm going to do nothing. I can't be held responsible for my reactions—what I say or what I do—when faced with a real life Martin Sandeke. He's the man equivalent of a gun to the head, except without the fear for my life aspect. I'll write him an email, tell him that he adversely affects my ability to function as a rational being. As such, our discussion this evening and all resultant agreements are null and void. I'm sure he'll understand."

I felt like I had stumbled into an alternate reality and was just now finding my way out of the rabbit hole.

Sam snorted. "Um, no. He's not going to understand. And, I doubt he'll take no for an answer. He's kind of a bully that way, or least he has that reputation."

This statement captured my curiosity; I turned in my seat to face Sam. "Wait, what do you mean? Does he—has he forced himself on—"

"No! God, no. I would never have teased you about getting his number if he forced himself on girls. That's not what I meant. He wouldn't need to do that in any case, as he has them lined up around the fraternity house with skirts up to their elbows, willing to bend whichever direction he prefers. I bet that's why he was hiding upstairs. It must get exhausting at some point..." Sam trailed off and I got the sense she was speaking mostly to herself.

I frowned at Sam. "Rape isn't about need, it's about power."

"Exactly. Sorry if I implied otherwise. Regardless, Martin Sandeke has a reputation for getting it on with a cornucopia of willing females."

"Then what are you talking about? How is he a bully? Other than making females he's slept with cry and getting into fist fights." I listened to the words as they left my mouth, realizing that those two facts made him enough of a bully to be labeled as such.

"I just mean he's used to getting his way, right? He has his own yacht. His. Own. Yacht." She stared at me, her eyebrows raised with meaning. "If he wants something, it's his. He doesn't even ask, he just mentions it."

I twisted my lips to the side and considered this information, not really understanding why it was pertinent to our discussion. "So? What has that got to do with me?"

Sam's eyelids drooped with disbelief, but her eyebrows stayed suspended. "Have you not been paying attention? I saw the way he looked at you, the way he held your hand all the way to the car, the way he kissed you before we left. He wants you. Martin Sandeke wants you."

I considered her, her words, and sighed. "I'm not a yacht."

"No. You're a girl. He's had hundreds of girls. But he has only one yacht." Then under her breath she added, "Well, he has only one yacht that I know of."

"Sam, weren't you the one pushing me to get his number?"

"Yes, but that was before I was told to stand outside while you went into his lair. That was before I saw the dazed look on your face when you emerged from the aforementioned lair. That was before I found out he wants you to go away with him for a week! I want you to get your freak on, but I don't want you to get your heart broken."

"I think you're overreacting. You said yourself, he has them lined up around the block. I'll politely decline his offer, and he'll move on to someone else. There is no need to become hysterical."

"I'm not hysterical and you are being purposefully obtuse."

"Fine. I'll sleep with him. I'll call him tomorrow and tell him I want to get it over with. Then, by your logic, he'll go away. Problem solved."

Sam growled. "That's not a good idea either."

"Well, what do you want me to do?"

"You should tell him face-to-face that you don't want to go. You should explain your reasons why and establish boundaries for future interactions. And you should have me there as your representative to make sure he doesn't try to zap you with his sexy ray."

"Zap me with his sexy ray?"

"You know what I'm talking about. I barely saw him and I'm feeling the effects. He's got like an…electromagnetic pulse of sexy or something. So does his friend, Eric. They're a menace. They shouldn't be allowed in public."

"That's not how electromagnets work."

"Whatever. You get my point."

"We're here." The driver's voice over the speaker interrupted our conversation and drew our attention to the view of our dorm outside my window.

I heard the sound of him exiting the car, presumably walking around to open my door.

Sam covered my hand with hers bringing my attention back to her. "Just think about what I said. Carter did a number on you, but his intentions weren't hurtful. This guy," she paused, her eyes moving between mine, "if Carter was a stick of dynamite, this guy is a nuclear weapon."

**

THE CAMPUS EMAIL directory was public information within the school's Black Board system. I could find any person's email address by conducting a simple first name, last name, year enrolled search. However, since it was so easy to find a person's email address, very few people actually used their on-campus email account, preferring Gmail or another alternative where spam wasn't such an issue.

I knew this. I knew the chances of Martin actually receiving my email were minute. Regardless, I reasoned I would have the moral high ground if I sent him an email as soon as I arrived home. Then, when he showed up the next day and I was missing, I could point out later that I did—in fact—send him an email.

It wasn't my fault if he didn't check his email.

Martin,

I hope you are well.

I appreciate your offer to accompany you on your travels during spring break, but I've reconsidered my response. Upon gaining distance from the situation, I see that I made an error when I agreed to go with you. I simply have too much school work to do this week. As well, I volunteer at a women's crisis center as their resident desktop support. I do not want to leave without giving them proper notice as they count on me to be here when issues arise. Therefore, please accept my apologies. I'm sure you'll have no problem finding an alternative.

As well, I would appreciate it if our future topics of conversation were limited to chemistry (and only chemistry) from now on. See you in the lab.

-Parker

"What are you doing?" Sam asked as she walked into our room.

When we arrived back to the dorm, I'd gone to the bathroom first to wash my face and brush my teeth while Sam changed. Then, she went to the bathroom while I changed. But instead of changing, I pulled out my laptop.

"Nothing."

She *tsked,* putting away her toiletries. "You're sending him an email. That's a mistake."

"It doesn't matter if he gets it. I sent it. That's what matters."

"That's not what I meant. You're giving him a heads-up. Now he'll be able to plan a counter attack."

I glanced at her from the corner of my eye. "Counter attack? This is not some exercise from Sun Tsu's *The Art of War*, this is me rejecting his free vacation offer. What can he do?"

"You'll see." She said this in a sing-song voice, switching off the light on her side of the room, and climbing into bed.

"Besides. I sent it to his school account. He probably won't even get it."

"Then he'll show up tomorrow and you'll have to deal with him in person."

"No. I'll be gone. He said he'd be here at eight. I'll leave at seven and stay at the library all day."

"Coward."

"Is a chameleon a coward because it can change its color? No. It's evolved and awesome. I like to think of myself in a similar fashion. There is nothing wrong with having a strong sense of self-preservation."

"Whatever. Do you want me to wake you up? I have tennis practice at six."

"Nah, I'll set the alarm on my phone." I closed my laptop and tucked it next to our shared nightstand, then stood to dress for bed.

After changing, I grabbed my phone to set my alarm for 6:30 a.m. I wanted to be gone long before Martin or one of his people arrived. I usually woke up around 7:30 a.m., therefore the alarm was necessary.

Upon glancing at the screen of my cell, I noticed I had two missed calls from my mother plus a text message. It read,

Just got home. Call when you can. I'll be up until 2.

My mother: senator, workaholic, efficient conversationalist, superhero.

Distracted by the message, I abandoned my alarm for the moment and dialed my mother's number. It wouldn't take long. Our discussions rarely lasted over three minutes. She answered after one point five rings.

"Kaitlyn. You have not communicated your plans for spring break. Is it your intention to join us in Monterey or are you remaining on campus?" my mother's brisk, businesslike voice sounded from the other end.

She had an agenda and talking points for every conversation. Growing up, she would hand me a paper copy and ask me to follow along. When I was very young, she used pictures in place of words and we'd discuss things like: *Three month review: Preschool. Scheduled: Haircut. Action plan required: Cleaning your room. Music: Interfering with scheduled playtime.*

Before I left for college, if one or both of my parents were traveling, the family meeting would be conducted via conference call. Now we typically held the meeting via conference call due to my physical absence from home. Topics for discussion ran the gamut of *Purchase Request: New Bike,* to *Family News: Your Grandmother has cancer,* to *Point of Concern: Time spent on music surpassing time spent on homework,* to *Scheduled Recreation: Yearly vacation options,* to *Kaitlyn News: Accepted to Harvard, Yale, Princeton, MIT, Caltech.*

"I am remaining on campus."

"Will Sam be present?"

"Yes."

"Do you require any funds?"

"No."

"Are you amenable to a visit with your father and me next Sunday? Brunch or lunch, Kartwell's Deli."

"Yes. Sunday. Brunch."

Even now, family meetings occurred on Sundays. My father and I would submit agenda items to George, my mother's PA (Personal Assistant) no later than Friday night. A draft agenda would be circulated Saturday afternoon for comment and the final version distributed Saturday evening. Attached to the agenda would be a copy of our individual calendars for the next month, updated weekly.

I'd fallen out of the habit of updating my calendar since leaving home. Agendas, schedules, and lists ensured we made the most efficient use of our time. I knew this. But my schedule only changed once a semester. My life was predictable, therefore I saw no need to send weekly updates.

"How is school?"

"Very well. How is work?"

To my surprise, she didn't provide her typical rapid-fire response of, "It is what it is." Instead, she paused then sighed and said, "Terrible."

My mouth opened and closed, I could feel my eyebrows jump on my forehead. "Uh…care to elaborate?"

"My Net Neutrality measure is not progressing to my satisfaction in The House, the Telecommunications lobbyists are growing rabid, and the FCC is being difficult. I am frustrated."

I immediately responded, "Net Neutrality is an important issue and worth the effort and frustration. You are doing the right thing." Every once in a while I served as my mother's cheerleader. Every so often she served as mine. These occasions were rare as we both believed in self-sufficiency unless circumstances were dire.

However, we loved each other. Neither of us were so austere as to withhold support when it was requested, but I appreciated and subscribed to her no-drama mantra. Energy should be spent on solutions to real problems—like the abysmal status of the US foster care system, or our strained foreign policy with Pakistan, or Telecommunications giants using Net Neutrality as a weapon against the public good—therefore, when she said she was frustrated it usually meant she was at her wit's end.

"Thank you. I appreciate your words of encouragement and I value your opinion." Her tone was softer. It was the voice she'd used when I was a kid and she'd read me the first three Harry Potter books before bedtime.

"Anytime."

She then surprised me further by saying, "You know I love you, right?"

Again, my mouth did its little opening and closing dance before I blurted, "Of course. Of course I know you love me. I love you too."

"Good...good."

She told me every Sunday that she loved me. It was the last thing my parents and I would exchange on our conference calls even though it wasn't listed on the agenda. A mid-week *I love you* hadn't occurred since my parents dropped me off at University my freshman year.

I was about to push her for more details on the source of her stress, because she was obviously out of sorts and had me concerned, but before I could, her efficient tone was back.

"Please send George your updated calendar with a weekly update for the period of spring break. You do not have classes next week, as such the calendar is incorrect."

"I will."

"Thank you. Goodnight, Kaitlyn."

"Goodnight, Mom."

She clicked off first. I held the phone to my ear for several seconds before lowering it to the nightstand, then distractedly readied myself for bed.

My mom was the daughter of a physicist (my grandmother) and an astronaut (my grandfather). My grandfather was also a physicist in the Navy. She'd been an overachiever her whole life and believed in goal-focused structure. She was a superhero. She was *my* hero. Therefore, moments when she allowed herself to display vulnerability were distressing. It was like watching Superman struggle through a bout of kryptonite exposure.

I returned to my pillow and comforter, both of which I loved; they smelled like lavender, and were so cozy, poems should be written about their epic cozy wonder. I snuggled against their softness and willed away the touch of anxiety I felt about my mom's strange behavior.

Eventually I fell asleep.

CHAPTER 5
Basic Concepts of Chemical Bonding

"PARKER."

Fingers were in my hair, brushing it away from my face. Then the fingers caressed a path over my shoulder, down my arm, and fit themselves around mine, squeezing.

"Parker... Time to get up. Time to go." A mystery male voice reverberated in my head. It was a nice voice. It made my insides feel like a warm marshmallow, sweet and fluffy and melting.

I lifted my eyebrows but couldn't quite open my eyes; I asked in a sleep mumble, "Where are we going?"

"We're going to the beach."

The words sounded faraway and my drowsy brain told me to ignore them. I began to drift.

"You're cute when you don't want to wake up." The mystery voice sounded both growly and amused. I liked the mystery voice.

I also liked the word *cute,* but not as much as its alternates. "Adorable, captivating, charming, darling…"

"What?"

"Synonyms."

"Okay. Come on, Cutie pie. Wake up." The hand was on my face, cupping my cheek. I noted that it felt exceptionally callused. A thumb brushed back and forth, whisper light touches over my bottom lip, sending little shivers down my neck to my spine.

I opened one eye, managed a squint at the fuzzy form, and recognized the owner of the mystery voice. It was Martin Sandeke. And it looked like he was sitting on my bed. I couldn't quite make sense of it.

"What's going on?" I rubbed my eyes with the base of my palms, still someplace between my dreams and reality, but closer to dreams.

This was a dream. I was certain. It was a dream within a dream or one of those dreams that felt eerily real. Maybe, if I was lucky, I'd be able to control the action of the dream and spend some naked time with Martin Sandeke's superior physique without the danger of his personality ruining things.

"I'm picking you up for our trip." His hand settled on my bare thigh.

The weight of it felt very real.

I stopped mid-eye rub, opting for motionless contemplation instead of a gasping shriek.

"Martin?" I asked to what I hoped would be an empty room.

"Yes?"

I jumped to a sitting position, my eyes flying open. "Oh my God, what are you doing here?"

Martin was sitting on the edge of my bed toward the middle. I stared at him; he was wearing dark, faded jeans, a white T-shirt, and a smile. He was so handsome I felt like filing a civil lawsuit against his parents, claiming punitive damages, pain and suffering to my psyche.

"I'm picking you up."

I reached for my phone to check the time. It was 7:00 a.m.

"What? What? Why? What?" was all I could manage, because my alarm didn't go off.

I had fallen off to sleep, but forgot to set my alarm... Gah!

So, Martin was one hour early and he was here. In my room. Sitting on my bed. Watching me like he wanted me for...things.

He leaned forward, his gaze on my mouth somehow both gentle and wicked. Horrified that he might try to kiss me first thing in the morning, I scrambled to my feet and ran off the bed, jumping from the mattress like it was a spring board. I'm sure I jostled him on my way.

I reached for my bag and pulled out my Wintermint gum, unwrapping three pieces, and shoving them into my mouth.

"It's seven," I said sloppily around the wad in my mouth.

"Yes. I'm early."

I glanced over my shoulder and found Martin Sandeke had stretched himself out on my bed, ankles crossed, leaning against my pillow, his laced together fingers resting behind his head.

Turning fully around, I aggressively chewed and stared at him. His eyes were moving up and down my body with a heated and slow appraisal. I glanced down at myself. I was wearing my Sponge Bob Square Pants tank top and sleep shorts. But I wasn't wearing a bra and my shape was easily discernable through the fitted shirt.

I crossed my arms over my chest and stiffened my spine. "How did you get in?"

"I have my ways..." He'd gone from appraising to ogling. He licked his lips. The action felt malicious. "Why don't you come over here?"

"I'm perfectly fine over here," I said primly, but the effect was ruined by the gob of gum in my mouth that was quickly losing its flavor. I reached for a napkin next to my food stuffs and daintily rid myself of the gum, tossing it into the trash two feet from my position. The nice thing about dorms is that everything is within reach.

However, I'd positioned myself on the side opposite the door. If I wanted to leave I'd have to walk by Martin on my way out.

Abruptly he said, "Bring the red pants."

"What?"

"When you pack, bring those red pants. I've been thinking about them a lot."

I sputtered, "I'm not bringing the red pants."

He shrugged, his hands still folded behind his head. "Fine. Don't bring the red pants. Bring nothing."

"I'm not bringing nothing, I'm not bringing anything!"

"Good. We're in agreement."

"That's not what I meant. I'm not bringing anything because I'm not going."

He squinted at me. "You promised."

"Under duress."

"I wasn't holding a gun to your head."

"No, just holding yourself to my body. That's quite enough to put me in a state of duress."

"My body places you in a state of duress?" Something wicked sparked behind his eyes.

"Of course. Of course it does. What a ridiculous question. Your body causes distress, disquiet, desolation, and puts me in a state of duress."

He grinned, sitting up in the bed like he planned to stand up. "Maybe I'll use it now."

"Please don't." I held up my hand as though it could stop him. It didn't stop him. He stood, reached for and closed the door, then whipped his shirt off. My mouth went dry. My heart thumped painfully. My girl parts forcefully made their opinion known.

Me want Martin flavored cookie! Me want cookie now!!

The sight was indecent because the sight immediately made me want to do several indecent things to him, around him, near him, on top, underneath, adjacent to—if it was a preposition, I wanted to do it with Martin.

"Ack! No!" I squeezed my eyes shut and covered my face with my hands. "Not the chest! Anything but the chest!"

"Anything?" I did not miss the wicked teasing in his taunt, nor did I miss the distinct sound of a zipper being undone.

"Okay, I lied. Shirtless is fine, just please, please, please don't take off your pants." I turned from him, still covering my face with one hand, and blindly reached for the door of the closet with the other. The closet ran the length of one wall and had sliding doors. I knew I would be able to fit inside. Maybe I could barricade myself until he left, or throw my shoes at him like missiles.

For the first time in my life I wished I owned spiky heels instead of mostly sneakers. I did have one pair of Doc Martins, however…

His pants hit the floor, the change in his pocket jingling on the descent, and I imagined he was now toeing off his shoes.

"For the love of Bunsen, please put your pants back on." My voice sounded desperate because I was desperate.

I slid the closet door open just as Martin's hands claimed my hips from behind. I stiffened because he pressed his bare chest to my back and his groin to my bottom. He was hard and I was soft, and I was convinced I was about to die of… something related to abrupt sexual desire. I released a tortured moan because I could feel his stiff thickness through his boxers—or briefs, or boxer briefs.

Unthinkingly I reached around me, my eyes still shut, and encountered the thin cotton of his boxer briefs just as he bit and kissed my neck. I yanked my hand back. "You're in your underwear."

"So are you."

"Oh my God. Who does that? Why would you do that?"

"I'm launching a counter attack."

"A counter attack? I haven't attacked. You can't launch a counter attack until the other person has attacked."

"Fine." Kiss. Bite. Tongue. Lick. "Then it's a preemptive strike," he said, hand under my shirt, on my stomach. Other hand over my shirt, kneading my breast.

Some instinct had me pressing my bottom backward and against him as I arched into the hand toying with my breast.

"You think I'm only interested in you for one thing. You're wrong," he whispered against my ear, hot breath spilling against my neck making me shiver, his hand on my stomach inching lower.

"This, what you're doing now, how you're touching me, does not give credibility to your words." My breath hitched, my brain disengaging.

"You're wrong. I'll prove it to you."

"I'm right. I'm right. I'm so, so, so right." I sighed, my hands abandoning the closet door and reaching behind me to touch his body. My center ached. My stomach fluttered. My skin was on fire. Lust and madness had descended.

"You're coming with me. There is nothing temporary about how I want you." His thumb was tracing a circle around my nipple. He pinched it roughly, causing me to suck in a startled—yet delighted—breath.

He was so talented at this. So very, very skillful. His movements were expert, practiced. Meanwhile, I was fumbling, a creature of instinct, reacting to his proficient petting.

"Do you like this?" he asked, his voice sounding dark and lovely against the shell of my ear. "Does it feel good?"

I nodded.

"Do you want more? Say yes or no."

"Yes," I gasped. "So much yes."

The fingers of his other hand delved into my panties, his long middle finger stroking my center. If I hadn't been lost to lust and madness, I would definitely have been embarrassed by the state of my nether region.

I was sure the girls he was used to had porn-star vaginas—waxed, smooth, bleached for color tone consistency, surgically enhanced to make them appear less like a forest floor—but I was au naturel downstairs. I'd never had a reason to do anything beyond trimming the hedge for hygiene's sake.

But I wasn't embarrassed. I was a little terrified and a lot confused, but mostly I was trapped in Martin's erotic haze. I was bucking against him because his finger had just entered me.

"Whoa!" I panted.

"Fuck," he breathed against the back of my neck, his teeth sharp as they bit my spine. "You are so tight. So fucking tight."

"That's because I'm a virgin and I'm aroused," I said unthinkingly on an exhale. "The vaginal canal swells when aroused."

His hands stilled—both at my breast and in my panties—though his penis seemed to push more insistently against my ass, as though raising its head and saying, *Tell me more about this vaginal canal swelling of which you speak.*

"What?" he asked, his tone sharp, exacting.

"It's true, it swells." I shifted restlessly when he remained motionless. "It also elongates."

"You're a virgin?"

It was my turn to hold still, a spike of some unpleasant sensation coursing through my body. I hadn't meant to admit that. I hadn't meant to ever tell him anything personal about myself, anything that could be tucked away and used to make me cry at some later date.

"Um...," I said, struggling to think of some way to hide that fact without flat-out lying.

Martin withdrew his hands and I felt the loss of him at my back; a few seconds later I heard the jingle of the change in his pants pocket. I closed my eyes again, my forehead hitting the closet door.

"Ah, barnacles," I whispered, my body cold and hot. I was tightly wound with both mortification and unspent sexual energy.

"You're a virgin," he said, this time not a question; it sounded like an accusation.

I nodded, took a deep breath, and glanced over my shoulder. He was buttoning his jeans, his expression thunderous. I glared at where his fingers gripped the waist of his pants.

"So what?" I said. If I pretended like it was no big deal maybe he'd believe me. "So what, I'm a virgin."

Finished with his button, he pulled the zipper up with a rough yank. "So you're a virgin and I'm not going to—" He growled, cutting himself off and reached for his shirt with a rough swipe. "I'm not a total bastard," he said, this to his shirt.

I glared at him, disbelieving what he'd just said, what he'd just implied. "What does my being a virgin have to do with anything? All girls should be treated with respect regardless of whether or not they're virgins. Being a virgin doesn't make me any more or less worthwhile than a non-virgin. Your seduction logic is flawed."

"It's not virgins I have a problem with. I've fucked plenty of virgins."

I winced at this and watched him pull his shirt on with jerky movements. Before I could recover from his harsh admission, he continued.

"But you being a virgin and you being Kaitlyn Parker makes me want to ensure our first time touching each other isn't some grope session against the closet of a dorm room."

"So if I hadn't been a virgin, then we would...what? We would have just, just..." I couldn't say the word *fuck*. I just couldn't. Instead I rushed to finish. "You would have impaled me with your penis while I face planted against the closet?"

"God, Kaitlyn. No!" His protest appeared to be equally appalled and earnest. "I wanted to tease you until you agreed to come with me. I wasn't going to let it go that far. Haven't you ever fooled around before?"

I think he knew the answer before he finished asking the question, because his eyes widened with realization as the last words left his mouth.

No. No, I have never fooled around.

I didn't want to admit anything. Yet I couldn't help but look away, stare unseeingly at the foot of my bed. I belatedly realized my small evasive action told him everything. My hands balled into fists and I crossed my arms over my chest. The weight and heat of his gaze, what he must be thinking about me, made my skin feel three sizes too small.

"Damnit, Kaitlyn! Was I your first kiss too?" He sounded angry and his words made me jump.

"No. Of course not." My cheeks and neck were on fire. I tried to lift my eyes to his but couldn't manage any higher than his chin. "I've kissed someone before."

"*Someone*? As in, one other person?"

For some inexplicable reason, I felt like crying. Tears stung behind my eyelids and my throat felt tight.

I knew it.

I KNEW IT.

I knew he was going to make me cry. It's what he did. Therefore, I didn't answer him. I just blinked at the foot of my bed and pressed my lips together, focused on my breathing.

He sat down heavily on the edge of my bed, his elbows on his knees, running his hands through his hair, and I heard him exhale a dumbfounded, "Fuck."

I muttered, "That word is unimaginative."

"You're completely inexperienced." He said this to the room.

He was probably thinking, *What is wrong with you that you've only been kissed by one other person? That you never made it past first base prior to yesterday?*

"I've read books," I said dumbly, clearing my throat, safely past the threat of tears. "And watched a number of pornographic videos. I took extensive notes. I've also read several enlightening journal articles on pubmed about the physiology of the sex act. I probably know more about the logistics of it then you do. I'm not an idiot."

"No. *You're* not the idiot," he said. Again, he sounded angry. He bent to put on his shoes and I noted that his jaw flexed, and he was grinding his teeth.

I shifted uncomfortably on my feet. The instinct to hide was strong. I considered stepping backward into the closet and sliding the door shut. Maybe he wouldn't notice. He'd just look up eventually and it would look like I'd simply disappeared.

I was about to put this plan into action when he stood abruptly. It startled me so I did a weird step forward then backward shuffle, similar to a jazz square. He crossed to me, his eyes fierce, his gaze intent. I retreated until my back hit the closet, lifting my chin to maintain eye contact.

"This is what is going to happen," he said, his hands moving like he was going to touch me, but then he yanked them back at the last minute and stuffed them in his pockets. "Pack your things, you're coming with me."

I opened my mouth to protest, but he cut me off.

"You promised, Parker. You said yes and you promised."

Not breaking promises was one of my life rules. If I made a promise, I kept it. Therefore I frowned at him and admitted nothing.

He studied me for a moment, his gaze growing thoughtful, introspective. His words sounded shaded with distraction as he said, "We're going to take this slow. We're going to start over and do this right."

I squinted at him, my mouth doing its opening and closing dance. "What? What are you talking about? Take what slow?"

"You like me." He said this matter-of-factly, with a hint of belligerence.

This statement did not answer my question.

"What?"

"You like me. You want to know me better."

"I most certainly do not want to know you better."

"I definitely want to know you better." His gaze flickered down then up meaningfully.

I gaped at him because—hot hottie from Hotsvillie—the growly and intense way he'd said, *I definitely want to know you better* made my insides flare into a frenzy of wanting that *wanted* him to know me better.

My immediate thought was, *Okay, let's do that. Let's just do whatever you want, just say everything using that voice, mmm-kay?*

He continued, "We'll have dates."

Because my mind was distracted, I didn't understand his meaning, therefore I said, "I don't like dates. They're too sugary and stick to my teeth."

His somber and fierce façade cracked, a small smile tugging at the side of his mouth. He leaned closer, resting his hand on the closet behind me, his face just inches from mine.

His truly magnificent eyes were bright with amusement and something else as they scanned my face. His truly magnificent lips formed a mesmerizing curve. His truly magnificent body was scant inches from mine, but touched me nowhere.

"Fine." His voice was quiet and laced heavily with intimacy. "We won't have dates on our dates. We'll have tacos."

"I like tacos." I said this because I did like tacos, but I was also mesmerized by the voodoo of his closeness.

"Good. Tacos. Promise me." He stuck out his hand.

"I promise." I took his hand, shook it, released it, then frowned. "Wait, what?"

His eyes darted to my lips and he licked his own, drawing the top one into his mouth and biting it. I think I fainted a little, which I know isn't possible—one does not *faint a little*. But his sexy lip-lick-suck-bite thing may have caused a head rush.

I thought he was going to kiss me, because he was staring at my mouth in such a way that lead me to believe he was hungry…for my lips. He appeared to be struggling, warring with himself; I held my breath.

The five seconds he hesitated proved to be the undoing of the potential kiss, because we were unceremoniously interrupted by a shrieking Sam.

"What the hell is going on?"

CHAPTER 6
Chemical Kinetics

"**FOOLISH, ABSURD, BRAINLESS**, crazy, preposterous, ridiculous, silly, stupid…," I muttered.

"What are you doing?"

I slid my eyes to my right where surly faced Sam sat, flipping through her political science textbook pretending to study.

"You know what I'm doing," I whispered.

"It's the synonym game, isn't it?" she whispered back, turning just slightly in her seat and dipping her head close to mine. "What's the word?"

"Foolish."

"Oh. How many do you have so far?"

"Uh, seven I think, maybe eight."

"Well…you need more than that." Sam turned and glanced over her shoulder.

I had the window seat. She had the aisle seat. Therefore, the boys were behind her. I'd achieved maximum willpower and hadn't looked at Martin for the last forty-five minutes. If this were a video game, I'd be on level one thousand, about to face the final boss, and my palms would be sweating with the anticipation.

My palms were sweating now.

Not looking at Martin every thirteen seconds was torture. He was so…lookable. And *lookable* wasn't even a word. It should have been, because he was definitely it. Easy-on-the-eyes was the closest phrase I could come up with that would be synonymous with the non-word *lookable*. Maybe mesmerizing?

Mesmerizing, hypnotic, irresistible, alluring, seductive… Hmm…

"Did you know that deductive and seductive are only one letter away from being the same word?" I asked.

Sam turned back to me and gave me a slight stink eye. "And conducive is conductive, but without a T."

"Huh." I nodded. That was interesting. I wondered how many –ductive words I could identify.

Sam continued on a whisper, "Are you ready to talk about it yet?"

"Talk about what?" I removed my eyes from her and stared at the vacant seat in front of mine. Since we were on Martin's dad's private plane, we had tons of space. Two seats were on each side of the aisle, and the plane had six rows with an open seating area in the back that included a bar, couches, and a big screen TV. In the front cabin, every other row faced backward which resulted in four seats facing each other.

When we boarded the plane, Sam insisted she and I needed all four of our seats and that neither Martin nor any of his boy-entourage were allowed to sit across from us. Since finding Martin hovering over me earlier in our dorm room, with clear intent-to-kiss posturing, Sam had been doing a lot of insisting.

Sam leveled me with a narrowed glare. "Don't play dumb, Kaitlyn Parker. Why are we on this plane?"

I folded my arms on my knees and buried my head in my arms.

I felt her tugging on my hair, not hard, just trying to get me to sit up. I didn't. A moment later she was leaning over me, whispering in my ear, "When I walked in on you this morning you were about to do something *imprudent*. Is that one on your list of synonyms for foolish?"

"No. I'll add it to the list." My response was muffled because I was hiding.

"Parker, why are we on this plane?"

I stared at the fabric of the jeans covering my legs within the dim cavern created by my head, arms, and hair. Blowing out a long, measured breath, I sat up slowly, straightening until my back was resting against the seat cushion again and my eyes were level with surly faced Sam.

I stared at her. She stared back, expectant.

"I promised him," I said.

Her eyebrows bounced up then down. "You promised him? That's it, that's why we're here? You promised?"

I nodded. "Yes. I promised him. I promised him last night and I promised him this morning and then you walked in and you freaked out and then he freaked out and then I thought about hiding in the closet, but I don't own any spiky heels, so I just agreed. Okay? I just agreed so the freak outs and the name calling would cease and desist."

Sam's eyes were half-lidded and her continued surly expression told me she was not impressed with my answer.

But it was the truth…kind of.

When Sam walked in, she'd pitched a fit and started yelling at Martin. Really, she overreacted because she loves me. She was pretty nasty to

Martin, called him some unpleasant names I won't repeat, but I will say they are synonyms for whoreson.

Then Martin, who has no problem yelling at females, males, turtles, grass, and furniture, yelled back. Really, he was defending himself from her overprotectiveness and nasty name-calling. To his credit, he didn't call her any names. Mostly he just told her to back off and to *"mind her own goddamn business."*

I stepped in and tried to calm them both down. In doing so, I reassured Martin that I would be going with him—because I did promise him more than once—but only if Sam could go too. Eventually he overcame the shock of my request and agreed. Once he confirmed our destination would have a tennis court, Sam agreed.

Then he did something weird.

He gathered me up in his arms like I belonged there, gave me a swift, closed-mouth kiss, and said he'd wait for me in the hall. Then he left the room and stepped out of the suite area and promptly waited…in the hall…for me…for a full hour.

I felt like Scarlett O'Hara after she was kissed by Rhett Butler, confused and anxious and swoony and wanting it to happen again.

Sam and I had a brief argument after that, and by some miracle she agreed to come with me. Honestly, I don't think she felt like she had a choice since I stubbornly insisted I was going, and she lacked the time necessary to argue me out of it.

However, all the arguing and promising and name-calling aside, a large part of me was strangely excited about the trip. I was nineteen years old and the dodgiest thing I'd ever done was drink peach schnapps and drunk dial my ex last summer. I'd never thrown caution to the wind before. I'd never done anything this nutty and spontaneous. It was equal parts thrilling, terrifying, and confusing.

So…here we were. On the plane, with Martin, his handsome friend Eric from the fraternity party, and seven other dudes, most of whom looked like they'd stepped out of an Abercrombie and Fitch photo-shoot; except they had clothes on, unfortunately. Sam and I were the only females if you didn't count the two flight attendants.

We'd been briefly introduced to the boys upon entering the plane. Martin had referred to a few of them by a number first, then by first name.

Interestingly, they didn't seem to be surprised by our presence. I was also pretty sure they were checking me out, but not in the, *I might hit that* checking me out. More like a, *Are you a Yoko Ono?* checking me out.

As I shook everyone's hand I was surprised to see that one of the seven guys was Ben, the cuss monster from my time spent in the science cabinet. I couldn't fathom why Martin would have him come along, especially given the fact he'd tried to drug then extort Martin the night before.

Maybe they'd man-hugged it out.

Boys were just weird.

I made a mental note to tell Martin the entire conversation between Ben and the unknown female, because Ben had basically admitted to drugging girls. And there was really only one reason he could be drugging girls. He was Ben the rapist as far as I was concerned and I wanted nothing to do with him.

Sam and I took a seat in the front of the plane after introductions and left the males to their bonding.

I felt the mounting pressure of Sam's glare; she pressed her lips together in my general direction, looking displeased and surly.

"I can't believe we did this, I can't believe I let you talk me into this. How did that happen? How did we get here? And now we're going to some private beach in the middle of the Caribbean? This is crazy."

"It is kind of crazy." I shrugged, feeling shell shocked by the fact I was on this plane and all the circumstances leading up to this moment. Less than twenty-four hours ago I'd kissed Martin Sandeke—or rather, he'd kissed me. And then it happened again…and again. He'd placed his hands on my body like he had a right to do so, and I let him.

My skin still remembered his touch. Just thinking about his hands on me made my breasts feel tight and heavy, and my neck, back, and arms break out in goosebumps. I was warm all over and felt a little drunk with excitement and fear.

"But," I started, stopped, gave my head a quick shake, then began again, "but…it's okay. We're okay. We're together. If we get there and we don't want to stay we can leave."

"And go where? Do what? Swim to Jamaica?"

I shook my head, fighting back the swelling tide of Martin-inspired lust.

"No. I sent George, my mother's PA, a message. George knows the flight information, where we are. Worst case scenario, I call him and he arranges for us to leave. We're good."

Sam looked at me for several soundless seconds, then blurted, "You told your mother?"

"Of course. Well, technically I told her personal assistant, George. As the daughter of a senator I have to inform her any time I leave the country."

"You don't think she's going to freak out?"

"No. Why would she? I'm using the buddy system. She knows where I am, and with whom, and for how long, and why."

Although, I was still a bit uncertain as to why...

"You ladies need any drinks?"

Both Sam and I glanced up to find handsome Eric hovering in the aisle, poised at the precipice to our secluded island of four seats. Sam stared at him, like she was confused by his presence.

"What?" she asked.

"Drinks. Do you need any...drinks?"

"No. No drinks." She crossed her arms and tilted her head to the side, her eyes narrowing as though she were inspecting him. "You're shorter than I remembered."

He returned her eye squint and raised her a smirk. "Maybe you're suffering from altitude sickness. You should probably get up and walk around, stretch your legs."

More squint staring ensued and now they were both smirking.

At length, Sam nodded and said, "I could stretch my legs."

I eyeballed her as she quickly unbuckled her seatbelt and stood, all the while her gaze affixed to handsome Eric. His smirk became a grin when she stepped into the aisle and his eyes visibly brightened when she moved a tad closer to him.

"Let me give you a tour of the plane," he offered helpfully like a boy scout. "You can lean on me if we experience any turbulence."

"Sure thing," she drawled, sounding surly and amused at the same time. "Lead the way, shorty."

Eric rubbed the back of his neck and breathed a laugh as the two of them walked off together to the front of the plane. I craned my neck and watched them depart with borderline rapt fascination.

When Sam laughed at something Eric said I could watch no longer without labeling myself a creeper. So I relaxed—as much as I could relax—back in my seat and stared at my hands.

"Parker."

I jumped at the sound of my name coming from Martin's lips and turned to face him. I also, for reasons known only to my subconscious, balled my hands into fists and lifted them between us, like I was prepared for a fist fight or a boxing match.

He studied my defensive posturing and smirked, taking the seat Sam had vacated without asking permission. Meanwhile I glared at him, my mental wall up and prepped, though my hands fell back to my lap. I had to do this because…super-hot boy alert level ten thousand.

"Sandeke," I said. I knew I sounded ridiculous, like I was greeting a sworn enemy, but I had to be on guard.

His gaze skated over my face then flickered to my hands, still fists on my lap. Then he gave my hands a smile. Apparently they amused him.

"Are you going to hit me?"

"I don't know," I answered honestly. "It depends on if you take your pants off again."

"You'll hit me if I take my pants off?"

"Yeah…I might give you a junk punch."

He laughed, very loudly and very suddenly, and with the complete abandon that comes from being surprised. But his laugh was a radioactive seduction and had a half-life of infinity. I wanted him to stop laughing never. It made his eyes crinkle and his mouth curve in a sinful smile, showcasing his excellent dental hygiene regimen.

He also looked so different. He usually wore an expression of perpetual unimpressed boredom. Perpetual unimpressed boredom was a good look for him, a very good look. As were all the other expressions I'd seen, like distrust, mischievous amusement, thunderous anger, unveiled interest, etc.

But laughter…he almost looked happy. Happiness on Martin was a revelation of beauty and physical perfection married to excellent and infectious good-mood vibes. I let my fists drop. Less than a minute into our first interaction on this trip and my carefully constructed defenses had been virtually blown to bits.

I might as well wave the white panties of surrender.

"Oh, well. Barnacles," I said to nothing and no one.

His laugh gradually receded and his eyes flickered over me. "No more fists."

"Nope. There's no use." I'm sure I sounded despondent.

"So you think I could take you in a fist fight?"

"I think you could take me whenever." I shrugged. "If you wanted to, and I really only have myself to blame."

Martin narrowed his eyes, and they sharpened, surveying me. "You don't look happy about this."

"I'm not."

"Why not?"

I stared at him for a beat then freely admitted the truth. "Here is the problem, Martin. I feel like I like you."

The sharpness in his gaze softened and his mouth curved into a lazy, satisfied smile. "That doesn't sound like a problem to me."

"But it is," I pressed. "Because the feeling originates entirely in my pants."

Martin choked a shocked laugh, and leaned away from me.

I rushed to continue. "Hence the problem, you see? I know you as my lab partner who won't help me tabulate findings. And I also know you as a bit of a—and pardon the expression—as a bit of a manwhore who is not nice to the girls he sleeps with and who gets into fist fights, and who is somewhat bitter and jaded despite having the world at his fingertips."

Martin clenched his jaw. His eyelids drooped into unhappy slits and he flinched just slightly. His long fingers tightened on his legs.

I ignored the outward signs of irritation, wanting to make him see reason. "We have nothing in common. You're in a fraternity, go to parties *on purpose*, own a yacht, and are the king of the universe." I pressed both of my hands to my chest. "And I'm an unapologetic nerd who thinks it's fun to spend Saturday nights playing my guitar and writing music. I like arguing about Doctor Who episodes, and whether Samwise Gamgee or Frodo Baggins was ultimately responsible for the destruction of the ring. I play video games. I limit myself to three cookies, but then always cheat and have seven. Meanwhile you look like you've never had a cookie in your life. I'm a virgin and you're only the second boy I've kissed... We just don't fit." I said this last part quietly, gently, hoping he'd see reason.

Martin's face was devoid of expression, but his gaze moved from the tip of my chin to the top of my forehead, then back to my eyes.

He was smiling...sorta. But it resembled a grimace more than a smile. I watched his chest expand with a deep breath before he said, "You don't even know me, how can you say we don't fit? That's not right, Kaitlyn."

"I—"

"The way you describe me makes me sound like an entitled asshole."

It was my turn to flinch, lean away. My cheeks heated and stung as though they'd been slapped. I gaped at him and his fierce blue eyes for a long stretch. When he said nothing more, just glared at me, I ducked my head and studied the armrest between us.

"I. I. I...you're right," I admitted on a sigh. "I don't know you, not really. And you're right that my conclusion we don't fit is based on my observations and assumptions, which are clearly limited to empirical data sources."

"I'm not suggesting marriage, Parker. I just…" He paused, though I felt his gaze on me and it felt heavy. "Look at me."

I braced myself, then lifted my chin to meet his eyes. I expected to find a glower or a scowl. Instead I found his stare to be oddly earnest and searching.

"I'd just like a chance to know you."

"But why?" I blurted, feeling offended on behalf of everything that was perfect and gifted and beautiful about him. "Why me?"

"Because you're not intimidated by me."

"Well, that's wrong. I am. You scare me."

"No, I don't."

"You kind of do."

"No, I don't. That feeling of fear and excitement? *That* originates in your pants. It isn't about who I am, it's about what I look like. I feel that for you too."

My brain stumbled to grasp his meaning. I lifted an eyebrow, pursed my lips, and considered this statement.

He continued before I was finished considering. "You don't care about my family."

"I care about your family as human beings, but I don't know your family," I said defensively. "I'm sure if I knew them I'd care about them."

"Exactly. That's exactly right, except you wouldn't. If you knew my family you wouldn't care about them, because you're smart." The cloudy frustration in his eyes began to dissipate and he looked like my answer pleased him.

"That's true. I am smart. But you are also smart, maybe smarter."

"And you're funny."

"You should know that most of the time the funny is not on purpose."

"And honest."

"That's not always a good thing."

"And fucking gorgeous—"

I paired a huff with dismissive snort-laugh. But then my expression sobered when I saw Martin was serious.

I swallowed with difficulty then cleared my throat. I couldn't quite bear the weight and intensity of his stare, so I glanced down again at the arm rest. I'd learned from my mother that when someone gives you a subjective compliment—meaning one that can't be disproven and is based on opinion—but that you find to be completely false, rather than argue, it's much better to just say *thank you,* or *I appreciate that* and strive to be that compliment.

Fools fight compliments, she'd said, and sometimes other people see you better than you can see yourself.

So I quietly said, "Thank you," to the armrest.

"You're welcome."

I tucked my hair behind my ears and wrestled to find the courage to look at him again. I made it as far as his neck.

"Are you going to give me a chance? Yes or no?" The way he spoke, with such severe directness, was off-putting and strangely alluring. He was entitled, or at least he came across that way, because all of his words were demands.

It also made me want to refuse what he was demanding.

"I'm…going to be open to the possibility of giving you a chance." When I finished, my eyes flickered to his. I discovered him watching me with a narrowed stare and a little smirk. He was really too freaking good-looking, it was the un-fairest of the unfair.

"Is that the best you can do?" he challenged, leaning forward.

"No. But how you speak to me sometimes makes me want to withhold what you want."

His eyes flashed and felt at once more penetrating. "How do I speak to you?"

"Like I owe you something, like you're entitled."

"That's just confidence. I'm not going to be self-conscious for any reason, and I'm not going to fake it to make you feel better."

His response was jarring, irritating, and oddly thrilling, so I volleyed back, "Maybe you should be. Maybe your confidence isn't based on reality. Maybe you're not infallible. Maybe you're not always going to get what you want."

He watched me as several long moments passed, his gaze growing increasingly inscrutable but somehow hotter. I held his eyes, maybe finding the courage because my feathers were ruffled.

"Okay," he finally said. "I'll try not to demand things of you…as often."

"Good." I felt strangely disappointed at this news, which made no sense. Did I enjoy it when he spoke to me like I was an underling assigned to obey his every whim? When I reflected on it I realized that maybe I did, because I certainly enjoyed rebelling, defying, and challenging his demands...

We stared at each other. I tried to look at him and his beautiful face with as much objectivity as possible. Who was this person? Who was Martin Sandeke really?

"Tell me something, Martin."

"What do you want to know, Parker?" Again my question seemed to please him, his features softening and settling into amused—dare I say enthusiastic?—curiosity.

"What do you think about the Samwise Gamgee versus Frodo Baggins debate?"

His smile flattened just a little and for the first time since he sat down, Martin glanced away. He cleared his throat, picked at a spot on his jeans, then returned his gaze to mine. "I have no idea what you're talking about."

This admission made me smile, then laugh belatedly because he looked uncomfortable. Martin Sandeke looked uncomfortable and it was because he was out of his depth, specifically, he was out of his nerd depth, and being out of his depth looked adorable on Martin.

"Well, let me enlighten you," I said with a bit of show-womanship, waving my hand through the air. I then turned toward him completely. I didn't try to dim my bright smile. "There is this book, it is called Lord of the Rings and it was written by a linguist w-a-a-a-y back in the twentieth century."

"I've heard of the Lord of the Rings." His lips twitched but his tone was deadpan. I took this as a good sign.

"Ah, good. Have you seen the movies?"

"No."

"But you've heard of the twentieth century? It came right after the nineteenth century."

He didn't respond, but his closed-mouth smile grew. His fathomless blue eyes were at half-mast, aquamarine, and glittering like the ocean at sunset.

"I'll take that as a yes. Anyway, in this book there are different kinds of races—elves, orcs, humans, blah, blah, blah, dwarves—but also, there is this race of beings called hobbits. They are little, short of stature, and usually considered insignificant. They have furry feet and they like to smoke pipes and live quietly. In fact, they live very quietly. But they have several breakfasts daily, so...awesome. Anyway..."

Martin cocked his head to the side as though studying me. I didn't know if he were actually listening or not, but his eyes were intent and focused, like I was providing him with a super important riddle he would have to solve at some point. It gave me fluttery butterflies in my stomach to have his complete attention like this. It also reminded me how much that area in my pants liked him.

"Anyway," I repeated, trying to focus. "The whole point of the book is to destroy this ring, because the ring is very, very bad."

"Why is it bad?"

"You'll have to read the book, and don't interrupt me. It's distracting enough looking at you. You've already derailed my brain train with your face several times."

Martin's mouth pressed together more firmly and I got the impression he was trying not to laugh.

"Back to the story, ultimately—spoiler alert—the ring is destroyed by two of these hobbits."

Both of his eyebrows jumped in surprise. "How did they do that? You said they're insignificant."

"Like I said, you'll have to read the book for the specifics, but the crux of my question has to do with the two hobbits who destroy the ring— Frodo and Samwise. Frodo bears the ring. He carries it. But," I lifted a finger in the air for emphasis, "Samwise is his trusted servant, and he is very trustworthy. He supports Frodo, he keeps Frodo from giving up. He even bears the ring for a short time. Plus there's this bit at the very end that…well, you'll have to read the book. So, the question is—who deserves the credit for the destruction of the ring? Who was stronger? Frodo or Samwise? The master or the servant?"

Martin frowned at me; I took it as a good sign because it meant he was actually considering the question. But then his frown started to worry me because his eyes grew cagey and guarded.

After a few minutes he asked, "Is this a test?"

I lifted an eyebrow at him and his tone. He sounded a little angry.

"What do you mean?"

"Just what I said, is this a test? If I answer incorrectly are you still going to give us a chance?"

Yep. Definitely angry.

It was my turn to frown. "Martin, it's a conversation. We're just having a conversation. This isn't a test. You said, and I agree, that I don't know you very well. This is my attempt to get to know you better."

"But if I answer in a way you don't like, what happens?"

I stared at him, my features likely showing my disorientation at his odd question. "Um," my eyes flickered to the side, because I was trying not to look at him like he was a crackhead, "nothing? I mean, we talk about it, each reviewing our own opinions and providing support for what we believe. But then, we can always agree to disagree at some point."

"Then after that?"

"I guess we could end it with a high five to show that there are no hard feelings...?"

His eyes narrowed at me, and he was looking at me like I was the puzzle; when he spoke next it was with an air of distraction. "That sounds nice."

I frowned, considering him, considering his reaction to a simple question. It made me wonder whether or not Martin Sandeke had ever had a conversation before, one where he was allowed to disagree without being made fun of or punished for his thoughts, where it wasn't a test.

I was about to ask him something along these lines when the pilot's voice came over the intercom. He announced we were approaching the airport, and should buckle in for our final descent. Meanwhile, I blinked at Martin and a dawning and disturbing realization took root.

Martin Sandeke wasn't used to freely voicing his thoughts and feelings...nor was he used to kindness.

CHAPTER 7
Molecular Geometry and Bonding Theories

MUCH OF SAM'S surly mood dissipated after her fifteen-minute plane tour courtesy of the handsome Eric. I was both pleased and distressed by this turn of events. Since Sam's attention was redirected—or best case scenario, it was split between me and Eric—this meant she wasn't quite as focused on her role as my spring break chastity belt.

A very luxurious stretch limo picked us up. Inside the car, I sat next to one of the seven other guys; his name was Ray, and his parents had immigrated from Mumbai, India, when he was two. He was a biochemistry major, and he was five seat.

"Five seat?" I asked, my head titling to the side. "What do you mean five seat?"

Two more of the boys entered the limo, sitting on the bench across from Sam and Eric.

"Five seat in the crew boat. I'm a starboard," Ray explained, flashing me a big smile when he saw I didn't quite understand what he meant. "We're all on the crew team together, in the same boat. I'm five seat, Martin is eight seat. He's the stroke at the stern, the back of the boat." Ray lifted his chin toward one of the other guys. "That's our coxswain, Lee."

I gave Lee a friendly smile. "What's a cocks-twin?"

Lee chuckled and shook his head. "It's pronounced cox-wain, not cocks-twin. Basically, I steer the boat and keep these guys from being lazy assholes."

"Lee also gets to stare into Stroke's dreamy blue eyes all day," Ray added with a grin. "You should probably be jealous."

I shrugged my shoulders convulsively, feeling acutely weird and self-conscious. "What…I…we…it's…I mean…what are you talking about?" I sputtered as my hands did weird things, jerky movements in the air in front of me. "I'm not jealous. Why would I be jealous? I don't even know the guy."

Ray, Lee, Eric, and another of the guys whose name was Herc—who had obscenely large leg muscles—all lifted their eyebrows at me in unison.

"You're his girl, right?" Lee glanced at his teammates as though to confirm his statement.

"That's right," Herc confirmed, his tone sure and steady.

I felt Sam tug at my shirt but I ignored her. At that moment three of the other guys entered the car; I'd recognized two of them as the pair of brown-eyed frat boys who'd been with Eric at the party the night before. The taller of the two, Griffin, had been handsy with me at the frat house. The other one, Will, had hit Griffin on the back of the head as they'd walked away.

The other guy's name was Tambor. He had blond hair, darker than Ben's, longish with pale highlights likely caused by the sun. He had deep brown eyes and an exceedingly stoic face. He and Herc were the shortest and the stockiest of the boys at an approximate and *measly* six foot one.

"So…where does everyone else sit? In the boat, I mean," I asked weakly, wanting to change the subject.

"As you know, Martin is stroke, which is eight seat." Ray then pointed to Eric. "Eric is a starboard, seven seat. Ben," he paused and looked around the inside of the vehicle. Ben and Martin were the only two not in the car yet. "Well, Ben who isn't here is port, seat six. We've already established that I'm starboard five seat. Griffin is behind me, port four seat. Then Will, starboard three seat. Tambor, port second seat. Last but not least is Herc. He's the bow, first seat, in the front of the boat."

"All the even seats are port seats, and the odds are starboard?"

Ray nodded. "That's right. Port and starboard have to do with the sides of the boat. My oar is rigged on the starboard side; whereas Martin's, Ben's, Griffin's, and Tambor's are rigged on the port side."

I nodded, picturing a crew boat I'd seen on TV during the summer Olympics. Now, considering how Martin had originally introduced everyone on the plane—referring to each of them as a number first before their names—this made a lot more sense. Their nicknames were their seat assignments, with Martin called Stroke and Herc called Bow.

Martin entered the limo just as Ray finished explaining port and starboard. I noted that a hush fell over the occupants; everyone seemed to sit a little straighter, the guys looking to him as though called to attention.

His did a sweep of the interior as Ben entered through the other door and shut it. Martin's gaze paused on me, which sent heat to my cheeks and set off a buzzing in my stomach. Eventually he glared at Ray and his eyes narrowed by an infinitesimal margin.

Ray's answering smile looked cautious. "I'll just move over this way…" Ray scooched away from me, leaving plenty of room for someone to fill the void.

Martin followed Ray's movements with his eyes, stared at him for a beat, then ducked and crossed to the now vacant seat next to mine. Martin then cast a dark glare around the limo, almost like he was warning them off his Chinese takeout leftovers.

Meanwhile I pressed my lips into an unhappy line. I was unimpressed with the dynamic of unspoken, but clearly understood, possessiveness.

Even if I were Martin's girl—which I wasn't—there was nothing amiss with me sitting next to Martin's friend. I felt abruptly as though I'd just been peed on.

I didn't want to be peed on.

***

THE REST OF the journey was eventfully uneventful. The limo's journey to the marina was fifteen minutes. At the marina, men appeared—as though from nowhere—and loaded our belongings onto a boat. Then the men disappeared. The boat journeyed forty-five minutes to another, much smaller marina situated on a spec of an island.

At least it looked like a spec at first. Upon closer inspection, I estimated it was about four miles long and at least a mile wide. The lush tropical forests were dotted with obscenely massive luxury homes—some directly on the beach, some higher up on hilly cliffs. I counted seven as we circled to the dock.

We then loaded into five all-terrain golf cart-like vehicles, two per vehicle. I traveled with Martin, Sam traveled with Eric. We traversed a well-maintained dirt road to where I surmised we'd be staying for the next week.

I didn't bring up Martin's inappropriate behavior; this was for several reasons. First, drama repelled me. I didn't want to start a conversation on the topic when others could overhear. Therefore I just put up with his hovering and the way he would stare down the other guys when they'd enter my radius.

Second, I didn't know how to start the dialogue. What if I was imagining things? What if I was being overly sensitive? What if this was what normal relationships were like? If we'd actually been dating, I think I might have been able to navigate through the conversation, but we weren't.

"Why are you so quiet?"

I'd been wrapped up in my thoughts and started a little at his bluntly spoken question.

"Uh." I glanced at him. He was splitting his attention between me and the road. "Because I'm thinking about something."

"What are you thinking about?" he asked. As usual it sounded like a demand.

I tried not to read too much into the tone of his voice; maybe Martin didn't know how to ask nicely, another thing I didn't like very much about him.

"I guess because I don't have much experience with boys, so I'm trying to figure something out."

"What is it? Maybe I can help." He nudged me with his elbow.

I shook my head, not ready to talk about it yet. "I'm not ready to discuss it. I need some time with my thoughts."

His intelligent eyes flicked over me, his expression growing distant and impassive. At length he shrugged, grim-faced, and gave his attention wholly to the road. We didn't speak again until we arrived at the house.

And by house I mean not a house at all. It was a behemoth.

Once inside I marveled at the opulence. The giant foyer steps were a blue marble, resembling turquoise, with inlay brass. A grandiose and gracefully curving staircase dominated the left side of the entrance, while a three-story single-paned window provided natural light and a breathtaking view of the ocean beyond. In the center of the space was a wide fountain with a surprisingly tasteful sculpture of a mermaid blowing water out of a conch shell.

Everything was overly detailed. The wooden carvings on the staircase had carvings. The brass inlay danced beautiful oceanic patterns over the floor. Glorious mosaics of blue and copper decorated the fountain.

It was all too much. It didn't feel like a house, it felt like the lobby for a huge, swanky hotel.

When I realized I was gaping, I snapped my mouth shut and glanced at Martin to see if he'd caught my oddball display of horrified amazement. He had. He was glaring at me. Again.

I was starting to wonder if I'd imagined his laugh back on the plane and if he were capable of anything other than heavily-lidded severe stares. Don't get me wrong, he still looked heavenly even when he was administering heavily-lidded severe stares, but that was only if one wasn't the recipient of said stare.

I was on the receiving end now, his focus on me, and he looked unhappy.

Therefore I gave him a buggy-eyed nose scrunch, followed by a full-on weird face—tongue out, eyes crossed, teeth bared like a rabbit—and then refocused on his features to see if it had made any effect.

It had. Now he was looking at *me* like I was a crackhead.

"Parker, what are you doing?"

"Making a funny face in an effort to make you stop staring at me like I murdered your beloved goldfish. What are *you* doing?"

I was pleased to see his eyes lighten with something like confused wonder, but before he could speak, the sound of voices entering the house pulled my attention back to the massive doors. I opened my mouth to announce where we were, but the words never came because Martin put his hand over my mouth—abruptly but gently—bringing my attention back to him.

He put a finger to his lips in the universal symbol for *shhh* then fit his hand in mine and pulled me around the fountain, down a hall, beyond the massive, three-story window overlooking the sea, through a large living room with a giant fireplace—fireplace? On a tropical Island? Rich people were crazy—and into a massive bedroom suite done all in sterile whites and shades of blue and sea-green.

He shut the solid teak door then backed me up against it, staring down at me, holding me in place with his eyes and the promise they held. My heart thudded painfully in my chest and I was drowning in his intense focus.

I opened my mouth again to say something, anything really, but it was lost because he was kissing me. The hot, urgent slickness of his tongue robbing me of my breath, his solid body against mine warming me beyond the humid stickiness of the tropics, permeating to my center.

We kissed and kissed then kissed some more. It wasn't until he tore his mouth from mine that I realized I was holding fistfuls of his hair and was on my tiptoes.

His forehead met mine and he growled, a low sound laced with frustration, before he said, "You are too fucking cute."

"You too."

He exhaled a disbelieving breath, and swallowed. "I'm cute?"

"As a button."

He chuckled, stealing another kiss. "I wish we were here alone. I wish…God, I just want you to myself."

A prickle of unease made the short hairs of my neck stand at attention. On one hand, it was a lovely thing for him to say. On the other hand, he'd just figuratively urinated a circle around me in his blatant display of caveman possessiveness. Maybe I was overreacting, but I had no baseline for comparison. This was all very, very new territory for me.

I needed time to think, away from his lips *and* mesmerizing looks.

Luckily, I was pretty certain this place had some nice closets.

***

"HE'S THE ALPHA male." Sam said this from my bed where she lay with her arms and legs spread out. I was next to her, my arms and legs also spread.

We weren't touching. The bed should have had its own zip code.

After my lovely kisses with Martin, he informed me that the gargantuan and beautiful suite was mine. The voices of our co-travelers grew louder, closer, and so he told me to stay put. He explained people would be bringing in my luggage as well as food. Then he left.

People did arrive with my bags. Again, random people seemed to appear out of thin air—an older man in a suit directed a younger man where to place my things. Then a woman about ten years older than me showed up with a tray of decadent food, sparkling mineral water, and asked if she could draw me a bath or arrange for a massage.

I politely refused both, but insisted on introducing myself to these apparitions. Ultimately I had to press them for names because at first they offered me only titles.

The older man was the staff director - Mr. Thompson.

The younger man was one of the groundskeepers - Peter.

The woman was the house manager - Mrs. Greenstone.

I tried to modulate my tone to offhanded and nonchalant as I asked how many other staff members were present at the house. After Mr. Thompson listed the cook, cook's aide, three other groundskeepers, and two maids, I stopped counting. The house staff outnumbered the guests.

Sam found me just as Mr. Thompson was taking his leave.

That's right, taking his leave…like some grand butler from regency England. I'd entered the bizzaro world of the obscenely rich where baths were drawn and leave was taken.

Now Sam and I were munching on the tray of food and staring at the vaulted ceiling. An immense, beautiful skylight showed me the late afternoon sky was a cloudless blue.

Sam continued voicing her theory while munching on grapes. "You know, like a pack of wolves. He's their alpha."

I grimaced and twisted my lips to the side to hide my expression, not that she was looking at me.

"That's silly," I said.

"No, it's totally not. They all…well…they all basically worship him, I think. Eric said that eight seat, Martin's position, is arguably the most important seat in the boat. He sets the rhythm for the rest of the boat, pushes them. Even Lee, who *freaking* steers the boat, follows his lead. They do what are called 'power tens' during practices and races. It's where they all row as hard as they can for ten strokes—well, Martin decides when and for how long. He's only a sophomore and he has the most coveted spot on the team, *and* he's team captain. The rest of the guys are juniors and seniors."

"Maybe it's because he's from such a fancy family," I said flippantly, because Sam was starting to make it sound like this stuff mattered. Granted, she was a competitive athlete, therefore I could forgive some of her wide-eyed expression and excitement in her voice.

Whereas I'd never understood sports and team dynamics. I'd tried playing soccer once; everyone was so serious about it. I kept thinking how silly it was to run around a grassy field, kick a ball into a net, and think of it as an accomplishment.

Finishing War and Peace, now that was an accomplishment.

"No, I asked Eric how Martin got his seat," Sam said, turning to face me, her elbow and hand propping up her head. "He said Martin has the best erg time—it has to do with the rowing machine they use, the ergometer or whatever it's called—and that he has the best form *by far*. Honestly, it's like Eric is brainwashed or has a crush on him or something. They talk about him like he invented the sport."

I shrugged, but my mind was caught on the "pack of wolves" metaphor, Martin as an alpha to a pack of hard-bodied rowers. It might explain why every time he spoke it sounded like a demand. As well, it explained the pack mentality in the limo and on the boat. He was younger than they were. I wondered if all his dazzling wealth had anything to do with why he was able to command their respect so completely.

I could feel Sam's eyes on me. I kept my attention focused on the sky.

After a while she said, "You are beautiful, you know."

My eyes jumped to hers and I automatically frowned, her earnestly spoken words catching me off guard.

"What you talkin' 'bout, Willis?"

She gave me a little smile then pushed on my shoulder. "You, being beautiful. You are beautiful. You don't focus on your looks or even seem to care about them, but you're really quite spectacular to look at."

I turned my head completely toward her and folded my hands on my stomach. "And you think this is why Martin is suddenly whisking me and my foul-mouthed friend off to private beaches? Because he thinks I'm beautiful?"

"It's definitely part of it. The boy has eyes and urges."

"Ha. Yes, he does..."

"But that's not why, or that's not all of it."

"Then what is it? Why am I here?"

Sam was quiet for a minute, then asked, "Why do you think?"

I glanced over her shoulder, my eyes resting on the magnificent view behind her. The entire back wall of the suite was glass and overlooked the beach. The house was some feet above sea level. If I'd been standing I would see the white, sandy shore. But from this vantage point, all I saw was blue sky kissing the blue ocean at the horizon.

"I think," I started, deciding to speak my thoughts out loud as they occurred to me. I needed to talk this through with someone and I needed to get out of my own head because I couldn't get any further than, *This makes no sense!*

"I think he wants someone to be nice to him," I blurted.

I brought Sam back into focus, saw her surprised expression, but then something like contemplation gripped her features.

I continued. "I think he's tired of people judging him or making assumptions about who he is based on who his family is. I think he wants someone to be nice to him, like him, and show interest in who he is because he's Martin, just Martin, and not because of who is family is, how much money he has…or what he looks like."

"That sounds…well, actually, that sounds plausible."

"I wonder," I propped myself up on my elbow, facing Sam and mirroring her position on the bed, "maybe he really just wants a friend. I think I could do that for him."

Her eyes narrowed on me. "I don't think he wants you to be his friend."

"But that's what he needs," I said, wrinkling my nose. "I think he trusts me because I don't want anything from him. I think he just really desperately needs someone to talk to, someone who is on his side, and he's confusing trust with…lust."

Sam smiled her amusement, her eyes dancing over my face. "Or he's confusing lust with trust."

I rolled my eyes and fell back to the bed, again staring out through the skylight.

"But seriously," she started, paused, then took a deep breath, "he's kind of possessive of you, right? Like, how he stared down Ray in the limo. And I thought he was going to bite Griffin's arm when he touched you while we were on the boat. It seems especially strange since you two aren't even really together yet."

Yet… O.o

"It is weird. I'm glad you said something because I wondered if I was just overreacting. And it's all so fast."

"No, not really. You've been lab partners for almost two semesters. From what you told me about your conversation with him against the pool table last night, for him, I think this relationship—in some form—has been going on for months, not hours. I suspect he's been thinking about you far more than you realize."

I covered my face with my hands. "How do I survive this? How am I going to get through this week? He needs a friend and all I can think about is doing very bad things to his body."

"You're starved for physical intimacy. He's starved for emotional intimacy. Maybe you can help him *and* help yourself."

"I don't want to use him like that. I think his whole life people have been trying to use him."

"I'm not talking about sex, Katy. I still don't think you're ready for that. You have a big heart and it would definitely get in the way of a no-strings arrangement. I'm just saying, there's nothing wrong with fooling around a little with a guy you're attracted to. Maybe…," Sam reached for my hands and pulled them away from my face. She then lifted her eyebrows and gave me a pointed look. "Maybe you can help each other."

CHAPTER 8
Bond Polarity and Electronegativity

SAM SPENT THE night with me. Having her there helped. But despite the heavenly bed and the sound of the ocean in the background, I didn't sleep very well.

Sam and I hadn't joined the boys for dinner. Instead we opted to sit on the balcony overlooking the sea and study. This was my idea. I needed more time to think, to consider, to plan my next move with Martin. I was certain he needed a friend much, much more than he needed a girlfriend, now I just needed to convince him of this fact.

Mr. Thompson stopped by to check in and make sure everything was to our liking. I asked about having dinner in the suite and he said he'd pass the message along. One of the maids brought us dinner. Her name was Rosa and she reminded me of my paternal grandmother; her big smile was sweet and she promised us cookies if we ate all our vegetables.

She also brought me a note from Martin. In his scrawling, masculine, chaotic script it read:

Parker,

I'll be down at the beach tonight. Come find me.

-Martin

I was relieved he didn't come by or press the issue of me taking dinner in my room. I needed space and time and...basically all the known dimensions available to me, maybe even the assistance of invisible dark matter. I wasn't ready for a moonlight stroll on the beach with Martin yet. The sky had too many stars to be anything but fatalistically romantic.

After eating, Sam and I studied some more. I opted for the giant shower with seven heads—despite the fact the bathtub was the size of a small swimming pool—then worked on a term paper until midnight when we went to bed.

It was early when I woke, the sun just making an appearance and the light still soft and hazy. I pulled on my bathrobe and walked to the window, wanting to catch the purples and oranges painting the sky before it surrendered to blue.

I got my wish and then some. The view was epically spectacular. The white sandy beach and calm water called to me in a way I'd never experienced. Suddenly, I wanted to go swimming. Right that minute. I needed to leave the manufactured luxury of the big house. The genuine beauty of nature called to me.

I quickly changed in the bathroom, careful to lather myself in super high SPF, and grabbed two oversized beach towels.

I also packed a canvas bag with a leftover bottle of water from the night before, my current book, a big hat, sunglasses, and other beach essentials. I exited out the balcony door and picked my way down the path to the beach. The path consisted of ten stone steps and a hundred feet of the finest, softest sand I'd ever touched.

Once there I dropped my belongings, discarded my T-shirt, cotton shorts, and flip flops, and walked into the salt water. The water was crystal clear, the temperature cool and refreshing, and was nearly as calm as a lake. It felt like heaven.

For at least an hour I floated, swam, searched for shells, and just generally enjoyed the alone time with my thoughts in this beautiful place. When my fingers became prunes, I reluctantly abandoned the water for the shore.

I arranged one of the towels under the shade of a big palm tree and rolled the other towel into a pillow for my head. Then, I read my book, drying in the sea air, and lazing about like a lazy person. This was the kind of unscheduled relaxing I'd embraced since starting college.

I was maybe four pages into my novel when I heard the noise; it was a chant—faint then louder—of baritone voices. Lifting onto my elbows, I set my book to one side, holding my place with my thumb, and peered around for the origin.

Then I saw them. All nine of the boys—looking remarkably like men— out some distance from shore; far enough away I couldn't quite make out individual faces, but close enough I could plainly see they were all shirtless. And it ought to be noted that they should always be shirtless. In fact, they should be disallowed from wearing shirts...ever.

They were rowing, their boat flying over the water. I strained my ears and realized they were counting backward from ten.

I followed their progress, marveling at how they moved so quickly and with seemingly so little effort in perfect unison. I wondered what that must be like, being part of something so perfect, so harmonious. It was...well, it was beautiful.

The closest I'd ever come to something like that was playing my music, losing myself on the piano, or jamming with my Sunday night bandmates. But we weren't perfect. We were far from harmonious, however sometimes we'd have a good night where everything felt right and effortless, like we were flying on the music we'd created together.

Just as suddenly as the rowers appeared they were gone. The boat went around the edge of the cove and their chant grew fainter, farther away. I stared at the spot where they'd disappeared for a minute then reclined back on my towel, watching the horizon.

"Holy crap. That was something."

I turned my head slightly and found Sam standing on the beach, her hands on her hips, and her attention focused on the bend of the cove. She was wearing an itsy bitsy bikini that showed how hard she worked on her tennis game.

"Hey, you there. Good-looking female," I called to her. "Why are you up?"

"Because I bought this damn bikini last year and this is my first chance to wear it." She sauntered over to where I reclined and spread out her towel. Her spot was somewhat in the sun, but I doubted she minded the opportunity to tan. I didn't want to take the chance of blinding someone, so I liked my spot in the shade. With my paper-white complexion, the glare off my thighs would likely burn retinas.

She turned to me to say something else, but then the chanting became audible again. Sure enough, the boat came back into view. Eight muscled rowers sweeping the water with their oars, Lee at the stern facing Martin. Their arms and shoulders flexing, their stomachs and backs rippling. The movement of their bodies was as mesmerizing as it was arousing. This time they were close enough I could almost see their facial expressions, see the sweat rolling down their necks and chests.

From where I sat, they looked stern, focused, maybe a little bit in pain, but still beautiful. Heart-achingly beautiful. My mouth went completely dry.

Sam and I watched them for almost a full minute before they flew past and were once more out of sight.

Then, she fanned herself. "Yeah. I am totally going to have sex with Eric. That was hot."

I said nothing, because once again my dirty thoughts were at odds with what I knew was smart, with what I knew was right.

Martin needed a friend.

I would be that friend.

I would.

And my pants hated me for it.

***

THREE OF THE groundskeepers brought brunch down to the beach under the oversight of Mrs. Greenstone. And by brunch, I mean they transported what looked like the equivalent of a fancy outdoor restaurant down to the beach. A large buffet was spread out on a huge wooden serving table, and beautifully carved dining tables and chairs with deep cushions were set up on the edge of the water. A sideboard with china, crystal, linen napkins, towels, suntan lotion—and basically everything else one might want for the beach—was set out with practiced and aesthetically pleasing efficiency.

To top it all off, several large arrangements of tropical flowers were placed on the tables along with little packets of aloe set on ice to chill.

I glanced sideways at the opulence, feeling out of place with my modest, black two-piece that was three years old, my turquoise Walmart flip flops, and my gas station sunglasses.

To be honest, the excess repelled me in much the same way the size and luxuriousness of the house had repelled me when we first arrived. I wasn't against people being rich. Nor was I against people owning and enjoying nice things.

I guessed the problem was that everything was too big, too much, too shiny, too new, too sterile, too impersonal. I felt like all the real details that mattered—the smell of the ocean, the sensation of sand beneath feet, the soft sounds of the sea meeting the shore, the rustle of wind through the palms—were lost in the ostentatiousness of the house and its sprawling splendiferous shadow.

Where Sam and I had set our towels was a good two hundred feet from the fancy buffet and beneath the shade of a palm; however, the spot was clearly visible from the trail. We were both on our stomachs and reading when Herc, Ray, and Ben appeared from the house path.

Ray gave us a little wave and an amiable smile, Herc gave us a little wave that I imagined was friendly for him, and Ben gave us a leering look and no other acknowledgement. I silently wondered again why Martin had invited Ben as all evidence pointed to the fact he was an unsavory sort. The guys crossed to the impressive brunch spread.

No sooner had they made it to the tables did Eric and Griffin jog past. Eric skidded to a stop when he saw us and gave Sam a bright smile. Griffin lifted his chin and waved politely, then made a beeline for the food.

"I'll be right back." Eric held out his index finger to us in the universal symbol for *give me a minute*. "I'm starving."

"Take your time." Sam shrugged, and I saw she was doing her best to appear unaffected. "It's not like we're going anywhere."

"Yeah. Good." Eric's eyes moved over her body—not in a leering, *I'd-hit-that* kind of way, but rather in a *damn-you-must-work-out-and-I'm-impressed* kind of way—his eyebrows doing an adorable double jump of appreciation as he scanned her. Then he shook his head as though clearing it and slowly turned away. In fact, his steps were almost halting as he walked to the buffet yet turned back and glanced at Sam twice.

Sam, however, was looking at her book. But I could tell she wasn't reading. When he was out of earshot, she asked in a near whisper, "Did he look back?"

"Yes. Twice."

"Excellent."

I smirked and looked up at the guys. Unable to help herself, Sam lifted her eyes as well.

They hadn't bothered yet with shirts and were still clothed in spandex shorts that ended just above the knee. Really, they should have been naked. Their outfits left nothing to the imagination.

I quickly refocused attention on my book, my cheeks red from sudden exposure to male fineness, but Sam gaped for a few minutes longer.

"Thank you, Katy. Thank you for being Martin Sandeke's lab partner. Thank you for having no idea how amazing you are. Thank you for driving him wild with your clueless indifference. Just…thank you for this moment."

I rolled my eyes behind my sunglasses and flipped onto my back.

"You're welcome. Never say I didn't get you anything, especially since there are four more shirtless rowers on their way."

"I will die happy here, today, in this spot," she sighed.

"In your puddle of lust."

"Leave my puddle of lust alone. Get your own puddle."

A few moments passed in relative silence, relative because the sound of the boys' conversation drifted to us, though none of the words were decipherable. I was actually able to concentrate on my book for about ten minutes before we were interrupted.

"Hey, so what do you think so far?"

I turned my head and found Eric kneeling in the sand next to Sam's towel, splitting his attention between both of us. I rolled to my side then sat up, pulling my knees to my chest. Sam, however, continued to lounge on the ground.

"It's really nice," I said with feeling, because it was nice and he was being nice, and it's nice to be nice.

Then, because I wanted to say something more than just nice, I added, "The beach is exquisite. I've never seen this kind of sand."

Eric gave me a friendly smile. "Yeah, this is our second year. Last year Martin brought us down for spring break and I've been looking forward to it since we left. I love this place."

"I can see why," Sam said, "it's gorgeous."

Eric's gaze rested on her for a beat before he agreed, "Yeah, gorgeous…"

My eyes flickered between the two of them, obviously sharing a moment, and I tried not to make any sudden movements. I adverted my gaze to the cover of the book I'd discarded and realized I had no recollection of what I'd been reading.

Eric was the first to speak, and he did so with a charming grin. "So, Sam. Would you mind helping me put suntan lotion on my back? I'd like to go for a swim but I'm sure the stuff I put on earlier is mostly gone by now."

"Sure," she responded immediately, then hopped to her knees, grabbed her lotion, circled behind him as they both stood, and applied a generous amount of liquid SPF and UV protection to his torso.

He was facing me, so Sam was behind him. Therefore I was treated to her facial expressions while she touched his body. At one point she mouthed the words *Oh my God*, her eyes growing large. I had to roll my lips between my teeth to keep from laughing.

After the longest lotion lathering in the history of forever, Sam moved to step away but he caught her hand.

"Want to go swimming?"

She nodded, a big smile on her face. All her earlier attempts to keep it cool must have melted away…for some inexplicable reason.

Without a backward glance or a wave or an, *I'll see you later* in my direction, the two of them took off for the ocean. I watched them go feeling a mixture of excitement on Sam's behalf, and worry, also on Sam's behalf. She obviously liked him a lot. And I supposed he was likeable enough. But neither of us knew him very well.

"Hey. Kaitlyn, right?" someone said from behind me.

I turned toward the voice at my back and found Ben—the cuss monster, would-be drugger, self-admitted rapist, and blatant leerer—hovering at the edge of my towel. My stomach tightened with trepidation.

"Yes. That is correct. I am Kaitlyn," I said, not meaning to sound as robotic as I did but unable to help it. This guy wanted to hurt and extort Martin, and that alone was enough to make me dislike him with the heat of magma.

"Hey, so," his eyes moved over me again, where I was curled into a ball on my towel, "I need help getting this stuff on my back." He held up the bottle of suntan lotion Sam had just discarded.

"Okay…?" I peered at him, not understanding why he was telling me this.

We stared at each other for a beat. He was quite good-looking, very well built, very tall, and he made me exceedingly uneasy.

At length he huffed. "So, I need you to put the lotion on my back."

My frown deepened and I shook my head. "Um, no thanks."

"No thanks?"

"That is correct. No thanks."

His eyes darted between mine and he appeared to be confused. "You're not going to do it?"

"Correct. I'm not going to do it."

Ben's confused expression morphed into a sneer. "What's the big deal?"

I tightened my arms around my legs. "It's not a big deal. I don't touch people I don't know, it's one of my life rules." The nice thing about having life rules is that you can make up new ones on the spot when it's convenient. Not touching people I don't know hadn't been a life rule before this minute, but it was definitely on the list now.

"We've met."

"Yes, but I don't know you and I don't want to touch you."

He stared at me for five seconds, but it felt like an hour, his pale eyes growing mean and angry. Abruptly, he blurted, "Why are you being such a bitch about this? I just need some fucking help here and you're acting like a fucking bitch."

I flinched at the words—even his expletives were redundant and unimaginative—and then pulled my gaze from his, opting to stare at the beach and wishing I'd forced myself on Sam and Eric. They were in the water, floating, talking, and probably not cussing at each other.

Even though you don't feel calm doesn't mean you can't be calm. My mother's words came back to me.

"Go away," I said. My heartbeat and the pumping of my blood roared between my ears. My body was beyond tense, like it was bracing for a physical blow, and I felt abruptly cold and removed from my surroundings, like I was in a tunnel.

"Fine, fatty. I don't want your fucking chubby-ass fingers on me anyway."

I closed my eyes, waiting for the sound of his departure and trying to calm my heart. But he didn't leave. I felt him hovering there, just beyond the little island of safety that was my towel. I was about to launch myself up and away to the water, when he spoke again.

"Yeah, glad you're having a good time. This place is pretty great."

I frowned my confusion—which had momentarily paralyzed me—but didn't open my eyes.

But then Ben said, "Oh, hey Stroke," just as I discerned a new set of footsteps approaching from behind me. Martin was walking over.

I exhaled a slow breath, my insides still feeling like icicles, and slowly opened my eyes. I kept my attention affixed to the shore as I didn't want to look at this Ben person again, probably never.

"Hey," Martin said from someplace nearby and over my shoulder. "What's going on?"

"Ah, not much. Just keeping Kaitlyn company." Ben's voice was remarkably different, friendly, affable. "But since you're here, I'll just go grab some food. Do you want anything? Can I get you something?" Ben was obviously directing this solicitous question to Martin.

I wondered briefly if Martin should invest in a poison tester of some sort. I wouldn't trust Ben with a snake I didn't like, let alone to bring me food that wasn't tainted with arsenic.

"No," Martin said.

I nearly laughed, despite my brittle state. Martin's simple *no* sounded like so much more than a *no*. It sounded like a warning and a threat, like a dismissal and a command. I was impressed how much disdain he'd managed to pack into a single syllable word.

"Okay, well…" At last I heard Ben's feet move against the sand. "I'm starving so I'm going to eat. See you two later."

I remained still even when I was sure Ben had left. I couldn't quite pry my fingers from where they held my legs tightly tucked against me.

Growing up, I'd struggled a bit with my size, but not in the way most people approach size frustrations. I struggled and worked to accept it. I wished I could be different, yet because I trusted my mother and her assurances there was nothing wrong with me or the way I looked, that the baby fat was normal for me and that my body would shed it eventually, I never fought against the rolls.

I was a pudgy kid and very, very short through most of my childhood; then, during my sophomore year of high school, I stretched out and grew four inches basically overnight. I grew another two inches in my junior year.

But I've never been lean and firm; rather, I've always been soft and curved. I did rather like the line of my waist, however, because it tapered dramatically beneath my ribs, then flared out again to my hips—an hourglass, my mother had said with a smile, defining it for me.

She told me I should be proud of my healthy shape and healthy body, and love and treasure it because it was mine. No one, she said, could tell me what to think of my body. If I let another person's opinion matter I was giving him or her control over me, and I had complete control over my self-image.

That's what she said.

But that wasn't the truth, not really. Because even though I knew Ben was a bottom feeder of the worst sort and his opinion mattered just as much as the coruscations in the sea, words like *fatty* hurt, no matter the source.

I felt Martin's eyes on me and I wished I had a shirt, a bathrobe, or a big plastic trash bag to cover the imperfections of my shape. Furthermore, I wished I'd junk punched Ben when I'd had the chance.

Martin moved, walking on Sam's towel and sitting next to me. I lifted my chin and kept my eyes on the horizon; I was not yet ready to look at him. I was still trying to gain control of my scattered feelings. I was also attempting to suppress the self-consciousness creeping from my chest to my throat and choking me. I was this awkward, pudgy girl, the color of chalk, sitting alongside a muscled and bronzed Greek god.

Martin stretched his long legs in front of him; he rested a hand behind me so his arm and chest brushed against the bare skin of my arm and back. The contact was a spark in my tunnel of frigid numbness. Then he leaned forward, nuzzled my cheek softly with his nose, and placed a gentle kiss on my jaw. Unexpectedly, I felt myself melt.

"Hey, Parker," he whispered, then kissed the hollow of my cheek. "What's wrong?"

I shook my head even as my body instinctively leaned into him, my shoulder resting against his chest. He felt good, solid, warm.

"Why is that guy here?" I asked.

Martin glanced over his shoulder to where his teammates were eating, then faced me again. "Did he say something to you?"

I cleared my throat then answered with another question, "Why would you invite him? After what he tried to do to you."

He exhaled softly, then brushed the back of his fingers down the length of my arm to my elbow; his eyes followed the path. He seemed to be studying my hand where it gripped my leg.

"Because he's strong and we, the boat, need him to win." His voice held an edge of ire, but I knew it wasn't directed at me.

I slid my eyes to the side, considered this news and Martin's expression. He didn't look happy about having Ben there. In fact, he looked angrily resigned. I got the impression he wasn't used to making compromises, and this one felt wrong and unwieldy.

"He tried to drug you," I stated with a fervor that surprised me, feeling outraged on Martin's behalf.

"I didn't say I trust him. I said we *need* him. Trusting and needing someone are usually mutually exclusive." Martin lifted his dazzling eyes to mine. This close I was startled to see they were the exact color of the ocean. Flecks of green, silver, and turquoise radiated from his pupil like a starburst.

"But sometimes, rarely…," he started, stopped, his attention drifting to my lips briefly, "you meet someone you need, who you can also trust."

He stared at me and I stared back, feeling muddled and disbelieving the implication of his words. He allowed me to struggle for a full minute, then he reached for my hand and pried it from my leg, holding it lightly, reverently.

"Kaitlyn, did Ben say something to you? Because if he did I'll get rid of him." Martin's eyes narrowed by a fraction and his gaze grew penetrating, searching.

I gathered an expansive breath and turned from Martin's probing stare. His obvious concern was doing strange things to me. His protectiveness didn't feel like possessiveness, and I wondered how often I'd lamentably mistaken one for the other.

I didn't want to lie. But if Martin could live with Ben trying to drug and extort him for the sake of team cohesion, then I guess I could live with a few nasty words.

Of course, there was the whole Ben drugging girls for undefined reasons issue...

I looked over the water as I spoke. "Martin, I didn't tell you this on Friday when I saw you at the party, but you're not the first person Ben has tried to drug. When he was talking to that girl, he made it sound like…like he's been drugging girls for a while. That can really only mean one thing, right?"

I peeked at Martin and his scowl was fierce. He said through gritted teeth, "Thanks for letting me know. I'll handle Ben. He won't—" he stopped, exhaled slowly, "he won't be doing that again."

"But what about what he's done so far?"

"I'll take care of that too."

"He's so awful. He's…he's like ammonium dichromate with mercury thiocyanate. He's the college boy equivalent of the bowels of hell."

Martin's smile was sudden and its unexpectedness seemed to take us both by surprise; he laughed lightly at my analogy, but he also looked concerned. "Hey, did he say something to you? Before I came over?"

"I don't like him," I said, then rushed on when I feared Martin would see I was being evasive. "He's unpleasant and creepy and I don't want to talk about him anymore. Let's talk about chemistry."

I felt rather than saw Martin's small smile because he'd leaned forward and nipped my shoulder, his lips hovering against my skin. "Yes, let's talk about chemistry. We have excellent chemistry."

I leaned a tad to the side and away because his soft lips, sharp teeth, and hot mouth were overwhelming to my chest, stomach, and pants.

"I meant our assignment. I brought all my notes, I think we should start on the literature search this afternoon."

"Na-ah." Martin lifted his head, placed my hand on his thigh, and then gathered several stray strands of hair away from my face. He tucked them behind my ear. "We're leaving. You and I have plans."

"Plans? What plans?"

"I know a place where we can be alone."

"Other than the fifty spare rooms back at the house?" I said, then immediately felt myself burn scarlet at the unintended insinuation. "Ah…I mean…that is…what I mean is…oh blast it."

He watched me struggle under his suspended eyebrows, a whisper of a smile on his face, then cut in when I tried to hide my face in my arm. "No, the place I have in mind is better. Lunch is packed. Come on." He squeezed my arm then pulled my hand as he stood, tugging me with him. "We need to get going."

I snatched my hand back and quickly covered myself with a towel.

I tried not to look at him, mostly because he was magnificent. Unlike the others, he was clothed in board shorts that ended at his knee. His shirtless torso was flawless and completely smooth. He looked like a golden statue, cast in hard relief by the sun, but warm to the touch. And that was just his torso! I didn't trust my gaze to venture downward to assess the flawlessness of his legs...or elsewhere.

My heart and the area previously defined as "my pants" both twisted and tightened at the sight of his perfect body. I felt pinpricks and tingles all over and a little lightheaded as I turned away from him.

"Let me get changed first," I mumbled without thinking. "I wish I'd invested in a burqa or a moomoo…"

Martin gripped the towel as I tried to wrap it under my arms, bringing my attention back to him.

His expression was again fierce, his eyebrows lowered in a frowny scowl. "What did you say?"

"Nothing."

"What are you doing?" His gaze flickered to the towel then back to mine.

"Getting my things."

He yanked on the towel and I held it tighter. His frown intensified. As he surveyed my face, I felt very much like I was being examined under a microscope.

Martin took three full, measured breaths, his hand now stubbornly fisted in the terrycloth, before he asked again through clenched teeth, "What did Ben say to you, Parker?"

"Nothing important." I tilted my chin upward and shrugged. When he looked like he was going to press the issue further, I let go of the towel, letting the weight of it drop in his grip.

Martin looked troubled, but his attention strayed as though he were compelled, as though he had no choice but to look at my body. I tensed, fought the urge to cross my arms over my chest, and glanced at the sky, letting him look.

It didn't really matter. We were at the beach for Bunsen's sake! Sooner or later he was going to see me in a bathing suit. I repeated my mother's sage advice, *If I let another person's opinion matter then I was giving him control over me; I alone had complete control over my self-image.* I held still for as long as I could.

Then I heard him sigh. "Fuck me…"

My eyes darted back to Martin and I found him looking at my body with a mixture of pained hunger and appreciation. The profanity had slipped from his tongue like an odd caress.

"Excuse me?" I questioned, though I almost asked, *Was that a request?*

His gaze jumped to my face and he stepped forward, tossing the towel to the sand. He didn't touch me except to fit the fingers of my left hand in the palm of his right. "It's an expression, Parker. It usually means a person is surprised."

I squinted at him. "What's surprising? Is it my ghost-like skin? Does it scare you?"

I saw his mouth tugged to the side just before he turned from me and pulled me toward the house path. "No. Your ghost skin doesn't scare me."

"Is it—"

"You're fucking, goddamn gorgeous, Parker," he said roughly, a half growl, and without looking back at me.

Startled, I snapped my mouth shut, as a pleased and pleasant warmth suffused my cheeks, chest, and stomach. For the first time in my life I found I didn't mind the use of curse words.

CHAPTER 9
Reactions in Aqueous Solution

I DIDN'T CHANGE clothes as I completely forgot that I wanted to change clothes. Therefore I continued to wear my relatively modest, halter-top, two-piece bathing suit on the ride from the house to this new and better place where Martin insisted we go…to be alone…

Being alone with Martin didn't freak me out at first. It felt like a very theoretical state of being; like being informed I was going to go become quark–gluon plasma (i.e. one of the theoretical phases of matter) or the winning contestant on American Idol. So, equally likely.

The truth was that my mind was slow on the uptake because everything was happening too fast. On Friday afternoon I was hiding in a science cabinet on campus. It was now Sunday afternoon and Martin was practically wooing me—insomuch as crazy handsome, billionaire, geniuses woo a girl—on a small island in the Caribbean.

I was not used to change and I was not good with surprises. The entirety of my past and all changes therein were well documented via the agendas prepared by George. I'd always had time to prepare.

But not this time.

Thus, I forgot to freak out until he was leading me by the hand down a sandy path and through a healthy amount of tropical underbrush. In his other hand he held a picnic basket. I glanced up and blinked at the broad muscles of his back and it abruptly hit me where I was and who I was with and what we'd done so far.

The kissing, the touching, the whispering, the shared moments *and* the heated stares. I'd made eye contact with him more in the last thirty-six hours than I had in the last six months as his lab partner. A shiver passed through me. Life was happening too fast.

I mumbled, "Fast, quick, rapid, supersonic, hurried…"

Martin glanced over his shoulder, his oceanic eyes sweeping me up and down. "What did you say?"

"Nothing."

His eyes narrowed on me. "Are you okay?"

I lied, "Yes. Good." Then deflected, "Where are we going?"

A glint of some devilry flashed in his gaze, curving his mouth to one side—devilry looked really good on Martin Sandeke—and he returned his attention to the path. "Just this place I know with a waterfall and cave. It's part of the estate, so no one else uses it."

"How nice," I said, bending as he held a palm frond out of my way, and added conversationally, "we have a garage at my house. It holds a car and some of my dad's tools."

Martin glanced at me, equal parts amused and confused. "Oh?"

"Yes. And a hammock in the back yard."

"Is that so…"

"Yeah."

"So, no waterfalls?"

"No. But this one time, when it rained a lot, the gutter broke. That was similar to a waterfall."

Martin laughed. I knew he was laughing because, though he was quiet, I saw his shoulders shake; and when he turned to look at me, his eyes were bright with humor and he was flashing a lethally bright smile.

"You're funny, Parker."

"Thank you." I looked away from the beacon of his smile. It was blinding. "You're also…humorous at times."

We walked another hundred yards or so in silence and I forced myself to study the surrounding landscape. The ground was sandy—light grey and white—and heavily littered with bleached shells. Tall palm trees provided the ceiling of the canopy. The path was littered with thick palm bushes and underbrush. All around us insects buzzed and hummed a constant symphony, and I could make out the faint sounds of rushing water. It grew louder the farther we walked but not overwhelming. The weather was warm, and would have been hot if we were in the sun and farther inland. But in the shade and so near the ocean, a cool breeze whispered over and cooled my bare skin.

Martin turned slightly, still holding my hand, though his attention was on a series of rocks before us that descended a stairway of sorts.

"Be careful here, just watch your step. It might be better if you do this barefoot. You're not going to need shoes anyway."

He released my hand, kicked off his shoes, and preceded me down the path made by the sandy boulders.

I, likewise, kicked off my flip flops and followed, keeping my attention on the trail. The sound of the rushing water increased exponentially as we descended. Then I stopped because Martin stopped, and I looked up and saw this place where he'd brought us.

And my mouth fell open.

He'd brought us to a very small cove, mostly shaded by palms and the surrounding rock face. It was about twenty feet in diameter. The crystal clear, turquoise water was mostly still, but rippled near the far end. Upon closer inspection, the cove appeared to be adjacent to a cave. The waterfall was unseen, but I heard it; I guess it must be behind the rock face.

It was like a little room, private, intimate, breathtaking.

I don't know exactly how long I stood there gaping at the small natural loveliness of our surroundings. But I became aware of Martin's gaze all at once, watching me; I darted a look at him, snapping my mouth shut.

"Do you like it?"

I nodded. "It's...it's stunning."

He grinned, obviously pleased. He'd set the picnic basket down at some point on a shelf created by the curving rocks, leaving both of his hands free. Martin with two hands free felt a little dangerous. I glanced at his hands, my heart skipping.

"Come on," he said, holding one of his dangerous hands out to me.

I accepted it, and he led us down into the water, his eyes holding mine. It lapped at my ankle, then calf, then we were submerged to our waists just three feet from the edge.

"How deep is this?"

"Uh, that's an entrance to the cave where the waterfall is." He indicated with his head to the far side. "It's relatively deep over there, maybe fifteen or twenty feet. But on this side," he pointed to my right, "it's flat and about three or four feet."

"Have you gone into the cave?"

He nodded, his eyes traveling over me. It was a slow perusal of my body that did things, unexpected things, like made me tremble, my stomach flip, and my nipples harden. The longer he stared the hotter and more intense his gaze grew. It felt like he was on the precipice of something, saying something.

I didn't want him jumping off any verbal cliffs, so I interrupted him, pulling my hand from his, before he could speak. "What's the plan, Stan? What's the deal, Neil? Is there a schedule for the rest of this week? Anything I should be aware of? I remind you again and in all seriousness that I have two papers to write and a vector calculus test to study for. Also, again, you and I do have that lab assignment we need to prep. I have you trapped here, therefore I expect you to help with the literature search. Also, I have two books I've been dying to read."

Martin wasn't smiling, but his eyes were warm and interested. "Do you always talk like that?"

"Like what? Like awesome?"

"Yeah, like awesome." His tone was serious, verging on earnest.

I felt pleased by the compliment despite the fact I'd self-deprecatingly complimented myself and he'd merely agreed. Because I did want to be his friend so it was important to be honest. "Actually, no. Truthfully, you make me nervous so I'm a little more jumpy and vociferous than usual."

"Vociferous. You have an excellent vocabulary." He pushed himself backward a few feet and began treading water near the center of the cove. His eyes seemed to glow, reflecting the sea-green of the saltwater.

"Ah, yes. That I do. I'm a big fan of synonyms."

He exhaled a soft laugh, peering at me like I was weird and wonderful. It made my smile widen.

"So, plan for this week? What can I expect?" I took small steps near the edge, not wanting to venture too close to Martin and his glowing eyes and dangerous hands.

"Well, team practice, like this morning. The waves are minimal on this side of the island because we're basically set in the middle of a large inlet. The Gulf is like a big lake. We'll be practicing and training in the mornings, so you'll get your quiet time." His voice was downright conversational. It was nice.

"Good." I tucked my hair behind my ears, this news settled my nerves somewhat. If he was training in the mornings then I could use the time to prepare my friend attacks.

"But in the afternoons and evenings…," he paused, licked his lips, his eyes flickering over me, "I want us to be together."

This news halted my progress around the rim of the cove. Paired with the predatory glint in his eyes and the slight undercurrent of a mandate in his words, my insides felt like a jumble of knots…made out of magma. That's right, magma knots. Perhaps if I hadn't skipped breakfast my stomach wouldn't have been so tumultuous.

"To have tacos?" Despite my best efforts, this question emerged somewhat high-pitched and breathless.

"Yes, tacos. And there will be parties and other things."

Parties.

Parties?

What?

I frowned. I'm pretty sure I scowled. This reaction was instinctual. I hated parties. Hate.

"Parties?" I may have curled my lip in a miniature sneer.

"Yeah, on the island, at some of the other houses, friends of mine. You know, the usual college scene stuff."

Usual college scene…just a bunch of billionaires' kids and their friends. It sounded delightful.

"Yeah, no thanks." I pulled my eyes from his, inspected the rocks. "I don't go to parties. It's one of my life rules."

"Life rules?"

"Yes. Good ideas to live by."

"You just made that up. Not going to parties isn't one of your life rules."

He was right, I had just made up not going to parties as a life rule, but he didn't need to know that. Therefore I ignored his last comment and tried to act blasé. "I don't want to go, but don't let that stop you from going."

"Parker."

I sighed, then met his gaze.

"I want you to come."

"No, thank you."

He ground his teeth. "Kaitlyn, you promised you were going to give this a try."

"I will…"

Once again he was giving me the severe stare down, likely because my weakly delivered *I will* didn't even sound convincing to me.

Managing to swallow around the sudden thickness in my throat, I squared my shoulders so I was facing him.

"Here's the thing, Sandeke. I am. I am going to give this a try. Despite my worries—"

"What worries?" He sounded exasperated.

I ignored his question. "Despite my worries and reservations, I'm going to give this the good college try. But I don't even know how to dance. I can tango like a pro, but I don't do the body wiggle weird thing. And isn't that what the kids do these days at parties? Dance?"

He lifted an eyebrow at my excuse—obviously unimpressed—and with two fluid strokes moved to join me.

I stiffened, my eyes wide, and backed up a step at his advance.

"What…what are you doing?"

"I'm going to teach you how to dance," he said simply, already on me, reaching for my body.

I stiffened further, feeling unaccountably breathless as his big hands slipped around my waist and settled on my hips and lower back.

"But there…but we…but—"

"Shhh," he said, pulling me closer. "Relax."

"Create cold fusion," I murmured in response, unable to relax and placing my hands nowhere, because placing them anywhere on Martin felt perilous to my well-being.

He glanced down at me, his eyebrows in a perplexed V. "What does cold fusion have to do with anything?"

"You tell me to relax, which is impossible. I tell you to create cold fusion, which is impossible."

His answering smile was crooked. "You can't relax?"

"No."

"Why not?"

"You know why not."

"Well, it might help if you touched me."

"That will not help."

"It might."

"It won't."

"Touch me."

I scowled at his chest, my hands still in the air at my sides. *Stupid perfect chest.*

"Parker, if we're going to dance you have to touch me." He sounded amused and his fingers flexed on my bare skin. I felt the roughened calluses of his palms just before he released my body to grab my hands. He brought them to his shoulders, pressed them there, then returned his own to my hips. I didn't miss the fact that his hand placement was now a bit more daring than it had been a moment ago, lower, closer to my bottom.

I swallowed thickly, glaring at my fingers where they touched his perfectly sculpted shoulder.

"Don't you want to touch me?" he asked, his inflection daring, teasing, but also something else. Something hesitant and uncertain.

I lifted my eyes to his; they were guarded, his smile looked bracing, almost like a grimace, like he was preparing himself for bad news.

I sighed. I knew I sounded resigned and a little pitiful. "Yes…"

His gaze thawed as it dropped to my lips. "Then you should…because I want you to."

"I don't know how," I blurted.

"I'll teach you." His voice was low, soft, and held a promise.

"I'm not good at this."

"We haven't even started."

"I don't mean the dancing, I mean the touching. I'm pretty sure I'll be good at the wiggle dancing once I apply myself, as I have excellent rhythm." Heat was beginning to build in the space between us where we didn't touch; my stomach and his, his chest and mine. I had the sudden sensation we were magnetized, and I had to make my body rigid to keep from plastering myself against him.

"Why do you think you'll be good at dancing? You're very stiff, you need to loosen up." He swayed his hips and mine to the left, then the right, then back, his movements measured and slow. I moved with him, trying to loosen up without succumbing to the magnetism.

"Because I used to ballroom dance and I play three instruments. Did you know that? And also the drums…so I guess four instruments."

His eyes, which were still on my lips, flickered to mine and his eyebrows ticked upward with surprise. "Really? What else do you play?" He sounded interested.

"Guitar mostly. But also the piano and saxophone and the aforementioned drums."

He smiled. I swear he'd been smiling so much it felt unnatural. Before now, I thought I'd seen him smile three times in the last six months and all three of those times the smile had been mean and hard because he'd been about to unleash a world of hurt on someone.

These were different smiles, relaxed and happy smiles. They were devastating and no less precarious to my wellbeing than his mean and hard smiles.

"I'd like to see that," he said after a beat. "I'd like to see you play."

"We can go back now and I'll show you. I think I saw a guitar in one of the rooms back at *the compound*." I said "the compound" in a deep, weird voice, hoping to cut through the raging tension building between us, making it difficult for me to breathe.

I made like I was going to move away. His grip on me tightened, staying my attempted retreat.

"No." He shook his head, the word sharp, and his eyes flashed with a warning. Then he brought me flush against him.

This was not a good idea. It drove all the breath from my lungs and I trembled, gasped, spikes of hot and cold rushing under the surface of my skin. I felt sensitized everywhere. Instinctively, my eyes shut, startled by the ferocity of the sensual, swirling, damning, overwhelming physical feels.

He half growled, half groaned then set me away, placing essential distance between us. My lashes fluttered open and I found him watching me with his jaw set and his eyes ablaze. His hands were on his hips and I saw his Adam's apple move with a thick swallow.

I shifted on my feet, not sure what to do with my arms. I decided to place them in the water at my sides. "Sorry."

"Why are you sorry?"

"I don't know. I guess I'm not sorry."

He growled, his eyes half closing, and he tugged a hand through his hair. He looked…frustrated.

His frustration made me frustrated because I didn't know why he was frustrated. I surmised based on his expression that I'd done something wrong, made some novice misstep, but I had no idea what.

I hated I was so clueless about boys. I didn't know anything about them other than what one can absorb from porn and pubmed articles. Otherwise they were a cornucopia of conundrums.

"What's going on?" I blurted, feeling lost and confused by the last sixty seconds, not to mention the last two days. My hands convulsively gripped my thighs in the water. "What are you thinking?"

His eyes lifted to mine and he stared at me, saying nothing, but his frustration was tangible. I could hear him breathe though, could see his chest rise and fall with his deep exhales. The longer he stared at me without saying anything the faster my heart beat; I felt like it was going to throw itself out of my ribcage.

Then he said, "Come here," causing me to jump a little, though his voice was quiet, almost lost amidst the combined sounds of the waterfall and the insect symphony. Even if I hadn't heard the words, I would have read the want—what *he* wanted—in his eyes. He looked a little wild with want.

I tried to take a deep breath but managed only a shallow inhale. Silently I obeyed, wading toward him until a foot separated us. I was glad my hands were in the water so he couldn't see them shaking, because they were shaking—just a little.

When I stopped, his gaze dropped to my body, to my chest, ribs, and stomach. My lower belly felt tight and my breasts heavy. Full. The force of his stare was physical—corporeal—and I shifted a half step backward under its intensity.

Maybe he thought I was going to turn and flee, or maybe he'd reached the limit of his patience. Whatever the reason, Martin closed the remaining distance between us. He gripped my waist again. This time the shock of sensation from Martin's rough calluses against my bare midriff sent a jolt to my center and up to my heart.

He held me firmly as though he didn't trust me to stay.

"I need to touch you."

"You are touching me," I whispered breathlessly, unable to tear my gaze from his.

Martin shook his head slowly, lifted one hand to the tie at my neck that was holding up my top. Without breaking eye contact, he tugged on the fastening, loosening, then releasing the halter. With a feather-light touch he brought the straps forward, the tips of his fingers on my neck and shoulder sending a shiver down my spine. His movements were slow and purposeful, and he didn't stop pulling, and his eyes never left mine.

He brought his other hand to the second strap, the backs of his knuckles brushing against the tops of my breasts—pulling, pulling, still pulling—until he delved with meticulously measured movements into the material of my bikini top and tugged it down with aching deliberateness, exposing my body.

His gaze dropped to my bare breasts and he blinked, his eyes half lidded, the rise and fall of his chest obvious.

Then he touched me with the backs of his hands and knuckles—my hardened nipples and the undersides of my breasts—until the top was lowered completely. My stomach twisted and my back arched on instinct. I was near panting now.

I felt crazed, overwhelmed, like I was on the precipice of a high cliff and needed to jump—I had to. I had no choice. I absolutely needed it. Whatever Martin was about to do, I needed it.

A small, helpless sound escaped my lips, something like a whimper, causing his gaze to sharpen and his body to sway toward mine. I realized his chest was rising and falling faster than it had been, and the sense he was close to a similar edge made me bold.

So I touched him.

It was just my fingertips against the hard ridges of his abdomen, but it made him flinch and release a growly sigh like I'd both hurt and pleased him.

"Kaitlyn..." My name from his lips was tight, choked, needy.

He shifted an inch closer; the water swirled around us. One of his hands slid back up my body and cupped me—reverently at first, like I was fragile—and his other moved lower, around my back, slipping into the fabric of my boy short bikini bottoms, inside, down, until he was gripping my bare ass with one hand and massaging my breast with the other, his thumb sweeping over the peak twice before pinching it.

I cried out, the spike of pleasure severe and unexpected and clearly wired straight to my core. My hands instinctively lifted to grip his shoulders and my back flexed, arching on instinct.

"Dammit." His eyes half closed, and he brought me against him with a jerky movement, as though it were a reflex he couldn't control.

Suddenly he bent at his waist and his mouth was on me. He licked, kissed, and sucked my nipple into his hot mouth, then grazed it with his teeth.

"Ah! Martin." My eyes drifted shut briefly and my hips bucked, my grip on his shoulders increasing. I felt taut and swollen and greedy for his touch, his hands, his mouth, his body.

"I have to touch you." His voice rumbled. He circled the center of my breast with his tongue before drawing it between his lips.

"You are touching me," I repeated, holding on to his neck and the back of his head, pressing him to my chest, and feeling a little insane.

"Not here," he growled, his caresses growing more aggressive, insistent, forceful.

He bit the underside of my breast and my ribs like he wanted to consume me, his fingers on my bottom digging into my flesh, severe and punishing. He pinched my nipple again, this time harder, and it hurt, but it also felt necessary. Then his hand in my bikini moved from my bottom to my front, his fingers parting and entering me.

Martin straightened, then captured my lips with his just as I cried out my surprise. His tongue mirrored the stroking of his fingers. His free hand grabbed my ponytail and he roughly positioned me how he liked, tilting my head to the side, opening my mouth just as he was opening my center.

My nipples grazed his chest. I flexed my thighs, my stomach, and my back tight. My nails dug into his shoulders and back. His fingers were inside me and it wasn't the soft teasing he'd employed in my dorm room.

This was rough, urgent, his fingers searching, uncomfortable and a little painful, but…God, it felt so good. So good. So, so good.

My body seemed to understand what my mind hadn't yet discovered and my hips rocked instinctively in time with his strokes. He bit my lip as I panted, his hot mouth moving to my jaw then neck as he yanked my hair, exposing the vulnerable expanse of skin to his teeth and tongue.

As though from a great distance, I heard him cussing and complimenting me. A steady stream of growled *fucks* and *beautifuls* and *gorgeous* and *damns* between clenched teeth, against my skin, hot breath spilling over my ear and neck. I became aware all at once that his erection was pressed against my hip and he was moving the hard length, rubbing against me, as I moved on his hand. My breath hitched as my stomach coiled tight. My jaw was tight. Everything felt tight and taut and close to breaking.

And then I did.

I broke.

In fact, I cried out.

Violent, sweet desolation tore through me, delicious spasms accompanied by fierce trembling. I was paralyzed by this vicious wave of beautiful destruction, strangling and releasing and suffocating me over and over. I became aware of his fingers stroking slower, softer, like they'd taken what they wanted and were now moving as a mere echo of their earlier urgency.

My body also instinctively relaxed without my telling it to do so, going almost limp. Martin's mouth was on my neck, sucking, licking, and biting. I felt his heart beating against my bare breast and its thunderous pace matched mine. My vision was blurry and I realized I wasn't breathing, so I gasped for air, swallowing a gasping breath as I buried my face below his neck, hiding.

I felt him shudder. His fingers inside my body, still stroking and petting—like I'd done something good and he was rewarding me with a gentle touch.

With plain reluctance, he slipped his hand from my bikini shorts and released my pony tail. At first I thought he was going to set me away again, but he didn't. He embraced me. His strong arms came around my body and he crushed me to him. Automatically I snuggled closer.

I wasn't confused. I was nothing other than my body. Blissfully satiated. My mind was completely blank, devoid of thought. I merely felt.

And everything about being in Martin's arms felt like bliss.

CHAPTER 10
Properties of Solutions

ONCE AGAIN, SAM and I took dinner in my room.

It took me a while to recover from…

MY VERY FIRST ORGASM!!!

That's how I thought about it in my brain.

MY VERY FIRST ORGASM!!!!!!!!

It was all capital letters, followed by a ridiculous number of exclamation points. In the past I'd tried to bring myself to satisfaction any number of times and always failed, which was why I'd done so much research about the sex act. I thought if I could read enough about the subject I would eventually find the key to…wait for it…

MY VERY FIRST ORGASM!!!!!!!!!!!!

I didn't expect it to render me speechless, but it did, and for several hours. Luckily and bewilderingly, Martin also seemed to require recovery time. Neither of us spoke afterward, not in the cove, not on the walk back to the golf cart, not on the ride back to the estate.

Although, some barrier between us had been shattered, because he seemed to feel at liberty to kiss me and touch me whenever and however he wanted, and I let him because I quite simply needed the post-orgasm reassurance and touching. It felt necessary and natural and I craved it.

Before wordlessly retying my halter, he lavished my breasts and shoulders with hot, wet kisses—fondling my body like it was his with which to play and explore as he liked. As we left the cove, he pulled me into his arms and kissed me until I was climbing him breathlessly. During the duration of the drive in the golf cart, he placed one possessive hand on my thigh, then caressed my bottom greedily as we walked to the house.

Once inside, he caught my hand and spun me around until we were pressed against each other from knees to chests, and he kissed me again, his hands smoothing down my neck, then shoulders, arms, waist, and hips.

When we finally separated, he wore a deeply satisfied smile and his eyes glowed like they had in the cove.

Then he spoke. "Go clean up. Take this."

I glanced down at the basket he was holding. It was the picnic we hadn't eaten. I took it then returned my gaze to his.

"You should eat something," he said.

I nodded obediently.

His smile grew. "Are you ever going to speak again?"

I blinked at him then shrugged my *I don't know.*

Speak? Speak? What was that?

He laughed, pulled me in for another hug, and kissed the top of my head. His eyes were happy as he sent me on my way with a low, "See you at dinner."

But I didn't see him at dinner. I ate in my room with Sam because my mind caught up with what had happened while I took my shower. I felt the soreness between my legs and reality crashed over me like a tempestuous waterfall. The world came into sharp focus. I reached for the wall of the shower to steady myself.

His fingers hadn't been gentle, hence the soreness. And as I reflected on the events in the cove, I recognized that everything about him—his touch, his words, his kisses—had been dictatorial, forceful, and domineering. He may have given me my very first orgasm, but he'd taken something as well.

And he knew it. He'd known it *while* it was happening.

Adding to my confused state, I saw in the bathroom mirror that he'd left bite marks and hickies on my skin - two on my neck, and one on the underside of my right breast. They looked like evidence. Like they'd been placed there purposefully.

I needed time to marinate in the events, to accept it had happened, to decide what it meant, to figure out why I'd let it happen, and to determine whether it was a good thing or a bad thing.

I didn't panic. But I did remember that the blood of a thousand virgins had been sacrificed at the altar of his sexual prowess.

A cold lump gathered in my stomach, comprised of confusion and uneasiness, and I dressed in sweatpants and a large T-shirt.

Sam stopped by about an hour later—found me curled on my giant bed staring out the window to the sea. Though I knew she noticed the purple marks on my neck, she seemed to sense I didn't want to talk, and I was grateful when she suggested we eat dinner then study in my room. I'd brought my class-specific notebooks, to which I had an unhealthy attachment, therefore I was all for getting down to study town.

My notebooks were soothing to me. Just seeing my hand-written notes was like going back in time to the day of the lecture. They gave me confidence. They made me feel like I might actually be capable of acing tests. They were the brain-spinach to my Popeye the sailor man.

As well, I didn't really want to face Martin's teammates with hickies, obvious evidence of what we'd done. I wasn't regretful or embarrassed, but it felt private, sacred to me. I didn't want to share what had transpired with a room full of near strangers, especially with Ben the leering douche-bucket.

Therefore, Sam and I sat on the balcony and munched on salmon cakes, garden salad, and asparagus, between chapters and class notes of vector calculus and European history. At sunset we went for a walk on the beach. She told me about her day, wherein she swam with Eric then convinced him to play tennis with her.

Of course she kicked his ass.

I didn't ask her whether she liked him and she didn't ask me what was going on with Martin. In a lot of ways Sam and I were similar. When real, weighty feelings were involved, we both found vocalizing unformed thoughts difficult. I think we both needed time to figure out our own stuff before talking it through with each other.

During our walk we decided to share my giant bed again, so she went off in search of her PJs, while I grabbed the tray with our dirty dishes and wandered around the house in search of the kitchen. I needed tea, not to mention cookies.

In the kitchen I encountered the chef—a red-cheeked, red-haired, red-nosed woman in her sixties named Irma, and her aide—a similarly red-cheeked, red-haired, red-nosed forty-something woman, Tamra—who I suspected was Irma's daughter. They gently admonished me for clearing my own dishes then promised to bring me up tea, milk, and cookies. I asked for directions back to my room, and Tamra offered to show me the way.

Upon my request, she was showing me the most direct path, rather than the scenic route, as I suspected I would make several stealthy trips to the kitchen during my stay. I probed her for answers about the house as we walked, and learned it had been acquired by Mr. Sandeke senior— Martin's father—ten or so years ago. The staff came with the house. I also learned Tamra was divorced and childless, and had moved down to work with her mother some four years prior.

They lived at the house in staff quarters year round and fed the rest of the staff daily—most of whom were also employed year round. However, Mr. Thompson and Mrs. Greenstone were also responsible for several other extensive family properties in England, Italy, Switzerland, Thailand,

Japan, New Zealand, and the United States. They traveled with the family and always opened the houses for Martin and his parents wherever they went.

We turned into the long hallway that led to my suite when Tamra stopped—walking and talking—suddenly, then took a step back.

"Oh! Mr. Sandeke." Tamra turned toward me, gave me a tight smile, then walked off without another word.

I watched her go, a bit perplexed by how suddenly she fled her employer.

When I turned back to my door I understood why. Martin's eyes were deep blue pools of unhappiness and his jaw was set in a firm, grim line.

"Where have you been?"

My eyebrows ticked upward—because his demanding question made me want to junk punch him—then lowered—because I remembered he now had carnal knowledge of me and I'd not joined him for dinner like we'd agreed.

Also, despite his grumpy tone and face, my body apparently wanted him to give me the rough treatment again, because it melted and hummed under his scowl of dissatisfaction.

I straightened my spine, giving my body a mental slap aimed at sobriety, and lifted my chin.

I was careful to keep my voice nice and steady. "I've been cavorting with the servants."

"Cavorting," he repeated, his tone flat. But I was pleased to see the granite-like edge to his jaw soften and his eyes lose their harsh glint.

"Yes. Cavorting for cookies. I wandered the halls for a while, got lost, then eventually found the kitchen." I said this while walking toward him as casually as I was able, then entered my room, leaving the door open behind me in a silent invitation.

He took the invite and closed the door as he followed. I heard him sigh before he demanded, "Why weren't you at dinner?"

"Sam and I decided to get some studying done. And I was tired." I crossed to the sitting area by the big window and plopped down in a chair, then gave him a small, friendly smile. "How are the boys? Quite recovered from the perils of traveling via private plane, limo and yacht, and practice this morning?"

Some of the sharpness re-entered his gaze and he crossed his arms over his chest. "You would prefer to fly commercial?"

"Of course not. I'd prefer not to fly at all. I insist you teleport me the next time we take a vacation to paradise."

He finally cracked a smile and crossed to where I sat. He examined me for a moment in silence, then took the chair next to mine. He eased into it, all fluid grace, long limbs, and coiled power.

"The next time?" he asked, and I was pleased to hear his voice held a hint of teasing.

"Of course. I've decided that you and I are going to be best friends, just as long as you keep me in a steady supply of salmon cakes."

"And cookies."

"Yes. And cookies." I bent my elbow on the high, cushioned arm of the chair and rested my cheek against my hand, let my eyes move over his handsome features and found him watching me, his eyes intent.

His mouth curved into a smirk that was mirrored in his stare. "And dancing lessons?"

I grew very still, my eyes locked on his, because by dancing lessons, I knew he meant orgasms. Probably mutual orgasms. And lots of them.

I swallowed thickly, and heat traveled up my chest to my neck. The cold lump in my stomach seemed to balloon and press against my lungs. I thought about the marks on my skin and the soreness between my legs, reminders of how physical intimacy with Martin had been exciting and satisfying, but also extremely intense and a little scary. Maybe too intense.

He reached for my hand where it rested against my cheek and I stiffened, straightened, and yanked it away, opting instead to twist my fingers together on my lap. I also tore my gaze from his and stared at the floor.

We were silent for a stretch as I tried to figure out what to say, how to respond. This was problematic as I didn't know what to say or how to respond.

"Look at me."

I tried to swallow again but experienced a swallow misfire, and released a shaky breath. "Martin..." I covered my face with my hands. My cheeks were hot and I shook my head.

"Kaitlyn, if you tell me you regret what happened..." His voice was low, sounded tight and barely controlled.

"I don't regret it," I blurted, because it was true. I didn't regret it. I liked it, a lot. And I wanted to do it again.

I peered at him from between my fingers, found him watching me, his jaw set and his eyes fierce. When I spoke it was muffled by my palms pressed to my mouth. "I don't regret it. But I don't know how to feel about it because it was a little scary."

His gaze grew introspective, like he was searching his memory, and I noted his forehead was marred with wrinkles of concern. "Scary? How so?"

I tried to distance myself from the conversation and approach it with pragmatic analysis. "Well, I think the first true 'sexual experience' for any girl is going to be frightening, so there is that. But also…well…I'm sore. And you left bruises on my hip and bites on my neck. You were quite intense and I liked that a lot, but you weren't very…gentle."

He blinked rapidly and a flicker of something like dismay clouded his features. He studied me with pensive unhappiness. Then his head fell backward to the cushion of the chair and his chest expanded with a large breath. "Goddammit."

He looked angry.

"Are you…mad?" I asked, my hands dropping to my lap as I studied his face for a clue. I couldn't believe he was angry. For heaven's sake, I was new at this, at *all* of this.

He closed his eyes for a full five seconds, then said, "I didn't mean to hurt you, not at all. I don't *want* to hurt you."

I examined him, how upset he was, and realized that irritation was pointed inward. "Can you be—I mean—is it possible for you to be less rough?"

He lifted his head, his eyes opening and I saw his determination before he spoke. "Yes. You have my word. That won't happen again."

I got the sense he was disappointed in himself…*very curious.*

"I didn't say that exactly. I mean," I cleared my throat, trying to quash my nervousness, because it was weird doing a post-orgasm analysis with Martin Sandeke, "so, just to be clear, it was good. It was all *very good.* I liked what happened…earlier. My pants liked it too. But, as much as my pants want to get this party started, I'm very new to all of this." I emphasized *all of this* by waving my hands over my pelvis then waving them in the direction of his entire body.

Some of his dismay gave way to amusement. "I know."

"I'm not saying the rough was bad, and I'm not ruling it out for future interludes—if there are future interludes—as long as I get to be rough sometimes too."

His gaze abruptly heated and his eyes narrowed, sharpened. I ignored this because the idea of getting rough with Martin was…epically arousing. I rushed to continue, "I'm just suggesting that, if this happens again—"

"When it happens again."

"—you go a little easier on me until I know how to do this thing."

He nodded and I was pleased to see him relax a bit more.

We stared at each other for a beat, and the air felt ripe and heavy. He was watching me as though he were imagining these future interludes, planning and preparing for them.

"I just wish—"

"What do you wish?"

A sudden idea occurred to me and I embraced it before I could think too much about the ramifications; I assumed he'd reject the idea outright, which is why I blurted it. "Heck, let's go all in. If we're going to give it a try, we might as well *really* give it a try. I think we should throw caution to the wind and label each other as girlfriend and boyfriend. Ala, *Have you met Martin? He's my boyfriend. I'm Parker, his girlfriend. We're together in the biblical sense of the word, sans the sacrament.*"

He stared at me for five full seconds, obviously caught off guard by my suggestion, but then he surprised me by reaching forward, and with a sure and smooth movement, pulled me onto his lap. I stumbled and basically fell into him. Meanwhile his hands cradled my face, his thumbs caressed the line of my jaw, and his eyes moved almost reverently from the progress of his fingers to my lips.

"Parker," his voice was a rumbly, growly whisper, laced with warning, "don't say it unless you mean it."

Well, crap. Bluff called.

I licked my lips—a nervous habit—which had the byproduct of turning his aqua eyes darker. He looked…greedy.

"Martin, this is nuts. You don't need or want a girlfriend."

"I want you."

Gah! Right in the feels!

He felt comfortable touching me, that much was clear. But I hesitated to touch him. I didn't want to touch him when he wasn't really mine; because *when* this was over, I wouldn't be allowed to touch him anymore. Then I would have lost something.

Therefore, I crossed my arms over my chest and shook my head.

"Let's talk about our differences," I said, hoping a well-reasoned argument would make some kind of dent in his crazy fixation.

Again, he ground his teeth; his hands slipped away from my face and his arms wrapped around me, as though to keep me from leaving.

"Yesterday, back in the limo," I said, firming my resolve, "and then on the boat, and then when we left the marina, you did this thing where you gave the other guys dirty looks for talking to me."

Martin stared at me, betraying nothing of his thoughts.

"I feel pretty confident in stating that you're…well, you're interested in me and it's not platonic. Therefore, your behavior felt as though you were marking your territory. I've never had a guy do that before, but maybe I'm misreading the situation…?"

He cleared his throat again. "You're not."

"I didn't like it."

"You didn't like it?"

"No. I didn't. It made me feel like, I don't know, like I was Chinese leftovers and you didn't want anyone to sample me."

"I don't want anyone to sample you."

"But I'm not food. I get to say who samples and who doesn't."

"I thought most girls liked it when guys were possessive."

"Really?" I asked this because I really didn't think so; then I shook my head. "No. At least…well, at least I don't think so, not like that. It's like, why would I want to be with someone who doesn't trust me to be loyal? I'm not a buffet. Guys can't sample the lo mein just because I'm standing there. I get a vote in who eats my noodles."

"I trust you," he said quickly, his gaze darting to mine then away. "After Friday night, what you did, I think I trust you more than anyone."

Oh, gah! He sounded so…sincere. I ached for him, because I believed him and it made me sad. How was it possible *I* was the most trustworthy person in his life? How heartbreaking was that?

Unable to help myself and spurred by a sudden desire to touch him, I placed my hands on his shoulders. "Martin, it's just, I don't have much experience with dating or having a boyfriend. I've had one, but he wasn't…well, he didn't count. I'm not really sure how it works—"

"I have even less experience than you."

I glared at him. "That's a lie."

"No. It's not. I've never…," he cleared his throat, "…you're the first girl I've wanted…like this." He sounded enormously frustrated and his fingers dug into my hip and ribs where he held me. When he spoke next it was through gritted teeth. "I just wish you'd be less stubborn."

"You can't always have your way."

"I know that. If I had my way we'd be naked right now in the ocean or…shit, doing anything other than discussing more reasons why you don't think this is going to work."

My instinct was to pacify him, reach forward and soothe his bad temper, promise I would stop being difficult and just give in to the fantasy of this being my reality. But I couldn't ignore reason and logic, even if I was strangely flattered by his caveman displays, possessive impatience, and apparent fixation.

And also…skinny-dipping with Martin = pre-bedtime imagery for the win.

Heat raced up my neck and over my cheeks and I squeezed my eyes shut, gathering a deep breath. I hoped to also re-gather my wits, because right that minute they were skinny-dipping with Martin some hundred yards away in the Caribbean.

"And now you're blushing." He didn't sound pleased about this. He sounded frustrated and resentful.

"What do you expect?" I asked, then opened my eyes. "I'm not used to this. It's going to take me some time to get used to the idea that you're interested in me. For cripe's sake, it's been forty-eight hours and we're not even dating—"

"We are dating. Remember, we're having tacos and soon we're going to have lots of dance lessons." His eyes drifted to the love marks on my neck and he smirked. It was a satisfied, pleased smirk.

A jerk smirk.

"Well, future tacos notwithstanding," strategically and stubbornly, I ignored his reference to dance lessons, "I know I'm not your girlfriend, and even if I were I wouldn't want to be peed on."

Martin choked on air then gave me a squirrely look. "Peed on?"

"You know, figuratively and—for the record—literally. If we got to a place where we became 'involved'," I used air quotes to emphasize *involved*, because it seemed like an odd word, but the most appropriate for the situation, "I don't think I'd be happy with you marking your territory, unless some guy was being inappropriate with me and I sent out the boyfriend bat signal."

He glared at me, his gaze searching. Then he nodded. "Fine. If I go all day tomorrow without…peeing on you," his lips twitched, but he quickly schooled his expression, "if I do that, then you'll come to the party with me tomorrow night."

What should have been a request or a question was once again a declaration. I stared at him. I really hated parties.

But he looked…oddly hopeful.

Oddly hopeful on Martin Sandeke made my heart melt. His expression, plus the feel of him all around me, meant I really didn't have much of a choice.

"Fine." I sighed, trying not to sound like a petulant teenager and *mostly* succeeding. "I'll go."

CHAPTER 11

Stoichiometry: Calculations with Chemical Formulas and Equations

MARTIN DIDN'T PEE on me. In fact, he didn't even look at me or talk to me for most of the day.

Like the day before, the guys were up early practicing, Sam and I assumed our spots on the beach, and they arrived in the early afternoon for food. I left as soon as Ben arrived. He made me feel uncomfortable and icky—and I knew that was on me. I should have been able to ignore him, but I couldn't. So I left.

I milled around the house, exploring, expecting Martin to show up. He didn't. I found the music room—yes, this compound of excess had its own music room, with signed gold records from rock and country music legends lining the walls, signed concert posters, and pictures of a tall, lanky, geeky looking dude alongside several notable musicians and celebrities.

I recognized the geeky dude in the photos as Martin's dad and noted they had the same thick hair and lips. They were likely the same height. But that's where the similarities seemed to end. After inspecting the pictures several times, testing out the baby grand piano—it needed to be tuned—and discovering three beautiful Gibson guitars along the wall, I went back to my room and read.

Then I did some chemistry homework.

Then I took a nap.

Then I woke up on a man.

I didn't realize it at first, because I suffered from post-nap confusion. When I did come to my senses I discovered I was half sprawled on a hard chest, and fingers were playing with my hair, brushing it back from my cheeks and neck, gathering it, twisting it, tugging it lightly.

I stiffened, shot upward, lifted my fists to defend my honor, and found Martin laying on the bed, his hands up like he surrendered.

"Whoa!" His eyes were huge and he gave me a startled smile. "Do you always jump up like that after sleeping?"

"Like what? A badass?" My voice was gravelly, still laced with sleep.

"Yeah, like a badass."

I huffed, let my fists fall to my lap. "No. Only when I find Martin Sandeke on my bed."

"Good to know." His lips twisted to the side and his eyes swept up and down my form. "I'll make sure to wear protection when I'm in your bed."

"You should probably wear it even when we're not in bed."

"I always use protection." He lifted an eyebrow meaningfully.

Pause.

Blink.

Oh...I get it.

Amazingly I didn't blush. I just gave him a half-lidded *I'm not impressed* glare which made him burst out laughing.

"You are such a guy." I gave him a reluctant smile.

"What do you know about guys?" He repositioned himself on the bed, scooching up and placing his hands behind his back against the pillows.

"Admittedly, not much. My dad isn't much of a *guy*."

"What's your dad like?" Martin sounded interested, his face suddenly sober.

"Well, let's see. He's a scientist. He's always losing things. His socks never match. He loves baseball, but he can't play it very well. He tried to get me to play softball. I'd always sneak my Gameboy in my practice bag then hide behind the bleachers and play Dr. Mario instead."

"So he pushed you a lot?"

"No. Not at all. I think he wanted me to do it because he likes cheering for me...to be honest. He's always the one taking pictures, at events, ceremonies, that kind of thing. He's hardly ever in the pictures. I looked back at my high school graduation photos and realized he'd taken over a thousand, but he wasn't in any of them. So I dressed back up in my cap and gown, did my hair the same, and—with George's help—arranged to have a photographer come to the house so we could get some good shots."

"Who's George? Your ex-boyfriend? The one who didn't know how to fool around?"

"No." I glared at Martin, shook my head at his antics. "George is my mom's personal assistant, he's like an older brother to me."

"Hmm..." Martin's eyes narrowed a fraction, considering me, then asked, "Did your dad like that? What you did?"

I nodded, smiling at the memory. "Yeah. He did. He cried actually. Not a lot, just a little. The last time I visited him at work, I saw he'd hung up no less than six of the pictures in his office." I laughed lightly, shaking my head. "He's a goof."

We were quiet for a long moment, sharing a stare. His mouth held a whisper of a smile as though he were living vicariously through my experience and found it a pleasant place to visit. It was…nice. Comfortable. Strange.

I cleared my throat, averted my eyes, finding this nice, comfortable, strange moment more disconcerting than the heated exchanges we'd shared so far. This felt like it could lead to something lasting and normal. We were Martin and Kaitlyn having a conversation, sharing things, like real people did. Not like billionaire playboys did.

"So, what about your dad?" I asked, because I was curious. I knew a lot about Martin's dad because his dad was a genius, sickeningly rich, and seemed to be in the news all the time dating some model or actress.

"My dad…" The smile left his eyes, and the one that lingered on his lips looked false.

"Yes. The man who raised you."

He barked a humorless laugh and his eyes closed. "He didn't raise me."

I studied his features—his full, delicious lips, strong jaw, high cheekbones, and thick lashes—his perfect features. So perfect. I wondered what it would be like to be perfect, or at least seen that way by the outside world. It seemed to me that perfect—the word and all its connotations— might feel a bit like a cage, a defined floor and ceiling.

"Tell me about him," I said, knowing I was pushing.

Martin opened his eyes and the bitterness that had been absent the last few times we'd been together was back. Jaded, jerk-faced Martin.

"He didn't come to my high school graduation."

I blinked at him. "Oh?"

"No. He said later that it was because I wasn't valedictorian, but I think it's because he forgot about it. It didn't rank in his priorities."

"Oh," I said, because I wasn't sure what else to say. His eyes were hooded, guarded, taunting—like he was daring me to feel sorry for him. I wouldn't though. Or, rather, I wouldn't show it.

"He's the smartest man in the world, did you know that? He's taken all the tests, whatever the fuck that means, and overall he's the smartest."

I placed my hand on his thigh and squeezed. "There's more than one kind of smart, Martin."

"That's true," he conceded, his eyes losing focus over my shoulder as he considered my words.

Feeling brave, I added, "I don't think any of those examinations tested for parent-smarts, or priority-smarts, or valuing-your-incredible-son-smarts, because if they did, he would have failed."

His brilliant gaze refocused on mine and I was somewhat surprised to see the bitterness leech out of his expression, leaving only sorrow and breath-stealing vulnerability.

"You're a good person, Kaitlyn." He was frowning at me, like I was a puzzle or a unicorn, like "good people" were the subject of fairy tales.

I opened my mouth, then closed it, then opened it again. "Thank you. You are too, Martin."

His answering smirk looked wry and his eyes moved to my neck, where I still had the purplish marks from our encounter in the cove.

Normal and comfortable conversation gave way to our baseline: sexual tension. His half-lidded stare grew hot, the intensity of it built a fire in the area of my pants. He was forever building fires in my pants. The figurative Bunsen burner forever alight.

"You've never lied to me before," he said, his voice sultry and teasing.

"I haven't lied yet."

"Parker." He gave me a knowing look.

"What?"

"I'm not so good. You know that, remember? You called me a jerk-faced bully."

"Well, so far you've been good to me, as far as I know."

"I'd like to do more good things, better things, if you'll let me..."

I was hot. My cheeks were flushed. I had to measure and regulate my breathing. The soreness between my legs was a lovely reminder of the good things he'd done, but so were the marks on my neck.

"No more hickies," I blurted.

His eyes widened though he grinned. "Why not?"

"Would you like me to give you a hicky?"

"Hell yeah."

I rolled my eyes. "I'm going to call your bluff. I will give you a hicky."

He held his hands out to his sides like he was offering himself to me. "Anytime, lambchop."

"I'll do it on your bottom and I'll make them so big, you won't be able to sit down." I narrowed my eyes and pointed at him.

He groaned like a starving man taking a bite of the most delectable dessert, as though the very thought was more pleasurable than he could process.

I scoffed at him, snorting. "*You're* a doofus."

Then he sat up and scootched to where I sat, one hand sliding up my thigh into the hem of my cotton shorts, his other tucking my hair behind my ear. His eyes felt cherishing and a little lost. The effect of his triple assault—earnest eyes, caressing hands, sexy smile—potent.

"I told you before," he paused, brushed a light kiss over my lips, leaving me breathless as he continued in a low voice, "don't say it unless you mean it."

I lifted my chin for another kiss, but to my surprise, Martin stood from the bed. I watched him, confused by his withdrawal, and wrapped my arms around my middle.

He glanced at me and must have sensed my confusion, because he explained as he walked backward to the door. "It's late, you've been sleeping for hours. You missed dinner, again. I'll get Rosa to bring you a tray before we leave, but we need to get going."

"Going? Where are we going?"

His smile turned smirky and victorious as he said, "To the party of course."

The party.

The bet.

I'd forgotten.

Well...barnacles.

***

MARTIN WON THE bet, even though he'd cheated, and therefore Sam was in my room getting me ready for the party. She saw me coming out of my room with my hair in a ponytail, wearing sweat pants, flip flops, and a raggedy stained T-shirt that showed Chuck Norris destroying the periodic table. It read, *The only element I believe in is the element of surprise.*

She didn't think my attire was appropriate.

Therefore she marched me back into my room, made me wait while she found some suitable clothes from her room, then dolled me up. She'd put me in a backless orange and purple paisley halter dress that made my boobs look fantastic. She also scrunched my hair with chemicals, separating my curls and somewhat taming the frizz.

To top it all off, she put makeup on my face. *Again.* It was some kind of personal record, makeup twice in one week. I gave her my resting bitch face while she applied mascara to my lashes.

"The straps of the halter covers your…," her eyes flickered to my neck, "…it covers your love marks."

I grumbled. "Just make me look pretty so I can throw myself off a cliff."

"You are being ridiculous."

"You know I hate parties."

"You didn't complain this much on Friday."

"That's because I had a mission. I had a reason to be there, an assignment. Get in, tell Martin about the plot, get out, go home. This time," I lifted my hands—and my newly painted purple fingernails—then let them drop noisily with a smack on my thigh, "this time I'm window dressing. I'm the paisley curtains."

"This dress looks great on you."

"I know, I'm sorry. You are being so nice. I just need to complain."

I wasn't kidding when I'd said I hated parties.

Hate!

I didn't understand them. They seemed to bring out the worst in people. People laughed too loud, talked too loud, exhibited odd behavior, pretended to have fun when they weren't having fun…or maybe that was just me. Maybe people *did* have fun at parties and I was the weirdo.

Despite my grumpy stance, I had to admit Sam was a miracle worker. I looked good.

We met the boys in the foyer; they were dressed casually in shorts and T-shirts, but they all seemed to have taken special care shaving, administering product to their hair, and applying cologne. It was a variable hurricane of smells—all flavored Proctor and Gamble manly.

Yet some of my surliness receded when Martin looked up and our gazes met. When his eyes widened a little and he appeared to be some degree of blindsided by my appearance. His lips parted and his eyes dropped, moving up and down a few times, blinking.

Sam nudged me and cleared her throat, saying just loud enough for me to hear, "It's not the dress and it's not the makeup, it's you." Then she walked toward Eric, addressing her next comment to him, "This time I want to drive."

"You drove last time."

"Your point?"

He smiled at her, looking handsome and happy, then shrugged. "Fine, drive now, ride later."

She hit him on the shoulder, but she laughed at his double entendre, and walked out the door. Meanwhile Martin pulled his eyes from me and I was a little perplexed to see a mask of boredom slip over his features.

"Hey Ray," Martin said. "You got Parker? Griffin is going to ride with me."

I felt like I'd just been pawned off and had no idea why. I didn't even want to go to this party, Martin had *insisted*, and now he didn't want to ride with me?

Ray glanced from me to Martin, then back again, his raised eyebrows and slightly parted lips betraying his surprise.

"Ssssure," he said, hesitating, frowning his confusion. Martin and Ray exchanged a glance as I fiddled with the pocket of my dress, all the good feelings upon entering the foyer dissipating in the face of this strange exchange. As well, Ben was there and I could feel his slimy eyes on me. I wished my boobs didn't look quite so fantastic in this dress.

Then Ray nodded with sudden vehemence. "I mean, absolutely." He turned a bright smile to me. I was relieved to see how genuine it looked, and he offered me his arm. "I'd love to."

"Thanks." I gave him a tight smile.

Boys were weird and I hated them. Except Ray. Ray was nice.

We left first. He chatted amicably on the drive over, making me laugh with a story about how he fainted in high school when he had to dissect a stingray. He also had a really engaging smile and an openness about him and made me think we were friends, or he was my ally, or I could trust him not to eat my Chinese leftovers even when I wasn't looking.

When we arrived at the house—another sprawling monstrosity, though slightly less sprawling—Ray ran over to my side of the cart and helped me out. We were the first to arrive, so he seemed content to loiter by the cart while we waited for the others.

Ray fit my hand in his elbow and gave me a big grin. "So, you and Martin, huh?"

"I don't honestly know. Doesn't make much sense to me," I admitted, shrugging.

"It makes sense to me." His words were quiet, softly spoken.

I looked up at Ray, surprised to find him looking down at me with equally soft eyes. "You're smart, beautiful—"

I snorted, rolled my eyes.

"Wait, listen, you're not pretty in a conventional way. You're not pretty at all. You're beautiful."

I pressed my lips together and frowned at him, saying flatly, "And I have a really great personality, right?"

He grinned at that, looked like he was trying not to laugh. "Yeah, you do have a really great personality."

"You're nice, Ray."

"No, *you're* nice, Kaitlyn. And you have a nice laugh and a great, weird smile with that cute gap between your teeth."

I mock-scowled at him, pressing my lips together.

He seemed to hesitate as he studied me, debating whether or not to give a voice to his thoughts. He must've decided in favor of the idea because he abruptly said, "You're the girl that guys like us, if we're smart and if we're lucky that is, you're the girl we marry. You're the marriage girl."

My jaw dropped and my eyes bugged out of my head. It took me three or four seconds to find my voice before I said, "What are you talking about?"

"I have two sisters, and I tell them this all the time. Be the marriage girl. Don't be the hook-up girl. Don't be her. She's stupid and shallow. Yes, she gets lots of male attention, dressing in her sexy lumberjack or sexy nun costumes...for a time. But then she's used up, hardened, disillusioned and desperate, because no one stays with the hook-up girl."

I blinked at him, pulled my hand from his elbow, and backed up a step. "You're disgusting and that's completely misogynistic. What if the hook-up girl is using you just as much as you're using her? What if she's just having fun? This is the problem with society. When a guy sleeps around, he's sowing oats. When a girl does it, she's a hook-up girl."

He held his hands up and shook his head. "I'm not going to defend society, I'm not saying it's right. I'm saying it's biology. It's evolution. It's programmed behavior."

"You do realize I'm nineteen, right? I may never marry. And I certainly won't be getting married any time soon."

"Doesn't matter. Your independence, the fact you aren't actively seeking your MRS degree—that the very idea is repellant—only makes you more of the marriage girl. You're the polar opposite of the hook-up girl."

I growled at him. He laughed at me.

"Listen, I'm not talking about the girl who wants to have fun and a good time with no strings attached. I'm talking about the girl who's looking for a free ride after the ride ends."

I snapped my mouth shut, scowling at him for real, and crossed my arms over my chest. I said nothing, because I knew that girl. Well, I didn't know her, but I'd overheard her plotting with Ben on Friday to drug Martin. *That* was what Ray meant when he was talking about the hook-up girl.

"Ah…I see you know what I mean."

I huffed. "I don't even know what we're talking about anymore."

"You. You're not the hook-up girl, you couldn't be if you tried. You're the girl we marry."

"How lovely for you, especially after you've spent your adolescence and early adulthood making girls like me feel like excrement."

He gave me a shrug that would have been charming ten minutes ago. "I'm just telling the truth. It might not be easy to hear, but that's the way of the world. You are the finest example of the marriage girl I've ever met. You're beautiful. From what I've seen, you're graceful under pressure, smart, capable, and drama free. You come from a family that's historically famous for being brilliant and exceptional. You're nice—like really, really nice—genuine, and you're hilarious."

"You think I'm funny now? Just wait until the party. There will copious pointing and laughing then."

Ray ignored me. "*That's* why you and Martin make sense. Because, if Martin is one thing, he's smart. He may not be nice, but he is fucking sharp as a Katana. He's never had to work for it, he's never had to work for anything. He's bored. He's had his fun. He's over the hook-up girls. He's ready for what's next and you are the Olympic gold medal, the Nobel Peace Prize, the Pulitzer Prize, and the Academy Award of marriage material."

The rest of the carts chose just that moment to show up. I heard Sam's squeals of glee as she and Eric swung around the corner. They parked neatly and tidily in the space next to Ray's. Herc and Tambor were next, followed by Lee and Will, Ben by himself, then Martin and Griffin bringing up the rear.

Meanwhile Ray was looking at me like an older brother might look at his sister, or a father might look at his daughter, after delivering a hard truth about life. Like he was apologizing for the way things were, but not sorry to have delivered the message.

He stepped forward and offered me his elbow. "Did I ruin your night?" His tone was sober and apologetic.

I shook my head, took his offered arm, and said, "No." He hadn't ruined my night because I was going to a party. There was no way to ruin something that was already ruined.

"I've known him forever," he whispered, as the engines of our companions' carts turned off and they spilled out onto the gravel driveway.

"How long?" I asked, careful to keep my voice low.

"Since elementary school."

I nodded, thinking about this, thinking about our bizarre conversation.

"He's kind of crazy about you, Kaitlyn."

My eyes cut to Ray's. His mouth was a grim line. Before I could question him further, the others were upon us and our strange heart-to-heart was at an end.

"Let's go!" Sam slipped her arm in mine and tugged.

Ray let me go with a small smile and a wave, and a look that said, *Let me know if I can help.*

I didn't know quite how to respond to that, what look to give in return. So I turned my attention to the mansion in front of me and the task at hand. I couldn't think about being Martin's marriage girl, not until I was safely through the evening with the odious party at an end.

Then and only then would I examine this new development and try to figure out what, if anything, I was going to do about it.

CHAPTER 12
Limiting Reactants

SOMETIMES I HATE it when I'm right. Sometimes I love it when I'm wrong.

Let me explain what happened. I'll try to keep it as emotion free as possible for the sake of all the people who can't deal with the ups and the downs, and the drama and the angst. This is because I'm one of those people. I can't deal with the drama. Admittedly, this is likely because I was raised in a drama-free household.

I once tried being dramatic when I was fourteen. My mother told me to add it to the calendar.

We arrived at the house, Sam and I arm-in-arm, the boys behind us. We walked in the door. Martin gave me a curt nod then left. That's right, he walked away. He disappeared into the crowd.

I stood there stunned for about twenty seconds before Sam pulled me closer and yelled over the music, "Maybe he has to use the bathroom or something."

"Or something," I said, feeling gargantuan levels of annoyed and hurt and confused. Boys were so epically strange and obviously placed on the earth to torture girls. Martin's behavior made no sense. I considered trying to sort it out, but ultimately decided the actions of men were beyond my comprehension.

I noted Herc was glued to Ben as they passed and were absorbed into the throng. I'd wondered if Ben would try to drug someone at this party, but now I suspected Herc has been assigned to keep an eye on him.

Sam, Eric—who, let the record show, stayed with Sam—and I took a brief tour of the party. We walked from room to room, surveying the surroundings, getting a lay of the land as it were. To me it looked like a party in a big house and nothing more exciting than that. So...not at all exciting.

The rooms were gargantuan and lavishly decorated and were getting trashed by partygoers. A DJ played loud house music. People were dancing and getting drunk, and talking loudly to hear each other over the music. The majority of the girls were dressed in string bikinis. The majority of the guys were dressed in shorts and T-shirts, or board short swim suits. The pool was huge and wrapped around one side of the house. It had a waterfall and three slides as well as four hot tubs.

Sam said she wanted to go swimming. I hadn't brought a swim suit. She lifted up a bag on her shoulder and informed me that not only had she brought me a swim suit, it was a string bikini. I thought I might die of happiness.

That last part isn't true. I was being sarcastic. Sorry.

Sam and I left Eric on the deck with a promise to return once we were appropriately attired. I numbly got dressed, refusing to look at myself in the mirror, because…why? Why would I do that to myself? Afterward, we walked downstairs. We walked on to the deck.

And I saw Martin kissing a girl.

That's literally how it happened. I took two steps out the door, scanned the space for Eric, and instead saw a leggy blonde with her arms around Martin's neck and her body plastered to his, and her mouth suctioned on his like she wanted to taste his dinner.

I immediately averted my gaze.

Even though you don't feel calm doesn't mean you can't be calm.

"I'm going to kill him." Sam's voice was low with menace.

I gripped her arm to keep her in place and I shook my head, letting her see I considered the whole situation ridiculously futile. I doubted my gaze of acceptance had been very effective because I could feel tears sting my eyes. I turned back to the door and walked away from…all of that hot mess.

I heard her growl at Eric when he started to explain and felt her close behind me as I wove through the crowd. She stopped me when we reached the far end of a huge kitchen.

"God, what an asshole!" I could feel her eyeballing me. "What do you want to do?"

I shrugged and rolled my eyes so I wouldn't cry.

I wouldn't cry.

Nor could I deal with the funnel cloud of feelings that tore through me, because…I just couldn't. I didn't know what to say or do or where to look so I glanced over her shoulder. Several guys were doing keg stands near the largest refrigerator I'd ever seen.

"Kaitlyn, what do you want to do? Do you want to leave?" Sam poked me.

"No," I said. I didn't want to leave. I wanted to find a closet and go chill with myself, calm the rising tide of emotion. "But I do have to go to the bathroom."

"I'll come with."

"No." I shook my head as I spotted Eric hovering behind her, about five feet away. He gave me a grim, apologetic smile. "No. I'm actually fine, I just need a minute. I'll come find you later."

"Kaitlyn…"

"Really, I'm fine," I yelled over the cheering keg standers and lifted my chin toward Eric, encouraging him to rescue me from Sam.

I did need a minute alone. Actually I needed several. Ironically, I was more likely to find alone time here, in this crowd, than I would if Sam and I left the party. She would want to rage against Martin, maybe pack up and leave the island tonight. I didn't want to do that. I wanted to gather my thoughts, leave the party in a few hours, and fulfill my end of the bargain.

Then in the morning, after a very calm, rational discussion with Martin Sandeke, wherein I spelled out all the very factual reasons he and I would never work—for example, how I now hated him with the fire of all the furnaces in hell, and that he was a lying liar who lied when he said he would never hurt me—I would leave the island.

I wouldn't cry.

I wouldn't accuse.

I hadn't really expected any better from Martin, so why should I be surprised now? Just because he gave me an orgasm near a waterfall. So what? It's not like he'd given me a unicorn. It was just an orgasm.

I would *not* cry. I would simply leave.

As soon as I arrived home, I would email my chemistry professor and request a new lab partner. And if I was very careful—and very lucky—I would never have to set eyes on jerk-face Martin Sandeke ever again.

Part 2: HEAT

CHAPTER 1
Thermochemistry

I WALKED THROUGH the house and the partygoers in search of quiet, space, and cleanliness. In the end, numbness descended and I embraced it. Basically, I decided not to care, and instead thought about my ideal party.

Give me a small intimate gathering of five people, a dinner party, where one-on-one conversations can be had, where people talk about current events, good books, good food, and weird news. That was my idea of a good time.

Not keg stands with a hundred people on a private island, with a DJ and underage girls puking in the bushes while venereal diseases were shared in the hot tub. Add to that Martin ignoring me and making out with random girls.

Not that. That was not fun.

I happened upon the library, or a room with a lot of books. It was packed with people and I'm pretty sure a few someones copped a feel as I tried to squeeze past the bodies in favor of the books. I scanned the shelves and felt a spark of something good, something nice as I spotted *Twenty Years After,* by Alexandre Dumas. I'd been meaning to read it for a while. It was about the three musketeers twenty years after their initial adventures.

To my right someone threw up on the carpet. I glanced at the guy and decided that if people were throwing up on the carpet then no one would care if I borrowed a book.

I pulled it off the shelf, clutched it to my chest, and went in search of a quiet space. I roamed the house for a bit, thought about going back to the souped-up golf carts and just waiting for everyone outside, but dismissed the idea. The available reading light would be insufficient. I also dismissed the bedrooms, as those would be occupied. A bathroom was an obvious choice, but not a good one because they'd be in high demand, and it would be selfish of me to tie one up so I could read.

I tried to find a closet with a light. At one point I almost tripped over a passed-out Ben in the hallway. I glanced around and found Herc hovering nearby, talking to several girls. He gave me a nod. I returned it and continued on my way. I decided my suspicions were correct: Herc had been following Ben around. I wondered if Ben had inadvertently consumed his own date-rape drug.

I made a mental note to contact the campus police department about Ben when I got home. Martin had promised to handle it—whatever that meant—but if *handling it* meant no jail time for Ben, I would step in and do something.

Shaking off thoughts of Ben the rapist, I ended up stumbling upon the laundry room quite by accident. It was actually perfect. There was a clean comforter folded on the washer and plenty of reading light. Therefore, I arranged the blanket and hopped up on the machine, leant against the wall with the cushy comforter at my back, and began to read.

It was a truly excellent book. I didn't know how much time passed—two hours, maybe three. That Porthos…I swear, he's a riot. His antics always make me laugh. Although Athos was my favorite. I think it was because of his tragic past. I was a bit of a sucker for a guy with a tragic past.

"What are you doing?"

I lifted my eyes at the sound of Martin's voice, but not immediately. I finished the paragraph I was reading, then I looked up, holding my place in the book with my thumb.

He was dressed in swim trunks and he was wet, with beads of water dripping down his chest. As such, he looked super hot. However, only the right side of his body was visible as the door blocked the other side. His hand was still on the doorknob and he leaned a tad to one side, into the room.

My eyes wandered over his form and I allowed myself to appreciate the beauty of Martin Sandeke like I might admire the beauty of a cold, soulless statue. Physically, he was a magnificent male specimen: corded muscle, long limbs, and rigid angles. Even his temples were drool worthy, especially since I knew his head housed a giant—albeit mismanaged—brain. Truly, he was one of our finest. His ancestors should really give themselves a big pat on the back.

A little pool of water had gathered at his feet, which made me wonder how long he'd been standing in the doorway. My eyes traveled upward again and I noticed he wore an angry expression. He looked livid.

I started a little at the heated annoyance in his stare. Then I glanced around the laundry room, searching for the source of his anger. I found that I was still alone. Therefore, I surmised his fury must be directed at me.

But, just to be sure, I said, "Who? Me?"

"Yes. You," he growled, then stepped into the room and closed the door behind him. "What are you doing in here?"

I raised the book and tipped my head toward it. "I'm reading."

Martin exhaled loudly, another growl. "I can see that, Parker. But why the fuck are you in here reading?"

I frowned at his use of profanity, my shoulders bunching with tension. I realized I'd gotten used to it, how often he cussed; I'd accepted it as part of him. But that was before he'd left me standing at the entrance to a party I didn't want to attend, and that was before I'd seen him kissing a random girl.

"It's the first sequel to The Three Musketeers. I've been meaning to read it. I found it on the shelf in the library—or living room, or whatever room. There are too many rooms in this house, so I don't know what half of them are called."

Martin gritted his teeth, and I got the distinct impression he wanted to strangle me. "Parker. This is a party. And you're in the laundry room? Reading?"

I paused a beat to make sure this wasn't a trick question. When I could find nothing amiss with his interrogation, I nodded slowly. "Yes. This is a party. I am in the laundry room reading."

"Why? What is *wrong* with you?"

My mouth opened and closed but no words arrived, because his questions continued to confuse me. Finally, I admitted, "Martin, I don't know what you want me to say or why you appear to be upset. I found the book when I was in one of the several rooms with lots of books. I've been meaning to read it. So I picked it up and found a quiet place. Why are you so angry?"

He charged at me and I ineffectually scrambled backward on the washing machine. In less than two seconds he'd pulled the book from my hands, slapped it on the counter at my left, and braced his arms on either side of my legs, leaning forward.

I realized he'd made me lose my page in the book. I decided to ignore my urge to vocalize this complaint, because his eyes were beyond heated.

They were incensed blue flames. I braced myself, my gaze wide and watchful, and flinched when he lifted a hand. I relaxed a smidge when he used it to push my hair off my shoulder.

When he spoke, his voice was low, strained, like he was trying very hard to control his temper. "I brought you here as my date. That was our agreement."

I nodded once. "Yes. I know."

"And, instead of talking to people or having fun, you're in here reading a book."

I kept my voice even and calm, tried to sound soothing. "I am having fun. I'm reading a book."

"You're trying to punish me for winning our bet, for bringing you here."

I shook my head, hoping he would see the honesty in my denial. "I'm not. I promise. I like to read."

"Who comes to a party, an entire mansion at your disposal, and reads Dumas in a laundry room? I've been looking for you for two hours."

He's been looking for me? For two hours? Why would he do that?

"If you've been looking for me then why are you wet?"

"This place has pools with caves, and I've been through all of them searching for you. You're avoiding me."

"Honestly, Martin…" I shrugged. "I didn't think you'd notice."

"You didn't think I'd *notice*?" he roared.

I winced. "That's right."

He blinked at me once, then held perfectly still. His features completely motionless as though his face were stuck in angry suspension. I could see something building behind his eyes, like how you can see a far-off storm gathering in the distance. Therefore, I decided it would be best to explain before he lost control of his temper.

"Earlier, after I changed," I motioned quickly to the string bikini I was wearing, "I went back to the deck and saw you had your hands full—and at one point, your mouth full of a tongue that wasn't yours—so I figured you were good. You know, entertained, taken care of, no need of my escort services."

He flinched, blinked rapidly during my explanation like I'd splashed water in his face, and his back straightened.

"You saw that?" He appeared to be surprised.

Lifting my hands up between us like I surrendered, I nodded and continued, "But, no worries. I understand that kissing random girls is in your wheelhouse. Which, like I've been saying all along, is another reason why we're not compatible. Because, as I've said—and no judgment—I'm not really into kissing guys who kiss other girls. *That's* not in my wheelhouse. So you should go return to your women folk. I'll be down here reading; no rush. But if you plan on spending the night, let me know so I can ensure to hitch a ride with Eric and Sam, or Ray. For your own safety though, please make sure the sheets are clean. I overheard one of the guys in the library say that he thinks he has ringworm. I didn't ask which bedroom he used."

Martin's eyes narrowed as I spoke and his mouth curved into an unhappy line. When I was finished he lifted his gaze to the ceiling, subtly shaking his head; he paired an eye roll with a whispered, "Fuck."

Again, I flinched at the profanity and scrunched my nose, my gaze moving back to the discarded book. I wondered how much longer this conversation was going to take, because Porthos's shenanigans were seriously cracking me up.

"Parker..."

My eyes jumped back to his, which were now once again on me. He didn't look as angry, but he did look frustrated.

"Yes?"

Martin lifted his hand like he was going to put it on my leg, but stopped when I stiffened. He cursed again. Shook his head, again. Gritted his teeth, again.

"Look," he said, "if you'd stayed, then you would have seen me push her away. I'm not interested in her." His expression relaxed, and I saw the flash of hopeful vulnerability. My heart leapt in response.

Stupid heart.

He cupped my cheek, his thumb tracing the line of my jaw, and added, "I'm not interested in any girl here other than you."

I pressed my lips together to keep from frowning, though I knew my eyes betrayed my disbelief because Martin's frustration visibly spiked.

Before he could continue, I interjected, "Martin, even if I believed you—which I don't—it doesn't really matter. You pawned me off on Ray for the drive over. When we walked in here, into this house, you left me. You walked away from me, and you didn't introduce me to anyone. You went off as though I wasn't there. I don't know any of these people and I'm terrible at parties."

His gaze turned thunderous. "Is that what this is about? Are you down here because you're pissed that I left? I thought I was doing what you wanted. You said that you didn't want me to be possessive and hover. Is this some kind of punishment? Because I don't respond well to that kind of mind-fuckery or passive-aggressive bullshit."

Despite my desire to stay calm, his words felt like gasoline on a fire I'd been carrying around in my chest, but had thus far managed to keep under control. My temper rose and with it the volume of my voice.

"No, Martin. I don't do passive-aggressive and I don't punish people. That *is* one of my life rules. I'm honest. If something upsets me, I'll let you know. But in order for me to be upset, I'd have to be surprised by your terrible behavior. What you did, leaving me in a room full of strangers and giving CPR to female partygoers didn't upset me, because I don't really expect more from you."

It was his turn to flinch. He sucked in a sudden breath and straightened away from me, his eyes cooling to frigid icicles. "What the hell is that supposed to mean?"

"It means you're used to getting what you want or who you want when you want it. And I couldn't care less if you were upstairs, right now, having a ginormous orgy with the ringworm gang. Because I've known all along that you are a jerk-face and you don't know how to treat people with decency."

His mouth fell open, presumably at my words and my hostile tone, and he stared at me. His expression was that of someone who'd been stunned speechless.

I didn't like losing my temper. In fact, I prided myself on how laid-back and in control of my reactions I was, and how I never lost my temper. Therefore, this loss of control was another irritating new development since spending time with jerky Martin Sandeke.

At length, he found his voice. Though, surprisingly, he didn't sound quite as angry. "If you don't like how I treat you, then why do you keep letting me kiss you?"

"Opportunity and lust."

Gah...that was spiteful.

He flinched like I'd kicked him and he glanced away. His reaction made my heart hurt, and therefore, I heaved a gigantic regretful sigh.

My words came out in a rush. "That's not true. I'm sorry. I shouldn't have said that. The truth is…"

He lifted his eyes to mine, and the raw emotion made me forget myself. It made me forget to be cautious. Without really thinking about it or planning to do so, I gave him the whole embarrassing truth.

"You're smart—in fact, you have flashes of brilliance which is a huge turn on for me—and you're funny and charming when you want to be. And sometimes, you treat me with kindness and respect. Also, you're a good kisser. I thought at first it was my lack of experience, but now I think you're just an exceptionally good kisser. I like kissing you. I like the way it feels. I love how you make me feel when you touch me. But what feels good isn't always what's good for me, and I'm not willing to settle for being with someone who *sometimes* treats me well. I'd rather be alone."

With the end of my unplanned speech the numbness returned. I peered at him in a way I hoped demonstrated my acceptance of the situation and the impossibility of us, and I reached for my book. I did all this while I tried to suppress my blush of mortification. "Now, if you'll excuse me, Porthos is rather charming and I'd like to finish this chapter before leaving."

Martin's glare moved from me to the book. Before I understood his intention, he'd reached for the book, pulled it from me, and tossed it over his shoulder. I yelped my surprised unhappiness, but couldn't retrieve the novel because he'd stepped forward again, crowding my space. He gripped my waist and yanked me forward so he was between my legs, and my chest was against his.

My mind might have been numbed to him, but my pants weren't. I sucked in a sharp breath at the contact, everything tightening and twisting and bracing for his touch.

He stared at me for a long moment, during which—I'm ashamed to admit—my heart rate quadrupled and my body responded by pressing more fully against him. When he did speak, his voice was a growly and hostile whisper. "Listen to me for one fucking second, okay?"

I also whispered, but only because he was whispering, "Only if you stop using the F-word like you get paid royalties every time you say it."

"I'll fucking use whatever fucking word I want to fucking use whenever I fucking want to," he whispered back.

I shook my head and spoke mostly to the other washing machine and two dryers lining the walls. "Again, proving my point, jerk-face."

"Kaitlyn, you are irritating."

"Feeling is mutual, jerk-face."

"Especially when you're right."

"Well, you can..." I paused, blinked at him and his shocking words. "Wait, what?"

His eyes moved over my face as he spoke and the tension in his body eased. Peripherally, I noted he was wrapping his arms around me, one hand sliding under the string of my bikini and against my bare back.

"I'm sorry." He was still using his growly whisper.

I narrowed my eyes, attempting to peer into and through his words, looking for trickery. As well, I was trying to ignore the wave of goosebumps that had spread outward from where his hot palm pressed against my back, and the fluttering butterflies in my stomach.

A beautiful man is the devil's most potent weapon.

A few seconds ticked by while we stared at each other. I wondered if I looked as hostile as he did.

I responded, "Do you even know why you're apologizing?"

"Yes." Another growl.

"Why? Why are you apologizing?"

"Because I shouldn't have left you when we got here. I should have kept you close to me, and I shouldn't have let Danielle close enough to touch me, not when we're together."

My brain stumbled on the word *together*, and I frowned my confusion at his accurate listing of offenses. "This seems like a miraculously sudden apology."

His jaw flexed. "Are you seriously going to give me shit about apologizing?"

I shook my head. "No. No, I am not. I accept your apology. Thank you for apologizing."

His eyes flickered between mine, then lowered to my mouth. "Now it's your turn."

"My turn?"

"Your turn to apologize."

My eyebrows bounced an inch upward. "What am I apologizing for?"

"For always assuming I'm an asshole."

It was my turn to stare at him while he filled the silence, his chin dipping toward mine, our mouths scant inches apart.

"I didn't leave you because I was trying to be a jerk. I wanted to give you your space. I thought I'd circle back around and find you…prove that I trusted you. I don't know how to be near you without being possessive, because every time a guy looks at you I want to rip his head off. I've never come to a party with someone before. I don't know girl-rules. This is new for me. And I wasn't kissing Danielle. She kissed me and I pushed her away, but you obviously didn't stick around for the half second it took me to tell her I wasn't interested."

My mouth opened and closed. I was shocked. His words shocked me.

He wasn't finished. "You promised me you would give this a try. But you've already made up your mind about me. Sitting down here, avoiding me, isn't trying. Seeing another girl kiss me, and then walking away, isn't trying. Assuming the worst of me isn't trying. Either you do this for real, or you break your promise. But don't put this all on me. I'm not a fucking mind-reader."

I sputtered, perplexed. "Okay, I'm sorry. I'm sorry I assumed the worst.

I shouldn't have done that."

"Apology accepted. Now kiss me."

I evaded his mouth by leaning to the side and bracing my palms against his chest. "Wait, just wait a minute. I don't know. What did you want me to do? Walk over and rip that girl's hair out?"

"Yes." He stated this emphatically and paired it with a single head nod, his eyes lowering to my breasts. The small triangles of the string bikini did very little to cover them; I felt like I was wearing pasties and floss. Martin seemed to both love it and hate it because he released a frustrated and distracted sounding sigh and lifted his gaze to mine. "Yes, if I matter to you, then yes."

"Martin...I'm..." I shook my head, having difficulty finding words. They were hiding in all the closets of my brain, the little bastards.

Finally I managed, "I'm not like that. I'm not going to enter a race I can't win."

His hand moved from the middle of my back to my waist, his thumb drawing a gentle circle on my ribs, tickling me, touching me, feeling me. "You totally could have taken her. She's not a good fighter. She favors her right side."

I laughed because what he said was preposterous and therefore funny, and I was relieved to see that even after our harsh exchange, he was trying to cut the tension with humor.

"That's not what I meant. I know I could have knocked her out. She probably hasn't eaten in days, the poor dear."

"Then what do you mean? Because you are the only boat in this regatta."

I shook my head, feeling high and low and everything in between. "I don't know how to do this. I'm the bow-out-gracefully kind of girl, not the brawling-for-my-man-at-a-party kind of girl. Not when my competition is a supermodel."

Martin's stare was severe and stern, and his thumb stilled on my skin. "If all I wanted was a supermodel then I wouldn't be here with you."

I scrunched my face at this. It sounded like a compliment, but it also sounded like an insult. I had no illusions I was supermodel material, but to my ears his statement emerged as, *If I wanted someone good-looking then I wouldn't be with you.* I knew that was wrong and unfair and twisting his words, so I threw that messed-up interpretation into the garbage where it belonged...but my sinking heart lingered.

He growled a sigh and rolled his eyes. "That's not...that came out wrong. What I mean is, yes—of course I want to be with someone who is beautiful. But you're so much more than that. Why would I bring a single scull to an eight-man race? I wouldn't."

"A single skull?"

"A scull. It's a boat with one rower and two oars. An eight-man racing shell would beat a single scull every time."

I squinted at him and nodded once, rolled my lips between my teeth, and tried not to laugh at his manly rowing analogy. I let him know I understood the gist of what he meant and that I wasn't going to hold the conversation hostage.

He continued, "But I need you to fight, not bow out gracefully. When you want something, you fight for it."

I lowered my eyes to his neck, watched him swallow. I inhaled and held the breath in my lungs, unsure what to say or how to proceed. This was not how I foresaw the discussion progressing.

"Look at me," he demanded, and I did.

"When you want something, you fight for it," he repeated, the pressure of his hands increasing on my body, telling me he wanted me, telling me he would fight for me.

Then he asked, "Do you want me?"

I stared at him for a beat, the answer having immediately formed in my brain, but I hesitated. I felt like admitting my want for him would give Martin power over me, power I wasn't ready to cede.

He must have seen my struggle because before I could speak, he volunteered, "You don't have to answer that right now. You tell me when you're ready, okay?"

I nodded, releasing an unsteady sigh. "Martin..."

"Shh, just...just listen to me." He licked his lips, his mouth scant inches from mine. His eyes told me he was interested and invested, the rest of his body communicating that everything he'd said was the truth. I might not have been a gazelle, but his body wanted my body.

Eventually he continued on a rumbly, seductive whisper, "Maybe you're right. Maybe I don't know how to treat people. But I meant it when I said that I...fucking hell, I want you. I like you. I'm all in. I'm not a liar and I'm doing my best here. You need to meet me part way."

I nodded, no longer feeling numb.

I read the intention in his eyes before he moved and I shivered in anticipation. He slid his hand from my ribs up to my neck and pulled the string holding my top up. He leaned just two inches away and the flimsy thing immediately acquiesced, the little triangles ineffectually supporting my D-cup fell, baring me.

"I need to touch you," he said even as he touched me, both of his hands sliding into place, massaging, kneading.

I sighed, arched my back, offering myself more fully to his wonderfully callused hands.

"I need you to touch me," I whispered on a gasp. His fingers tugged on my nipples, sending liquid fire straight to my core.

He bent his head, bit my neck, then gently kissed the two love bites he'd left yesterday. "I like these. I like seeing my mark on you."

He used his knuckles, brushing them back and forth over the tight peaks. I tried to press myself tighter against him, needing his palms, not the light, maddening, teasing sweeps of the back of his hands.

He tongued my ear, making me tremble, before his hot exhale spilled against my jaw and neck. "I want to taste you."

I had a flash, a thought, an image pass through my mind and it made me groan. Martin, bending over me, kneeling, his mouth at my center, licking, sipping, tasting, sucking, as I reclined on the washing machine and his blue eyes watched me. Some dark, pleasure-seeking part of myself became obsessed with this idea.

"Oh, please do," I panted. Obviously the time for pride was at an end.

He chuckled. It sounded wicked, throaty, and really evil. Unsurprisingly, wicked and evil were really hot on Martin Sandeke. Desperate for what my body wanted, I brushed my fingertips down the front of his chest, lower to his abdomen, and lower still into the material of his swimsuit.

He sucked in a stunned breath and I felt his muscles tighten, grow rigid as I cupped his length, gripped it. The feel of it, the hardness, the thickness thrilled me. It was the greediest part of him and a surge of aroused power made my sex pulse.

"Fuck me," he exhaled, his eyes closing, his hips moving in an inelegant, wild movement.

"Surprised?" I asked. I was surprised. I was surprised by my vixenish boldness.

He laughed, it was tight and tortured sounding. "You have to stop," he said even as he pressed himself more completely in my hand.

"Or what?"

"Or I'm going to come all over your tits."

I thought about that. I'd seen something similar in a porno last year. At the time I'd cringed, somewhat grossed out. But with Martin it sounded really sexy. I didn't see a problem.

"Okay."

"Don't say it unless you mean it." He looked wild, feral, and I knew he was trying to control some dark impulse to take without asking.

"I mean it."

He growled, then covered my mouth with his, devoured me—his lips and tongue bruising, desperate, almost angry. He pushed his swim shorts down then moved one of his hands to cover mine where I held him. Guiding me, he gave himself a rough stroke. I felt him shudder, his mouth separating from mine as he inhaled a shaky breath.

"Fuck, fuck, fuck…" he said.

"Say my name," I whispered. The constant *fucks* were seriously getting on my nerves. Therefore I thought I'd offer him an alternative. "Say Kaitlyn instead."

His eyes flashed. Hips grinding into my palm, jaw clenched, he growled, "Kaitlyn."

I smiled. My smile made him groan. His head fell against my shoulder and his hands grabbed fistfuls of my bottom. He chanted, "Kaitlyn, Kaitlyn, Kaitlyn…" and, honestly, it got me hot. Soon I was panting.

One of his hands released me and returned to my breast, giving it rough treatment, grabbing and pinching while he bit my shoulder with his sharp teeth and thrust into my hand.

"Oh God, Kaitlyn." The words were tight yet uncontrolled. Every one of his muscles strained, flexed. His hands on my body tightened, his grip so hard I wondered if he'd leave bruises, and I finally understood what people meant when they said, *Come apart in my hands.*

Because Martin came apart in my hands. He came apart all over me, and yes, part of the coming apart landed on my breasts. Basically he came apart on everything but my hand. I gasped, not at all prepared, then laughed my surprise.

Sure, I'd seen pornos and money shots. But Martin's semen seemed to launch out of him—and there was a great deal more of it than what I'd seen in the dirty films.

His breathing was ragged and he sagged against me, his grip now loose, the tremors receding and leaving him gasping. I brought my other hand up to his back and stroked him from his shoulder blades to the base of his spine, then back again. I felt and heard him sigh. It sounded content. I did it again and again, soothing him.

He placed a kiss on my shoulder, lingered there as his heart slowed.

"I didn't know it was going to do that," I said suddenly, voicing my thoughts.

He stiffened—not much, just a little—and leaned just far enough away to bring my eyes into focus.

"You didn't know what was going to do what?"

"Your..." I hesitated, feeling unaccountably embarrassed. It was strange, I didn't mind doing it, but talking about it made me feel squeamish and uncomfortable. I cleared my throat, determined to soldier on and not be a ninny. So I said bravely, "I didn't know your ejaculate was going to shoot out like that."

His eyebrows jumped and he gave me a surprised, crooked smile. "My ejaculate?"

"Yes. Like a cannon blast of semen, and there was—is—a lot of it. It's everywhere."

Martin gave a surprised laugh, looking at me like I was weird and wonderful.

But then he sobered suddenly and asked, "Are you...are you uncomfortable?" He shifted like he was going to grab one of the washcloths folded neatly on the dryer.

"No. Not particularly. But it's getting a little cold."

He stared at me. I stared back. I didn't know what I was supposed to do, how to let his penis go, because my hand was still around it. So I tried stroking him again. He winced, jumped away, and gulped air.

"Kaitlyn, no, no, don't do that."

"Sorry. I didn't...I mean, I don't know what to do after..."

He exhaled, placed his hands on his hips, and dropped his chin to his chest, but not before I saw his small smile.

Meanwhile, I did what I think anyone would do in my situation. I leaned back on the washing machine and gave him a good once-over because Martin Sandeke was naked. He was completely naked. And he was crazy beautiful. I'm not an idiot, so of course I was going to exploit this moment.

I sighed then bit my lip, because I was still aroused and he was naked. This was more pre-bedtime imagery for the win.

He lifted his head at the sound, his eyes moving over my body with what felt like a hungry compulsion. He must've noticed me doing the same because he smirked. Martin sauntered forward, grabbed a washcloth and wiped off my stomach and chest, taking more time and care than necessary.

At some point during his careful ministrations I began to feel inhibited—not because I was ashamed of my body—because I wasn't used to being on display. I wasn't used to being looked at while naked, with desire or otherwise. I'd always been modest, and therefore, as he tossed the dirty washcloth to the floor I moved to cover myself.

Martin intercepted, then covered my hands with his, halting my progress.

"What are you doing?"

"I'm covering up."

"Why?"

"Because..." I glanced around the room, feeling oddly embarrassed, then answered with simple honesty, "Because I'm not used to this, to being exposed like this."

Martin released my hand and I finished tying the strap, but then he slipped his fingers into the cup of my bikini and massaged, caressed, possessed—almost like he was communicating that it didn't matter whether I covered myself. My body was his to touch how he liked. This was confusing because it thrilled me. I felt dominated and I liked it. He loomed, hovering, peering down at me, all tall and strong and powerful...and naked.

"You have the most luscious breasts." He whispered this, then nipped at my lips, his tongue darting out to taste them.

"Oh? The most?" I panted.

I felt his smirk return. "Yes. The most."

"Luscious?"

"And delicious."

"Really? Are they flavored?"

"Yes. Kaitlyn flavored...and now Martin flavored. I wonder what the rest of you tastes like."

My eyes flickered to the door behind him as sounds of partygoers being loud and ruckusy ebbed and flowed, cutting through this little world we'd created in the laundry room. I gathered a deep breath, swallowing down my desire. I'd already ventured quite far out of my comfort zone for one night. I needed time to think and regroup.

So I shook my head, returning my eyes to Martin's. "No, no. I'm good."

He lifted a single eyebrow, clearly surprised. "You're...good?"

I nodded. "Yeah. That was fun...watching you and, um, touching you during. I'm good."

He studied me, his eyes narrowing. "What if I'm not good?"

I glanced to one side, then the other, trying to figure out why he wouldn't be good. "Did I not do it right?"

"No, no. Not at all. You did great. That's not what I meant. What if..." He paused, his eyes moving down the length of me, blazing a path that left goosebumps in its wake. He reached for my hand and brought my middle finger to his mouth. I was transfixed as he sucked it into his mouth, his tongue swirling. I moaned. I did. Because the inside of his mouth felt like the gateway to heaven.

"Oh, Martin, what are you doing?"

He withdrew my finger and rubbed the pad of it back and forth over his bottom lip. "I need to taste you, Kaitlyn. I want to fuck you with my tongue."

I shivered convulsively and had no idea how to respond to that, so I said, "I have no idea how to respond to that."

"Say yes. Say: Yes, Martin. I want you to fuck me...with your tongue."

"I don't think my mouth can say those words out loud. I'm not that outgoing."

He grinned, bringing my knuckles to his mouth and slipping the aforementioned tongue against the back of my middle and index finger, licking the space between them where they joined. I gasped because the spot seemed to be a wormhole; he'd bent time and space creating a shortcut to my clitoris.

I yanked my hand away, hopped off the machine, abruptly standing, forcing him to take a step back. He moved to reach for me but I placed two hands on his chest—*stupid perfect chest*—holding him at bay.

"Just...just give me a minute."

"Kaitlyn—"

"No, no, no. I need a minute."

"Let me—"

"I don't think I'm ready for that, okay?"

He caged me in, his hands on the machine behind me. "You seemed ready for it earlier." His voice was teasing, held sensual promise that my pants really liked. I think my pants are the president of the Martin Sandeke sensual promise fan club.

I shook my head, staring up at him, my words rushing out of me. "I wasn't. I mean, I wanted to and I want you to, but I don't think I'm ready...yet. I mean I just had my first orgasm yesterday afternoon. We just kissed for the first time on Friday. *Friday*. I can't move this fast. I need time to acclimate to changes, process what they mean."

His scorching gaze subdued, grew thoughtful, and he straightened, giving me space.

I continued, "If I keep giving in while we're in the moment then none of this has meaning."

This last statement seemed to make a huge difference. He rocked back on his feet then took two steps away; to my surprise, he was nodding. "That makes sense."

I clasped my hands and returned his nod. "It does, right? I mean, we could jump each other's bones now, in this laundry room, but what would it really mean? It would feel good—really, really good—but—"

"But it wouldn't have meaning for you," he finished for me, his eyes searching mine. Martin's voice deepened and his gaze grew open and earnest. "I want it to have meaning, Parker. And I'm fine with waiting for some things, but I still need to touch you."

I gave him a little smile, my hands on my hips. I felt a tad silly standing in front of him, talking about giving meaning to physical intimacy while the barest remnants of his sperm dried on my stomach and chest.

"And I still need you to touch me, Martin. That's part of this whole dating thing...I think. The point is, we're trying to figure it out, right? And I think we can."

"Good." He rushed forward, like he needed to be close. His hands moved to touch my waist, stalled, then settled benignly on my shoulders. "Good. We're on the same page."

"Good." I grinned, feeling excited.

It was, I realized, the first time I'd truly entertained the possibility that things might actually work between us. Before this moment I'd kept my guard up, trying to prove the null hypothesis, ready for Martin to mess up or for him to realize his interest in me was transitory and misplaced.

He must've seen some shift in my expression because his answering smile was soft and hopeful.

He asked, "You want to have some tacos?"

"What? Here? Now? They have tacos?"

"Yeah." Martin's eyes skated over my face and they lit at my delight. "They have a taco bar."

"Oh my God." I stared at him for a beat, my mouth agape, then nodded vehemently and declared, "Best party ever!"

CHAPTER 2
Chemistry of the Environment

I WOKE UP the next morning struck by a sudden idea of super genius.

Actually, it was almost noon when I woke up, so I guess I woke up the next afternoon struck by a sudden idea of super genius.

It had to do with something Martin had said the night before, just before we'd eaten our tacos.

Last night, after Martin grabbed a clean beach towel from the dryer, we left the laundry room of sensual promise. We held hands as we navigated the party; navigating the party with Martin was quite different than navigating it on my own. The sea of bodies parted—people catching sight of him or sensing him, all moved out of his way.

He steered us back to the deck, then continued his hasty strides toward the pool. Along one of the walls were three outdoor shower stalls. Martin turned on a shower, set the temperature to warm, and pulled me under with him, rinsing the last of our encounter from our skin.

This left me feeling both cleaner and dirtier. Cleaner for obvious reasons. Dirtier, because he made no attempt to school his expression as he looked at me. Clearly, he appreciated my form; his eyes followed the trail of water as it flowed over my shoulders, between my breasts, down my stomach and legs. Under the burden of his scorching gaze, I attempted to remind myself of my feminist ideals, that I was not put on this earth to be attractive to men.

But those ideals felt really faraway, maybe a little naïve, and a lot inconvenient.

Being desired and desirable was a heady feeling. It was addictive; it felt really, really good. And the way Martin looked at me and desired me, with forceful concentration and barely restrained intensity, made me wonder if Oreos and yoga pants were all that great after all.

That thought felt like sacrilege.

Then he bent and whispered in my ear, "All I can think about is touching you."

At the time, the comment made me hot all over because all I could think about was Martin touching me.

But in the clear light of early afternoon it made me realize that the touching—though verra verra nice—might actually be the problem.

Sam was, once again, sleeping in the bed with me. I'd tried to explain what had happened with Martin at the party, the PG version, and how we'd misinterpreted the kiss. She interrupted my explanation to tell me she already knew we'd misinterpreted the kiss. Apparently Sam had taken it upon herself at the party to confront the leggy blonde, Danielle, on my behalf. Danielle admitted that Martin wasn't interested. Sam then spent most of the night trying to find me to tell me the news.

Once she spotted me eating tacos with Martin she figured he'd found me and we'd worked it out.

However, Sam made it a point to insist that she and I sleep together. I think, in a way, we'd become each other's chastity belts. If we were sleeping with each other then we couldn't be doing more than sleeping with anyone else.

I left the bed quietly, showered, changed into shorts and a T-shirt, then went in search of Martin. I found Ray and Griffin first. They were on the multi-level balcony that ran the length of the back of the house. To my surprise, they were studying.

Ray informed me that Martin might not be up yet as it was one of the only mornings they'd planned not to practice.

"He tries to sleep in for as long as possible if there's no practice," Ray explained. "But I can tell you where his room is. I don't think he'd mind if you woke him up."

"Hmm…" I hesitated. I didn't want to interrupt his sleep, especially if he rarely had an opportunity to sleep in.

"I don't think he'd mind at all," Griffin added with a dimpled grin, his brown eyes moving in slow appraisal from my ankles to my eyes.

I gave him a narrowed glare. He looked like the type to eat lo mein leftovers if given the opportunity.

"Sure, okay," I said to Ray. "Can you draw me a map?"

While Ray pulled out a blank piece of paper to draw a diagram of the house, Griffin returned my suspicious gaze with a teasing twist of his lips.

"So your grandfather is an astronaut?"

I nodded. "Yep."

"And your mom, she's the senator, right?"

"That's right."

"Didn't your grandma work on the atomic bomb, or something?"

"Something like that." My maternal grandmother was a physicist. She didn't work directly on the Manhattan project, but she did help the US government equip the earliest nuclear submarines.

"Must be weird coming from such a famous family."

I wrinkled my nose. "We're not famous."

"That's not true. You're like American royalty. Isn't your dad the president of something?"

"No. He's a dean at a college of medicine."

Griffin blew out a low whistle, his gaze growing less appraising and more introspective. He sat up straighter, his face and tone becoming serious, almost reverent. "So, you're like really smart then, right? What are you going to do? What's your major? You'll probably cure cancer or something."

I stared at him for a beat, not wanting to respond. I was proud of my family, but their accomplishments were not my accomplishments, their ambitions were not my ambitions.

For better or for worse, our ceiling and our floor are initially judged by our ancestry. People expected me to reach for the stars.

I was smart, but I wasn't a genius physicist working on nuclear submarines, or an astronaut, or the dean of a college of medicine. I didn't have the drive for greatness. I lacked the patience required for that kind of pressure. I had the drive for normalcy and anonymity and playing around on my guitar.

I shifted my gaze to Ray's and found him watching me, his eyebrows suspended over his eyes, as though to say, *See. You're the ultimate marriage girl.*

I ignored Griffin's question, giving him a tight, noncommittal smile, then affixed my attention to Ray. "So, Ray, how close are you to being done with that map?"

***

MARTIN WAS ASLEEP when I found him. He was shirtless, all tangled up in his simple brown sheets and comforter on a twin bed that looked too small for him. He held a pillow to his chest, another was at his back, and another under his head. The twin bed was pushed against a corner; he'd surrounded himself on all sides with cushy comfort, like he was being embraced while he slept.

The size of the bed surprised me. I was also surprised by how small his room was. It was maybe double the size of just the king bed I'd been sleeping in and was sparsely furnished, like a real bedroom might be. In addition to the twin bed, there was a dresser with no mirror, a desk with a simple wood chair, and a side table. Stuff littered the surfaces like a person really lived here.

It was the opposite of the palatial suite he'd put me in. My room was a fantasy of sterile white and luxury, the kind of room you'd see in a fancy magazine. His was cozy, messy, and real. It reminded me of my room at my parents' house.

I watched him sleep for a full minute, hovering at the entrance to the room like a creeper. This thought made me smile. Instead of being a hovering, indecisive creeper, I decided to close the door behind me and sit at his desk, be a full-fledged lurking creeper instead, maybe give him a little fright when he woke up and found me staring at him. This thought made me laugh with sinister glee.

I pulled out the chair and was just arranging myself when Martin scared the crap out of me. He sat up, grabbed me, pulled me into his arms, and brought me to the bed. He then rolled me under him and pinned me to the mattress.

"Ohmygod, Martin!" The wind was driven from my lungs by fright. "You scared me!"

He was planking on the mattress, his eyes piercing yet laughing, touching me only where his hands held my wrists above my head. "Good morning, Parker."

"How long have you been up?" I scowled at him, willing my heart to calm and the brief spike of adrenaline to recede.

"For about five minutes. I was up when you knocked and I heard the door open." He grinned down at me. His voice was deliciously roughened by sleep.

"Do you always grab girls and throw them on your bed when you wake up?"

"Only if that girl is Kaitlyn Parker."

I appreciated that he'd just used my own line against me and I shook my head at his shenanigans. This seemed to make him happy because his eyes lit with menacing satisfaction.

But then the longer we stared at each other the thicker the air grew between us, and the more difficult it became for me to breathe. His gaze also changed and lit with a new flame, both ominous and hungry. I momentarily forgot why I was there and what my super genius idea had been. All I knew was that his look held the promise of something that was going to feel fantastic.

"I like you here," he whispered, his eyes half lidded as they moved to my mouth, lingered there.

"You like me where?"

"In my bed. Being in my bed every morning should be one of your life rules."

"Oh…" Every inhale felt painful, tight.

"All I can think about is touching you," he said, lowering himself to kiss me.

It was the key phrase and it sparked my memory. I remembered why I was there. I remembered my super genius idea.

"Wait!" I said, turning my face to the side.

"Wait?"

"Yes, wait. I have an idea and it involves you not kissing me."

"That sounds like a terrible idea." He nuzzled my neck, licking my throat, using his hot breath to make me squirm.

"It also involves you letting me go."

"Another terrible idea."

"But it's not. It's really genius…oh!"

Martin nudged my legs apart with his knee then settled himself on top of me, grinding his *good morning* wood into my center.

"You are so sweet," he said, biting me then tasting me with his tongue. "I can't get enough of you. I dreamt about you last night, under the shower—"

"Seriously, listen to me." My words were weak and I'd closed my eyes so I could focus on all the sensations associated with Martin above me, Martin licking me, Martin touching me. Instinctively I tilted my hips to cradle him. "This is really important and I think it'll…oh…oh, that feels good…"

His laugh was rumbly and pleased. "Are you going to give in, Kaitlyn? Do I get to taste your sweet pussy? Or should I make you come like this?"

"No." I shook my head, squeezing my eyes shut, my words breathless. "No. I want all of this to matter. I want it to last."

Martin stilled his movements, his mouth on my throat ceasing its exploration, and I felt his lithe body stiffen briefly, then relax.

"Ah…damn." He sighed, placing a soft, closed-mouth kiss to my collarbone then rolling to the side, releasing my wrists.

I pulled in a huge breath, filling my lungs with cool air, and pressed my knees together. My pants hated me. Hated. Me.

Damn was right.

Darn, damn, dammit, shoot, gosh darn it, heck.

We lay next to each other for a full minute. Our bodies touched, but we weren't actively touching each other. Our breathing similar degrees of harsh and ragged. I covered my face with my hands and found it flushed. I was not surprised. I felt hot all over.

"Martin..." My palms muffled my words, but I had to keep my hands on my face. If I didn't I might jump him and demand he provide my pants with satisfaction. "My super genius idea is as follows: I think we should institute No-Touch Tuesdays."

He said nothing for a long time, so long in fact, I wondered whether or not he'd heard me. I was about to repeat myself when I felt him shift so he was lying on his side. I glanced at him from between my fingers, found him leaning on his elbow, his head propped in one hand, his face contorted in horror.

"I don't think that's a good idea." He placed his other hand on my stomach, slipping his fingers under the hem of my shirt to connect with my bare skin as though to emphasize his words.

"Let me explain."

"Let me see your face."

"Fine." I hesitated then drew my fingers away, folding them over my chest. "Here is what I am thinking. Neither of us have ever really dated someone before, correct?"

He squinted at me. "I thought you said you had a boyfriend."

"He was gay."

Martin frowned. "What? How is that possible?" His eyes swept down, then up, then down, then up my body. Again, he looked horrified.

"It's not like I can turn a person gay. Obviously he was gay before we got together. He...well, I was his beard."

"And you went along with that?"

"No. I didn't know."

He studied me, his eyes searching. "How long were you together?"

"Four years."

"And you didn't know?"

"No. I didn't. I guess I had a very Disney-like perspective of dating before college, very neutered and naïve. We kissed, mostly at parties in front of other people. We held hands, hugged. But when we were together we hung out, had a good time. We were good friends. This is consistent with my parents' relationship. They love each other, but they're good friends first and foremost. I can count the number of times I've seen them kiss on one hand."

"You didn't want…I mean, didn't you want…"

"More? Yes. I did."

"And he…?"

"He said he wanted to wait until he was married."

"Why didn't you break up with him?"

I opened my mouth to respond, but then snapped it shut. I thought about Martin's question. I mulled it over for close to a minute.

Then I responded with the truth. "I don't know. I guess I thought…I don't know. It made sense at the time. We were good friends. We liked each other. We supported each other through a lot. I was there for him when his parents divorced and later when his father died of cancer. I was thirteen when we got together. We were Kaitlyn and Carter. People just expected us to be a unit."

"So you never did anything but kiss? For four years?"

I nodded.

He whistled out a breath from between his teeth, his eyes losing focus as they moved to a spot on the bed over my shoulder. "No wonder you need time…what an asshole."

I huffed a laugh. "He's a nice guy. He was just confused and I'm glad I could be there for him."

Martin's gaze moved back to mine and it sharpened as he frowned. "No. He's an asshole. He used you, he messed you up, made you think there was something wrong with you, that you aren't sexy, that you aren't goddamn gorgeous and fucking hot as hell. If he was a nice guy he would have broken things off so you could get felt up in the back of a car by someone who thought about nothing else but getting in your pants."

I wrinkled my nose at him. "That sounds delightful. I'm so sorry I missed out on some horny teenager using me to get his jollies."

"You mistake my meaning. I'm not talking about someone who was going to use you, who just wanted a warm body. You're too smart for that. You would've spotted a user a mile away. I'm talking about the guy who wouldn't have been able to stop thinking about *you*, because he wanted *you*, not some indiscriminate jerkoff."

"My purpose on this earth is not to be desirable to a man." The words slipped out of my mouth, the thought second nature.

Martin reared his head back and he stared at me—nay, he glowered at me—for several seconds. "What the hell does that mean?"

I shrugged, trying to think how to explain something so obvious to me. "It means I don't care if I'm desirable or not."

"That's bullshit. I call bullshit." Martin pressed his lips together and shook his head. The look he gave me made me laugh. It was so ridiculous on his face; like *Giiiiiirl, you crazy!*

"It's not bullshit!" I insisted through my laughter. "I don't want my decisions to be about what will make me more appealing to the opposite sex. I want my decisions to be about making a difference, being a good person."

"You do care," he said flatly. "Everyone cares. Every single person on his earth wants to be desired, wants to be wanted."

"Okay, let me rephrase then. I don't want to care. I strive to *not* care."

"Now that's something different," he conceded, his hand on my stomach moving lower, his fingers touching the skin just below my belly button as though feeling my skin were compulsory for him. "But don't you think it's about balance? And finding someone who…someone where it's good *to* care? Where their opinion matters because they matter? And being desired by that person, striving to be more desirable to that person, makes you better?"

Now it was my turn to stare at him. I didn't glower, though. I stared. His words were deep, verging on philosophical, a complete shock and a total turn on coming from this guy I'd labeled as a jerk-face.

"Martin Sandeke," I shook my head, my lips parted in surprise, "I was wrong about you. I'm sorry."

He grimaced. It was subtle, but it happened, and he glanced away toward the ceiling. "I don't know if you were wrong about me so much as the fact that everyone I've ever met in my entire life—before you—pissed me off."

I couldn't help it. I laughed again.

His eyes slid back to me and I saw a reluctant smile curve over his lips.

"Everyone?" I asked, teasing him and poking him in the ribs for emphasis.

"Not everyone, just most people. I don't like being framed by other people's expectations. Growing up, I was public property to my parents."

"Even your mother?"

"Especially my mother." He rolled his eyes and the tilt of his chin was resentful. "She wanted to be loved by everyone, but no one in particular. She wanted to be worshipped, but didn't care if people knew her."

"She was an actress, right?"

"Yes." He nodded once, his eyes going back to the ceiling. Martin flopped on his back next to me; his hand searched for mine, found it, brought it up so he could see it, and held it between both of his. "She died when I was thirteen."

"I'm sorry."

"Don't be. It was a relief."

"God, Martin." His callous remark sent the wind from my lungs. I drew myself up so I could look at his face. "That's a terrible thing to say."

"It's the truth. She was a user, an addict. She used me for publicity and stupid stuff all the time. She tried to get me into show business, modeling. I hated it. I didn't want to do it. She did...other things." Suddenly, he heaved a frustrated sigh. "I...I don't want to talk about this."

I pulled my hand free and draped my arm over him, laying my head on his shoulder, and gave him a squeeze. "Then we don't have to talk about this."

He gripped my arm, pressed it to his chest. "It's depressing, and I don't want to associate lying in my bed with you with depressing stuff. I want to associate it with hot, sweaty, naked stuff."

Despite the gravity of our conversation, his comment sent a wave of awareness through my body. I was amazed at how quickly, with just a few words, he was able to get me fired up.

"Well, we're not doing that today. Today is No-Touch Tuesday."

"We're touching now."

"You know what I mean. We're going to do fun stuff."

"I thought you said we weren't going to touch."

I smacked his shoulder. "We can do fun stuff that doesn't involve touching."

"Can you touch yourself? I don't mind watching."

That comment deserved a pinch. I lifted my head, leaned over him, and I pinched the skin of his ribs below his pectoral.

"Ow!" His hands flew to the spot where I'd assaulted him.

"That's what you get for your sass."

"Holy crap, Parker! That hurt. Fine. What did you have in mind?" I saw that he was rubbing his skin; his tone and expression were those of a petulant adolescent, though he looked like he was fighting a grin.

"I'm going to teach you how to dance and you're going to teach me how to row."

"I thought you didn't know how to dance?"

"I know how to ballroom dance. I'm going to teach you the tango."

He lifted an eyebrow; it was an eyebrow of suspicion. "You know how to tango?"

"I do."

"Hmm."

"And you'll teach me how to row."

"Hmm...I'll have to touch you to teach you."

"That kind of touching is fine, it's instructional touching. It's not done with carnal intentions."

"Parker, every time I touch you it's with carnal intentions." His voice was flat and his eyebrows arched.

I huffed and was proud of myself that I didn't roll my eyes or smile. "Well, you'll have to learn to control yourself for one day."

"Why are we doing this again? Why is this a good idea?" His eyes lowered to my breasts where they were pressed against his shoulder.

"Because we don't really know each other."

"I do know you."

I ignored this statement because it was nonsense. "We agreed last night that we want this to last, yes? Beyond this week?"

He nodded, distracted, still looking at my boobs.

"Gah...are you listening to me?"

"Yes. You want me to last."

I pinched him again.

He jumped. His eyes lifted to mine, and he grabbed my hands. "Stop pinching me."

"Stop being a horndog."

He tried to hold it together, but in the end he lost his battle with laughter. "You are so easy to tease."

"Oh? You want me to tease you back? 'Cause I can tease you back." My voice held a threatening edge, low and laced with threatening intent; it made me proud.

He stopped laughing. His eyes grew wide and sober. "Parker..."

"I think I still have that string bikini somewhere. Maybe I could help out by lathering up and washing the golf carts..."

He sighed—more like a growl—and his eyes shut. He released my wrists and pressed the base of his palms into his eye sockets. "That's not nice."

It was the first time I'd used my sexuality for anything...ever. I was so used to relying solely on my brain. Exploiting my femininity was kind of fun. *Who knew?*

Of course, this thought was immediately followed by guilt. My guilt reminded me that the generations before me—like my mother—had worked tirelessly to free women from the bonds of sexuality as the primary source of female importance.

Women were more than the status of their hymen or their dress size.

Then my sexuality bitch-slapped my guilt. Then my guilt sucker-punched my sexuality. I mentally took a step back, leaving them to fight it out amongst themselves, like a giant squid and a sperm whale in the depths of the ocean.

I shook my head before I spoke, trying to disentangle myself from my dichotomous thoughts. "Then listen to me and stop teasing. If you actually want a relationship with someone you need to know them, and not just physically. No-Touch Tuesday is a good thing. It will give us some no-pressure time to find out more about each other."

"I know you." His eyes were still closed and he said this to the room.

"No. You don't. What do I like on my pizza?"

Martin was silent. I took this as a good sign. But he also looked despondent when his eyes opened and tangled with mine.

Obviously I needed to remind him that No-Touch Tuesday wasn't going to last forever.

"And then tomorrow..." I trailed my fingers down his chest, stomach, to the waistband of his boxers. He caught my wrist before I could slip my fingers inside.

"And then tomorrow, what?" he growled, his eyes glinting with a dangerous edge.

"And then tomorrow is Wednesday. Maybe we could play chess, or work on our chemistry assignment."

He shook his head slowly, his voice low and thick. "I don't think you understand how badly I want you."

Again, another wave of awareness spread through my body, sending pinpricks of sensation everywhere, but especially to my pants. Reflexively I clenched my thighs together.

"Martin—"

He sat up and bent forward, the movement silencing me, so that I lay back; basically we switched positions and he was hovering over me.

He held my gaze until the last possible second as he leaned forward and whispered, "So many ways..." He kissed my cheek, his hand gliding down my stomach, his fingers pushing into the band of my cotton shorts and teasing my curls, petting them, petting me. I tilted my hips, a visceral reaction to his touch; but I knew in my heart I needed to keep things from escalating.

"It's No-Touch Tuesday, Martin," I breathed, reaching for his wrist.

His hand stilled, and his face fell to my neck. "Fine. No-Touch Tuesday. But then tomorrow is going to be Wet-and-Wild Wednesday, and the next day will be Tongue-and-Teeth Thursday, and Friday..." He bit me, his teeth sharp—*why were his teeth so sharp?!*—then licked the spot. "Well, I think you can guess what's going to happen on Friday."

CHAPTER 3
Aqueous Equilibrium Constants

NO-TOUCH TUESDAY was a huge success and a huge literal pain in my gluteus maximus.

I'd only been going over the basics of the tango for ten minutes when Eric and Sam caught us in the act. Our twosome became a foursome and this was a good thing, because the tango is not a dance for platonic, getting-to-know-you discussions. I showed Martin the correct hold position and he looked at me like he hated me a little.

Therefore, I paired with Eric, Sam paired with Martin, and at one point, Martin paired with Eric and tried to dip him.

Seeing Martin's silly side with his friend was a huge revelation. Also revealing was that he couldn't dance without taking over, even when he didn't know the steps very well. He could not cede control. He was incapable of allowing anyone else even a short period of leading. But he was also a fast learner and surprisingly graceful, and was soon taking Sam around the room with sure steps.

...typical. He's good at everything, except maybe being nice.

Rosa announced lunch on the balcony and I was starving. The four of us joined a few of the others and sat on the highest level, overlooking the ocean. Notably, Ben the rapist was absent. As was Herc. Apparently they'd both stayed the night at the party and hadn't yet returned.

When the rest of the guys heard my plan to learn how to row, it was met with overwhelming excitement and enthusiasm. Though they didn't know me very well, it appeared rowers are always trying to convert other people into becoming rowers. As such, the group decided to take one of the boats out. Since two people were missing, Sam was drafted to replace Ben.

They also decided to take out a wooden boat—an antique they called Pocock—instead of the sleek carbon fiber Vespoli typically used for practice. Eric explained it would be easier to "set"—i.e. balance—with two new rowers as it was much bigger and didn't sit so high in the water.

They walked it out from the beach until the water reached their hips. Sam and I were too short to be much help with the boat because they carried it over their heads; therefore we brought out the oars.

Martin instructed me how to "rig" my oar, making sure the oar lock was completely fastened, then took me through the motions of rowing with just my arms—the catch, the sweep, the release, the return—making sure I said the words legs, body, arms; arms, body, legs as I moved. He also stood behind me, his arms around me, as we… *ahem* stroked.

O.o

"Rowing is about physics, specifically torque. It's about getting the most out of each stroke," he explained, whispering into my ear. His bare chest was at my back, his legs brushing against mine in the water. He made the act of rowing sound like a dirty, wonderful thing.

"How come you didn't teach me like that?" Ray asked. Both Martin and I turned toward Ray where he stood in the water by five-seat position. He lifted his chin and indicated to how Martin held me in his arms. "Why didn't you hold me like that?"

"Because you've got that rash," Martin said, completely deadpan.

"Oh…yeah. That's right." Ray nodded, chuckling. "Good point."

Once the guys felt sure we had the full motion of the stroke committed to muscle memory, they put us in the boat. I sat in Martin's seat—seat eight, the stroke seat at the stern—and Sam sat at the bow in seat one. We placed our feet in the shoes, stretchers is what they called them, and practiced rowing and balancing, sliding the seat, moving through the catch to release to return.

The guys held the boat in place and kept it level until Sam and I got used to being in the water on such a narrow craft. Then, when I was sure I had everything mostly right, Martin taught me how to feather my oar.

"Like this," he said as he showed me how he twisted his wrists, making the blade of the oar perpendicular to the water at the catch and sweep, but then after the release and during the return he instructed me to turn the oar so it became parallel to the water.

I nodded, gave it a try a few times. It felt clumsy at first, but after a while more natural. Logically it made sense. Leveling the blade during the return would cut down on air drag—again, relating it back to physics. I noticed that the soft pads of my hands were starting to hurt, so I paused and glanced at my fingers.

I blinked, frowned, blinked some more. I had a blister.

Though I had calluses on the tips of my fingers from playing the guitar, there was something really hardcore about having a bleeding blister on one's palm.

"Huh," I said to my hands. I thought it was pretty cool, as it kind of made me feel like a badass.

I'd noticed that all the guys had really rough hands, like *really* rough. Martin's palms and fingers—especially near the joints—were hard. They looked like manly-man hands and I'd made a note of them last semester during one of our lab assignments. I had wondered how this spoiled, entitled rich kid could have such plebeian hands.

He must've noticed my diverted attention because he reached for me, turning my palm toward him for inspection. When he saw the forming blister he frowned severely, lightly touching it with his thumb.

"Damn," he said. I was surprised by how upset he sounded. When he lifted his eyes to mine he looked regretful and troubled.

I gave him a little smile. "I don't mind."

"I do. You should never be hurt."

That statement, and the earnest, stern sincerity with which it was stated, surprised me. Then it laid siege to the remaining defenses around my heart and gently annihilated them. I felt myself melting.

Martin ended up wrapping my hands with medical tape so I wouldn't get any more blisters. Between watching him dreamily, I thought about protesting, but then he made a good point when he said, "That blister is going to tear off and bleed if you don't tape it. If you don't tape them, you won't be able to use them today or tomorrow."

"Why don't you use tape?" I asked as he wound the tape around my fingers.

"I need my hands to be tough. I row almost every day. If you row all the time it's better to let your hands bleed for a while than covering them with tape to protect yourself. If you use tape then you'll have to use it all the time."

"So rather than taking the time to cover your hands, you just toughen up instead? Until you stop bleeding, and you can't get any more blisters because you have so many calluses."

He nodded absentmindedly. "Something like that."

Well...*there* was an apt analogy if I'd ever accidentally stumbled over one. Martin Sandeke was basically his hands. I tucked that thought away for a later discussion.

After hand taping and another half hour of practicing, finally, *finally* they let us row on the open water.

I took Eric's seven-seat, sitting right behind Martin. Eric took three seat so Sam could sit behind him in two-seat. The boat went fast but our movements seemed slow. Martin was careful to set a measured pace, therefore I don't know how fast we were actually traveling. But it felt very fast. It was unsettling at first. I was sure, though I didn't voice it, that I was going to fall into the water. But I didn't.

I didn't even *catch a crab,* which is what it's called when you try to feather your blade too soon or too late and it gets pulled under the water. I was told this usually ends with the oar handle hitting you somewhere on your torso or in your face, or completely throwing you out of the boat (or any combination of the above).

We also turned the boat in a circle using various methods, under Lee's excellent direction.

It was a lot of fun. It was a crazy amount of fun. It was epically fun. When we all moved in unison I felt like I was flying. I loved it. And I could see how rowing might become addictive. There was something about being one with your teammates and the boat, the water and the sky. Something about feeling the rush of the wind, all the while moving your body.

It. Was. Awesome.

But apparently it was also a lot of work because my legs, arms, back, and stomach felt like rubber when we made it back to shore. Sam and I put away the oars as the guys moved the boat. Eric suggested we all go swimming, so we excused ourselves to clean up.

When I finished my shower—my painful, painful shower—I found Sam in her bikini, lying on my bed like she was never going to move from the spot. I put on my swimsuit with a great deal of effort, then collapsed next to her.

"I hurt. I hurt so bad." She said this dramatically, like she might cry. Sam was face down, spread eagle on my mattress. She was clearly exhausted.

"But you had fun." I was also exhausted and lay limply on my side.

Her blue eyes focused on mine, then she gave me a mischievous grin. "It was worth it. I ogled Eric the whole time. I think his back muscles have muscles." Then she added, again sounding in pain, "But I think I'm too sore for sex and that makes me sad."

I laughed, and then winced, my abdominal muscles protesting.

"It's like dating boot camp," she said.

"I think boot camp hurts less."

"That's not what I meant. This, being with Eric all the time, it's like dating boot camp. We've only known each other since Friday but I'm having conversations with him that I never had with any of my previous boyfriends. It's…it's intense."

I nodded—or tried to—thinking about her analogy. "I have no basis for comparison, not really. But you're right. I feel like everything is being rushed, like we're cramming weeks and months of relationship interactions into hours and days."

She gave me a weird, searching look. "Is Martin pushing you?"

"No. But we're…getting close."

"Oh?"

"Yeah."

"And how is that? Are you still convinced he needs just a friend?"

"Yes…and no."

"And…?"

"And what?"

"Don't be coy, I've seen those hickies on your neck. You might be flexible but you didn't give them to yourself."

I narrowed my eyes at her, unwilling to move any other part of my body. "Yes, obviously we're being more than friendly."

"Don't let him pressure you, Kaitlyn."

"It's honestly not like that."

She snorted and rolled her eyes with disbelief. "Yeah, right. I've seen how he looks at you. He wants to have a penis party in your vagina."

I pressed my lips together so I wouldn't laugh, because laughing was painful. "I told him I want to take things slow because, well, I'm the queen of inexperience."

"And he agreed?"

"Yeah. He said he wants us to last, he wants what we do to be meaningful."

"Whoa! He said that?"

"Yes. So we both agreed to slow down, hence the dancing and rowing lessons today."

She smirked, her eyes lighting with mischief. "But he got you off, right?"

Now I rolled my eyes. "Sam…"

"He did. I can tell. You don't need to answer."

"How can you tell?"

"Because you're looking at him like you want him to have a penis party in your vagina."

"Ugh."

"Was it good? Did he use mouth, or hand, or both? I like it when they use both."

"I'm not answering that."

"But it was good, right?"

I blinked at her.

She grinned. "*Niiiice*. Let me know when you're ready to shed your repressed modesty and discuss the baser details. I can tell it was good because of how you're blushing."

"I'm not blushing. It's just warm in here."

"Whatever. I'd high-five you if I could move my arm."

"How do you think I feel? You're already an athlete, I hurt in places I didn't know existed."

"You're the idiot who wanted to learn how to row. Why, Kaitlyn. Why? Why would you do that? Why would you ask that sadist to teach you how to row? Why?"

I tried to shake my head but I couldn't. "I don't know. Shut your whore mouth. I just want to die."

A knock sounded from the door; Sam and I said in unison, "Come in."

Martin poked his head in. I moved only my eyes because even my neck muscles were sore.

"Hey, you ready?"

"No. I've decided to die instead."

He considered me, assessing, then asked, "Are you sore?"

"I would nod but I'm too sore."

Martin strolled into the room, stopping where I lay on the bed, his eyes conducting a slow perusal of my body. "You're going to be sore for a while," he said thoughtfully, his lips twisting to the side. Then he bent down, scooped me up, and brought me to his chest.

"Oh God, I don't even care." I lay limply in his arms, dead weight. "Do whatever you want. I can't even move."

He laughed a little, kissing me lightly then nipping my lower lip. He strode out of the room, calling over his shoulder to Sam, "I'll send Eric in with an anti-inflammatory."

Sam's response was weak and barely audible as he carried me down the hall. "God bless you, Martin Sandeke, even if you are a sadist."

***

THE FIRST THING he did was carry me to the lowermost balcony. I didn't even know it existed. It was hidden and down a short path, away from the house. Then he set me gently in a hot tub. The next thing he did was turn and leave.

That's right, he left me. But he was soon forgiven because the hot water felt amazing, my knotted muscles relaxed. Furthermore, he returned with anti-inflammatory medication, a giant glass of water, and a plate of assorted yummy food.

He slipped into the hot tub next to me, seemed to hesitate, and then pulled me between his legs.

I said nothing. I didn't get a chance to say anything because Martin was using his callused hands to massage my back, neck, and shoulders.

I sighed and just gave into it even though it was a definite grey area for No-Touch Tuesday. He might have meant it to be a helpful respite for my sore muscles, but it was making me feel really good in other places.

Like, as you may have guessed, in my pants.

Therefore I groaned. With pleasure. It was a definite pleasure groan. I didn't mean to groan, but it happened, so there it is. I'm a groaner.

His hands stilled; his thumbs were pressing expertly into my lower back and his fingers were wrapped around my waist, massaging my bare stomach. I felt his quads flex at my hips.

"I can't do this if you're going to make those sounds."

"Please, don't stop." I exhaled. It felt so good. I didn't want him to stop. Maybe never.

It was his turn to groan. His forehead met my shoulder. "And you can't say that kind of stuff."

I wiggled, pressing my bottom and spine backward, trying to get him to move his hands again.

"Kaitlyn, you can't move like that either."

"You have a lot of rules," I complained, lifting my hands and placing them on his thighs, trying to get better leverage to push myself into his skilled fingers.

He lifted his forehead from my shoulder, his hands sliding from their relatively benign positions on my body to much less benign positions— like slipping into the cup of my swimsuit top and my pants. I gasped.

When he spoke next his whisper was more growl than whisper. "I know you don't want to be desirable to a man, but it's too fucking late. So stop making me crazy. If you don't want me to touch you, you need to stop teasing me."

Instinctively, I leaned back, my shoulder blades connecting with his chest and my arms coming up out of the water and reaching for his neck.

"I swear, I'm not trying to tease you, and I never said I don't want to be—"

"I heard you earlier, in my room. I heard what you said. It doesn't matter, because I meant it when I said that all I can think about is you." He bit my ear, like he couldn't be close without tasting me, and added, "Honestly, you should be a little scared. I want you in so many ways, and I can't stop thinking about it."

I swallowed past the rising, choking lust that filled my lungs and sent liquid, aching heat to my center. My breathing was shallow, and as such my words were hushed and labored. "Martin, you don't even know me. We've been here for three and a half days. Three and a half days isn't a lot of time."

He released a humorless laugh and it sent an odd chill down my spine. Slowly, very slowly, almost like it was meant to be more of a caress than a withdrawal, he removed his hands from the sweet spots where he touched me and his fingers closed over my upper arms. He lifted me up just slightly so he could move to the other side of the hot tub, placing as much distance between us as was possible in the small space.

He swallowed, focusing on some spot over my head for a long time, gathering himself—his thoughts, his self-control—before bringing the full weight of his gaze back to mine, pinning me in place.

When he spoke, his voice was hypnotic, soothing, and darkly unapologetic. "Parker, you've been the star of all my wet dreams since the first day of lab in the fall. I'm beyond caring whether you know…I've been watching you. I know you drink your coffee black and always from the same Doctor Who mug. Your favorite band is Weezer, or you just have an incredible amount of Weezer concert T-shirts. I know you mumble synonyms to yourself and it's fucking adorable. I know you look for ways to help people, like giving that girl in lab a safety pin when her shirt ripped, or offering your notes to that douchebag, Kenneth."

"You remember that?" My eyes moved between his, fascinated, enthralled, shocked.

"Yes, and all the other quiet acts of kindness over the last six months. As well as the fact that you're the only girl who has ever refused to give me her phone number."

I was struck by an unhappy thought. "Is this…am I just some kind of challenge for you?"

He shook his head, looking disappointed in me for asking the question.

"No. You are not a challenge to me or a problem to be solved. I want to be *with* you, all the time. Did you think it was just a coincidence we were paired as partners two semesters in a row?"

My mouth fell open and I'm sure my eyebrows were doing strange things on my forehead. A little squeak of disbelief escaped my lips, but overall I was speechless. This was…this was…I was…

Shocked, stunned, surprised, bewildered, confused, bemused, befuddled.

I would have been distressed, except for the fact that Martin had been starring in all my dirty fantasies since the first day of lab in the fall.

I cleared my throat as I thought this over, considering how best to respond. When I was on the precipice of taking too long, I blurted, "I have to be honest, Martin. If you weren't so hot, this would be really distressing. But, for some reason, the fact that you're hot negates the creepiness factor."

His mouth tugged to the side, though his eyes and voice were hard. "Lucky me."

"And also in the spirit of honesty, I've been thinking about you too, mostly your body and face and eyes…but I didn't like you very much before this trip."

"I know. I was always trying to think of ways to get you to see me, talk to me, but you were always looking the other way."

"But I *did* see you. I saw when you fought that guy in the dining hall last semester, and I saw you yell at that girl outside the Basic Sciences building in October and make her cry."

Martin stared at me, some of the glacial frigidity thawing as he considered me. Then he said, "No wonder you thought I was an asshole."

Before I could think better of it, I shrugged and said, "You kind of are an asshole."

He exhaled a surprised laugh, but amazed me by saying, "Yeah. I guess I am. But I don't like to be used, Parker. Do you know how often people ask me for money? People who I considered friends? Do you know how many girls want to throw themselves on my dick? It's not about me. It's about greed. I'm not bored of it. I *hate* it. I've had a lifetime of people trying to leverage me to get what they want. And if I'm an asshole it might have something to do with that."

I nodded, remembering the conversation I'd overheard just a few days ago in the lab cabinet, the catalyst for all of this. That girl was going to drug him, assault him, rape him, and hope to get *pregnant*—all for money. She didn't want him. She obviously didn't even know him.

I added absentmindedly, "Kind of like the calluses on your hands."

"What?"

I stared at him for a beat, wondering if he'd appreciate or be irritated by the analogy. I decided this was No-Touch Tuesday, and tomorrow was Wet-and-Wild Wednesday. If I was going to decide whether or not to participate, then I needed to be as honest and forthright as possible now.

"The calluses on your hands. They're purposeful, meant to protect you in the long run. They're armor, so that you can't be hurt. Just like how you treat people…callously."

His eyes narrowed on me, grew meditative, introspective, but not hostile. He said nothing.

I continued, "You're callous because you have to be. Because otherwise you'd be bleeding all the time."

Martin's face did a funny thing then; he looked like a wounded animal. His eyes flashed, grew at once guarded and distant. His sudden reaction and the gathering ferocity in his stare set my heart hammering. I'd obviously touched on a nerve, because he now looked slightly dangerous.

I tried to think of something to say that could diffuse this change in his demeanor, but before I could, he asked, "What about you?" The tone of his voice told me he was very close to losing his temper.

"Me?"

"Yeah, you."

"Uh, what about me?"

"What about your calluses?"

I turned my face to the side, administering him a sideways look. "My calluses?"

"Yes. You're not exactly a very feeling person." He said these words quite callously, the wall between us now feeling like an actual, tangible thing.

"I'm not…? What?" The hairs on the back of my neck rose, but I didn't know if it was because his question was confusing or because my subconscious was warning me that I was venturing near a trap. "I'm a feeling person. I care about people."

"I'm not talking about empathy for other people. I'm talking about *you*…feeling." His eyes darted over me and when he spoke next it was as though he were speaking to himself. "You're controlled, childish, and repressed."

My mouth dropped open; I pointed to myself with my thumbs and my voice was dripping with incredulity. "Repressed? Childish?"

"Sponge Bob Square Pants pajamas?"

"So? What's wrong with Sponge Bob? He's funny."

"Don't you want to feel sexual?"

Now my scalp was itching, my throat was tight, and I could hear the blood rushing between my ears. I had to take a calming breath before I could speak because I was angry, and I didn't know why I was angry.

"Of course."

He shook his head slowly, surveying me. "I don't think so."

"Why? Because I wasn't ready for you to…to…put your mouth on my private area?"

"See. You can't even say it."

"I can say it." I crossed my arms over my chest, the hot tub suddenly felt too hot.

"Then say it, Kaitlyn." He grinned, and it looked wolfish. "Say the words. Say *fuck me with your tongue.*"

I gathered a deep breath, glared at him and his predatory smile, and prepared myself to say the words. Then I held my breath. Then I gritted my teeth. Then I narrowed my eyes.

"You can't say it," he whispered, looking triumphant and sad—not for himself, but for me. I comprehended that he felt sorry for me.

I released the breath and looked away, my blush now crimson. My anger was multiplied by mortification, my stomach a storm of dismay and disappointment. Why couldn't I say it? What the hell was wrong with me? I squeezed my eyes shut then covered my face with my hands. I felt like crying, it was so ridiculous.

Seconds passed in relative silence while I tried to get myself under control. But it wasn't working. I was going to cry.

Abruptly Martin said, "I wish you wouldn't do that."

"Do what?" I snapped.

"You always cover your face when we talk."

I sensed rather than heard him draw closer. When he put his hands on my wrists, I jumped, startled even though I knew he'd crossed the barrier between us.

"Let me see you." His grip tightened—firm but not hurtful—and pulled my hands away.

I was crying. Not big messy sobs, because that's not how I cried. When

I cried it was silent and usually into my pillow. And I didn't cry often. The last time I'd cried was when my cat died in my junior year of high school. My mother had added an item to our weekly agenda: *New cat for Kaitlyn - Pros/Cons.*

"Why are you like this?" Martin's voice startled me because it was so…gentle.

I lifted my watery eyes to his and had to bite my bottom lip to keep my chin from wobbling; his gaze matched his gentle tone. He looked a little concerned and a lot curious.

"What's so scary about being seen?"

I cleared my throat and glanced over his shoulder. "Just because I'm not ready to take the next step in the physical intimacy pyramid doesn't mean I'm afraid to be seen."

"I agree, it doesn't. But you *are* terrified, Kaitlyn. Everything is logical discussions with you, everything is so reasonable and analytical. Don't you feel passionate about anything?"

"Of course."

"What?"

"…I love my parents." I said this lamely, because it was lame. Not that loving one's parents is lame, but rather the only thing I could come up with that at all resembled passion was loving my parents.

"That's not what I'm talking about and you know it."

I slid my teeth to the side, not sure what to say.

Martin turned, bringing me with him, and settled into a seat. He pulled me, his hands moving on my body to position me as he liked, until I was facing him, my legs straddling his hips. And I let him because I felt lost. This conversation was confusing.

Passion…was a confusing concept to me, which was—in and of itself— a weird thing to be confused about. I chided myself, feeling abruptly clumsy and stupid, and yes, childish. How could passion be so foreign? I'd read enough books about it. I knew, theoretically, what it involved. I felt a degree of passion for books and geek culture, shortbread cookies, and my favorite bands. As well, I'd felt something close to passionate about music once upon a time.

My mother and I had talked through why this passion for music was both good and bad.

It was good to have an appreciation for the arts. As a whole, the arts enriched society.

But it was bad to be passionate, focus energy on something, when I had talents in other areas of greater need, talents that were scarcer and in greater need by society.

She explained that the world didn't need more musicians. But it did need more female—especially female—scientists, mathematicians, politicians, physicians, and leaders. I was good at my music, but being just good would likely never yield the results necessary to support myself as a musician. Nor would I have a directly positive and lasting benefit to society as just a good musician. It was much better to focus on math and science, areas where I was already gifted, areas where I could make a tangible difference.

I was lost in these thoughts, my tears having ebbed, when I became aware that Martin was staring at me, watching me. I felt his gaze scan my form. He'd paused, as though considering me, then brushed his knuckles over the swell of my breast.

My breath hitched and my gaze jumped to his.

"There," he said, his eyes searching mine as he touched me again, this time also tugging the strap of my top down and baring my breast. His other hand trailed along the column of my throat to my shoulder then collarbone, tickling me. I shivered and sighed. "There it is. You have it, and when I touch you like this, it's there."

I could only look at him in response. I didn't want to move even though we were breaking the No-Touch Tuesday rule. I was caught in rule-versus-want purgatory. Ultimately, I decided not to move, and No-Touch Tuesday could go help itself to jumping off a cliff.

His hands slid down my sides, stomach, and hips. Under the water, he used the backs of his fingers on the inside of my thighs and I tensed, paying no heed to my sore muscles.

"I understand that you're not ready for me to fuck your sweet pussy with my tongue. I do. I understand." His whispered words sent a lightning strike of white-hot longing through me. I felt like I might break in half.

He continued, all the while his fingers stroked back and forth, each time coming closer to my center. "If you help me soften my calluses, I'll help you soften yours."

I swallowed, feeling dazed. "How?"

"Be passionate."

I shook my head, a dizzy denial spilling from my lips. "I'm just not built that way."

"From where I'm sitting, you are." Martin growled this then leaned forward to steal a quick kiss, his mouth leaving a trail from my jaw to my neck, whispering after biting my ear, "You are. You've just…turned it off, buried it for some reason."

"Why do you even care?"

"Because, Kaitlyn, and I don't know how many times you're going to make me say this, I care about you, I want *you*."

"But why—"

"Why do people care about each other? What is attraction? I can't give you a list of reasons why I react to you like I do. This isn't an equation to balance. You're the one I'm always thinking about. It's you. It just is."

"You need to rethink that list, because what if I'm just…asexual?" I felt unsteady and sensitized; the hot, balmy, bubbly water licking my bare breasts and back. As such my words were breathless, labored.

He leaned back, captured and held my gaze before speaking. "This isn't about sex, Parker. But for the record, you're sexy as fuck. I'm talking about passion. Wanting something. Loving it. I'm passionate about rowing, and I'm passionate about knowing how everything works and telling other people what to do." He smirked at this last thought, then his eyes grew staid and thoughtful. Martin's knuckles skimmed up my inner thigh and finally, *finally* touched my center. He rubbed the back of his middle finger up and down the apex between my spread legs, whispering, "And I'm passionate about you."

My breath hitched, needy and painful spikes of pleasure originating from where he touched me, singing through my body. These sensations were unwieldy, unmanageable, and I realized it was because I believed him. I believed he was passionate about me.

"Touching you right now is meaningful for me. Tasting you, taking you now, here, would be meaningful for me." He removed his fingers and my thighs tightened. Ignoring my reflexive protest, he lifted his hands out of the water, and then pulled my bikini straps back up my shoulders. He covered me as he said, "But it's not going to be meaningful for you…unless you're passionate about me."

CHAPTER 4
The Discovery of Atomic Structure

IT WAS PAST midnight and I was lying in the middle of my giant bed, staring out the skylight to the stars above.

Neither Martin nor I spoke much after we left the hot tub. I couldn't. I guessed he sensed that I couldn't, so he let me be.

Sam was not currently with me in my super-huge king-sized bed tonight. I saw her briefly at dinner, but then she and Eric and a few of the other guys decided to go for a moonlight swim. I'd been mostly quiet during the meal and didn't want to go to the beach. I felt...morose.

Therefore I excused myself, ignoring Martin's watchful glare as I left, and hid away in my gigantic suite.

Martin was right. I was analytical—overly so—and I'd been using it as a way to suppress passion. Everything could be reasoned away or made to look silly with enough rational scrutiny. Faith, love, hope, lust, anger, sadness, compassion—everything.

And that's what I'd been doing with every feeling and emotion that was confusing or difficult to control. Except, when Martin touched me I felt a little out of control...or rather, a lot out of control. I felt unsteady, I felt uncertain, I felt...

I *felt*.

I rolled to my left side; instead of staring out the skylight, I stared at the wall of windows overlooking the beach.

Passion and being passionate were not bad things. Just like arsenic isn't bad, even though it can be used to murder a person. If passion wasn't bad, then why was the very idea of *being passionate* so terrifying?

I sighed, rearranged myself in the bed—again—and punched my pillow. My pillow was seriously getting on my nerves. It wasn't reading my mind and supporting my neck like I needed. I considered breaking up with my pillow, but then decided to give it one more chance. Settling back on the mattress, this time on my right side, I squeezed my eyes shut and willed myself to go to sleep.

I couldn't.

My body was sore, yes. But it wasn't why I couldn't sleep. I felt restless, I felt irritated, I felt dissatisfied, I felt...

I *felt*.

Abruptly I sat up in bed and threw the pillow across the room. I *felt* like it was giving me inadequate neck support and I hated it. I hated that pillow with passion.

We were never ever, ever, ever getting back together.

I tossed the covers to one side and bolted out of the gargantuan suite. Its largeness was overwhelming and I needed small. I needed safe. I wandered around the house for a bit, intent at first on a visit to the kitchen because...cookies. But at the last minute I took a right instead of a left, went up the stairs instead of down, and found myself in the room with the piano and the guitars.

I hovered at the door and stared at the piano. It was a Steinway grand and it was gorgeous - black and sleek and curvy. Moonlight spilling in through the windows gave it a shadowy, secretive appearance. I wanted to touch it. For some reason, in that moment, it felt forbidden.

It made no sense.

You're being silly, as it's just a piano, I thought. But then I pushed that thought away because it felt too rational. Instead I embraced the sensation of *feeling*. This act, coming here in the middle of the night to touch and play the piano, excited me because it felt forbidden. So I let it be something dangerous, even if in reality it wasn't, because it made my heart beat faster and my breath quicken.

I closed the door behind me and tiptoed to the instrument. I sat on the bench, wincing when it creaked just slightly under my weight. I set my fingers on the ivory keys and closed my eyes. Inexplicably— irrationally—they felt warm to the touch, soft and smooth.

Then I played the piano.

At first I played a few songs from memory—Chopin, Beethoven, Strauss—then I bluffed my way through a jazzy version of *Piano Man*, by Billy Joel. Then I bluffed my way through something new, slow and morose, a composition of my own making that had no beginning and no end. It was nonsense because it was the middle, and everyone knows songs have to have a beginning and end.

My lack of adhering to common sense and established norms also felt forbidden and dangerous. It was dangerous because it was altering. Altering me. I felt myself change, shift in some fundamental way as I played entirely in the bass clef.

It was my song.

So what if it never started or ended?

So what if it was nonsense?

So what?

It was mine and its lack of rationality was seductive. I loved it. It was beautiful to me.

"Prudence," I said to the empty room, my left hand moving unhurriedly over the keys. "Practicality, good judgment, reasonableness, rationality, realism…" Each word was punctuated with a chord in the key of B minor.

Schubert was said to regard B minor as a key expressing a quiet acceptance of fate, but I was using it now as a battle cry. My right hand joined my left to marry treble and bass, the sweet descant like cries and sighs of melancholy.

But then I realized the cries weren't coming from the piano. They were coming from me. I was crying. I *for real* cried, loud and messy and angry. I gave myself over to it, and the piece became *incalzando*—louder, faster—and it felt good to lose control. Like a release. Like unearthing something essential, but up to this point buried.

I didn't angry-cry for very long; my tears reached their crescendo and so did the song…and then I just couldn't play anymore. I stopped mid stanza, folded my arms on the music rest, then buried my head and cried.

They weren't my normal sedate tears, however. They were still messy and raw. Uncontrolled and unsteady. Restless and irritated. Dissatisfied. They were tears of passion.

Someplace, closer to the surface than I would like, a version of Kaitlyn Parker was rolling her eyes at my dramatics, wanting to point out all the ways I was being epicurean and childish.

I was able to keep her at bay because I wasn't being childish. In fact, I was finally *not* being childish. I was waking up from a deep slumber, where the only two things that mattered were being smart and being safe. I was taking the first step toward leaving that behind for something infinitely frightening, for a kaleidoscope of feelings.

The hand on my shoulder made me jump and scared the bejebus out of me. I sucked in a shocked breath, but then immediately released it in a whoosh of relief when I found Martin was the owner of the hand. He was idling behind me.

I huffed another breath, my heart still beating staccato as I calmed myself. I glanced up at him and pointed out the obvious, "You scared me."

He didn't respond. I couldn't see his face very well, but from what I could discern he appeared to be staring at me with something like violent absorption. It was…unnerving. I wiped tears from my cheeks and laughed a little, giving an inch into the instinct to feel silly.

"I don't even know what I'm doing here," I said, shaking my head.

"Parker, you said you could play the piano."

I nodded. "Yeah. I mean, yes. I dabble mostly."

"Dabble?"

I pressed my lips together, liquid feelings still leaking out of my eyes. "Yes. Dabble."

"That's not dabbling. That's mastery."

I flinched at his compliment, then immediately shrugged it off. I began to rise, turn away from him. He caught me by the shoulders and turned me to face him, my bottom hitting the piano keys and making a clumsy chord.

"You are an *artist*." He shook me a little as he said this, his eyes darting between mine like this—what he was saying—was of vital importance. "Why aren't you a music major?"

I automatically scoffed and he pushed the bench to the side with a swift nudge from his knee, then stepped into my space, annihilating the distance between us. The hollow, awkward notes from where my backside still pressed against the keys created an eerie, off-tune soundtrack to what was quickly feeling like another confrontation.

"I'm pretty good, but I'm not amazing."

His gaze searched mine again and his features twisted until they communicated that he thought I was crazy.

"Why are you lying to yourself? What kind of bullshit is this? What I just heard, that wasn't *pretty good*. That was…that was spectacular. That was once in a lifetime."

My chin wobbled, and Martin was growing blurry as new tears filled my eyes. I shook my head in denial but I couldn't speak. I felt too raw. I felt too vulnerable.

I *felt.*

Martin's eyes were devouring my face, like he was seeing me for the first time, or he was seeing a new me, and he was afraid that this vision was fleeting.

"You," he breathed on a harsh sigh, like the word was torn from deep inside him. I watched him swallow and he appeared to be struggling, fighting against some invisible monster or tide, rising above him and preparing to wash his world away.

He said nothing else, though he looked like he wanted to. Instead he caught my cheek in his palm, and pressed an ardent kiss to my lips. His other hand settled firmly on the base of my spine and brought me against him.

My movement was restricted because he held me so completely; therefore I slid my hands under the hem of his shirt and gripped his rigid sides, loving his smooth, taut skin. I rubbed myself against him, sought to deepen the kiss, a little wild with the irrationality of just feeling.

But then he pulled away, turned away, and crossed to the far side of the room. I slouched, trying to catch my breath, and I heard him curse viciously. Yet almost immediately he turned back and charged at me, muttering another curse before he pressed me more completely against the piano, insinuating himself between my legs.

Again, the discordant music caused by my bottom and thighs was nonsensical and jarring. Nonetheless, my heart swelled at the harsh melody, because it *felt* real and honest. Martin rocked into me and I sucked in a surprised breath. His erection was unyielding—granite, hard and covetous—and he rubbed himself against my center with an impatience that felt forbidden, dangerous, and seductive.

As well his hands were everywhere, searching, grabbing, wanting, and grasping as though he would remain forever disgruntled with settling for just one place, one touch. They slid under my shirt, pushing it up, insisting I discard the offensive garment. I lifted my arms to assist and he whipped it off, his mouth tasting and biting my collarbone.

His hands cupping my bottom, Martin lifted me off my feet and turned, supporting my weight entirely. He brought me to the side of the instrument. Abruptly he lifted me higher, then relinquished my weight to the piano. He buried his face in my breasts while he showered them with all good things—some painful, some tender, all wonderful—then pushed me gently backward until my back met with the cool lacquer of the instrument. My legs dangled off the side.

"Martin, what—"

"Let me," he said, his thumbs rubbing a controlled circle around the tight peaks at the center of my breasts, then sliding his hands down my stomach, to the waist of my plain, grey sleep shorts. He curled his fingers around the band, then moved to my bottom, lifting my hips. He tugged the band lower, pulling my shorts and underwear over my hips, bottom, and thighs.

I stared at him as he did this and his gaze didn't deviate from mine. When my pajamas hit the floor his hands slid up my calves, the backs of my knees, the underside of my thighs, lifting my legs as he went until he'd positioned my heels on the edge of the piano, my legs immodestly spread.

Then his gaze flickered away and he looked at me. I held my breath. Waiting. Watching.

Martin licked his lips, his thumbs at my center opening me. Then he bent and placed a cherishing, closed-mouth kiss directly on my clitoris, his soft, full lips lingering at my apex.

"Oh God."

I panted. I tensed. My hands gripping the smooth surface of the piano and finding no purchase. Every part of me sore and throbbing from my earlier exercise, yet singularly focused on where his lips loved my body. He leaned away slightly and kissed the inside of my thigh, nipped at the skin, then soothed it with his tongue, trailing a wet path directly to my slick center. He licked me, softly, reverently. Then he licked me again, and again.

He tasted me over and over; wet, lapping noises that struck me as tremendously carnal married with my harsh breaths and moans. The combination was discordant, awkward, and clumsy; yet like the accidental and inharmonious tones of the piano as he'd pressed me against the keys, the sounds were real and they were honest.

They were the sounds of sex, of desire.

If I hadn't been lost to my passion, if I'd heard the sounds separate from this act, they might have struck me as lascivious and animalistic, repugnant. But passion changed them. Passion changed us. Passion changed *me*.

His fingers whispered over the backs of my thighs, making my legs shake. I threaded my fingers through his hair, pressing him to me, needing to hold onto him. Then he did something shocking and wonderful. Keeping his lips on my center, his tongue lapping me loudly, hungrily, he moved his index and middle finger into my body and stroked.

My breath hitched, my hips lifted off the piano, and I felt my insides shatter into a million shards of pleasure. It felt so good it hurt—the sharp edges of my release cutting through me, leaving a trail of ruin and stunning anguish. My lungs seized as I tried to hold on to the sensation, willing it to last and last.

But it didn't. It couldn't. And when the shards dissolved and disappeared, leaving me cut and wounded and satiated and defenseless, I realized I was crying again.

Not big messy sobs.

Just quiet, joyful tears.

I didn't think about them, whether they made sense or what Martin might think. I didn't try to reason them away or analyze the pros and cons of tears after cunnilingus.

I felt cherished.

I *felt*.

And it felt like perfection.

***

I SLEPT NAKED in Martin's bed. Yep. True Story.

Well, Martin slept. I didn't sleep much. I couldn't.

After our early morning inauguration to Wet-and-Wild Wednesday, Martin wrapped me in a blanket and carried me to his room, leaving my clothes strewn all around the piano. I was deposited on his twin bed. He then pulled off his shirt—but left on his pajama pants—and climbed under the covers next to me. He wrapped an arm around my torso and pulled my bare back to his bare front, slipped his leg between mine, and cupped my breast with his palm.

Then I felt him sigh. It sounded content and it made me smile. I had to bite my bottom lip to keep from laughing because the noise made me so happy.

"What?" His voice penetrated the darkness, sounding curious and maybe a little concerned. "What's wrong?"

I shook my head, willing myself not to laugh.

"Tell me."

I mimicked his sigh, but said nothing.

He stilled, waited, his hand at my breast toying with it, with me. I tried to ignore the lovely stabs of pleasure caused by his ministrations, coiling again in my lower belly.

Out of the blue he blurted, "We should move in together."

My eyes flew open. All thought was bulldozed straight out of my brain by Martin's statement.

"I...what?"

Martin pinched my nipple, rolling it between his thumb and forefinger, causing me to hiss and tense, then he smoothed his hand from my shoulder, down my ribs, over my side, over my hip, until it cupped my bottom. He caressed me there, like touching my body was his favorite thing to do.

This time when I sighed it wasn't meant to mimic. It was a sigh of pure contentment. Who knew that lying in Martin's bed, having one's bottom stroked could feel so good?

"I said," he whispered against my ear, "we should move in together. When we get back we'll start looking for places."

"That seems terribly impetuous and likely to end badly." My voice was lazy, soft, and not at all argumentative.

"It won't end at all, Kaitlyn." He kissed my shoulder, then smacked my backside once. "Now I need to get some sleep or else I'm going to be dead for practice tomorrow."

And with that he resumed our position—bringing me against him, hand at my breast—and fell quickly asleep.

Meanwhile, I did not.

It was one thing to be passionate, it was quite another to let passion be the sole driving force in my life. Reason and rationality still had a place at the table, even if passion wanted to have sex on aforementioned table.

So I spent at least another hour and a half reasoning my way through this latest and unexpected minefield. Because I wasn't going to move in with Martin unless I trusted him completely, unless ground rules were established, discussed and negotiated, unless we were both on the same page. *Unless I was in love with him.*

And I didn't and we hadn't and we weren't. And I wasn't…at least, not yet.

CHAPTER 5
Simple Organic Compounds

I KNOW I fell asleep because I was eventually woken up, and the waker-upper was a demon sent from hell.

"What the actual fuck is going on in here?"

This question was shrieked very loudly, and startled me into a sitting position on Martin's bed. Instinctively, I grabbed the sheet to cover myself. I blinked through my sleep and glanced frantically around the room, worried it was on fire or about to explode—because why else would someone be yelling at me?

I brought the shrieker into focus and frowned at her. I had no idea who she was. I wondered for about two seconds if I was still dreaming and in my dream I was being harangued by an insane wet T-shirt contestant, or a woman made homeless by her penchant for elective plastic surgery.

"Pardon me…I'm…what?" I asked her sleepily, figuring if she were merely a figment of my imagination she would disappear.

She didn't disappear.

"I said," she ground out between clenched teeth, her hands coming to her slim, Barbie-doll like hips, "what the actual fuck is going on in here? Who the actual fuck are you?"

I blinked at her, knowing definitely this was not a dream. I would never dream a person who used the phrase "the actual fuck" unless that person was a parrot trapped in a human's body and didn't know any better.

"I was sleeping," I answered honestly, pushing my hair out of my face. I shook my head to clear the cobwebs as I looked around. I was in Martin's room and the events of the prior night abruptly rushed back. I didn't have any time to organize my thoughts because the woman was still glaring at me, so I continued, stating the obvious. "But now you're yelling at me and I don't know who you are."

Her head did this strange bobbing/pivot thing on her neck, which really made her look like a parrot. This of course surprised me, though I successfully fought the sudden urge to burst out laughing.

"*You* don't know who *I* am? What the actual fuck?!" she shrieked.

I took a deep breath and leaned back against the headboard of the bed. I clutched the sheet to my chest as I surveyed her, noting this was definitely one of those occasions where passion served no purpose.

She was tiny, maybe five one, and very tanned. She was also wearing platform sandals that added four or five inches to her height. She also had very small hips and very thin legs. But her boobs were as big as mine, maybe a little bigger, and truly gave her the unnatural proportional appearance of a Barbie doll. Her eyes were pale blue, her hair was bleach—and I mean *bleach*—blonde; it fell like straw around her shoulders and likely reached her tiny bottom.

She was wearing blue eyeshadow and pink lipstick and there was just something really wrong about her lips and lack of facial expression. Though she was shrieking her face never seemed to alter its expression. It was eerie.

"I'll tell you who I am, and then you're going to get the actual fuck out of Martin's room, leave this house, and never talk to him again." She sounded angry. Her words told me she was angry, but her dead-face was distracting and fascinating.

She pointed to her sternum, the place between her giant, balloon-shaped boobs. "*I* am Mrs. Sandeke, Mart-*tin*'s stepmother…? You see? I own this house and you need to leave."

I didn't like how she said his name. It was…possessive, and…creepy.

"Oh," I said, nodding. "Nice to meet you." I cringed after the automatic words left my mouth, because they would likely sound insincere given the situation; therefore, now flustered, I rushed through the rest of my thought. "Um, well, if you'll give me a few minutes to get my things then I'll be out of your—"

"No." Martin's voice thundered from someplace down the hall and pulled Mrs. Sandeke's attention over her shoulder.

He wasn't running when he entered his room—seemingly careful not to touch her as he slipped past where she hovered at the door—but he sure was walking fast. His eyes held mine as he approached the bed, then he bent down, cupped the back of my head, and gave me a quick, soft kiss.

"Hey, you okay?" Martin looked genuinely concerned, maybe a little panicked, and his eyes darted between mine. I barely had time to nod before he said, "I'll take care of this, don't worry about a thing. You're staying with me."

"Mart-*tin*! What the actual fuck?" This time she didn't shriek. She whined.

Martin's eyes rolled back and I saw he gritted his teeth as he straightened and stood, turned and faced his stepmother.

"Can you get her to stop saying that? It's really irritating," I muttered to his back, hopefully low enough that only Martin would hear.

"Patrice," he said, crossing his arms over his chest, "you need to get out of my room."

Everything became very, very still.

Leave it to Martin to intone so much with slowly and softly spoken words. They dripped with icicles, icicles of hate. I actually felt the temperature of the room drop at least five degrees. I hoped he never spoke to me like that.

"But...but Mar-*tin*..." Her voice became very baby-like, high pitched. It was weird.

I couldn't see her because Martin was blocking my view, but I imagined her expression didn't alter because...dead-face.

"You know you are *never* allowed in any of my rooms."

"But," she sighed softly, like a bird cooing, "you know you don't mean that."

"You disgust me. You're repulsive. You married my father for his money and have been trying to fuck me ever since. Climbing in bed with a fourteen-year-old boy is not okay, Patrice."

I flinched, and my mouth fell open in shock, my eyes expanding to their maximum aperture. There was family dysfunction, and then there was Martin's family. This was crazy. This was Jerry Springer meets Lifestyles of the Rich and Famous meets The Count of Monte Cristo.

"Why...what...why..." Patrice huffed and puffed, sounding lost and alarmed. "I don't know what you're talking about."

"I want Kaitlyn to know. I want her to know what being with me means, what disgusting baggage I carry in the form of family members."

The room fell silent, and I felt another shift in the temperature of the room; it grew even colder.

"Fine," Patrice said, her voice now alto, sounding *entirely* different...like a completely different person.

Instinctively I leaned to the side to see if a new woman had taken her place. It was still her, but her posturing had changed. Her shoulders were thrown back and her chin was tilted stubbornly upward. Other than that, her face looked the same, because...dead-face.

Patrice crossed her arms over her chest and added, "But you should do this skank someplace else, not in my house."

"This isn't your house. This is my house. All the houses are *my* houses. Everything is in *my* name. Everything was put in my name before my father married you, because he knows you'd divorce him, screw him over in a heartbeat if you thought you could walk away with more than a few hundred thousand dollars."

What the what? His house?

This statement—or reminder, I was guessing—didn't make her happy. The room temperature dropped again. I wondered if it would snow.

Obviously feeling cornered and nasty, Patrice decided to go for the personal approach. "You like this type of girl? The chubby ones do it for you?"

"Don't." The single word, again softly and slowly spoken, sent chills down my spine. It was more than a warning; it was a threat and it sounded lethal.

She held her hands up. "Whatever. I don't care. But I will enjoy tearing her to pieces and making her life hell and using your money to do it."

He chuckled at this. "That's funny, Patrice."

She cocked her head to the side as he laughed. "What? What's so funny?"

"This girl right here," he motioned to me, sounding proud and coldly amused, "this girl is Kaitlyn *Parker,* as in *Senator* Parker's daughter. You know, potentially the first female president of the United States in the next election cycle? As in the granddaughter of Colonel Timothy Parker, the *astronaut*. She's untouchable. She's a national treasure. You do something to her, the entire fucking world will bring pain to your doorstep."

I'd never thought of myself in these terms, not really. Nothing he said was untrue, but living the reality of being a perceived national treasure and accepting it were two entirely different states. Therefore, hearing this declaration come from Martin's mouth—like *he had* thought about it— made my brain stutter and a spike of alarm shoot up my neck.

Patricia's eyes slid to mine and, miracle of miracles, her expression did change. The color left her face and her eyes seemed to dim. Meanwhile I sat motionless in the bed, not sure what I should be feeling.

Then Martin added, obviously enjoying himself a great deal, "That's right. She's a goddamn national treasure, and she's my girlfriend, *and* you need to get the fuck out of my house before I decide to stop being so nice to you."

CHAPTER 6
Dimensional Analysis

UNBELIEVABLE.

That's the word that kept flying around my stunned brain. I couldn't even play the synonym game with the word. It was just all completely, totally, entirely, wholly, and absolutely unbelievable.

It was, the entire exchange was, epically unbelievable.

Patricia Sandeke—fourth, latest, and longest-lasting wife of Martin's father—was…truly a different species. I know it's not PC to think ill of my fellow females. In fact, one of my life rules is to try to assume the best of people, but—I'm sorry and I'm not sorry—the woman was a miserable excuse for a human being. She was a caricature, the epitome of a scheming, blonde bimbo gold digger.

Maybe she had hidden layers and a secret pain that explained away all her terrible behavior.

Maybe I was being a petulant and judgmental harpy.

Or maybe there were no hidden layers or depth. Maybe there weren't two sides to this story. Maybe she was a black hole of vapidity and greed.

And Martin…

I tried to swallow. My mouth was dry, and therefore my throat was parched. I hazarded a glance at him but then quickly looked away before he saw my sneak peek.

I didn't honestly know what to think about Martin.

At present he was staring straight again, the set of his jaw grim, the clouds in his blue eyes menacing. We were speeding away from the house via a fancy speedboat.

I didn't know anything about boats, but I knew this one was super fancy for a speedboat. It was like a mini yacht. We were in an enclosed cabin aboveboard that looked over the bow; Martin was sitting in the elevated captain's chair and I was in the co-pilot seat to his left. Both chairs reminded me of splendidly plush, leather barstools with armrests.

The vessel even had a downstairs bedroom with portal windows for undersea viewing. The space was much larger than I'd expected from first glance of the boat hull; it had room enough for a double bed, dresser, desk, bathroom, efficiency kitchen, two closets, and a respectably sized sitting area.

He hadn't said more than two words since we left the house. But before we left, in his room, he explained that he'd cut morning practice short when Mrs. Greenstone radioed Lee in the boat about Martin's father and stepmother's unexpected arrival.

After the showdown at the *I'm not OK Corral*, otherwise known as Martin's bedroom, he gave me one of his shirts and a pair of his shorts so I could get dressed. Then he left and told me to lock the door after him.

To me it all felt clandestine, cloak and dagger, high dramatics.

To Martin however, I suspected it felt like a Wednesday.

He returned ten minutes later with my things and informed me I would be sleeping with him for the duration of my stay. I opened my mouth to question this, but then he added that the gargantuan suite was the master suite, and Mr. Sandeke had claimed it for himself.

I wanted to point out that there were other rooms in the house, but Martin's severe and distracted scowl made me back off. I decided to just go with it…for now.

I changed into my own clothes before we left, but I made him turn around while I dressed. Being naked at night with a happy Martin felt different than being naked during the day with an angry Martin. Yes, the odd modesty rules were likely my own dysfunctions rearing their ugly heads, but I didn't have time for self-psychoanalysis. Martin wanted us to leave the house, and do so as quickly as possible.

He busied himself by stuffing some of my things and his things into an overnight bag.

When I was finished changing, I risked his ire by asking, "What about Sam? We can't leave her here."

"Eric has Sam. He's taking her to the cottage on the other side of the island. We're going to meet them there tomorrow. Everyone else, all the other guys, are flying back today." He didn't look at me as he said this, as he was too focused on his task of merging the essentials of our belongings into one small bag.

"Tomorrow? She's staying?"

"Yeah, I figured you wouldn't stay without her, so…" He sighed, picking up my chemistry book. After considering the cover for three seconds, he put it in the bag.

I guessed he didn't want to chance another encounter with his wicked stepmother. Or maybe it was his father he dreaded seeing. Or maybe both.

Sitting next to him now, while he steered his fancy speedboat with livid concentration, I didn't know what to say.

When I thought about relationships, I had thought the role of the significant other was to know what to say. My parents always seemed to know what to say to each other. But then, my parents had been married for thirty years and hadn't been raised by evil people.

I'd only been conversing (about topics other than chemistry) with Martin for six days. Granted, those six days had included quite a lot of conversing. Sam had been right when she'd said this week was relationship boot camp. I was certainly getting bang for my time buck.

But the fact remained I didn't know Martin well enough to know what to say, or if I should say anything at all. So I fretted instead until he slowed the boat to an idle, stopped it, then cut the engine.

I glanced around us. We were some distance away from the southernmost tip of the island and no other boats were nearby. We were completely alone.

"This was a mistake."

Martin's distracted statement drew my attention. I studied him for a beat, wondering if he were planning to continue unprompted.

When he remained silent, his eyes examining the gauges on the dashboard in front of him, I decided to ask, "What was a mistake?"

"Bringing you here, to the island. We should have just stayed on campus; my father wouldn't have bothered us there. But I thought..." Martin absentmindedly covered his mouth with one hand, lifted his eyes to the horizon.

I didn't wait to see if he was going to continue. I slipped from my chair and closed the short distance between our seats, standing in front of him, and placing myself between his legs. I wound my arms around his neck as he lowered his eyes to some spot on the floor. His hand dropped to his knee but he made no move to touch me.

"Martin..." I tried to use the voice my dad used when he attempted to explain the unexplainable. It always made me feel safe and comforted; in fact, I repeated my father's words now because they seemed right for the situation and it was the best I could do.

"We can't change the past. But we can change how much importance we allow it to have over our future."

His lips tugged to the side and his eyes drifted shut. He shook his head slowly, but I was gratified when his hands settled on my hips.

"Who told you that?" he asked without opening his eyes; his tone told me he was reluctantly amused.

"My dad, when I didn't study for a trigonometry test in high school and then subsequently failed it."

Martin's laugh burst forth with a *tsk* and a wonderful scoffing noise; it was adorable because it sounded involuntary. Best of all, when he opened his eyes and gazed at me, he didn't appear to be angry.

He looked a little helpless, a little lost, a little hopeful, and a lot vulnerable.

"Oh, Martin." I stepped all the way forward and pulled him into a hug, which he returned immediately. I felt a surge of fierce protectiveness for my Martin. It took my breath away, caught me off guard.

My Martin...oh, sigh.

In that moment I hated his father—a man I'd never met—and his stepmother for their treatment of him. I hated them for being too blind or evil to recognize how sacred his heart was, how he needed tenderness, care, and love. My heart broke a little as I wondered whether he'd ever experienced genuine affection from another person.

Given what I knew so far, I thought the chances were slim.

Yet, there was something about him that made me think he knew what *normal* was; he seemed to want normal for himself. He knew that mutual respect, honesty, and affection were essential, even though those closest to him had never demonstrated any of those character traits.

His enemies were now my enemies. I hoped he knew that, no matter what happened between us in the long run, whether we ended as friends after all this was over, he had a safe place with me.

After several wordless moments, I kissed his neck then spoke against the spot. "We have several strange conversations queued up for today's agenda, but for right now I say we just hug it out for a bit, then maybe go swimming."

He *tsk*-laughed again, a little longer this time, then pulled away so he could look at my face. I gave him a bright smile; my heart didn't hurt quite as badly now he was looking less lost.

"Also, I hope you brought food because I'm hungry." I patted his shoulders. "Please tell me there're cookies."

"Are you always like this?" he asked, his eyes narrowing in mock suspicion.

"Like what?" I pretended to be confused. "Amazing?"

"Yeah," he nodded, finally smiling, "amazing."

***

AT THE STERN of the boat, we ate at a table that popped up from the deck. Martin set some fishing poles up and left them in these neat fishing pole holders that buzzed when there was a bite, then reeled the fish in on the line. I didn't even know that kind of thing existed.

"You mean you don't have to hold the pole in order to fish?"

"Nope."

I felt slightly outraged. "But…that's the whole point of fishing, to hold the pole, to reel in the fish."

"The point of fishing is to catch fish."

"That's cheating. You're cheating at fishing."

He shrugged. "Outcome is the same."

A light breeze picked up his hair and tossed it about a bit, playing with it, as though the wind couldn't resist touching him. Behind Martin was the endless green-blue of the Caribbean and the endless, cloudless soft blue of the sky. The unmistakable, but not unpleasant, salty smell of seawater made the palette of greens and blues feel sharper somehow. Martin's gorgeous eyes almost glowed on his tanned face.

I smiled at him, because he'd just placed the last of the grapes from lunch on my plate. "Well, where did you even find this infernal contraption? At the lazy fisherman dot com?" I teased.

"No," he said, "but that's a good domain name. I invented it."

"What?"

He popped a grape into his mouth, chewed, then took a drink of his bottled water before finally answering. "The lazy fishing pole. I invented it."

I stared at him. I couldn't decide if I was outraged or proud.

"When did you do that?"

"It was my eighth grade science fair project. The first mock up was very crude since I'd built it myself. But I did a Kickstarter for it my junior year of high school and they're now manufactured in Switzerland."

"Oh." I didn't know quite what to say, so I studied the grapes.

He was so full of surprises. He was unexpected, and not at all who I thought he'd be. Yet at the same time, who he was made total sense. Martin seemed to really know himself, have a level of comfort and confidence in his own skin. This confidence was wrought by multiple trials by fire, and it manifested as not caring what anyone else thought.

I envied that. I envied him.

Everyone I met always presumed to know who I was because of who my family was, and therefore, what I would do with my life. I had huge, impressive, worthwhile shoes to fill—so obviously that's what I would do.

But rather than think about my own shortcomings, apropos of nothing, I blurted, "I don't think we should move in together."

Martin's hand stopped midair as he reached for another grape on my plate and his blue-green eyes told me I'd caught him off guard.

"Really…" he said, like he was stalling for words.

"First of all, Sam is counting on me. As well, I'm very regimented about things like dishes and messes and such. I wouldn't want us to be roommates and find that we can't stand living with each other. Sam and I keep a chore list and we're both really good about sticking to it. Would you be that kind of roommate? Also, there is the matter of cost, size, and personal taste. I don't mind living in a small space, I actually kind of like it. I also like how inexpensive it is compared to an apartment. It's likely that where you'll want to live wouldn't suit my budget or my size preference. As well, the opposite is probably true…"

Martin watched me through my well-reasoned speech. His surprise at my subject choice changed to a leveling glare of cynicism, then frustratingly, complete withdrawal.

"If you don't want to move in with me you can just say so."

I wrinkled my nose at his frosty tone. "No, Martin—it's not about wanting or not wanting to move in with you, it's about thinking through all the pros and cons of any proposed action."

His jaw ticked. "Do you want to be with me after this week is over?"

"Yes. We're dating. We're officially two dating people who are dating each other, at least that is my understanding. We are dating, right?"

He nodded coolly, but said nothing.

I tried to pacify his sudden surly mood. "We don't have to move in together in order to be dating, or be in a relationship, or see each other."

"When?"

I frowned at his question because I didn't know what he was asking and he looked extremely frustrated.

"When what?"

"When are we going to be together? When will I see you when we get back?"

"You want specific dates and times?"

"How often? Will I see you every day? Or will it be once a week?"

"Martin—"

"Maybe we should make a chore chart for it." He stood abruptly, looking menacing and angry. "Then you can allocate just the right amount of time to maintaining an adequate relationship."

I stood as well, heat spreading from my chest to my neck. "That's not how it would be."

"I'm going for a swim." Martin turned from me and pulled off his shirt; he shook off his sandals as I rounded the table, trying to reach him before he jumped off the boat.

"You're overreacting. Just stop for a second and think about this. I know if you think about this you'll see that I'm right."

Martin's attention was on his watch as he removed it from his wrist. "All I know is that I'm completely crazy about a girl who doesn't want to move in with me because she's worried I'll be messy."

"That's an oversimplification of the issue, Martin Sandeke. You can't let your passion make every decision for you."

"No, you're right." He stilled and glanced up at me then, his eyes glinting like daggers, his voice hard. "It's much better to be a musical prodigy, to love something passionately, but give up and *bow out gracefully*. To not fight. To talk yourself out of caring about what matters to you, because then you'll have all those fine deeds and reasonable decisions and logic to keep you warm at night."

My mouth moved but nothing emerged. He was being completely crazy and irrational and I had no idea how to interact with someone who was being completely crazy and irrational.

But then I looked at him more closely as he placed his watch on the table and saw the unhappy curve of his mouth. I realized I'd hurt him.

"Martin." I placed my hand on his bicep to stay his movements. He winced a little at the contact, but I took heart in the fact he didn't shrug me off. "I'm not trying to hurt you. I just want us to be—"

"Smart," he finished for me, his resentful gaze softening as it moved over my face. "I know. You always want to be smart and do the right thing. But the problem is, Parker...I just want you."

CHAPTER 7
Covalent Bonding and Orbital Overlap

MARTIN WENT FOR a swim. A really, really long swim. I was a little jealous of the water.

I distracted myself by finishing up my last term paper.

He returned and I tried to keep from gawking or drooling as he pulled himself onto the boat. He was wet, so very, very wet. As such, all the oxygen seemed to abruptly disappear from the atmosphere. He dried himself off and I pretended not to watch. Eventually, mostly dry, he disappeared into the captain's cabin.

I sighed unhappily then distractedly studied for my math test. Then I heard a strange buzzing and clicking and realized it was coming from Martin's infernal lazy fishing pole contraption.

He'd caught two yellowfin tuna by proxy and I had to make a split decision: I could go get him and risk losing both fish, or I could try to haul up the smaller, more manageable of the two. I was successful in bringing up the one, but the other broke loose and swam off in the three minutes it took to get my fish netted, unhooked, and deposited in a huge cooler of sea water set on the deck.

"You're pretty good at that."

I looked over my shoulder and found him leaning against the doorway to the upper deck cabin, watching me as I bent over the cooler and untangled the fish from the net. He was still shirtless and droplets of water were clinging to his hair.

"I lost the bigger fish." I straightened and said this apologetically. "I didn't think I could bring it up by myself and I didn't want to lose them both."

He shrugged and moved away from the door, walking to me until he crowded my space. His hands slipped under my T-shirt and caressed the expanse of my stomach.

"Hi," he said, looking down at me. He looked a little cagey and regretful.

"Hi," I said, then lifted on my tiptoes to give him a kiss. It was just a soft press of my mouth to his, but I needed it. When I went back on my feet I saw he needed it too.

"I'm sorry," he said.

"You're forgiven," I said.

He smiled, and those thorny feelings in his gaze gave way to relief. "I haven't told you why I'm sorry."

"You're still forgiven."

His thumbs dipped into the waistband of my shorts, rubbing down the line of my hips. "I did overreact. And all your points are valid ones. I just don't want to get back to campus and for this to go away. I need to see you, often."

I wound my arms around his back and pressed him to me. Really, I wanted to feel his skin against mine, but for now I decided to settle for just his warmth.

"This isn't going away. I don't think I'm going to disappear into a chemistry lab cabinet when we get back. And besides, if I did, you'd know where to find me." I kissed his collarbone. Damn he was delicious. Being so close to him had my hormones throwing a parade and making a Slip 'n Slide out of my pants. It would have been embarrassing if I'd cared, but I didn't. I'd grown to love the way he made me feel.

"Promise me that when we get back, maybe in a month, or when finals are over, you'll reconsider moving in together."

The idea of dating Martin—or still dating Martin—during finals made what we were doing here feel very real, and it gave it a sudden gravity. It was a fixed time point in the future. I thought about meeting him for study sessions in the library and coffee shop. How it would be. How he might spend the night with me on those odd weekends when Sam went home.

I realized, or understood better, why he wanted to move in together. If we shared an apartment our default would be together—like it had been here—and he didn't want to give that up. Neither did I.

"Where are you living over the summer?" I asked, smoothing my hands up and down his back just so I could feel more of him.

"I was already planning to move out of the house in April. I was thinking of an apartment downtown."

"So far away?"

"Yeah, but then I can catch the train to New York easier."

"What's in New York?"

He hesitated for a minute, watched me, and his hands stilled. "A project I'm working on."

"What kind of project? A class assignment?"

He shook his head, his fingers moving around to the back of my shorts.

"No. It's not for class. It's a…a venture capitalist thing."

My eyebrows bounced up and down as I oscillated between surprised and impressed. "Just a little venture capitalist thing, in New York?"

He huffed a laugh, his voice low, rumbly, and delicious as he said, "Yeah. Something like that."

"Does it have anything to do with your cheating fishing poles? Maybe a golf club that plays eighteen holes all by itself?"

"No, it has nothing to do with fishing. It's, uh, it's satellites."

"Oh." I nodded, made sure I looked like I thought satellites were as impressive as a finger painting. "Oh, satellites. Who *doesn't* have a little venture capitalist side project in New York about satellites? I have twenty at least."

He was full on chuckling now, looking at me like I was cute and hilarious. "Really? We should compare notes."

"How much money are you trying to raise for this little cosmic endeavor? Five? Ten million?" I'd thrown the figures out there because they sounded preposterous.

He shocked me by responding seriously, "Sixty and some change, but I have a way to raise the capital, so we're golden."

My mouth fell open and I struggled not to choke on my bewilderment. "Who *are* you? Why are you even going to college?"

"College is good for making contacts, meeting the right people—smart people who I might be able to employ later— and networking." He shrugged, like the college experience was one big social networking conference or a giant job interview for all of his classmates in the inevitable Martin Sandeke Empire. He added, "I also like to row and I like to win."

I couldn't help but tease him. "Am I one of your right people? Are you planning to employ me later?"

"No." He grew sincere, introspective, and his tone mimicked his expression. "You were a complete surprise and you might ruin everything." Then he added as a distracted afterthought, "You might ruin me."

I felt a little stab of sober hurt just under my heart. "I wouldn't," I implored, my fingers flexed into the muscles of his back. "Martin, I would never ruin you."

"You wouldn't do it on purpose," he soothed, looking resigned. "But you could if you wanted to."

"I won't want to."

He merely smiled wryly in response and let me look at him. Then he took advantage of me being distracted by reaching into my shorts and swimsuit and touching my bare skin.

"Let's go downstairs."

"Why?"

He bent to my jaw and kissed it, then kissed a path to my ear. "I want to do very bad things to this bottom." He growled, grabbing and massaging me, making my breath hitch and liquid heat race to very nice places…in my pants.

"What kind of things? Give me some details. Maybe a numbered list." I was teasing him but my voice betrayed me, as it was breathy and uneven.

He lifted his head from where he'd been biting me; his gaze was heated, hooded, and full of sexy promise.

"Let's get you naked and I'll show you."

***

I WAS NAKED. He was not.

He'd kept his swim shorts on all day, then changed into boxer briefs and pajama bottoms for bedtime.

I wasn't comfortable being naked in general. Over the course of my life I was only ever naked right before, during, or after bathing/a shower or changing into a bathing suit; therefore, being naked while alone with Martin specifically, felt like an epic skydive outside of my comfort zone.

I briefly wondered if this made me an odd duck. Did other nineteen-year-old girls—less sexually repressed girls—spend minutes and hours alone with themselves naked? Admiring their knees, becoming acquainted with their elbows, discovering the dots and indents of their backside? Somehow I doubted it, at least not girls from the United States of America.

This was the country where Janet Jackson's inadvertent boob exposure during the 2004 Super Bowl led many to believe it was a sign of the Apocalypse. Movies frequently displayed death, violence, and gore with a PG-13 rating, but *god forbid* a nipple be exposed, or an ass crack. Cuss and swear and maim and kill, but the sight of the human body is lascivious, offensive, and shameful.

Really, in the USA, there were only two sure ways one could ever see a human male penis without having sex: porn, and anatomy/physiology 101. Part of me wondered if zoos were so popular as a direct result, giving kids an opportunity to assuage their curiosity with animal anatomy, and therefore labeling the experience as educational.

Presently, I was naked and being spooned. Martin was spooning me. It felt very surreal and far-fetched, just like almost every other moment during this week. It was on the tip of my tongue to yell to no one in particular that I was snuggling with Martin Sandeke, as in: I AM SNUGGLING WITH MARTIN SANDEKE!

But instead I asked, all calm and cool, "So, tell me, do you prefer to be the spoon or the spooned?"

His lips were against my upper back, where my neck met my shoulders, and I felt his mouth curve into the barest smile. "I don't know, I've never done this before."

"What? Spooned?"

"Yeah."

I allowed this to sink in. Once it did, I grinned into the dim cabin and said with no small amount of wonder, "Kaitlyn Parker has popped Martin Sandeke's spooning cherry."

I felt his smile grow just before he said, "It's only fair. I hope to pop your forking cherry."

I sucked in a shocked breath, but then burst out laughing, half-heartedly covering my face. After a moment he joined in, and I felt his chest shake with laughter.

It felt good, talking to him, joking with him. I couldn't pinpoint when we'd grown to this level of comfort with each other, but it was a bit strange to think I'd let him touch my body with intimacy before I'd felt confident I could tease him about spooning.

We'd spent all day fooling around, then swimming, then eating, then talking, then fooling around some more. He liked me on my stomach, lying on the bed, his fingers between my spread legs, biting my back and sides and neck and bottom.

He also liked me straddling his face while he lay on the bed, his fingers digging into my hips and thighs while he tasted me.

He also liked me straddling his hips while we just made out like hormone-addled teenagers, necking, touching, and petting, learning each other's sweet spots.

Despite how the day had started, I admitted to myself that it had quickly ascended to one of my favorite days of all time. I felt happy. *So happy.* Giddy, excited, joyful, thrilled, and carefree in a way I'd never felt before. Just lying with him was exhilarating. We were a team and I felt certain I could rely on him, and I wanted him to rely on me.

"That, sir," I referred to his forking joke, "was hilarious and well timed.

You win today's Witty Wednesday contest."

"I didn't know we were having a contest, and I thought today was Wet-and-Wild Wednesday."

"A Wednesday can be more than one thing, it doesn't just have to be wet and wild. It can also be witty, or wistful, or worrisome. That's the beauty of Wednesdays."

"What did I win? What's my prize?"

"Just the knowledge you've won, and that you have my respect."

He squeezed me. "How many people have your respect?"

I thought about this, my lips twisting as my eyes narrowed. "Forty-seven...and a half."

"Who is the half?"

"It's not a half, it's two three-fourths, and they belong to John F. Kennedy and Richard Nixon. I three-fourths respect them."

"You respect historical figures?"

"Yes, after careful vetting."

"Richard Nixon? Really?"

I nodded. "Yes. He did a lot to normalize our relationship with China. As well he pulled us out of Vietnam. But then...the whole power-hungry arrogance, lying, and being too much of a dweeb to wear makeup on TV stuff brings him down to three-fourths."

"And JFK? What were his deficiencies?"

"I don't like how he treated women, especially his wife. He didn't practice what he preached and that made him slimy. Also, the Bay of Pigs fiasco and groupthink, *ugh*. Don't even get me started."

"Okay, I won't get you started." He squeezed me again.

"How about you? How many people do you respect?"

Martin sighed. I felt his exhale against my neck as it sent several of my hairs dancing over my shoulder, tickling me.

"Let's see," he stalled.

"Too many to count?"

"Five...no, four."

"Four? Only four?"

"Yes."

"Well, who—pray tell—are these pillars of humankind?"

"Unlike you, historical figures don't have my respect, not actively anyway. If I've never met a person I can't respect them."

"You sound so serious."

"It is serious."

"Now I really want to know." I shifted my legs and turned my head so I could peer at him over my shoulder.

"You, of course."

I smiled, but then quickly suppressed it. "Of course."

He still appeared serious as he continued, "Eric."

"Your teammate?"

He nodded.

I turned my head back to my pillow, pleased to hear that Martin respected Eric since I was pretty sure Sam really, really liked Eric.

"And my business partner."

"For the satellite venture capitalist thing in New York?"

"Yes."

"Who is the fourth?"

"Your mother, Senator Parker."

I frowned, blinked rapidly several times, my tone betraying my surprise. "My mother? You've met my mother?"

I felt him nod as his arms tightened around my torso.

"Martin, when did you meet my mother?"

"Three years ago, in Washington, DC."

"What…how…when?" Unable to settle on a question, I turned completely around so I could see his face. "Okay, start from the beginning. What happened? How did you meet her?"

He shrugged like the fact he'd met my mother *before* he'd met me was not a big deal. "I was in DC with my father. We were at a restaurant having lunch with a team of telecom lobbyists, and your mother walked in with a few members of her staff."

"And you respect her because…she ordered the hamburger instead of a salad?" I squinted at him, trying to understand how one brief encounter with my mother three years ago could garner his respect, how she could become one in a short list of four.

"My father stopped her as she walked past, suggested that she join us for lunch." Martin's gaze moved to a place over my shoulder, his eyes unfocused as he recalled the scene. "It was the first time I'd seen my father be polite to *anyone*. And she looked at him like he was scum." The side of his mouth ticked upward at the memory.

"What did she say? Did she have lunch with you?"

He shook his head and smiled softly. "No. She said, '*No, thank you,*' and tried to walk away; but he stepped in her path and pushed her about it. Then she said, '*I'd rather eat glass than suffer through one second of your corrupt and tedious company.*'"

Martin's smile grew as his eyes shifted back to mine.

"Holy rude comeback, Batman!" I exclaimed on an exhale.

"I know. And she was fierce, in control, cold even. She made him look small and insignificant by comparison." He said this like he admired her, how she'd cut down his father. "After lunch I found out who she was, looked up her voting record, and then it all made sense."

"How so?"

"Because she's the chairwoman of the Commerce, Science, and Transportation Committee in the senate. She's sponsored or co-sponsored every pro-consumer and anti-Big Telecom bill that's been drafted in the last ten years."

I felt the need to defend her. "That's because telecom companies in the US hold a monopoly and enter into informal non-compete agreements with each other to keep prices artificially high, which means no one can ever get Sandeke Telecom, or Brighthouse, or Version to actually provide competitive rates let alone appropriate customer service. Is it too much to ask for reasonable Internet speeds that cost less than $100 a month? Or a service call window that doesn't span eight hours? Who has time for that?!"

Martin chuckled, grabbing my wrists; I hadn't realized it but I'd started gesturing with my hands to demonstrate my frustration.

"I know, I know. I agree," he said, trying to pacify me, rubbing the inside of my arms and kissing me softly. "Your mother does good work in Washington."

She did. I knew she did. She was amazing and I loved that my superhero mother was on his short list. He had exceptionally good taste.

Regardless of our agreement on her awesomeness, I squinted at him again, pursing my lips. "It feels weird talking about my mother while I'm in bed with you."

"Then what do you want to talk about?"

I blurted the first thing that came to mind, "What was Martin Sandeke like as a kid?"

He lifted an eyebrow in response. "Talking about your mother is weird, but talking about me as a kid isn't?"

"Just answer the question."

Martin considered me for a moment before responding. "I was…quiet."

"So you were a watcher."

"A watcher?"

"You were one of those creepy kids who watched the other kids play."

"I wasn't creepy."

"I was. I was a creepy watcher. I watched the other kids play—quite creepily—and tried to make sense of their games. Mostly the girls. They seemed to do a lot of fighting with each other. And crying. And making up. And whispering."

"But you didn't?"

"No." I remembered how it had hurt at first, being snubbed when I was seven and eight and eleven and sixteen, but then my mother told me I shouldn't waste energy on average people because they would never amount to anything beyond ordinary. *"You don't need to befriend them in order to lead them,"* she'd said.

I continued, pushing away the memory. "They didn't let me play their reindeer games, mostly because I was creepy, but also because I was always trying to make them stop fighting. I tried to make lasting peace. But encouraging harmony between little girls is like trying to negotiate a Middle East peace treaty."

Martin exhaled a laugh and tucked a strand of hair behind my ear and shoulder. "I wanted everyone to get along and they just wanted to be dramatic. But that was okay. Their rebuffs allowed me to perfect the art of hiding at a very young age."

"Why did you hide? Did they make fun of you?"

I shook my head. "No. They ignored me. I think I hid because hiding made it my choice. You can't be ignored if no one can see you." I was talking from a stream of consciousness, having never really thought about why I hid before. The revelation of my motivations made me feel acutely uncomfortable, so I cleared my throat and changed the subject. "What were you really like as a kid? Other than quiet?"

"Stubborn."

"Ha! I'm shocked." Then I added under my breath, "I'm lying. I'm not shocked."

Martin pinched my rib, just enough to make me squirm. "I was quiet, stubborn, and shy."

"Shy?" I settled into the mattress, my cheek on his arm, and frowned at this last adjective. "I cannot imagine you being shy."

"Why? Because I'm so outgoing now?"

I thought about this—a shy Martin—as my eyes searched his, thought about his behavior for as long as I'd known him.

He'd barely spoken to me as my lab partner, though he'd apparently been thinking about me for quite a while. I remembered the time he'd asked for my phone number last semester and how he wouldn't look me in the eye while he spoke. At the time I thought it was arrogance. I recalled that at the party last Friday he'd been upstairs playing pool instead of downstairs getting drunk and engaging in merriment.

This prompted me to think and ask at the same time, "Martin, do you like parties?"

His eyes narrowed, but he said nothing.

My eyes widened, and I proclaimed, "You don't like parties! You sneak!"

He caught my wrists before I could do anything—like tickle him or pull away or smack his shoulder—and he brought my hands to his bare chest.

"No. I don't like parties."

"Then why did you make me go?"

"Because I liked the idea of showing you off as my date."

My nose wrinkled. "That makes no sense."

"I didn't say it made sense, it just is."

Now my eyes crinkled. "But you left me when we arrived."

"We've already been over this. I left to show you I wasn't going to…what did you call it? Pee on you? I looked for you twenty minutes later and couldn't find you. You went and hid in the laundry room. Instead of showing you off as my date, I spent half the night trying to find you."

"Is that why you were so pissed when you found me?"

"No. I was pissed before I found you, because I thought you might have gone off with someone else. I was relieved when I found you, but then pissed because you preferred to read a book over being with me."

"Poor, poor Martin." As much as I could with him holding my wrists, I petted his chest. "I will kiss your ego and make it better."

He lifted a single eyebrow. "I don't want you to *kiss* it."

I flattened my lips and blinked at him once, very slowly. "Are you always thinking about sex?"

"Yes."

I snorted.

"More accurately, sex with you."

I stilled, and watched him as he watched me. Before, when he'd joked about *popping my forking cherry,* it had felt like a joke. But now...not so much.

I didn't think I was ready for that, not yet. We'd been together less than a week. I'd given him my trust less than three days ago. This might have been dating boot camp, but I was still trying to wrap my mind around the concept of passion. Having sex with Martin before it was making love to Martin would be a bad idea.

I didn't want to confuse one with the other.

"Martin, I don't—"

"I know. You're not ready yet." He nodded, his eyes darting between mine, his body shifting closer in a deliciously lithe movement as one of his hands released my wrist and smoothed down the length of my body, from my shoulder to my hip.

Then, making me both smile and scowl, he added, "Maybe tomorrow."

CHAPTER 8
Transition Metals and Coordination Chemistry

THURSDAY MORNING DAWNED and I found myself one half of a tangled mass of limbs. In Martin's defense, I was totally crowding his side of the bed. I was basically sprawled on top of him.

Aaaaand, I was still naked.

Diffused sunlight filtered through the undersea portals; I had no idea what time it was. I disentangled myself from Martin, careful not to wake him, and went about getting dressed and making breakfast. Then I took a cup of coffee up to the deck and studied for my upcoming math test, feeling all warm and fuzzy and happy with life in general, especially and specifically because of the sexy boy downstairs.

Martin joined me sometime later, bringing me a new, hot cup of coffee. Wordlessly, he gave me a toe-curling kiss good morning—even though it was already afternoon—and, looking smug and satisfied by my breathlessness, took the chair across from mine. He opened his laptop and began working on something or other, likely something serious and important and poised to make him millions.

We didn't talk. We sat together in companionable silence. It was…really great. Comfortable and easy. Every once in a while I'd catch him watching me. He would smile his pleased smile when our eyes met, but he'd never look away.

I began to daydream about what life would be like if I did agree to move in with Martin, and that was dangerous because smart Kaitlyn knew it was too hasty. But silly, prematurely falling in love Kaitlyn wanted to doodle our names together on notebooks and take cooking classes together on weekends.

Maybe he would come see me play my jam sessions on Sunday nights. Maybe I'd take the train and meet him in New York for lunch on days when I didn't have class. Maybe I'd write songs for him and about him. Maybe we'd sleep together every night, having fun and taking comfort in each other's bodies. Maybe he'd sleep naked too at some point.

But I was only nineteen, and college wasn't a networking conference for me. I didn't know who I was or what I wanted to do with my life. I suspected that music was going to have to be a major part of it—not because I believed I was a prodigious talent, but because something had shifted within me on Tuesday night, and I couldn't stop thinking about it.

Whether I was good or magnificent or merely adequate didn't matter. I recognized music as a passion, one that I'd been repressing. Of course, I hadn't given the matter, the how and when, enough thought yet. I still had a great deal to sort through.

The idea of falling in love with Martin (if I hadn't already) before I had my head on straight about what I wanted to do and who I was made me feel uneasy. He was always going to be the alpha of his pack, as he didn't know any other way. I didn't want to get lost, lose myself before I'd been found, in his flock of admirers.

I was staring at him, lost in my ruminations, but didn't realize I was staring until he asked, "Hey, everything okay?"

I blinked him back into focus, and shook my head to clear it. "Uh, yeah. Fine."

He studied me, looked like he wanted to ask or say something. Eventually he did. "What do you think, Kaitlyn?"

"About what?" I gave him a friendly smile as I closed my notebook. I couldn't study anymore; there was no use pretending.

"About us."

I flinched involuntarily because his question was almost eerily attuned to my current musings; I wondered tangentially if—in addition to everything else—Martin Sandeke was a mind-reader.

I looked away from him and studied the horizon. It was another beautiful day.

"I think we're having a lot of fun."

He was quiet and I felt his eyes on me. The silence didn't feel quite so comfortable anymore.

Then, very softly, he asked, "What's going on in your head?"

Out of nowhere and as a consequence of nothing, I said, "I'm afraid of letting everyone down."

He paused for a beat then asked, "What do you mean?"

"My eighth grade science fair project was a solar heater and it was made out of tin foil, black paint, and a shoe box."

"So?"

"So," I returned my gaze to his, "I'm never going to be a great scientist or a world leader."

He watched me like he was waiting for me to continue. When I didn't, he prompted again, "So…?"

"So? So?! You said it yourself yesterday to that vile woman. I'm

Kaitlyn Parker; my grandfather is an astronaut; my dad is the dean of the college of medicine at a very excellent medical school; my grandmother outfitted the first nuclear submarines with freaking nuclear weapons; my mother might be the first female president of the United States in the next ten years…and I'm not brilliant."

He laughed. At first it was a short laugh of disbelief. Then it became a full on belly laugh when he saw I was serious. He was wiping tears from his eyes and shaking his head.

"It's not funny," I said, even though I fought a smile. Of course, it was funny; and I didn't mind laughing at myself.

I was smart. I knew that. I had no reason to complain. I came from a loving—if not comparatively regimented and sterile—family. I had all my fingers and toes. I had everything to be grateful for.

And yet…

I knew who I was supposed to be, but I was not that person. As well, I had no idea who I actually was.

When he finally stopped laughing, he sat back in his chair and considered me with glittering eyes over steepled fingers. A warm smile lingered over his features.

"Kaitlyn, you are very intelligent, and besides that you're a musical prodigy."

I shook my head. "I know you know what I mean, and I didn't say what I said because I was fishing for compliments—though, if I were fishing for compliments, I would want one of your cheating fish pole holders."

His smile widened, though he persisted the point. "Why do you think you have to be a scientist or a world leader? Why not focus on your music instead?"

I glared at him. "Come on, Martin. Don't play dumb. You know it's what everyone expects. I may love music, but aren't there enough musicians in the world? If I have even the smallest talent or aptitude for politics or scientific endeavors, and the connections, don't I owe it to society to at least try?"

"What other people expect doesn't matter. You don't owe society anything. Screw society! You should do what makes you happy."

"That's ridiculous. Life isn't about making yourself happy. Life is about exploiting your talents for humanity, in order to make lasting difference for good when and where you can, and for as long as you are able."

"Is this one of your stupid life rules?"

"Don't call them stupid. My life rules keep me from making avoidable mistakes."

"What a load of self-sacrificing, martyring bullshit."

"It is not! There is great value in self-sacrifice."

"And you think you can't 'do good' with music?"

"No. Not as much as I could by stepping up and becoming a leader like my mother or a scientist like my grandmother. Even you respect my mother."

"Yeah, but I don't want to fuck your mother."

I felt a spike of anger at his crass reply. "Are you telling me that who my family is has nothing to do with why you like me? That it doesn't make me very attractive girlfriend material?"

He held my glare and his grew increasingly heated, the earlier amusement giving way to stony severity. He took his time answering, like he was debating with himself, and eventually his non-answer seemed to speak for itself.

I felt abruptly hot and cold and adrift.

"Martin…?"

"Of course not, Parker," he finally said.

I exhaled my relief, but the back of my neck tingled. Something about the way he was looking at me, how long it had taken him to respond, didn't feel honest.

"You misunderstand my meaning." His tone was firm, unyielding, like he was trying to lead me to a certain conclusion. "I meant, of course I'd never tell you that who your family is has nothing to do with why I like you so much, because that statement would be a lie. Who your family is has a great deal to do with why you're very attractive girlfriend material. Of course I want you because of who your family is."

My hesitant relief became stunned incredulity at his admission. He was watching me closely, though giving none of his own thoughts away.

I stood abruptly, filled with sudden restless energy, and a fierce need to reject his words. My hands came to my hips, then fell to my legs, then pushed through my hair. Stunned incredulity grew into a cauldron of boiling anger.

"How can you say that to me? You know better than anyone, better than *anyone* else, what it's like to be wanted because of who your family is."

"Because it's true," he answered, watching me carefully.

"What? This is…"

…you are the Olympic gold medal and the Nobel Peace Prize and the

Pulitzer Prize and the Academy Award of marriage material. Ray's irritating words from Monday came back to me in a rush accompanied by the thundering sound of blood rushing between my ears.

Distractedly, I said, "Ray warned me about this."

"Ray?" This got his attention, he sat up straighter.

"Yes. Ray." I glanced at Martin, feeling equal parts anger and confusion. "He said that you liked me because of my credentials, that I was the girl guys like you married after you finished sowing your poison oats—or some such nonsense—but it wasn't nonsense because he was right. He was right." I muttered this last statement to myself.

"He was right," Martin confirmed, again stunning me. This time the wind truly was knocked from my lungs.

"No, he wasn't." I shook my head, making the denial on his behalf because I didn't want it to be true.

"Kaitlyn, Ray was right. He knows what kind of girl I want, what I've been looking for."

I felt like he'd slapped me across the face or sucker-punched me in the stomach. Therefore, I didn't think much about the next words out of my mouth.

"You, Martin Sandeke, are a complete and total jerk-face! How dare you... How dare you! Why would you...and I thought..." I screamed this at him in fits and starts, which felt weird because I'd never screamed at anyone before in my life.

I decided just to go with it.

The line of his mouth became contemplative as he looked at me, but he said nothing. This only served to increase my frustration.

"What the heck is wrong with you?" I continued my tirade. "Aren't you going to defend yourself? Or are you just going to sit there and stare at me?"

"Do you want me to defend myself?"

"Yes!" I immediately responded, loudly and on instinct, the single-word admission ripped from some insurmountable desire to be wanted and seen for who I was, even if I didn't know who that person was yet.

"Why?" He was on the edge of his seat and his gaze was filled with a strange hope.

"Because..." My voice cracked and so did my heart. Stupid tears flooded my eyes.

Tuesday night's crying was cathartic, necessary, and I'd embraced it.

But I didn't want to cry now. I didn't want to show weakness to someone who, by his own admission, cared more about who my family was than who I was as a person.

I kept thinking, *I knew it! I knew he would make me cry! Stupid Kaitlyn. Stupid passion. Stupid trust. Stupid jerk-face Martin Sandeke.*

I turned away from him before he could see my face crumble. I needed to hide. The desire was brutal. Thus, I tried to bolt for the cabin below deck, with my ultimate goal one of the two closets. But, somehow detecting my intentions, Martin had other plans. I listened to his chair hastily scrape against the deck, his quick steps circle the table.

He was hot on my heels as I descended the stairs and he intercepted me before I could grab for the handle of the closet door.

Martin gripped my shoulders and he turned me to face him.

"Let me go!"

"Christ, Kaitlyn. Calm down for a minute. You wanted me to defend myself, so listen."

"I hate you!" I yelled this, but I didn't really mean it. Besides feeling wonderfully dramatic and perfect in the moment, I wanted to hurt him. Because I was hurting.

"No, you don't. You're falling in love with me." He looked stunned by my outburst, but sounded almost pleased by it, like my reaction was part of some big plan, a game of strategy he'd been playing.

Damn it all, he was such a bully. I knew this, but I must have forgotten it someplace between his mouth and his hands and his eyes and his words.

I responded to this accusation through clenched teeth, sounding not at all convincing. "No, I'm not."

I fought his grip and pushed against his granite chest. Of course this did nothing but make him change his hold so I couldn't continue hitting him.

"Listen to me, Kaitlyn. Just—would you listen?"

I took a deep breath and forced myself to calm down.

Even though you don't feel calm doesn't mean you can't be calm.

I stilled. I closed my eyes so I couldn't see him. I needed to distance myself. I needed to either reason or bluff my way through this. My urge to cry dissipated as I thought through my action plan.

I would…I would just freeze him out. I could do that. I'd been doing it for months before he found me in that science cabinet and everything went to hell.

I cleared my throat, testing the steadiness of my vocal chords. "I changed my mind. I'm not interested. I don't care."

He laughed at this, though it sounded completely frustrated. "Shutting me out, are you? How convenient that you're able to just turn your feelings off so easily."

I kept my eyes shut and repeated over and over, *even though you don't feel calm doesn't mean you can't be calm.*

I had no reason to answer him, so I didn't. I just pretended he wasn't there. Eventually he'd have to let me go. When I was eleven, I spent seven hours in a closet waiting for a babysitter to leave. I didn't like her because she cheated at Monopoly.

Martin hadn't cheated at Monopoly, but he did just admit that he was using me because of who my family was. In some sick way it made sense. By his own admission, college was one large-scale job interview of his classmates for the future Martin Sandeke conglomerate. Why wouldn't he also be interviewing girls for the role of girlfriend?

In the game of life this made him one of my least favorite people. *He* was manipulating me. The very thing he detested in others. He knew I was falling in love with him. *He knew.* Was I the first girl he was going to *test*? Martin Sandeke's Girlfriend 1.0?

"You are so stubborn." Now he sounded upset. "Open your eyes and look at me."

I didn't. Instead I built the case against him in my mind. Everything he'd said and done became damning evidence and I felt myself grow numb.

"Fine. We'll do it this way."

Martin's hold changed, and he was walking me backward. The high mattress of the cabin's double bed hit my bottom and before I quite understood what was happening, he lifted me into his arms and placed me on the bed.

I did open my eyes then, scrambling away from him to the far corner of the mattress. I glared at him, hoped to communicate that I would kill him dead if he touched me with intent to arouse.

He seemed to understand the silent threat because he lifted his hands up and said, "I'm not going to touch you, not if you don't want me to. I'm just going to sit here, on this side. But you have to promise me that you won't cover your face or close your eyes again. I need you to see me when I say this. And I need to see you."

I said nothing. I wasn't going to make him any promises.

He paused, indulging himself in a moment to examine my face. At length, he said, "You're so good at that. You'll have to teach me how to do that, hide in plain sight. It's a handy skill." These words were surprisingly bitter, approaching the intersection of sarcasm and spite.

I pulled my knees up to my chest, wrapped my arms around my legs, and said nothing. Though I got the distinct impression he was stalling. I briefly wondered why, but then became irritated with myself for my curiosity. I shouldn't care.

He sat on the edge of the bed in the opposite corner, facing me. His features were hard, verging on resentful.

Abruptly, he released a breath and with it the words, "I'm in love with you, Kaitlyn."

I said nothing, but I did flinch. As silent seconds ticked by, feelings welled within me, ballooning past the numbness, and I could barely contain it. I felt like I was being stretched beyond my capacity, my chest tight and heavy, my stomach intermittently twisting and pitching. I was dizzy.

As well, I found I couldn't quite hold the enormity of his gaze paired with his admission, so earnestly spoken. I believed him and I couldn't quite handle this truth, so I removed my eyes from his and swallowed. It didn't help. I was shaking.

He cleared his throat, politely ignoring my turmoil, and said, "Who your family is, it's a part of you. Just like my family—all their fucked-up spite and bullshit—is also a part of me. We've been shaped by them but they don't define us. I'm not them. I don't have to be like them. You're not your illustrious ancestors. You don't have to be like them. You can be whoever you want. Our families couldn't be more different, but—because of who your family is—you understand what it means to have…expectations. To have people prejudge you or want to use you for who they are, what they've done, and what they have. That's what I meant when I said who your family is has a great deal to do with why you're very attractive girlfriend material."

I slid just my eyes to his. They were stinging and I felt like crying. I was overwhelmed but I was unable to keep from surveying him to discern the veracity of his words. He appeared to be completely sincere and I felt the gravity of his blue-green gaze to my bones.

Before I could catch myself, I blurted, "So you like me because I can empathize with you?"

"No…yes, that's definitely part of it, but…" His frustration was a tangible thing, curling around his strong body and filling the air with tension. "I *like* you because you are Kaitlyn—genuine, beautiful, brilliant, amazing Kaitlyn—not because you're Kaitlyn Parker. And I'm *in love* with you because I can't help myself."

Oh well...barnacles.

That struck me right in the feels.

I knocked my feels on their collective swooning asses for a moment because I needed to focus on the real issue. "But, upstairs you were trying to make me think you were using me. Why make it sound like you were just using me?"

He leaned forward, but made no move to advance closer, his voice rising with every word. "Because you're so controlled all the time. I ask you to move in with me and you make a pro/con list, as though we'd be *just* roommates, but make no reference to what you feel for me, like it doesn't factor. I'm in love with you and I have no idea what you feel for me, if you feel anything at all!"

"How can you say that? How can you even think it? Who was upstairs yesterday giving you a hug and trying to comfort you after your wicked stepmother showed up?"

"You. You were upstairs." His tone held a hard edge, ripe with unhappiness. "But you would have done that for anyone; you would have tried to make things right for any random person. I don't want to be just anyone to you."

I couldn't believe this. I couldn't believe him. "Then who has been on this boat with you since yesterday morning? Who was all up in your junk yesterday afternoon? And who woke up naked, tangled up with you this morning in this bed? You are not any random person to me! I've never done anything with anyone before! I've never let anyone so close. And these things, all these things we've been doing, and not just the physical stuff, the sharing of...of myself, of our dreams and our fears, this means something to me. None of this has been done lightly."

"I needed to be sure."

I hoped I was misunderstanding him somehow, because the alternative was completely cray-cray.

"So, help me understand this. Earlier, on the deck, just now...you misled me as some kind of test? To see if I'd be upset?"

"Yes." He nodded, looking unrepentant.

My brain was going to explode.

"That's messed up, Martin. You know this is a sore spot for me, if not *the sorest spot.* Your need for certainty does not matter more than my feelings. You don't purposefully hurt people you care about. You can't do that. That's not allowed!"

He flinched and abruptly stood, turned away, like he couldn't stand looking at me with the knowledge that he'd hurt me. He tugged his fingers though his hair and sighed, stalking back and forth from one side of the cabin to the other.

"I never wanted to hurt you. I didn't think I *could* hurt you. I didn't expect you to freak out like you did. You never freak out about anything. I just wanted to see how you would react. I wanted to see if I mattered."

"Well, looks like you have your answer. You matter. Happy now?"

"No. I'm the opposite of happy," he yelled back, then exhaled like he was out of steam. His gaze moved over me with such raw longing that I couldn't stand looking at him anymore. I closed my eyes *and* I covered my face.

A moment later I heard something crash followed by, "God*dammit!*"

I jumped at the sound and blasphemy, but kept my face buried. I was all mixed up and not one thought or feeling seemed to rise to the top.

"Kaitlyn, will you look at me?"

I gathered a fortifying breath then peeked at him between my fingers. It was the best I could do.

He was now glaring at me, likely irritated by the hands still covering my face.

Then he broke the stony silence. "I'm sorry," he said, then waited like he expected me to respond in a certain way, like we were following some script I hadn't been given. He growled impatiently, "So?"

"So what?"

"So, am I forgiven?"

My hands dropped from my face in my shocked outrage. "No!"

"What?" He was surprised.

How can he possibly be surprised?! Gah!

"What you did was not okay. You just purposefully hurt me as some dysfunctional litmus test." I scrambled off the bed and pointed at him, then waved my finger through the air to indicate his entire body. My face was screwed up in anger. "You're not forgiven, mister. Not by a long shot."

He turned and fell back on the bed. He groaned. He covered his face with his hands then rubbed furiously. "Tell me what I'm supposed to do and I'll do it."

"Lots of begging," I blurted and crossed my arms. Now I was pacing the cabin. My mind was a jumble. He was either a sociopath or just really clueless about basic human decency.

He chuckled. It only sounded half frustrated. "I don't know how to beg."

"Figure it out."

He removed his hands from his face and lifted his head, his eyes trailing up then down my body. "You don't want me to beg because you know I'm not going to beg. You want something else."

"I guess you'll just have to keep apologizing until I'm ready to forgive you."

"What was I supposed to do? It's Thursday. We leave on Saturday morning. I only have one more day."

I waved my arms through the air and may have resembled a bird struggling to fly. I appealed to any shred of sanity within him. "You could have just asked me, you fucking asshole jerk-face!"

Whoa!

My brain was shocked by the curse words and how good and necessary they felt given the circumstance. Perhaps cussing had its time and place…

Martin looked surprised as well, but instead of focusing on my foul language, he said, "I tried to do that."

"Really? I don't remember you saying at any point today," I lowered my voice to mimic his, " '*Hey, so, I love you. Are you in love with me?* ' "

He sat up and stared at me, then shocked the hell out of me by actually saying, "I love you, Kaitlyn. Are you in love with me?"

CHAPTER 9
Organic and Biological Chemistry

WE'D REACHED A stalemate after our big fight. I couldn't answer his question. He wouldn't let me hide in the closet.

But we'd also reached a ceasefire, which was a very good thing because we were at least ten miles from the island and were utterly alone, with each other, for the rest of the day.

As such, things became strained, but also exceedingly polite. We went back above deck, ate lunch in relative silence. I cleared the dishes while he washed them. *Please* and *Thank you* were used in excess. But not *You're welcome.* For some reason, through an odd silent accord, we'd both agreed that *You're welcome* was off limits. Instead I'd say, *No problem.* Or he'd say, *My pleasure.*

Strained politeness became complete silence as he focused on fishing—actually holding the pole!—and I laid a towel on the platform of the bow and pretended to read my book. Instead, I thought about the nuttiness of the last few days and hours and what I was going to do about it all.

It was weird being with Martin and not talking to him. Therefore, when the sun approached the horizon and Martin asked if I wanted to head to the cottage and meet up with Eric and Sam, or stay on the boat for the night, I surprised both him and me when I responded that I wanted to stay on the boat. I also asked that he call Sam and Eric and let them know our plans.

Even though we'd been gone since Wednesday morning, I didn't want to go to the cottage when he and I weren't on more than polite speaking terms. Tomorrow was our last day. There was too much left unsaid. Regardless of whether we returned as friends or as more than friends, I wanted us to be in a good place.

Martin needed a friend. He needed a safe place. I wasn't in love with him...*or maybe I am...or maybe I'm falling in love with him... I don't know! Gah!*

But he mattered to me. Once the urge to hide in the closet passed, I was determined we not abandon what we'd started. I wanted to see it through.

When he learned I wanted to stay the night on the boat, Martin's mood shifted. He became less stoically polite and more actually polite.

He touched base with Eric via a satellite phone and I spoke to Sam for about three minutes, just long enough to assure her I was perfectly fine and I'd see her tomorrow in the afternoon.

Then he asked if I wanted to go for a swim, and I said yes. So we did. I did my best to ignore his body, because it still put me in a state of duress and gave me lusty pants, and he did an admirable job of keeping his hands to himself.

I made a salad and he made sashimi for dinner from a second yellowfin tuna he'd caught during the day. I was super impressed he knew how to make sashimi from whole tuna until I realized it was just cutting up the pretty part of the fish. I'm lying. I was still impressed. He was really good with his knife.

I praised his fishing and fish-cutting prowess. As well, we found a topic that was perfectly safe to discuss - our chemistry assignment. Therefore, after dinner we spread out the chemistry text, my notes, divvied up the tabulations and analyses, and set to work.

That's right, ladies and gentlemen, mark this day on the calendar of your life. Martin Sandeke helped with the tabulations and analyses.

If anything says, *I'm sorry I hurt you earlier by making you think I was using you for your family because it didn't occur to me to just ask how you felt about me*, helping with laboratory tabulations and analyses will do the trick.

Of course, it helped that he could do the work in a fraction of the time it took me. Then, maybe as a peace offering or maybe because he found himself enjoying the task, Martin offered to finish my portion of the tabulations. I let him.

I stretched as I stood and glanced at the half moon in the sky and the gathering clouds. It looked like it was going to rain.

I cleared the table and did the dinner dishes while he finished our lab work. While rinsing suds off the plates I was struck by a peculiar sensation of melancholy and mourning.

Tomorrow was our last day.

It was hard to believe that Martin had found me hiding in a science cabinet just last week. It felt like a lifetime ago. And yet, the week had flown by. Everything was different. I was different. I wondered how it was possible to live one's life, week in and week out, with nothing of consequence occurring.

But then suddenly, over the course of seven days, my entire world shifted. Just seven days that could have been like any other seven days.

This really was relationship boot camp. Through this fight—or whatever it was we were in—I'd learned more about Martin, understood him better than I had during the first six days of the trip combined.

1. He was damaged in ways I might never understand.
2. He was used to getting what he wanted—whether that be information or acquiescence—through manipulation.
3. He was in love with me, or at least he thought he was.
4. He was willing to learn from his mistakes.
5. He didn't want to repeat his mistakes.
6. He feared rejection.

The last revelation made him very, very normal. The first two, however, were sources of extreme concern. Numbers four and five gave me hope.

But the third made me feel weak every time I remembered him saying the words. It made my heart swell, it made it hard to breathe, it made the Bunsen burner in my pants go on alert level one million, and it made me willing to forgive him for almost anything.

That was the truth of it. I wanted to forgive him. I wanted to trust him again. I did trust him before the fight, because he'd earned my trust with sincerity and honesty. I also wanted him to trust me enough to risk his heart without trying to tear mine out in the process.

"Hey."

I glanced over my shoulder. Martin was in the doorway to the kitchen, holding two glasses, watching me. I took both from him with a tight smile, and turned back to the sink. I washed them, rinsed them, set them on the towel to dry.

Then he said, "I'm sorry."

I nodded, giving him my profile and another tight smile. "I know."

He moved into the small kitchen and stood behind me. I felt his warmth at my back and braced for his touch, my body tensing in anticipation.

But then music started playing from what could only have been a cell phone speaker. The sound quality was not good, but not terrible. I recognized the song within the first ten notes.

"Stevie Wonder?" I asked, turning completely around and glancing at the cell phone Martin held in his hand.

He nodded then reached around to place it on the towel next to the two glasses I'd just finished washing. "I thought you might like some music."

"*Overjoyed.*" I said the name of the song, and I'm afraid I was looking at Martin like he had three heads—all still devastatingly handsome, but three nevertheless. "You like Stevie Wonder?"

He nodded, not touching me with anything other than his penetrating gaze. "Yeah. He's one of my favorites. I like to rock out to *Sir Duke* or *Superstition* when I run."

"You like Stevie Wonder," I repeated, this time as a statement, because it was so odd. Then I laughed my astonishment and covered my huge grin with my hand. "This might be one of my most favorite things about you, Martin Sandeke."

His lips twisted to the side with a sardonic smile, his eyelids lowering. He reached for my hand, revealing my grin, and threaded his fingers through mine. "Don't cover your mouth, it's one of my most favorite things about you."

Butterflies and dragonflies held conference in my stomach then fluttered to the four corners of my extremities. Everything felt dreamlike, hazy—likely the effect of exploiting Stevie Wonder as a soundtrack to this conversation—and I found myself leaning toward him, lifting my chin.

He brushed his lips against mine, then tasted me with his tongue. It wasn't enough, yet he didn't deepen the kiss.

Instead he whispered, "I love you, Kaitlyn."

He leaned away, his eyes burning into mine, like he wanted to make sure I'd heard him and that I understood.

He released my hand.

Then he turned and walked out of the kitchen, leaving me with Stevie Wonder telling me how he'd built his castle of love, just for two, though I never knew I was the reason.

***

I COULDN'T SLEEP.

Where last night sleeping with Martin had been wonderful and filled with conversations about everything, tonight it was weird. We weren't touching. Instead we were relegated to the two sides of the bed, lying on our sides away from each other.

I was pretty sure he wasn't asleep either.

This suspicion was confirmed when I heard him sigh, then mutter, "Fuck this shit," under his breath, then shift, reach for my body, and pull me across the great divide into his arms and against his chest.

I smirked into the darkness.

"I can't sleep with you and not touch you," he said by way of gruff, unapologetic explanation. "So if you don't want me to touch you then I can go sleep on the couch."

"No." I snuggled backward, into his embrace. "No, stay. It seems I can't sleep either unless you're touching me."

He gave me a rumbly grunt of acknowledgement, then we settled into the stillness and the gentle rocking of the boat. Feeling cozy and warm and safe, I was approximately a half minute from drifting off to dreamland when Martin whispered against my neck.

"Please, Kaitlyn... Don't punish me."

I stiffened, the words confusing and alarming. I turned in his arms because I had a fierce urge to see his face.

I searched his eyes in the dim light before I spoke, and found him both weary and guarded.

"Martin, I've told you before. I don't punish people. You can expect honesty from me."

He lifted his hand and brushed his knuckles against the side of my cheek, then pushed several strands of my hair over my shoulder, following the progress with his eyes. "You haven't forgiven me yet."

"No. I haven't. But that doesn't mean I'm punishing you. I promise, I'm actively working to forgive you. I just need time."

He nodded his understanding, his gaze on my shoulder. He was touching me there, his thumb tracing a circle on my skin.

Then he returned his eyes to mine, ensnared them. His gaze and voice were laced with challenge as he asked, "Will you let me...can I make you feel good?"

The butterfly and dragonfly conference was back in my stomach. My heart was banging like a gavel, calling the sexy meeting to order. I flexed my thighs then pressed them together in automatic response to his request, my lower belly twisting, hot and liquid, my nipples tightening into stiff peaks.

Yes, I wanted to say. *God, yes. Please.*

I didn't quite trust myself to speak as my heart lurched painfully toward the vicinity of his heart, so I said nothing. But then I was struck with sudden inspiration.

"No," I breathed, not really believing I'd turned him down, yet found the wherewithal to add, "but I'd like to touch you."

His eyes widened and his handsome mouth parted. Everything about him softened and it was clear he hadn't been expecting my request. Holding my breath, I sat up in the bed and peeled the covers off his chest then pulled them completely away.

I reached for the waistband of his pajamas and he, as though coming back to himself, suddenly gripped my wrists to stop my progress.

"What are you doing?"

"Touching you."

His jaw was tight, his eyes betraying his confusion.

"Why?"

"Because I like touching you." I shrugged.

"Kaitlyn," he growled. He looked like he was in pain. "Don't tease me."

I waited for him to really *see* me, and I hoped he saw my sincerity. I hoped I didn't have to make verbal promises. I hoped he'd just simply trust me.

Eventually, and with a shaking breath, Martin released my wrists, though he looked fierce, dangerous as he did so. The glint in his eyes again reminded me of a wounded animal. I knew I had him in a vulnerable position and that was a unique prospect for him.

I curled my fingers around the band of his pajamas again, one hand on either side of his hips, and pulled them down his legs. He helped by lifting his hips, though his eyes never left mine.

I tried to make my expression as unconcerned as possible, even though I had no idea what I was about to do. Trying to feign confidence, I moved my eyes to his middle and gazed upon his very long, thick, and remarkably shaped penis. It was an anatomy 101, textbook penis—very normal looking in the best way possible, just longer and thicker.

Therefore, I had no idea why the sight of it got me so excited. It was a penis. There was nothing special about this penis—excepting being longer and thicker than the average representation of penises everywhere—other than the person to which it was attached.

Inexplicably, I wanted to taste it.

I bent forward to do just this when Martin stopped my progress by gripping my shoulders.

"What the hell, Kaitlyn?"

I looked at him then his penis. It jumped. He growled.

"No," he said. "No, no, no." He leveraged his grip on my shoulders to pull me back to where I'd been lying on the bed just minutes prior. He climbed on top of me, pinning me down. "You're not going to do that."

"What? Why? Do you not like it?"

"Of course I like it! But you've never done it." He was hovering over me, naked, nearly yelling because I wanted to give him my first blow job.

"You think I'll suck?"

He blinked at me, stunned for a moment, then groaned. His forehead hit my shoulder and it was then I realized the double meaning of my words.

"Oh snap, sorry. Of course, you *hope* I'll suck."

He groaned again. "You're trying to kill me."

"No." I laughed, because I couldn't help it, wishing I could touch him but he was holding my wrists. "I'm not. I just...I just want to make you feel good."

He didn't lift his head. "Right. You want to give me a blow job after I made you feel like shit this afternoon, and you still don't forgive me for it. Because that makes sense."

I didn't want to tell him that the reason I hadn't forgiven him yet was because he obviously didn't trust *me*. Him not trusting me to put his penis in my mouth was evidence enough. I thought it was a truth universally acknowledged that all men love blow jobs, beer, and again, blow jobs. Who turns down a blow job? Martin Untrusting Sandeke, that's who.

I huffed. "Listen, Sandeke. I would like to place your very picturesque penis in my mouth. Yes or no?"

He groaned, buried his head in my neck, bit me.

I bent my head to the side reflexively, little waves of wonderfulness spreading through me originating from where his mouth loved and tortured my neck.

"Yes or no?" I squeaked.

He lifted himself up, planking above me. His erection pressed into my belly and I tried not to squirm because I knew that would likely set him off again.

"Why are you doing this to me?" His tone was subdued, but his eyes glared menacingly.

"Yes or no?"

He swallowed, his gaze moving in a deliberate trail from my eyes to my mouth, neck, then breasts.

"Fine," he said, and I could tell he didn't think I'd actually do it. "But you have to take your shirt off."

"Why?"

"Because I don't want you to swallow this time. If you swallow your first time you'll never go down on me again, because cum tastes nasty."

"And you know this how?"

"Girls tell me so. Lots and lots of girls."

Now he was just being crude, trying to push me away instead of giving me an opportunity to demonstrate I was trustworthy. But I was stubborn.

I lifted my chin and asked, "I still don't understand why I need to take my shirt off."

"Because I like seeing my cum on your beautiful tits."

If he was trying to freak me out, gross me out, or shock me, his words had the opposite effect. My lungs filled with fire and my breath hitched. I don't know what possessed me to do it, but I repeated the words he'd already used on me twice.

"Don't tease me," I whispered.

His eyes widened as they searched mine. I'd surprised him again. Wide eyed, mouth slightly parted, looking at me like I was a sexy alien creature, Martin released my wrists and lay back on the bed.

I sat up again, pulling my shirt off and arranging myself near his middle. His hands had balled into fists at his sides. I guessed this was a byproduct of trying not to touch me.

I bent forward and reached for his shaft with one hand, holding his erection still because it was jumping, straining as I came closer. I licked my lips, breathing on him, and he groaned. He sounded so tortured. I felt a desperate spike to ease his suffering so I opened my mouth and slid my lips and tongue over his penis, accepting him into my mouth, suckling him.

He cursed—a steady stream of panting expletives intermixed with my name.

I moved up and down, remembering a porn movie I'd watched with Sam last semester while eating seasonally appropriate pumpkin-spiced kettle corn. Sam spent twenty minutes critiquing the girl's fellatio technique. She'd even paused the video, stood up, walked to the TV, and used my yardstick as a pointer.

"See here," she'd said, indicating to the girl holding her own breast, "she should be using that hand to tickle his balls, the inside of his thighs, or the backs of his knees. What's it going to do on her breast? Nothing. That's a misuse of resources."

I tried to recall the rest of her pointers, and knew that if I tried to bring him in too deep then I would gag. I wasn't ready for that yet, gagging being something I didn't enjoy, so I tried to focus on doing what felt good to me, what I enjoyed.

I was surprised and not surprised to learn that what I enjoyed, he also seemed to enjoy. When I groaned because I liked the salty taste of his pre-cum, he answered with a groan of his own. When I twisted my fingers around his shaft and swirled my tongue around the head of his penis, every muscle in his body tensed and he held his breath.

It was like having a salty Popsicle that never melted, attached to a lovely, sexy man who derived both pleasure and pain from my experimentation. It made me feel oddly powerful and light-headed. The skin was soft—impossibly soft—and so, so hot.

And quite abruptly it was over.

"Kaitlyn stop, stop…fuck, I'm going to come." He pushed me away, gripping himself.

My eyes widened at the sight of his big hand gripping his big dick. It was the absolute sexiest thing I'd ever seen. I wiped the back of my hand against my mouth, transfixed.

"Okay," I said, "tell me what to do. Should I lay down and you get on top?" Of course I was referring to the logistics of him releasing his semen on my breasts.

But it was too late. Martin gave himself two strokes and that was it. He spilled on his own stomach, angling himself down, his hand moving back and forth with jerky movements. I watched him as it happened. His body tense, his muscles cut in sharp relief, his face twisted for a very long moment in both agony and sweet relief, almost like he was confused and angry and listening to a choir of angels only he could hear.

Then he released a shuddering breath, brought his other hand to his face. He pressed the base of his palm against his forehead, like he was trying to keep his brain from exploding.

I smiled at him, waiting with anticipation for the post-BJ analysis. I found my shirt and wiped my hand dry, then placed it gently on his midsection; nevertheless, he flinched when the soft cotton connected with his still erect penis.

I cleared my throat, watched him absentmindedly clean himself, his breathing still labored. The pulse point on his neck pounded out a furious rhythm.

When he didn't move my smile waned. I was tired of waiting.

I poked him gently. "Martin…are you asleep?"

"No."

I waited for five seconds, then asked, "How was I? Did I suck?"

He laughed and it was mostly a good sound, velvety, seductive and satisfied; it wrapped soft tendrils of tenderness around my heart and squeezed, like a hug. It also rolled out the Slip 'n Slide in my pants and put up a sign that said *Ready for business time, only Martin need apply within.*

But it was also a smidge melancholy, and this smidge of melancholy made me feel nervous.

He sat up and swung his legs over the side of the bed, pausing only briefly before standing and walking to the bathroom. I watched him toss my shirt to the corner and leave, the sound of his laugh still vibrating in my ears and heart.

The water switched on and off. Martin returned almost immediately and reached for his discarded pajamas.

I considered him, then asked, "So, seriously, how did I do? Any pointers for next time?"

His movements faltered at this last question, then he finished pulling on his pants and said, "There won't be a next time."

His words were confusing and sad. He also looked a little sad.

"Why not?"

He ground his teeth and swallowed before answering, "I'm not doing this."

His words broke my heart, he sounded so raw.

"What?"

"This." He lifted his chin toward me.

"You have to be more specific."

"I'm crazy about you—"

"I'm crazy about you, too." I moved to stand, but his next words gave me pause.

"Stop!" He sliced his hand through the air, his voice harsh. He appeared to be struggling. "You know what I mean, Kaitlyn. I'm in love with you, and you're not...and I don't know why you did what you just did, but this is...this is so fucked up."

Martin pushed his fingers through his hair and turned away from me.

My heart took a kamikaze leap in his direction. "Martin—"

"No." He shook his head. I saw his eyes were closed, like he was trying to block me out, and I understood why he hated it when I closed my eyes or covered my face.

He continued, and I was relieved to see he did so with open eyes. "I don't want to be a pity project. And I don't want to push you into doing things you obviously aren't ready for."

"What makes you think I'm not ready?"

He faced me and gestured furiously to the bed. "Because you shouldn't be giving blow jobs to guys you aren't in love with. That's not who you are."

"What if I am that girl?"

"You're not! This, what we've been doing, every time I touch you, it means something to you more than just getting off. I can see it and I don't want that to change. I *need* it to mean something to you! I can't...I'm not doing this anymore."

"But what if I am in love with you?" I didn't think about the words before I said them. For better or worse, I just said what I felt at that moment.

He stiffened, winced.

"Don't..." I saw his eyes narrow, flash in the low cabin light. "Don't say it unless you mean it."

I stood from the bed and walked to him, driven by the momentum of our week together, our beautiful week. I felt that everything we'd done, all of our discussions and fighting and joking and challenging each other had led to right now.

My legs were unsteady, but I felt the crazy, nonsensical rightness of this moment in each of my nerve endings. I took his hand in mine and placed his palm on my left breast. My heart was beating sure and steady, but deep and hard—like my blood was viscous and my heart was working with effort. Then I covered his heart with my hand.

"I'm in love with you, Martin. And I'm saying it because I mean it," I whispered.

His gaze darted between mine and he blinked with hesitation, like I might disappear if he closed his eyes. Suddenly I was crushed to him, encircled in his strong arms, his mouth on mine, and he was walking me backward with stumbling steps to the bed.

"I want you," he said between kisses, my back hitting the mattress as he rose above me.

"I want you too," I said.

"God, I love you. I love you so much." He trailed a licking, biting, sucking path to the valley between my breasts, then back to my neck, frantic movements that told me he was overcome, wanting all of me at once. I was all waves and spikes of sensation, longing, and wound, taut desire.

"Say it again," he demanded.

"I love you," I breathed. And then again, this time for myself, because I felt it, "I love you."

He growled harshly, his hands tightening on my body in response.

"Please," he said, biting my neck, hot breath making me shiver, his hand at my breast, kneading. "Please, I need to be inside you."

I tilted my head back, offering him more of my neck. "I thought you didn't beg."

His hand skimmed from my breast to the waist of my shorts, sending a shock of goosebumps in its wake. His fingers pushed into my panties and between my legs, parting me, rubbing a tight circle over my clitoris, and making me cry out.

"I'm not begging," he said, entering me with his fingers. "I'm asking nicely."

I laughed, but then abruptly sucked in a sharp breath as Martin removed his fingers, grabbed my shorts, and pulled both my pajamas and my underwear down my legs. He took advantage of the moment to also shed his pants then reached over to the nightstand. When he returned I noticed a few things at once.

He was straddling me, his penis fully erect, entirely recovered, and jutting out from between his legs, not quite resting on my belly. The sliver of moonlight filtered through the underwater portholes, casting his beautiful body in blue-ish white relief. I reached for his sides, gripped him just above his narrow hips, loving the smooth texture of his skin over the hard planes of his muscles.

Glaring down at me, he brought a foil packet to his teeth and ripped it. My eyes widened at the sight because…sex.

We were going to have sex.

I was going to have sex.

In about two minutes or less I was no longer going to be a virgin.

Holy crap.

I wasn't sure what I thought was going to happen when I told him I loved him, and I wouldn't take it back because it was true, but immediate post *I love you* sex hadn't even entered my mind. According to Martin, one minute I wasn't ready to administer blow jobs, the next minute I was ready to lose my virginity.

"Whoa! Wait, wait a minute!" I held my hands up between us.

Martin didn't exactly wait, nor did he exactly move forward with the pending deflowering. Rather, his hands stilled right before he rolled the condom over his dick. Then he grabbed my wrists, held them down on the bed at my sides, and loved my breasts with his hot mouth and tongue and teeth.

"Tell me what you want," he said between inhibition-demolishing kisses, suckles, and bites. "Do you want me inside you?"

"Ah," I breathed as he released one of my wrists and brought his middle finger to my mouth; he dipped it inside. Instinctively I sucked on it, swirling it with my tongue. Then he trailed the wet tip from my chin, between my breasts, over my abdomen, and finally, *finally* parted my thighs and entered me. His middle finger stroked up and down, circling my center yet never quite touching where I needed.

"Because I want you, I want you so many ways." He bit the underside of my breast, making me jump. "Do you want me?"

I was going to say *yes*, but what came out instead was a breathy, "I'm on birth control."

He stilled. Groaned. His forehead dropped then pressed against my ribs.

"Fuck me," he said. Then I sensed him throw the condom to the floor. Sliding up my body to cup my cheek, his voice soft and serious as his eyes searched mine, "I'm clean, I promise. I would never take a chance with you."

I nodded and swallowed. I trusted him. I loved him. His body was heavy over mine and I felt less in control than I'd ever felt in my entire life. He must've read the fear in my face because he gave me a soft kiss then nuzzled my ear.

"You want me to eat your sweet pussy first? I'm going to taste you and make you come with my mouth. If you want more of me inside you, then you'll have to ask nicely."

My breathing was coming fast, pants of trepidation and anticipation. I had the fleeting thought that it hardly felt fair, leaving the entire decision to me when I wasn't the one who was experienced, when I could never be fully informed of what losing my virginity would feel like until after it happened.

He nipped my bottom lip then moved to explore his way down my body, but I caught his arms before he could go far.

His eyes came back to me and I knew mine were wide with alarm. "Wait...how bad is it going to hurt? On a scale from one to ten?"

He gave me a cherishing smirk and smoothed my hair away from my face, his eyes sobering, losing a bit of their haze of desire. "It doesn't feel great, Parker. There's a lot of bullshit out there. I've never heard of a girl getting off her first time."

"But you said you had, and I quote, '*fucked plenty of virgins...*' end quote. None of them have ever, you know, orgasmed? During their first time?"

Martin cleared his throat and glanced away, exhaling a little laugh. "You want to talk about other girls right now?"

"Yes and no. I don't need to know their names or what color their nail polish was or whether you loved any of them, but I'd like to hear at least some empirical data so I can make an informed decision."

"I didn't love them," he said suddenly. Frowning, he added, "But no, none of them orgasmed the first time."

"And other confounding variables?"

His frown softened. "Such as?"

"Were you wearing a condom?"

"Always."

"And did they love you?"

He hesitated. I could see he was thinking, and then answered with impressive honesty, "Yes. I think one of them did."

I bit my lip, my eyes blinking furiously. For some reason that thought made me feel numb.

He studied me, his fingers absentmindedly playing between my legs, like he couldn't help himself. I was alternating between aroused, very aroused, very scared, very concerned, and—finally—very aroused.

Then, on the vein of continuing his impressive honesty, he added, "I've never fucked anyone without using a condom. I've never thought about anything but protecting myself and getting off, and how good it feels while it's happening. It felt better if the girl is really into it, but it wasn't required. I've never...made love to anyone, and I've never been concerned about the girl's enjoyment more than mine. But, I swear to God, Kaitlyn," he licked his lips, his eyes darting between mine, "I want to make this amazing for you. I want you every day for the rest of my life. I don't want to hurt you, but I do want your body—just like I want your heart and your mind—and I do want to feel you lose control while I'm inside you."

I sighed, breathing out some of my fear and inhaling courage. I nodded, pressing my lips together. He kissed me, pressed the tip of his middle finger against my center, then whispered, "I'll make this so good for you, the next time you'll get on your knees and beg me for it."

I moaned, arching my back, which made him chuckle and place a wet kiss on my right breast.

"So beautiful," he said, trailing more slippery kisses against my skin, sending coiling heat to my core. "So fucking perfect." He bit my hip. It hurt, but it also felt wonderful.

He spread my legs wide, placing his large hands on the inside of my thighs and holding me open. He breathed on my center then licked me—hot and soft and slippery. He tongued my opening and slid the tips of his fingers along the inside of my thighs, tickling me and sending a new wave of shivering goosebumps racing over my skin.

He proceeded to tease me, his touches, lapping, licking, and stroking never enough to push me over the edge, but more than enough to drive me crazy.

I felt empty and needy.

So I reached for him, threaded my fingers through his hair to his temples, and said, "Please, please…"

Martin didn't ask for clarification.

He lifted to his knees, his rock-solid, imposing form rising above me. He wiped the back of his hand across his mouth. His eyes were hooded as they surveyed my open legs, my reaching hands, and my skin. I was bare to him. His right eyebrow quirked, just a little, and his smile was more sexy smirk than grin.

With measured, lithe movements, he stalked up my body, aligning himself at my entrance. I felt the swollen tip of him nudge me as he hovered above, watching me with avid, almost fascinated interest.

"Please, Martin," I moaned, my hands on his hips. My belly and pelvis felt aching and hollow. I angled my hips up, sliding against him.

I saw him shudder and heard him release a low growl. Then, seemingly out of patience, he lowered himself and kissed me—a soft, yielding, searching kiss—and a split second later, while his mouth was still loving mine, he pushed himself into me with one swift thrust.

I stiffened, a pinching, harsh, acute pain between my legs, and I whimpered.

"I love you," he whispered, his eyes holding my shocked, rounded gaze. He withdrew then pushed deeper.

I felt myself stretch. It was impossible and uncomfortable and I couldn't breathe. It hurt.

But each withdrawal was twice or three times as long in duration as his invasions and I was grateful. The slow, sliding movements brought me back to the pleasure he'd built with his mouth and hands.

Part of me just wanted it to be over, wanted to push him away, make it stop.

Yet his eyes, so cherishing and concerned, hopeful and reverent, grounded me. Then he dipped his head to my neck, releasing hot breath just under my ear, biting me and loving away the sting.

Whispered again, "I love you, Kaitlyn. I love you. You're perfect, and your body is perfect. I love you."

Finally, the inward strokes didn't hurt as much and, though I still felt uncomfortable, I didn't feel sharp pain.

With each careful rocking of his pelvis he placed a soft kiss on my face—my chin, my nose, my cheeks—the feather-light touches making me feel loved and utterly cherished.

I was nowhere near reaching my peak, but curiosity and some instinctual rhythm roused me from my paralysis and had me lifting my hips to meet his.

His hand pressed into my hip to still my movements.

"Kaitlyn, don't do that. If you…fuck, I'm going to…I can't…"

I spread my legs wider and flexed my inner muscles, enjoying the fiery—resentment? Warning? Desire?—in his eyes. I responded by narrowing my gaze and undulating my hips quicker, forcing him to match my rhythm.

"Stop, Parker, you have to… Oh God…"

Then his thrusts became inelegant and demanding. He became rigid. He grit his teeth and groaned.

And I watched all this, how he completely and totally lost control, with a roaring feminine satisfaction that was an excellent runner-up to an actual orgasm.

His body fell into mine like more than just gravity pulled him downward. He fit his hand between my back and the bed and embraced me, his breathing labored. I didn't mind the temporary, crushing weight of him or the slickness of his heated body. Being surrounded on every side by Martin was perhaps the best feeling of all time.

He lifted his head, his gaze searching and serious. He slipped one of his hands from beneath me, pushed his fingers through my hair and cupped my cheek.

"Are you okay?"

I nodded, giving myself a moment to be thoughtful about the matter, then said, "Yes. I'm just fine."

His gaze turned dark. "You're just fine?"

I nodded and patted him on the back. "You did good, Martin. It was painful. I'm not going to lie. But I'm not at all traumatized."

He stared at me for a beat, looking equal parts offended and amused. When he spoke, however, his tone was laced with demanding determination.

"We're not leaving this boat until you have multiple orgasms on my dick."

I felt my forehead wrinkle as my eyebrows pushed upward. "Multiple? Is that even possible? I'm pretty sure I read that was a myth."

"Parker…" He dipped his head to my neck, nibbled my earlobe, making me shrug my shoulder reflexively and shiver with delight.

He continued on a whisper, "If multiple orgasms are a myth, then you can call me Hercules."

CHAPTER 10
Multiple Bonds

THE SKY WAS overcast when Martin woke me up with kisses and bites on my shoulders. He insisted we go for a swim right then just in case it started to thunder or rain.

I later found this was also a slick kind of strategy because he jumped into the ocean naked.

I did not.

I dressed in the string bikini, daintily dipped my toes in, and then climbed down the ladder at the back of the boat. Martin eyed me over the gentle waves for about ten seconds while he treaded water. Then he lunged at me, chased me, caught me, easily discarded my bikini, and proceeded to feel me up.

We didn't make it as far as the bed. Instead, both of us feeling an irrational sense of urgency, we attacked each other in the water, then on the ladder leading to the deck, then on the deck. He pulled me down to his lap, straddling him, as he sat on the cushioned bench at the end of the stern. My breathing and movements were frantic, erratic, and when I came down on him we both cursed.

I'm not going to lie, it still hurt at first. But something about being naked under the sky, sticky and wet with sea water, learning each other, seeing the love and lust in his eyes, lubricated all the right spots. He guided my hips until I found a natural rhythm.

But I was distracted by the soreness between my legs and how my breasts bounced and swayed as I moved, until Martin leaned back on one elbow, his thumb moving to my apex, his eyes devouring me, and growled his appreciation. "This, you, here, now—hell, Kaitlyn. This is it, this is everything."

I did my best, but I wasn't proficient in the art of man-riding. I knew I was driving him crazy because he'd closed his eyes, obviously trying to hold off for as long as possible, his brow wrinkled into a severe frown of concentration which I would forever think of as the *don't come don't come oh God, don't come* face.

I'd been close for a while, but I was frustrated with my body's lack of accelerative progress. It was starting to feel nice, but I wasn't going to climax. Therefore I leaned forward and whispered, "Don't worry about me."

His eyes flew open and he stared at me with a ferocious kind of challenge. "What the hell does that mean?"

I lifted myself up then came back down, enjoying the sexiness of the act but somehow resigned that this time was going to be another miss.

He must've seen something in my eyes he didn't like, because before I could explain my meaning, he surprised me by standing, picking me up with him, and carrying me to the table.

"Lay down," he commanded.

I did.

He pulled out, spread my legs wide, knelt on the ground, and proceeded to have me for breakfast. It didn't take long before I was near spiraling, my lower belly tight with the promise of sweet, torturous relief. My hands gripping the edge of the table.

And I started chanting, "Oh God, oh God, oh God!"

And I came.

But then before I'd quite crested the wave, Martin stood and filled me, his thumb still circling my clitoris mercilessly in rhythm with his thrusts. And I came again—harder, better, faster, stronger—the rhythm of my blood thundering between my ears. The soreness between my legs adding a layer of exquisite pain to our combined pleasure...intensifying it. My mind was lost to everything except the sweet, overwhelming searing sensation.

I think I actually screamed, or yelled, or yodeled. I don't know what I did, but my throat hurt from the effort afterward. I hoped it wasn't a yodel...

He came a very short time later, looking overwrought, confused, and spent. Again he fell forward like a force other than gravity brought our bodies together. But this time he held himself up with bent arms and kissed my neck, chest, and shoulders hungrily.

My nerve endings felt fried so I let him play with my body, lick my skin, nip my nipples, and tongue my belly button as he slipped from me. His breathing returned to baseline after three or more minutes.

Then he said against my right ribs, "I love you. You're the most beautiful thing...so perfect."

I huffed a laugh, my hands reaching for, finding, then playing with the damp hair on his head. "I'm not perfect, but I'm glad you think so."

He brought himself back over me, so we were face to face, his gaze both curious and irritated. "Why do you do that? Why do you shrug off compliments? You are fucking goddamn gorgeous, Parker. You. Are. And you are a fucking goddamn musical prodigy. The fact you're not making music every day is criminal."

I gave him a sideways look and a small smile, wanting to choose my words carefully because he looked like he was considering some method of torture in order to push me into admitting my amazingness.

"I love that you think so, Martin."

"Kaitlyn—" His tone held more than an edge of warning.

"No, listen." I framed his face with my hands and lifted my head to rub my nose against his. I left a soft kiss on his lips and said, "I *am* glad you think I am all those things, and I believe you. But I'm not going to magically think I'm beautiful or perfect or talented just because you do. I have to get there for myself. I have to believe those things for myself—not because I have a boyfriend who values me and thinks I invented airplane neck pillows. If I base my self-worth on someone else's opinion or view of me, then I will also base my lack of worth on that person's opinion as well. And *that* has the potential of tearing me to pieces."

His eyes narrowed a fraction, but I saw reluctant understanding ignite behind his expression.

"Are you always like this?"

"Like what? Brilliant?" I teased.

"Yeah…brilliant."

***

I CAUGHT MARTIN staring at me no less than twenty times during the next few hours. And each time he looked a little dazed, like he was caught in the web of his own imagination. Sometimes I'd stare back, narrowing my eyes and administering a mock suspicious look. He'd smile—slow and lazy and sexy—then kiss me.

One thing was for certain: Martin Sandeke was using his big brain to work through an issue of enormous proportions.

Meanwhile, I worked on my last term paper in between conversations with Martin. He told me about his vision for the future of telecommunications and how satellites were going to play an essential role.

Science may not have been my passion, like I was wondering if music truly was, but I had a great deal of interest in science related topics. He told me all about the seventeen—SEVENTEEN!!—patents he held. Although, when I'd asked him if he was going to use the money from his inventions as the source for the sixty million he needed for the venture capitalist project, he'd laughed.

Inventing stuff, he explained, was fun. It was his hobby, but none of his inventions would ever bring in enough money.

When I asked him what he defined as enough money, he responded grimly, "Enough will be three times whatever my father is worth at any given time."

Seeing as how his father was a billionaire, this answer struck me as supercilious and off key. Making enough money sounded like an unhealthy obsession and dissonant with happiness.

I didn't voice this opinion.

By mid-afternoon the boat was ensconced in a torrential downpour, I'd grown used to his dazed stares, and—sadly—it was time to head back to the island.

We weren't going back to the big house, as we were going to the aforementioned cottage on the opposite side of the island, where Eric and Sam had been since Wednesday. I hoped she wasn't too irritated at me for my lack of communication…

I felt guilty about it, like a bad friend.

At present, Martin was in the captain's chair, steering us back, and I was trying to catch him unawares by lobbing rapid-fire questions at him, attempting to get him to admit something embarrassing.

"Favorite movie?"

"Wall Street."

"Favorite food?"

"Black licorice."

I paused, his answer surprising, but then pressed forward. "Favorite color?"

"Black."

"Black?"

"Yes."

I thought about this, then asked because I felt compelled, "How can it be black?"

"Most people's favorite color is black, but they're too fixated on what others think to admit the truth, even to themselves. Think about it, what color is represented in your closet more than any other? Is it blue? Green? Red? No. It's black."

"But black is depressing, it's the color of funerals and dark rooms and despair."

He gave me a half smile and almost rolled his eyes, but not quite. "In

Japan, the color associated with funerals is white. Dark rooms can be fun. Also, black feels like something new to me, like the sky right before dawn."

"Martin Sandeke, that was almost poetic."

"You're easy to talk to." He didn't sound precisely happy about this.

"You say that like it's a bad thing."

"It might be. I say things to you I've never said or told anyone." He looked serious as he admitted this, gazing down at me with either resentment or longing, I couldn't tell which.

So I tried to disarm the sudden tension by saying, "That's because you *loooove* me."

He rolled his eyes. But he also smiled.

***

"SPILL IT."

"What?"

"*Everything.*" Sam elongated the word, over-pronouncing each syllable. "Spill it all. Spill it all over the place. Dump it out—on the floor, on the ceiling, on the duvet—spew it all, every last bit of it, because I am so far past interested, I've entered the neighboring territory of obsessively curious."

I glanced at her from the corner of my eye. She was staring at me, wide-eyed, mouth in a tight line, jaw set. It was her game face. She meant business.

It was nearly dinner time. We'd arrived about a half hour ago. Martin had anchored the boat and tied it to a small wooden dock adjacent to the cottage, then we'd raced through the rain to the cottage.

The cottage was actually everything I thought of when I thought *beach cottage*. It was cozy and small, had two bedrooms and one bathroom, a postage stamp kitchen with a breakfast bar, and a combined family room/living room. The place was also decorated in nautical themes. Crafty mosaics of sea glass and shells lined the walls, and a big, rusty anchor hung above the front door.

Sam and I were currently in my room—well, the room Martin and I would share for the night—and I was going through my things. Sam and Eric had brought most of my stuff from the big house, but several items were missing; so far one of my textbooks, a folder of class notes, and several shirts. The textbook and the shirts were no big deal, but I needed the folder.

Also, it gave me an excellent excuse to postpone responding to Sam's questioning.

"Kaitlyn...you're stalling."

"I'm trying to figure out if all my stuff is here."

"You're stalling."

I huffed, turned to face her, and threw my hands in the air. "Yes. Yes I'm stalling."

"Why are you stalling?"

"Because I don't know how much I'm ready to share with you. I haven't decided."

"How much? How *much*?" she sputtered for a moment, her eyes sweeping up then down my body. "Well, how much happened?"

"A lot."

"Are..." Her eyes narrowed a bit as she considered her words. "Are you okay?"

"Yes."

"Are you and Martin okay?"

My serious face slipped as an involuntary and dreamy smile arrested my features. "Yes."

Her eyes went wide again. "Are you and Martin officially together? Like girlfriend, boyfriend, committed exclusive relationship, *I'll go bat-shit crazy and burn all your stuff if I find you with someone else* together?"

"Yes." I sighed as I said this, and it was a girly, wistful sigh.

However, Sam's expression was growing more anxious, pensive. "Did you...?" She licked her lips then nibbled on the bottom one, not finishing her question. Yet, the implied meaning was there. It hung over us both, the word *sex* in capital letters followed by a giant question mark.

I nodded, shifting my weight between my feet, unable to stand still.

"Oh my God." Her eyes lost a bit of their focus briefly and I couldn't tell what she was thinking. Then she blurted, "Please tell me he used a condom."

I felt a niggling bit of guilt or regret, which I pushed away immediately, instead deciding to roll my eyes. "Sam..."

"Kaitlyn, don't you *Sam* me. Please tell me you were safe."

"I'm on birth control," I whispered. I didn't know why I was whispering.

"So? Birth control doesn't stop genital warts."

"Sam…" Apparently my only defense against her commonsense facts was to roll my eyes.

"Kaitlyn, you are not stupid. So why are you acting stupid about this?"

"I trust him," I said without thinking, and shrugged.

Sam's eyes widened then closed, her chin dropped to her chest; I heard her exhale then say to the floor. "You think you love him."

I didn't respond. At my silence she lifted just her eyes. She looked sober, concerned, bracing.

I shrugged because, though I could guess the source and reasoning behind her anxiety on my behalf, I didn't share her worry. My feet were too far off the ground. I was basking in post-boat bliss. Martin loved me. I loved him. And the genital wart-covered world could go hide itself in a chemistry lab cabinet for all I cared.

"I do. I love him. I'm *in* love with him."

"Oh." She tried to smile, but it looked more like a grimace. "Well, that's…great."

I laughed at her effort to be supportive. "I know what you're going to say—"

Really, there were so many warnings she might give, concerns she might voice given the situation and how little she knew about Martin.

But instead she held up her hands to keep me from continuing. "I'm not going to say anything. Other than I hope you know that I will always be here for you should you ever need anything. Anything at all. *Anything.* And that includes a visit to the gynecologist or the name of a hit man."

I smiled at my friend because there was no doubt in my mind that she did love me. "You're a good friend."

She returned my smile, but worry still rimmed her eyes as she spoke, "You too, Kaitlyn… And you deserve the best, especially from Martin Sandeke."

Sam crossed the room and pulled me into a hug, and added in a whisper, "Never accept less than his best."

***

DINNER WASN'T UNCOMFORTABLE at all. It wasn't. Really, it wasn't.

Sure, Sam gave Martin the *I will cut you* glower at random intervals, but all in all, our foursome got along quite well. Her periodic awkward stare-downs were actually kind of funny because she'd typically pair them with ominous statements and dubious double entendre, like:

"Are you going to use the mustard, Martin? Or do you not use condom...mints?"

Then she'd lift her eyebrow meaningfully.

Another of my favorites was when we were discussing travel, places we'd like to go. Eric said he wanted to go to Australia and Sam blurted, "How about you Martin? Ever gone *Down Under*? Or is south of the equator not to your tastes?"

I noticed that Eric had to hide his smile and/or laughter behind his napkin on more than one occasion.

Martin didn't smile. Instead he'd answer her questions plainly, as though they were just normal questions; but I could see through his poker face that he thought she was equal parts funny and irritating.

After dinner and dishes were done, Martin pulled me away from Sam's suggestion that we play a game, setting his arm firmly around my waist.

"We're tired," he said.

"We are?" I glanced at him beseechingly, then back to where Sam was setting up Risk. Man...I loved board games. Especially games of world domination.

"We *are*." Martin narrowed his eyes at me and I wasn't so oblivious to realize he wanted more alone time.

I sighed my disappointment, then turned back to Sam. "I guess we're tired."

Her mouth was pinched and her eyes—appraising and unhappy—were moving between us, like she wanted to say something, but was quite literally biting her tongue.

I felt a small pang of guilt and mouthed, *I'm sorry*.

She gave me a small smile and shrugged as she packed up the game. "Don't worry about it. Maybe you can play another time...when *Martin* isn't so tired."

The pang of guilt blossomed into something else, something resembling unease. I didn't respond. Partly because I wasn't sure what to say, and partly because Martin was already leading me out of the room. But I finally found my voice when we made it back to our bedroom.

"Are you tired? Because I'm not actually tired. And, something you may not know about me, I really enjoy a wholesome game of vicious world domination every once in a while."

"I'm not tired." Martin pulled me into the room, shut the door, pushed me against it, and moved in for a kiss. His hands were already everywhere, like an octopus with opposable thumbs.

I turned my head at the last minute, bracing my hands against his chest. His lips landed awkwardly on my jaw, but he wasn't deterred by the misfire. Improvising, he kissed a wet path down my neck while his deft palms massaged my breasts through my bra.

"Hey, you." I tried to keep my tone light and conversational. "Maybe we could, um, slow down a minute and have a discussion regarding your feelings on world domination."

Martin's thumb swept over my nipple then he pinched me, hard. It felt good, sending spikes of Martin-juju-arousal-fog to the four corners of my body, but it also felt like a punishment, or retaliation.

"No," he said.

"No?"

"No."

The back of my head fell against the door and I huffed, liking everything he was doing, but disliking how single-minded he was being. In attempt to get his attention, I pinched the skin over his ribs.

"Ow!" He flinched a little, then laughed. It was a low, rumbly, sexy sound. Not at all the outcome I was going for. "Do you want to be rough?"

"No." I pushed *that* alluring thought away with all my willpower. "I want you to listen to me."

"And I want to bite you and lick you and fuck you and make you come."

"Ah, Martin—"

"Kaitlyn, stop talking." He moved his mouth to my ear and bit me before whispering, "I need to be inside you."

My body trembled with a little pleasure earthquake as his hands slid to the band of my shorts and down into my underwear, stroking me. I began to melt against him. My objections—and whether I actually had objections—grew muddled and distant. But then as he pushed inside me with two fingers I felt more than a twinge of soreness. I winced in response to the discomfort and I shoved at his chest.

"Wait. Stop, that hurts."

He stilled immediately, removing his fingers but not withdrawing his hand. Martin lifted his head and stared down at me, his green-blue eyes searching.

"That hurts?"

I nodded, swallowing before rushing to explain. "My pants aren't used to frequent invasions, or any invasions. It's been a busy week for my pants. As such, my pants need time to adjust, acclimate. My pants still like you a lot, but I think my pants need a rest."

He was so close, crowding me against the door. I could've counted his eyelashes.

"Your pants?"

I nodded.

"We're calling your pussy, 'pants'? That's what we're calling it?"

"No. I mean, we can…I guess. But 'pants' doesn't necessarily conjure the most alluring images. I'm open to other names if we have to name it. Why do we have to name it?"

His hand in my much-discussed pants slipped around to my bare bottom, caressing and squeezing. "We don't have to name it. I just thought you were naming it."

"No. I'm not naming it." I shook my head. "I was just saying, or trying to say, that the area in my pants that is required for sexual intercourse is—"

"You mean your pussy."

"Yes."

"Then say it. Say, *my pussy*."

I scrunched my face at him even as his hands continued to glide over my body and his hips rocked into me, making me feel muddled all over again.

"What? Why?"

"I just want to hear you say the word." Martin unclasped my bra.

"Why can't I say *vagina*?"

"No."

"Vag?" I tried, half serious.

He made a face then shook his head, pulling my shirt and bra from my body.

"How about my *nether region*?"

The side of his mouth quirked just before he took a step away to discard his own shirt, his fingers then moving to unbutton his jeans. "No."

"Dewy petals?" I batted my eyelashes at him.

"Ugh, what the fuck does that even mean?" He stepped out of his jeans, leaving his long, lithe, fine form in nothing but black boxers. He reached for me, and I let him.

"I have a ton of these." I grinned at his reaction. "I play this game, really it's a strange coping strategy, where I repeat synonyms for words—"

"I know. I told you, I heard you do it all the time during lab."

"Oh, that's right. Well, I know *lots* of euphemisms for the female anatomy."

"Don't tell me, I don't want to know." Martin turned us, marched me backward until my legs connected with the mattress, then eased us down using one arm wrapped around my middle and a single knee on the bed.

It was an impressive display of upper body strength and core muscles. In other words, it was hot.

"Just one more?"

His hand slid from my collarbone, between my breasts, and down my abdomen; he hitched two fingers into my shorts at my hip and paused.

"Okay, just one more."

"Meat curtains."

He frowned in a way that wasn't a frown, pressing his lips together valiantly before speaking mostly to himself. "This is what I get for falling in love with a girl who hides from me in lab cabinets instead of someone who wants to use me for my money."

Martin's eyes were bright with teasing, but they were also hot and focused. I could see his intentions before he licked his lips, his attention moving to my mouth.

So I blurted, "I need my vector calculus folder!"

"What…" He frowned at me, plainly confused, then asked, "Right now?"

"No. Not right now, but before we leave. I think I left it at the big house. I need it, as it has all my notes from this semester."

"Ah, well…I'll call tomorrow before we leave, see if Mrs. Greenstone can find it and bring it to us at the marina."

"Why don't we stop by on our way in the morning? I'm not one-hundred percent certain where it is."

"No. We aren't going back there." Ice entered his words; his declaration was almost hostile.

"But what if Mrs. Greenstone can't find it?"

"I'll call tonight. If she can't find it, I'll go over there by myself."

"That's silly. I'll be able to find it faster."

"If I can't find it then I guess I'll just have to tutor you in vector calculus."

I grimaced. "Seeing my own handwriting takes me back to the moment when I took the notes and the lesson. It's the only way I can study. I have an unhealthy attachment to my class notes."

"Hopefully you also have an unhealthy attachment to me."

"So, how do you feel about me using you for your brain instead of your ties to massive wealth or the magnificence that is your body? I'd like to use it, often."

"What do you mean? Use what often?"

My back was resting on the bed now and he was over me, his bare chest against mine. I wasn't going to be able to think in this position, especially since I could feel his erection against my hip, so I smiled hopefully and pushed him until he was lying on the bed and I was hovering at his side.

"Listen, I don't want to mislead you. I *do* want to use you for your body, just so we're clear. But I'd also like for you to put that big head of yours to use."

He stared at me, and I realized too late that what I'd meant to say was brain…not head. Not. Head.

Martin fought a smile, and just looking at his handsome face made my stomach do a sudden backflip. He said smoothly, "Tell me more about what you'd like me to do with my big head."

I scowled at him. Surprisingly, I didn't feel a huge amount of embarrassment, just slightly flustered.

"Quit your backtalk or else I may have to pinch you again."

"I wouldn't mind, as long as I get to pinch you back." His hand moved to my breast and he fingered my nipple, making my breath catch and his already stiff erection tent his boxers.

"Stop it for a minute, I want to talk to you. I'm trying to be serious."

Martin's heated stare turned into a petulant glare and he removed his hands, sighed, and folded them behind his head. He blinked at me once, then moved his eyes to the ceiling. "Fine. What do you want to talk about?"

I didn't roll my eyes at his somewhat dramatic withdrawal, but I wanted to. Instead I pushed myself up and sat on the bed facing him, hugging my knees to my chest and started again.

"What I'm trying to say is that…I like *you*, Martin. I like your brain." I blurted the last part, not knowing exactly what I was about to say.

Just his eyes slid back to mine, the lines of his face thawing as he searched my face.

I tucked my hair behind my ears then rested my arms on the top of my knees, heartened by his open interest. "I like you. I like you for who you are, even though you're callous and don't quite know how to treat people. You're clever and funny. I admire the way you move and how you can't help but lead. I like how driven you are, and passionate. It's fun to watch. I also think there's a good heart in there, but I feel like it might be bruised and neglected..."

After I said the words I knew it was true. His heart was bruised and neglected. He needed mending, care, and comfort. He needed someone to trust.

I shook myself, realized I'd trailed off and we'd been sitting silently for a long moment, and turned my attention back to Martin. He was peering at me, waiting for me to continue.

I took a deep breath before speaking. "The thing is, I've been wanting to tell you this since Sunday. You have a friend in me. No matter what happens between us, I want you to know that if you ever need me—as a friend, as someone you can trust—I'll always be there for you. I'll always be your safe place."

Martin considered me for a moment, his gaze flickering over my face as though searching, before saying, "I don't think I'll ever want to be friends with you."

I must've made some outward expression that mirrored my inner surprised hurt because he gripped my leg to keep me in place and rushed to add, "I mean, I don't think I could ever be *just* friends with you. I could never be disinterested enough."

"Disinterested? You think friends are disinterested in each other?"

He half shrugged, his eyes moving to the right. "Yes. I have friends, but I'm not interested in them."

"Do you have any female friends?"

He nodded. "Yeah. My business partner is a woman. I'd consider her a friend and I couldn't care less who she's out with. But with you, I don't think I'd be able to see you with someone else and not go crazy."

"So, what? If we break up then you'll just cut me completely out?"

"I would." He nodded, looking very serious.

"Because you think you'll never be disinterested?"

"I know it."

"And by stating that you'll never be *disinterested* in me, you mean that you'll always want to..." I waved my hand in the air to finish my sentence.

His eyes moved back to mine and he grinned. "I'll always want to...?"

He was being obnoxiously obtuse, trying to force me to use his language.

"You'll always want to have intimate relations with me."

He shook his head like he thought I was cute, and clarified using his own vernacular, "Yeah, I'll always want to fuck you."

I scowled at him. "You know, it's one thing to use that word when we're," I waved my hand through the air again, "when we're in the middle of copulation. But it's completely different when we're sitting here and I'm trying to have a conversation with you about serious matters."

"Why? Why does it make any difference?"

"Because, it's crass and ungentlemanly."

"Ungentlemanly?" He looked like he was about to burst out laughing.

I increased the severity of my scowl. "Yes. Ungentlemanly. How you speak to me during everyday discussions matters because it's a direct reflection of how you see me and whether or not you respect me. Using bad language—yes, bad language. Don't give me that look."

He'd rolled his eyes and ground his jaw, like he thought I was being ridiculous. So I pointed my finger at him and wagged it.

"Using bad language tells me you don't have enough respect for me to use good manners or think about the implication of your words before you say them."

"Kaitlyn, you know I respect you."

"Yeah, you respect me so much you want to fuck me—not make love to me, not be intimate with me. Fuck me."

He grew still, the amusement and rebelliousness waning from his features, and he studied me. Though I got the impression he only half saw my face, and was mostly lost in his own thoughts.

At last he said, "I didn't mean it like that."

"But it's what you said."

His jaw ticked as he processed this information. A calculating gleam entered his eyes and they narrowed. "All right, how about this. I'll use more *gentlemanly* language during our everyday conversations if you use more *bad* language while we...during our periods of intimacy." He said this last bit in a flat tone, like he couldn't believe he was actually saying it in place of his favorite four-letter "F" word.

I considered his terms for less than five seconds. Really, there was nothing to consider. Using his bad language during lovemaking made sense...might even help me loosen up. Therefore I nodded and stuck my hand out for him to shake.

"Deal."

He smiled, fitting his hand in mine. "Parker, I love you."

"Sandeke, I see your love, and I raise you a secret handshake."

CHAPTER 11
Line Spectra and the Bohr Model

MARTIN RECEIVED A call in the morning that Mrs. Greenstone couldn't find my notebook.

Therefore, the next morning—after a forty-five minute argument, copious seething glares from Martin, and two hours of him giving me the silent treatment—we were all on our way to the big house to get my folder.

I couldn't take the chance he'd be unable to find it or abandon the search prematurely. I wasn't kidding when I told him I had an unhealthy attachment to my class notes. I was convinced the notes were the only reason I was getting As in all my upper-level courses.

Yes, my notes might have been somewhat of a security blanket for me, but so what? I needed them. I believed I needed them in order to succeed. I wasn't leaving the island without them.

We drove the rugged golf carts across the island, Martin and Eric in one, Sam and I in the other. The all-terrain vehicles were loaded up with our luggage and I was splitting my attention between Sam's chatter and her roll case threatening to fling itself off the cart with the slightest bump or provocation.

When we arrived at the mansion, Martin walked over and offered his hand to me. When I accepted it, he gripped mine tightly and studied my features; his were stormy and uncertain. When he made no move toward the house, I lifted my free hand and smoothed it over his cheek, lifted on my tiptoes, and brushed a soft kiss to his mouth.

"Hey, let's get this over with. We'll go in, get my folder, and get out. Maybe steal some cookies from the kitchen."

I watched him swallow. His features still stormy and undecided.

"If we run into my father, just do what I say. Just…" He sighed, closed his eyes, and ground his teeth. "This is a bad idea. You shouldn't be here."

I didn't know how to make this better for him, so I took three shuffling steps toward the house and tugged him after me. "Hurry up. I need those notes and we have a plane to catch."

He opened his eyes, giving me one last pained stare, then overtook my lead, pulling me after him. He paused just briefly with his hand on the door handle, as though mentally preparing himself, then opened the door quietly. We walked into the entrance and Martin searched the space briefly, loitering on the foyer steps. He seemed extremely reluctant to venture farther.

Before I could make an attempt to soothe his obvious tension, one of the most irritating sounds in the known universe halted our progress.

"Heya, Stroke."

Ack.

I knew that voice.

It was the cuss monster.

I looked to the left just as Martin did the same, then I glanced up at Martin's face. He was clearly perturbed and confused.

"What are you doing here? Why didn't you go back with everyone else?" Martin's grip on me tightened just a fraction as we turned to face Ben.

"Didn't see a good reason to go back yet," Ben said, before taking an obnoxious sip of what appeared to be a strawberry daiquiri through an oversized straw.

"Because I told you to leave. How about that for a good reason?" Martin's tone was flat, hard, and irritated.

I pressed my lips together to keep from making any kind of facial expression.

Meanwhile, Ben shrugged again, but sounded positively elated as he said, "But your dad invited me to stay, so I did. Besides, I've decided to quit the team, so you can go fuck yourself."

I felt tension roll through Martin—gathering—tangible in how he stood and the measured way he drew breath. But before he could respond, we were interrupted.

"Marty." This came from the top of the wide staircase and echoed through the foyer. The man waited until both Martin and I looked at him before continuing. His pale blue eyes rested on me. "I thought you'd left the island."

Denver Sandeke, Martin's father, was taller than I thought he'd be. Taller and not nearly as scrawny. He wasn't a good-looking man; his chin was almost non-existent and his nose was oddly shaped, thin and long. As well, he was either a member or the president of the hair club for men.

And with his entrance I felt a shift.

Whereas before Martin was and had always been the center of focus, the "alpha of the pack" as Sam put it, now his father's presence demanded the spotlight. In truth, neither of them clearly dominated the other. It wasn't shared power; it was dual power that co-existed very, very badly, like when two acid-base reactions are after the same proton.

"No," Martin said. The frost in the single word seemed to lower the temperature of the room by several degrees. It seemed that Denver, like his wife, brought out the Abominable Snowman in Martin.

Denver didn't respond to his son. Instead he sauntered down the steps, his eyes still on me, a friendly smile affixed to his lips. I noted that the shape of his mouth was similar to Martin's.

"You're Joss Parker's daughter." He sounded immensely pleased. Meanwhile something about the way he used my mother's first name made me want to pluck out all his nose hairs.

I started to respond, but Martin tugged on my hand and shifted so he was half blocking me from his father, like he was protecting me with his body. "We're leaving."

Denver ignored his son and offered me his hand. "It's so nice to meet you. I know your mother quite well. She is," he chuckled to himself, "she is certainly a force."

"Don't touch her." As Martin said this he moved me completely behind him, and with one hand on my hip, guided us a step back toward the door. I noted that he still faced his father, almost like he knew better than to turn his back.

My view of his father was obscured now that the mountain of Martin was between us, but I heard the change in Denver's voice as he addressed his son.

"You finally did something useful, Marty. You're still the village idiot, but at least your dick makes smart choices."

I heard Ben fake-suppress an obnoxious guffaw, but I barely registered it as my brain was still trying to grasp the venom that had erupted from Martin's father's mouth.

His father!

And yet, even knowing what I did about Martin, even knowing he had a history of callous indifference toward the feelings of others and had no qualms about yelling at men, women, children, and turtles, I was completely unprepared for his response.

"Better the village idiot than the village pervert and impotency expert. By the way, Ben here used your entire stash of Viagra earlier this week. You two flaccid assholes have so much in common."

Martin's father *tsked* and responded coolly, "Careful, Marty. Or I might decide to break your new toy."

"You even fucking look at her and they won't find your body." Martin took another step back, taking me with him.

This was completely crazy. I thought the run-in with his stepmother was vicious—this took vicious to a whole new level.

"You forget who bankrolls your life, *son*." I winced as Denver said the word *son*. In context, coming from Denver's mouth, it sounded more like *whore*. "Your toys are my toys, and I'll use them whenever and however I please. Now step aside, you're not going anywhere until I say so."

I felt Martin tense. He released my hand and I saw both of his were balled into fists. He shifted on his feet, his stance bracing, like he was about to throw a punch. Martin was big, but his father was also big; as well, Ben the rapist was clearly on Team Evil's side. Two against one was hardly fair. I might be able to call for Eric before the situation escalated, but that was unlikely.

Tangentially, I wondered how many times Martin and his father had come to blows, but pushed the thought away for later contemplation. I couldn't stay where I was, silent, hiding. Now was not the time for me to hide, not when Martin was putting himself into harm's way on my behalf. I needed to *do* something.

Now was not the time to bow out gracefully. Now was the time to fight for Martin.

Since Martin was no longer holding me behind him, I stepped to his side and slipped my left arm around his right elbow.

Placing a thin smile on my face, I addressed Denver. "You'll forgive me if I don't shake your hand. As I've met your wife and see the company you keep," I nodded toward Ben, "you'll understand if I'm wary of communicable diseases. As Ben will tell you, not touching people I don't know is one of my life rules."

I was gratified to find my small speech had stunned all the testosterone in the room into inaction. Three sets of male eyes stared at me as though I were a strange creature.

I cleared my throat and continued, "I have no interest in knowing you, Mr. Sandeke. All I want is my vector calculus folder and then we'll be leaving."

Though Denver's eyes were on me, he spoke to his son. "I'm looking at her now, Marty. What are you going to do about it?"

Martin shifted restlessly at my side but I tightened my grip around his arm and responded for both of us, my voice conversational. "Again, I'll just take my vector calculus notebook and we'll be on our way."

"No. You won't." If Denver's wife had dead-face, Denver Sandeke had dead eyes.

Channeling my mother, I drew myself up straighter and glared at him square in his beady dead eyes. "Actually, we will. You see, Martin told me before we came over that you were a wee little worm of a man. Therefore, I made a call to my mother's security team. You may have heard of the US Secret Service? ...Yes? ...No?"

Mr. Sandeke shifted a half step back, his gaze narrowing on me.

"Ah. I see you've heard of them. Despite all their guns and shooting and whatnot, they're actually very nice men." I moved to side step him and pulled Martin with me, careful never to give him our backs. "Now, we'll just be getting that notebook then we'll get out of...well, we'll get out of your hairpiece."

***

ON THE UP side, I had my folder. I also managed to collect my missing textbook and clothes—so, double bonus.

On the down side, Martin had barely spoken since we'd left the mansion. He also wouldn't look at me and had made no move to touch me beyond helping with my bags, offering me his hand on the boat, and guiding me to my seat on the plane—so, double whammy.

Also, his father was basically Satan, but with no chin.

Regardless, I didn't regret meeting the man. Meeting Denver swiftly explained many things about Martin, brought so much of his behavior and motivations into painfully sharp focus.

Now, as I eyeballed Martin from my seat, I noted that his face was red, flushed with color, and his eyes were a bit wild. I knew he was still thinking about his father and I knew his emotions were very, very near the surface. His seething anger radiated from him, like a billowing cloud of dark rage.

Honestly, I felt like one wrong move, or word, or glance, and he might trash the inside of the private jet...or scream at me. As such, all four of us had been silent. Even Sam saw fit to keep her sarcasm bottled up as she thumbed silently through a magazine like it held the answers to the perfect tennis game.

I was again faced with the reality that I didn't know the right thing to say to my boyfriend. As I stewed in this realization, I further recognized that being held hostage by his anger bothered me more than the possibility of getting yelled at.

My nagging disquiet grew as I watched him, his jaw clenching and unclenching, his breathing purposefully slow. He was so alone, entirely focused inward, lost in a dark place. This was where Martin Sandeke lived and how he'd learned to survive. I couldn't stand it.

I loved him.

Watching him fumbling through the labyrinth of his wrath was akin to my unreachable itch, except this time it was in my brain and heart.

Therefore, and acting completely on instinct, I unclicked my seatbelt, crossed to him, and sat on his lap. He stiffened, his razor eyes cutting to mine, laced with a fevered fury and severe warning. I ignored them.

Instead I encircled him with my arms, threading my fingers and nails into the hair at the nape of his neck, and whispered in his ear, "I love you, Martin. I love you."

He grew rigid for a split second, but then he embraced me. Really, he crushed me to him with his powerful arms and his forehead fell to my shoulder. We sat like that for several minutes—me gently scratching the back of his head and placing soft kisses everywhere I could, given my limited range of motion, and him holding onto me like a life raft. I silently rejoiced when I perceived the inflexibility wane, ease, relax, and his breathing grow normal, less measured.

He broke the silence with a growled, "I hate him."

"I can see why." I wanted to add that hating his father was counterproductive, as it gave his father all the power. But I didn't. I figured we'd have plenty of time in the future for me to help Martin deal with his poorly controlled rage where his father was concerned.

"He sent Patrice." He said this against my neck, his voice a broken whisper.

"On Wednesday morning? When I was in your room?"

"No. When I was fourteen. He sent her…to me."

My eyes narrowed with confusion and I stared at the side of his head. "I don't understand. What do you mean he sent her to you?"

I felt Martin gather a deep breath before he lifted his face from where it had been sheltered in my neck. He avoided my eyes, opting instead to stare at the cabin's ceiling and rest the back of his head against the headrest.

"After my mother died, I moved in with my father. I'd never…I'd never spent time with him before, but I'd always thought of him as a way to escape my mother's manipulations. During the first year he ignored me. Then something changed when I was fourteen. Everything was a test, all of our interactions were mind-games and I was always failing, and he always let me know how much of a disappointment I was. I wanted to prove myself to him. I thought I could earn his respect."

Martin's eyes darted to mine and he gave me a wan smile shaded with bitterness as he continued. "I was so fucking stupid, naïve. I thought no one could be worse than my mother, and I'd worshiped my father. But I was wrong."

I studied him, thought about what it must have been like for him as a shy, beautiful boy to be at the whim of a fame-seeking mother, then thrust upon his unfeeling, manipulative father. I'd been allowed to hide in closets. He had not. My heart broke for him.

As well, his earlier statement, about his father *sending* Patrice to him nagged at me, filled my stomach with dread.

I prompted gently, "What did you mean, your father sent Patrice to you when you were fourteen?"

He heaved a sigh. "When I was fourteen she climbed into my bed. She was naked. I was asleep. She put my hands on her body and kissed me, touched me…" He said this like the words were sour and swallowed. "I woke up and realized what was happening, so I pushed her out of the bed and my room. The next morning I went to my father and told him what happened—this was before they were married, so I figured he'd leave her. Instead he laughed at me. He told me he'd sent her, that it was a test, and that I'd *finally* passed a test."

"Test? What kind of test?"

Martin held my gaze as he explained, his tone hollow. "He had to marry her, she has something incriminating on him, but I'm not sure what. But he wanted to keep his money out of her reach, so it was a loyalty test. I think he liked the irony of using her to ensure her undoing. Shortly after that he transferred all his property into my name using a trust."

"What about his bank accounts? Surely she can just raid those in a divorce?"

He shook his head, adding impassively, "No. In their state of residence, draft accounts existing prior to marriage, even new deposits, aren't community property, nor are retirement, stock options, and savings. That's why the houses—the ones he owned and the new ones he's purchased—are in my name. They're in a trust until I turn twenty-one."

"So…next year?"

"No. Four months."

I stared at him, nonplussed. I'm sure my eyebrows were drawn together in a severe frown of equal parts anger and disbelief. I shook my head at this elaborate scheming, the disgusting test of loyalty that had obviously humiliated and scarred Martin, and felt the acidity of furious indignation rise in my throat, building a concrete structure in my chest.

But before I could vocalize my horrified amazement, Martin added in a voice so quiet I could barely make out his words, "Then he told her. He told Patrice she could use me if she wanted."

"He what?!" I blurted. Actually, it was more like a shriek.

"She didn't—she tried, but she didn't get a chance. I wasn't at the house much after that."

I was so angry. My eyes were burning and fury choked my throat. Therefore, without meaning to, I expelled my acrid thoughts. "What a goddamn, motherfucking sonofabitch."

He laughed a little, obviously surprised, and his answering smile was small and sad. "I don't know. I never met my grandmother."

I huffed a laugh, but my features twisted with sadness and anger, and I wanted to make everything better for him. Yet I felt completely helpless. I noted he was avoiding my eyes again; as well, his earlier rage had dissipated and seemed to be replaced with a simmering and fierce determination.

I moved my hands to frame his face and feathered a soft kiss over his lips. "I wish I could drop a house on your father," I whispered.

His mouth tugged to the side, so I kissed the side of his mouth.

"No...I'll make sure he gets what he deserves."

I lifted an eyebrow at this statement and leaned back just far enough so I could look in Martin's eyes. "What he deserves is your apathy."

His eyes flashed and I felt his fingers flex on my body as he contradicted through clenched teeth. "No. What he deserves is to be ruined and humiliated."

My gaze moved over Martin's features and I saw passion there. It was dark passion, potent and fathomless. I was certain he was absolutely intent on being the instrument of his father's destruction.

It hadn't occurred to me until that moment that he might not want to work through the issues with his father. Rather, it appeared his zealous loathing for his father might currently be the driving force in his life.

"Martin—" I started, but stopped, unsure how to proceed but needing to say something. I swallowed as I searched his eyes for some thread of sanity and reason where Denver Sandeke was concerned. I found none. "Martin, maybe take a step back from this. I understand your father is a horrible man who has done horrible things, but what can be done? He's very powerful."

"He's not untouchable," he was quick to point out, his eyes growing a darker shade of blue as he added, "and I have a plan…"

"But why waste your energy on him? Why not forget him, cut him out of your life like the cancer he is, and move forward with your—"

He shook his head while I spoke, his jaw tight with steely determination, and interrupted me. "No. Fuck no!"

I flinched and his grip tightened on my body as he continued with a harsh whisper, "Nothing else matters other than making him suffer. *I'm* going to be the one to destroy him. Seeing him humiliated is all I've thought about and planned for since I was fourteen. If I achieve nothing else in life, if I do nothing else…" He ended there, his eyes losing focus as his thoughts turned inward to a dark place I couldn't follow.

My disquiet spread, trepidation ballooning with the dawning comprehension that Martin had allowed this passion—this hatred for his father—to define him.

And most of all, more than the tragic and twisted tales of his childhood, this realization broke my heart.

CHAPTER 12
Factors Affecting Solubility

THE PLANE LANDED and I was in a mood. An introspective, anxious, overthinking-the-situation mood.

Whereas Martin's mood had lightened considerably.

When we stepped off the plane and piled into the limo, my mood did not improve. Eric and Martin discussed what to do about Ben's abdication from the team. Sam tossed me searching looks. I stared out the window.

When we arrived at the dorm and the boys carried our luggage into the building, my mood did not improve, not even when Martin pulled me into an abandoned study room on the first floor and motioned for Sam and Eric to go on ahead. Not even when he backed me up against the door, crowded my space, his eyes dark and hot with intent.

Not until he said, "I told you because I trust you, Kaitlyn. I don't want anything—least of all my fucked-up past—coming between us."

I held his gaze and felt some of the tension ease from my shoulders, leaving me feeling merely melancholy. "Thank you for trusting me. I'm just…I'm just so sorry you had to go through that. I know trusting can't be easy for you."

"You make it easy." His eyes lit as he caught my wrists, and used his body to press me against the door. Martin's voice dropped an octave as he added, "Being with you, listening to you play music, calling you on your bullshit…"

I lifted an eyebrow at this, feeling acutely peeved and opening my mouth to protest. He grinned and spoke faster to keep me from interrupting. "…touching you, kissing you, watching you come, making love to you…you make everything right."

I felt my cheeks warm as he held my gaze and his lips slowly descended to mine. I lifted my chin to meet his mouth, anticipating his kiss, hungry for it.

Martin released my wrists as his mouth slid over mine, his greedy hands moving under my shirt to the bare skin of my torso. When we parted, my fingers were twisted in his hair and I was breathless; as well, he'd built a fire in the vicinity of my pants.

He was basically an Eagle Scout of pants fires.

So I groaned and pleaded, sounding silly and pathetic to my own ears, "I miss you already. Will you stay? I could spend some time calling you on *your* bullshit, or we could study chemistry."

"Or make out."

"Isn't that what I just said?"

He laughed, stole a fast kiss, and then hugged me to him. I returned his embrace and felt him speak against my hair. "I have to go back to the house, make a few calls, take care of some business. But then I'll come back and stay as long as you want me to stay."

I nodded, nuzzling his chest, and smiled, thinking how intoxicatingly wonderful it was to have the promise of an evening with Martin in my immediate future.

***

I WAS IN a much better mood when we walked into the suite area of my dorm room, and right into the tall, straight, hard chest of a secret service agent.

No one ever expects the secret service.

I backed up, excusing myself, and stepped on Martin's foot as he was following close behind me. He held my shoulder with one hand, and shifted us both away from the agent. My mind went around the Ferris wheel of confusion only twice before I realized that the presence of the secret service could only mean that my mother was someplace nearby.

I was expecting her for brunch on Sunday, as per our earlier discussion.

Her plans must've changed.

"Oh, hello," I said automatically, reaching out my hand to the man, "I'm Kaitlyn Parker."

The man was dressed in a black suit, black tie, and white shirt; his sunglasses were tucked in his coat pocket and I caught my reflection in half of the lens peeking out of its home.

"I'm Stevens." Stevens accepted my hand for an efficient shake, his dark brown eyes skating over Martin then back to me. His tone was equally efficient. "Ms. Parker, the senator is waiting for you in your room."

"Okay." I nodded and glanced at Martin over my shoulder as I searched for the handle of my suitcase behind me. "Hey, you want to meet my mom?"

His eyebrows jumped and he shifted on his feet, relinquishing the luggage to my care. "Uh...sssssure."

It was easy to see he was caught by surprise, so I waited for a beat, turned, and studied his face. "You don't have to. You can go make your calls and come back later. There is no pressure here. She can be kind of intimidating."

He gave me a bantam smile, really just a hint of one whispering over his lips, and his tone turned teasing. "Really? Intimidating? I hadn't heard that about your mother…who is a *US senator*."

I narrowed my eyes at him and pressed my mouth into a flat line to keep from laughing; I turned back to the agent and asked, "Do you need to frisk him? I can do it for you if you want."

Martin made a choking sound behind me.

The agent did not smile. "Yes, ma'am. I will need to search him before he approaches the senator."

I nodded and walked around the secret service agent, then turned and walked backward toward my dorm room door.

"See you inside," I said cheerfully. I also winked at him.

He scowled at me, but then had to move his attention to the agent who was instructing him to put his hands out, palms up.

I snickered and walked into my room. I found my mom sitting in the chair next to my microwave talking on her cell phone. She was dressed in her typical outfit: an expensive, nicely tailored pantsuit accessorized simply with an American flag lapel pin. The cut and style remained constant, but the color varied between blues, black, and greys. Today she was in black.

Her eyes lifted to mine as I entered and she smiled warmly, pointing to her phone then lifting her index finger in the universal sign for, *give me one minute*.

I nodded and placed my suitcase on my bed, returning her smile. I unzipped the bag and began emptying its contents to keep myself busy…because I found I was equal parts nervous and excited. I really, really wanted her to like Martin—so, nervous. And I was certain she would like him—so, excited.

Everything with Martin had happened so fast; in some ways I was still on that speeding train, because it didn't occur to me that my mother meeting Martin would yield anything but stellar results.

Turns out, she really did only need a minute to end her call. In fact, I think she clicked off without saying goodbye.

As she stood and pulled me into a quick hug, she said, "I hope you don't mind, I asked Sam and her friend if we could have the room for a few minutes. She dropped her things off just a moment ago."

I shrugged and returned her fast embrace. "No, no. That's fine. I think she has to go check in with her tennis coach anyway."

She released me and folded her hands in front of her. She never crossed her arms. When she stood still she always folded her hands. She told me once that early in her career folding her hands kept her from fidgeting. Now she did it out of habit.

"Good. You must be wondering why I'm here a day early and without your father." Her gray gaze moved over me searchingly, like she was cataloguing changes in my appearance.

"I told George I wouldn't be back until today when I called him last week. I hope you got the message."

"Yes. Your unexpected trip. That's partially why I'm here." My mother's eyes finally settled on mine and I detected a slight hesitation in her usually confident voice.

I frowned, casting her a sideways glance. "Is everything all right?"

Her eyes softened in an alarming way, and she opened her mouth to respond. But then she quickly snapped it shut and glanced at the door over my shoulder. I followed her gaze and found Martin hovering at the entrance to my room. I couldn't help my giant smile.

"Oh!" I reached for his hand, not really registering the stoic mask that had slipped over his features as I tugged him into the room and turned back to my mother. "Mom, this is Martin Sandeke. Martin, this is my mom, Joss Parker."

I knew I sounded positively giddy as I made the introductions, but I couldn't help it. I was so excited. I loved my mother, and was so proud of her. She was my superhero. I was her biggest fan.

And now I was introducing my Martin to her, this boy I loved so much.

I figured that since they were both amazing and brilliant, and had wonderful thoughts about the future of Big Telecom and technology, the two of them would immediately fall into a stimulating conversation on the subject. I ignored the fact that Martin's intentions weren't entirely altruistic because the outcome of his plans would benefit society just the same.

I glanced between them as they shook hands, grinning, waiting for the stimulating conversation to begin.

It didn't begin.

Instead I watched as my mother became Senator Parker, her gray eyes adopting their steely and coldly assessing glint as she looked Martin up and down.

"Senator Parker," he said.

"Mr. Sandeke," she said.

My stomach sank at their mirrored frowns and frosty posturing. I winced and tried to swallow, a thick, foggy numbness unfurling in my stomach as comprehension struggled to dawn and silence stretched.

No one said anything for a full minute. Actually, no one said anything *verbally* for a full minute. Instead they stared at each other and a form of silent communication passed between them. My heart thumped uncomfortably as I struggled to find words to make everything better, explain that Martin was a good guy, that he wasn't his father.

But just as I opened my mouth to voice this as fact, Martin bent, gave me a soft kiss on my cheek, and whispered in my ear, "I'll see you tonight."

He gave me a tight, apologetic smile that didn't reach his eyes. He turned away. He left.

I stared after him, blinking at the door, wondering how everything could have gone horribly wrong in one and a half minutes when absolutely nothing had been said.

My mother's soft sigh pulled my attention back to her and I struggled to speak. Finally I blurted, "He's wonderful. He's really wonderful. He hates his father, and you're going to love him. He has ideas about satellites and he invented lazy fishing poles…and I don't understand what just happened."

She gave me a sad smile—hers didn't reach her eyes either—as she crossed the three steps to the door and shut it; she turned back to me and folded her hands.

"Kaitlyn, Martin Sandeke is why I am here, one day early, and without your father."

I frowned at her, searching her face for a clue but found only patient concern; at a loss, I vocalized my confusion. "I don't understand."

She sighed again. She hardly ever sighed. I felt a nagging sense of disquiet.

My mom placed a hand on my shoulder and guided us both to the bed until we were sitting, facing each other; then she said in her normal, businesslike tone, "My office received a call from a reporter at the Washington Post yesterday asking me to comment on my conflict of interest regarding the affordable telecom bill. He questioned my ethics if I remained in the chair position on the Commerce, Science, and Transportation committee because my daughter is in a serious relationship with the son of this country's largest telecom provider's CEO."

"Wait...what?"

"It seems he has pictures of you and Martin during your vacation and sound bites from one of your fellow students, a Mr. Benjamin Salsmar, who was with you this last week, indicating that the two of you are very serious, and that our families are quite close."

Benjamin Salsmar. Benjamin. Ben. Ben the bottom-feeding rapist, cuss monster!

UGH!

"Ugh." I shook my head as my face fell into my hands. *"That's* why Ben was still there this morning...what an asshole."

I heard my mother clear her throat. I hadn't thought before I spoke; I was pretty sure this was the first time she'd ever heard me cuss. To her credit, she made no comment about it, even though she'd told me when I was younger that curse words weren't adult language and had been mischaracterized as such.

She'd once explained that curse words were used by the idiots, and unimaginative members of our society, individuals who never learned actual adult language—i.e. multisyllabic descriptive words—and flung curses around during childish temper tantrums.

Nevertheless, Ben *was* an asshole.

But aside from Ben's assholery, what he'd said—what he'd told the Washington Post—was fifty-one percent true. Martin and I were in a relationship. I was not ashamed of it or of him, but I was now beginning to see that our relationship might cause some professional problems for my mother.

After several seconds she asked softly, "What is going on with you and Martin Sandeke?"

I gathered a calming breath and straightened, letting my hands drop from my face. I met her eyes and told her the truth. "Martin and I are dating."

"I see..." Her thoughtful expression didn't change except that her eyes narrowed just slightly. After a short pause she asked, "How long has this been going on?"

"About a week."

"Oh. Then it's not serious."

"No. It is serious."

"After a week?"

"Yes," I responded firmly.

She inspected me for a long moment, her gaze searching and tinged with slight confusion, but then she conceded with a nod. "Okay. If you say it's serious, then it's serious."

I stared at her. She stared at me. I waited for her to say something, to give me the right answer.

When she didn't, I blurted, "Mom, I can't just walk away from Martin. I think I'm…I mean, I've fallen in love with him. We're in love with each other. I love him."

My mother's face softened at this news, but her eyes held pity and worry. "Oh, Kaitlyn." She placed her hand on my shoulder and squeezed, her gaze moving over my face. "Honey, from what I know about Martin Sandeke, he's not the kind of boy who is going to be gentle with your heart or appears to do anything without an ulterior motive. As such, I find this news worrisome."

I tried to give her my best responsible young adult face. "Yes. I can guess what you've discovered about him. But I've spent a week with him—with just him for the most part—and he is not who he appears to be. He is…he is amazing and so kind."

"He's kind?" Her tone held a note of disbelief.

"He's kind with me."

"But not with everyone." This wasn't a question. It was a statement of fact.

"No, not with everyone. But if you knew—"

"And you've fallen in love with a person who doesn't feel it's necessary to be kind to anyone else but you?"

I pressed my lips together and swallowed. She didn't sound judgmental or even upset. She sounded curious. It was always this way with my mother. Her curiosity was why she won every argument, and why people always listened to her and took her advice.

She was exceedingly reasonable. She was never malicious or pushy, never condescending or irritated. She was only curious. She'd poke holes in terrible proposals and theories with her curious questions until it was clear to everyone that the proposal or theory was garbage. But she'd never, ever come out and say it.

I'd learned that the best defense against curiosity is honesty.

"Yes. I'm in love with a person who doesn't feel like it's necessary to be kind to anyone else but me."

"I see." She nodded thoughtfully, her eyes narrowing as she examined me. I could see her brain working, considering all the data, working through the scenarios.

I prepared myself for a detailed curious onslaught. Instead, she surprised me.

"Kaitlyn, I trust you. You know what's at stake." Her tone was firm, almost hard. "I've explained the situation and you are exceedingly bright. You understand the ramifications of staying in a relationship with Martin—and not only to my career and me, which is really the secondary issue here. The primary issue is what this does to the American public. You understand that Martin's father is using this relationship to expel me from the chair position of the Commerce, Science, and Transportation committee. He will succeed because he is right."

"But…but how is he right? How can he do that?"

"He is right because I will have an intrinsic bias if my daughter is in a serious relationship with this country's largest telecom provider's Chairman of the Board and CEO's son. That is a fact. I will resign before I am forced out, because perception of bias is just as damaging as actual bias. Mr. Sandeke has been positioning Senator Neimann to take my position for the last two years, both with the Vice President and the President pro tempore of the senate. He is the handpicked replacement and he will kill or bury the affordable telecom act—you know this is how Washington works—and those Americans in rural areas will continue to be unable to access affordable high speed services, thereby placing them at a prolonged disadvantage over those living in urban city centers."

I blinked at her, at all her facts, and ground my teeth. "So I can break up with Martin until the bill passes or stay with him and ruin the lives of millions of people?"

Her expression turned sad. She took a deep breath like she wanted to say something but hesitated, thought better of it.

"What? What do you want to say? Just say it."

She sighed. Again! And her next words surprised me because they sounded shockingly maternal. "You know I trust your judgment, Kaitlyn. But…I'm worried about you. I wonder, have you considered the possibility that perhaps Martin's feelings for you are not what they seem?"

I stiffened, leaned slightly away from her. "What is that supposed to mean?"

She pursed her lips, and her eyes darted to the door then back to mine. "Martin's father is a very intelligent man, and he's equally calculating. He has acuity for industrial strategy like I've never seen. As well, he's known to use those closest to him as part of his strategy. Seven years ago his wife—yes, his current wife—was at the center of a sex tape scandal with Senator Peterson from Wisconsin. You likely don't remember because you were only twelve or thirteen."

She paused and I noted she looked extremely uncomfortable. She took a deep breath, and her eyes searched mine. "Senator Peterson was the chair of the Commerce, Science, and Transportation committee at the time, the position I hold now. This bill that Martin's father has been fighting so hard to bury is a reimagining of Senator Peterson's bill from seven years ago, before an ethics panel removed Peterson from the position during the investigation."

I frowned at this news and the obvious conclusion I was supposed to make. "That's not what's going on here. Martin isn't dating me because his father told him to."

"Are you sure?" she pressed. "Because I've been under constant scrutiny from the ethics board since I took this chair position. Your father and I have been audited three times by the IRS. Denver Sandeke and his lobbyists have been relentless. The last time I saw him he actually suggested we open negotiations for affordable service. I was stunned and I took that as a victory—because he's never given an inch before last month. I assumed it was because he's been unable to discredit me…but now I'm wondering if this trip you've just taken with Martin was part of his plan."

I stared at my mother, my stomach made queasy and sick by her suggestion. "You think it's so impossible Martin would just be interested in me for me?"

Her eyes widened, then her entire stance changed. She looked horrified. My mother grabbed my shoulders and turned me so we were facing each other directly. "God, Kaitlyn…no. No. Absolutely not. You are a treasure, and I'm not saying this just because I'm your mother and I'm proud of you. I'm saying this because it is the truth. It is very likely that these two issues—Martin's feelings for you and his father's manipulations—have nothing to do with each other. But I needed to ask the question. Based on historical data, how Mr. Sandeke has conducted himself in the past, the question had to be asked. You understand that, right?"

I nodded, believing her, but saying nothing.

She sighed again and I could feel her frustration with the situation. Actually, she looked frazzled. I'd never seen her so discomposed and my stomach soured further because *I* was the cause of her worry. I felt like a disappointment.

"Kaitlyn, we can only try to do our best. I am trying to do my best here.

The situation is impossible for me to solve, and that's why I'm leaving it in your hands. You have all the facts. There will be hundreds of bills, and there is always good work that needs to be done. If I resign from the committee and this bill fails, then I will refocus my energy on something else. But," she paused to make sure I was looking at her as she finished, "I have only one daughter."

I pressed my lips together, feeling miserable and conflicted.

My mother must've seen my struggle because she lifted her hand and cupped my cheek in an uncharacteristic display of affection. Her eyes were reassuring, yet resigned. "I'm not going to insist on making this decision for you. You have to decide what's wrong and what's right for yourself."

CHAPTER 13
Vapor Pressure and Boiling Point

AFTER MY MOTHER left, leaving the crushing weight of this decision in my hands, I spent the next hour fretting and chasing circular logic in my head. I had no right answer, but I recognized I had two options.

I could hide in the closet and wait for everything to resolve itself.

Or I could talk to Martin, lay it all out there, and insist we work together to solve this conundrum.

In the end, I realized I couldn't go back to being the closet girl. Over the past week something within me had fundamentally shifted. I would never be content as a closet-dweller again. I was out of the closet…in a manner of speaking.

So, really, I had one option.

Once I decided Martin and I would work through this together, I absolutely could not wait to discuss the matter with him. Therefore I grabbed my jacket, ran down the three flights of dorm stairs, and jogged to Martin's fraternity house.

I was still very much in my own head when I spotted Griffin on the front porch, carrying a ladder to where three other guys waited with nails and a sign. Paying the other three no notice, I jogged straight to Griffin.

"Hey, Griffin."

"Kaitlyn, hey. Are you here to see Martin?" He handed the ladder off to one of the three and gave me a warm smile.

"Yes. That's why I'm here. Can you take me to him?"

"Yeah, yeah. Sure." He didn't hesitate. He turned for the door to the house and assumed I'd follow. I did.

We climbed two sets of stairs and navigated through a tangle of hallways, all with dark wood floors and beige paint. No art donned the walls; I tried to make a mental topographic map just in case I arrived to visit Martin in the future but encountered no friendly tour guide.

At last Griffin stopped at one of the doors—much like any of the others—and knocked three times.

"Hey, it's Griffin—"

"Go away."

"—and I've got Kaitlyn with me."

Griffin gave me a small grin and a quick wink when the last part of his announcement was met with silence followed by approaching footsteps.

The door swung open, revealing a shirtless, sweaty Martin Sandeke. He was dressed only in shorts, socks, and shoes, and he'd obviously just returned from a run. Martin's eyes landed on mine immediately and he appeared very pleased to see me. I was very happy to see him, sweat and all.

Actually, his chest was so perfect it glistened.

I had a boyfriend that glistened, and not in a weird shimmering kind of way. In a manly, super sexy, flawless kind of way.

Oh...sigh.

I smiled at him, because that's what one does when faced with a glistening, shirtless Martin. You just do it. It's a law of nature, like gravity or eating cookies when they're hot out of the oven. No. Choice.

I was about to say hi, but he cut me off by reaching forward, grabbing my hand, pulling me into his room, and shutting the door.

I was about to say hi again, but I was cut off by the sound of Griffin's muffled voice from the hallway. "Okay then, you're welcome. I guess I'll just get back to what I was doing."

"You do that," Martin responded absentmindedly, his gaze moving over my face like he hadn't seen me in days instead of hours.

Finally, hearing Griffin's retreating steps, I laughed lightly and was just about to say hi again, when Martin kissed me. He braced his hands on the door at my back and devoured my mouth. I lifted on my tiptoes and tilted my chin to provide better access, but when I reached for his body he pulled away.

"Don't." He stopped the progress of my hands by holding them between us. "I need a shower. I just got back from a run."

"I don't care." I shrugged, knowing my traveling stare was somewhat hazy and a lot greedy as I scanned his torso; and then, because I finally could, I said, "By the way, hi."

At my good-natured greeting, I saw his shoulders visibly relax and he returned my smile. "Hi."

"It's good to see you." I exhaled, feeling better about...everything now we were face to face. My back was to the door and he was standing in front of me, holding my hands in both of his.

"It's good to see you, too." His tone was relieved, sincere; but I noted he appeared to be somewhat cagey, bracing. "How was the visit with your mother?"

I closed my eyes briefly and shook my head, opening them again before responding. "It was…troubling."

He released my hands and crossed his arms over his chest. "I don't think she likes me."

"When she gets to know you, she will like you."

Martin's smile was crooked and my allusion to the future seemed to comfort him. He nodded, like he believed me. "Yeah, eventually she'll come around."

"Yes. Eventually. I'll just have to bring you home with me over summer vacation. You and my dad can talk nerd stuff."

"You talk nerd stuff, too." Martin turned and crossed to his dresser.

"Well, then all three of us will talk nerd stuff at the same time. It'll be a nerdy conversation trifecta." I took three steps into his room and surveyed the space. It reminded me a lot of the room back at the island where he slept: small, cluttered with personal things, small twin bed, comfy comforter and pillows. I liked the absence of sterile and fancy appurtenances.

He was rummaging through his drawers, obviously looking for something in particular, when he called over his shoulder, "So, you said her visit was troubling? What happened?"

"Oh, ugh!" I rolled my eyes, remembering the purpose of my visit was unfortunately *not* to ogle Martin's glistening chest of perfection. Flopping on his bed I didn't try to disguise my aggravation with the subject. "That's actually why I'm here now instead of waiting for you tonight. I need your help."

He stopped his search and turned toward me, his forehead marred with obvious concern. "What can I do?"

"Well, it's…the whole thing is completely bizarre. But I think we can figure this out together."

"Parker, what's going on?"

I heaved a big sigh, gave him a small smile, then proceeded to detail the gist of the conversation I had with my mother. When I got to the Ben part, his eyes narrowed and he ground his teeth. He looked irritated, but not exactly surprised.

"He's always been a fuckwad," Martin ground out, slamming his dresser drawer shut.

"Yes, well…rapists tend to be unsavory in most facets of their life, but—forget Ben for a moment—the real issue is what we're going to do about my mother and the Washington Post reporter."

Cagey Martin was back and he glared at me from across the room with his hands on his hips. "What do you want me to do?"

I heaved another big sigh and admitted, "I don't know. This is why I need your help. I need you to help me figure out how to make this right."

He shrugged, his tone growing distant. "Make what right? I don't see the problem."

This gave me pause because I felt like the problem was obvious. Giving him the benefit of the doubt, I decided to spell it out for him. "The problem, Martin, is that your father is using our involvement with each other—"

"We're not *involved*. You're my girlfriend."

"He is using our relationship to discredit my mother. He's already given two interviews where he alluded that she is softening on the Net Neutrality bill because of me, because we're dating."

"So?"

My eyes widened at his flippant response and I was struck slightly speechless; I parroted, "So…? So? So, this is very bad. We need to make him stop."

"It's none of our business." Martin scratched his chin, sounding aloof, and shrugged again.

I was really beginning to dislike his shrugs.

I was also starting to lose my temper.

What the hell?

I stood from the bed and paced, ranting to all four walls. "Of course it's our business. It's everybody's business. Net neutrality is *everyone's* business! Just because you've never had to work for anything in your life doesn't mean it's not your business."

Martin's expression grew stony and fierce, his jaw set. I regretted the words as soon as I'd said them.

"Okay, sorry." I reached my hands out between us then let them fall to my sides when he continued to glare at me. "I didn't mean that how it sounded. But you don't get to ignore important issues that affect everyone but the top one percent just because you're in the top one percent. It's irresponsible."

"What do you suggest that I do?" The question was clearly meant to be equal parts rhetorical and sarcastic. "You've met my father. He's not going to listen to me. He won't listen to anyone. And if I go against him, he'll cut me off."

"Martin, what's left then? Hmm? I can't let my mother step down because of bogus charges. If you can't get him to listen to you then the only other option is…is…" *For us to break up.*

I didn't say it, but I might as well have said it because it was obviously the only remaining option.

Martin immediately grasped my unspoken meaning because his entire body went rigid and his eyes grew thunderous. His menacing denial was softly spoken.

"No. No fucking way."

"Then give me another solution."

"No, that's bullshit." He charged toward me, but I held my ground as he quietly raged at me. "This has nothing to do with us. You're looking for an excuse. This is just an excuse to shit all over everything we've built. You've been looking for a reason to run away, and this is it."

I reached forward to touch him but he twisted away, stalking back to his dresser and slamming another drawer.

I didn't like the pleading edge that entered my voice, as I said, "No. This is me standing up for what I believe in. Your father is discrediting my mother, damaging her reputation and people are *buying into it.* She has worked her whole life against corruption. She has fought for good and justice and peace and prosperity."

Martin scoffed, his words mocking. "She's not superwoman, Parker."

"She is to me. And I'm not going to do nothing while your dad uses me to make her look like a corrupt flake."

He shook his head, clearly frustrated. "Listen to me. What could you possibly do to make Denver Sandeke change his mind? He never changes his mind. Talking to him is useless. Arguing with him just makes him happy. He gets off on other people's misery."

"We have to stop him."

"We can't."

"So…what? Am I supposed to just let him say these terrible things?"

"What choice do you have?" He turned completely around, finally facing me again and giving nothing away with his expression.

"I'll give an interview. I'll call the reporter from the Washington Post."

"It won't make a difference. We *are* dating. We are together. Our families aren't close, but that doesn't matter because perception is all that matters. Why would anyone believe you over my father? They wouldn't." I saw that he was trying to talk me down from getting my hopes up, and he was trying to be gentle and break the reality of the situation to me, the fruitlessness of it.

But he was wrong, because there was one person that could discredit Denver Sandeke...

"But you *could*."

Martin stared at me, his gaze becoming increasingly calculating and guarded. When he responded his words were measured and slow. "No. I couldn't. Like I said, he'll cut me off, and I am so close. I'll be twenty-one in less than four months. I will not do anything to risk losing access to that money."

"Martin, I could...I could help you. We could move in together, share expenses. You don't need your father's money. You're a freaking genius, and you have all those patents. You don't need his money."

His eyes were now slits and he was shaking his head slowly. "No. You don't understand. My father has forgotten about the trust, and I need that trust. I need those houses. I have plans, I can't just abandon them."

"What plans?" I reached for him but he pulled his hand from my grasp and turned away, so I spoke to his back. "Tell me the plan. What are you talking about?"

He walked to his desk chair; his big, powerful hands gripping the back of it, and gave me his profile. "The venture capitalist deal in New York. The houses all over the world. The sixty million dollars. The satellites. The plan, everything I've been working for to completely screw him over. If I discredit him now then he'll look for ways to make me miserable, and he'll remember the trust. Then I'm cut off and it all goes away."

I stared at the side of his face, my mouth open but no sound emerging, because I was mostly confused. After a moment I found some words. I wasn't sure they were the right ones, but they were the only words I had.

"I'm sorry, I don't understand what you're talking about. What do houses all over the world have to do with sixty million dollars? And how are satellites going to screw over Denver Sandeke?"

Martin exhaled but it sounded like an impatient growl. "The houses, Parker. His houses are all in my name and I am four months away from accessing the trust when I turn twenty-one." Martin faced me, his stance inflexible. "I have buyers for six of them, and I'm confident I'll have buyers for the other eleven soon. That's how I'm getting the sixty million."

I blinked furiously. "You can't do that, those aren't your houses."

"They're in my name."

"But—"

"And, all together, they're worth well over sixty million. And I'm selling them and he doesn't know a goddamn thing about it. And when I've sold them, I'm investing the money into launching telecom satellites that will replace traditional landlines, DSLs, and—in some cases—fiber optic cable. I'm going to break the telecom monopolies that Sandeke Telecom holds. I'm going to give the people in his service areas an alternative source for their Internet and phone. I'm going to drive my father out of business and make billions in the process. But I can't do that if he cuts me off now."

My face scrunched and twisted. This was…this was unbelievable. This was global scale corporate warfare and so beyond my frame of reference.

"It can't, I mean, it can't be as simple as that. If satellites are the answer to the great telecom monopoly debate, then it seems to be that someone else would have solved it by now."

Martin's frown was severe, his eyes cutting, almost mocking. "Have you ever heard of Elon Musk?"

"Yes. Everyone knows who he is."

"Not everyone."

"He's the CEO of Tesla and a genius philanthropist," I supplied blandly.

"Yeah, well look up his work on alternate sources of Internet delivery. It *is* as simple as satellites, but there is nothing simple about these satellites."

I huffed then growled, punching my hands through the air as I fought to control my temper. "Well…so…fine! You have your 'fancy satellite plan'! It's going to work. You'll screw your father and break up his monopoly. Where does that leave us?"

"Right where we are. Nothing between us changes!" He was yelling again.

"What does that even mean?" I was also yelling and appealing to the ceiling, throwing my hands in the air.

"Us. Together. And we ignore my father."

"But we can't. We can't ignore him. If we do nothing, then my mother steps down and her life's work is over."

Martin shrugged, scratched the back of his neck, and said with infuriating ambivalence and granite resolve in his eyes, "Not. My. Problem."

In that moment I wanted to punch him in the face, because I felt like he'd punched me in the stomach. Resentment filled my mouth, choked me as we glared at each other, our rapid-fire argument over and nothing resolved. I was twisting in the wind and he didn't seem to care. To my infinite irritation I felt the first signs of tears—stinging eyes, wobbly chin—and was powerless to fight it.

I couldn't control the shakiness in my voice as I whispered, "I trusted you."

"You *can* trust me." His voice was steady, yet clearly laced with frustration. "I would do anything for you…except this. You can't ask me to do this, to go against him publically, when I'm *so close* to seeing this through."

Again we stared at each other and neither of us gave an inch. I swallowed the building thickness in my throat, creeping despair twisting its fingers around my chest and making each breath painful. Yet I had to give us one more shot. I was trying my best to fight for him, fight for us. I gathered a deep breath and tried once more to appeal to him.

I was careful to keep the volume of my voice low, though I struggled to keep it steady. "If you love me…" He closed his eyes with a slow blink and he turned slightly away. Martin shook his head, stared at the floor, with his jaw set, and his powerful arms once more crossed over his chest. "If you love me then it *is* your problem, because I can't let my mother do that. I can't let her step down because of me and my choices."

"There is nothing you can do, Kaitlyn." His tone was flat and entirely patronizing.

And he was wrong.

There was one thing I could do, one finite solution that would solve the problem, but that was also going to break my heart. I felt a new, more powerful wave of tears build behind my eyes as I stared at his outward expression of indifference.

A single thought bubbled to the surface of my mind: *he's betrayed me.*

I'd flung myself off a cliff, trusting that he'd be there to catch me, but he let me fall. I hadn't realized until that moment how completely I'd trusted him. I was so stupid.

I felt my heart slow and sputter, thump and crack. The dam broke and gave way to a flood of bitter tears.

I mimicked his stance, crossed my arms over my chest and lifted my chin, hoping the posturing would give me the bravery I needed even as fat drops of saltwater spilled from my eyes.

"You're wrong, Martin. There is something I can do."

Martin became very still, quiet. His eyes cut to mine and they were sharp, focused.

"I'm breaking up with you." I made no move to wipe away the wet tracks because...what was the point?

"Kaitlyn." My name sounded like a plea and an accusation. I firmed my jaw. He shook his head. "Don't say that."

"What other choice do I have?" I was screaming at him, my anger reaching a boiling point. "If we break up then this goes away, there is no bias because we're not together."

"But we'd...what?" He searched my face. "We'd see each other in secret?"

I stubbornly shook my head, feeling the physical effects of misery. Yet grim, soothing resolve crept its way up my spine, wrapping my heart and mind in a blanket of numb certainty. He must've seen something shift, some change in my expression, because he rushed forward and gripped my arms.

"No...no, no, no. That's not going to happen. You are not doing this."

I released a pained breath that sounded more like a sob and looked at the wall over his shoulder, sniffling. Tears fell freely and I barely felt the cold trails they left on my cheeks. This desolation was like bee stings on every surface of my skin, my stomach rolling and clenching. I felt like I was being torn apart.

When I responded, it was without emotion, because I already knew what his answer would be. "I don't think I really have a choice here, unless you can think of another solution."

"You're just going to give up? Just like that?"

I twisted out of his grip, walking backward several steps, and spat at him, "You make it sound like this is easy for me. This isn't easy. You won't give up your fancy satellite plans and I can't let my mother suffer because of your father's lies. You're asking me to choose between right and wrong. I have to choose right."

"That's bullshit!" I winced because his voice was loud and severe, his eyes flashing, his expression livid as he closed the distance between us and jabbed his finger in my face. "If you don't want to be with me then own it. Don't blame it on some higher cause. You own it!"

"I do want to be with you! I lo—" I turned, covered my face before he could see it crumple, and walked three steps away, biting my tongue.

This was madness. I thought we loved each other, and yet...

Reason reared its affable head and politely suggested that one does not fall in love with a person over the course of a week. What I was feeling was the infatuation of newness; it was his smile and the way he touched me and the way he looked at me.

Love was lasting. Love finds a way. Love endures.

But we'd had a week. One week. Only a week.

"A beautiful week," I said through my tears, not immediately realizing I'd spoken out loud.

"What?"

"We had a beautiful week," I whispered, as I finally wiped the wetness from my face and dropped my hands, reason reminding me that just because I didn't feel calm, didn't mean I couldn't be calm.

I would be calm.

I would not be hysterical.

I would walk out of this room, walk away from him, and never second-guess the decision, because it was the right thing to do.

Therefore, I lifted my chin, mentally preparing myself for what came next, and dug deep for courage. "I'll always remember it. I'll always…think of you."

My vision blurred again. I needed to leave before more tears fell, because once I really started, it was going to be an epic sob fest. Multiple boxes of tissues were going to be used.

He spoke through clenched teeth; I knew he was furious, but he also sounded desperate. "I swear to God, Parker, if you leave, if you do this then that's it. I swear, I'm done. I can't forever be trying to prove to you that what I feel for you, what I want from you is real."

"I believe you," I said without turning around. I couldn't look at him. I needed to leave. I wrapped my arms around my middle and after a short pause, walked to the door.

"Don't," he said quietly, his voice roughened with an edge of desperation. "Now I am begging, please don't do this. I love you." He exhaled this last part, the last word ending abruptly like he'd swallowed it, like it'd cost him.

A shock passed though me, his words were physical, possessed the ability to electrify the air, reach out to me, into my chest and squeeze my numbed heart. My steps faltered, my shoulders curved forward, and my arms held me tighter. I felt as though I was holding myself together. If I moved my hands I might shatter to pieces.

I turned, tried to gather a deep breath but found I couldn't, the pain was too sharp, too acute. I met his gaze directly; the force of it, the pleading and prideful ferocity nearly knocked me over.

"Then help me," I begged in return. "Please help me find another way. I don't want to do this. Help me fight your father."

His eyes were despairing, tortured as they moved over my face. He pleaded, "We can see each other in secret."

"No. Someone would find out, and then it would make my mother look even worse."

"He will cut me off, Parker." Martin shook his head, pain and frustration and helplessness casting a contorting shadow over his features. "I can't go against him, not yet."

I released the breath I'd been holding. My voice was watery but firm. I shrugged, then said, "Then...I guess this is goodbye."

CHAPTER 14

Atomic Weights

I COULDN'T STOP crying.

I just physically could not.

I hurt. I hurt so completely. And every time I closed my eyes I saw his face and I hurt more. I was choking on it, asphyxiating, drowning in it.

I was not this person, or at least, I'd never been this person before right now. I was calm and detached; I abhorred drama. I never understood girls who cried about boys. But I did now. I totally freaking got it. I had no control over this agony, I had no choice but to feel it, all of it, and it sucked.

So I buried myself under my covers and cried like it was my job and I was hoping for a promotion. I cried until my pillow was soaked and the only thing that came close to the hurt in my heart was the throbbing in my head.

And this is how Sam found me that night after breaking up with Martin.

She paused when she opened the door to our room, the light from the suite area spilling across my bed, and I met her eyes as they scanned my splotchy, swollen face. The corners of her mouth turned down as she pressed her lips together.

"Anyone die?" she asked.

I shook my head and pressed my face to the damp pillow, my words muffled, as I responded melodramatically, "No. But I want to."

"You want to die?"

"Yes, I want to die."

"Why?"

"We broke up."

Aaaaand more crying. I hiccupped on a ragged sob.

"Well…shit." I heard her sigh, then say gently as she rubbed my back, "I'll be right back with stuff for ice cream sundaes."

The door clicked shut behind her. So I cried and wrapped myself in the chaotic thoughts that had plagued me since leaving Martin.

Maybe I was being selfish.

Maybe Martin's revenge was more important than my mother's reputation and providing affordable Internet service to millions of people.

Maybe we could see each other in secret and no one would find out.

Maybe we were just taking a break for four months and we'd pick right back up once his master revenge plan was set in motion.

Maybe I was turning into a pathetic creature grasping at straws because I missed him with every cell in my body and the thought of never seeing him or talking to him again made me want to light myself on fire.

Not *actually* light myself on fire, but do something drastic because I just freaking hurt so very, very bad.

And it had only been five hours.

Sam returned sometime later while I was in the middle of replaying my conversation with Martin in my head for the hundredth time and therefore second-guessing my decision for the millionth time.

She flipped on the light, making me groan, wince, and wish more fervently for death.

"Katy, take the pink pills by your bed and drink some water. You're probably dehydrated."

"What's in the pink pills?"

"Ibuprofen."

I struggled to sit up, reached for the pills, and started to cry. "Okay," I said through my tears, "I'll take the pills, but nothing will *ever* make me feel good *ever* again."

Sam *tsked* sadly and I heard the clatter of dishes and spoons, the rustling of a plastic bag, and the sure sounds of an ice cream sundae being prepared. After I finished taking a gulp of water and Sam tossed me a new box of tissues, she placed the bowl in my hands.

"Eat your ice cream and tell me what happened."

I shrugged, squinted at the mint chocolate chip and fudge in my bowl. "I don't know what to say."

"Do I need to hire a hit man?"

I took a bite. It tasted good. I was numbly amazed that anything could possibly taste good. "No. I broke up with him."

"You broke up with him?"

I nodded, pushing the ice cream to one side so I could get a spoonful of fudge.

"Does this have something to do with your mom?"

I nodded again, my throat tight. Suddenly I didn't want fudge because fudge wasn't Martin, and fudge would never be Martin.

Stupid fudge.

Holding her own bowl, Sam insinuated herself next to me on the bed and wrapped an arm around my shoulders. "Kaitlyn, tell me everything. Talk to me. Let me help."

"Nothing will help." I knew I sounded emo and morose but I didn't care. Being dramatic was the only thing that felt right.

"Then tell me because I'm nosey. Tell me what happened."

So I did. I told her all about Martin's pariah parents and how he'd grown up being used and humiliated—though I didn't share the specifics—and about the impossible situation with my mother, and a vague description of Martin's plans for revenge.

It took me an hour because I had to stop every once in a while to sob like an infant. Talking about it was reliving it again and I experienced fresh pain with each word. However, when I was finished, when my tale of woe was complete, I felt somehow different.

I didn't feel better. I just felt less…despairing.

Despairing, desolate, dejected, depressed, hopeless, inconsolable, miserable…

"I'm sorry if this makes things weird with you and Eric." I said this to my melted bowl of ice cream because it hurt to lift my eyeballs.

"What do you mean?"

"I'm just saying, I hope this doesn't put you or Eric in an awkward situation. You shouldn't let my break up with Martin affect your relationship."

She was quiet for a moment, and I felt her eyes on me. "Kaitlyn…Eric and I aren't in a relationship."

Even though it hurt, I lifted my scratchy eyes to her, knew my face betrayed my confusion. "You're not?"

"No, hon. We're not dating."

"Then…then what happened last week?" My voice was nasally and a little squeaky.

She shrugged. "Nothing of significance. I mean, yeah…we had a good time together, but we're not dating."

"Did you sleep with him?" I didn't know I was going to ask the question before I asked the question, and I winced because it was rude, and sounded judgmental and demanding.

Her half smile was just north of being patronizing. "Yes. We slept together. And we hung out and made out and had a lot of fun. I like him a lot, but I'm not looking for a relationship and I told him that at the beginning of the week. Between school and tennis and now needing a summer job, I was looking for a good time. So we had a good time, but I doubt I'll see him again."

New tears flooded my eyes and I blinked them away, tangentially amazed that I could still cry. "Am I a bad feminist? You can tell me the truth."

"What are you talking about?" Sam chuckled and tried to untangle a patch of my hair near my ear.

"Because I fell in love with Martin. I started falling in love with him the moment he kissed me in the chemistry lab. I am totally weak for him. And the thought of sleeping with someone without being in love...I don't know. It makes me want to throw up."

"Kaitlyn, you and I are two completely different people with completely different temperaments, experiences, and personalities. Not all women can—or should—have casual sex. Just like, believe it or not, not all men can have casual sex. And your inability to have sex without deeper feelings doesn't make you a bad feminist any more than my love for lace panties and the color pink makes me a bad feminist. Do you see what I mean?"

I nodded, still feeling like a bad feminist. But more than that, I still hurt. The absence of Martin screamed in my ears and the acute pain of sudden loss tortured my soul...*ugh!* Now I was contemplating my tortured soul. I was pathetic.

I groaned. "What is wrong with me? How can I be this upset over a guy I was with technically less than a week?"

"First of all, stop beating yourself up for what you're feeling."

"I'm pathetic. I'm a drama llama. I'm *that* girl. I've spent years judging that girl, and now I'm her and I feel so terrible for judging her because, if she felt one tenth of the agony I feel right now, then I need to write her an apology letter. I should punch myself in the face for being so judgey."

"Kaitlyn, we are all *that* girl sooner or later. You can't know or understand another person's pain until you've lived through a similar experience. You fell hard and you fell fast. It was dating boot camp on that island, and you were all in. Girl, you just lost your virginity two days ago! Give yourself some time to adjust."

"Oh, Sam, how am I going to make it through the rest of my life when almost six hours post breakup I'm already contemplating death by fire as a preferable alternative to the ache in my heart?"

Sam sighed and wrapped her arms around me. She laid her head on my shoulder and said softly, "Kaitlyn, stop and think about this, really, really think about what's going on. Think about what you know about this guy."

"I know he loves me and I broke up with him and I don't even really know why."

"You know why. You broke up with him because he was unwilling to do the right thing."

"But he loves me and—"

She made a sound in the back of her throat that reminded me of Marge from the Simpsons and interrupted my whiny tirade. "Here is the truth, and I'm sorry if it hurts, but here it is: Martin is never going to choose anyone—even you—over himself."

I winced because... *Gah, right in the feels.*

I pressed a damp tissue to my face. "Gee, thanks."

"I'm not saying this to be hurtful. You are beautiful and amazing and so smart." Sam paired this with a squeeze. "And did I mention beautiful? But the thing is..." she lifted her head and searched my face, "the thing is, he doesn't know how to love. He doesn't. You said it yourself, his parents are pariahs. He knows all about self-preservation, and he's thinking only of revenge. He's the Count of Monte Cristo."

I gave a pitiful laugh and shook my head. "I know you're trying to help, but you don't know him like I do. I *know* he loves me."

"I'm sure, on some level, in Martin's universe of one, he's willing to make room for you. I'm sure he does love you, as much as he's capable. But, that's just it. It's a universe of one, and giving you a corner isn't what you deserve. You deserve a universe of two, and a pedestal, and cabana boys to peel your grapes."

Tears squeezed out of my eyes even as I snorted. I wiped them away with my tissue, which was basically just lint at this point.

"I don't want cabana boys. I just want...I want..." I glanced at the ceiling and shook my head.

"I know. You want Martin Sandeke to choose you over his mastermind revenge plot, a revenge plot that's occupied his mind since he was a teenager and toward which he's been working since he reached the age of reason."

I nodded and added sarcastically, "Yes. Exactly. Why can't I be more important to him than a life-time ambition?"

Sam wasn't at all sarcastic when she squeezed my hand and said, "But don't you see? You *should* be. You're not asking him to do anything wrong or illegal, you're not asking him to choose you over his convictions. You're asking him to do the right thing, the good thing, the honorable thing. If he really loved you, really and truly loved you, then *you* would be more important to him than revenge."

I stared at her until she grew blurry in my vision and added absentmindedly, "But I'm not."

"But you're not," she echoed, giving me a sad face, then pulled me into a hug, whispering again my ear, "And you should be."

***

I TEXTED MY mother on Monday and told her that Martin and I broke up. She texted me back that she would arrange through the chemistry department for me to finish my lab credits without a lab partner. She also said she was looking forward to seeing me over summer break.

When I received nothing else from her—no call to ask how I was, no thank you or recognition of what the break up cost me—I became irrationally angry and played 'Killing in the Name' by Rage Against the Machine on my acoustic guitar until 2:37 a.m. I only stopped because Sam came home from a late night study session and needed sleep. When she left the next morning, I picked up my guitar and played it again.

But playing angry music on an acoustic guitar is completely dissatisfying, so I stopped. What I needed were drums.

The next week was really strange. Sam said I was in mourning, but somehow I felt like the one who was dead. Life became mostly periods of calm detachment infrequently interrupted by flashes of intense and painful chaos.

Toward the end of this endless week of insignificant moments, I wondered why anyone would want to fall in love. Falling in love sucked—figuratively, it sucked the life out of me, left me hollow, a desolate wasteland of suckage.

Except when I played my guitar.

So I played my guitar, but instead of playing angry music, I played guitar suites—mostly classical—but somehow made them sound angry.

I also ignored George's messages about the Sunday family agenda. As well I skipped the Sunday call, though I did give my cell phone the double finger salute when it rang. Then I played my guitar.

On the Monday one week after the break up, I was a hot mess. I hadn't been showering…much. But I took comfort in small accomplishments, like brushing my teeth once a day and making it to my classes.

Going to class gave me something to focus on. As well, before my vector calculus class, I received a huge shock when I overheard that someone in Martin's fraternity had been kicked out of school and arrested for attempted rape and assault of a minor.

"Who?" I asked loudly, not caring that this question would label me as an unabashed eavesdropper.

The two guys glanced over their shoulders at me, apparently found me harmless in my sweatpants, tangled hair, and stained Lord of the Rings T-shirt, then turned toward me so I could be included in the conversation.

The ginger spoke first. "One of the crew guys, Salsmar. His picture is in the paper if you really want to know and there's supposed to be a video. They're not releasing the name of the girl 'cause turns out she's underage."

Benjamin Salsmar. Ben. Ben the rapist.

Oh my God!

My stomach dropped. I felt like such a terrible person. I should have called the police about Ben as soon as I arrived back on campus. But I'd forgotten and given myself over to personal drama and now someone had suffered because of me.

Ugh...just, ugh!

"Just another fraternity fuckup," the darker-haired boy said derisively. "It would be news if this kind of shit didn't happen all the time. Show me a fraternity guy who doesn't rape girls, that would be a shocker."

"Yeah," the ginger nodded, adding, "it'll be newsworthy if Salsmar actually gets convicted. Usually these guys get a bailout from their daddy and a slap on the wrist."

"But with the video?" I pressed. "If they have a video, then surely he'll see some jail time?"

They both shrugged, like power, money, and influence mattered more than hard and tangible evidence. Then class started and our impromptu gossip fest was over.

But I couldn't focus on class because I had ants in my pants. I was sure Martin had orchestrated Ben's arrest, or at least had been responsible for making sure it was caught on tape.

***

BY THE END of the third week after the breakup, I was showering semi-daily and I hadn't cried in seven days. I'd also lost fifteen pounds...not even cookies could hold my interest. I hadn't returned any of my mother's calls, nor had I participated in Sunday family meetings.

I was once again hiding in closets. After class I would walk back to my dorm, step into my closet, and shut the door. Sometimes I would bring my guitar and play my own compositions and improvisations. All the songs were morose.

I hadn't seen or heard from Martin and everything still hurt. His absence was everywhere. Therefore, sitting in the darkness and enjoying the lack of sensation, the lack of feeling was a relief.

I was not getting better; things weren't getting easier. Life was various levels of *blah* and horrifically painful.

As such, things went from blah to horrifically painful in the middle of the afternoon on Thursday. I was walking home intent on spending some quality time in the blackness of my closet when I saw him.

My feet stopped moving on their own, and I told myself not to blink or breathe, just in case he was a mirage. I didn't realize until that moment how hungry I was for a glimpse of him. Even though it hurt to the depths of my melodramatic and tortured soul, I stared at Martin.

He was sitting in the student union at a circular table. His big hands were in his hair and he was studying papers on the table before him. Next to Martin sat a very pretty blonde in a grey business suit, a black leather attaché case on the chair next to her. I noted that she looked about ten or so years older than me, but I wondered how much of that was the suit and makeup and air of professionalism.

Meanwhile he looked just the same. His hair was a little messy, but that was probably because he'd been pulling his fingers through it. But his color was fine. He looked fine. He looked perfectly fine.

I forced myself to take a breath and move to the wall, out of the flow of pedestrian traffic. My brain re-booted after close to a minute of standing and staring like a crazy person at my…at my Martin.

But he wasn't my Martin.

A fresh wave of pain pierced my chest and I struggled to inhale. It felt like someone had stabbed me, right through the heart. Every beat was a sluggish ache.

He wasn't *my* anything. And he looked perfectly fine. He was fine and I was a mess because he'd never loved me and I'd allowed myself to fall completely in love with him…like a complete idiot.

Cold certainty and acceptance was a bitter but necessary salve to the open wound I'd been carrying around. It was just as Sam said: he wasn't capable of love. I was wasting my time, both staring at him now and pining for him over the last three weeks. Everything about my time with Martin Sandeke had been a waste of time.

A truly desolate yet comforting numbness wrapped around me like a blanket. I embraced it. Hell, I slathered myself in it and wanted to have its babies. It was armor and a weapon, and finally, finally a tool to combat feeling like an exposed nerve. I was so tired of being vulnerable and helpless.

At last, after indulging myself with one more look—noting with calm detachment that he was now smiling at the woman, and she was laughing at something he'd said—I shook my head to clear it of his image and turned away.

I hadn't smiled in over three weeks. But I hadn't cried in seven days and I wasn't going to cry today. Furthermore, I decided I was never going to cry over Martin Sandeke again.

I decided to take the long way through the student union building rather than walk within feet of his table. The long way took me by a cluster of vending machines, so I stopped and decided to grab a bottle of Dr. Pepper and some peanut M&M's. I couldn't actually remember the last time I'd eaten and that was completely unacceptable. I loved food and I'd allowed Martin-anguish to eclipse every facet of my life.

I was putting a stop to his joy-sucking right now and I was going to use the magic of food to do it.

I fished two crisp dollar bills from my wallet and had just claimed my lunch of champions when I felt a hand on my shoulder.

I glanced at the owner, expecting to find a fellow student asking for change. Instead my eyes connected with Martin's. I was surprised, but so completely numb at this point that I'm sure my expression betrayed nothing but indifference.

I did note that he looked great. Really, really great. Beautiful even. He glowed, like he always had. He was dressed in a black T-shirt, the graphic image on the front depicted some rowing scene, and dark jeans. I noted that he never wore skinny jeans; this was probably because his thighs were too muscular and skinny jeans were for skinny guys. He would never be skinny.

Granted, his expression wasn't happy, but he didn't look like he'd been suffering. He wasn't fifteen pounds lighter and white as a sheet. His eyes weren't bloodshot. His hands weren't shaking. He appeared to be angry but nowhere near heartbroken, at least not the version I saw in the mirror every morning.

I felt like throwing up.

Averting my eyes, I tried to step around him, but he countered and halted my progress.

He moved as though he were going to grab my wrist so I stopped and yanked my arm out of his reach, rocking backward. Since I was basically trapped in the vending machine alcove, I turned my face to the side, inspected the wall, and gave him my profile.

At length he asked, "Will you look at me?"

I tensed. Hearing his voice did something terrible. It broke through this new barrier, the detachment I'd embraced. Therefore I didn't want to look at him again. I was finally exhibiting control over my feelings and I couldn't take the chance. I suspected looking at him now would hurt like a motherfucker.

And apparently, in addition to discovering that just seeing someone can cause physical pain and illness, I was discovering the cathartic and necessary nature of curse words. Despite my expansive vocabulary, there existed no other way to describe how much it would hurt to look at Martin.

In my peripheral vision I sensed movement and I flinched away before he could touch me. I crossed my arms over my chest.

"Goddammit," he seethed. His anger and frustration settled over us, a dark, accusatory fog.

We stood like that for a minute and I imagined I was building an actual wall of bricks between us. I'd volunteered for three summers during high school with Habitat for Humanity and I could build a heckofa brick wall.

He broke the stalemate. "Talk to me, Parker."

I shook my head and closed my eyes, pressing my lips together in a firm line. Despite the sounds of college life around us I could hear him breathe. He wasn't breathing loudly, it's just I could hear it. And it reminded me of the times he'd held me on the boat. I pushed that thought from my mind before it made me cry—because it would make me cry—and turned my attention back to the fictional brick wall.

"You look like shit," he said.

Yeah, it was a crappy thing to say. But it was so Martin. So thoughtless and candid. I did look like shit. And I realized that Martin wasn't a very nice person, not even to me. He was honest first and foremost; sometimes his honesty meant he said nice things to me. But he was never nice for the sake of being nice, or polite because he wanted to spare my feelings. Not once.

I wondered if it even occurred to him that I had feelings...

"Have you been eating?" He shuffled a step forward, his tone nonchalant, almost friendly. "You need a sandwich, let me buy you lunch."

I opened my eyes, affixed them to the floor, but remained silent. Seeing him had satisfied some fundamental—and likely unhealthy—need to witness how he was dealing with the breakup. Was he as tortured and ruined as me? I had my answer and now I couldn't wait to never see him again.

Unexpectedly he blurted, "If you don't talk to me I'll go crazy."

His words were quiet but rough, as though torn from his chest. They certainly had the effect of tearing at my chest. Searing pain flared in my stomach and I had to count to ten before I could breathe again.

I said nothing. Had this happened before today, had he approached me even one hour earlier, I likely would have burst into tears and begged him to take me back. But, for better or for worse, seeing him moments ago looking so well had flipped my off switch. I'd finally accepted we were over—mostly due to the fact that we never truly were.

"I love you." He exhaled the words and I almost believed him. He was so close I could feel the breath fall over my face, a whispered caress that pierced my heart and stomach, ripping and shredding. He repeated, "I love you."

Then he touched me, his hands cupping my face.

"Don't." I tried to jerk my head away but he held me tighter, stepping into me and backing me against the wall.

I lifted my eyes but couldn't raise them above his neck as he tilted my chin up and pressed his lips to mine. He kissed me. I didn't kiss him back, holding onto my earlier resolve and numbness like a lifeline. His forehead fell against mine and he held me there, breathing my air.

"Please talk to me. Please."

"There is nothing to say." I was gratified by the hollow quality and steadiness of my voice.

"I need you."

I shook my head in denial, because I knew he didn't. If he needed me then he wouldn't have let me go, he would have chosen us over revenge. If he needed me then he wouldn't have been able to smile at pretty blondes and look exactly the same as he had three weeks ago after a vacation in the Caribbean.

"You need to leave me alone," I responded through clenched teeth.

"I can't." He pressed his lips to mine again, taking another kiss, lingering there like he was afraid to move, like it would be the last time. He spoke against my mouth. "I can't leave you alone. It's been almost a month and you're all I think about."

"That's a lie."

"No, goddamn you, it isn't! Haven't you noticed me following you? Haven't you seen me outside your dorm, waiting for you? Fucking hell, Parker, you *never* see me, you never have, but that doesn't mean I'm not there."

I gripped his wrists and pulled his hands from my face, twisting away and seeking to put distance between us. His words were confusing because I did see him, just moments ago, smiling at someone else and appearing completely fine. I didn't want his words. I didn't want anything from him.

Despite my certainty and earlier pledge, I felt the beginning of a chin wobble and a stinging moisture behind my eyes. "If I'm all you think about then are you ready to tell the world your father is an evil asshole and being with me is not an alliance between our families?"

This was met with silence and the silence fed my detachment.

I huffed a humorless laugh. "Yeah, I thought so."

"Kaitlyn, there is no reason why we can't be together in secret, if you would only—"

It was the same argument; nothing had changed, so I interrupted him. "If we're seen together then all of this has been pointless. My mother—"

"Fuck your mother," he growled.

I winced, stared at the floor because I didn't want to see him, and when I spoke my voice was unsteady. "This is pointless. You need to let me go."

"What if I can't? Hmm? What if I don't? What if I call the Washington Post and tell the reporter that we're still together, that our families are closer than ever?"

I finally lifted my eyes to his so he could see how serious I was, and that—in that moment—I hated him a little. I looked at him even though it hurt like a motherfucker.

Somehow I managed to say, "That's blackmail."

"If that's what it takes." He punctuated this with a belligerent shrug.

I shook my head, mostly at myself for thinking we were ever a team. "Martin, there's a time to fight, and there is a time to bow out gracefully."

"You never fight," he spat, his mouth twisted in an unattractive sneer, his eyes dark blue flames.

I fleetingly thought of how I'd fought for him in front of his father, how

I'd fought for him and for us in his room three weeks ago. But what was the point? Arguing would get us nowhere. *We* didn't exist.

Instead I said, "What do you want me to do? Do you want me to blackmail you? Issue threats? Call your father and tell him about your plan to sell his houses?"

He winced like I'd struck him, blinking several times in rapid succession. "You wouldn't do that."

"No. I wouldn't. I respect your decision, even if I think it's a mistake."

"So you bow out gracefully, like a coward."

"You're wrong. You're so wrong. I'm fighting for what I believe in, I'm going to do the right thing—"

"Self-sacrificing, martyring bullshit!'

"—and I'm not going to change my mind. So it's time for you to find the self-control to bow out gracefully and let me go."

Eyes flashing, Martin shifted on his feet, his stance telling me he was preparing to launch another verbal volley, so I quickly added, allowing a hint of pleading in my voice, letting it waver and shake, "If you ever had the slightest feeling for me, you will respect my decision. You will walk away right now and you will leave me alone. I need you to *leave me alone*. You are ruining me."

His blue-green eyes were glassy and raw with pain as they searched mine. I recognized his hurt because it was an echo of the suffocating agony I'd been carrying with me every day.

After a long moment he nodded once, his mouth a flat line. His eyes fell away, searching but not looking at any one thing. I saw his chest rise and fall, heard the end of an unsteady exhale, before he turned and left.

His stride (as expected) was confident as always. Every step of his smooth gait just proved that Sam had been right. He was a universe of one and I wasn't enough.

I watched him go, watched the back of his head until he turned a corner.

Then I ran home. I sat in my dark closet. And I cried.

Part 3: CAPTURE

Prologue

A Molecular Comparison of Gases, Liquids, and Solids

-Six months post-breakup-

"I DON'T KNOW how to do this, Kaitlyn. You're going to have to help me."

"Do what, Dad?"

The phone was silent for a beat before he said, "Talk to you about your mother."

I grimaced and picked at an imperfection on the kitchen table. Four months ago, when Sam and I had moved off campus, we furnished our apartment with thrift store purchases. The shellac was peeling away from the Formica and I was making it worse.

"I don't know what there is to say." I shrugged, biting my lip to keep my chin from wobbling. The truth was that I missed her. My dad and I had been talking regularly over the phone, but I hadn't been participating in our Sunday meetings for the last six months and I missed having a connection with my mother.

"I think she hurt you. Am I right?"

I shrugged even though he couldn't see me. Part of the reason I hadn't contacted her was definitely because she seemed to be indifferent to my feelings about breaking up with Martin.

The other part was because of my fear she'd be disappointed in me. During my summer of discontent after my breakup with Martin, I'd decided to switch majors—from chemical engineering to music—and take the fall semester off school.

Taking a semester off school was the Parker family equivalent of giving up on life. I'd made the decision rather flippantly, and without consulting my parents. However, my determination to change majors had deeper roots and was the impetus behind my current gainful employment as the piano player in a special events band.

After a week of psyching myself up, I'd auditioned in July and was now officially a paid musician. The group played mostly weddings. They also performed at Bar and Bat Mitzvahs, swanky business receptions, and office parties anywhere between Boston and New York City. My evenings and weekend afternoons started filling up fast, especially when we'd have to travel into the city for a job.

Being around music almost daily—either as part of the band, or the time spent alone composing—made me realize I had to pursue it. I had to live it. It was my passion and ignoring what gave me happiness and peace was unacceptable.

Instead of admitting the whole truth about why I was avoiding my mother, I said, "I don't even really understand why I'm so upset with her. She didn't do anything. Not really. And I know she had good intentions. It's just...I feel like she doesn't care about me sometimes, I guess."

"Well, you're wrong. She does care about you. She loves you."

"Then I don't think I understand what love is. I thought I knew. I thought it was this great thing where two people support each other and work together to solve problems. I thought it was about trust and loyalty, being honest, kind, being a team. But now I have no idea. In fact, I'm doubting that love exists. Maybe, as a society, we made it up to explain and justify our unhealthy desire for co-dependence."

He was silent for a moment and I knew he was thinking about what I'd said, processing it. One of the coolest things about my father was that he listened to understand, not to react.

"I actually agree with you to a certain extent, if I'm understanding your meaning correctly. We humans, most of us, are co-dependent and it's often unhealthy. It's up to the two people within the relationship to keep the co-dependence healthy. But, you are assuming there is only one kind of love, Kaitlyn. I can tell you there are as many kinds of love in the world as there are stars in the sky."

"That was very poetic, Dad."

"I bet you didn't know I used to write poetry for your mother."

This made me start and I sat up straighter in my chair. "You did?"

"Yes. And it was pretty good, for a medical student who was infatuated with an unobtainable ice queen. It made her melt...a little."

I heard the smile in his voice and it made me nostalgic for his sweet sappiness.

"What happened?"

"I asked her to marry me, not expecting that she would say yes, but she did. So we got married, and I was in very deep infatuation-love with her. She was so...good. So driven. She was talented at inspiring people and surprising them with how smart she was—because she is, she's brilliant. And she's very charismatic."

I thought about this for a second, mildly horrified that I was attracted to guys who were like my mother.

He continued. "But then I became disillusioned because she belonged to the world just as much as she belonged to me. And I didn't like that."

I considered this for a moment, thinking about my father being jealous of the world. I couldn't imagine my father being jealous at all. He was so…nice. Even tempered. Sweet.

"What did you do?"

"I told her I wanted a divorce. I told her I couldn't be with someone who was always putting me second and that I'd made a mistake."

I sucked in a sharp breath. "Why did I not know about this?"

"It happened before you were born."

"What did she do?"

My father sighed, as though he were releasing memories from long ago. "She begged me to stay, which shocked the hell out of me, but she did. She offered to leave politics and even went so far as to drop out of her commissioner's race without telling me. She tried to make herself into a different person, because she didn't want me to go. She didn't want to lose me."

"That seems…very unlike her."

"It was. It is. But love—the kind of love she felt for me—makes people do crazy things. It twists them up and can make them question their own choices."

"So, you stayed, obviously. But then how did she get back into politics?"

"I realized I was ruining her with my jealousy. She tried to change for me, and not for the better. The parts of her I loved the most—her brilliance, charisma, goodness, fierce desire to correct injustice—these were not compatible with my jealousy. And I also realized that she didn't belong to the world, and she didn't belong to me. She belongs to herself. We all belong to ourselves, until we have children. Then our children lease us for as long as they want."

I exhaled a laugh and shook my head.

"Never doubt that your mother loves you, Kaitlyn."

Feeling ashamed as I contemplated my father's wise words, I forced myself to stop picking at the Formica.

My father continued, "But she does everything in the extreme. In your case, she respects you and trusts you in the extreme, so she trusts that you'll come to her when you're ready. Meanwhile she's bitten off all her fingernails."

I thought about this for a stretch, feeling a bit of panic at the thought of facing her and being a disappointment.

"What if I'm never ready?"

"Then that would make you stupid, and you're not stupid. You're stubborn, but you're not stupid."

"I don't know how to do this, Dad. How do I make things right?"

"Come home for Thanksgiving. Talk to your mother. Or yell at her. Just do something with her. You two need each other and I can't take another Sunday call without you, so call in for the next one. Just…be brave."

***

-Seven months post-breakup-

BETWEEN YOU AND me and the tree, I think we should have our own Thanksgiving before you leave." Sam was folding our clean laundry while I sorted through my desk, purging it of old classwork and notes. I'd decided to go home for Thanksgiving and was leaving in three weeks for the long weekend. I had an abundance of restless energy. I used the energy to clean my room.

My father was correct. It was time for me to make things right with my mother.

I'd rejoined the Sunday calls at the beginning of October, yet none of us had broached the subject of my months-long absence.

As well, she and I hadn't spoken yet about my decision to take a semester off school, and I was glad. When I brought it up on a mid-October call, I'd tried to explain and defend my position. She told me to wait.

My mother had said, "You need time."

And she was right. I'd needed the time to figure things out without dwelling on the fact that I must be a disappointment.

"Is your mother going to make Tofurkey again?" I asked Sam.

Her only response was to make a gagging sound.

I chuckled at this. Her mother was a strict vegan. Sam loved steak.

"Hey Sam, do you think I could get a job at your restaurant? Not as a server of course, since I don't have any experience, but maybe I could bus tables or wash dishes."

I was re-enrolling at the university in the spring, but now as a music major. I'd applied and auditioned for the music program, probably setting my graduation date back by two or more years. As well, this meant likely losing my academic scholarship. My dad had offered to pay for tuition; therefore I was determined to get a second job, pay for my living costs, and pitch in for the school expenses.

"I can ask…" She peered at me for a long moment, biting the inside of her lip as she considered me. "But have you thought about maybe applying for a job at The Bluesy Bean? I hear the lady there only hires musicians as baristas because she makes them serenade the customers."

I chuckled. "Ha ha, that's funny."

I tossed a stack of papers into the paper bag I'd set aside for recycling and then shifted my attention to the bookshelf. I had so many textbooks. I thought I'd need them for reference; I should have just sold them back for cash. The room fell into silence, which wasn't unusual for us these days.

Which was why I was surprised when Sam blurted, "So, I think it's time that you talk to me about what's going on with you."

I glanced at her over my shoulder, and found her watching me with her hands on her hips.

"What do you mean?"

Her jaw was set, her eyes narrowed into determined slits. "I mean, you didn't speak to me—or anyone else—for months, until you got that job with the band last July. Hell, even when we picked out this apartment it was like pulling teeth trying to get you to voice an opinion. And don't get me started on the weird, angry acoustic guitar music."

I gave her an apologetic half smile. I knew this conversation had to happen eventually. Sam had been so patient with me. I was better, so much better, and now was as good a time as any to bring everything out into the open, to clarify my headspace over the last few months.

I faced her, crossing to the bed. "I know. I'm so sorry about the angry acoustic guitar music."

She continued like I hadn't spoken, as though some dam had broken and she needed to get all her thoughts out. "I know you don't like me mentioning *his* name."

I rolled my eyes at my dramatics from months ago, when I'd told her I never wanted to speak of Martin Sandeke ever again; but it also made me realize I'd been greedy with my thoughts.

"And then you joined the band and started drinking Red Bull. Next you decided to change your major and take a semester off school—which I'm totally for, by the way. It's just that you never talk to me about anything. You're in your head all the time. And I want to know, it's been almost eight months since the two of you split and I think it's time for you to tell me. Are you over *him* yet? Is Kaitlyn back? Is it okay for me to ask you questions and voice my unsolicited advice?"

I took a deep breath, gazed at her affectionately, then patted the spot next to me on the bed. She eyeballed me, then the bed, then plopped down beside me.

"Okay," I started, trying to figure out how to give her a Cliffs Notes version of what I'd been going through. The words would be difficult, so I decided to use terminology with which I was most comfortable. "Let me start from the beginning, with the solid state of matter."

She lifted one eyebrow at me, her chin falling and issuing me a look of disbelief. "Solid state of matter? What are you talking about?"

"Let me finish. So, after M-Martin and I broke up—"

"So we can say his name now?"

"Just listen. After Martin and I broke up, I admit I did not take it well. I was an immovable mass of low energy. I kept thinking that if I didn't think about it, then I would never have to deal with it."

"So, you were in denial."

I laughed a little at her apt simplification. "Yes. Basically, I froze everyone out. I was a solid. This lasted for a long time, because I'm stubborn. As well, you know I like my pity parties and self-recrimination soirées."

"Yes, it lasted two months. You went to class, sometimes you went to your jam sessions, but mostly you just hid in the closet."

I cleared my throat, remembering this dark time, and grateful I'd moved past it. "So then this brings us to the liquid state of matter. You know how I started loosening up once we moved into the apartment?"

She nodded. "Yeah, but you still wouldn't talk to anyone. You just sat in your room listening to Taylor Swift's angry-girl music."

"Yes, but I was angry. I wasn't frozen anymore, I was just really, really pissed off. I think the new apartment was the catalyst for my shift in state from solid to liquid. It felt like a new start. Away from the dorms, away from the college atmosphere. It was a reminder that life existed beyond school. I was only nineteen—almost twenty—and, I realized that I have decades left on this planet. I couldn't keep hiding in closets…"

I reflected on my feelings at the time. Yes, I couldn't keep hiding in closets, but this thought made me angry. I'd been happy hiding in closets before Martin had ruined everything and scratched my itch.

I hated him for it.

During my liquid state I'd redoubled my efforts to avoid all mentions of, or references to, Martin Sandeke. I wasn't ready to accept he existed in the world, and yet might as well be Hercules as far as I was concerned. I would never see him again—never in person—but maybe in a magazine or in the news. Our breakup had been my choice and it was the right decision, but it still pissed me off.

As well, I wasn't ready to accept that *I* certainly no longer existed to *him*.

Sam sighed. "So, this angry phase, this *liquid state* as you call it—this is when I tried to get you to read that fitness magazine interview Martin gave over the summer?"

I nodded. "Yes. Sorry for snapping at you about that."

She shrugged. "It's okay. I get it. So, if I recall my high school chemistry correctly, the gas state comes after the liquid state."

"That's right. Though I like to think of it as the nitrous oxide, aka laughing gas, phase—otherwise known as the *I-don't-give-two-poos* phase."

"Oh! That's when you started drinking Red Bull and boxes of wine. I still can't believe you're drinking the demon liquor even though you're not yet legal. Shame on you."

I tried to give her my best *girl, you crazy* face. "Sam, you're the one who buys me the boxes of wine. You're my supplier. But I make no apologies and I have no regrets. I've discovered I like my boxes of wine and I'm not giving them up for the next six months before I turn twenty-one. They're stackable, like Tetris. All beverages should be stackable."

"I agree, beverages should be stackable, it saves on shelf space. And it's not my fault I'm older than you are and enjoy enabling your illegal activities, especially if it means I'm not drinking boxed wine by myself. But back to you and your states of crazy, the boxed wine phase was when you started going to those music meet-ups. I remember that phase."

"But, if you remember, it was around this time that I decided to take the fall semester off school and switch my major to music."

"And you started hanging around those druggies at the Fourth Avenue bar. But that only lasted a week."

"Yes, it only lasted for about a week." I studied Sam for a beat before continuing, marveling at how perceptive she was and how lucky I was to have her as a friend. "I'd made a deal with myself: I would be carefree and act my age. If I were carefree then I would forget about Martin and be happy."

"The boxes of wine do seem to make you happy," Sam agreed.

What I didn't say, because it was difficult to admit my irresponsibility, was that everything became a joke. I didn't *need* Martin. I didn't need anyone. I could live outside the closet of obscurity just fine on my own. I needed nothing.

"You're right though, it wasn't sustainable for me. I'm far too practical and reclusive. Firstly, Red Bull tastes like excrement."

"It does! Right?"

"And secondly, as much as I enjoyed the time I was actually playing music, I had no patience for druggies."

Watching people actively choose to destroy themselves felt like watching Martin choose revenge over living his life free from his father. It was during this time I recognized revenge was Martin's drug and he was an addict.

"So, solid state is denial. Liquid state is anger. That makes the gas state the bargaining stage."

I cocked my head to the side, studying Sam. "What do you mean?"

"The five stages of grief," she explained matter-of-factly. "Next is depression."

I looked at my friend for a long moment, realizing she was right. She was *so* right. The next state was depression.

"Oh my God, you're right." I gave her a sad smile. "Yes, otherwise known as the plasma state of matter."

Sam's gaze became sympathetic as it held mine, her features softening with compassion. "Toward the end of the summer, when you started crying again."

"You heard that?"

"Yes. I heard the crying. And the sad music you were composing in your room. It's beautiful, by the way. Much better than your Red Bull-slash-gas-slash-bargaining phase music."

I gave her a soft smile. "Thank you. It was very…cathartic. It allowed me to reflect on the months that came before it. But mostly I think I was trying to wrap my mind around how and why I'd allowed one week—one solitary, singular week—to completely change the course of my life."

Why had I given Martin Sandeke so much power over me? And why was I continuing to give him power? I hadn't seen or spoken to him since that terrible day on campus. He hadn't once tried to contact me, but I hadn't expected him to try.

And yet…I missed him. I thought about him and our week together all the time.

Sam's mouth turned down at the corners and she gave me a sincere and sympathetic look. "Kaitlyn, you fell in love with Martin over that week. You trusted him…you slept with him."

I nodded, glancing down at my fingers. "I know…"

I know I missed the depth of feeling, the loss of control, the surrender to passion, the being lost and found all at once. Being seen. He was still wrapped around my heart and I had no way to evict him. I wasn't sure I could.

I added, "I know that, before Martin, before our week together, I'd been repressed, stuck without knowing it. But then after we split things were even worse."

Sam pulled me into a hug as I continued my confession. "He became my compass, my beacon. And before him, I'd been a girl desperately trying to follow the footsteps of expectations even though the shoes didn't fit."

"And he helped you see beyond family expectations?"

I nodded against her shoulder. Over spring break I'd started to become a woman who was excited about forging her own path.

I pulled away from my friend, but continued to hold her hand. "Then I left him and he left me. We abandoned each other before I'd discovered what I wanted or who I was. My compass was gone. I couldn't go back to hiding in closets even though I tried."

She chuckled at this, adding, "Boy, oh boy, did you ever try."

I smiled at her. "But the closets don't fit anymore. Nor do I know how to move forward blindly. I want to be something else, someone else, not Kaitlyn Parker who hides in closets and does what everyone expects."

"But not everyone has the benefit of a compass or a guide. Most people go blindly into their future."

I nodded again. "Yes. I figured that out."

I'd figured out that people did this by trusting their heart.

"Well, we've already covered denial, anger, bargaining, and depression. Does this mean you've moved on to acceptance?" Sam gave me a wide, hopeful smile that made me laugh.

"Kind of." I shrugged, my gaze moving over her shoulder as I focused my thoughts. "Think of it this way. The fifth state of matter is a theoretical state—"

"Really? We're still using the chemistry analogy?"

I continued as though she hadn't spoken, because the word *acceptance* didn't feel quite right. "One could argue the fifth state of matter isn't theoretical, that it's a class of states that occur under unusual or extreme circumstances, like Bose–Einstein condensates or neutron-degenerate matter."

"I have no idea what you just said."

I pressed my lips together so I wouldn't laugh, but returned my gaze to Sam. "But for the purposes of my stages of grief, I'm going to label the fifth stage as quark–gluon plasmas. It's a state of matter that is believed to be possible, but remains theoretical…for now."

"Theoretical?"

"Theoretical because my fifth stage of grief has to do with me getting over Martin, which I admit hasn't happened yet. And it also centers on finding my purpose, but using only myself as a compass."

"You can also use me as a compass, you know. I'm very good with the aforementioned unsolicited advice."

If I hadn't realized it before, I realized now that Sam was a singularity of awesomeness. "I know, and I will. But it's more than just moving on from Martin. It's a stage where I become comfortable in my own skin, happy with where I am, what I'm doing, and who I'm doing it with."

"So, it's theoretical."

"Yes." I nodded, finally returning Sam's hopeful grin. "It's still theoretical. But it's possible."

***

-Eight months post-breakup-

I FOUND MY mother in the garden.

She was home for the Congressional Thanksgiving recess. Growing up, I'd always thought it funny that the US government took a *recess,* like little kids took recess in primary school. I imagined the Speaker of the House hanging upside down on monkey bars and the majority leader shaking down junior senators for lunch money.

I knew we'd be seeing each other because it had been on the Sunday agenda for the last month. I'd been mentally preparing for this meeting. She'd said I needed some time before we discussed my months-long absence from her life and my decision to take a semester off school.

But the time had come. I needed to talk to her about it, even though it was messy and unsettled. I needed her to listen without trying to fix.

When I found her in the garden, I announced to her back, "I want to be a musician. I want to pursue music and major in it and I don't want to be a scientist or a politician."

My mother turned as I spoke, stared at me for a beat, her forehead wrinkling slightly, probably because I wasn't prone to outbursts. Then she nodded and said, "Okay."

I waited for her to continue, maybe add a, *But you're on your own...* or *But when you come to your senses...* or something similar. She didn't.

When she just continued looking at me, my suspicions burst forth. "You think this is a phase, right?"

My mom took a deep breath, glanced briefly at the ground, then returned her gaze to mine. "Maybe. Maybe not."

"You're disappointed in me? Because I took off this semester? Because I'm not following in your footsteps? Because I'm—"

She held up her hands and cut me off. "Kaitlyn, stop. Stop. Stop putting words in my mouth. I'm not disappointed in you. I'm disappointed in myself."

I frowned at her, studying my mother in her navy pants suit, and light blue shirt, and the little United States flag on her lapel. Finally I asked, "Why?"

"Because you obviously need my support and I have no idea how to give it to you." She crossed to me, her eyes searching, then pulled me into an unexpected hug.

When she spoke next I felt her chin move against the side of my head. "I'm not...I've never been very good at being maternal."

I laughed, partly because I hadn't expected her to say it and partly because it was true.

She squeezed me. "I'm good at being rational, methodical, and solving problems with logic and analysis. But, try as I might, I've never been able to figure out how to provide the comfort that you've needed. And I'm sorry."

Every one of my internal organs flooded with the warmth of relief that accompanies hope. I squeezed her in return, unable to help myself. "You're forgiven."

She stepped back, but her hands remained on my arms. She was clearly frustrated. "I don't know how to help you or be what you need, Kaitlyn."

"Can you listen?"

"Yes. Of course."

"Without trying to problem solve or find a superior solution to my issues?"

She hesitated, her eyes narrowing, looking incredulous. "You mean, just listen?"

I nodded.

She stared at me, appeared to be firming her resolve, then said, "For you, absolutely."

***

-Nine months post-breakup-

"ARE YOU EVER going to go out with Fitzy, or what?"

I let my befuddlement show on my face by widening my eyes and looking from side to side.

All I wanted was a bottle of water.

"What you talkin' 'bout, Willis?"

I enjoyed asking my bandmate this question, mostly because his name was actually Willis. Usually no one my age had any idea that the question was a reference to a 1980s TV show I used to watch with my dad called *Different Strokes.*

Willis glanced over his shoulder to where Abram the bass player, Janet the lead guitarist and saxophonist, and Fitzgerald our singer and second guitar—aka Fitzy for short—were finishing the sound check. Since Willis held my water bottle hostage, I followed his gaze and found Fitzy watching us. When he saw our attention focused on him, Fitzy averted his blue-eyed stare and began messing with his mic stand, his shaggy brown hair falling adorably over his forehead.

Willis turned back to me, leveled me with his dark brown eyes. Like the rest of us, Willis was dressed in a tuxedo, bowtie, cummerbund, the whole get up. Unlike the rest of us, Willis was in his mid-forties and never minced words.

Unfortunately, he chopped his words instead, usually with a dull blade or a mallet. Willis's thoughts were often sporadic and hard to follow; as well his analogies didn't quite make sense.

"Listen, Cupcake. He's got it bad for you, like a porcupine and a balloon. Now, I don't care what y'all do in your free time, but I'm tired of losing good people because you kids can't keep your seatbelts fastened. We lost Pierce, our last pianist, when Janet and he refused to work together after six weeks on a mattress tour. They drew straws and he came up espresso—you see?"

I nodded, trying to follow. "So, Janet and Pierce, your last piano player, were a thing? And it didn't end well?"

"It *never* ends well." Willis narrowed his dark brown eyes and pressed his mouth into a flat line. He was bald, his head completely shaved, and the collar of his dress shirt didn't quite hide the tattoos on the back of his neck. This didn't affect our squeaky image since he was our drummer and sat at the back of the stage. Also, he was my boss.

Willis lowered his roughened voice—made gravelly by years of smoking and drinking and laughing too loud—and squinted at me until his pupils were barely visible. "Musicians are like lightbulbs, they burn hot and bright, but can't be screwed more than once. If you two need to get it out of your system, that's fine. But you're a great kid, real goddamn talented, pretty, look good on stage. But Fitzy is also pretty and will be hard to replace—you get my meaning?"

"I think so. You don't care if Fitzy and I get together, but you don't want it to impact the dynamic of the band. Right?"

He nodded, looking irritated. "Isn't that what I just said?"

"Yes, absolutely. I understand loud and clear. Not dating bandmates is one of my life rules."

What I didn't vocalize was that Willis didn't need to worry. Although Fitzy was super hot, super nice, and super talented, I felt no attraction to him beyond the surface of his skin and the attractiveness of his voice. This was because Fitzy wasn't very bright.

If he were an actual lightbulb he'd be a twenty watt fluorescent. Hard to look at—because he was so pretty—but too dim to make a noticeable difference in any given room.

Abram the bassist, however, was a completely different story. His face wasn't classically good-looking—with his long brown hair, hazel eyes, big jaw, and hook nose—nor was he book smart. But he was tall and broad and manly-handsome. As well he was shrewd, and wicked sharp. He had a razor wit and twisted sense of humor.

He also always had one or two women in the audience who waited for him after our sets. It didn't matter if we played a country club wedding outside New Haven, a dive bar in Queens, or a high-rise in Manhattan. Without fail, he never went home alone. As well, at times his jokes were shaded with bitterness; it was easy to see he was jaded.

I was undoubtedly attracted to Abram—the talented, witty, sexy bassist. But I wasn't attracted to Abram—the serial dating king of the bitterness squad.

I'd come to the conclusion that intelligence was my catnip, followed closely by charisma. And, thanks to my romantic history, I'd realized that just because a person was intelligent and charismatic didn't mean they were good for me. The brighter the brain, the greater the gravitational pull, the more wary I was.

Therefore, Fitzy was harmless.

And furthermore, I was careful to stay out of Abram's orbit.

What I needed was a nice guy who understood my jokes. Someone who was friendly rather than charismatic. Someone who was bright, but wasn't so brilliant he was blinding.

"Get on your perch, lady bird. It's almost time." Willis walked past me to his place behind the drums.

I grabbed my bottle of water and followed Willis to the stage. Avoiding Abram's level stare, I gave Janet a friendly head nod and waved at Fitzy. He waved back, giving me a big, white, perfect smile.

Tonight we were playing a Christmas party at a New York City location we knew well. It was a converted fire station, now a moderately sized concert venue—very popular spot for weddings and office parties. I liked it because the interior was original red brick with cool Norwegian-looking tapestries lining the walls, likely placed purposefully to help with acoustics.

Also, the stage was set back from the dance floor. Though I'd been playing publicly for several months, being close to or surrounded by the audience still felt overwhelming. I liked being in the back, with the piano between me and the audience.

The set started with the basic cocktail hour fare: heavy on the piano, vocals, and saxophone; light on the drums. We would play five sets, each growing progressively louder and edgier as the older crowd left, leaving the young people who wanted to dance.

Nothing was special about this event. I had no expectations, indications, or signs from above (or below) that this event would be any different from the dozens of other office parties I'd played over the last several months. I was cool. I was collected. I was fine. I was doing my thing and wondering if I still had bacon in the fridge, because I had a severe hankering for a BLT.

Then, amidst my bacon preoccupation, my ponytail holder snapped during the fourth set and the bobby pins I'd placed to fasten my bun were no match for the weight of my hair. I was forced to perform the remainder of the set with curls in my face.

It was irritating and distracting. As well, and inexplicably, the snapped ponytail holder was the catalyst for an intense and abrupt wave of self-consciousness. The sensation started with a nagging tingle on the back of my neck. I ignored it. It persisted.

I lifted my gaze to Abram and found him watching me with a smirk. I rolled my eyes and turned my attention back to my fingers as they flew over the keys, writing off the tingle as Abram-related. A moment later I glanced back at Abram, feeling irritated I could still feel his stare, but he wasn't looking at me.

Yet, I felt eyes on me. I felt watched. It was a weight, like a hand, and I couldn't shake the impression. My heart thudded uncomfortably in my chest as I scanned my bandmates. I found them all focused on their instruments.

I told myself I was being silly, but the feeling persisted. It was unnerving, like walking down a dark hallway and hearing the echo of footsteps.

When the set was finally over, I twisted my hair over my shoulder and out of my face. I glanced at the audience as I stood from the piano, scanning the crowd for the source of my discomfort, half expecting to find nothing.

But I did find something.

I found blue-green eyes on a familiar face, dressed in an immaculately tailored suit, with a tall brunette on his arm, a drink in his hand, and his penetrating gaze firmly anchored to mine.

CHAPTER 1
Resonance Structures

"I'M SORRY, WILLIS. I need a minute…I don't feel well." I was sitting on an upturned bucket backstage, my hands on my knees. My voice was weak and I truly, truly did not feel well.

Janet was rubbing my back and Fitzy hovered nearby with a plate of food. Abram was leaning against the far wall, his feet crossed at the ankles, his hands shoved in his pockets as he watched me.

Seeing Martin again—just *seeing* him across a crowded room—had been so much more flustering and mind-bending than I could have predicted. My thoughts on repeat were:

He's here.

He's here with someone.

I kind of still hate him.

But I hope he doesn't hate me.

I think I'm still infatuated with him…

Surprisingly, the loudest and most pressing thought: *He's seen me naked.*

Martin, plus my dad—when I was an infant—were the only two men in the entire world who had seen me naked. Really, only Martin actually counted, because I didn't have boobs or pubic hair or a girl shape when my dad used to give me raspberries on my tummy. Plus, he was my dad.

Only Martin…

That pressing thought served to confuse me and increase the potency of my awkward feels. Perhaps I needed to fix that. Perhaps I needed to find another guy and show him my girl stuff, widen my audience, so that being in the same room with Martin didn't turn me into a skeevy, nudity-obsessed wacko.

Perhaps diluting the meaningfulness of intimacy would lessen the impact of his presence. Then I could look at him and think, *Hey, you're one of the guys who has seen me naked. So what? Who hasn't seen me naked?*

"Do you think you can play? It's just one more set," Janet asked softly, pulling me from my thoughts. She was a nice girl, very maternal, with a heart entirely too soft. A direct contradiction to the image she projected with her dyed black hair, pale skin, icicle eyes, and copious piercings.

I nodded and closed my eyes. I could play. I would play. I just needed a minute to stop my hands from shaking.

I wondered if there was a broom closet nearby where I could chill out for five minutes. I wouldn't hide all night, just until it was safe. Maybe Fitzy could join me and I could show him my boobs.

"Jarring, unsettling, startling, alarming, disconcerting, distressing, disquieting."

A pause followed my mumbling, and then Willis asked, "What are you doing?"

"She's chanting synonyms." Abram's voice carried from across the room. I opened my eyes and met his gaze. He was watching me with interest. "It calms you down, yes?"

I nodded, frowning. He was entirely too shrewd.

Willis grunted. "Well, okay. That's…as weird as a loan shark with debt. But we got another ten minutes before rodeo time."

I held Abram's gaze for a moment longer, then stood—a little wobbly on my feet—and turned to Willis. "I think I'll take a short walk."

Fitzy leaned forward and began to volunteer, "I'll go—"

But Abram lifted his voice and talked over him, "I'll walk with you. Come on. Let's go."

The tall bassist pushed away from the wall and crossed to me, wrapped his hand around my arm just above the elbow, and pulled me out the back door.

"Be back in five minutes!" Willis called after us.

"We'll be back in seven," Abram countered, steering me down the alley to the street and away from the stink of the dumpster.

I pulled out of his grip when we reached the sidewalk and folded my arms over my chest, not really feeling the cold of the last November evening because my mind was racing, trying to keep pace with my heart. I was definitely not going to show Abram my boobs. That would be like jumping from the frying pan into the beer batter, then back in the frying pan.

When I saw Martin across the room, I just stood there, my fingers still on the edge of the baby grand piano. It didn't feel real and I was sure he was going to disappear if I blinked.

So I didn't blink.

Eventually, Fitzy pulled me off the stage and I had no choice but to blink. Yet when I looked back and Martin was still present—still standing at the bar with his beautiful date next to him, surrounded in a thick cloud of arrogance, still staring at me—I almost blacked out.

He didn't disappear. He was real. And he most definitely saw and recognized me.

"You feeling better?"

I realized Abram and I had already walked a block and a half. The distance was a surprise. "Yes. I feel better. We should go back."

Lies, all lies. I didn't feel better. I felt like throwing up. *Will the drama never stop?!*

We continued forward.

"Sometimes you sound like a robot when you speak." He didn't appear to be annoyed as he made this comment; rather, it was simply an observation, maybe meant to distract me.

"Do I?"

"Yeah. Mostly when you talk to me."

"What can I say? You bring out the artificial intelligence in me."

I heard him chuckle as he took my arm again, bringing me close as we skirted a crowd of rowdy young men, all dressed in New York Knicks jerseys, likely on their way home after a game at Madison Square Garden. When we were past the boisterous crowd, I moved to pull my arm out of his grip, but he didn't release me. Instead he tugged me into a small doorway and turned me to face him.

"So, who's the guy?"

I lifted my eyes to his, found him studying me with moderate interest. Moderate interest for the perpetually sardonic Abram felt like a laser beam pointed at my skull.

"What guy?"

"The guy at the bar. The stockbroker, or hedge fund manager, or whatever he does."

I squinted at Abram, setting my jaw, but said nothing.

He lifted a single eyebrow and I noticed he had a scar running through the center of it. The scar paired with his hooked nose—likely broken more than once— and long hair, gave him a rather ruffian-like appearance, a pirate prone to fights.

"Ex-boyfriend," he stated. He'd clearly pulled the answer from my brain with his ruffian voodoo.

I grimaced. "Yes…kind of."

His lips pulled to the side as his eyes skated over my face. "Kind of?"

"We need to get back." I didn't move.

"Are you afraid of him?"

I ignored this question because it was entirely too complicated for me to answer. Instead I said, "It's been five minutes at least."

"Did he hurt you?"

I closed my eyes, leaned back against the brick of our little cave, and murmured, "We hurt each other."

We were silent for a stretch and I felt his gaze on me, but I hardly noticed. My mind and heart were twisted up in a battle of wills, and yet neither of them had decided what to do, how to feel, or what to think.

"Come on, let's go."

Once again, Abram encircled my arm with his long fingers and tugged me down the street. This time I made no effort to pull away. Once we reached the first stoplight, he slipped his grip from my arm to my hand, lacing his fingers with mine. Even in my fog I definitely noticed. Usually, I would have withdrawn by crossing my arms over my chest in the universal body language code for *not interested in you touching me*, but instead I let him hold my hand. I let myself take some comfort from the connection, even if he wasn't really offering any.

Honestly, I had no idea what to think about Abram, whether he was actually offering comfort, why he was holding my hand…so I didn't think.

Soon we were back in the alley and entering the back door of the venue. Willis was the only one left in the backstage area; he stopped mid-pace as we entered. "You're late as a Chevy to a fuel efficiency contest. It's been ten minutes."

"We're not late. We're early," Abram drawled, squeezing my hand then releasing it. He crossed to the cooler and pulled out a Coke while I sunk back to the bucket I'd been sitting on earlier.

"Early? You said you'd be back in seven minutes. It's been ten."

"Yeah, but I meant fifteen." Abram paired this by lifting his broad shoulders in a shrug, then adding an unapologetic and crooked smile.

Willis turned his scowl to me. "Are you ready?"

I opened my mouth to respond but Abram cut me off, "No. She threw up twice during the walk. She can't play, unless you want her tossing chunks all over the stage."

Again, I opened my mouth to interject. This time Willis cut me off. "No, no! You stay back here, I can't have glitter at a confetti party." He rubbed his bald head and stomped toward the steps, muttering as he went, "We'll figure it out."

"You're welcome," Abram said between swallows of Coke, bringing my attention back to him.

"Why did you do that?"

"So you'll owe me one."

This only served to intensify my frown. "I don't owe you one. I didn't ask for your help."

"Fine. Then I did it because I'm a nice guy."

I shook my head. "You're not a nice guy."

He grinned, looking positively wolfish. "No. I guess I'm not. But you're a nice girl. You bring out my altruistic side."

"Hmm..." I squinted at him and said nothing else, but I felt a little bit better.

This, this right here, this exchange between Abram and me was likely the source of my improved spirits. If I'd met Abram last year I likely would have run in the other direction. But now I was talking to this smart, charismatic, undeniably hot musician and hadn't once considered that I might be reduced to a blubbering fool.

I was officially *adulting*.

I was engaging in discourse with a guy to whom I was attracted, but whom I would never consider dating. Bonus: I wasn't trying to change the subject to musical theory, or some other tactic meant to distract.

Abram mimicked my squinty stare—though his was joined by an amused smile—and tossed his empty Coke bottle in the trash. "Wait for me after the set, I'll take you home."

"No thanks, I'm taking the train."

He stopped in front of me on his way to the stage and straightened his bow tie before sliding his long-fingered hands—bass-player hands—down the front of his suit jacket. The suit wasn't tailored very well and was baggy around his middle. Obviously he'd sized up so the shoulders would fit but hadn't invested in tapering it to fit his torso.

"You'll wait. Remember? If you're too sick to play the piano, then you're too sick to take the train."

"I live in New Haven. That's a long drive."

He shrugged, turned, sauntered to the steps, and called over his shoulder, "I like long drives."

I heard the recorded music cut off and Fitzy announce the last set followed by an upbeat number. I stayed on my bucket, my arms folded across my stomach, for three and a half songs, considering my options and trying not to think about Martin.

I ultimately decided I would think about Martin, but not yet. I'd wait until I was at home, just in case thinking about Martin made me cry. Also, thinking about Martin often led me to compose music. I was not above exploiting my memories of him or the feelings associated with unexpectedly seeing his face in the crowd for my own purposes. I liked to think of it as *channeling my angst.*

Yes, thinking about Martin later with a blank sheet of music and boxes of wine and tissues was definitely for the best.

Furthermore, I decided Abram could enjoy a nice, long car ride all by himself. I was going to take the train.

I pulled on my jacket, hooked my bag over my shoulder, grabbed another Coke from the cooler, and left via the backdoor. I didn't feel it necessary to leave a note; rather I would call Willis in the morning and apologize for flaking out.

I was ten steps from the backdoor when I saw him, or rather, the silhouette of him. The city lights were at his back, his face cast in total shadow.

I stopped. Everything stopped, or slowed, or suspended. It was a moment out of time, a singularity.

Then Martin moved and everything started again.

My heart slammed against my ribs, making me flinch and flush as he straightened away from the corner of the building. And I regretted my decision to postpone thinking about Martin. I should have sorted through my feelings inside, because now the momentum of my emotions choked me, leaving me defenseless. I couldn't actually form words. Martin hovered at the end of the alley, waiting, like he expected me to speak first.

But what could he possibly want to hear from me? We were together for one week and we'd ended badly. I'd purposefully avoided all mention of him—online and elsewhere. Even so, I couldn't help but know some details. Those details told me he'd withdrawn from college last semester and moved to New York. I guessed the rest—he was doing splendidly as a boy wonder venture capitalist.

Our mutual silence stretched and I grew certain he definitely expected me to break it, like we were in the middle of a conversation and it was my turn to speak, the ball in my court. Eventually it must've become obvious I wasn't going to be the one to modify the state of our conversation inertia.

He cleared his throat as one of his hands came to his jacket and he touched the front of his coat.

"Parker," he said. I felt the single word in my bones, though it sounded like a casual greeting. But it struck a chord because I never thought I'd hear his voice again.

I shifted on my feet, also cleared my throat, and tried to mimic his unaffected intonation. "Sandeke."

Another long moment passed where neither of us made a sound or movement. It was a bizarre situation to find oneself in for many reasons, not the least of which was all the busy goings-on surrounding us—people rushing by on the sidewalk, cars and buses and taxis whizzing behind him. I heard and felt the subway beneath my feet, the muffled music behind me, horns blaring, sirens whining. But we were still and silent.

Then abruptly, walking toward me, he said, "Do you need a ride?"

I shook my head. "No. No, thank you."

"I have a car. Do you live in the city?"

"No. I'm still in New Haven."

"I see…"

He stopped, now some five feet away. His gaze traveled up then down my body and he stuffed his hands in his pants pockets, his exquisite eyes remote and guarded when they landed on mine. I could see him clearly now beneath the light of the alley, and what I saw made my chest ache with the unfairness of him. I couldn't help but devour his features, recommitting his face, both familiar and unfamiliar, to memory.

He looked older, more like a man, and there was a new hardness in his face. He also might have been an inch taller, or maybe not. Perhaps he just carried himself differently. I didn't know how it was possible, but he felt even more imposing than he had before, and the gulf between us felt wider than ever.

This was hard. My heart hurt.

I thought I'd matured, grown from a repressed girl into a woman with an adequate amount of aplomb, worldliness; but I could see now that I still had a long way to go. Or perhaps I was always going to be part doofus. Perhaps it was in my genetic makeup to be a perpetual kid. Just standing near him made me feel like an imposter, like a poser trying to play grown up.

He was inspecting me. I could see the calculating gleam in his eyes; I was a problem that needed to be solved. I felt the heavy heat of embarrassment surge uncomfortably from my chest to my neck. Old Kaitlyn raised her hand and suggested I should hold very still and close my eyes until he got the message and left me alone, or thought I'd transformed into a large rock or a living statue.

Old Kaitlyn sure was a nut.

Whereas new Kaitlyn suspected that the chances of making it through the next ten minutes without bursting into tears were about three percent. New Kaitlyn was also very frustrated because she wanted to be over Martin Sandeke. She wanted to be able to see him without becoming an emotional pendulum.

However, both new Kaitlyn and old Kaitlyn wanted nothing to do with drama or angst or unwinnable arguments. I was over being a hot mess and wallowing. I had no idea why he was here, but every instinct told me to extract myself as soon as possible if I wanted to avoid future pitiful behavior.

I decided to embrace new Kaitlyn's frustration. Old Kaitlyn's suggested antics would get me nowhere. Whereas I could channel frustration into something useable, maybe even transform it into false bravery.

"Well, I'll see you around." I gave him a flat smile, thankful the alleyway was dim because it would mostly hide the impressive blush burning my cheeks, nose, forehead, and ears.

I moved as though to walk past him, and he quickly countered by stepping to the side, blocking my path. "Do you want to get a drink?"

"Oh, no thanks. I have a drink." I held up my Coke as evidence, trying to keep my voice steady and polite.

The corner of his mouth tugged to the side. "I meant, do you want to go somewhere to drink? Coffee?"

My eyes cut to his. "What about your date?"

"What about her?"

"Well, would she come with us?"

His gaze searched mine. "Would you be more or less likely to say yes if she did?"

This question hurt my heart and sounded like a riddle, so I ignored it. "Nah, I have work in the morning and I'm pretty tired."

"Work? Another show?"

"No." I pressed my lips together, not wanting to admit I was basically restarting college in the spring, and worked as a singing barista at the Bluesy Bean. But then I decided I was being a ninny and had nothing to be ashamed of. Martin had always been meant for a different world than mine. We were opposites, we always had been, always would be.

I lifted my chin and glanced beyond him as I explained, "You know that coffee shop with the blue bean hanging over the door? The one next to the row of bars on Crown Street?" I forced myself to meet his gaze again, adding, "Well, I work there now. I'm one of the singing baristas." I was pleased I was able to admit this without a fresh wave of embarrassment. As well, my voice sounded conversational and entirely normal.

His eyebrows furrowed, transforming his achingly handsome face into a sexy scowl. "You're working at a coffee shop? Why?" he demanded.

I shrugged. "Why do people work? To make money."

"Did your mother cut you off? After—"

I interrupted him, not wanting to hear what came after *after*. "No. Not at all. Nothing like that. I just—"

I stopped myself from explaining, abruptly wondering why we were talking at all. What was the point of this exercise in masochism? I had a nine-month-old wound that felt remarkably fresh. A dull ache had set up camp in my chest and was expanding, inflating to my throat, and pressing against my ribs.

"Listen." I sighed as I glanced beyond him again, my eyes beginning to sting. Now that the shock was wearing off, looking at him was becoming increasingly difficult. "I need to go. I have a train to catch."

"I'll drive you."

"No, thank you."

"Parker, let me drive you."

"No."

"Why not?" he asked quietly, sounding less pushy than curious.

I was about to respond with the truth, that being around him made me feel like I'd made no progress over the last nine months; that I was at a minimum infatuated with him if not still completely in love with him; that I had no desire to cry in his car. I had no desire to cry anywhere ever again.

But we were interrupted by the sound of a door closing, sauntering footsteps, and Abram tossing his arm over my shoulder.

I glanced up at my bandmate, confused by his sudden closeness. "Because she already has a ride," he drawled.

CHAPTER 2
Acid-Base Equilibria

IT TOOK MY brain five stunned seconds to engage and realize the ramifications of Abram's appearance and announcement. In the sixth second I pushed Abram off and away.

First of all, the implication was clearly that we were together.

In order to clarify, I announced loudly, "He's not my boyfriend. We're not dating."

Secondly, Martin was no longer looking at my face; he was looking at the spot where Abram's hand had rested on my shoulder.

And thirdly, my life was officially a cliché. I wondered if there were some unseen director just around the corner saying things like, *Okay, cue the new love interest. That's right, we want him to walk onto the scene at the worst possible moment.*

"But you still want me to give you a ride?" Abram asked, his tone chock full of zealously good-natured solicitousness.

"No. I don't want a ride. I don't want any rides. No rides for this girl." I pointed to myself with my thumbs, burning a brighter shade of red.

Martin's eyes flickered to mine and narrowed. I was being scrutinized.

Abram chuckled and nudged me flirtatiously with his elbow. He turned his smile to Martin. Martin was not smiling.

"Hi. I'm Abram. Katy's *bassist.*"

I shook myself and realized I'd made no introductions. "Right. Martin, this is Abram. He plays bass in the band. Abram, this is…Martin."

"Pleasure to meet you, Martin," Abram said, like it truly was a pleasure and offered his hand.

Martin's glare focused on the offered hand—the same hand that had seconds ago rested on my shoulder—then he lifted his gaze to Abram's. He reached forward and accepted Abram's hand for a shake. It was one of those weird, man handshakes that last too long, and where the hands turn a little white at the knuckles.

After several seconds I couldn't take it any longer. This was Martin Sandeke, grand Jedi Master of the short-tempered fist fight. *Ye Martin of old* never needed a reason to lose his temper. Granted, I hadn't seen him in almost nine months. But the last thing I needed was Abram with a busted jaw or—worse—a hurt hand. Willis might never forgive me.

So I reached forward, pulled them apart, and tugged Martin toward the street. "Aaaand we're done. Martin, would you be so kind as to drive me to Grand Central station?"

"You've got an impressive grip for such a pretty stockbroker," Abram yelled after us.

"I'm not a stockbroker, asshole." Martin's voice was low and belied the intensity of his irritation; I could feel hesitation in his steps, like he wanted to turn around and show Abram the meaning of an impressive grip, so I linked my arm through his and increased my pace.

Abram's laughter followed us as far as the street and I turned right even though I had no idea where his car was parked. Being so close to him was disconcerting and set my heart racing. We made it to the end of the block before Martin used my hold on his arm to stop us and pull us to the corner, out of the pedestrian traffic.

"Where are you going?"

I released him and took a step back, grateful for the space. "I don't know. I just wanted to get you away from Abram."

Martin's gaze swept over my face. "Why? Does he bother you often?"

"No, not at all. He's fine, and we get along fine. I think he was just trying to be helpful, in his own weird way."

He was still scrutinizing me as he shifted a step closer. "You two...ever...?"

I released a pained sigh when I understood what he was asking, deciding the evening had taken a sharp turn in the direction of completely preposterous. I closed my eyes, fought the urge to cover my face.

I won. I didn't cover my face. But I did take a minute to collect myself before saying, "That's none of your business. You said you didn't mind giving me a ride to the station." I opened my eyes but didn't manage to lift my gaze above his chin. "Will you please take me to Grand Central station so I can catch the train home?"

I could tell he wanted to say more, he wanted to yell, scream, and rage, and I couldn't wrap my mind around the implications of his short fuse, why he might be angry. I reminded myself that this was Martin Sandeke, who always expected people to jump when he said so, who'd never had a problem yelling at females and males and turtles and grass and furniture. I braced for his tantrum.

Instead he took a deep breath, silent but visible in the rising and falling of his chest, and nodded. "Yes. It would be my pleasure to give you a ride to the station."

I squinted at him, at his oddly polite words and tone. "Martin...?"

"Parker."

"Is there anything else you'd like to say before we're within the confines of your automobile? Anything loud perhaps?"

He shook his head and pulled his leather gloves out of his coat pocket, his tone soft, gentle even. "You should wear these. It's cold."

"You want to say something. What is it?"

"Weren't you the one who always told me..."

Martin reached for one of my hands and I lost my breath when his skin came in contact with mine. I'm not going to lie, my pants went a little crazy, and my heart did a flip then thumped uncomfortably—all signs I was still intensely in lust with him. He hesitated, his thumb drawing a gentle line from my wrist to the center of my palm, then he slid the large glove over my fingers with more care than necessary. They were warm from his pocket.

When he'd slipped both gloves in place he lifted his bewitching eyes and finished his thought. "I can't always have what I want."

***

THE CAR RIDE lasted less than fifteen minutes and was spent in wordless silence. Of note, it was also spent in a super fancy luxury automobile. I didn't know the make or model, but the dials were in Italian, the seats were buttery-soft leather, and when he accelerated it made a really satisfying *vroooom* sound.

I'm not ashamed to admit I took off one of the gloves just so I could caress his taut...leather seats.

When we arrived at the station I turned to him, taking off the second glove, and said benignly, "Thank you for the ride."

He gave me his profile as he nodded, his tone casual and polite. "No problem, any time."

Confused by his weird politeness, and feeling remarkably empty though my heart had set up camp in my throat, I placed his gloves on the armrest between us and opened the door to leave.

Then he said, "I read The Lord of the Rings."

I paused, my car door half open, and twisted to face him. "You did...?"

"Yes." He cleared his throat then met my stare; his was guarded, bracing. "I did."

"What did you think?"

"It was good…" Martin's eyes lost focus and moved to the headrest next to my face. "Slow at first. I thought they were never going to get out of that Hobbit village."

"Ah, yes. It only took them ten thousand pages and three thousand verses of elf songs."

He smirked. "Give or take a thousand."

I smiled, glanced down at my fingers where they twisted the strap of my bag.

I was surprised he'd read it and wasn't sure what it meant, if it meant anything. I was still pondering this revelation when his next words shocked the heck out of me.

"I don't think Frodo was responsible for the destruction of the ring."

My gaze jumped to his and I found Martin watching me attentively, again as though he was scrutinizing me. I struggled with my bewilderment for several seconds at his referencing our conversation from so many months ago.

Finally I managed to sputter, "You…you think Sam is ultimately responsible then?"

"No," he answered thoughtfully and then paused; he seemed to be memorizing my expression before continuing. "I think one couldn't have done it without the other. I think Frodo needed Sam as much as Sam needed Frodo, maybe even more."

I don't know why, but my eyes misted over even though I wasn't in danger of crying.

I gave him a soft smile, letting him see my pleased astonishment, and agreed quietly, "I think so, too."

We stared at each other and I felt something pass between us. I surmised it was closure because it felt peaceful and good. We'd shared a beautiful week. Because of him I was on a new path, a path I loved. He'd woken me up, even if I was kicking and screaming the whole time, and even if it broke my heart in the process.

Maybe we weren't meant for each other, but I finally realized that our time together wasn't a waste. It changed me and I would always be grateful to him for that, even if we'd parted under painful circumstances.

"Thank you," I said suddenly, breaking the moment.

"For what?"

I realized I couldn't say, *Thank you for waking me up to my passion* without sounding wacko, so instead I said, "For reading the book, I guess. And for the ride to the station." I tossed my thumb over my shoulder, my hand landing on the door to push it farther open.

"Right." He swallowed, glancing behind me. "You're welcome."

"I should go."

"Right." He nodded, giving me a flat smile and his profile.

"Goodbye, Martin."

I paused for a second, waiting for him to say goodbye, but he didn't. His jaw was set and his eyes were studying his rearview mirror. So I opened the door all the way and climbed out of his fancy car, shut it, and turned to Grand Central station.

I didn't hear him pull into traffic, but I didn't look back to check. I'd already spent too much time looking backward.

CHAPTER 3
Concentrations of Solutions

SAM LIKED TO go '80s dancing on Thursday nights with several of her tennis pals. I'd never gone with her because I had no level of confidence in my non-ballroom dancing skills. But part of my theoretical state included opening myself up to new experiences, but not being so open-minded that my brain fell out.

Therefore, on Thursday night when Sam asked me if I wanted to go '80s dancing, I said yes.

I discovered that club dancing was basically just moving around however the heck I wanted; furthermore, I discovered it was a lot of fun. Sure, weird guys would sometimes sidle up to our cluster and try to cop a feel or insinuate themselves in the circle, especially since girls outnumbered the guys in our group. I quickly learned how to avoid stranger danger behavior by latching on to one of the three male tennis players who tagged along until the uninvited dude moved on.

This worked perfectly until the end of the night when Landon, one of the three tennis guys, asked for my number. I panicked and gave it to him as Sam watched on with an amused smirk.

As soon as we were back in our apartment, Sam started sniggering.

"What?"

"You're a good dancer," she said, eyeballing me.

"Thanks...?"

"What did you think of Kara?"

I had to really, really concentrate to remember which of the girls she was referencing. "Was Kara the one with pink hair?"

"No, Kara was the one with the Dungeons and Dragons mini dress."

"Oh! Kara, yes. I liked her."

"Well, she's looking for a place to stay next semester. How do you feel about another roommate?"

"Would we move?"

"Yeah, but I think there's a three-bedroom becoming available in our building sometime in February."

I scrunched my face, wrinkling my nose. "Can I think about it? You know how particular I am. Can I meet her a few more times? Hang out? See what she thinks of the chore chart and angry acoustic guitar music?"

"Sure. That makes sense. I'll set something up after New Year's." Sam began eyeballing me again. "Speaking of you being particular—sooooo Landon, huh?"

I gave her a pained look. "I didn't know how to say no. He's the first guy in my twenty years on this planet who has ever asked for my number."

"Technically he's not the first."

I grumbled, but said nothing.

"You didn't have a problem saying no to Martin last year in chemistry lab when he asked."

"But I thought Martin was a jerk. It's easy to say no to a jerk. Plus he never helped with tabulations so I felt no guilt. Landon seems like a nice guy. It's hard to say no when a nice guy asks so nicely, and he spent most of the night helping me keep creepers at bay."

"So you gave Landon your number because he was helpful and nice?"

"I don't know…maybe? I feel like I should reward his nice behavior." I hung my jacket up in the hall closet, noting I had two jackets on the rack and the rest were Sam's.

Sam shook her head, walking past me to the kitchen and calling over her shoulder, "When he calls don't go out with him. He's actually a douche canoe. And he's a big baby on the court."

"Then why did you invite him?" I followed her, abruptly in the mood for Cheesy Poofs dipped in Nutella.

"Because he's tall and menacing looking. His face reminds me of the eagle news reporter from the Muppets."

"He does have thick eyebrows, I should give him the name of the lady who waxes mine." I crossed to the cabinet and searched for the ingredients for my junk food fix. I was still down seventeen pounds from last year. I'd gained some back over the summer, but running around at the coffee shop and playing gigs at night kept me busy and cut into my cookie time.

"They're like caterpillars sitting on his face, I bet they're fuzzy…but forget Landon for a minute. What I want to know is, does this mean you're finally over Martin?"

I lamented the contents of the cabinet pitifully, partially because there was no Nutella and partially because I hadn't told Sam about my run-in with Martin over the previous weekend.

"What's wrong?"

"There's no Nutella, and I'm in the mood for Cheesy Poofs dipped in Nutella—"

"That's disgusting."

"—and I saw Martin last Saturday."

"Whoa! Wait, what?" She spun on me, her mouth open, her eyes wide.

"There's no Nutella—"

"Don't be clowning me. You know I want to hear about Martin, not your Nutella woes. You saw him? Where? When? How come you didn't tell me?"

I grabbed the Cheesy Poofs from the cabinet and turned to face her, feeling weary and wary of the subject already. "I don't know why I didn't tell you. I guess I needed to…no, that's not right. I think I didn't tell you because we kind of gave each other closure and I needed a few days to process it."

Her eyes abruptly narrowed. "He gave you 'closure'?"

"Yeah. At least I think he was trying to. Anyway, it doesn't matter. Seeing him was a total fluke. He was at a gig we were playing in New York. We talked a little, he drove me to the train station, then we said goodbye."

Actually, I said goodbye. He didn't say anything. But I'd assumed his goodbye was implied. As such, I felt comfortable with my version of the story.

Sam looked me up and down, her face twisted in a way that betrayed her disbelief and/or confusion with my story. At length she said, "Huh…that's weird."

"Why is that weird? Honestly it was kind of nice. We were both *adulting* like adult adults who behaved like adults."

"It's weird because of that one interview he gave in the fitness magazine over the summer. I think it was in Men's Health. Did you ever read that, by the way?"

I shook my head, taking a bite of a poof and lamenting the obnoxiously crunchy sound it made; I spoke around my chewing, orange cheesy food dust puffing from my mouth like a cloud. "No. Never read it."

"Hmm…"

I ate another poof as she studied me. *Crunch, crunch, crunch.*

I was just about to stuff my face with another when she said, "It's about you, you know."

"I… What?" I did not eat the poof. Instead I held it in front of my mouth as I frowned at my best friend.

"The interview, it's about you. Well, not the whole thing. Just…half of it."

I choked on nothing and could feel my eyes bug out of my head. "Wait, what? What? Why? What?"

"If you're feeling over him then it might not be a good idea to read it."

I stared at her, my mouth opening and closing as I struggled for words. Finally I settled on, "What did he say?"

"Are you going to read it?"

"Should I?"

"Are you over him?"

Was I?

Not knowing how to answer, I ate the suspended cheese-rice-puffed-food. This time the crunch felt satisfying instead of obnoxious, like an exclamation mark.

"Don't read it," she said suddenly.

"Maybe I want to."

"Then read it."

"Maybe I shouldn't."

She grinned. "Then don't."

***

I DIDN'T READ Martin's interview. At least, I hadn't read it as of Saturday night.

Friday and Saturday were busy; we played four gigs. Two afternoon holiday parties in Boston, one evening wedding in Yonkers, and one crazy late night Bat Mitzvah on Saturday in New Haven.

As well, I had a very odd conversation with Abram after the third set at the Yonkers wedding; it started with him saying, "What you need is a rebound guy."

I glanced over my shoulder, found him standing just to my right, facing me, his mouth curved in its perma-smirk.

"You mean for basketball?"

His smirk became a grin. "No. Not for basketball. For getting over that stockbroker douchebag."

I scrunched my face at Abram and sipped my Coke. "What are you talking about?"

He shifted a half step forward, lowering his voice. "A warm body, someone who's good at kissing and fucking. You need a rebound lay."

"*Oooohhhh…*" His meaning finally sank in, which only made me nervously gulp my Coke. My eyes grew wide as I tried to look everywhere but at him and my brain attempted to figure out how to extract myself from this conversation. His comment sounded a lot like, *Hey, I'd like to have sex with you to help you get over your boyfriend. Use me.*

"I'm not offering," he clarified, correctly guessing that my abrupt bout of anxiety had everything to do with my assumption he wanted to be my rebound guy. I relaxed a bit, but then he added, "Though I wouldn't mind being the guy after the rebound guy."

I choked on my Coke.

He laughed, a deep, baritone laugh that sounded more sinister than merry, and he patted my back. "Hey, are you okay?"

I nodded, sucking in air through my nose, then coughing again.

"Did I surprise you?" His dark eyes were warm and still held his earlier laughter.

I continued nodding as his hand stopped patting my back and switched to stroking it instead. I shivered, because his hot palm and capable fingers against the thin material of my tuxedo shirt felt good and was sending little tingles along my spine; as well he was standing in my personal space, his magnetic maleness making me a bit dizzy.

I stepped away and caught his arm, halting his movements.

"So, I'm…that is to say, I'm—"

"You're not over the douchebag," he supplied, which wasn't what I was going to say; nevertheless it was the truth.

"No. I guess I'm not." My voice was raspy from my coughing fit.

"Then take my advice and get laid. Let someone else make you feel good. Hell, I bet Fitzy would cream himself at the thought."

I winced. "I don't like the idea of using people." Plus I didn't like the idea of having sex with someone when I wasn't in love, but if I'd said that to Abram, I assumed he would make fun of me.

"You need to. Sure, be upfront about the arrangement. Let him—whoever him is—know that it's a no-strings kind of thing. But do yourself a favor, and find a rebound guy. Otherwise it'll be years before you get over your ex."

I studied Abram for a long moment, releasing his arm and leaning away, wanting to really see him. He wasn't teasing; in fact, he appeared to be speaking from experience.

"How many rebound girls have you been with, Abram?"

His smirk was back, but it was somehow less sharp. "I've lost count."

"And have they helped?"

"Yeah. I mean, they *have* helped. I'm not nearly as miserable and pathetic as I was before…" He trailed off, and his smirk waned, his eyes turning serious. "But I'm not going to rebound forever."

"When will you stop?"

"When I see someone who's worth hurting for again. Someone worth the risk." He lifted his hand and tucked several strands of hair behind my ear, his fingers lingering on my throat. "Or she finally sees me."

***

BY THE TIME my alarm went off on Sunday morning for my shift at the Bluesy Bean, I was cursing Sam for telling me that Martin's interview was about me, or half about me.

I was also cursing Abram for planting strange ideas in my head—about a rebound guy, about him as a potential post-rebound guy. I was all mixed up. I was attracted to Abram, but hadn't allowed those feelings to deepen beyond passing interest. But what if I let myself actually get to know him? What if I *liked* him?

I was relieved to find my co-worker Chelsea already on the register when I arrived.

"You're early," she sang, giving me a bright smile.

"I thought I was late."

"No. Ten minutes early. It's been really quiet so far." She pulled her long, thick, blue-tinted braid over her shoulder.

I fastened my apron and took stock of our milk supply. "If today is anything like last Sunday, we can expect a mad rush with all the

Christmas shoppers."

"That means Christmas carol requests. You'll have to sing with me." Chelsea gave me a wink and a smile.

I gave her a smile that likely looked more like a grimace. "Oh…yay."

She laughed, then turned her attention to the front of the store where two early morning customers had just entered.

I kind of loved Chelsea…from a distance. I think everyone loved Chelsea from a distance. She was charming, incredibly talented, clever, and crazy fun. As well, she had one of the most beautiful soprano voices I'd ever heard. She was also thrice divorced at the age of twenty-eight. Given the Marilyn Monroe resemblance of both her face and body, men loved her. They loved her a whole lot.

But I suspected Chelsea loved the stage and the thrill of admiration. When she wasn't singing for wages at the local community theater, she was singing for tips at the Bluesy Bean, flirting with her legion of admirers. I was grateful that she craved the spotlight; her willingness to be the center of attention allowed me to settle into a comfortable zone.

And speaking of zones, since starting at the coffee shop three weeks ago, I found it was easy to zone out while making lattes and cappuccinos. Cooking in general, and making coffee specifically, was a lot like chemistry lab. Thus, as I set to work, I was able to meditate on the carousel of pros and cons circling around my brain.

Pro - if I read Martin's interview, then I could stop obsessing about whether or not I should read the interview.

Con - if I read Martin's interview, I might start obsessing about the content of the interview.

And so the day proceeded in this way and all was well. More precisely, all was relatively normal until just after the mid-afternoon rush died down. I was cleaning up the mess associated with coffee grounds and drippings accumulating over time on a tile floor when I heard Chelsea say under her breath, "We've got a Chris Pine at twelve o'clock."

Chelsea had a labeling system for men.

She told me she was looking for a Brad Pitt (older version) or a Chris Pine (younger version). Someone charismatic, beautiful, smart, wealthy, and dedicated to a cause other than himself. I asked her if she'd ever considered looking for a Neil deGrasse Tyson or a Francis Collins. Someone who wasn't necessarily physically stunning, but whose brain and goodness more than made up for any external lack of overt attractiveness.

She'd snorted at me, rolled her eyes, and said, "If I have to have sex with the guy, I don't want to have to do it in the dark all the time."

It was an interesting perspective…one which I found disturbing. On one hand I understood why attraction was an essential element of chemistry between two people. But her inability or unwillingness to appreciate attractiveness beyond the skin and see the person as a whole made me feel a little sorry for her.

Presently, curious about her Chris Pine, I straightened from my task and tried to nonchalantly glance over the coffee makers. That's when I spotted Martin walking into the café.

My eyes widened in surprise and I ducked back behind the espresso machine, shock and a strange panic keeping me motionless for several seconds while I had a silent argument with myself:

What in the name of the cosmos is he doing here?

Perhaps it's a coincidence.

What am I supposed to do???

…just act normal.

What's normal?

I briefly considered staying hidden for as long as possible, but then I realized it would be weirder to suddenly appear once he ordered his drink than to gradually straighten now.

Maybe I could pretend I was cleaning the floor…which is what I was doing just moments ago, before he walked in.

Or maybe I could actually finish cleaning the floor.

This idea seemed to make the most sense, so that's what I did.

Unfortunately, cleaning the floor only took me five more seconds. So when I straightened, I struggled to act normal. I didn't know what to do or where to look and had abruptly forgotten how to breathe and stand with my arms at my sides. Yet even as a fierce blush lifted to my cheeks, I was determined to make the imminent encounter as benign as possible.

"Welcome to the Bluesy Bean. What can I get you?" I heard Chelsea say using her husky voice.

I decided I just needed to go through the motions of normalcy, do what I would normally do. So I picked up the towel I'd been using to mop the floor. I turned and deposited it in the bucket under the sink, then moved to wash my hands.

"I'll have a large Americano." Martin's voice caused a shiver of awareness to race down my spine. I endeavored to ignore it.

"Room for cream?"

"No."

I finished washing my hands and turned back to my machine, refilled the espresso grounds, and set the dial. In less than ten seconds I was going to have to reach over and grab his cup and I would be fine. I didn't know why my heart and brain were freaking out so much.

"Really? How about sugar?" In my peripheral vision I saw Chelsea leaning on the counter. She often did this to take full advantage of her low-cut top.

"What? No. No sugar."

"Oh. I was just curious how you take your coffee. I like mine sweet and creamy."

There was a distinct pause, a thick silence difficult to ignore. It lengthened, grew, then suddenly felt untenable. So I glanced up and found Chelsea watching me, her eyes narrowed in confusion. Then I glanced at Martin. He was watching me, too.

His stare was pointed, like he'd been watching me for longer than a few seconds and was waiting for me to look at him.

All at once I felt caught.

"Oh... Hi, Martin." My acting skills were pathetic, but I tried my best at genuine surprise. It might have helped that I was feeling a little out of breath.

"I was hoping you'd be working today." Still looking at me, he passed Chelsea a twenty.

Her eyes bounced between us, narrowing more.

"That's right, I forgot. I told you I worked here."

"Are you going to make my coffee?" He grinned, leaving his twenty on the counter for Chelsea to pick up, and floated closer to where I was mostly hidden by the machines. But I wasn't really hidden from him because he was so tall. He could easily see over the row of contraptions. Realizing this, I stopped twisting my fingers and reached for a large cup.

"Yes. I am your barista at this fine establishment. It is my pleasure to make you coffee." I lamented the fact that, due to my uneasiness, I sounded like an android.

He must've noticed my odd speech pattern too, because he asked, "Do you always talk like that?"

"Like what? Like Mr. Roboto?"

"No, like awesome."

My lips parted and I blinked at him, his comment catching me completely off guard. When his eyes began to dance and his grin widened, I realized he was using our past to tease me. This might have pissed me off two weeks ago, Martin thinking he had the right to tease me about anything, but the fact that he'd given me his gloves when I was cold and read The Lord of the Rings somehow made his teasing not...bad.

"You're weird," I blabbered unthinkingly and shook my head at him and his bizarre teasing. But I had to twist my lips to the side to keep from returning his contagious smile. "Why are you here, weirdo?"

He seemed pleased with my name-calling and drifted closer until he was directly in front of me, only the machines between us. "I want to talk to you. Do you have a break soon?"

"Umm..." I stalled by commencing coffee creation; I flipped the brew switch and moved two doppio cups under the dual espresso dispenser.

I was way overdue for a break. Chelsea had taken three, and I'd taken one. I glanced at Chelsea, found her watching us with a frown. It wasn't an angry frown or a sinister frown; rather, it was a *the world has ceased making sense* frown. Her brain was obviously working overtime trying to figure out how I knew her Chris Pine, aka my Martin Sandeke.

"S-s-s-sure. Let me finish your Americano and I'll make myself some tea. Go grab a table." I tilted my chin to the one by the window, in the center of the café.

"Good. Will you please bring me a muffin? I haven't eaten since breakfast."

I could only nod and stare at him, again caught off guard by his conversational tone—like we were old friends—as well as the use of the word *please*. The smile he gave me before he departed was softer, smaller, but somehow more devastating than his others. As I watched him ignore the spot I'd indicated in favor of a very private table in the corner, I mulled over his strange behavior.

The smiling.

The teasing.

The manners.

The lack of bluntness and demands.

It was all very disconcerting.

Disconcerting, distressing, confusing, alarming, perplexing, odd…

***

"YOU MAKE GOOD coffee." Martin sipped his hot beverage, his eyes watching me over the rim.

"Technically I just press the buttons." I was having difficulty relaxing beneath his gaze, so I fidgeted with my tea cup and spoon.

"Parker, just take the compliment and say thank you."

"I won't. I won't take it because I don't deserve it. The machines make good coffee, as do the bean growers and bean roasters."

His face told me he thought I was being ridiculous. "Fine, then you're an excellent button pusher."

"Thank you. I accept the compliment and acknowledge that I excel at pushing buttons."

"Especially my buttons." He paired this with a smirk and an eyebrow lift.

I huffed, irritated I'd walked right into that verbal trap, and yet reluctantly amused by the word play. "Very funny, Sandeke."

His smirk became a smile. Then he laughed and my heart gave a little leap.

Suddenly, it was nine months ago and we were on a plane headed for the island. I was faced with the heady sight of a happy Martin. It was a reminder that happiness on Martin was a revelation of beauty and physical perfection married to excellent and infectious good-mood vibes.

But this time I didn't laugh. My heart felt tender and wary of this Martin, because he was so easy to like. So I crossed my arms over my chest, protecting myself from the onslaught of his magnetic charisma, and waited for his laughter to recede.

When he saw I wasn't charmed, his smile faded and he straightened in his seat, clearing his throat as though he were about to speak.

I spoke first, wanting to get right to the point. "Why are you here? What do you want to talk about?"

He must've read something in my expression, perhaps a hardness in my eyes that told him I was low on patience, because when he spoke next, everything about his demeanor changed.

His eyes grew sharp, the set of his jaw rigid, and his shoulders leaned back in the chair, making him appear taller, more imposing, and yet relaxed at the same time. Based on this body language and what I knew about power dynamics from watching my mother, I surmised we were about to enter into a negotiation.

I was quickly proven correct.

"I want to discuss the terms of our friendship."

I stared at him, careful to keep my face devoid of expression, even though I wanted to yell, *WHAT THE HELL ARE YOU TALKING ABOUT?*

Instead I said, "What friendship?"

"The one you promised would always be mine if I ever wanted it, no matter what happened between us."

This made me blink several times, succeeded in cracking my calm exterior, but I managed to say in a steady voice, "You can't be serious."

"I am. I'm completely serious. You promised I would always have *a safe place* with you, and now I want that safe place."

This was the Martin I remembered. This was the unyielding, demanding, blunt boy that had stolen then broken my heart.

I gritted my teeth and willed the rising tide of so many different emotions to stay buried. Obviously anger was the first, the strongest to swell in my chest and try to choke me. Again, he must've seen something shift or build in my expression because, and to my astonishment, he leaned forward and his austere business façade yielded, his eyes turned beseeching.

"Listen, I'm not here to take more than you're willing to offer. Obviously you can tell me to go fuck myself. All I'm asking for is a chance to be your friend. Because, even though things between us didn't end well, I still trust and respect you more than anyone I've ever met. You are," he paused, gathered a deep breath, his gaze searching as it skated over my face, "Kaitlyn, you are incredibly honorable, and reasonable, and good. I could really use your advice. I could really use some honorable and good in my life."

"But not reason?" I questioned, stalling, not sure what to make of this impassioned speech.

"No. I have plenty of reason. But without honor and goodness, reason isn't worth much."

My lips parted in surprise and I felt my mask of indifference slip at his shockingly wise words. He looked earnest and focused and I knew I was already teetering on the edge of acceptance.

But the acrid taste of past heartbreak and the bitterness of his previous betrayal held me back, keeping my altruistic instincts from taking over.

And something else, something petty and entirely based on vanity.

When we had this conversation in the past, at the cottage on the island, he'd told me at the time that he could never be indifferent enough to be my friend. That he would always want me too fiercely to settle for just friendship.

If he wanted to be friends now, that could only mean he'd become indifferent to me. He didn't want *me* anymore. And that made my vain, selfish heart hurt. This realization stung, because I couldn't imagine being able to achieve the same indifference toward him.

"You don't have to answer me now." His gaze and tone were steady, sensible.

I wanted to tell him he'd hurt me too deeply, that this newfound indifference toward me that allowed him to ask for friendship was hurting me now. But I couldn't. Because that would be giving him the knowledge he still had power over my feelings.

Instead I opted to make the decision his and, by doing so, I hoped it would push him away. "Let's say I only agree to be your friend if you tell the world your father is an evil asshole and that our families were never close, that he never had influence over my mother. What would you do?"

I didn't expect Martin to grin, but that's what he did as he quickly replied, "Parker, I already did that. I did that, like, two months ago."

Again I felt my mask slip and I blinked at him in astonishment. "You did?"

"Yes. The interview was in the Washington Post. Haven't you read any of the interviews I've given?"

I shook my head and answered honestly, "No. I haven't. I've been avoiding them."

"None of them?" Something like dawning realization cast a shadow over his features.

Again I shook my head. "No. I didn't…" I took a deep breath and forced myself to continue the thought, "I didn't want to know about you. I didn't want to know what you were doing."

This was mostly because given how well and unaffected he'd looked the last time I saw him, and how wretched and heartbroken I'd been, I assumed he'd quickly moved on with his life, maybe even dated other women. In fact, given the fact he had a date last week at my show, I was now certain he'd dated other women.

I didn't need to see magazine spreads and page sixes of Martin Sandeke, the most eligible bachelor of the universe, hitting the town with his legion of admirers.

Meanwhile I hadn't been able to move on.

He stared at me for a long moment, his grin waning into a pensive frown.

"Are you going to read them?"

I shrugged, tried to look unaffected. "Probably not."

Martin's open gaze morphed into an irritated glare at my statement.

Abruptly he said, "I searched everywhere trying to find out about you, what you were doing, how you were. That's how I found your band."

"My band? Wait, what?"

"I hired your band to play that party last week. Well, my PA did. It was for a group of startups focused on rural technology education initiatives. It's a new project of mine."

I didn't hear anything after, *I hired your band to play that party last week.*

"Why would you do that?"

"For the same reason I'm sitting here right now." Martin sounded like he was on the border of exasperated and angry.

My gaze drifted to the table between us as I tried to sort through this mountain of surprising information. He hired my band? Why? To have the opportunity to talk to me? But then he brought a date to the event? What the what?

But before I made it very far, he stood, drawing my attention and focus back to him. He'd pulled out his wallet.

"Listen, you take some time. You think about it. Here's my number."

I accepted his card without looking at it as I was too busy staring at him with muddled incredulity.

Dumbly I said, "You have a card?"

"Yes. It has my personal cell phone number. If I don't hear from you I'll stop by again next week."

"So…you what? Have other business cards that have a different number on them? Ones without your personal cell phone number?" Leave it to me to be caught up in the details.

His frown intensified, as though I'd asked a trick question, then he eventually responded, "Yes. My other cards have the number of my PA. So what?"

"You realize you're a twenty-one-year-old with two different business cards, right? And a PA. And likely a corner office someplace." This was all coming out of my mouth stream of consciousness, as I was thinking and speaking at the same time.

He blinked at me, shook his head like he didn't understand my meaning, like *of course* he had a corner office.

"That makes you both impressive and ridiculous. Please tell me your towels aren't monogrammed."

Martin set his jaw as he recognized my meaning, but I could see the reluctant smile in his eyes as he peered down at me.

"They are monogrammed, aren't they? And you've probably taken to calling them 'linens.'"

His lips pressed together in a firm but rueful line. Martin crossed his arms and said, "Is this what I can expect from our friendship? You giving me shit about my linens?"

"Absolutely," I said, then indicated to his wrist with my chin, "and your fancy watches."

"So, is that a yes?" he pushed, lifting a single eyebrow.

"It's a...it's a maybe."

CHAPTER 4
Avogadro's Number and the Mole

NOW THAT I was working, I typically didn't have a chance to look at the agenda for the weekly family call until ten minutes before I was supposed to dial in. We'd shifted the time due to my new work schedule, which was nice. But it also meant I was rushing around just before, and I never seemed to have enough time to review the materials.

This wasn't usually a problem. However, today, five minutes before I was supposed to call into Skype, I read the agenda and I spotted a new item.

Benefit and Campaign Fundraiser - Kaitlyn to perform.

I frowned at the topic. But there was nothing to do about it, no reason to ask for clarification ahead of time since our meeting was just about to start. So I highlighted the line and wrote a big question mark on my paper copy of the agenda. Then I opened the Skype session and dialed in.

"Hello?" I heard George, my mother's PA, on the line. He hadn't activated the video yet.

"Hey, George. It's Kaitlyn."

"Yes. I see you. Let me switch on the video." I heard some rustling as he added, "Your mother is on the phone with Senator Peterson, trying to talk him off the ledge. She'll be right back and then we can get started. Your father was called into surgery."

"Sounds good." I scanned the rest of the agenda. Everything else looked fine. Once his face popped up on my computer screen I asked, "Hey, George. I have a question about one of the new items on the agenda, the one about the benefit and fundraiser."

"Oh, yes. Your mother has a campaign fundraiser coming up in May. The week after is a benefit concert for Children's Charities. Both are in New York. She thought it would be good for you to perform at one or both."

I saw my expression in the little box located in the bottom right corner of my computer screen. I looked just as surprised as I felt. But what my expression didn't show was the spike of panic. The idea of performing in front of a crowd of people who knew who I was, who my mother was, held absolutely no allure for me. Being just another member of a random band meant I was anonymous. But being Senator Parker's daughter, on stage in front of hundreds or thousands of people sounded horrible and terrifying.

"Really? That seems strange." My voice cracked a little.

He shrugged, scratching the top of his bald head. "No. Not if you think about it. You've always been gifted with music. I remember when you were thirteen and you taught yourself all of Beethoven's sonatas without sheet music. When music was just a hobby for you, asking you to perform would have been an exploitation of your private life. But now that it's your chosen career, this will be beneficial for you both."

That's what I liked about George, he was a straight shooter, never minced (or chopped) words, just said things plain and simple.

My mother popped into the picture and gave me a wide smile as she adjusted the computer so they were both visible. "Did George tell you about William?"

"Yes, Dad was called in," I said.

"Since he can't make it today we'll skip over the house stuff and hold it until the next meeting," my mother clarified, still smiling warmly. She looked so happy to see me.

"Sounds good." I smiled back.

This was only our second week using Skype instead of a dedicated conference line (with no video) and I really liked it. I liked seeing my mom and dad (and George); it made them feel more real. I liked they could see me and see I was doing well.

"We were just talking about agenda item four," George said, drawing my mother's attention to a piece of paper he had placed in front of her on the table.

"Oh, yes." Mom glanced at me, her smile even wider. I could see the excitement in her eyes. "Let me tell you about this, I think it's a great opportunity for you."

"George already filled me in on the basics. You want me to perform in front of people for a campaign fundraiser and for a benefit, both in New York in May?"

"Yes, well, that's the gist of it. There will be a large number of industry professionals present, people from Broadway and Hollywood at both events. I know you have your little wedding band, but I also know you're capable of so much more than that. Just think of it as a way to network and make connections for your career."

I tried to keep my face from betraying the pang I felt when she'd said *little band*. I know she didn't mean anything by it, because—to her—it was a little band. Whereas for me it was a giant leap of self-actualization.

I had to clear my throat of emotion before responding. "Would I be performing with others? As part of an ensemble? Would there be practices leading up to the performances?"

"No. You'd be solo, and hopefully playing one of your own compositions if you can have that ready in time. I'm sure it won't be a problem for you." She was distracted as she answered because her cell phone was ringing again; she didn't see me sit back in my chair or the color drain from my face.

"I'm so sorry, Kaitlyn, but I have to take this call." She turned an apologetic and frustrated gaze to the computer screen. "We'll hold the rest of the agenda until after the holidays."

I nodded, relieved I would be given a reprieve from having to give her an answer. She stood up again as she answered her cell phone, leaving George and I on the call.

"Next week is Christmas," George noted absentmindedly. "Did you mail your packages yet? Do you need me to send you a shipping label?"

"I'll mail everything on Tuesday, before I head to New York. A label would be nice," I answered distractedly, trying to imagine myself playing one of my own compositions in front of industry professionals. I grimaced, feeling slightly sick. It's not that I lacked confidence. It's that I disliked people. I especially disliked people looking at me with expectations and judgment. I just wanted to play music.

"Sounds good. I have the address of where you'll be staying next week in Brooklyn while you're up there playing shows. According to our last call, you are planning to stay with your bandmate, Janet Deloach, and her two friends, the Mr. Bergmans. Is that still correct?" George asked, obviously running down his list of questions.

"Yes."

"Your father will be calling you this week just to talk. He expressed his extreme disappointment that he had to be absent from today's call and wished me to tell you that he loves you and misses you very much. Is the calendar you send for this week still valid?"

I smiled at my dad's words—as read by George—and answered his question, "Yes. There haven't been any changes to my calendar."

"Okay, then I think we're finished." He glanced up and gave me his trademark, flat and friendly George smile. "Merry Christmas, Kaitlyn."

I mustered up enough wherewithal to return his smile with one of my own. "Merry Christmas, George."

Then we ended the call.

**

"Sam, can I ask you a question?"

"Do it." She was studying her menu. We'd opted for Italian tonight; she could never decide between the lasagna and the chicken carbonara.

I put my menu down and folded my hands, readying myself to ask a question that had been forming in my mind for the last several months.

"When did you feel like it was okay—like, it was appropriate—for you as a girl or a woman or whatever, at what age was it that you felt comfortable, or wanted to dress and act, and I guess be perceived as—"

"Spit it out already. Just ask the question."

"Fine. At what age did you feel like you wanted to be sexy?"

Her eyes darted to mine, grew wide, and she stared at me from across the table.

"Is sexy a difficult word for you to say out loud?"

I shook my head. "No. But it's a difficult concept for me to contemplate and not be confused. I don't think I fully understand sexy."

She nodded thoughtfully, her eyes drifting back to her menu.

We were on our Monday night date...with each other. We'd started doing this after we both secured employment over the summer. It was an excuse to get dressed up because otherwise I would spend all my time in either a tuxedo uniform, or baggy jeans and a men's concert T-shirt.

I was trying to explore the concept of traditional femininity—perfume, makeup, matching lacey undergarments, dresses, jewelry, pretty shoes— because I didn't want to dismiss dressing up having never given it a real chance.

Yes, I recognized that "traditional femininity" was historically steeped in misogyny. However, I also recognized deciding to eschew traditional femininity because of chauvinism was just as flawed as subscribing to lace underwear just because men seemed to like it.

I wanted to explore this part of myself for me, not in spite of or because of another person. If I was going to change my style or add to it, I wanted to do it because of how it made me feel. Not because I wanted to make someone else feel better or view me differently.

At least, that's how it had started. But after seeing Martin last Sunday, and realizing how hurt I'd been by the fact he now viewed me as a platonic friend, I was starting to wonder if I had deeper, subconscious motives for exploring my femininity.

An example of one of my less than healthy thoughts: *Maybe if I'd been sexier and more traditionally girly, Martin wouldn't have been able to get over me so fast.*

So…yeah. Not healthy. Which was why I still hadn't looked up or read any of Martin's interviews. I didn't want him to be the motivation for my decisions.

Of note, I still hadn't decided what to think about Martin's offer of friendship or about wearing makeup and frilly garments.

Regarding the clothes, at first everything itched and I felt like my movement was restricted. After a while though, after four girl-dates, I began looking forward to glamming it up, and found myself noticing other peoples' makeup and clothes with appreciation.

"Hmm," she said at last, still studying her menu. "That's a really interesting question."

I took a sip of my water and waited for her to answer.

"Do I want the lasagna or the carbonara?"

"The carbonara."

"Okay. Decision made." She placed the menu on the table and closed it, giving me a searching stare. "So you want to know when I started to feel sexy or when I started wanting to feel sexy?"

"Were they different ages?"

"Yes."

"Then tell me when you started wanting to feel sexy."

"I guess I was fourteen."

My mouth fell open. "Fourteen?"

"Yes. Or maybe thirteen, or twelve. I remember wanting to be sexy like the girls in the magazines."

"What magazines?"

"Vogue, Glamour, Cosmo."

"You read Cosmo at twelve?"

"Yes. When did you start reading Cosmo?"

I sputtered for a moment, then admitted, "Never. I've never read Cosmo."

"Most of it is garbage, meaningless fluff, stupid stuff. But they sometimes have brilliant articles and short stories. Also, it's how I learned to do the cat-eye."

"You mean that black eyeliner thing?"

"Yeah. They had step-by-step instructions with pictures."

I thought about this, the fact she'd been twelve when she'd first wanted to be sexy. Meanwhile I wasn't sure if I wanted to be sexy, even now.

"Do you feel like twelve was too early? Too young?"

She shrugged, wrinkling her nose. "I don't know. I got my period at ten. Five hundred years ago women were getting married at fourteen or fifteen. In some parts of the world they still do."

"But in modern times and western culture, our context being the here and now, do you think it's too early?"

Sam squinted at me. "Yes and no. On one hand, I think it's natural to be curious about sexuality. But on the other hand, I think girls are caught in this terrible net of perpetual disappointment. We're not really allowed to talk about sex, or ask questions about it, or be interested in it. If we are interested and if we like it, then we're labeled as *easy* or *sluts*. If we're not interested, then we're frigid and repressed...we're prudes. It's like, we see images of women being objectified everywhere. And then we're told to act and dress like a man at work and school, or else no one will take us seriously—even other women won't take us seriously. Basically, women are fucked."

"That's depressing."

"Yes. Yes it is. How about you? When did you first think about being sexy?"

I gathered a large breath and shook my head slightly. "I guess the first time I thought about being sexy was when I was seventeen."

"Wow."

"Yeah. So that makes me a frigid, repressed prude?"

"Yes. Absolutely. And I'm a whorey slut. Why seventeen?"

"Honestly, it was only because I could never get Carter—"

"Your gay boyfriend."

"Yes, my gay boyfriend who I didn't know was gay. I could never get him to do anything but kiss me, and only in front of other people. He never wanted to do anything when we were alone together. I thought maybe it was because I wasn't sexy."

Sam watched me for a bit, considering this, then asked, "But...didn't you ever want to be sexy for yourself? Just to feel good?"

"What do you mean?"

"Like, put on a new outfit or eye shadow? Not because someone was going to see you, but just because you wanted to dress up and feel pretty?"

I began shaking my head halfway through her second question. "No. Never."

"Hmm…" she sat back in her chair and inspected me, then pressed, "And you're sure you like guys?"

My mouth fell open in startled outrage and I leaned forward to loudly whisper, "Sam, just because I'm not a girly-girl doesn't mean that I…that I'm—"

"That you prefer mares to stallions, I get it. I just don't understand it. I always thought you wanted to dress that way because you didn't like attention."

"What way?"

"You know, frumpy."

"I dress frumpy?"

"Kind of, actually, yes. Yes, you dress frumpy… frumpily… whatever."

"Because I don't wear form-fitting clothing or clothes that bare my skin and highlight my body?"

"Kaitlyn," she gave me an *oh, come on* look, then continued, "baggy, shapeless clothes that cover your body is the definition of dressing frumpish. Hell, your tuxedo for work makes you look hot in comparison, as at least it shows off your ass."

I opened my mouth to protest but then realized she was right. Baggy T-shirts, oversized jeans with the cuff cut off…on most days I dressed frumpily.

Do I want to dress frumpily? Should I even care? What is wrong with me that I never realized I dress like a frump?

As if seeing my internal struggle, Sam quickly added, "If you want to dress in baggy clothes then dress in baggy clothes. If you like it, then to hell with what everyone else thinks, including me."

"But, I don't… I mean…I—"

"Ladies? Are you ready to order?" Our waitress chose that moment to return to the table, giving me a brief reprieve from trying to verbally untangle my thoughts.

"I'll have the lasagna and she'll have the lobster ravioli." Sam picked up both of our menus and handed them to the server. I usually didn't mind that she ordered for me, because I always ordered the same thing.

But for some reason, this time I was incredibly irritated by her assumption I would order the ravioli. What if I wanted the steak? Or a salad?

"Actually," I interjected, giving the waitress an apologetic smile, "I'll have the duck ziti."

Our server nodded, like it was no big deal, then left us to our discussion.

Sam lifted an eyebrow at me as she raised her water glass to her lips, saying before sipping, "The duck ziti, eh?"

I nodded firmly. "That's right. The duck ziti."

"Not the lobster ravioli?"

"No. I'm tired of lobster ravioli."

She studied me for a long moment, replacing her glass, crossing her arms, and narrowing her eyes. I mimicked her stance and her glare.

"That's fine. Don't get the lobster ravioli if you don't want it. Try duck ziti, try the steak."

"I will."

"But just know, no matter what you order and no matter what you eat, it's your decision. If you want the lobster ravioli every day for the rest of your life, there is nothing wrong with that. Don't change your order just because you think you're supposed to, because society tells you it's weird to order the same thing every time. You have to live with your entrée, not society, not me. You."

"But how will I know whether I like the duck ziti if I don't try it?"

She paused, considering me, her mouth a flat, thoughtful line. Then she sighed, saying, "I guess you won't. I guess you do have to try the ziti. I just don't want you feeling pressure to change, because you're pretty awesome just how you are. It would make me sad if you started ordering steak when you really want ravioli."

"This analogy has officially gone too far. We both know we're talking about my tendency to hide. It doesn't matter if it's a closet or it's baggy clothes. I can't keep hiding from new things."

"But, you're not. Look at you, you're all dressed up. You have your eyebrows professionally waxed and shaped. You're in a band. You're a singing barista. You try new things."

"Yes. At a snail's pace I try new things. When I feel completely safe, I try new things. When I'm with you, I try new things." I gave her a small smile, leaned forward, and put my hand on the table, palm up. She fit hers inside mine and returned my grin.

"Sam, you're a good friend. I want to try new things, even when those things don't feel entirely safe. I want to try new things before I'm even certain I want to try those new things. It's time for me to take some risks."

"You're not talking about drugs, are you? Because, smack is whack."

I laughed and rolled my eyes. "No. I'm talking about buying a T-shirt that fits. Maybe a new dress, so I don't have to keep borrowing yours."

What I didn't add, because I hadn't yet told her about seeing Martin at the coffee shop, was that trying new things also included agreeing to a friendship with Martin Sandeke.

***

THE NEXT MORNING Sam was out of the apartment.

Even so, I shut the door to my room in order to achieve maximum privacy. I was going to call Martin.

I'd thought about making the call from the bathroom, just in case Sam came home unexpectedly, but I decided that was taking things a bit too far.

I gathered several deep breaths as I psyched myself up. Then, feeling an odd surge of courage, I grabbed my phone, tapped in his number, and lifted the cell to my ear.

It rang three times.

I was trying to figure out whether or not I should leave a voicemail— should it come to that—when it was answered.

"Hello?" asked a female voice on the other end.

I frowned, glancing at the card he'd given me, wondering if I had the wrong number or if I'd been given his PA's phone number instead.

"Hi. Hello, um—I'm sorry. I think I might have the wrong number. I'm calling for Martin Sandeke."

"No. You have the right number." Her accent was British.

"Oh. Okay. Is this his PA?"

"No. This is Emma Cromwell, his partner. Who is this?"

Partner. Partner? Oh! ...partner. Well, barnacles.

I closed my eyes and released a silent sigh, felt my stomach fall painfully to my feet. I sat on my bed and cleared my throat before responding, "I'm...Parker."

"Kaitlyn Parker?" It might have been my imagination, but she sounded a little irritated by this news.

Which meant she knew who I was. That was just lovely. Now I felt like an evil usurper. Here I was, the ex-girlfriend, calling *her* Martin. I was pretty sure that if I were in a committed relationship, I wouldn't want my boyfriend's ex calling him.

How did I even get here?

I nodded, then realized she couldn't see me, so I said, "Yes. Kaitlyn Parker. If now is a bad time, you can just have him call me later. But no rush."

"He's just getting out of the shower, so I'll have him call you back when he's not busy."

I nodded again, my heart joining my stomach, beyond my feet, falling down to the center of the earth. "Sure. Like I said, no rush."

"Mmm-hmm. Goodbye."

"Good—" I didn't get to say 'bye, because she'd already ended the call.

***

I WAS COMING to recognize I was probably still very much in love with Martin. Maybe I always would be. This thought made me want to cry, but I didn't.

Instead I decided to go shopping because I had Christmas presents to buy. If there was one thing I'd learned over the last nine months it was the importance of going through the motions. Sam called this: Fake it 'til you make it.

This last week leading up to the big holiday was going to be crazy busy. We had two or three gigs a day, starting tomorrow. Last minute office parties, hotel feature events, themed weddings, and holiday brunches. As they were in New York, I was planning to stay in the city for the week with Janet (my bandmate) and two of her friends.

I was an efficient shopper, mostly because I'd always been ambivalent to shopping. I quickly grabbed the items on my list and was finished, ready to head back to the apartment after two short hours. But for the first time in perhaps my entire life, I didn't want to go back to the apartment and be alone. So I window-shopped for a bit.

Strangely, window shopping turned into store buying, and after another two hours I was back at the apartment with three new pairs of women's jeans, several fitted but delightfully nerdy tops, four matching bra and panty sets—because they were on super sale—and two new pairs of shoes. I also bought myself some cozy socks with Abraham Lincoln on the calves, because he was my second favorite president.

Once home, I unpacked then repacked my bag, deciding to take some of my new stuff with me, then went to the kitchen in search of hot chocolate.

That's when my phone rang. I didn't look at the number before answering because I was still thinking about how much I'd enjoyed my morning. I was floating in my new-clothes-euphoria.

"Hello?"

"Kaitlyn?"

Aaaand…now I was crashing back down to earth.

"Hi, Martin." I endeavored to ignore the familiar ache in my chest.

"I hoped this might be your number. You called earlier? You should have left a message."

This gave me pause, but then I started speaking and thinking at the same time. "I did leave a message."

"Really? I didn't get a voicemail."

"No, I left a message with your…" I tripped over the word, but then forced myself to say it. I knew it was better to rip the bandage off than to try to peel it back slowly. "I left a message with your girlfriend."

He was silent for a beat, then asked, "My girlfriend?"

"Emma."

"Emma? No. No, no, no. Emma is not my girlfriend. She's my partner."

"Partner, girlfriend, significant other, sensei—whatever."

"No, Kaitlyn." I heard him laugh lightly, like he was both relieved and anxious. "Emma is my *business* partner. We've never…we're not like that."

This gave me pause. I was fairly certain Emma had sounded irritated on the phone earlier when she'd discovered my name. Perhaps I'd been imagining it.

"Anyway, you called?"

"Yes. I did. I called." I glanced around the kitchen as though it might help me figure out what to say next. My mind hadn't quite reconciled the fact that Emma wasn't his girlfriend; my heart and stomach were looking to me for direction on whether to soar or switch places, and I had none to offer.

Should I feel happy? Relieved? Ambivalent? Unsurprisingly, the kitchen offered no guidance.

I must've been quiet for too long, because Martin asked, "Are you still there?"

"Yes. Sorry, I'm here. Yes, I called. I wanted to talk to you about the terms of our friendship."

"Our friendship?" I heard the smile in his voice.

"Yes. I was thinking, you and I…I mean, even though we only spent a week together, I feel like—on some level—we became friends. And I liked our friendship, I liked you." I closed my eyes, winced, and covered my face with my hand, feeling mortified and glad he couldn't see the monster blush creeping up my neck.

"I liked you"…really? You are so bad at this.

But then Martin surprised me by saying, "I liked you, too. If you remember, I liked you a lot."

This made me laugh my relief, pleased I wasn't the only one risking part of myself and my pride.

I answered quietly, "Yes. I remember." Now I was blushing for an entirely different reason.

"So, terms?" He prompted, "What days of the week do I get custody? And for how long?"

"Custody?"

"When do I get to see you?"

"Martin, we don't need a schedule. If you want to see me or talk to me, just call me."

"What about today?"

Again I glanced around the kitchen; it had no advice to offer.

I sputtered, "Uh…well…I guess…sure. If you have the time. I'm heading up to where you are in a little bit, as we have a show in the city tomorrow morning."

"I'll take you out to dinner tonight."

Going out to dinner felt too much like a date. I didn't think I was ready for anything that my heart might misconstrue and pin hopes upon.

"Or we could meet at the MET and grab a bite there." The cafeteria at the Metropolitan Museum of Art had great food and was extremely public. Plus, it felt like a neutral spot, like something platonic friends would do together.

He was quiet for a few seconds and I could almost hear him thinking. Finally he acquiesced, "Sure. That's fine. Where are you staying tonight?"

"In Brooklyn, with my bandmate, Janet, and a few of her friends. We're actually staying there all week. I have, like, three shows every day this week."

"You're not going home for Christmas?"

"No. I went home for Thanksgiving. Plus the Christmas season is a very lucrative week for the band. I promised Willis I'd be available."

"Willis?"

"My boss."

I heard the creak of leather, like he was shifting in his seat, and when he spoke his words sounded measured, carefully casual. "You could stay with me, if you wanted. I have plenty of room and I'm in Manhattan."

My heart sped up at the offer. *Hmm, let me see. Spend a week with Martin on an island. Why did that sound so familiar and hazardous?* It actually sounded amazing, at least my pants thought so…but also like a really, really terrible idea.

"No, thank you. I wouldn't want to soil your linens." I was pleased to hear him laugh at this while I continued, "But that's really nice of you to offer."

"I'll pick you up from the station."

"No need. Janet and I are riding over together, then we're dropping our stuff off in Brooklyn. I'll take the subway to the MET and meet you there for food."

"The offer still stands." I could tell he was grinning. "Feel free to stay with me anytime."

I realized I was grinning too, like a love-sick goof.

And I also realized that this, a friendship with Martin, was either going to help me get over him and be my best idea of all time, or I was going to fall even harder and it was the worst mistake I would ever make.

CHAPTER 5

Phase Changes and Heating Curves

TURNS OUT MY worst idea ever of all time was deciding to stay with Janet and her twin, aspiring actor friends.

As soon as we walked in the door I knew something was amiss, mostly because of all the drug paraphernalia scattered around stinking up the studio—including, but not limited to bongs, bags of weed, bent and burnt spoons, lighters, syringes, and what I was fairly certain was the hydrochloride salt form of heroin.

One of the twins was passed out on the couch. The other was on the floor, shooting up.

I paused in the doorway just long enough to absorb the general splendor of these idiots ruining their lives before turning around and marching back down the last flight of stairs we'd just hiked up.

"Katy, wait. Where are you going?" Janet called after me, but did not follow.

"I'm leaving."

"But—wait, wait a minute." Now she was following me. I'd made it to the second landing before I felt her hand on my arm making me stop. "What do you mean you're leaving?"

I faced her, my eyes darting back to the open door, her bags still in the entry. "Just that. I'm leaving. I'm not staying with druggies."

Her lip curled as her eyes moved up and down, as though she were seeing me for the first time. "Is this because your mother is a politician? Are you afraid of ruining her rep? Or are you just being stuck up?"

"I guess I'm just being stuck up. This has nothing to do with my mother. Even if my mother were a singing barista, I wouldn't spend one second more in that apartment. I don't like drugs. I don't want to have anything to do with them."

"Come on, they're not bad guys." Her expression softened and she smiled warmly. "Come back—we'll order a pizza and ignore them."

I shook my head before she finished speaking. "No. It's one of my life rules. I have no tolerance for drugs or for people who do drugs."

"Does that mean you have no tolerance for me?" Janet stood straighter, her chin lifted in challenge.

"Do you do drugs?"

"Hell yes."

I shrugged. "Then I guess you have your answer."

Her mouth opened in shock and I took advantage of her momentary stunned surprise to walk down another two flights of stairs.

I heard her call after me just before I exited the building, "Good luck finding a place to stay the week before Christmas, every place is booked. And don't come back here with your judgmental bullshit!"

The door slammed behind me, cutting off any additional tirade she might be flinging in my direction. I took a deep breath, filling my lungs with icy air, and reminded myself, *just because I don't feel calm, doesn't mean I can't be calm.*

I walked toward the subway station, holding my sleeping bag to my chest and shifting the weight of my backpack. Even though I'd packed relatively light, the bag was still heavy. Janet was right. Finding a place to stay for the night was going to be nearly impossible, especially a place I could afford.

I basically had two options.

I could call my parents and ask them if I could borrow money for a hotel room. I really, really didn't want to do that.

I wasn't going to live my life having my mother and father support *my little hobby.* It wasn't a hobby to me. I wanted to be treated like an adult. I was making my own decisions about my future, I should be able to make my own way. I would accept their help with tuition, but then I promised myself I would be on my own in all other facets of my life.

The second option was catching a train back home tonight, then catching another train back to the city early in the morning. This wasn't a great option either since it was going to be incredibly expensive to take the train back and forth every day, not to mention exhausting.

Debating my options, and knowing ultimately I really only had one option if I wanted to be truly self-sufficient, I took the subway back to Grand Central Station.

Once I was no longer underground, I texted Martin.

Kaitlyn: *Sorry. I have to cancel our MET meet up. I'm not staying in the city and need to try to catch a train back home before they're all sold out. Maybe next time.*

I was standing in front of the departures board when I felt my phone vibrate, alerting me to his response.

Martin: *Are you already in the city?*

Kaitlyn: *Yes, but my arrangements fell through, so I'm going back home.*

Martin: *Don't go. Stay with me.*

I stared at this message for a full minute, my heart accelerating then dipping then twisting as I thought about this potential solution I hadn't considered. Earlier, from the comfort of my living room in New Haven, this suggestion had seemed ludicrous. Now, faced with the reality of a train ride back home and another in the morning, this idea felt a lot more plausible. We *were* friends after all.

Maybe I was staring for longer than a minute because Martin texted again.

Martin: *I'm hardly ever at my place. You'd basically have the apartment to yourself.*

I felt like this last message was an unbreakable code...

If he was hardly ever there, did this mean he had a girlfriend? Emma the business partner wasn't his girlfriend, but he didn't deny *having* a girlfriend. What about the brunette at the gig last week? Maybe she was his girlfriend.

Did he spend the night at this theoretical woman's place all the time?

Could I be any more psycho and weird about Martin Sandeke?

Feeling like I needed to know for certain whether he had a girlfriend before I agreed to spend a night in his apartment, I debated how to respond to his latest text.

If he had a girlfriend then I was leaving for home tonight and the answer was a firm no. I didn't want to see him with anyone else...ever. As well, how fair would it be to this hypothetical girlfriend if I was lusting after her boyfriend for a week while in his apartment? It wouldn't be fair at all, and it was against the cool-girl code.

But I felt strange about texting him and asking him, so I tried to cleverly extract the information instead.

Kaitlyn: *Does this mean you're a workaholic or is your social calendar just impressively full of hot dates?*

Martin: *A workaholic. My social calendar is mostly work stuff.*

Kaitlyn: *So, you're out late only because of work?*

Martin: *Usually.*

Kaitlyn: *Any other reason?*

There was a significant pause in his text messages. I waited, watching the clock on my phone. I was about to do a google search for "Martin Sandeke girlfriend" just to put myself out of my misery when he finally responded.

Martin: *Are you more or less likely to stay the week if I have a girlfriend? Because I can get one if I need to.*

Once again I was staring at my phone, surprised by his text. But I shouldn't have been surprised. Martin had nerves of steel and balls of titanium. Before I could text him back, he sent another message.

Martin: *There is no one. Stay with me. It'll be the most exciting thing that's happened since I bought a PS4.*

He didn't have a girlfriend…!

I couldn't help myself, I did a jig, right there in front of the departures board at Grand Central Station. It was an instinctual, involuntary jig.

After the fact, I recognized I did a jig for no reason because nothing was ever going to happen between us again. He'd had his revenge on his father. He existed in his universe of one. He'd moved on. And I wasn't likely to trust him enough to let anything happen. Regardless, the fact he was single felt like a victory, so I did my jig.

I read his message again and my attention caught on the very last part.

Kaitlyn: *Wait, you have a PS4?*

Martin: *Yes.*

Kaitlyn: *Do you have any Lord of the Rings games?*

Martin: *Yes. Middle-earth: Shadow of Mordor.*

Kaitlyn: *What's your address? I'm on my way.*

***

M ARTIN LIVED IN the Upper West Side. Finding his building was no big deal and was basically a relatively short subway ride with one transfer. When I arrived, the doorman seemed to be expecting me because he greeted me as *Ms. Parker* and ushered me into the lobby to the desk of a friendly concierge. Her name was Mae and she was extremely cheerful.

"Aren't you lovely, dear? Mr. Sandeke called ahead and said we should be expecting you. I'll show you up to his apartment."

"Oh, I don't mind waiting until he gets home."

"Nonsense, dear. He was particular about you going up right away. Besides, who knows when he'll be home?" She leaned close to me as we boarded the elevator and whispered, "He keeps odd hours, so you might be waiting until midnight."

Martin lived on the sixth floor and his place was at the very, very end of a long hallway. Mae made chitchat the entire time and, to be honest, I had no idea what she was talking about. Staying with Martin when I was tired, hungry, and stranded seemed like a reasonable alternative to catching trains daily back and forth between New York and New Haven.

Now, faced with the reality of Martin's apartment, I was beginning to question my judgment. I wondered if I should add a new life rule: never stay at an ex-boyfriend's place.

Mae unfastened the lock and opened the door, practically pushing me inside when I loitered a little too long at the entrance. However, she did not enter the apartment. I took a few stumbling steps into the space and greedily absorbed the surroundings.

The first thing I noticed was that Martin's apartment was not ostentatious, at all. Other than its size, the impressive view of Central Park, and the fact he had an actual patio with chairs and a table—currently covered in snow—everything else was rather modest. And cozy. And homey.

The visible walls were plain white, but mostly the room was lined with honey-colored wooden bookshelves, all of which were full of books. He had a worn-looking, dark brown leather sofa in the center of the living room, two matching club chairs in the same leather, a Shaker-style coffee table, and an antique looking drafting table in the corner; it was covered in papers with sketches tacked to a corkboard to one side.

He also had a stone fireplace; the hearth was free of decoration, but a large painting of an eight-person crew boat done in a Norman Rockwell style hung above the mantel. It was the only art or picture I could see. The living room looked like a comfy library.

"Okey dokey. You're all set." Peripherally I heard Mae call to me just before the apartment door clicked shut. I turned around and found that she'd gone, leaving me alone in Martin's home.

My back twinged and I was reminded of the heavy backpack I'd been carrying for the last few hours. Sighing, I placed my sleeping bag on the couch and relieved myself of my luggage, letting it fall to the sofa as well. Then I realized I needed to relieve myself of…other things.

I decided I wasn't going to feel weird about invading Martin's space since I'd been invited, and set off to find the bathroom. The first door I opened was to a very tidy, very large bedroom. The walls were white and within was a bed with no headboard or footboard. The comforter was sky blue. The side table and dresser were a distressed, Shaker style. If I didn't recognize the craftsmanship of the woodwork, I would've assumed they'd been purchased at a garage sale. Both were completely bare of stuff. This was obviously a guest bedroom.

The next door was to a closet with sheets, blankets, pillows, and towels, or as I would call them later in order to tease Martin, linens. I checked to see if his towels were monogrammed. They were. I smirked.

The next door was to a bathroom. I flipped on the light and sucked in a surprised and delighted breath. The bathroom was very vintage and very cool. The tilework was checked black and white, a pedestal sink stood to one side, and the nobs appeared to be antique porcelain.

The shower was a stall with a glass door and the toilet looked old and new at the same time. Perhaps it was a reproduction of antique-style toilets. I had to pull a chain hanging from a ceramic box in order to flush it, which I honestly thought was exciting.

I would have to make a special effort to keep from flushing the toilet for no reason.

But like the bedroom, it was entirely free of clutter. The only items in the bathroom other than the fixtures were two white towels, toilet paper, a soap dispenser, and an empty trashcan.

I walked back to the living room and decided to send him a text, let him know I made it.

Kaitlyn: *I am texting from inside your apartment.*
Martin: *Are you going through my things?*
Kaitlyn: *Yes. And I've soiled all your linens.*

Martin: *Just stay away from my fancy watches.*

His last message made me laugh, and then I caught myself. Texting back and forth with Martin was fun. It made me remember conversations we'd had during spring break, the quick exchanges, the teasing. The messages reminded me of how easy and right it had felt between us.

My phone vibrated again and I had to blink several times to bring the screen into focus.

Martin: *I'm almost home and I have pizza. Your room is the first left down the hall. Get comfortable.*

My heart sped at the thought of seeing him so soon and I told it to calm the frack down.

We were friends now. If I was going to be seeing him I was going to have to learn to control my body's reaction. I was going to have to learn how to become indifferent. That meant no more celebratory jigs and no more heart races.

Lugging my backpack from the couch to the sparsely decorated room I'd spied earlier, I unpacked. While hanging my tuxedo in the empty closet—which was strange to see, who has empty closets?—I walked by a mirror and caught my reflection. My hair was in two thick, long braids on either side of my head. I was wearing an extra-large men's concert T-shirt, a very baggy pair of cargo pants, and Converse. This outfit was great for travel because it was comfortable and I didn't care if it became dirty.

But it was undoubtedly frumpy. I did not like how I looked in it.

I decided to change into one of the outfits I'd bought earlier: a dark pair of (women's) jeans, a fitted long-sleeved, red and white rugby-style shirt with Avogadro's number on the back. I thought this was hilarious.

The lady at the store didn't know what Avogadro's number was, but she told me I wasn't supposed to button the placket at the collar because it was meant to be a deep V-neck; she said that leaving it open would highlight my cleavage, that it was sexy.

I glanced down at my chest, saw that just the edge of my black bra was visible. I decided leaving it unbuttoned was, indeed, sexy. However, I also decided that buttoning just one button would make me more comfortable, so I did. Glancing in the mirror I assessed myself. I was comfortable, but I was not frumpy; I also felt good about how I looked instead of merely ambivalent. I liked that I could incorporate my inherent nerdiness into my new style. I liked it all.

I'd just started pulling my hair out of the braids when I heard the front door open.

My heart wanted to race like a contestant at the Kentucky Derby, but I yanked it back, taking several deep breaths. All of the floors in the apartment were wood and creaked, so I could hear Martin's steps as he moved through the apartment. Satisfied I wasn't going to act like a spazz, I walked calmly into the living room while I pulled my fingers through my hair.

"Hey," I called, searching for him, "what kind of pizza did you get?"

"Who are you?"

I turned toward the sound of the voice—a British female voice—and found a beautiful woman dressed in an expensive black skirt suit, black high-heeled boots, and long wheat-colored hair, glowering at me.

"Oh, hi. I'm Kaitlyn. You must be Emma. We spoke on the phone earlier." I reached my hand out to shake hers.

She glanced at my fingers like she was a vegan and they were greasy pork sausages. She didn't shake my hand.

"How did you get in here?" Her irritation was obvious, and not just because she wouldn't shake my hand. It dripped off her…she was leaking ire.

I let my hand drop and shrugged. "Through the front door."

She gnashed her teeth. "Who let you in? Why are you here?" She was practically snarling.

"Whoa, just, calm down for a moment. There's no reason to be upset."

"I'm not upset!" She yelled this.

I widened my eyes and took a step back, holding my hands up between us. "Okay, my bad. You're not upset. You always walk into other people's apartments and yell at their guests. This must be a normal Tuesday for you."

Her eyes narrowed and her lip curled into something like a snarl. "You are a dimwitted—"

And, thankfully, Martin chose that moment to walk in the door. "Emma? What the hell?"

We both turned our faces to him as he swept into the living room and deposited a large pizza box and a plastic bag on a table behind the sofa, then quickly crossed to stand next to me.

As usual, he was more than just a tall good-looking guy. He was a presence. A swirling, atmosphere changing force, a magnetized center of attention—or at least he was to me. I felt my heart do a few jumping jacks and I told it to sit still.

Emma took a step back as he approached. She swallowed, looking just a tad worried, and crossed her arms over her chest. I noted she was good at masking her nerves as she lifted her chin in a stubborn tilt.

"Really, Martin? Really? You think this is a good idea?"

"Emma." He shook his head, his jaw set, and his eyes flashed a warning. "It's none of your business."

"Your business is my business, and *she* is bad for my business." Emma indicated to me with a furious wave of her hand.

Well, this was awkward. I thought about slowly backing away. To that end, I furtively glanced behind me to see how successful I might be sneaking out of the room without either of them noticing.

"You're going, now. And leave the key." Martin's tone was low, monotone. Yes, he appeared to be angry; more than that he appeared to be disappointed.

"If I don't have a key, how am I supposed to pick up your planning documents for the foundation? How about your *sketches*?"

She said sketches like most people say poop. I surmised she was not a fan of his sketches.

"We're not talking about this now because you're leaving."

Her brow pulled low and she hesitated for a bit, searching his face before asking, "Does she even know what you did for her? What you gave up? Did you tell her? Is that why she's here?"

I turned my attention back to the argument, and again my eyes widened.

I stared at Emma, really looked at her, and I realized she wasn't jealous, not in a love interest, girl longing for a guy kind of way. Rather, she was extremely frustrated—and definitely jealous—but for a different reason.

Martin drew himself straighter, his face stone and his eyes unyielding icicles. "You need to leave before I sever our partnership, because we've already had this discussion, you're too fucking stubborn to listen, and now you're really pissing me off." He was furious and his voice was beginning to lift. I remembered facing his temper and I could see he was close to losing it now.

Emma coolly studied him for a long moment. "Fine. I'll leave." She reached into the satchel slung over her shoulder and pulled out a ring of two keys. "Here is your key." She held it to him and he took it out of her hand.

Her eyes slid to mine and her gaze narrowed as she spat, "You are selfish. But worse, you are naïve and ignorant and stupidly obstinate—just like your mother."

I opened my mouth to say something, but it didn't matter because she'd already turned on her heel and marched out of the apartment, slamming the door behind her.

Martin and I stood perfectly still for several seconds. I was trying to wrap my mind around everything that had just happened and the odd verbal exchange I'd witnessed. I arranged my questions in order from most pressing to simple curiosities, and turned to Martin to gauge his mood.

His mouth was curved into a decisive frown and he was staring at the spot where Emma had just been standing.

I gathered a deep breath, preparing to pose the first of my questions, when he turned toward me. His eyes, how they moved over me, made my breath and words catch in my throat.

"You look different," Martin said, his attention on my hips, moving to my thighs then back up to my stomach, breasts, neck, lips, then hair. If I wasn't mistaken, he looked appreciative of the changes in my wardrobe. "What's different about you?" This question was softly spoken and teasing.

I shrugged, pretending I didn't know what he was talking about. "I don't know. I'm using a different moisturizer for my face now."

His gaze met mine and narrowed. "That's not it."

"I switched from Crest to Colgate." I showed him my teeth.

"No." He smirked.

"My hair is longer."

"Maybe…"

I lifted an eyebrow at him and wondered if he were stalling, trying to distract me from the issues at hand—such as Emma's mention of me being the reason Martin had given up…something big.

"Why don't you tell me what your business partner meant when she said—"

Martin turned away, drawing his heavy coat from his shoulders. "Can we not talk about that tonight? Can we just…" I heard him sigh, "can we just hang out?"

"I don't think so. I won't be able to focus on anything else until you tell me what's going on."

My eyes moved over him as he walked to the entryway closet and hung up his coat. This left him in an exceptionally well-tailored, dark gray, three-piece suit. His tie was cobalt blue and matched his current eye color.

"Kaitlyn," Martin paused, facing me, loosening his tie and unbuttoning the top two buttons of his crisp business shirt, "I've been looking forward to seeing you all day."

This admission made my insides flood with warmth and I marveled at how open he was with his thoughts, how fearless. I surmised our friendship would be similar to our previous courtship; I'd never have to wonder what he was thinking or feeling about me. He would be direct and honest.

In truth, I admired this about him. I wasn't nearly as fearless. By comparison, and especially with him, I was a feelings and thoughts hoarder.

"I don't want to talk about Emma or her constant nagging. I want to sit on the couch, drink a beer, eat pizza, and talk about shit that doesn't matter—and laugh."

He looked older than his twenty-one years; his suit was partially to blame. However, he also just looked tired—really, really tired. Upon further study I saw that his color was off, paler than before; his eyes were rimmed red, the dark circles beneath giving his face a drawn appearance. As well he was sporting a stubbly, late-afternoon beard.

I studied him, his obvious exhaustion, and felt like a compromise was in order. "Okay, fine. We don't have to talk about it right now."

He gave me a grateful, and tired, half smile. "Good."

I held up a finger and pointed it at him. "But once you've recovered from your day, and you've had your beer and eaten your pizza, and we've talked about things that don't matter, we will discuss the meaning of the ominous and mysterious conversation with your partner."

He'd removed his suit jacket and vest, and was now unbuttoning his cuffs. "Fine."

"Fine. I'll get plates."

"And beer."

"And napkins."

He nodded once and stumbled toward the hallway. On his way he stopped directly in front of me, paused for a moment, then scooped me up in his arms and gave me a tight hug.

"I'm so glad you're here."

I hesitated as my chest had grown tight, confusing emotion momentarily choking me. I wasn't expecting us to be *hugging friends*. But then I returned his embrace because…Martin.

And also because his arms around me were like chocolate chip cookies for my soul. He felt strong, sturdy, warm, snuggly, good, right—delicious.

Yet my heart ached for him, he sounded so weary.

"Are you okay? Is something going on?" I soothed my hand up then down his back.

"No, not the way you mean. Nothing serious. I just…" I felt him exhale and relax a bit more into my arms. "I just missed you."

Gah! Right in the feels.

***

"THAT'S IT. I'M going to make a list of all the TV shows you need to watch." I was sitting cross-legged on his couch, facing him and resting my head on the back of the overstuffed sofa. Martin was sprawled on the other side, holding his beer on his stomach and fighting to keep his eyes open.

"I own the Sherlock Holmes books."

"The BBC show is awesome. Have you read the books yet?"

"No."

"Maybe try reading them."

"I will. Didn't I read The Lord of the Rings?"

"Yes. But Sherlock has maybe the best sidekick in the history of forever." I glanced behind him and found the clock on the wall. It was almost 10:30 p.m.

This conversation—about books, movies, pop culture, international current events, Internet memes, and music—was entering its third hour, although it felt like we'd just started talking, like no time had passed.

"I liked Sam, Frodo's sidekick," he said, stretching his legs. He was dressed in pajama pants and a gray T-shirt. I tried not to notice how delicious he looked. I tried and failed. His deliciousness paired with our easy conversation was somewhat intoxicating. I was feeling giddy.

"If you like sidekicks, then you have to watch Doctor Who." I sipped my tea and studied the tea bag. "The Doctor has several companions, which is unusual but really works for the series."

"I think you're a sidekick person."

"You think I'm a sidekick?" I glanced at him over the rim of my cup.

He peered at me. "No. I think you like sidekicks and side characters, maybe better than main characters."

I thought about this for a moment before nodding. "Yeah. I can see that. I feel like sidekicks aren't as well developed as the main character in a story, but they're essential in defining that main character. And the protagonist needs the sidekick more than the sidekick needs the protagonist. Sometimes the villain is just as important."

He lifted his beer toward me and said before taking a sip, "But every sidekick and villain is the main character in his or her own story. Everyone is the main character in their own story. Even if the person is an asshole."

This made me laugh. "Are you thinking of a person in particular?"

"No." His eyes narrowed on me. I watched him take a deep breath, then amend, "Actually, yes."

"Really? Who?"

"Do you remember Ben?"

I searched my memory and quickly registered the name. "Ben Salsmar, the drugging rapist," I supplied. "Yes. Unfortunately, I do remember him. He's responsible for the figurative potato sack of guilt I carry around."

"What do you mean?"

"I mean, I should have gone to the police when we got back from the Island. Instead I… didn't."

"Kaitlyn, there is nothing you could have done about Ben. You need to free the potatoes."

"I overheard at the end of last year that he was arrested for sexually assaulting a minor, and I might have done something before he had a chance to—"

"Well, that's not exactly true. He didn't sexually assault her because he was stopped before he could do anything beyond drugging her and dropping his pants."

I felt an immediate warm relief spread through my veins.

Martin studied me before continuing, "Just know that you couldn't have stopped him. It would have been your word against his, and you had no evidence. But did you hear anything else?"

"Just that there was video proof."

"Yes, there is a video. Actually, there were a few videos, from several different vantage points. He was arrested for the drugging, assault, and attempted rape. He was also expelled once the video was shared with university administration."

I hesitated for a moment, then asked, "Was he convicted?"

"He will be. A few of the guys on the team will testify. Plus there's the videos. His dad tried to delay the proceedings and, because of the delay, a few other girls have come forward. As of now it looks like he'll be facing more than one rape charge."

I felt sickened by this news—that several girls had been abused—but also heartened they had come forward. "Well, that's good, right?"

"Yes. That's good."

"Well…good. I'm glad he was stopped."

"Me, too." Martin stared at me for a long moment and I knew he wanted to say something more. I was just about to prompt him when he said, "I don't think I ever thanked you for that night, when you came to the fraternity house and told me what he was planning."

I gave him a half smile. "It's no problem. Did you ever find out who the girl was?"

"No… but thank you," he said solemnly. Then, he added just as solemnly, "I promised you I'd take care of him, and I wanted you to know I kept my promise."

My left eyebrow lifted of its own accord. "*You* took care of him?"

His expression grew cagey. "Technically, he did it to himself. I just installed the cameras…"

I studied him, guessing he'd likely been more involved than just installing cameras.

Martin heaved a heavy sigh, settling deeper into the cushions of the couch. "Like I said, everyone is the main character in their own story. Even villains."

I shook my head. "I don't know… Not necessarily. I mean, sometimes the story is bigger than the characters, like Jurassic Park. The Park was really the central focus of the story, and all the characters were secondary to the Park. Their only purpose was to react to the Park."

Martin yawned, set his now empty beer on the coffee table, and closed his eyes. "That's because dinosaurs are awesome. We're all sidekicks to dinosaurs."

"Or dinner."

"Or dinner," he slurred, issuing me a sloppy nod.

I watched the rise and fall of his chest, noted he appeared to be completely relaxed. If I was very quiet I knew he'd be asleep in less than sixty seconds.

But the conversation—or confrontation—with his business partner earlier was still nagging at me. If he fell asleep I'd have to wait another day to get my questions answered.

"Sandeke," I whispered. "Why does Emma dislike me so much?"

He shifted, his head lolling to the side, and heaved a sigh. "She doesn't know you."

"That's why she doesn't like me?"

"Yeah…if she knew…you…she'd…really like you."

Aaaand he was asleep.

I studied him for a long moment, but knew I didn't have the heart to wake him. He'd been so tired. As we talked I saw the tension ease from his shoulders. He needed a night off from whatever genius high-stakes shenanigans he'd been up to.

I set my tea on the coffee table, then remembered the blankets in the linen closet. I tiptoed to the hallway and grabbed one, laying it gently on his sleeping form and tucking it between his hip and the sofa cushions so it wouldn't slip off. Standing back, I surveyed Martin. Unable to help myself, I threaded my fingers through the hair at his forehead and pushed it gently to one side.

He turned his head toward my hand, pressing against my lingering touch. The simple action, the way he instinctively sought affection and warmth made me smile sadly. I'd forgotten how lost Martin was, how completely used and abandoned he'd been by his family. In my own grief surrounding the breakup, I'd forgotten he didn't have many friends, and trusted very few.

This made my heart hurt in a new way, one focused outward instead of inward, and I felt the weight of my childish selfishness.

He needed a friend, someone who truly cared about him.

I still cared about him a great deal. I was maybe (definitely) in love with him. So shouldn't that mean I wanted what was best for him? Shouldn't I want to see him happy? Even if we didn't find happiness with each other?

I let my palm press against his cheek for a few more seconds before drawing slowly away, and I made a decision. I was going to give our friendship a real chance, and not just use it as a way to get over Martin

Sandeke. He deserved better than that. He deserved human kindness and consideration.

I was going to shelve my persistent feelings of romantic attraction and be a good friend to him. I was going to be his safe place, the friend he needed.

CHAPTER 6
Periodic Properties of the Elements

MY PHONE ALARM announced the end of happiness (sleep). It was obscenely early in the morning. For a moment I was confused by my surroundings, but then I remembered whose apartment I was in and the happenings of the last twenty-four hours. This served to wake me up quite effectively.

It was still dark outside. My first show for the day was at a fancy tree-trimming party in a penthouse not far from where Martin lived. It would be just Fitzy and me, and for that I was grateful. I wasn't ready to discuss rebound guys with Abram, or heroin as a viable life choice with Janet.

Tossing the covers to one side and grabbing my clothes, I planned to tiptoe to the bathroom as quietly as I could, not wanting to wake Martin at this ungodly hour.

As it turned out, I didn't need to worry about waking him because he was already up and leaving his room just as I exited mine. But he was dressed in workout clothes whereas I was still in pajamas. He didn't see me at first because his attention was on his phone.

"Martin," I whispered—as I was prone to do early in the morning when regular speaking volume is blasphemous—wanting to get his attention before we collided in the hall.

He lifted his eyes, frowning as though he were confused by my presence, and took a step back. "What are you doing up so early? Did I wake you?"

"I have a show." I indicated with my chin to where I held my tuxedo.

"Ah." His gaze skimmed over me, probably taking in my sleepy and rumpled appearance.

I decided then and there that something about the way he looked at me would always make me feel awkward. It wasn't his fault. It was just him being Martin: the shade and intensity of his eye color paired with the brilliance and acumen behind his gaze; the sharpness of his bone structure; his towering height; the graceful line of his form and movements—he couldn't help causing my self-consciousness any more than I could help the reaction.

I made a decision to just accept it rather than fight it. Maybe if I accepted that my body would respond to him no matter what my head and heart might prefer, then I would be able to move beyond the sensations until they felt commonplace.

"You're off to work out?" I asked unnecessarily, still whispering.

"Yeah. I meet a few guys at the Hudson boathouse and we try to get in a few thousand meters before breakfast. The river isn't frozen yet, so we still have a few weeks. Why are you whispering?"

I cleared my throat, managed to lift my voice slightly, though it was still low and sandpapery from sleep. "I don't know. I just always do this early in the morning. It's like my ears aren't ready for sound yet."

This made his mouth curve into a small smile. He walked slowly forward until he was standing between me and the bathroom. Martin leaned against the hallway wall and peered down at me.

"I know what you mean." His answering voice was soft, low, rumbly, and delicious. Again, I allowed the sensations of being close to him in a dark, small space and speaking with him in low, intimate tones wash over me. Accelerated heart rate, warming cheeks, fluttery stomach. No use fighting it.

I tried to redirect the conversation back to him and his morning routine. "So, you're still rowing? That's great."

He nodded, his eyes on mine, but he appeared to be distracted, torn. "I could...I mean, I could cancel if you want company this morning."

"But if you cancel how will they row the boat? Doesn't every seat need to be filled?"

"Technically they need an even number of rowers. So, most of them— six plus the coxswain—would be able to go, but someone might have to sit out."

"Then go row your boat. Don't worry about me. I have to leave soon anyway."

Martin glanced at his phone again. "I can stick around for another ten minutes. Come out here." He motioned for me to follow as he pushed away from the wall and walked past me. "I'll make you coffee and I have muffins."

I watched his back while I considered this offer, and followed him into the kitchen. I deposited my clothes on the couch as we passed. He was being awfully solicitous, maybe he wanted to talk about the Emma situation.

"Is ten minutes enough time for me to ask you my questions about yesterday? What happened with your business partner?"

He shook his head, giving me his profile as he fiddled with the coffee machine. "No. No—I do want to talk to you about all that—but we don't have enough time this morning. I don't," he paused, apparently struggling over his word choice, "I don't want to be rushed. A lot has happened and ten minutes isn't enough time to explain everything. What's your schedule today? Could we have lunch?"

"Not unless your office is in Harlem. I have a gig up there all afternoon. Dinner?"

"No." He frowned, turning to face me while he leaned against the counter, the coffee machine coming to life. "I have a dinner meeting tonight until late."

"Well, I'll be here all week. I'm sure we'll have a chance to catch up at some point."

He appeared to be a tad frustrated; it was plain irritation at the situation, not irritation with me.

"Thanks for the break last night. But I want to know what's been going on with you. What have you been up to? What have you been doing? Any big changes?"

I gave him a half smile. "You mean any big changes I can adequately summarize in eight minutes or less?"

"Yeah. Good point." His grin was surprising because it was somewhat self-deprecating. Self-deprecating at 5:05 a.m. looked really adorable on Martin Sandeke.

But then, that was the crux of my problem. To me, *every* smile looked good on Martin Sandeke. Every expression, anytime, anyplace. I simply adored his face because—despite our history and his past assholery—I still adored *him*.

"Well, I'll give you the Cliffs Notes version then we can discuss in greater detail later, sound good?"

He nodded. "Sounds good."

"Okay, let's see." I sorted through the last nine months, filtering out the epic sob-fests, chronic melodramatic closet visits, and angry acoustic guitar music. "Sam and I moved off campus at the beginning of the summer. I auditioned for the band in July. I decided to change my major around the same time and take a semester—the fall semester—off school so I could audition for the music program."

For some reason, the fact I'd switched majors felt like a really momentous proclamation, especially saying it out loud to Martin. I slid my eyes to the side to gage his reaction and I found him grinning at me.

"That's," he started, stopped, looking a tad overwhelmed. He leaned away from the counter and crossed to stand in front of me. "That's fucking awesome news!"

I laughed, partly as a release of nervous energy and partly because his voice was much louder and he sounded so excited for me. Really, he sounded ecstatic.

"Thank you." I dipped my head to the side, feeling a bit too pleased by his reaction.

"Really, this is great." He was beaming with happiness, his smile now enormous. Obviously unable to help himself, Martin grabbed me from where I loitered at the entrance to the kitchen and pulled me into a tight hug.

I laughed at his effusive display of excitement and wrapped my arms around his waist. "Yeah, well, I know I want to play music and I know I love to compose, but I'm not sure what I want to do exactly."

He leaned away, his hands shifting to grip my arms above the elbows, seemingly wanting to see my face as I relayed the rest of my thoughts.

"Do I want to teach? Write for record labels? Score soundtracks? I have no idea." My stomach twisted with unease; my mother would be asking me about performing at her fundraiser and benefit again as soon as the holidays were over. Eventually I would have to make a decision.

Martin mistook my grimace of anxiety for nerves about switching my major, and said, "But you'll make a lot of good contacts in the school of music, people who can help you figure out what to do next. Don't hesitate to exploit them for their knowledge."

"Yes. Exactly. I like the idea of expert unbiased input."

His smile widened again as his gaze skated over my face, his eyes were positively glittering. "That's a very Kaitlyn Parker thing to say."

Of course I returned his smile, his happiness for me was heady and infectious. "So you mean it was an awesome thing to say?"

"Exactly."

His coffee maker beeped or chimed or made some odd musical notation to announce that my coffee was ready. The sound was very official. Martin didn't release me immediately and for a second I thought he might pull me back into another hug. Instead he sighed—a happy sounding sigh—and let go, moving to a cabinet and grabbing a coffee cup.

"You know, we should go out and celebrate."

"Celebrate my switch in majors?"

"Yes. And hopefully other things, too."

"Like what other things?"

He placed the cup on the counter in front of me, looking a bit distracted, pensive.

He hesitated before answering, but when he did his eyes were sharp and sober, and his tone told me he was a smidge frustrated. "It might speed things up if you read some of the interviews I've given over the past few months. Then when we have time this week to talk you'll know...everything."

"Sure. Fine. That makes sense." I nodded, sipped my coffee.

This seemed to both relax him and stress him out. I watched him gather a deep, bracing breath. "Good," he said, sounding like maybe me reading the interviews was both good and bad. Abruptly he pulled out his phone and frowned. "I'm late. I have to go."

"Okay." I gave him a reassuring smile because he seemed to need it. "I'll see you later."

Martin loitered, just looking at me, his expression unreadable. Again I experienced an involuntary reaction to his *looking*. And again I just accepted my body's flutterings and warmings as one of life's truths.

Then Martin nodded once, turned, and left.

He just...left, the sound of the apartment door shutting punctuating his abrupt departure.

I stood in the kitchen for a full minute staring at the doorway where he'd disappeared so unceremoniously. He hadn't said goodbye.

The longer I stared the more the early morning silence felt harsh and loud, so I gave myself a mental shake—deciding he must've been in a hurry—and crossed to the counter where I spied the aforementioned box of muffins.

Grabbing one—and my coffee—I decided that now was a good time to start reading the interviews he'd mentioned. Now that I had food and caffeine, I didn't need the extra time I'd allotted to secure both before my gig nearby. I left my breakfast on the kitchen table and returned with my laptop, figuring I had a good twenty minutes of reading before I absolutely had to take my shower.

I bit into my delicious banana nut muffin, pulled up my Internet browser, and typed *Martin Sandeke interview* into the search field.

What popped up made the delicious muffin in my mouth taste like sand.

Picture after picture of Martin and a redheaded woman wallpapered the results page—a very pretty, petite, smiling redheaded girl about my age or a little older. She was always smiling, either at him or the camera. The photos dated as far back as August and as recently as three weeks ago.

They looked so pretty, the two of them, so young and vibrant and *suited*.

My heart thundered between my ears and I forcefully shut my laptop, blinking rapidly at nothing in particular. This wasn't like seeing him briefly with the brunette at my show last week. This was very different. All those feelings I'd been trying to avoid for the past nine months, the fear of irrefutable evidence that he'd moved on, seeing Martin with someone else, were finally realized and made my chest feel vice-grip-tight.

And yet, as I sat there, having my freak out, calming my breathing, and staring at nothing, a little voice reminded me that he'd texted me the day before and stated he didn't have a girlfriend. He wouldn't have lied to me, not when it would be so easy for me to discover the truth. And besides, Martin hadn't ever knowingly lied to me before, he wasn't a liar.

Perhaps she was a friend. A really good friend. A friend who he'd been photographed with a lot, since August. A friend he saw all the time.

Then another little voice asked me why it mattered, because he and I were over. And that little voice made me immeasurably sad.

I briefly contemplated opening the laptop and continuing my search. But instead, I decided I didn't have time to contemplate Martin, the pretty redhead, and my jumbled feelings on the matter and still make it to work on time. I could always go back to the search later if I was feeling brave enough.

I gulped my coffee and threw the muffin away, then grabbed my laptop and clothes from where I'd discarded them earlier. I had all morning to consider my next course of action. There was no need to make myself late.

***

THE TREE-TRIMMING party was fine.

I spent the entirety of the three sets obsessing about the pictures of Martin and the redheaded girl. But the time obsessing was ultimately productive as I came to the conclusion that I was definitely not ready to read his interviews or see the pictures. I knew my limitations, and seeing Martin happy with someone else—even if he didn't have a girlfriend now and they weren't together anymore—was not in my wheelhouse. Not yet.

I had no desire to read about his relationship status via the Internet.

I decided that my questions about his business partner and her insinuations, as well as my new questions about the girl in the pictures, would just have to wait until Martin and I found the time to talk. I felt good about this decision. Less ragey—*ragey* because I couldn't think of an equivalent real word to describe what I was feeling—and flustered. More in control of my mental state.

The show in Harlem with the entire band was also fine.

Although things between Janet and me were still frosty. Willis called us on it and wanted to know what happened. I think she expected me to air her dirty laundry—telling him about the drugs and her druggie friends—but I didn't.

Instead I told Willis that she and I were having a disagreement about whether Jimi Hendrix or Jimmy Page was the most influential guitarist of the modern rock era.

He said he understood, as we both had good points, but that we needed to work through our differences like a knife cutting peanut butter...or mayonnaise...or something else that didn't make any sense. He really had the nuttiest analogies.

Once he walked off, Janet turned her glower back to me, but it wasn't quite as hostile. "Why didn't you tell him?"

"Tell him what?"

"You know what."

"Why would I? It's none of my business. You want to ruin yourself, that's your business. But I don't have to watch you do it."

Her glower softened into a suspicious glare. "Why are you so weird about this stuff? Did something happen to you?"

"No. But the fact you think I'm being weird because I have no tolerance for heroin is a bit distressing. The truth is, I have very little patience for people who choose to waste their potential and destroy themselves in the process."

"Hmm..." The glare melted away, leaving only an uncomfortable frown. "See now, I completely disagree. Heroin helps me see the world differently, it opens up my mind. It makes me feel free. It doesn't destroy me, it improves me."

I shrugged noncommittally, because her words sounded crazy. I'd never done drugs, so I couldn't comment with any authority on her personal experience. Plus we had fifteen minutes until show time; now was not the time to point out all the extensive research that proved heroin destroyed peoples' lives. Plus, you know, it kills people.

Instead I pulled my bowtie from my bag, excusing myself to the ladies' room. I could have affixed my bow tie in the backstage area, but Abram had just entered and I found his presence highly distracting. And agitating.

I was avoiding him.

He liked me. I knew that. His suggestions I get a rebound guy notwithstanding, I wasn't so clueless that I could miss the giant neon sign he'd dropped on my head last Saturday. According to Abram, he'd been waiting for me to see him, to notice him.

The more I thought about his words, the more they reminded me of similar sentiments expressed by Martin in the past.

It occurred to me that perhaps I'd been so busy hiding, trying to keep myself from being seen, that I hadn't been paying adequate attention to the world around me. I was the one who wasn't seeing others clearly. Maybe I needed to stop focusing inward and start paying attention to what was in front of my face, starting with Abram.

I was never going to be a jump-in-feet-first, flash-the-Mardi-Gras-crowd-for-beads kind of girl. I knew it would take me some time to actually *do* anything about Abram. But I was now willing to entertain the possibility.

***

YES, I WAS spending the week with Martin on an island. But that was basically where the similarities to our spring break week ended.

After our pre-dawn chat Wednesday, I saw him zero times over the next few days. When I woke up in the morning, Martin had already left. By the time I came home, Martin was either already asleep or not yet home. I hadn't talked to him other than a daily exchange of handwritten notes.

This started on Thursday morning, when I woke up and found a simple note on the kitchen counter,

Breakfast stuff in the fridge if you're hungry. I'll be home late. –Martin

Actually the fridge was stocked with every good thing. Because I had the time, I made myself eggs benedict and bacon, with a raspberry and banana fruit salad. I also baked chocolate pecan cookies, and was sure to clean up all my mess. Admittedly, I might have been stress baking. My drama-prone side wondered if Martin would be home late because of his redheaded friend. But my pragmatic sided quickly assaulted my drama-prone side and gagged her.

I left the cookies in a sealed plastic container on the same spot where I found his note with a message that read,

Eat me. –Cookies

When I arrived back to Martin's apartment that night, I found his suit jacket on the arm of the couch and the door to his room closed. I surmised he was already asleep; but he'd left me a note on the counter that read,

I'll eat anything you tell me to eat. –Martin
P.S. Did you read the interviews yet?

I noted that the plastic cookie container was empty. He'd eaten all the cookies.

Not allowing myself to get caught up in a marinade of uncertainty (where the ingredients were: my lingering feelings and resultant confusion, the unknown nature of his relationship with the pretty redhead, and his business partner's mysterious insinuations) I jotted down a quick response,

Martin,
I have no time for reading interviews when cookies need to be made. Instead I've decided to wait until we have time to talk/discuss. I'd like to hear everything from you rather than the Internet.
-Kaitlyn

And so the next several days passed, and our note exchange proceeded as follows:

<u>Friday morning</u>

Parker,
Make me more cookies.
–Martin

Martin,
Here are more cookies.
–Kaitlyn

<u>Friday evening</u>

Kaitlyn,

What's in these cookies? Magic?
–Martin

Martin,
No, not magic. But I do use unicorn blood to make them chewy.
–Kaitlyn

<u>Saturday morning</u>

Kaitlyn,
Unicorn blood? You can find that in Manhattan?
–Martin
P.S Make me more bloody cookies.

Martin,
You can find everything in Manhattan...except affordable rent.
–Kaitlyn
P.S. Here are your bloody cookies.

<u>Saturday evening</u>

Parker,
Move in with me. I'll accept unicorn cookies as rent payment.
–Martin

Sandeke,
I haven't seen you in so long I'm beginning to think you're a figment of my imagination, except that you keep eating my cookies. Are you avoiding me because I smell like denture cream?
–Kaitlyn

<u>Sunday morning</u>

Kaitlyn,
Merry Christmas Eve. Do you have to work tonight? I thought I might take the afternoon/evening off if you're off. Do you want to hang out? If you can't today then how about tomorrow?
–Martin

P.S. I didn't want to say anything about the denture cream, but yes. The smell is why I'm avoiding you.

Martin,

Merry Christmas Eve to you as well. I have shows today from 2 p.m. until 1 a.m. But, miracle of miracles, I have nothing on Christmas except for a short late afternoon gig that's over at 4 p.m. We should hang out tomorrow morning. Also, know that I have burning questions you haven't yet answered. We could make food, then eat it...since we have no tree maybe I could pick up a Yule log?

–Parker

P.S. I will stop using the denture cream, but then you will have to chew my food for me...

I was actually grateful Martin and I hadn't seen each other for several days. The notes allowed us to settle into our friendship without all the looking at each other getting in the way and making things tense. He was still so completely and brain-meltingly *lookable*, as my pants liked to remind me whenever we shared the same space.

As well, it gave me time to contemplate and accept the very real possibility that the girl in the pictures had been his girlfriend. I decided I should feel happy for him, that he'd been able to move on so completely. I *decided* this, but I didn't *feel* it. So I worked on feeling it, I worked on moving on as he'd obviously moved on.

Therefore, I stopped avoiding Abram.

And once I stopped avoiding Abram, he and I actually had a fantastic time together. We hung out backstage and discussed mostly music and our childhoods.

We ate meals together between shows and sets, and I learned about all his (visible) tattoos, what they meant and why he'd had them done.

After gigs I played a few of my compositions for him and he played a few of his for me. We were talking and enjoying each other's company and it felt so very, very good to let myself like someone. Almost liberating.

As the week drew to a close I was feeling like things were moving in the right direction. Martin was my friend. Abram was my maybe future more-than-friend. Though I still had bucketfuls of residual feelings for Martin, all-in-all it had been a good week.

The plan was to head back to New Haven on Monday. I'd found a good price on the train ticket; tickets on December twenty-six were almost three times as expensive as they were on Christmas day.

Christmas Eve morning was actually my first and only chance to explore the city. I made a list of places I wanted to check out and crossed my fingers they'd be open. On the way I called my parents and wished them a Merry Christmas. It was a nice conversation, as they both sounded happy and relaxed.

My first stop was an independent record store in Greenwich Village that also served beer. Since it was only 10:13 a.m. when I arrived, I abstained from the beer, but I dug into the vintage collection of vinyl.

I found a few treasures to add to my record collection. As I was checking out, a discounted cover caught my attention. It was an original edition of Stevie Wonder's album *In Square Circle*, dated 1985. I checked the song list on the back and was gratified to see *Overjoyed*.

Not wanting to overthink the gift, I added it to my purchases then left the shop. My next stop was a book store, also in the Village, that was supposed to have antique medical textbooks. I'd already sent my dad his Christmas gifts, but he was always looking for wall hangings for his office.

Again, after finding something for my dad, I stumbled across something for Martin. Actually, it was a signed edition of *The Princess Bride,* one of my favorite books and movies of all time. I was caught up in the desire to share my book joy with him and since the hardcover wasn't a first edition I could actually afford it.

Then I went to a candy store famous for saltwater taffy. I bought more than I needed, deciding to wrap the extras up for Martin.

On my way back to his apartment, I passed a craft store and maker's space that had handmade Christmas stockings in the window. Again on a whim, I ran in and purchased a stocking with a crew boat and eight oars on the front in a very unusual black graphic design on red cotton. They also sold ceramics; I grabbed him a Hobbit soap dispenser for his guest bathroom that looked like a garden gnome with big feet.

Then spotted an awesome, handmade coffee mug with the picture of a bass guitar that read, *All about that bass*. It made me chuckle so I picked it up for Abram.

Before checking out I found some cool stationery; the desk set that immediately called to me had a fishing pole in the right corner and read at the bottom, *I'm not lazy, I just like to eat fish*. So, of course it was perfect for Martin. So, of course I grabbed that, too.

I maybe spent more money than was prudent, but I figured Martin had let me stay in his home for free; the least I could do was pick him up a few cool things for his apartment. Plus, I felt strongly compelled to buy him these items. I saw them and I felt an undeniable compulsion to give them to Martin.

I was juggling my bags and trying to fish out the key to his place while navigating the lobby of the apartment building, when I heard a familiar voice call to me from behind.

"Kaitlyn, may I speak with you?"

I stopped and tensed, waiting a beat before turning and glancing over my shoulder. The voice belonged to Emma Cromwell and—good news— she wasn't looking at me like I was responsible for Ebola.

But she did look determined.

CHAPTER 7
Atoms, Molecules, and Ions

I FACED HER, feeling caught and a little confused regarding what I ought to do next. "Um, hello, Emma."

I'd always been raised to say, *Nice to see you.* But in this case I didn't feel like it was appropriate because I didn't want to lie. She crossed to me, her eyes moving over me and to the bags in my hands. She smirked. It wasn't a nice smirk.

"Spending Martin's money already?"

I sighed, because she was already being distasteful. "No. I don't spend other people's money."

Her eyes narrowed as her attention moved back to my face. "Not even your parents' money?"

"That's a terribly rude question, Emma. Why do you feel like you have the right to be rude to me?" I asked this calmly because I was calm. She hadn't upset me, but I was curious as to why she felt like attacking me constantly. As far as I knew I hadn't salted the earth around her house or erased her DVR.

Her eyebrows notched upward and her lips parted. I'd obviously surprised her with my direct question.

"I…I…" She struggled for a few seconds, then finally her expression lost its hard edge. "I'm sorry. You're right. That was rude."

"You're forgiven. Do you want to come up for tea? I can't figure out his coffee maker, it has too many buttons. I feel like I might launch it into outer space."

I didn't wait for her to respond, instead I turned and walked toward the elevator. This was mostly because I was losing circulation in my fingers due to the heaviness of my bags. I knew she was following because her heels clicked on the lobby's marble floor.

Once inside the elevator I waited until she boarded before pressing the button for his floor. A few other passengers also filtered in, so we remained quiet for the duration of the ride. As well, we walked in silence down the hall, and she stood silently as I used my key to unlock the door.

She grabbed two of my bags and helped me carry them into the living room. I didn't miss how she peeked inside as she set them on the table behind the couch.

"Tea first or talking?" I asked, unburdening myself of my winter coat.

"Talking. I don't want tea."

"Fine." I shrugged, tossing my coat to the couch and claiming a leather club chair. "What's on your mind?"

She didn't sit. I noted she was bursting with restless energy. "Aren't you even a little bit sorry? A little ashamed?"

"Sorry about what?"

She huffed, like I was being purposefully irritating. "About Martin? About what he's done for you?"

I studied her, cocking my head to one side. "Here's the thing, Emma. I have no idea what you're talking about."

She snorted and crossed her arms. "Yeah, I find that hard to believe."

"I don't. I haven't been keeping up with Martin, I haven't been searching out news stories about him. In fact, I've been avoiding them."

"But you read the news, right? You keep up with current events?"

I shook my head. "Nope. I've been spending the last nine months avoiding the world, outside of music and work. I haven't read a newspaper or a headline in almost a year."

Something behind her glare loosened as I spoke and she blinked at me several times, like she was seeing me with new eyes. Her arms uncrossed and fell to her sides. Emma slowly sat down on the couch, her gaze growing introspective.

"You don't know about...anything that's happened?"

I shook my head.

"And Martin, didn't you ask him?"

"I haven't seen him since Wednesday morning, and he didn't want to talk about it then, so I didn't push."

"You haven't seen him since Wednesday?"

"Nope."

"But aren't you two back together?"

"Of course not."

"Why of course not?"

Now I huffed. "Would you please tell me what's got your piano out of tune? Because I need to leave for a gig in about a half hour."

She studied me for a beat, her eyes narrowing, but with thoughtfulness, not suspicion. At last she said, "Do you know about the houses?"

I shifted in my seat; this topic was a bit of a sore spot for me. "You mean the houses Martin was to gain as part of the trust his father set up?"

"He did, he got them. And then he sold them for approximately one hundred twenty million dollars."

This wasn't a surprise, given what I'd seen of the house in the Caribbean. "And then his father...? Did something happen?"

She shook her head. "He could do nothing about it. By the time he found out, the houses were sold and the money was offshore. Though he tried to file an injunction, a petition to sue for the proceeds, it was thrown out."

"How nice." I gave her a flat smile and she issued me a questioning look; I clarified, "How nice for Martin, that he got his revenge."

"His revenge? Hardly." She rolled her eyes, scoffing at me.

"What do you mean? He sold the houses, didn't he? He launched his fancy satellites?"

"He sold the houses, sure. But, so what? What's a measly one hundred twenty million to a man worth billions? Nothing. Denver's injunction was half-assed at best. Honestly, I think Denver had been looking for a reason to cut Martin off. As of right now, Martin is Denver's only child. He stood to inherit over twenty billion if he'd just been patient and quiet."

"Twenty...billion?" My mind had trouble comprehending that much money. It might as well have been a googolplex of pirate gold.

"Yeah." She nodded once, then added with an impressive amount of derision, "The money was invested into the satellite project, but instead of using these first satellites to drive Sandeke Telecom out of business— which was the whole purpose of his involvement and investment—he's proposed to the board that the satellites focus on delivering Internet to areas with the most need."

"He what?"

"Nothing about selling the houses has gone according to the original plan," she said, mostly to herself. "He gave the money away!"

I tried not to show my interest, but I was interested. Martin's plan and his unwillingness to deviate from it had been—at least in my mind—why we'd broken up.

"Gave the money away? What do you mean?" I picked a piece of lint off the knee of my jeans.

"He donated the sixty million." She said this like the words tasted sour.

I stared at her for a very, very long time, and she stared back. Her eyes were greenish and she was watching me with avid interest, as though keenly interested in my reaction to this news.

Certain I'd misheard her or misunderstood, I finally asked, "I'm sorry, what? He donated sixty million dollars? To whom?"

"To a non-profit foundation, one which he established early last summer. It provides funding for startups that focus on training rural educators, both domestically and internationally in the use of the latest classroom technology and web interfaces."

"I don't understand. He sold the houses for, what? A hundred and twenty million?"

"More or less, yes."

"And he donated half, and then invested the other half into the satellite project?"

"No. The donation and the investment are the same sixty million. He still has the other half—or thereabouts—in some offshore bank-account."

"I'm confused. You just said that he invested in the satellite project."

"No. *He* didn't invest in anything. The foundation he established owns what would have been his share of the 'satellite project'. He forfeited his profits. All the profits go to the foundation and will be used to purchase equipment for schools and students, and will fund initiatives to train teachers."

I sucked in a slow breath, trying to wrap my mind around this story she was telling me. "So, he...what? He gave away sixty million dollars to a foundation he founded?"

"Yes."

"So, the satellites will still be launched?"

"Yes."

"But the foundation owns his share?"

"Yes."

"And he'll...receive no profits?"

"He'll receive no profits. He's given up billions of dollars and probably his only chance to get revenge on his father."

I shook my head because I felt muddled. "Why would he do that? Why would he give it away?"

She smirked. I recognized it as her not-nice smirk. "Why do you think?"

I kept shaking my head. "I have no idea. It doesn't make any sense."

"For you. He did it for you."

I stopped shaking my head; instead I made a very unflattering scoffing noise that sounded a bit like a gurgle. "What? No. No…did he say that? Did he tell you he was giving away sixty million dollars because of me?"

Her smirk fell away and she looked suddenly tired, older. "No. But he didn't have to. We'd been planning this for three years. Then he meets you and everything changes. Of course you're the reason."

"No. That doesn't make sense. We're not together."

"He wanted you back. That's why he did it."

"Did he *say* that he—"

"No. We never talk about shit like that. We're not gal pals, we're business partners. But I have a working brain and I saw him after you broke his heart. Then suddenly all his plans changed and he's giving up his future because Joss Parker's daughter filled his head with bullshit altruistic nonsense? Yeah…he wanted you back, at least he did then."

I only half heard her tirade because I was lost in my own head. I started speaking, but honestly I'd forgotten she was in the room.

"We haven't been together since March, and then it was only for a week. He never called me, never tried to contact me. Not until a week and a half ago, and he didn't say anything about it. He hadn't said anything to me about this. Nothing. If he did this for me, then he would have called or tried to get in touch." My attention drifted back to Emma and I appealed to her simply because she was the only other person in the room. "Right? He would have called me and told me, if he wanted to get back together. He wouldn't have waited for months. That's not how Martin does things, that makes no sense…"

She shrugged, pursing her lips. "Well, I have no idea what he wants now. I mean, I believe he was seeing that intern from RER, Rural Educational Reform—that do-gooder think tank in Washington—another bleeding heart martyr type. But now I don't know, since you're here."

I involuntarily winced at this news, confirming my suspicions he'd been seeing someone else. I felt like all the air had been sucked out of the room and my heart was being stabbed with a fork. I rubbed my chest, the spot over my heart.

"He's…he's seeing someone?" I had trouble not choking on the words.

"Yes. I don't know how you missed it, they've been all over page six since August. They can't cross the street in each other's company without getting photographed. The problem is that they're just so pretty together. Her family is like yours. You know, lots of impressive ancestors with impressively good deeds." Emma's eyes moved up then down my form before she added, "You don't look anything like her, but he definitely has a type."

"What does she look like?" I asked, my question spewed forth unchecked.

Emma rolled her eyes. "I don't know, petite, *really* pretty, red hair, delicate. Who cares?"

It was the girl I'd seen earlier in the week in the pictures, when I'd made the mistake of googling Martin so I could read the interviews he and Sam kept talking about.

"Forgive me if I have no tolerance for gossiping and giving relationship advice to the person who stole my profits."

"Your profits?" I asked lamely.

"Yes. My profits. I was to receive a percentage of his share. And so now you see it's all gone. Instead he offers me a position at the goody-two-shoes foundation and a share of his third world broadcast rights."

"His what what what? Broadcast rights?" I forced myself to re-focus on the conversation, the real issue, not who Martin had been dating...or had recently dated. Honestly, I was only able to re-center myself because Martin had point-blank texted me he didn't have a girlfriend and I trusted him to tell me the truth.

Of course, that just meant he didn't have one right now. But it didn't mean he'd been celibate since we split. This thought made me queasy, more fork stabbing to the heart, so I pushed it from my mind.

Emma released a derisive snort. "Some crazy idea he has, and invested three million of his remaining monies." She waved her hand through the air like his idea was a gnat and she was trying to swat it. "He purchased broadcast rights for basically all of the third world. He has a virtual monopoly on Internet streaming of syndicated shows for the next fifty years, as well as the big sites, like Netflix, Amazon, etcetera." Then she added under her breath, "A lot of good it will do him since no one in those areas owns a computer and they can't get Internet."

I stared at a spot over her head as a picture arranged itself in my brain; unthinkingly, I spoke my stream of consciousness out loud. "Broadcast rights for the third world will never yield a profit...unless underserved areas can get cheap access to Internet. Or free access."

"And are given computers," she added unnecessarily.

My gaze flickered to hers, held it, and my mouth dropped open because Martin was a genius.

"You mean, if they are given computers by a goody-two-shoes foundation? And trained to use them, by the same foundation? A goody-two-shoes foundation that receives funds from the profits of satellites delivering cheap or free Internet to underserved areas?"

Her frown turned thoughtful, then startled, then amazed. "Oh my God."

I nodded, grinning at his cleverness. "Hasn't he discussed this with you? Don't the two of you talk about anything?"

"No. I wouldn't…I was so angry, I didn't want to talk about it."

"And you didn't figure it out?"

"No." She laughed a little, shook her head disbelievingly. "Martin always said you were smart, and he was right. I mean now that you point it out, everything is so obvious. I guess I was just so angry that he didn't follow through with the original plan, plus that stupid foundation… Oh my God. We're not going to make anything close to what we would have made if he'd directly invested in the satellite venture, and he'll never be anywhere near as rich as his father, but wow. We might break a billion. Maybe two."

"It might take a bit, but yeah. In about ten years, once the foundation does its thing and the satellites are buzzing around up there, giving people in rural Africa and the rainforests of Brazil high-speed Internet service, he'll be the only one making money off streaming video in what used to be the third world."

She looked at me and smiled. It was the first time I'd seen her smile since meeting her. Her eyes were bright with excitement and every bit of bitterness had melted away. It was almost a nice moment.

But then she had to ruin it by sighing happily and saying, "God, I love that man."

***

EMMA DID STAY for tea, and she was chatty. She also had a habit of tossing her long, perfect, wheat-colored hair over her shoulder in excess. It wouldn't have irritated me so much if she weren't so suddenly effusive about how much she admired Martin.

Really, he was all she talked about: how smart he was, how intelligent, how he was going to change the world. How he was Steve Jobs and Bill Gates and Mark Zuckerberg, except being born into wealth, and therefore able to make a substantial difference earlier in his life, not having to wait for pesky things like investors.

"You know Mark Zuckerberg created Facebook when he was nineteen? And Steve Jobs founded Apple at twenty-one?"

"Hmm." I did know this. I think everyone in my generation knew this information—or at least every person with any geek persuasions. Except I also knew that Steve Jobs was just a smart enough and pushy guy who exploited his friend (Steve Wozniak), pilfered his ideas, and passed them off as his own.

"There's no one like Martin, though. No one who thinks about strategy like he does, who sees the whole picture. He's completely brilliant." Her eyes scanned me, up and down, like she was expecting me to do a cheer for Martin, maybe suggest that we dedicate a fan site to him, and was irritated I didn't seem to share her enthusiasm.

I couldn't decide whether I liked Emma or not. Furthermore, I couldn't decide if it mattered. Perhaps it was the naïve do-gooder in me, but I was disappointed she saw no merit in Martin's foundation until after I pointed out his plan and the foundation would ultimately bring her millions. I also didn't like that her loyalty seemed to hinge on how much money she could make off him.

Plus, I couldn't stop thinking about the very pretty redhead he'd allegedly dated and with whom he'd been photographed countless times. I reasserted the prudence of my decision to never search for any news story or interview related to Martin until I was completely over him. Just thinking about him with someone else made me want to throw a month-long drama parade.

"Did you know I used to work for Martin's dad?" Emma asked apropos of nothing.

I shook my head, surprised. "No. I didn't know that. What happened?"

"Have you met Denver Sandeke?"

"Yes...unfortunately."

"Exactly. He's a complete ass. He's brilliant, but he's an ass and that means he's arrogant. And he's known for sexually harassing his female staff. Once you get used to it, it's...bearable. Mostly I just ignored that part of my job. But my work with Denver is how I met Martin. He was a junior in high school and I was arranging a corporate event at Denver's house in Santa Monica. Martin definitely didn't look like a seventeen-year-old. I knew who he was so I tried to be nice. He started asking me all these questions about what I did for his father, and I thought to myself, *This kid is brighter than his dad. He's going places!* It also helped that he was completely disinterested in me other than my knowledge. Unlike his father, he seemed more interested in what I had to say than my cup size."

"So how did you become Martin's business partner?"

"Well, I had access to information Martin did not. So Martin pulled me aside at one of the parties and asked me how I liked working for his father. I was careful at first, but eventually I saw that he had a plan. And, honestly, I liked the idea of screwing over Denver Sandeke—he is so awful. I agreed to stay on with his dad and pass Martin any information that might be useful. I figured once Martin trusted me enough, he would share his plans with me. He did and the rest is history."

"Hmm…" I studied her. "You placed a lot of faith in a teenager." Not to mention she'd just admitted to corporate espionage like it was no big deal.

"I did," she admitted soberly. "But there's just something about Martin, right? Do you know what I mean? He inspires confidence. People *want* to follow him. I thought about my position with his father and knew—other than gaining work experience—I had no growth potential at Sandeke Telecom. Denver runs it like a good-old boy's club. I was doing the work of an executive and being treated like a 1950s secretary."

"That does sound awful."

"I trusted Martin and he never made me feel like he was interested in anything from me other than my brain. I can't tell you how refreshing that was."

"I bet." I nodded, studying her and finding her to be sincere. Emma may have been a corporate shark, but she was a well-reasoned, capable corporate shark. I understood better why Martin had singled her out.

"What do you think of this place?" She indicated to Martin's apartment and sipped her tea, changing the subject and issuing me a friendly smile.

"I like it. It's very Martin." I hadn't thought about it until she asked, but it was very Martin. It was no fuss, but not sterile. Comfortable. It felt like a home.

I don't think she heard me, because she followed her question with, "I keep telling him he needs to move into a better space. We can't have dinner parties here. This apartment is…okay. But he should be in a penthouse. Did you know he picked out all the furniture himself? I tried to get him to use a decorator." She shook her head, like he was a silly child. "Sometimes I forget how young he is, how much he still needs to learn about the corporate environment. Eventually he'll see things my way."

I opened my mouth to ask why he couldn't have dinner parties in this apartment—it seemed fine to me—but then she started talking again.

"Maybe you could help me. Together we could get him to see reason. I'm sure you have a good perspective, with your parents being who they are. You're probably even better suited to persuade him than I am." She giggled meaningfully.

I tried to keep the abject horror I was feeling from painting itself on my face. I decided it was time for her to go.

She left when I mentioned I needed to get ready for work. Of note, she was diligently nice to me as she departed, asking if she could take me to lunch the next time I was in the city.

"I think it would be really great for Martin if you and I became friends," she said, then added as though to clarify, "that way he won't feel torn about his loyalty to either of us."

I gave her a noncommittal smile and nod, but felt like she was communicating in a different language. I didn't know how to speak corporate politics and networking.

Once Emma left, I made quick work of wrapping Martin's presents, stuffing as many as would fit into his stocking, hiding everything under my bed, then leaving for my gig.

I tried not to let myself get caught up in the idea that Martin had established the foundation and made sweeping, philanthropic changes to his grand plan as some sort of gesture to win me back, as Emma had suggested originally. If he wanted me, the Martin I'd known would have just shown up on my doorstep and demanded we reconcile.

No. There was more to the story of the foundation. I was sure of it. Maybe it had something to do with the pretty redhead he'd been dating...

Again, this thought made me queasy and was accompanied by forks piercing my heart, so I pushed it from my mind.

I decided I would wait to draw any conclusions until after I had all the facts, after I questioned Martin.

CHAPTER 8
Chemistry of the Nonmetals

CHRISTMAS IN NEW YORK is magical.

It's also a time for drunken holiday party hookups, engaging in yelling matches with co-workers after imbibing too much holiday cheer, and sloppy make-out sessions behind fourteen-foot plastic Douglas fir trees.

By the third set of the night I felt like the audience was much more entertaining than our band. We were playing a Christmas Eve party for some huge conglomerate at a skyscraper downtown. Willis told me they were originally supposed to have *a real band*, but then that real band backed out two weeks ago. A real band meaning recording musicians who wrote and sold their own compositions.

And so they were stuck with us and we were stuck with them and that set a very surly, rebellious tone for the evening. Willis decided we would end our third set with *I Wanna Be Sedated* by The Ramones.

When we walked off stage it was the first time they had applauded, and I even heard a few whistles of appreciation.

"We're playing punk, loud, and defiant for the rest of the night," Janet said as she fished a cigarette out of her bag.

Abram pulled out his own pack of cigarettes and his voice was tight and angry when he spoke. "Those fuckers out there are pissing me off."

"Agreed." Willis marched over to Janet and put his hand out for a cigarette. I'd never seen him smoke before; in fact, I was pretty sure he'd quit several years ago.

"Katy, you want to go take a walk?" Fitzy gave me a hopeful smile. He really was cute, handsome, nice. And yet he did nothing for my pants.

I was beginning to suspect that my pants were actually my brain.

Before I could respond, Willis laughed at Fitzy's suggestion. "Where are you going to go for a walk? On the roof? You'd be pacing a small square and shivering your nuts off. We have to be back out there in fifteen minutes, bucko."

"No thanks, I think I need to find the ladies' room," I tossed over my shoulder and didn't wait for anyone to respond. Rather, I exited the backstage area through a giant steel door in a rush because I actually really needed to use the facilities.

I walked through a window-lined hallway, the sounds of recorded music from the party following me most of the way. I stopped when I encountered elevators and a fork in the path. Shrugging, I decided to go left into a new hallway. One side was glass, looking down on an atrium several floors below. The other side was lined with offices.

Soon I found I'd gone in a circle and was back where I started. This was bad news as my bladder was sending up the yellow emergency flag and I was doing the pee-jig to keep myself together. Thankfully, I encountered a pair of intoxicated women who appeared to be on a mission. On a hunch, I followed them and sent a silent thank you to the heavens as they stumbled into a nondescript—and unmarked—women's bathroom with several stalls.

At this point I was cutting it close, so after my business was finished I jogged back to the backstage area and rushed through the door just in time to hear Fitzy say, "She's not even with you! Katy is none of your business—"

I halted, my eyes flickering over the scene before me. Abram was smirking at Fitzy, leaning his shoulder against the brick wall. Fitzy was standing in the middle of the room and appeared to be quite riled up. Willis was between them, apparently keeping them apart. And Janet was nowhere to be seen.

All eyes turned to me as I entered; I didn't know quite what to do. The only person who didn't appear to be upset was Abram. In fact, he looked positively pleased.

At a loss, I stared wide-eyed at the trio and gave the room a little wave. "Hey, guys… What's up?"

***

ABRAM DIDN'T STOP casting sinisterly pleased looks in my direction through most of the fourth set. I assumed this had everything to do with getting under Fitzy's shirt collar, so I ignored his antics.

But then abruptly, his expression sobered during the last song and turned irritated, his eyes narrowing on me as we wrapped up the last stanza. No sooner was I off the stage, I felt his hand on my upper arm leading me out the steel door I'd used earlier on my hunt for the bathroom.

"Where are you going? We have one more set!" Willis called after us.

"Just for a quick walk," Abram called over his shoulder, practically pulling me behind him.

Once the door closed behind us, I demanded, "Let go of my arm, this is a very uncomfortable way to walk."

He didn't turn, but his hand slid down to mine. Abram threaded our fingers together and continued leading me forward.

We came to the fork in the path and I volunteered, "It's a circle. No matter which way you go we'll end up back here." I was honestly too tired to give his strange behavior much consideration.

He pulled me to the right and finally spoke. "Your boyfriend is here."

"My boyfriend?"

"The stockbroker." His eyes slid to mine, his big jaw working, his brown eyes dark and unhappy.

I stumbled, forcing Abram to stop. "Martin? Martin's here? Where? I didn't see him."

"He showed up at the end of the last set."

"He did?"

"Yeah. Now, why would he be here? I thought you two were over."

I tugged my hand from Abram's and crossed my arms over my chest. My heart was racing now.

"We are over. But we're…we're friends. I'm staying with him."

"You're staying with him?"

"This week. I've been staying at his place in Manhattan for the week."

Abram's hands moved to his hips and he released a frustrated sigh. "If you needed a place to stay, you could have called me. You don't have to stay with your douchebag ex."

I scrunched my face, not liking that Abram was calling Martin a douchebag. I knew this reaction was silly as he'd done it before and I didn't object. But things between Martin and I had changed. I'd always cared about him, yes. And now that I'd let go of my anger about our breakup I didn't want people calling him names.

"Listen, he's not a douchebag. Like I said, we're friends. It's no big deal."

"And nothing's happened?"

I grew very still, but felt compelled to ask, "Why is that any business of yours?"

He grit his teeth, his eyes abruptly dimming. "I guess it's not. It's none of my business."

We stared at each other for a long moment in silence and I could see him building a virtual wall between us. He was making his mind up, having a conversation in his head, while I stood here and waited for him to give me a real response.

But he didn't. He closed himself off, burying his thoughts and feelings, and I realized Abram and I were extremely similar.

He wasn't fearless. We were both feelings hoarders.

He may have suggested a few weeks ago that I sleep with Fitzy, or use him as my rebound guy and whatever that entailed, because I wasn't in any danger of falling for Fitzy. And then Abram wouldn't be my rebound guy. He wanted to be with me, but wanted everything to be just right, just perfect, and all sorted before really putting himself out there.

I briefly wondered if the scene I'd walked in on earlier was Abram trying to push Fitzy in that direction.

I felt a smile of ironic understanding claim my features and I exhaled a small laugh, realizing that if I wanted bravery and honesty, it was going to have to come from me.

"Look, I think I like you. And I think you like me, too. I don't need a rebound guy. In fact, I don't *need* any guy. But I would *like* a partner. I would like to be part of a team."

Abram's cold expression didn't change but I did see something pass behind his eyes, a flicker of acceptance, of understanding.

He cleared his throat, his gaze moving to the carpet then back to mine. "It's none of my business, I know. But we've had, at least I've had, a really good time with you this week. So, what are we doing here? Are you back with your ex?"

I shook my head. "No."

"Are you over him?"

I hesitated, my attention moving to a spot behind Abram as I thought about the question, how to answer it honestly. "I don't know. He was my first everything. I'm starting to think it's not possible to ever truly get over that person, the first person who made you feel like... But maybe it is possible to move on."

He was silent for a beat, then acknowledged quietly, "I get that. I know what you mean."

We gave each other quick, commiserating glances and flat smiles. I twisted my fingers while he stuffed his hands in his pockets.

"Katy...do you want to be over him? Do you want to be with me?"

My eyes collided with Abram's and I saw it cost him something to ask the question. As much as I wanted to respond, *Yes, I want to be over Martin. Yes, I want to be with you*, I couldn't. Because my feelings were so much messier than a yes or a no.

He nodded, just a subtle movement at first, as though I had spoken, as though I'd already given my answer and he was processing it.

Before he got too far ahead of me I rushed to clarify, "I don't like feeling this way. I don't like being stuck in limbo and wanting two completely different things. Yes, I want to be over Martin. I know he's moved on, as he's had a girlfriend since we broke up—at least one that I know about. And, honestly, I don't trust him not to hurt me again. But part of me feels like things aren't finished."

"That's just you wishing." He didn't look upset, he looked resigned. "But I get it. I do. Because I didn't feel like things were finished with me and my ex. I hadn't moved on and I kept wishing things could be different."

"Did you tell her?"

"No. I was a coward." He uttered this with no bitterness, just a matter-of-fact assessment of himself.

"When did you stop? When did you feel like things were finished?"

"Not 'til recently. Not until I met you."

I sighed. His words, made with his powerful and deep voice, his soulful brown eyes, caused my heart to ache.

"Abram—"

"Does he know?"

"Know what?"

"That you're still wishing?"

I didn't answer. I didn't need to. Abram gave me a sardonic smirk and shook his head, his eyes teasing but also a little sad, like he felt sorry for me.

"You and I are a lot alike, Katy."

I returned his smirk and shrugged at my weakness. "I don't know how to tell him. I feel so paralyzed. I don't want to ruin our friendship."

Abram closed the distance between us and threw his arm over my shoulder, tucking me close to his broad chest and steering us back for our last set.

"If he hasn't moved on and he's wishing too, then you need to put him out of his misery and tell him what's going on in your head. Be brave."

"Ha! Says Abram. Self-professed coward."

He continued as though I hadn't spoken. "But if he has moved on, you need to know for sure. Because then you can move on, too."

***

MARTIN WAS IN the audience. He was standing by the bar and was surrounded by people. I spotted him almost immediately when we took the stage; I explained away this phenomenon to myself, reasoning that he was several inches taller than everyone else.

But really, I found him so fast because he was Martin. I think my blood chemistry had changed when we were together, because locating him in the crowd had been exceptionally easy.

His eyes lifted and found mine, and he held them until I looked away. I felt his gaze on me for the duration of the set. At first it was distracting. But then I settled into it, accepted it, and it began to feel oddly comforting.

When we finished the last song I think we were all surprised at the round of applause we received. The night had not started well, but Janet's idea of punk and rebellion seemed to do the trick. I lifted my attention to the audience, again my eyes immediately finding Martin. He lifted his cell and gestured to it. I interpreted this to mean, *check your phone.*

Backstage, Fitzy was waiting and jumped between my bag and me. "Hey, so, you want to grab a drink?"

I walked around him. "No thanks. I'm really tired."

"And she's got someone waiting for her," Abram chimed in, pulling on his heavy coat.

Fitzy glanced between us. "Who? You?"

"Nope." Abram's eyes met mine and I was impressed by all the different sentiments I saw there: humor, regret, acceptance, exhaustion, and a subversive pleasure in giving Fitzy a hard time.

I checked my phone, saw that Martin had sent me two messages; the first provided directions on where to meet him. The second read,

Martin: *Don't go out with the band, I'm driving you back to my place. I haven't seen or talked to you all week.*

I frowned at this second note, felt like it was an unnecessary addition. The more I studied the text, the more it looked like a command. I rolled my eyes. Typical Martin. I quickly typed out a response.

Kaitlyn: *You're not the boss of me.*
Martin: *I know. But sometimes I act like I am.*

Kaitlyn: *Why?*

Martin: *Because you like it.*

I stared at his last message; it set my heart off at a gallop. I did like it. I liked arguing with Martin, challenging him, bucking under his attempts to boss me around. Or, I had liked it when we were together.

Abram was right. I was still wishing. And yet, there were still so many things unsettled between us. Even if I told him I still had feelings for him and he returned them, would it matter? All of the reasons we split before seemed to have evaporated except for the biggest one: he'd chosen his revenge over us...or maybe he hadn't.

The way Emma described the situation, it sounded like Martin hadn't put his revenge plan into action. And yet, he'd let me walk away in the spring. GAH! I was confused. I didn't *know* if I could trust him.

Nevertheless, there was the girl in the pictures. Even if he'd ultimately abandoned his revenge, he'd still been able to move on with someone else and I hadn't.

Absentmindedly, I gathered my things and left the backstage area, only peripherally aware that Fitzy and Abram were still talking and that it might have something to do with me. I easily found the elevators, the sounds of the remaining party fading the farther I walked from the event space.

But then I became aware that someone was behind me and I turned, finding Willis. He looked grim.

I gave him a questioning look, stopping and facing him. "What's up?"

"I thought we talked about this."

"About what?"

"You and Abram. You and Fitzy."

I breathed my relief. "Nothing is going on with Abram. He and I are friends."

"What about Fitzy? He's looking at you lately like a sushi roll with no tuna."

"Nothing is going on with Fitzy and me either, at least not on my side."

He crossed his arms. "Don't shit on my leg and tell me it's frosting."

The elevator dinged, announcing its arrival.

Meanwhile, I did an admirable job of not laughing at the mental image of me defecating on Willis's leg then trying to pass it off as chocolate frosting.

"Again, nothing is going on."

"I told you before, I don't want you going on any mattress tours. This stuff between you and the boys needs to stop."

"Willis, I have no part in their boy-angst. Whatever they're arguing about is between them."

Willis nodded thoughtfully, but then his attention snagged on something behind me. I twisted to see what it was and found Martin standing just inside the elevator, his eyes narrowed and focused on Willis.

"Oh...oh!" I turned completely around, feeling my cheeks flood with warmth while I wondered how much of that conversation Martin had overheard.

"Do you want something?" I heard Willis ask.

"Yeah. Her." Martin lifted his chin toward me as he leaned forward, grabbed my arm, and pulled me into the elevator.

Willis snorted. "Take a fucking number."

"Hey!" I objected.

Martin ignored me, moving me behind him, obviously misunderstanding Willis's meaning. "You don't talk about her that way."

I heard Willis sputter, "I'll do whatever the fuck I want, *son*."

Uh oh... Of all the things Willis could have called Martin, son was probably the worst.

"Those are big words coming from a little man who's all washed up. So listen, grandpa, you treat her with respect or I'll—"

"You'll do nothing. He'll do nothing." I jumped in front of Martin, covered Martin's mouth with one hand and pushed the close-door button with the other. "Bye, Willis. See you tomorrow," I squeaked as the doors slid shut.

When the elevator finally started its descent, I let my hand drop from his mouth and leaned heavily against the wall behind me, letting my head fall back with a *thud*.

"That guy is an asshole," he said. No, actually he growled it.

I sighed, closing my eyes, "Martin..."

"What?"

"That guy is my boss."

"You need a new boss."

"Can you try being a little nicer?"

"What did I do?"

"You weren't very nice to Willis."

I heard Martin move, the rustle of his coat. "He deserved it."

"You misinterpreted the conversation."

"Really? I misinterpreted, 'Take a fucking number'?" He sounded really angry.

I sighed again, opening my eyes and sliding them to the side, peering at him. "Yes. Willis can be crass. But he wasn't insulting me. I promise."

"Doesn't matter. I don't like that guy."

"Just because you don't like people doesn't mean you can go around treating them like crap. What is so hard about being nice?"

"It's time-consuming." He said this completely deadpan and of course it made me laugh.

"Oh, Martin…" I wiped tears from my eyes. I was laughing so hard I was crying, but also I was just completely exhausted.

After a minute of watching me laugh at him, he reluctantly smiled and shook his head. "Besides, I'm nice to you."

"Is that supposed to make me feel special? That you deem me worthy of kindness?"

"Yes."

The doors opened and Martin grabbed my bag, hoisting it to his shoulder and leading me out of the lift with a hand on my lower back.

"Well, it doesn't," I said tiredly. "My self-worth does not rise and set based on your treatment or opinion of me. I want no special treatment, I insist you treat me like you treat everyone else."

"That's not going to happen."

"Why not?"

He didn't answer at first. In fact, he didn't speak for so long I started to think he wasn't going to respond. He guided me out of the building's main entrance to where his car was waiting. A man stood next to it, like a valet or a guard and had been waiting for us. Martin opened the passenger door for me, took my hand, and helped me inside.

But right before the door closed I heard him say, "Because you're Kaitlyn."

CHAPTER 9
Liquids and Intermolecular Forces

WE DIDN'T TALK in the car, mostly because I fell asleep during the quick ride. I woke up briefly when Martin lifted me from the car and into his arms. I curled into him because I was drowsy and he smelled like Martin. On the short walk to the elevator I fell back asleep, but this time I dreamt.

We were back on the boat. The sun was setting. The air was hot and salty. Martin carried me down the steps to our cabin. His hands were loving, caressing, amorous, as were his looks. We were both dressed in almost nothing, scraps of bathing suits, the feel of his skin against mine, and our combined warmth was intoxicating. He laid me on the bed, climbed over my body. He slipped his callused hand into my bikini. He touched me. I sighed. I trusted him. His oceanic eyes captured mine. He leaned down to kiss me…

I woke with a start in the present as he laid me on the bed in my room in his apartment and moved to take off my shoes. My body was humming and confused. My mind was still preoccupied with my dream, of us together, and all the ways I desperately wanted him.

"I've got it." My voice was unsteady as I bent my legs and sat up a bit, pushing my hair out of my face, needing him to leave before he saw my disorienting desire and embarrassment.

"Go back to sleep." He grabbed my right foot and took off my shoe.

"No, I got it." I wiggled my leg, trying to break free from his grip.

"Kaitlyn," his hand slipped into my pants leg, caressed my calf, making me freeze but also sending a lava flow of *Yes, please* to my center, "go back to sleep. I'm just taking off your shoes."

I couldn't respond. His hand on the bare skin of my leg meant I was rendered speechless. His eyes were visible even in the inky darkness and I couldn't look away. How pathetic was I? Martin inadvertently touches my leg, looks at me in the eye, and I'm mentally begging him to take off his pants. *Then my pants. Then our underwear. Then...*

But he doesn't. He holds my gaze as he takes off my shoes. He sets them on the floor at the foot of my bed. He turns. He leaves. And I experience a sensation I imagine is akin to falling off a very tall building.

As soon as I heard the soft click of the door, I lay back in the bed and stared at the ceiling, restless and overwrought, my center throbbing, aching. I tried to bring my breathing under control as well as the intensity and sharpness of my longing.

And the strangest thought occurred to me.

Really, it wasn't that strange. I'd touched myself in the past, but not since being with Martin. Before, it had basically been an experiment, an exploration of sorts, born out of detached curiosity. I'd wanted to make myself orgasm at the time because I wanted to know what it felt like, what all the fuss was about. My experiment had never yielded anything, just me feeling immeasurably silly.

But now—the specter of my dream and his lingering scent filling the room—the idea didn't feel silly at all. In fact, I could still smell him on me, expensive soap and aftershave. My desire, my craving for him felt abruptly overwhelming; I couldn't breathe. I was suffocating with it.

I knew he was in the apartment. I could hear him moving around. I closed my eyes and pictured him. I unbuttoned my shirt, unhooked my bra at the front, then let my other hand drift down my stomach to my pants, under the waistband, into my panties. I was on autopilot, my movements compulsory.

I was already wet. And when I touched myself I was shocked at how sensitive I was, how responsive. I glanced down—my fingers on my bare breast, my smooth stomach illuminated only by the city lights, my wrist disappearing into the waistband of my tuxedo—and imagined Martin watching me, seeing what I was seeing.

Maybe he was sitting on the edge of the bed, telling me to do this. Instructing me, giving me praise and loving—yet dirty—words of encouragement. Just the thought of him seeing me this way and liking it made my breath become ragged, and I felt myself edge closer to release.

Impatient, I unzipped my pants and spread my legs. This time I imagined he was in the chair at the end of the bed; he could see me, all of me, and he was silently watching. Maybe he was dressed in his suit, his pants unzipped and open, stroking himself…

Aaaand, that did it. I came. And I had to turn my head into my pillow to keep from crying out. Though I continued the fantasy, envisioning that imaginary Martin had also reached his release and was holding my gaze as we came together.

I sobered relatively quickly, the experience leaving me spent but unsatisfied. I removed my hands from my body and turned away from the door. I pulled my shirt closed, tucked my knees to my chest and stared out the window overlooking Central Park, at the tall buildings with their twinkling lights in the distance.

A cold lump of nothing settled in my stomach. I finally understood why Abram had been trying to get me to consider a rebound guy.

A warm body. A soft touch. A gentle kiss and whisper. It would have made a difference. True, they wouldn't have filled the void, but they would have softened the fall.

My chin wobbled and I tried to breathe normally. My eyes stung. I fought the urge to cry by biting my bottom lip fiercely, focusing on the voluntary pain I was inflicting with my teeth rather than the gaping hole in my chest that never showed signs of healing.

But then I started and tensed, because I heard the unmistakable sound of my bedroom door opening. I held my breath and squeezed my eyes shut, thankful I now faced the window.

"Kaitlyn?" he whispered. Goosebumps raced over my skin at the sound of his voice, but I couldn't speak.

Heck, I couldn't breathe. I didn't want him to see me. I felt certain if he saw my face, the front of my clothes, he'd know what I'd been doing. I didn't want him to know. If he looked into my eyes he'd know I was still crazy for him. And if there was even a chance he'd look at me with pity, I didn't want to see it.

So I said nothing.

I felt him move closer. He hovered at the edge of the bed. Martin set something on the side table…it sounded like a glass. My heart was hammering between my ears and I fixated on it, ignoring the urge to turn toward him and make a fool of myself, to tell him I didn't care if he'd ever loved me. I loved him. I wanted him. I needed…

I was concentrating so hard that I flinched my surprise when I felt a blanket fall gently over my shoulders. My lids opened automatically, startled, and I found Martin standing in front of me, covering me with a duvet from the closet.

"Go back to sleep." Again, he whispered this, his attention following the line of the blanket, perhaps to make sure I was completely covered.

But then his eyes moved to mine and our gazes collided, or at least it felt that way to me, like a head-on collision. His movements stalled then stilled. He looked surprised.

"What," he started, stopped, then stared at me. He seemed confused by what he saw. "Are you still angry with me about Willis?"

I shook my head. "No. Just tired." My voice was rough, uneven.

He frowned, lifted his chin slightly, and I could tell he didn't believe me. His eyes moved over my body where it was now covered by the blanket and narrowed with obvious suspicion.

"What were you doing—"

I cleared my throat, interrupting him. "I'm tired. Goodnight, Martin."

I turned my head into the pillow, my hair providing a concealing curtain. Especially right now, looking at him made everything harder, more painful.

He didn't leave immediately. Several seconds ticked passed, my heart rising higher in my throat with each passing moment. But then I heard him leave—his feet on the wooden floor, the soft click of the door.

And for the first time in several months, I cried.

***

I WAITED UNTIL I heard Martin's bedroom door close. After another ten minutes, I wrapped myself in a towel and tiptoed to the bathroom. My face was red and splotchy, and my eyes were itchy from my odd bout of tears. Standing under the hot spray of the shower did wonders for my peace of mind. I took my time washing my hair and soaping my body, feeling warm, soothed, and much calmer when I finally turned off the water.

Back in my bedroom I quickly dressed in yoga pants pajamas, one of my Death Cab for Cutie concert T-shirts that had been regulated to sleepwear, and my Abraham Lincoln socks. Just as I was climbing back into the bed my foot connected with something beneath it. I turned on the light and bent to peer under the mattress.

It was Martin's stocking and presents. I'd completely forgotten about them in my sleepy—then aroused, then depressed—haze. I pulled them from their hiding place and flipped off the light switch. Clutching the gifts to my chest, I held my breath and listened for any sounds of movement coming from elsewhere in the apartment. As far as I could discern all was quiet.

Again, I tiptoed out of my room, this time intent on the fireplace. I figured I could hang his stocking somehow then put the rest of the presents on the hearth. But when I entered the living room I stopped short and my mouth fell open in surprise.

Martin had procured a tree.

It was a small, Charlie Brown type of tree, no larger than four feet tall. The baby tree was in a tin bucket draped in white lights, yet held no other ornamentation, not even a star at the top.

However, the tree wasn't responsible for my paralysis. The reason why I was standing just beyond the hallway, still clutching Martin's gifts, with an expression of shock and awe, was because of what the tree sat upon.

His unfussy Christmas tree rested on top of an antique Steinway upright piano. The piano had a huge red ribbon and a bow wrapped around it. I couldn't move. It was the prettiest picture I'd ever seen. The little minimalistic tree, the classic piano with a big red bow, both sitting next to Martin's gray stone fireplace in his warm, cozy, bookish living room. Windows on the other side of the fireplace showcased a snow-covered New York City beyond.

I felt like I was looking at an image in a magazine. If I'd seen this image in a magazine I would have paused on the page, maybe even ripped it out and filed it under *my ideal life*. I couldn't move because I didn't want to move. I wanted to stay in this picture forever.

"What are you doing up?"

I yelped, jumped, and ungracefully twisted toward the sound of Martin's voice, gulping in a large, shocked breath. I struggled to keep hold of the packages in my arms, having momentarily flailed and loosened my grip. Martin rushed forward, seeing I was just about to drop a box, and caught it with one hand while steadying me with the other.

"Oh my God, you scared me." I closed my eyes, my heart hammering in my throat as the rush of adrenaline subsided.

His hand slipped from my waist to my shoulder, squeezing. "I thought you were tired."

"I was. I mean, I am. But I was waiting for you to go to sleep."

"I heard you take a shower so I couldn't sleep."

"You couldn't sleep because I was taking a shower?"

He ignored my question and asked me instead, "Are you okay?"

I nodded, laughing a little, and peeked at him through one eye. "You just missed Santa Claus. He dropped this stuff off for you, but left in a huff when he found no cookies."

He shrugged, giving me a brilliant smile. "Those bloody cookies are mine. Fat man needs a diet."

This made me laugh harder, and we both ended up laughing together for several minutes. As the hilarity and enjoyment of our own jokes subsided, I caught Martin eyeing the presents in my hands.

"What's all this?"

"Just some stuff I saw that I thought you might like."

His gaze lifted, his smile growing softer as his eyes searched my face. He asked in wonder, "These are all for me?"

"Yes. But you weren't supposed to know about them until morning. Congratulations, you've ruined Christmas."

Martin pressed his lips together and gave me a look reminiscent of our time on the boat last spring, like I was perfect and strange. "Technically, it's already morning."

"Oh, well, in that case," I stepped forward and dumped the cornucopia of wrapped presents into his arms, "Merry Christmas, Martin."

He accepted them gingerly, shifting to the side to make sure none of them fell. "Jesus, Kaitlyn!"

"That's right, Jesus." I nodded. "Jesus is the reason for the season."

This only made him laugh again while he struggled to keep his grip. "I mean—help me carry all this stuff to the couch."

Grinning at him, I took the boxes most precariously perched and turned for the couch, stumbling a little when I caught sight of the piano and tree again. A rush of uncertain happiness spread from my stomach to my extremities.

"Do you like it?" he asked from behind me, obviously noticing where my attention had snagged.

"Is it for me?" I asked, a rush of emotion — confusion, hope, hopeful confusion — making my throat tight.

I heard him deposit his stuff on the couch and felt the heat of his body directly at my back just before his arms wrapped around my shoulders, his cheek brushing against my temple.

"Of course it's for you." His voice was a rumble above a whisper.

I placed my hands on his forearms and squeezed, glad he couldn't see my face because I was overwhelmed. My hopes and my questions were assembling themselves, trying to partner up so I could begin to understand what this gift meant. I had to clear my throat before speaking.

"I…I don't understand."

"What's to understand? It's a piano. The guy tuned it yesterday and it's all ready for you. You should play something."

"Now?"

"Yes. Now."

I couldn't do that. I didn't want to touch it. If I touched it then I'd want to keep it and nothing in this apartment was mine to keep. And when the time came for us to part, which felt inevitable, I would lose something.

No. The piano wasn't mine any more than Martin was mine.

So I shook my head, clearing it of these maudlin thoughts, and decided to tease him instead. "You got me a piano for your apartment."

"Yes."

"So I have to visit in order to play it."

"That's the idea."

"So it's blackmail."

"It's an incentive."

I let my head fall back on his shoulder and looked up at him. "It's bribery at best."

He grinned down at me. "It's an enticement."

"Don't try to out-synonym me. Let's settle on enticing extortion."

"I'm fine with that."

"But you don't have to buy me a piano in order to ensure I'll visit. Friends visit each other. If you want me to visit, just ask me."

His arms tightened then let me go. I felt him draw away, heard him sigh quietly. "Do you want something to drink?"

"Are we going to finish this conversation?" I turned to watch him disappear.

"Yes. But I need some scotch to finish this conversation," he called from the kitchen.

"Scotch? Are you drinking scotch?"

"Yeah. It's good. You'd like it."

"Monogrammed towels, business cards, fancy watches, corner office, and now scotch. It's like I don't even know you anymore. Are you golfing now, too? Pretty soon you're going to retire and move to Miami."

He barked a laugh and reappeared with two glasses and two bottles of unlabeled red liquid.

"Fine. No scotch. How about sangria?"

"Oh! I'll take sangria."

I moved all of his presents to the center cushion of the couch and claimed one end while he poured us both a glass and settled on the other side. The sangria was really, really good. It didn't even taste like it had alcohol in it, except maybe a little red wine.

I sipped mine.

Meanwhile, Martin gulped his then refilled his glass.

"So…" I peered at him while he studied his loot. "Like I said, just ask me to visit."

"I will."

"You don't need to buy a piano."

He took another gulp of his sangria then set it to the side. Selecting a box, he tore through the wrapping, and said offhandedly, "I know I don't *need* to buy you a piano, but I like hearing you play—and more than that stuff you play in the band. I want to hear your music, the stuff you compose."

He grinned as he discovered what was inside the wrapping paper and held it up. "I like this. I'm going to use this when I send you letters."

It was the lazy fisherman desk set. My chest filled with warmth, the kind caused by giving someone a gift and seeing that they love it. Plus… letters from Martin.

"Open the rest." I bounced in my seat, caught up in the excitement of opening presents, and tossed him the hobbit soap dispenser—but I surreptitiously held back the Stevie Wonder vinyl. I felt a little weird about the record. When he'd played *Overjoyed* for me on the boat, it felt like he'd been trying to communicate with me. But this record was just a record, right? Or maybe it wasn't.

I pushed my anxiety away and took a large gulp of the sangria.

He dutifully opened his gifts, smiling and laughing and just generally having a fantastic time. I soaked it all up—the wonderful feelings and his expressions of happiness—storing it for later, hoarding it for when I would need the memory. I also drank two glasses of sangria, and began to suspect it contained quite a lot more alcohol than just red wine.

"The Princess Bride?" He opened the first few pages of the book, his eyebrow lifting in question.

"You're going to love it. It's full of awesome sidekicks and side characters, like a giant who rhymes, and man who is hunting another man who killed his father and has six fingers, and—"

"Isn't this a movie?"

"Yes. They're both great, but you should see the movie after you read the book. And look," I leaned forward, flipping the pages back to the beginning and pointing to the swirling signature, "it's signed by the author."

I gave him a satisfied grin, which he returned. As I sat back in my seat I was feeling warm and a little dizzy, the sangria and lack of sleep was going to my head.

"Thank you," he said softly. "I'll read this next. Then you'll come over for pizza and we'll watch the movie."

"Sounds good." For some reason this thought made me melancholy, a future that involved me visiting him in a few weeks to watch The Princess Bride.

With a silent sigh, I handed him his last present, feeling unaccountably nervous about the record, and grateful he'd suggested drinks before presents and conversation.

Part of me hoped that when he opened the gift he would see it merely as a record of a musician he liked. Another part of me hoped he would read more into it and tell me that he'd been wishing, too—but I wasn't holding my breath. Martin wasn't the wishing type. When he wanted something, he took it; or at least he was vocal about it.

If he wanted me still, then he would have done something, said something already. Therefore… not holding my breath.

He pulled back the paper, his big grin in place. Then his eyes moved over the front of the album and his grin fell away. He blinked at it. My blood pumped hot and thick through my veins and I fought the urge to cover my face with my hands. I didn't hide though. Instead I braced myself, deciding I would take whatever came next like an adult.

He seemed to stare at the front of the record for an eternity, and when he did look at me, he lifted just his eyes. Something raw but also detached made his stare feel like a brand. He examined me. The air in the apartment shifted, became heavier, hotter.

"Do you regret it?" he asked, glancing away, his voice cool and calm. He set the record on the coffee table along with the other gifts.

I swallowed thickly and managed to croak, "What?"

"Do you regret what we did?" His gaze swung back to me, held mine as he pushed, "That I was your first? The first guy you—"

"Engaged in gland to gland contact with?"

His grimace told me he didn't like my word choice. But the phrase had slipped out in a poor attempt at protecting my heart, some instinctual need to keep the conversation from becoming too serious.

Martin corrected, "Made love with."

I stared at him, giving my aching heart a moment to settle, wondering if I should be flippant or honest. In the end I decided on being flippantly honest, because sangria made me brave, but not brave enough to risk everything.

"No. No, not at all. I don't regret it at all. First, you are quite handsome, you know. Hot even. I'll never regret getting me some of all that." I pointed at him then moved my index finger in a circle, making him laugh lightly and roll his eyes.

Reluctant, slightly embarrassed laughter looked damn good on Martin Sandeke.

"And secondly, you really seemed to know what you were doing, how to make things easier, better for me. Since I was going to lose my virginity at some point, of course I wanted to lose it to an expert."

He stopped smiling then, the merriment in his eyes waned, and his mouth curved into something that wasn't quite a frown.

"And lastly…" I started, stopped, then decided to abandon being flippant and just be completely honest—however I kept my eyes fastened to my yoga pants.

"Lastly, I was in love with you. I wanted you—and not because of all that," again I pointed to him with my index finger, moving it in a wagging circle, "but because I wanted *you*, Martin, and all that you were, and how you made me feel, and how I hoped I made you feel."

I paused, gathered a breath for courage then met his gaze again, adding, "I wanted you."

"I was in love with you, too."

His words made me feel like someone had deflated all my birthday balloons. I gave him a flat smile, my eyes flickering away from his, but I said nothing, because I knew he'd never actually loved me. This knowledge was now bone-deep.

If he'd loved me then he would have chosen us over revenge.

If he'd loved me as I'd loved him, then he wouldn't be feeling platonic indifference toward me now; he wouldn't be able to settle for being my friend. He would be struggling as I was struggling.

If he'd loved me as I'd loved him, then a Martin Sandeke google search wouldn't have yielded pictures of him and a pretty redhead, who I was now convinced—after speaking with Emma—was his last girlfriend.

I glanced at my glass. It was empty again.

"What?"

"What, what?"

"Why did you give me that look?"

"Because I'm out of sangria."

"No. Before you looked at your glass." His eyes narrowed with suspicion. "You don't believe me." He stated this as though the thought had just occurred to him.

I gave a non-committal shrug and reached for the bottle at my left, intent on pouring a larger glass so it wouldn't run out quite as fast.

"You don't believe that I loved you." He stated this as fact and I felt the mood in the room shift from friendly to antagonistic.

"Meh…" I shrugged again. "What does it matter? It's in the past."

"It matters." His rising anger was tangible.

I felt a spike of furious indignation and tried to distance myself from my feelings on the subject, because, if I didn't, he was going to end up with a face full of sangria.

Instead I attempted to be pragmatically truthful. "Well, if it makes you feel any better, I'm certain you liked me a lot. And it was obvious you made a valiant—but failed—effort to feel more."

"Wow." He breathed, then exhaled again, like I'd knocked the wind out of him. "That's a really shitty thing to say."

Yep. He was super-duper mad.

But I couldn't feel sorry about what I'd said—a little twinge of guilt perhaps, but not sorry. He was the king of blunt (and sharp) honesty. He *never* pulled his punches. If he didn't like or couldn't handle my honesty then that was just too damn bad.

Regardless of the certainty of my own righteousness, discomfort and disquiet made a camp in my chest. I forced myself to look at him. "Listen, twisty britches, listen to the facts—"

"Fuck your facts." His eyes burned like an inferno, but his voice was surprising low and quiet.

"Well, see, here we go." I gestured to him with my refilled glass but averted my gaze. "This is an example. Your language. You see no problem talking to me like that, you never did. That's not how you speak to people you love."

"It is when you're passionate about them."

"No. It's not okay. It's disrespectful."

"We can't all be frigid robots."

I ignored this statement, obviously made with the intent to wound, in favor of pointing out the other facts. "And then you chose revenge on your father over us."

"And you chose your mother's career over us."

I nodded. "Yes. Yes I did. Because it was the right thing to do."

"And God forbid you do anything for yourself. God forbid you be selfish for one single, fucking second and give into your passion, take what you want." This was said through clenched teeth; I could tell his temper was rising and he was struggling to keep his voice from rising with it.

"At the expense of good, innocent people? That's not love, Martin. Love is supposed to make you a better person, love is supposed to…to…" I moved my hands in a circle, some of the wine dripping on his leather couch. I wiped at it with the bottom of my shirt as I searched for the right words. "It's supposed to improve your character, not demolish it. If you loved me—if you wanted what was best for me—then you wouldn't have wanted me to destroy my mother's career due to my own selfishness."

"I wanted you to choose me." He wasn't yelling, but I could tell he was barely controlling his impulse to intimidate with volume.

I responded quietly, "And I wanted you to choose me."

He looked away, the muscle at his temple ticking, the lines of his jaw and lips severe.

I shrugged. "So I chose reason, and you chose passion, and nary the twain shall meet."

"I chose passion?"

"Yes. Revenge against your father."

He nodded slowly. "Yes. I was passionate about that." His words a reluctant confession as his eyes focused over my shoulder.

"It's the love of your life." The words slipped out before I could catch them and I wished them back immediately. It was one thing to be honest, it was another thing entirely to bare my bitterness. Martin winced like I'd struck him.

I hadn't meant it to be mean, but it was mean. My heart constricted with a sharp ache—because I saw my blurted statement caused Martin pain. I didn't want to hurt him. That was the opposite of what I wanted.

"Barnacles," I said, shaking my head, trying to figure out how to apologize without sounding even more like a wicked witch. "I'm sorry, Martin. I'm sorry. I shouldn't have said that."

"That's right. That's who you see, and that's who I am." His tone was frosty, laden with animosity and sarcasm. "You still think I'm an arrogant asshole, and that's all I'll ever be to you." This last part sounded as though he were talking to himself.

I grimaced. "I don't want to hurt you."

"Waaaay too late." This statement was paired with a sardonic chuckle.

Another piercing stab nailed me through the heart and I felt cold and a little nauseous. "Okay, well then I'm officially the asshole. I accept the title and all the death stares that accompany it." Again, I couldn't meet his eyes; I busied myself by draining my glass.

"Parker." He sighed, obviously frustrated, rubbing his hands over his face. "Can we move past this?"

I nodded, still swallowing, and eventually was able to answer in earnest—but perhaps a little too loudly and with slurred speech. "Yes! Yes, let us never speak of the past again."

"That's not what I mean."

"Sandeke," I leaned forward, depositing my glass on the table and tucking my legs under me on the center cushion, kneeling directly in front of him, "despite my awfulness, I really do want us to be frie—"

"Are you drunk, Kaitlyn?" He cut me off, his eyes glinting with a dangerous mixture of exasperation and barely contained fury.

"No. Just tipsy enough to say what's on my mind without overthinking it."

"What were you doing earlier, in your room, before I walked in?"

I held very still and stared at him, a shock of flustering embarrassment crashing through me. His question was unexpected and made me chase my breath. I'm sure I looked guilty because I felt guilty. He was staring at me with contemptuous certainty, like he already knew the answer, like he thought I was a coward.

I felt caught.

Even so, I would never tell him the truth. "I...I was—"

He didn't give me a chance to lie. "If I kissed you right now, would you remember tomorrow?"

"Why would you...why would you kiss me?" I couldn't keep up with this conversation.

"Because you're beautiful. Because I want to." His gaze was on my mouth and he sounded completely belligerent; meanwhile, my heart was in my throat.

"Do you? Do you really? Or are you just tipsy enough to be feeling nostalgic?"

"No. I'm just tipsy enough to say what I want without overthinking it." He mimicked my earlier words through clenched teeth.

I couldn't help my next question because I needed to know, "Would it mean anything?"

"Kissing you always means something to me. Would it mean anything to you?" Despite his anger, he appeared to be choosing his words carefully.

"I guess it would confuse me. Are we...would we still be friends? After? If we kissed?" I couldn't choose my words carefully; they tumbled out of my mouth in a mass of disoriented chaos.

He shrugged, like he didn't care, but his gaze had turned sharp, menacing. "If you wanted to be."

I felt his response like a punch to my stomach, because I didn't want to be his friend, not really. I wanted him to love me. I wanted him to still wish like I wished. Yet I did want to be his friend, because it was the right thing to do. Because I cared for him. Because I wanted him to know he had a safe place.

This exchange hurt, and the rush of dismay bubbling to the surface of my psyche made my throat feel tight. And yet I couldn't help the desperate desire twisting in my lower belly at the idea of just one kiss, just one more time. I wanted him so badly.

Martin leaned forward, his eyes capturing mine, though they were sullen, verging on hostile. He placed his hand on my thigh as he advanced, his thumb rubbing back and forth drawing all my awareness to the heat of his palm.

"What if we kissed, and I touched you? What if we fucked? Would you remember tomorrow?"

"Yes, I would remember. But I don't understand why you're doing this." A hint of pleading had entered my voice and my eyes stung. Martin paused his forward momentum, now just ten inches separating us, his eyes searching mine.

"Would it mean anything to you?" he questioned softly, then his voice grew a bit rough as he asked, "or would it be sex between friends? No strings? Could we just make each other feel good for one night?" Martin's hand inched higher on my thigh, taking the heat of his fingers closer to my center. It was obvious he was very angry with me, as his touch felt vindictive, punishing in its gentleness.

I shook my head, though my body—and especially the vicinity of my pants—was on fire for him, for his touch, for his attention. The ache was physical, and made forming words difficult.

"I'm not built that way," I admitted clumsily, my voice unsteady as I balled my hands into fists because they were beginning to shake. "I think one more night together, just for the purpose of making each other feel good, would be the end of our relationship."

By the time I finished speaking my whole body was trembling with the effort to hold myself away from him.

I read hunger in his eyes, but I also saw resentment and malice. His fingers on my upper thigh drew away, and I captured his hand before he could retreat completely. I cradled it in both of mine and he let me.

My voice was wobbly, and my vision blurred as I gathered my remaining courage and said, "Martin, I am sorry for what I said. I can see you're mad at me and I hurt you and I'm sorry. But I don't want to lose you completely. Not again."

The rancor in his glare softened, but didn't quite disappear. He nodded and ground his jaw, his eyes falling away.

He used my grip on him to tug me forward but I resisted, feeling raw. I didn't trust him, and I certainly didn't trust myself to resist him.

His gaze lifted back to mine at my reluctance. He studied my face, likely saw my confusion, hurt, and apprehension, because his eyes filled at once with what looked like a rush of remorse.

"I'm sorry, Kaitlyn. I'm…God, I'm such a fucking asshole. I'm sorry." As he said this, Martin raised the hand not holding mine and wiped two tumbling tears away from my cheeks with his thumb, his palm moving back to my jaw and cradling my face.

"Come here." He swallowed, and I saw he did so with effort. He tugged on my hand again and this time I let him bring me to his chest. He moved both of us down the couch until he was laying horizontal and I was half on top of him, snuggled between his body and the couch.

I was so confused.

"I'm sorry," he said again. "I'm sorry."

I sniffled. "Me too. I'm sorry too. I wasn't trying to hurt you."

His arm squeezed me. "You're forgiven and obviously you were right, I'm still an asshole."

Something about the way he said, *I'm still an asshole* made me laugh lightly, but uncertainty and the lingering ache in my chest kept me from relaxing against the length of him. His suggestion that we use each other's bodies felt like an assault, like an affront against the sacredness of what we'd shared—at least on my side—and the tentative friendship and trust we'd been building.

And yet…

I felt him stroke my hair lovingly, his other hand held mine and he toyed with it. He lifted my fingers to his mouth and brushed feathery, cherishing kisses on the tips and knuckles. Eventually I forced myself to relax, and turmoil gave away to melancholy, and finally to exhaustion.

My cheek rested against his chest where his heart beat, and I listened to it slow then even, lulling me to sleep.

CHAPTER 10
Chemical Equilibrium

I WOKE UP in my bed with a Martin mattress.

Meaning, we were in my bed and I was sprawled on top of Martin. I frowned, searching my memory, getting ready to stone myself if we'd had wild monkey sex and I'd blacked out in the middle of it. But then I remembered everything from last night/early morning, and I sighed—both in lusty disappointment and levelheaded relief. He must've carried me into my room and decided to stay with me until I woke up; and I'd been so exhausted I didn't wake up.

A very Martin-esque move. He was smart, so he knew—after last night's awkwardness—I would avoid him this morning. But I couldn't avoid a Martin in my bed.

"Are you awake?"

I nodded against my pillow, turning my face toward his. I cracked open my eyes and studied him. It was obvious he'd been up for a while. I took stock of where my hands were, where his hands were, etc. None of our touching was technically friend-inappropriate, but I took the opportunity to stretch and shift my leg so it wasn't quite as insinuated between his.

"Yes. But barely," I mumbled, yawning.

"Good. I'm starving."

He lightly pinched my rib, making me jump and squeak. Taking advantage of my involuntary spasm, he rolled above me, planking, and captured my gaze with his, reminding me of the moment right before I'd lost my virginity nine months ago. My throat was Sahara desert dry. I blushed scarlet, but couldn't look away.

He was sexy. Epic, unlawful levels of sexy. I was suddenly very awake and quite incapable of moving.

"Parker, what happened earlier this morning—and I'm not talking about the Hobbit soap dispenser—it doesn't change anything." His tone was stern, as though he were commanding me to not feel awkward. "I was a jerk-face and I am really sorry. You made it clear that you don't want to risk our friendship and I'm going to try to respect that."

I blinked at him and nodded, giving him my best brave smile.

"Me too," I croaked.

A momentary frown pinched his features, and he faltered, studying me, his gaze straying to my lips. But then he gathered a large inhale, rolled off and away, and then strolled out of the room.

He called over his shoulder, his voice tight, "You make music, I'll make breakfast."

***

BREAKFAST WAS SOME sort of delicious egg casserole with onions, bacon, spinach, and more bacon. The smell of it cooking filled the apartment causing my mouth to water.

While he was in the kitchen I eyeballed the piano, found myself caught in its gravitational pull. It was so pretty, so magnificently alluring. The keys were real ivory—which meant the antique upright was over fifty years old—and were warm to the touch. I pressed middle C and found the sound rich, full, and beautiful.

"Play it."

I glanced at him.

He must've visited the muffin man and the danish man yesterday, because he brought me a very fresh-looking cherry and cheese danish, a banana nut muffin, as well as a lovely cup of black coffee. Martin placed his offerings on a table beside the piano then straightened, giving me a stern look, but his words were gentle.

"Please, play it."

I saw it meant something to him, so I sat, gathered a breath for courage, and teased out a tentative melody. Meanwhile Martin hesitated next to the bench. Then, as though abruptly making up his mind, he bent down and kissed my cheek, his morning stubble scratching my face and leaving a warm mark on my skin.

"You need to visit me all the time." He lifted his voice as he disappeared back into the kitchen, "Think about moving in. I was serious about accepting cookies as payment."

I smirked reflexively, my tune becoming light and silly, and thought about becoming Martin's roommate. As long as we both dated no one else, were celibate, and never drank sangria around each other, it sounded like a winning idea.

I allowed myself to get lost in an improvisation, though it was mostly based on a song I'd written over the summer after drinking a Red Bull and being unable to sleep for forty-eight hours. The composition was originally manic, but I slowed it down, added a few bass clef-only stanzas, and closed my eyes.

When it felt finished, I released the keys, pressing down on the sustain pedal with my last chord, allowing the notes to go on and on until they faded and reverberated like the memory of an echo. It really was a magnificent instrument.

When I opened my eyes I realized Martin was sitting in one of the nearby club chairs, his elbow on the arm rest, his thumb brushing back and forth against his bottom lip, and his eyes watching me intently.

I straightened, blinking at him and the room as I came out of my daze. "Sorry...how long was I playing?"

He didn't respond right away and I noticed he was also lost in a bit of a daydream.

"Martin?"

He shook himself, his gaze focusing sharply on me. "Yes?"

"How long was I playing?"

His eyes flickered to a spot behind me on the wall. I turned and followed his gaze, found a wall clock that told me I'd been at it for over forty-five minutes.

"Gah! Is the casserole ready?" I reached for my coffee, found the tumbler tepid and I pouted. "Cold coffee."

"Don't worry, I have more coffee." His voice was stiff as he plucked the cup from my grip and disappeared into the kitchen. "And breakfast is ready."

I followed him, loitered at the entrance, and appreciated the sight of a fine man moving around the kitchen like he knew what he was doing.

"How and where did you learn to cook?" I asked, as he opened the oven set to warm and withdrew a casserole dish.

"Mother had a cook. Her name was Esmerelda. She taught me."

"Hmm..." I grabbed my coffee cup from where he'd left it on the counter and dumped the cold coffee into the sink. "Can we play forty questions while we eat breakfast?"

"Forty questions?"

"Yes." I rinsed the cup then moved to refill it with fresh coffee. "Emma stopped by yesterday, and—"

"Emma was here yesterday?" His tone told me he wasn't happy.

"Yes, no big deal." I sipped the hot beverage, placed it on the small kitchen table, then turned to the cabinets to seek out dishes for breakfast. "We talked. It's all good. But she deposited a lot of information in my brain and I think it's going to take at least forty questions for me to gain the answers I seek."

"What kind of information did she deposit?" In my peripheral vision I saw he was grabbing knives and forks.

"Well now, you can play forty questions too. I ask you a question, you ask me a question. There's no need to keep tally of how many, it's just that I'd like to clear up as many unknowns as possible before heading home this evening."

He was quiet for a beat as we set the table, then said, "That's right. I forgot you're leaving today."

I took stock of our progress, found everything to be satisfactory, and sat next to him as he served the casserole.

"I'll start—I'll answer your question about what kind of information Emma shared."

He nodded, glanced at me warily, then grabbed a muffin and tore it in half. By the time I was finished relating the story of Emma's visit the day before, he'd eaten three servings of casserole, two danishes, and a muffin. As well, he was on his second cup of coffee and third glass of orange juice.

I stripped the conversation of all my emotions, tried to relate just facts, but he interrupted me a few times and asked for clarifications, making my tale longer. I decided to leave out the part where Emma and I discussed his last girlfriend as I felt like her existence wasn't really pertinent to the issue at hand.

At last I was able to question him. "So my question is, why did you set up a foundation as the controlling shareholder in the venture capitalist company instead of keeping the profits for yourself?"

He shifted in his seat and I saw he was considering how best to answer this question.

"You can tell me the truth, Martin, whatever that might be."

"I know." He drank some more coffee, examining me over the rim of his cup. "There were actually several reasons."

"Okay, what was the biggest reason?"

"How about I start with the most important business reason?"

"Fine."

He cleared his throat and set the coffee cup on the table, leaning forward. "After what my father did—with your mother, trying to use us to control her—I realized that if I invested directly into SAT Systems, the venture capitalist company launching the satellites, then there was a small chance—but a chance nevertheless—that he'd be able to take legal action against my investment. So I established the foundation. Its non-profit status cleaned the money, basically, and meant he had no claim to it. I didn't want to put the project in jeopardy."

"But you gave up sixty million dollars and subsequently billions of dollars in revenue."

"But that didn't matter to me as much as following through with SAT Systems. I mean, I'm the head of the foundation. I have the same voting power at SAT Systems that I had before. Only the profit doesn't come to me, it comes to the foundation."

"So," I tried to understand his motivations, "launching the satellites was more important than the money part of your revenge plan? Sorry to use the term, but I thought the main ambition of your revenge against your father was to eventually ruin him and make yourself three times as wealthy in the process."

He stared at me, gritting his teeth, his jaw ticking for a long moment, as though debating with himself. But then abruptly stated, "When you walked out, the *revenge plan,* as you call it, didn't hold much meaning anymore. It took me a while, but I figured that out by June, three weeks before my birthday, before I had access to the trust. You were right. Focusing my energy on fucking over Denver Sandeke was a waste. And you would have known all this if you'd read any of my interviews."

I sat up straighter, surprised, feeling like I'd been slapped—but not in a violent way, more so in a reprimanding, wake-the-fuck-up kind of way.

Before I could stop myself—riding a rising wave of resentment—I said, "Listen, I would have read the interviews, but when I did a google search all that came up were pictures of you with your girlfriend—or ex-girlfriend."

Martin frowned at me, his face scrunching in a way that told me he had no idea what I was talking about; in fact, he said, "I have no idea what you're talking about."

"Red hair? Petite? Pretty? Ring any bells? Emma also mentioned that you two were dating."

His lips parted and he blinked at me as though seeing me in a completely new light.

I couldn't hold his gaze any longer because I felt an abrupt spike of fear that his eyes would soon be clouded with pity. Instead I stabbed at my casserole and tried to fight the swelling distress that I'd just exposed myself.

I mumbled, "Like I told you last week when you came to the coffee shop, I avoided news about you for a reason."

He didn't respond right away, but I felt his eyes on me, considering me. Peripherally I was aware that he'd placed his fork on his plate and was leaning his elbows on the table.

"I'm considering Dr. Patterson as my replacement at the foundation for operations. Rose Patterson, the girl in the pictures, is his daughter." His voice and words sounded careful.

I took a bite of the delicious casserole that no longer tasted delicious, careful to keep my eyes averted. "Oh?"

"Yes."

"Okay." I was determined not to cry. I would not be that stupid girl who cries when she talks to her ex-boyfriend about his current exploits. Therefore—to ensure that I did not cry—I distanced myself from him, his words, and my feelings.

He was silent for a beat, still watching me. "I told you last week, I'm not dating anyone."

I shrugged. "It's really none of my business."

"Rose was a way to meet Dr. Patterson."

I nodded, cleared my throat, found that I really, really didn't want to talk about this. After ensuring that the buttresses around my heart were completely fortified, I lifted my eyes back to his and tried to bring the conversation back to its original focus.

"So, you were saying about the interviews?"

"Kaityln—"

"You decided revenge wasn't worth it?"

"Damnit, just listen for a second."

"Fine. I'm listening." I leaned back in my chair and crossed my arms over my chest, giving him absolutely nothing.

"I wasn't ever really with Rose. I needed to meet her father. She was..." Martin looked frustrated and seemed to be searching the kitchen table for the right way to explain.

Watching him struggle I suddenly understood the situation, and I supplied for him. "She was a means to an end? You used her because of who her father is?"

For some reason this thought made me feel both better and worse.

Martin gritted his teeth. "Maybe it will make more sense once I explain more about the foundation."

"Okay, tell me about the foundation."

I watched his chest expand with a large breath and his eyes settle back on mine; but now they looked as guarded as I felt.

"The actual plan—alternate source of Internet delivery for rural areas—still made sense, even without the ultimate goal of revenge on my father. So rather than focus my energy on Denver Sandeke, I turned my attention to how I could work with the team I'd assembled to make this venture meaningful and profitable. We're not doing this to drive my father out of business—although that may eventually happen, and at the very least, Sandeke Telecom and the rest of the big monopolies will have to cut their prices drastically—we're doing this because it makes sense. It's a unique opportunity, and, yes, it will make a difference."

His mouth was a flat, stern line, and he was glaring at me.

"I see," I said, because I did see. As Emma had suggested, Martin had truly given up revenge. I thought about telling him I was proud of him, but couldn't quite bring myself to do so.

Sighing, Martin glanced at his plate and shook his head. "I sold the houses—with Emma's help. She made that happen before Denver found out. I sent half the profits offshore and I donated the rest to the foundation. The foundation invested the money in SAT Systems. Emma explained to you what the foundation does, right?"

I nodded.

"Well, Dr. Patterson currently leads a think tank in Washington called Rural Education Reform. He's dedicated his life to trying to equalize the opportunities for children in underserved areas. I know I'm not the best person to lead the operations of this foundation if I truly want it to succeed—and I do, I need it to succeed. He is a content expert and he's passionate about the subject. I think he might be the best guy for the job."

"So you met him through his daughter?"

"Yes. I befriended her because I wanted to meet him." This admission held no note of an apology.

"So, you're friends?"

I noted that Martin's gaze was veiled before it fell away. He studied his plate, but I knew he didn't really see it.

Finally he said, "I used Rose to get to her father. It worked. He's probably going to take the position."

I felt my heart sink. I thought about asking him to clarify the extent of his relationship with Rose, but ultimately I decided against it. If he wanted to tell me, he would tell me. And he wasn't my boyfriend; we weren't involved. It wasn't my place to ask.

His eyes lifted back to mine; they held a new edge, like he was bracing himself for my reaction.

I shrugged, feeling frustrated but resigned to my place. "So, the foundation. You need it to succeed?"

He sighed and I couldn't tell if he was relieved or disappointed I didn't press the Rose issue.

Nevertheless, he answered my question. "Yes. Although the mission of the foundation is noble, ultimately I'm leveraging the work they do to make money for myself. Lots and lots of money."

I nodded again. "I figured that out when Emma told me you'd purchased the broadcast and streaming rights for the next fifty years in underserved areas."

"Good. I'm glad you understand that. Because, I'm never going to become a person who is selfless. If I see an idea to exploit, I'm going to exploit it." His tone was harsh, like he was trying to communicate something of great importance to me, like he *needed* me to see that though he'd let go of his plans of revenge, he hadn't suddenly become a philanthropist.

"Well then, I'll cancel the application for sainthood I filed on your behalf." I gave him a wry smile that didn't quite meet my eyes, hoping he'd see I never expected him to be a saint.

But he didn't.

"Kaitlyn…" He looked discontent, pushed his plate to the side, and rested his forearms on the table. His frown was pensive and severe. "I'm never going to be a person who thinks about honor before personal gain; it's not second nature to me, like it is to you. I might do things in the future that you don't agree with. But I hope that—"

I stopped him by covering his hand with mine. "Stop, listen for a second. I know you're not perfect. No one is perfect. I know that how you were raised means you're a survivor. You needed to be. I understand that. But revenge was a choice, protecting yourself is instinct."

His eyes were solemn, yet I saw he understood my meaning. I squeezed his hand then continued, "You said to me a few weeks ago at The Bluesy Bean that you had plenty of logic, or reason, or something like that. But you also said that you wouldn't mind having my self-sacrificing, martyring bullshit input either."

"Did I say that?" he deadpanned, fighting a smile.

"Basically. More or less. My point is, this friendship is good for both of us. I make lots of mistakes. So do you. And maybe we can get to a place where we trust each other enough to be a mirror for the other person. I'll let you know when you need more saintliness in your life. You let me know when I'm being a self-sacrificing martyr. How does that sound?"

His mouth crooked to the side as his gaze wandered over my face. "That sounds good."

"Also, I'll tell you when you're crossing the line between hot young executive, and an uptight corporate sell-out."

"Are we talking about my towels again?"

"You mean your *monogrammed linens*? If so, yes."

He huffed a laugh. "They were a house-warming present from Emma."

"I'm burning them."

"That's fine."

"And I'm replacing them with Lord of the Rings beach towels."

"That's fine too. I don't give a fuck about my towels as long as they dry me off."

"Good to hear. Then I'll also be adding some My Little Pony ones as well."

We shared a small smile and I released his hand, taking the pause in conversation as an opportunity to steal a chocolate chip muffin. As I did so, I noticed Martin fingering his calluses, rubbing the pad of his thumb over the tough patches of skin.

I guessed he had more to say, so I prompted, "Anything else I should know? Did you get a tattoo over the last few months?"

"No. Did you?" His eyes shot to mine.

"Yes. It's a centaur mounting a unicorn on a rainbow." I took a bite of my muffin and smiled.

He looked horrified. "Really?"

"Maybe."

His eyebrows jumped and his eyes automatically moved down my body, as though he could see the hideous hypothetical tattoo through my clothes.

Suddenly, catching himself, he closed his eyes, pressed the base of his palms against his forehead, and shook his head. "Actually, there is something else you should know. There's another reason I set up the foundation instead of taking the profits directly, and that has to do with your mother."

"My mom?"

He opened his eyes again, giving me a very direct and pointed look. "Yeah. The activities of SAT Systems fall under the jurisdiction of her senate committee. But my broadcast and streaming rights do not, especially since most are for international areas. The foundation is non-profit, and isn't regulated as one would regulate a for-profit corporation. Different rules apply."

"Okay…"

"Meaning," he paused, watching me intently, "meaning that you and I can have this…friendship, and your mother can't be accused—with any legitimacy—of having a conflict of interest or bias."

***

"YOU DON'T HAVE to come."

"I want to."

"You want to spend your Christmas afternoon at a senior center in Queens?"

Martin shrugged, switching gears. His car went *vroooom*.

Meanwhile I was still mulling over the information he'd detonated during breakfast. I was still wondering what the exact nature of his relationship with Rose Patterson had been. Plus I couldn't stop thinking about the fact he'd purposefully structured his involvement with the satellite project, and established the foundation so our *friendship* wouldn't compromise my mother.

I didn't want to read too much into the action, but it seemed like this meant he'd been thinking about me, and some future relationship with me, several months ago when he'd established the foundation. And this simmering thought process twisted me up into a ball of confusion.

Because I didn't know what his actions months ago meant for us *now*.

In fact, I opened my mouth to ask this question when Martin broke the silence with his own question.

"Why are you leaving tonight? Stay an extra day." He glanced at me briefly, his question and slightly demanding statement pulling me from my thoughts. He returned his attention to the road. "I'll take the day off tomorrow, show you around the city."

"That's nice of you, but train tickets tomorrow are really expensive. But I did want to ask you about—"

"I'll drive you home."

"No." I scrunched my face at him, shook my head. "Don't be ridiculous. That would be four hours of driving for you. Plus I promised Sam I'd be home tonight so we can have dinner together. She's been alone all day, and we have a plan."

"A plan?"

"Yes. We're going to exchange gifts, drink wine from a box, and binge watch the last season of Doctor Who."

He nodded and I noted that the corner of his mouth was curved downward into a frown. I could tell he was lost in thought. Meanwhile I was re-gathering my courage to ask him about the foundation.

Suddenly he asked, "When are you in New York next? When's your next show?"

"Oh, well." I cleared my throat, flexing my fingers over my knees. "Not until the end of January, as far as I know. Plus, with school starting up again next semester and all the new departmental requirements, I might have to cut back with the band."

"You seem...happier." Martin's eyes flickered to me, his gaze sweeping over my face.

His words and how he watched me as he said them, like he respected and valued me, made my chest feel airy and light. I recognized he was trying to be a good friend. I glanced down at my hands, feeling self-conscious beneath his steady and apprizing scrutiny.

"I am happy." I nodded at this assertion.

I was happy.

Even without Martin I would be happy and this realization caused a burst of gratefulness to warm me from my head to my toes—for him, for our week on the island, *and* for our odd Christmas in New York.

Because I wanted him to know he'd helped me and that I would always be grateful, I continued unprompted, "I love music, I love playing it and composing it. You were right to push me. You made a difference in my life and I don't think I've thanked you for that yet. So," I glanced up, found him watching me with avid interest, "thank you, Martin. Thank you for finding me in that chemistry closet and seeing me in the first place. Thank you for helping me see myself."

We were at a light and Martin studied me for a long moment. His jaw ticked pensively and he seemed to be working through a problem of some importance. I allowed him time and silence to ponder.

At last he said, "I'm sorry."

Or, at least I thought that's what he said. But the chances of Martin Sandeke saying *I'm sorry* out of the blue felt really slim. More likely he'd said, *I'm starry* or, *I'm a Ferrari*.

I sought to clarify. "What? What did you say?"

"I'm sorry," he repeated, his eyes moving over my face while his lips curved into a small smile, possibly because I looked so entirely incredulous.

The light turned green and we were off. As he spoke his eyes never strayed from the road.

"I let you down, and you'd trusted me. I thought...after spring break, I thought I could wait you out. I kept expecting you to change your mind, kept thinking you were bluffing, that eventually you'd agree to see me in secret—that way we'd both get what we wanted. But when I chased you down in the student union and you told me I was ruining you...I saw that you were right and how fucking stupid I'd been to wait. It didn't occur to me that we were over until you asked me to walk away. And when you did, I realized I was too late."

The sobriety that accompanied an unpleasant memory and serious matters chased away my smidge of warm fuzzies, and replaced them with a simmering discontented heat and a renewed flush of discomfort. I remembered that day with vivid starkness, like it had just happened. I remembered how well he'd looked at the time, how unchanged, until I'd practically begged him to leave me alone.

And then he'd looked destroyed. His agony a tangible thing, and a mirror of mine.

I stared at his profile, really looked at him. He was the same Martin, but different. We were both so different. I wasn't hiding in closets and he wasn't losing his temper.

"You deserved better," he said quietly. He sounded like he was talking to himself.

Martin pulled into the senior center and parked the car. His movements were jerky, like he was irritated with himself, or regretting his words, or the memory. Whatever it was, he was agitated and distracted as he exited the car. Meanwhile I felt incapacitated by the puzzle pieces arranging themselves in my mind.

He'd looked fine that day at the student union because he hadn't thought we were over. And this realization made me feel hollow, because I'd misjudged him.

And *he'd* deserved better.

CHAPTER 11
Molecular Shapes

MARTIN STAYED FOR the show, but things were tense.

Willis glared at Martin.

Fitzy glared at Abram.

Janet glared at the senior citizens. I surmised she wasn't a fan.

And Abram…well, he played his guitar and ignored the ire.

Luckily the show was only two sets of classic Christmas hits. When it was over, most of the band went their separate ways in record time and with no pleasantries. I hoped the weighty tension was due to spending a week together almost non-stop, and we'd get our groove back after a break.

Abram lingered, taking his time packing up his bass. Once we were alone, he walked over to where I was stuffing my tie and jacket into my bag and stopped just in front of me.

"Hey," he said, his smile small and genuine, but as always with a hint of smirkiness.

"Hey." I peered at him through one eye. "You look like you're up to no good."

"Me? Never." His grin spread as he reached for my hand and pulled it face up between us. Then he placed a small bunch of greenery tied with a white ribbon in the center of my palm.

"What's this?" I split my attention between him and the little package.

"It's mistletoe." His smile became lopsided and his dark eyes danced merrily. "For granting wishes."

I laughed, though I'm sure it was shaded with dejection, and I sighed. "You're good people, Abram Fletcher."

"So are you, Katy Parker."

I stared up at him and he stared down at me. I knew he perceived my melancholy because his crooked smile became a questioning frown.

"Hey…everything okay?"

I didn't know how to answer, but in the end I didn't have to, because Martin picked that moment to walk into the room. Both Abram and I turned our heads at the interruption. Martin's gaze narrowed as he assessed the scene before him, his eyes settling on where Abram still held my hand between us.

Before he could slip a mask over his features, I saw a range of emotions flicker behind his eyes, but none were permanent. In the end it was just an unreadable jumble.

Eventually, he straightened, standing taller, and his gaze meandered back to me, cool and aloof.

"Are you ready? I don't want you to miss your train." His tone was as flat as the line of his mouth.

"Yeah, almost." I turned to my bag and placed the mistletoe gently in the front pocket then retrieved the gift I'd purchased for Abram and handed it to him. "Here, this is for you."

His eyebrows lifted into sharp arches and his small, genuine smile was back. "For me?"

"Yep. You don't have to open it now. Put it under your tree and save it for when you need a mug."

He laughed and rolled his eyes. "Well, thanks for ruining the surprise."

"You're welcome. And thanks for the…other thing."

"You're welcome." Abram gave me a gracious nod then lifted his chin toward the door where Martin waited, his eyes never leaving mine. "Now go. I don't want you to miss your train."

***

MARTIN CARRIED MY bag to the car, which was silly because it weighed almost nothing. But I let him because I got the distinct impression that carrying my one-pound bag meant more to him than it did to me.

Plus, he was scowling.

My suspicions regarding his mood were confirmed as soon as he pulled into traffic. He was driving really fast, and aggressively, *and* impatiently. I checked the security of my seatbelt.

It was one of those situations where I felt like, had we been meant for each other, then I would know the right thing to say. But I wasn't sure whether he was upset about his sudden confession on the drive to the senior center, or if he were irritated about something else.

Regardless, I felt compelled to break the silence and *say something*. I wasn't okay with stunted communication between us.

"So, my mother wants me to perform at a fundraiser she's having." I allowed my eyes to flicker to him, watched as the hard lines of his profile didn't exactly soften, but almost.

"Your mother wants you to perform? So she's okay with the change from chemical engineering to music?"

"I didn't really give her a choice to be honest. I just decided, then told them about my decision. I then started working two jobs to make sure I could cover myself financially."

"Because you thought they might cut you off?"

I shook my head before he finished asking the question. "No. I wasn't ever concerned about them cutting me off. It's just, it was important to me to prove I could support myself financially, that music was my career and not a hobby funded by my parents."

He nodded and I noted that most of the tension had eased from his shoulders. Maybe distraction had been the right approach.

"I can understand that. I mean, if you think about it, you're more self-made than I am. All of my money, all the money I've invested, has come from my father, even though he didn't willingly give it to me."

"Does that bother you?" I tried to keep my voice low and gentle so he didn't think I was judging him, because I wasn't.

He shrugged but said, "Honestly? Yes. He used me. I used him. I'm so fucking tired of being used and using people. I'm..." he paused, his chest rising and falling with the silent breath, "I'm just tired of it."

"So, stop using people," I said before I thought better of it.

Martin glanced at me then back to the road, his expression a cross between incredulous and amused. "Just stop using people?"

"Yes. And don't let them use you."

I watched the corner of his mouth reluctantly curve upward as he gave an almost imperceptible head shake. "Okay... Maybe I'll try that."

His easy acceptance of my suggestion made me feel brave, so I pushed, "Maybe even apologize to the people you've used."

I watched as his eyebrows lifted and his smile faltered. "You want me to apologize to my father?"

"Oh, *hell no*! Not him, never him. But maybe...Rose?"

Martin's smile completely fell away. We were quiet for a moment and I could tell he was giving my suggestion serious consideration. Again I left him to his thoughts.

Then abruptly—and I suspected mostly to himself—he said, "We weren't involved, but she was a friend and I did use her. She wanted to be more than friends, but I wasn't...I didn't. At least I was honest about that from the beginning."

I bit my top lip because, inexplicably, I felt like smiling. It was likely the vain, selfish part of me; the part that did jigs in Grand Central Station. I was relieved, so very relieved, that he and Rose had never been involved. Because, obviously on some fundamental level, I was a selfish harpy and never wanted Martin to find happiness if I wasn't the source of it.

But instead of giving into the smile, I suggested, "Then tell her you're sorry and make an effort to not be that guy. Be a good friend."

His smile was back as he watched the road, but this time it was softer. "I think I will."

"Good."

It was a nice *friend* moment for us. It felt...pleasant, meaningful. We fell into a companionable silence, the earlier strain between us seemed entirely forgotten.

Martin's eyes darted to mine then away, and I watched his hands tighten on the steering wheel. "I'm so glad you changed your major."

I gave him a mock suspicious stare. "Why? Because I sucked at chemistry?"

"No, no. You excel at chemistry. Plus you excel at sucking..." Martin's smile turned sly and he glanced at me. Then he winked.

The villain was flirting with me...!

FLIRTING!

WITH ME!

AFTER OUR FRIEND MOMENT!!

Hot outrage flooded my system with an unexpected violence. I couldn't believe he was bringing up friends with benefits again after our conversation last night, after how much it had hurt me. I couldn't do that with him. Before I could catch myself, I reached over and pinched the inside of his thigh, just above his knee.

"You're a dirty, shameless flirt!" I spat.

"Ow!"

"That didn't hurt, flirt."

"I'm driving. Are you trying to kill us?" His words had no effect since he was smiling and trying not to laugh.

"No more flirting." I crossed my arms over my chest and scooched lower in the seat, tucking my chin to my chest, seething.

I felt him eyeball me before he demanded, "Why?"

"Because it—" I caught myself, gulped a large breath of air, and glanced out the window.

The silence was not companionable. It was tense and unwieldy. I fought my desire to reach over and pinch him harder.

"Why?" he asked again, this time his tone was softer, curious.

I heaved a heavy sigh and tried to release some of the potentially irrational anger that had built a home in my chest.

"I loved you, Martin. You were my…" I had to pause again, clear my throat before I could finish. "You were my first in every way that matters, and losing what we had was a big deal for me. That month, after we broke up, I lost twenty pounds. I felt no joy. I didn't even like cookies. Things didn't improve and I didn't start moving on at all until August."

Silence stretched again. He downshifted, turned on his blinker. The car decelerated. We stopped at a light. I heard him gather a breath like he was about to speak.

Still staring out the window, I cut him off before he could. "I don't think I'm ready for you to flirt with me. It…hurts. I need us to be one thing or the other. In between stuff just confuses me. So don't flirt with me. And don't suggest that we have no-strings sex."

"Kaitlyn, I'm doing this all wrong—"

"Then stop. Just," I glanced at him, allowed a hint of pleading to enter my voice, "stop confusing me. Be a good friend."

He nodded solemnly, his jaw working, and returned his attention to the road. Once again, tension hovered and surrounded us, permeating the inside of the car.

I tried to push the melancholy from my mind. I tried and failed. Therefore I felt remorseful relief when we pulled up to Grand Central five minutes later.

He opened my car door and helped me affix the large backpack in place. He remarked on the size of the backpack. We loitered for a few moments at the trunk of his car, continuing our benign discussion until uncomfortable conversation gave way to uncomfortable silence.

I stared at my shoes for five seconds then forced myself to look at him in the eye.

"Well," I said louder than necessary, nodding for no reason, "I guess I'll see you later."

His jaw ticked as his eyes moved between mine, searching. "Yeah…"

I stuck out my hand, gathering a bracing breath and feeling some unknown emotion rise in my chest, making it tight. He hesitated, then fit his hand in mine. Neither of us shook our combined hands. We just stood there, our hands suspended between us, sharing a strange stare.

"When will I see you?" he asked.

"I'll call you when I have the dates for our next show in the city. Maybe we can grab pizza."

He nodded, not exactly frowning. "We could watch The Princess Bride."

"Yeah, that sounds good."

"And you can visit your piano."

I gave him a half smile and moved to withdraw, but he tightened his grip, halting my progress. I glanced at our hands then back at him.

"I have to go."

"Right." He nodded again, again not exactly frowning; he let my fingers slip away, took a step back, and repeated, "Right."

"Goodbye, Martin." I reached into his trunk for my sleeping bag, my gaze flickering to his once more. He wasn't looking at me. His hands were in his pockets and his attention was on his shoes. I waited for a beat.

When he said nothing, I turned and walked toward the station. But this time, because I felt oddly and irresistibly compelled, I looked back.

He was still there, right where I'd left him, and he was watching me walk away. So I waved. He waved back, stuffed his hands in his pockets, but he made no move to leave.

After a long moment, I tore my gaze from his and entered the building.

CHAPTER 12
The Atomic Theory of Matter

AFTER NO CONTACT for a week, during which I tried my best to ignore all non-friend feelings for Martin, I received a very nice text message from him on New Year's at exactly midnight. It read,

Martin: *I wish you were here so we could start this New Year together.*

It was painfully sweet.

And confusing.

I didn't reply right away because I didn't know what to say. Was that a friend message?

My heart was scrambled and tangled in my chest, and I had difficulty sleeping because I was obsessing about his text. I waited until the next morning to respond. In the clear light of day I read his message again. Pragmatic and sober Kaitlyn decided I'd inferred way too much from the simple message of well wishes, and I opted to tap out a benign and friendly reply.

Kaitlyn: *Happy New Year! I wish you'd been here so I could show you your new towels. Look for "An Unexpected Party" to arrive this week.*

I stared at my screen afterward, but then set my phone aside when he hadn't replied after ten minutes. Really, it was the perfect friend response. I couldn't figure out why it made me feel so lame.

I didn't know how to navigate these waters with Martin. Yes, I was doing this blindly. But I realized late in the afternoon on January first—after reading his text message at least twenty times—that I was not following my heart. Eventually I meandered to my keyboard and tried to arrange music as a conduit for my chaotic feelings.

A thought began to form, that felt suspiciously like the beginning of a plan, which I assumed was the start of a decision. I was going to have to come clean with Martin. I was going to have to put it all out there, all my messy and disorganized wishes, and be brave. I was in the limbo of uncertainty and I was tired of it.

"I'm giving you my copy of Cosmo. Can you put it in the kitchen when you're finished?"

I blinked at Sam's sudden appearance in my room then at the copy of *Cosmopolitan* she'd just tossed on my bed.

"You're giving me your copy of Cosmo?"

"Yes. To borrow. There's a stupid quiz I want you to take on whether you and your best friend are compatible."

"If it's stupid then why do you want me to take it?"

"So we can make fun of it later. Also, remember my friend Kara? The one we went dancing with? The one who needs a place to stay?"

"Ah, yes. The potential new roommate."

"That's the one. Let me know what night next week we can all get together so you can interview her and share your chore checklist. We need to make a decision soon."

I studied Sam for a bit as she thumbed through our mail. "Sam…do you like the chore checklist?"

She shrugged, not looking up. "It doesn't bother me. I know you like it, but you're a lot tidier than I am. Dirty dishes don't give me hives."

With that statement she meandered out of my room.

My eyes drifted back to the magazine on my bed; a heavily photoshopped and airbrushed model graced the cover—more a manufactured pixilation than an actual person. I twisted my lips in distaste at her unrealistically long legs and the unnatural curve of her waist and boobs.

Basically, magazines wanted Jessica Rabbit—the animated character—not real women. Heck, even supermodels weren't good enough anymore. Real women didn't sell magazines. Unrealistic and unhealthy images of female beauty sold magazines. And in this men were not to blame, because the female readership dictated and perpetuated the cycle of dysfunction, not men. Women.

In many ways, women were the enemy of realistic representations of beauty. We sabotaged our own self-interests…and that was sad. I sighed at the model and flipped open the magazine, scanning the contents, noticing with no interest that there was an interview with *America's Next Top Model's* latest winner.

And then I remembered.

I remembered I'd been derelict in reading Martin's *Men's Health* interview from over the summer. Now that his relationship status with Rose Patterson had been clarified for me, I felt no trepidation at the thought of being faced with images of them together.

Sucking in an anxious breath, I jumped from my bed, and in my haste to scramble for my computer, tripped over a chair. It took a bit of browsing through smiling pictures of Rose, but I finally managed to locate the magazine article.

It had been given a month before his birthday and published the month after. His wasn't the feature story. In fact, the interview was rather short and toward the back of the magazine. There were several pictures of him—shirtless of course, and in spandex of course—looking pensive and muscular, staring out over the water with a blue sky behind him.

The first half was about him being the youngest team captain in the American Collegiate Rowing Association. But, as Sam had warned, the second half was about me.

Interviewer: We have to ask you about your love life now, as a service to all our female readers. Any special girl in the picture?

Martin: No. Not anymore.

Interviewer: Not anymore?

Martin: Nope.

Interviewer: Care to elaborate?

Martin: Nope.

Interviewer: You were at one time romantically linked with Kaitlyn Parker, Senator Joss Parker's daughter. Any credibility to that rumor?

Martin: Yes.

Interviewer: But you two split up?

Martin: Yes.

Interviewer: Did it have anything to do with Senator Parker's politics?

Martin: No. It had to do with me being an a__hole.

Interviewer: Whoa! Should we take this to mean Kaitlyn Parker is *The One That Got Away*?

Martin: If you want, but I prefer to think of her as simply *The One*.

Interviewer: Okay then. You should know you've just broken a lot of hearts with that statement, but let's move on. So what's next for Martin Sandeke?

The first time I read it I didn't absorb half of what it said. The second through hundredth time, I paused at the part where Martin said, *If you want, but I prefer to think of her as simply The One,* and my chest constricted.

If I thought I'd been obsessing about Martin before, then I hadn't known the true meaning of the word. I tried to remember every look, every conversation we'd had over the last few weeks. Basically, I chased my tail in a racetrack of circular logic, ala:

If I was The One, as Martin had said, then why didn't he try to contact me before December?

Because you told him to leave you alone, that's why. So he left you alone.

But now he's, what? He's over me? He wants to be friends? Then that means I was never The One.

That's right. You're not The One.

Then why did he say that in the interview?

Maybe you were The One over the summer but he changed his mind, or maybe you are The One, but he's waiting for you to give him a sign.

A sign? Like what? Ye Martin of Old would have just told me how he feels! What am I supposed to do?

I don't know! Ask him!! I HAVE NO ANSWERS FOR YOU BECAUSE I AM YOU!!

Stop yelling at me...

Going to sleep that night I was still epically muddled.

However, I was also experiencing a growing sense of responsibility for the current state of my relationship (or non-relationship) with Martin.

***

JANUARY SECOND ROLLED around, and I was very happy to be back at the Bluesy Bean making coffee and going through the motions, though—admittedly—still obsessing about Martin Sandeke. But instead of obsessing about *what ifs*, I'd moved on to obsessing about my plan to confront him.

I was going to do it.

I was going to arrange to meet him in a neutral spot and point blank ask him about the interview and the text message on New Year's. I was going to put on my bad-ass-girl trucker hat and "adult" like an adult.

That's why, when Martin Sandeke walked into The Bluesy Bean that afternoon, an immobilizing shock coursed through my body and I dropped the glass measuring cup I was holding. It shattered on the floor, making a really obnoxious *crash*.

Chelsea sucked in a sharp breath and jumped back from my inadvertent mess, possibly because she was wearing brand new, soft-soled leather slip-ons and didn't want shards of glass near her feet.

"You startled me!" She pressed her hand to her chest, fluttering her eyelashes like she might faint.

The male customer who was at the counter (and with whom she'd been flirting for the last ten minutes) gave me a harsh glower and reached forward, gripping her upper arm.

"Are you all right? Do you need to sit down?"

"Yes. Yes, I think so." She nodded and gave him a grateful smile.

She turned to face me so she could sit on the counter. Just before she swung her legs over, Chelsea gave me a conspiratorial wink, then turned into the waiting arms of the man. He was a Brad Pitt. Or, at least that's the label she'd given him when he'd walked in.

Luckily the place was empty except for Chelsea, the Brad Pitt, Martin, and me.

Martin didn't walk to the counter. He took a beeline to where I was standing behind the machines, his eyes moving over me as though searching for injury.

"Are you okay?"

I nodded, releasing a weary laugh. "Yes. Just…clumsy."

He gave me a half smile. "Let me help you clean this up."

"It's okay, I can get it."

But he was already walking into the back closet and returned quickly with a broom. "I'll clean, you make me an Americano."

"Martin—"

"Don't argue with me, just once. Just once, please."

I pressed my lips together, showing him I was displeased.

He mimicked my expression, but it looked ridiculous on him. Then he made the strangest face. His eyes crossed and he bared his front teeth as though he were a rabbit.

I blinked at him. "What are you doing?"

"Making a funny face in an effort to make you stop staring at me like I murdered your beloved goldfish. What are you doing?"

Of course, this made me laugh.

The problem was, I couldn't stop laughing once I started. It was absurd that he was reminding me of our time on the island, using my own lines and strategy against me so he could clean the floor. But it worked. It distracted me from the mess and it also distracted me from my Martin Sandeke obsession. It felt good to laugh, a necessary release. I had to hold on to the counter because I was laughing so hard. Basically, I had laugh-paralysis.

He chuckled and squinted his eyes at my inability to control the hysterics, but took advantage of my arrested state to sweep the glass and deposit it in the trash.

As soon as I could breathe again, yet still wiping tears, I turned from him and grabbed a paper cup to make his Americano. I figured I couldn't be trusted with anything breakable at this point.

When he finished, he replaced the broom and dustpan then moved back to the other side of the machines, waiting for me to finish.

"Feel better?" he asked.

I nodded.

"Can you take a break?"

My gaze flickered to his then around the shop. No one new had entered.

"Yes." I sighed and paired it with a nod. "But just until we get a customer."

"Good. I'll be over there." He indicated with his head to the table we'd used the last time he was here, then added, "And grab some cookies."

***

I BROUGHT ENOUGH cookies to share plus a muffin with butter, his coffee, and a cup of strong coffee for me. Really, I needed hard liquor, because I was going to do it. I was going to confront Martin Sandeke. I was going to demand answers.

However, no sooner had I sat down, he asked, "Now that we're friends, can I ask you for advice?"

I sputtered for a moment, then finally managed, "You want to ask me for advice?"

"Yes."

"Uh…sure. If I don't know the answer I'll look it up on consumer reports."

"Consumer reports?"

"I have an online account. I bought a mattress based on their recommendation, sight unseen until the delivery day, and it was the best decision of my entire life."

"Really?" He was smiling, his eyes shimmering at me with happy amusement, and he wasn't even trying to hide it. "The best of your entire life?"

"Yes. Of my entire life. It's so comfortable, and when I'm at home I'm basically in bed the entire time. I'm going to marry it and we're going to have twin beds together."

"When we were together we were in bed most of the time, too." He uttered this with no intonation in his voice, and his eyes were free of mischief, as though he was just making innocent conversation.

"Yes, well." I had to clear my throat, feeling off kilter, not knowing how to segue this conversation into the discussion I was determined to have. As well, my pants never let me forget how much they liked that time in bed with Martin, so I was feeling a bit hot and distracted. "We weren't sleeping much that week. In my new bed all I want to do is sleep."

"I think I hate your bed. If we ever get back together, you'll need to get rid of it." Again, his tone was conversational.

I tripped over my words, my heart in my throat, thumping wildly. The time was now, this was my chance to confront him and decide things between us.

However, before I could form the pointed question that would serve as the key to unlocking our conversation, he said, "So, let's say I like this girl..."

My mouth dropped open and I felt like I'd been tackled from behind, my breath leaving me with a *whoosh*. I blinked at him. The room tilted.

"Kaitlyn?"

"Yes?" I managed to breathe, though the room continued to dip precariously. I realized I was gripping the table and forced myself to release it, my hands falling to my lap.

"Are you..." his eyes narrowed on me, "are you all right?"

Just because you don't feel calm, doesn't mean you can't be calm.

I nodded. "Yes. Fine. So you like a girl." I sounded like a robot.

"Yeah. And I need your advice about her."

"You need my advice about her." I was careful to keep my expression unruffled and unconcerned, even though my brain was abruptly on fire. I noted there was a butter knife on the table and I briefly imagined stabbing him with it.

Really? Two days after that text message, he was going to ask me advice about another girl? Really?

Wow.

WOW!

Boys are stupid. I needed to explore becoming a lesbian. I needed to add this to my to-do list and bump it up to the top.

How had the male gender managed to survive millions of years? Given that Martin, as a sample of his gender, thought asking me—his ex-girlfriend, the one who he'd spent Christmas with, snuggling on the couch, the one he'd bought a piano for—about another girl was a good idea, the male portion of the human species should have been extinct by now.

Of course, I knew he was going to date someone else eventually, and I wanted him to be happy, but…

JERK-FACE!

Did he have to ask *me* for advice? Where was Emma? Where were Eric and Ray? Couldn't he pay someone to do this?

And yet…though my heart felt like it had suffered a new fracture, I couldn't help think I'd just narrowly escaped a brand new broken heart. I'd been on the precipice of being brave, and nothing can make a person more foolish and vulnerable than bravery.

He was interested in someone else. He'd just provided me with the definitive answer to all my questions. Martin Sandeke was officially over Kaitlyn Parker. I had my answer because I was never *The One,* and now I could stop wishing.

"Kaitlyn?"

"Hmm?"

"What do you think?"

I blinked my confusion at him and shook my head. "I'm sorry, what did you say?"

I must've zoned out, what with the planning to become a lesbian and eradicating the world of men and whatnot. I allowed myself to feel the hollow hurt, but would be damned if I showed it.

His eyes narrowed and he gave me a look of intense suspicion. "What was the last thing you heard?"

"You were saying something about your…girl?" I was very proud I didn't end the sentence with, *and then I was about to stab you with my butter knife.*

"Yes, and then I asked you how I should go about informing this girl that I'm interested in her."

Now I issued him a look of intense suspicion. "Martin Sandeke, you can't be serious."

"About what?"

"You don't need advice from anyone on picking up girls." I cleared my throat after I said this because I didn't like how melancholy I sounded, how weak. I just needed to get through the next five minutes then I could finally close the book on our relationship. Now I definitely knew he wasn't wishing for me.

He was wishing for someone new.

"You're wrong, I do. When I'm interested in someone—actually interested—I'm terrible at it. I come on too strong, say the wrong thing, act like an asshole, push for too much too soon. I'm tired of fucking everything up. I want to do this right."

"Because women usually throw themselves at you and you've never had to work for it?" I was pleased I sounded more like myself.

He frowned, examining both me and my words, didn't commit one way or the other for a long moment, then shrugged. "Basically, yes."

I snorted. "You are so arrogant."

"Parker, both of us know why these girls throw themselves at me and it has nothing to do with my big head."

"Or your itty-bitty, microscopic heart."

He laughed, reluctantly at first, then just gave himself over to it. His eyes crinkling, the rumbly sound infectious and thrilling. I laughed too, shaking my head.

This felt weird, laughing with him now. It's hard to laugh with a person when your guard is raised. Laughing can be just as intimate as touching. Given the fact he was *definitely* moving on, I didn't want to be intimate with Martin ever again, so my merriment tapered off before his did and I searched for a way to let go of my jealousy, and actually help him.

In the end I decided to fake and force my good intentions.

I was jealous of this hypothetical girl. I was *insanely* jealous. I had no way to get around my jealousy other than to pretend I wasn't jealous. And the thought of him trying to woo someone else didn't just make me murderous, it made me nauseous. I pushed away the cookies.

I tried not to show how flustered this conversation was making me and forced a steadiness into my voice I didn't feel. "Okay, so…you like this girl and you don't know what to do, how to let her know you're interested without coming on too strong, saying the wrong thing, and acting like an asshole."

"Yes. Exactly."

I peered at him, trying to approach this from a strictly problem-solving perspective and quell the ache in my heart. He stared back, his gaze intent and watchful, like the next words out of my mouth would solve all known mysteries of the universe.

I straightened in my seat, trying to distance myself from thoughts of Martin with someone else, because emotion was starting to clog my throat. "Pragmatically speaking, a lot of women like the whole caveman thing. You might be able get away with just being yourself, not changing your approach."

He looked disappointed, maybe a little frustrated. "Because I'm a caveman? That's how you see me?"

"No, no. Not at all," I said automatically, then sought to clarify, "I mean, we're…we are definitely friends now, things are different. Before, when you were interested in me, you were domineering and demanding."

"You liked that, I know you did."

"Sometimes I liked it…" I trailed off, thinking about how much I did like it when Martin would take charge when we touched and were intimate. I also liked debating with him, that he wasn't a pushover, so I added, "I liked that you challenged me and pushed me outside my comfort zone, pushed me to see that passion mattered. But I didn't like it when you were heavy-handed, or tried to manipulate me by yelling at me. No one likes being yelled at. I also didn't like how callous you were sometimes to my feelings. I appreciated your honesty, but it's important to be honest without being mean. Does that make sense?"

He nodded thoughtfully, his eyes losing focus. "That makes sense."

"Ultimately though, when I had a problem with how you were acting, I let you know. Like you said before, you aren't a mind reader. No one is a mind reader—Lord knows I'm still terrible at picking up on things even when they're staring me in the face. I think you changed that week, or tried to. But given the fact it was only one week, I really think both of us tried our best to hear each other and change for the better."

"That's what I'm talking about. Do you remember what you wished I would have done differently from the start? How do I approach this girl and not make the same mistakes I made before?"

I stared at him for a beat, wrestling with myself, my heart hurting with every beat. I wanted to lash out at him, scream at him for wanting to do things right with this girl and using me and our time together in order to make that happen; as such, I couldn't stop my acerbic remark.

"First, make sure her mother isn't a senator, so there's no external conflict of interest should you find an idea to exploit."

His jaw tightened as he ground his teeth and he focused his attention on the untouched cookies. There was a long pause, during which Martin looked like he wanted to say something but was remaining admirably quiet.

"I'm sorry, that was a stupid thing to say. I don't know what's wrong with me."

I tried to smile and make up for my regrettable sarcasm by adding earnestly, "Why don't you try asking her if she's busy over the weekend? Just ask, *Do you have any plans this weekend?* And if she says no, then ask her out for a movie or dinner. Not everything has to be flying to private islands for a week of dating boot camp."

"With us, it was too much too fast. I pushed you," he said with equal sincerity, his eyes ensnaring mine.

"Yes…and no. I mean, I doubt I would have given you much of a chance unless we'd been stranded on that island. But you're different now. You've changed." My words were honest because I was growing increasingly uncomfortable. I needed him to leave so I could process the end, *our* true end, without his tremendously brilliant eyes watching and assessing me.

"What do you mean?" He leaned and reached forward, pressed his palm to the surface of the table just two inches from where my hand rested next to my cup, but he didn't touch me.

"Well, you haven't yelled at me once since we've been friends. You've cussed, but you haven't yelled. You're…different. More mature, respectful. You seem calmer. Content."

"And that's good? You like the changes?"

"Yes, of course." I smiled because I couldn't help it, and even now, even when I knew our ship had sailed, I wanted to reassure him, because I cared about him. "Yes, I do. Contentment and self-control look good on you."

"Happiness and passion look good on you." Martin's hand inched closer to me, his knuckles brushing mine—like he was testing how receptive I'd be to his touch—before he captured my hand in his and entwined our fingers on the table.

I let him, because HOLY CRAP it felt so good, like hot cocoa on a snowy day…with lots of Baileys. During Christmas we'd been in a bubble; hugging, lying together, and holding hands had felt natural. I'd missed his touch over the last week. I'd missed it so much. I hungered for it. And now, knowing this might be the last time we touched like this, the connection felt startling, necessary, and oddly provocative.

Maybe my body craved his body because I'd never been with anyone else. Maybe his touch intoxicated me and set my heart racing because he knew me so intimately. He touched me with an understanding of my strengths and weaknesses, of my desires, of who I became when I lost control.

I stared at our combined hands, pressed my lips together and rolled them between my teeth, because I thought I might whimper. This was bad. Very, very bad. We were just holding hands. How was I going to move on like he had if I couldn't even hold his hand?

And now he wanted to be with someone else.

He wanted me to help him, give him advice on how to woo another girl. If I continued to be his friend, this time I would be solely responsible for breaking my own heart, no assistance from Martin required.

I could feel myself starting to crack. My blood roared between my ears. Unable to maintain my calm under all the swirling and torrid emotions, I yanked my hand away and stood abruptly, my chair scraping against the wooden floor as I backed up two steps.

"I have to get back to work." I whispered this to the cookies because…self-preservation.

"What time do you get off?"

"Work?" I questioned dumbly, my eyes darting to his then away when they connected with his steady gaze.

But I did catch his smirk before he clarified, "Yes. Work."

"Not 'til late." I stepped forward to stack our cups and clear our dishes.

"What are your plans for the weekend?" he asked.

I shrugged, careful to not pick up the dishes from the table until they were pre-bussed so he wouldn't see my hands shake. "Um, I have shows Friday and Sunday at night. Mostly I just need to get stuff together for classes." I tucked the plates close to my chest and turned for the kitchen.

"Do you want to hang out on Saturday? Celebrate your change in major?" He stood as well, grabbing the last of the dishes and following me.

"Where? In the city?"

"No, I'll be here. We'll have dinner."

I thought about this for a split second, but then realized I needed more time to decide whether I could truly be friends—just friends—with Martin. I had no idea. Therefore, I decided that one dinner wouldn't hurt. At the very least it might give me an opportunity to truly say goodbye.

"Sure. Pizza?" My voice cracked.

"No. Something more formal. Wear a dress."

I dumped our empties into the sink, still feeling flustered and distracted.

"A dress?"

"Yeah, if you don't mind. I want to try something."

I turned and faced him, my hands on my hips, and gave him a questioning frown; I was a little breathless as I was trying to keep pace with our conversation and the dizzying thoughts in my head. "Like an experiment?"

He nodded, his eyes trapping mine, pulling me further under his Martin Sandeke magic. "Yes. Exactly like an experiment. I'll even help you tabulate the findings after."

I exhaled a laugh that sounded more nervous than genuine. He needed to leave so I could figure out what to do without the dazzling interference of his presence.

I hurriedly agreed, "Sure. Fine. Saturday. I'll wear a dress. We'll experiment."

"Good. I'll pick you up at seven."

Before I comprehended his intent, he grabbed my upper arm to hold me in place, bent forward, and kissed me on the corner of my mouth. I was still paralyzed by shock—wondering if he'd meant for a cheek-kiss and had misaimed—when I caught his scent.

He smelled good. Really good.

Like a guy who showers with expensive, French-milled soap scented with sandalwood as well as something so completely him. It was the *him* part that hijacked my brain, because it took me back to a boat in the Caribbean where we'd laughed and fought and spooned…and forked.

It took me back to snuggling with him on the couch in his apartment, hugging him, and waking up with him Christmas morning. Liquid emotion stung my eyes and I felt overwhelmed by the fact he was unquestionably no longer mine. He wanted someone else.

Meanwhile Martin was in motion. He'd crossed to his chair, grabbed his coat, tossed a fifty on the table, and left without another word. The door chime alerted me to his exit. It broke me from my trance just in time to see him turn to the left and disappear from view.

He didn't look back.

CHAPTER 13

Thermodynamic Quantities for Selected Substances at 298.15 K

"**EXPLAIN TO ME** what's happening with you and Martin, because…I don't understand."

"I told you, we're going out to dinner as friends." I mentally gave myself a high five because I sounded convincing and not at all brittle. And that was a miracle.

Despite the fact Martin had moved on, I had not. I could not be friends with Martin Sandeke.

I couldn't.

I wouldn't.

I wanted more, and I would likely always want more.

After a great deal of thinking since seeing him earlier in the week, I'd decided to go with my original plan of confronting him. I was going to adult like an adult and tell him I was still in love with him. Then I was going to ask Martin if, despite his interest in someone else, whether or not he still had feelings for me he wished to explore via a relationship.

After that, I had no concrete plan.

"As friends?" Sam sounded and appeared skeptical.

"Yes. As friends."

"*Riiiight.*"

"It's true. In fact, right before we made dinner plans, he asked me to give him advice about another girl." I shrugged. I was getting good at this, at *rising above.*

"Oh…" Sam's face fell, then to herself she said, "Well, that's kind of a shitty thing for him to do."

"It's fine. I'm fine."

I wasn't fine.

I was the opposite of fine.

But I would be fine…eventually.

Either he said yes, he still had feelings for me. In which case we would hammer out the details of our reconciliation and move forward.

Or he said no, that he'd moved on. In which case I would tell him I could not continue to be friends with him, but would wish him well.

At least I would know for certain. At least I would be moving forward one way or the other.

"I'm not fine, in case you were wondering," Sam announced, pulling me from my thoughts. "I'm not fine at all. Who is she? Is she smart? Pretty?"

"If the girl is who I think she is, his business partner Emma, then yes. She is very smart and pretty." I'd decided the hypothetical girl was either Emma or Rose, both of whom were most definitely beautiful.

And that was fine.

That was actually truthfully fine, not fake fine. I was completely at peace with being beautiful to myself rather than being pretty in comparison to someone else.

"I hate her."

I laughed at my friend. "There's no reason to hate her."

"Why are you being so okay about this? Martin was your first love. You *loved* him. You were in love with him. You cried for months after it was over in an uncharacteristic display of emotion."

"And why are you trying to make me not-okay with this?"

"I'm not. I'm just..." Her face scrunched up with pensive dissatisfaction. "I'm just worried about you."

"Don't be."

"I can't help it. I don't want you hiding in closets again."

I tried to give Sam a reassuring smile, noting that this—her worry—was precisely why I hadn't shared my plan with her. As far as she knew, Martin and I were platonic friends and I was over (or almost over) him. After what I'd put her through during the summer there was no reason to give her cause for anxiety now.

I turned my attention back to the mirror and frowned at my reflection.

"I can't wear this dress."

I liked the dress a lot in the store. It was a complicated dress. A beige silk sheath was beneath. Layered above was black, open-work lace crochet. The dress clung to my body—over my breasts, torso, and thighs—highlighting the smallness of my waist in comparison to my generous hips and bustline.

At the time, I also liked that it had a square cut neckline, and the fact it ended just below my knees. In my opinion, there weren't enough square cut necklines. Large boobs always looked nice in a square cut and it showed my collarbone and neck to best advantage.

In truth, I'd bought it just for this dinner with Martin. I felt good in it, confident. But now I was questioning the choice. I worried it was too sexy. I didn't want to come across as desperate or manipulative, not when I was planning to have a serious conversation with him about whether or not our future relationship was in the cards.

"Why? You look hot. It's sexy. I'd do you."

"Because it might be too sexy. And it's always catching on things." I moved my arm back and forth over the openwork lace and my bracelet caught. I stilled my movements so I wouldn't pull the thread and ruin the dress.

"See. My bracelet is caught."

"Of course, when you try to get your bracelet caught it's going to get caught." Sam rolled her eyes then crossed to me, helped me disentangle my arm, and removed the bracelet. "Just wear a different bracelet. Or no bracelet at all..." Then she added under her breath, "Less for him to take off when you both succumb to passion."

I flattened my lips into an unhappy line and affixed a scowl to my face. "I want him to be sensible, not succumb to passion."

Sam glanced up at me, her face said, *bitch, please.*

Then she said, "Bitch, please."

"It's true. I...I need to talk to him, get some things straight. And besides, like I said, he wants someone else."

"*Wanted* someone else, past tense, after he sees you in this dress."

I grew frustrated because Sam's sentiment was the opposite of what I wanted. I wanted Martin to want me, *want me*. Not want me because of the dress. I wanted him to think of me as *The One* because despite everything, he was still my *One*.

Gah! This is so confusing.

"That's it, I'm changing."

"No! There isn't time. He'll be here any minute. It's almost seven."

Oh. Shoot.

I stiffened, glanced at the clock next to my bed. "Oh shoot!"

"What?"

"I'll be right back." I scoured the room for my black shoes. "I'm going to run down to the cleaners and get my tuxedo before they close."

"What? Why?"

"I have that show tomorrow and I forgot to pick it up today. Shoot! They close in ten minutes and they're closed all day tomorrow."

I slipped on one of my flats, deciding the dress was just going to have to be okay.

"No! You can't wear those shoes!" Sam lunged for me, ripping the second shoe out of my hand. "It's a crime against fashion. I won't let you do it."

"Sam, I don't have time for this."

She turned hastily and marched out of the room—holding my shoe hostage—and returned seconds later carrying sexy, black silk stilettos. I was stuffing my black clutch with my wallet, Chapstick, and cell phone.

"Here. Wear these." She held them out to me.

"I can't wear those. They're too…too—"

"It's fine." She knelt down and picked up one foot, then the other, elevating me by three inches as she slipped the shoes on. "See, they fit. They're perfect."

I didn't check in the mirror. If I didn't hurry, the cleaners would be closed and I would have to wear my dirty tux instead. It smelled like sweat and barbeque sauce. I tucked my clutch under my arm and spun for the door.

"You want me to go? He'll be here any minute," she asked.

"No, it's fine. I'll just run across the street and do it really fast. I doubt he's taking me someplace that requires reservations or anything."

"I don't mind," she called after me as I sprinted down the hall to the front closet.

"I got it," I called back.

"Okay, fine. I have to go drop a load anyway," she announced, and I heard the bathroom door shut.

I smirked as I stepped into the closet and felt for my formal coat. Of course mine was at the back. The last time I saw it was when I unpacked it two days after we moved into the apartment. I wasn't even sure it was in the closet.

I pulled the chord to turn on the hanging bulb above because the door had creaked shut behind me, cutting off my light source.

I shifted through the coats—all twenty plus of them—and reminded myself to ask Sam why she needed so many coats. There was one in each color of the rainbow plus four or five black ones that looked exactly the same.

"Weirdo," I said to the coats, shaking my head.

Then a knock sounded at the door and I stiffened, my brain shouting, *Oh barnacles! He's here!* I turned to abandon my coat search, my hands shaking a little, but found I couldn't move. I twisted, frowning down at myself, searching for the source of my immobilization.

The crochet dress was caught in at least three places on three different coats, by the buttons at the cuffs.

Blast!

"Coming!" I heard Sam call, the bathroom door opening and the sound of flushing toilet following her.

"Wait, Sam!" I whispered, reaching for the door, then realized my mistake too late. She couldn't hear me if I whispered behind a mostly closed door.

It was too late, because two seconds later I heard her open the front door and say, "Who the hell are you?"

I breathed a sigh of relief, glad it wasn't Martin after all, then turned to untangle myself from Sam's army of coats.

My relief was short-lived because, after a beat, Martin's voice responded, "I'm Martin. And you are?"

Ooooohhhh mmmmmyyyyy Ggggooooooodddd!!!!

I froze.

"Ha-ha, come in. Parker just left to run an errand, she'll be right back."

"An errand?"

"Yeah, she had to grab her dry cleaning from across the street. It should take her, like, literally less than ten minutes. They close in ten minutes, they're closed all day tomorrow, and she has a gig tomorrow night, so...you see how it is," Sam explained as she shut the door.

"Where's she playing tomorrow?"

"I don't know, some really fancy to-do. She has that tuxedo uniform for all the shows."

"Does Kaitlyn work every day? Does she ever get a day off?"

"Starving artist has to make a living somehow, you know?"

"Hmm..." His answer sounded non-committal, but also rang with frustration, like he was irritated I had to work every day. But I wanted to work, to prove I could support myself as a musician. It was important to me.

And I didn't know why I was obsessing about this since I was stuck in the closet and there was no way to exit gracefully. I glanced back at the coats holding me in place, deciding I was just going to call out and ask for help when Sam spoke again.

"Martin, are you still in love with Kaitlyn? Or are you just here to break her heart into a million tiny pieces again?"

I froze. My call for help stuck in my throat.

"Again?" His tone was dry. "I didn't know that happened. When did that happen?"

"Don't fuck around with me, hot stuff. I'm not impressed by your GQ good looks, your Scrooge McDuck money vault, or your genius brain."

"Then what impresses you?" I knew he was smiling…with his sharp teeth.

"Honesty," she said.

I could picture her face as she said it. Her eyebrows would be raised in challenge, like she didn't expect him to be honest, like she was daring him.

I opened my mouth again, but then stopped, squeezed my eyes shut, then turned to the coats. I couldn't call for help. It was too late. The only thing I could do was disentangle myself and try to sneak out undetected, praying Sam would lead him into the living room.

Instead I heard her press, "Why did you drop out of school? You didn't even try to contact her. That was kind of an asshole thing to do."

Then I heard Martin, who was by now, very close to the door, ask, "You want the truth?"

"No, Martin. Lie to me. I love it when boys do that." Sam's tone was flat and would have made me laugh if I hadn't been caught in the closet by her coats.

He did laugh, but it sounded forced. "Sure, fine, here's the truth. I left because if I hadn't, I wouldn't have been able to stay away from her."

"So you dropped out of school, out of college, abandoned your teammates, because you couldn't stay away from Kaitlyn?"

"Sure."

"And now? What are you really doing here?"

He didn't answer immediately and, stupid me, I was holding my breath, eavesdropping like a freak.

At last he said, "That's not really any of your business."

"But she is my business. If you have malicious intentions then that's my business. She's my BFF, do you know what that means? It means: Boy I will fuck up your face if you mess with my girl."

"Wouldn't that be BIWFUYFIYM…WMG?"

"No, nothing counts toward the BFF acronym except Boy, Fuck, and Face. It's a TLA."

"TLA?"

"A three letter acronym."

"Of course."

"Back to my original question, what are your intentions?"

"Sam…"

"Are you still in love with her?"

Silence.

"You are!" She sounded excited, like he'd answered, but I knew he hadn't. "You're in love with her! Of course you are. But is this some kind of revenge plot?"

Silence.

"It's not!" It sounded like she was jumping up and down. "Oh my God, you're in love with her and you…want her back?"

Silence.

"Hmm…you don't want her back. That's odd."

"I didn't say that."

"Ah ha!"

"I didn't say anything."

"You don't have to. I can read it all over your love-sick face."

"Shouldn't she be back by now?" His voice was tight, impatient.

"So, you're still in love with her, you want her back, but…what? Why haven't you just told her?"

Silence.

"Hmm…you're afraid."

Silence.

"No, no. That's not it. You're not afraid."

He sighed.

"You're with someone else. You've got another girl and—I can't believe I'm saying this out loud—you're too honorable to call things off with Emma."

"Emma? Did Kaitlyn mention Emma?"

I clenched my hands into fists, my heart jumping around my chest. I was going to kill Sam. She was going to die.

"Yes. She told me about adorable Emma. Kaitlyn thinks she's pretty and you two make a pretty couple."

"I'm not interested in Emma."

I covered my mouth with my hand to keep my gasp from being audible. I wasn't going to kill Sam. I was going to buy her a car.

"So you broke up?" Sam asked.

"No. We were never together."

"But you let Kaitlyn think you were together."

"No." He paused, then I heard his footsteps move away. When he spoke next he sounded frustrated. "I'm not discussing this with you, Sam. I need to make a phone call."

"Sure, sure. You can use Kaitlyn's room to make your call, it's at the end of the hall."

I heard his footsteps move farther away followed by the sound of my door closing. I stood, again frozen, for several seconds, making sure the coast was clear. I was about to turn back to the two coats still holding me hostage when Sam flung open the door to the closet.

"Oh my God!" she whispered, with feeling. "Did you get all that? He loves you! He's not with Emma!"

"Sam," I whispered back, scowling fiercely. "You knew I was in here the whole time."

"Yes. Of course, I didn't hear you leave so I figured you were hiding."

"No. I'm caught in the web of your superfluous coats and I was trapped."

She grinned, glancing down at where I was tangled in the cuff buttons of her garments.

"Ha-ha, that's funny. Here, let me help." She slipped in and quickly untangled me, then pushed me out of the closet.

Like a clothes ninja, she immediately found my formal black coat and yanked it off the hanger. She tossed it to me then pulled the string to turn off the light. As I frantically tugged on my jacket, she tiptoed to the front door.

She opened it.

She closed it.

She said loudly, "Oh. You're back."

I gave her a panicked look, untucking my hair from my collar, and whispered, "What are you doing?!"

"Were they already closed? You don't have your dry cleaning."

"Stop it," I whispered frantically. All my hope for bravado and planned bravery was scattered.

Meanwhile Sam smiled like a harpy.

The door to my room opened and I stiffened, my eyes closing briefly. I inhaled a steadying breath, repeating to myself, *Even though you don't feel calm, doesn't mean you can't be calm.*

Feeling only slightly more centered, I turned toward the hall and affixed a welcoming smile to my face. Martin's eyes collided with mine as he stalked toward me, making me take an instinctive half step back. It was the force of it, the force of him.

He was devastating, dressed in a black tailored suit, a slim black tie, a slate-blue shirt that hardened his eyes into steely blades. His heavy coat was folded over his arm. He must've just taken it off. I tried to get my heart to stop jumping on the bed of my lungs before I fell down and broke my head, but it wouldn't. It took a kamikaze leap in his direction, sending spreading warmth from my toes to my temples, making my knees weak.

Stupid kamikaze heart.

"Hey." My voice cracked, so I cleared my throat as he approached. "Sorry about that," I said, sounding a little more steady. I tossed my thumb over my shoulder. "My, uh, uniform is at the cleaners and I need it for tomorrow."

He didn't stop walking until he was almost on top of me, then he bent down and placed a soft kiss on my cheek, one of his hands coming to my upper arm to hold me in place. It was an echo of the kiss he'd given me earlier in the week, and again I was assaulted by his smell and closeness and warmth.

I thought I might swoon.

Once again, it was over before I completely comprehended what had happened. He took a step back, but didn't release my arm for two more seconds.

Once his hand fell to his side his gaze swept over my face then down to my closed coat. Then it traveled back to my eyes. They pierced me. "No problem, I just got here. You ready to go?"

I nodded. "Uh-huh." Even though I wasn't ready, because all my courage was still in the closet with Sam's jackets.

His mouth tugged slowly to the side as he looked at me and pulled on his coat.

Sam chimed in, "Well, have fun, you crazy kids. She has no curfew,

Martin. But it would be nice if you bring her back *all in one piece*, if you catch my meaning."

His eyes slid to Sam and his expression darkened. "Goodbye, Sam," he said as he reached for the front door and held it open for me.

"Goodbye, Martin." She smiled at him, like a harpy.

***

I WAS WRONG.

The place he took me for dinner definitely needed reservations.

Despite my shaky start to the evening, once we got to his car things felt a bit more natural, easy. He asked me about work. Instead of talking about the band or The Bluesy Bean, I told him I'd abandoned my twenty or so venture capitalist projects in favor of investing heavily in science cabinet futures.

He laughed and the tension was mostly cut.

We talked on the way over about his Spotify playlist and what books we were reading. His handsomeness and brilliance felt less like a death ray aimed at my heart and more like *Oh...look, it's Martin.* I half convinced myself I could still move forward with my plan to settle things between us.

But now that we'd arrived at our destination and the restaurant was actually super swanky, I felt a renewed spike of discomfort. I was sure the dinner was going to cost more than half my paycheck. I couldn't afford it because I'd just spent my whole paycheck on the awesome dress I was wearing.

Distractedly, I let Martin take off my coat as my eyes moved over the setting. It was intimate. There were maybe six tables visible and all of them were mostly hidden behind privacy screens. The lighting was dim but not dark, cozy but not complacent. Everything screamed elegant boudoir—the plush red walls, the dark furniture, the heavy, striped, crimson velvet drapes. It was romantic.

Scratch that.

It wasn't romantic.

It was sexy.

And it looked very exclusive, like you needed a membership card to gain entrance. I swallowed thickly, pressing my lips together, and gripping my clutch.

Completely preoccupied by my distress, I surmised—based on the overt sensuality of the restaurant—that Martin had brought me here tonight in order to try the place before he took *her* here. Last week he'd said that tonight would be an experiment. Of course, he would want to test the restaurant before he brought his *real* date.

Dejectedly, I realized there was no way I would be able to confront Martin during our dinner. I couldn't be brave in a place like this, especially not when I was a stand-in for the girl he hoped to win. I suddenly wished he'd taken me bowling instead.

So distracted by my dismay, I almost didn't hear Martin's whispered, "Fuck me..."

I turned to look at him and found his eyes moving in a slow, stunned sweep up and down my dress—or rather, my body in my dress—and I cocked my head to the side. "That means you're surprised, yes?"

"Jesus Christ, Kaitlyn." His eyes lifted and searched mine, then he leaned forward and whispered in my ear, "This dress makes you look like you're naked under that black lace."

I shook my head and whispered back, wanting to defend myself, "I'm not naked, though. It's just skin-colored silk. Here, stick your finger through one of the holes."

"Oh God," he groaned and leaned away, shaking his head and gritting his teeth, his eyes on the floor as the maître d' approached.

I grimaced, wondering if my dress was obscene. I tried to stop my blush before it started and took a step back, letting Martin deal with the man while I dealt with my embarrassment. I wished I'd changed, but it was too late now.

Hell, I wished I'd stayed in the closet.

Soon we were being led to a very private table, completely hidden from view by several cleverly placed screens. Martin's hand was on my back and I felt stiff and unsteady. The maître d' moved to pull out my chair but Martin frowned at him, then stared him down until he backed away. Martin moved to pull out my chair; as he did, he looked fierce and a tad frustrated.

I took my seat hurriedly then accepted the offered menu, only half paying attention as the maître d' recited the chef's specials. I was too busy looking for prices. There were none. My stomach sunk.

Then we were alone.

I glanced up at Martin and found him concentrating on his menu. He was frowning and his eyes were darting over it too fast to be reading.

"Are you upset?" I asked, unable to stop myself.

He moved just his eyes to mine, his jaw set.

I continued, explaining, "I honestly thought the dress was fine. Sam told me it was fine. You know I'm not so good with dresses. This is the fourth dress I've owned in my entire life. The first time you saw me in a dress it was borrowed and—"

Martin lifted his hand and waved away my explanation. "Kaitlyn, it's...it's not the dress. I mean, it *is* the dress, but it's not the dress. Everything is fine. You look beautiful."

I twisted my lips to the side. "Is it obscene?"

He gave me a half smile, it was shaded with regret. "No. It's great. I'm sorry if I made you feel uncomfortable. I was just...surprised. You look very different tonight." His eyes swept down then darted back up.

I tried to return his smile. "You expected jeans and a concert T-shirt? Or my tuxedo?"

His half smile turned into a full smile, though it was small. "I was hoping for the red pants."

I sighed my relief and laughed, feeling better, seeing he was being sincere and wasn't upset.

The grin disappeared from his face when I laughed and he stared at me. I felt my smile wane as I stared back. All sound was replaced by the rushing of my blood through my heart.

Martin opened his mouth, was about to say something, but then the waiter appeared and broke the odd moment.

Our server repeated the specials and asked for our drink orders. I indicated that the tap water in my glass was perfectly fine. Martin frowned at me then ordered a bottle of wine for the table. It had a lot of consonants and sounded really expensive. I was surprised when I wasn't carded.

When the man left, Martin considered me for a beat, then said, "Dinner is on me tonight."

I was sipping my water when he made this proclamation, so I swallowed quickly and shook my head. "No. Absolutely not. We're splitting it right down the middle."

"I'm not asking, Parker."

"Don't be silly. We're f-friends. Friends split checks." I stumbled over the word *friends* because it felt deceitful. I didn't want to be his friend. I tried not to wince at the uncomfortable pang in my chest caused by my dishonesty.

He huffed. "Then who doesn't split checks?"

"I don't know. Everyone should split checks. I've never not split my check."

"Even on dates?" His tone was aloof as he asked the question, but I noted his eyes narrowed slightly.

I considered how to respond, because I hadn't been on a date. I didn't consider the dates my gay high school boyfriend and I had gone on to be dates; besides Carter and I had always split the check.

Martin and I had never gone on a date, and I'd turned down all offers from others since. I thought about being evasive and saying, *Yes, even on dates*, because that wasn't technically lying.

But it was stupid and childish and I didn't want to play games, even though I'd just spent ten minutes inadvertently eavesdropping while hiding in the front closet of my apartment during which my roommate drilled him with twenty inappropriate questions.

Distressed by this thought, I revealed, "I've never been on a date."

He was staring at me again. I stared back and gave him a tight smile.

"You haven't....? Since we broke up?"

I shook my head. "No. There's been no one."

"What about that guy in your band? Adam?"

"Abram. And no. We're not dating. We haven't dated."

He nodded thoughtfully and he shifted in his seat. "I think he's interested in you."

I shrugged, getting a weird premonition I was about to say something monumentally stupid in an effort to be honest, but without the wherewithal to stop myself. I was still caught in the tailwind of my earlier evening calamities.

Calamities paired with my abandoned confrontation plans meant that there was no telling what would erupt from my mouth.

"Oh?" I said, reaching for my water again.

I could feel it coming; it was like the shark in Jaws…circling…circling.

"Yeah. If you gave him even a small sign, I bet he'd ask you out."

I replaced my glass. "Well, I can't date anyone right now."

"Why not?"

Oh God, I was going to say it. Oh God.

"Because I'm still in love with you."

There it is!

Time slowed, then screeched to a halt.

I'd surprised him.

Hell, I'd surprised myself.

Of course I wanted to tell him, but not like this.

Not like this.

Not. Like. This.

NOT LIKE THIS!!!

Then all at once, time lurched forward.

His mouth parted slightly and his eyes widened; they moved over my shoulder and searched the screen behind me. I'd caught him completely off guard. I could see he was shocked, stunned speechless.

Meanwhile I was feeling the aftereffects of handing him my heart. I thought I was prepared. I wasn't. I was so definitely and definitively NOT PREPARED!

I felt immediately bruised and dirty. As well, I was experiencing honesty and courage remorse. The words hung out there, like underwear with skid marks on a clothesline.

The waiter returned at just that moment and asked if we were ready to order. Martin blinked furiously then turned his attention to the man and I saw he'd mostly recovered. He cleared his throat before gesturing to the menu to ask a question.

I stared at him while he ordered an appetizer, my stomach falling further with every calm syllable from his mouth. Meanwhile the single word running around my brain was: *escape. Escape. ESCAPE!*

Martin's eyes lifted, connected with mine, and in that split second I could read nothing of his thoughts—probably because mine were in such turmoil.

The waiter turned, poised to ask me if I wanted anything. Instead I stood abruptly, my chair almost falling backward.

"I'm sorry," I said to Martin first, then turned to the waiter. "I'm sorry, where is the ladies' room?" My voice was higher pitched than I would have liked, but I wasn't going to complain because the fact I could speak at all was a miracle.

The waiter smiled politely and had just finished his instructions when Martin stood as well, drawing my attention to him.

His eyes were narrowed, like he suspected foul play, and he said, "Kaitlyn…" His tone held a warning, and he paired this with an almost imperceptible head shake.

I gave him a tight smile, not quite making eye contact because…devastation.

I nodded noncommittally as I darted out of the privacy screens. "I'll be right back."

But that was a lie.

There was no way in hell I was going back.

In that moment I knew with a sudden, implacable force that I had been right. I would never be able to be *just friends* with Martin Sandeke. I would never be able to see him and not want everything from him. I would always be drawn to him. I also knew that being with Martin wasn't necessary for my happiness, but I could never be happy as just his friend.

I was passionate about him, and I couldn't be unselfish or reasonable *or* calm where he was concerned.

As I threaded my way through the twists and turns of the screens, I felt the first stinging tears behind my eyes. Finally I made it to the front and I plucked my coat from the rack by the front door, then bolted out of the restaurant.

My feet didn't hurt, but they would, because I was going to have to walk at least four blocks to find a taxi.

CHAPTER 14
Nuclear Chemistry

"**DO YOU WANT** to talk about it?"

I shook my head and blew my nose.

It was stuffy.

I'd been crying.

But I wasn't crying now.

Yet my nose was still stuffy.

"No."

"At least tell me what happened!" Sam shook her fists at me in frustration, grumbling, "I'm dying here. You have to give me something. Do I need to take a hit out on Martin Sandeke? I will, you know. I have some Russian cousins who need an outlet for their aggression."

I gave a pitiful laugh and shook my head. "No. It's not his fault. I just...I just said something stupid, then regretted it, then left."

"Oh." Her eyes moved over me. Sam seemed to be planning her strategy as I pulled off the shoes she'd loaned me and placed them next to the bed.

After escaping from the restaurant I flagged down a taxi six blocks away, started to cry, then paid the exorbitant cab fare, and started to cry even harder.

I snuck into the apartment. Sam didn't hear me as she was singing loudly in the shower, then lay on my bed and cried. I cried into my pillow, quietly, just like old times.

Despite my carefulness, Sam heard me and came to the door dressed only in a towel.

Now we were in my bedroom and I was a pitiful mess. So much for trying to be strong on my own.

"I never want to see him again," I said to no one. "Just thinking about the possibility makes me want to join the Peace Corps and fly to a far off third world country. Hopefully they'll have closets."

"What did you say? It couldn't have been that bad."

"I told him I was still in love with him."

"Oh…oh!" She gripped her towel tighter, her eyes large as saucers. "Holy shit. What did he say?"

"Nothing. He ordered an appetizer."

"*What?*" Now she sounded pissed.

"So I got up and excused myself for the bathroom, but I left instead. He was probably relieved when he figured out that I left. God, I am so stupid." My chin wobbled again and I held my forehead with my fingertips.

Yes, I felt remorse and the pain of rejection, but I also felt relief. At least now it was over. At least now I knew for certain. Despite the clumsiness of my confession I'd finally freed myself.

Now I could move on and stop wishing. I could pick my crumpled heart off the floor and stop stepping all over it.

Sam took a deep breath and was possibly about to give me some words of wisdom, but a pounding on the front door interrupted her.

We both sat up straight and stared at each other.

Then we heard Martin's raised voice.

"Kaitlyn, open the door. I know you're in there."

I stood abruptly, my hands balled into fists, a thunder bolt of white hot mortification slicing through me. I was suddenly sweating.

"Oh my God. What do I do?" I whispered, which was silly because he wouldn't be able to hear me all the way in my bedroom.

Sam looked at me, stunned. "Open the door…?"

I shook my head frantically. "No. No, I can't. I can't face him. Please don't make me."

She gave me a sad look. "Oh, Kaitlyn—"

"I mean it. Open this door," he bellowed from the hall. He sounded really, really angry.

"I'll just tell him to go away, that you don't want to see him," Sam offered.

"No. That won't work. I have to hide." I nodded at this thought because I was crazy. "Tell him I'm not here."

"You want me to let him in?"

"Yes. You get the door. Tell him I'm not back yet. He'll…well, he might want to wait for a bit, but you tell him to leave. He won't stay in the apartment if you—"

"I'm going to count to ten and then I'm going to break this door down."

We both jumped at the sound of his threat.

Sam shook her head, her mouth curved in a frown of knowing better. "He won't be able to break the door down," she whispered, "it's reinforced steel."

"Okay, I'll go hide—"

"One."

"—in the front closet."

"Two."

"You let him in."

"Three"

"Tell him I'm—"

"Four."

"—not here, not back yet."

"Five."

"He'll leave."

"Six."

"Then—"

"Seven."

"—we'll be all clear."

"Eight."

She nodded her understanding and I tiptoed out of my room, running as lightly as possible. Sam loitered behind.

"Nine."

Sam called out, "Just a minute, Sandeke. I was in the shower. Hold your ball sack!"

I went to the hall closet where I'd been hiding earlier and shut the door behind me, pressing myself backward into the folds of the coats. My hands were shaking.

"Ten."

I heard the door swing open.

I heard his steps thunder into the apartment.

I heard Sam shut the door.

I heard her follow him, shouting, "What are you doing?"

"Where is she?"

"Who?"

"Sam..." His voice sent a shiver down my spine. He was really mad. I didn't think he'd be angry.

"What?"

"Where is Kaitlyn?"

"Why? What did you do to her?" Sam was also angry.

They sounded faraway, so I guessed they were in my room. I also noticed Sam was trying not to lie if at all possible.

"I know she's here, Sam."

His steps came closer then farther away. In my mind's eye I saw him marching into Sam's bedroom, coming up empty, then moving on to the bathroom, kitchen, then living room.

"If she's here, then where is she, Martin?" Sam was staying on his heels. They walked past the closet again. It sounded like he was going back to my room.

There was quiet and I held my breath, clutching my hands in front of me. Then a really terrible, terrible thing happened. It made my blood run cold and my entire body freeze.

"If she's not here, Sam..." his tone was glacial, beyond incensed, "then why are the shoes she was wearing earlier next to her bed?"

Sam said nothing. I covered my face with my hands and closed my eyes. I was such an idiot. In the dictionary next to the word idiot was a picture of me. But it didn't matter. Nothing really mattered because he was going to find me and then I was going to expire from a broken heart and embarrassment.

Embarrassment, mortification, chagrin, unease, discomposure... GAH! The synonym game wasn't helping!

I heard footsteps.

He was coming.

I heard a hand on the doorknob.

He was there.

I heard the door swing open.

It was him.

I heard the light click on.

I couldn't open my eyes. I'd exhausted my courage earlier in the restaurant. I had none left.

But when I heard the door shut, I dropped my hands and I found myself face-to-face with a very irate Martin Sandeke.

That's right. He was in the closet with me and he'd just closed the door. I stared at him. I knew I looked panicked because some of his irateness ebbed and became cautiousness.

At length he said, "Parker."

"Sandeke," I responded automatically.

"What are you doing?"

"Uh…" I released the breath I'd been holding. My eyes darted to the door behind him and I betrayed the truth of it. "I'm hiding in the closet."

His brow was still furrowed, but his gaze relaxed slightly. When he spoke, he spoke very slowly, like he was trying not to frighten me. "Why are you hiding in the closet?"

"Why does anyone hide in a closet?" My voice was very small, my chin wobbled, and as new tears flooded my vision, he began to blur a little.

Martin lifted a single eyebrow and stalked closer, raising then showing me the palms of his hands. He was less than a foot away when he gently wrapped his long fingers around my upper arms.

"Do you hide in the closet often?" His voice was soft and his eyes moved over my face, likely taking in the smudged mascara and resultant raccoon eyes.

I realized abruptly that we'd had this conversation before. Except it was in a chemistry lab and I'd been unable to scratch an itch. Maybe I hadn't made as much progress as I thought. Maybe all these months of trying to be someone different, better, stronger, more passionate had been futile.

Or maybe it was Martin. Perhaps I'd always be the girl hiding in the science cabinet, hiding from Martin Sandeke.

"Sometimes." I choked on the word, my jaw clenched, and I willed the tears to recede. Instead one spilled down my cheek. His eyes followed its progress then moved back to mine.

"Is this an everyday thing?" he asked in a near whisper, his thumbs brushing lightly over the sleeves of my dress.

He was confusing me and I heaved a sob, my chin falling to my chest and said, "No. Only on special occasions, like when I make an idiot of myself and tell Martin Sandeke that I'm still in…in…in—"

I didn't finish because he slid his finger under my chin, lifted my face to his, and kissed me.

Oh boy, oh boy, oh boy, did he ever kiss me.

It was a devouring kiss, a hungry kiss, a demanding, a claiming, a merciless kiss. He crushed me to him and swept his tongue into my mouth, leaving me no chance to breathe or recover or think.

And it went on and on. Martin dipped his head to one side then the next, his hands roaming over my body, grabbing and squeezing and reaching for the hem of my dress, sliding his hand against the soft silk. It was only when his fingers connected with the straps of my garter belt did he lift his head and let me breathe. And that was only because he wanted to release a string of expletives as he confirmed I was, in fact, wearing thigh highs; and I was, in fact, wearing lacy panties.

"Fuck me," he finished, his eyes moving back to mine, turbulent yet determined.

Meanwhile I was trying catch my breath. "Martin, I—"

"Parker, I fucking love you. I've always loved you. I never stopped."

I could hardly believe his words. I felt suddenly weightless, overwhelmed, and bursting with such intense levels of joy I just barely contained my instinctual desire to do a jig.

He continued, sounding stern yet tender, "And you really, really pissed me off when you left tonight."

"I'm sorry I did that." I nodded, smiling because I was level one million happy.

"I forgive you." He returned my grin.

This made me frown. I wasn't the only one who'd been an idiot, so I pointed at his chest with my finger. "But, in all fairness, you ordered an appetizer."

"So?"

"So? So I tell you I love you and you order escargot."

Martin, still grinning, bent and kissed my neck, then bit it. It hurt a little and it felt wonderful. His breath was hot against my skin. "You shocked the hell out of me. I didn't know. I had no idea. I never know what you're thinking. You hide everything behind those gorgeous gray eyes..."

I'd missed his sharp teeth and leaned my head to one side to give him better access, pressed against him. I couldn't think. All I knew was we were in a closet kissing, his amorous hands were up my skirt, and the figurative Bunsen burner in my pants demanded satisfaction.

"Martin—"

"There has been no one else since you. No one." His mouth was hot on my skin, devouring me. "You're all I think about, all I want. You are everything."

Oh, gah! Right in the feels!

I braced my hands against his chest before he could capture my mouth again, needing to tell him the whole truth. "Listen, wait, I know we have a lot to discuss and this is all very sudden, but—"

"Sudden?" He reeled back a bit. His contemptuous tone and slightly horrified expression told me he disagreed.

"Yes, I mean—one minute we're friends, or we're working on being friends, and the next minute I'm telling you I'm still in love with you..." I searched his eyes, made sure he was really looking at me. I wanted him to understand this wasn't temporary, that my feelings weren't going to change. "But, you need to know, this wasn't sudden for me. I made up my mind last week, after you explained things in New York, but before you came to the coffee shop. I want to be *with* you. I don't want to be just friends. That's not going to work for me."

His mouth hitched to the side and his hands on me tightened. "Kaitlyn, I decided we were never going to be just friends the moment you walked into chemistry lab last year. We were *never* going to be just friends. That wasn't ever going to work."

"But. But. You said—"

"I lied."

My mouth fell open.

He shrugged, showing me he did not regret this lie. "I was tired of waiting. I needed you to forgive me, show you I've changed, but I knew you wouldn't listen to me if I showed up at your door and demanded we get back together—which is what I wanted to do. Christmas was extremely frustrating because I saw you were taking my offer of friendship seriously, and you were trying to do the right thing."

"I did take it seriously. I wanted to be your safe place," I admitted with a new rush of emotion that stung my eyes. "I love you, I care about you, and I wanted to be there for you even if you didn't love me... But my pants kept getting in the way."

Martin smiled very briefly at the mention of my pants, but then he scowled. His tone became fierce and angry as he leaned farther away. "Don't ever think that I never loved you."

"I—"

"When you said that to me in New York, when you told me you didn't think I'd ever loved you, I swear to God I wanted to strangle you. I've never felt like such a failure."

"Oh, Martin, I promise, I didn't say it to hurt you. I didn't." It was important he believe me.

"I know. You didn't think I cared. I figured that out later, when you were asleep on top of me on the couch, after I acted like a fuckwad and suggested sex with no strings, wanting to hurt you back. I *am* sorry about that," he whispered, sounding truly remorseful.

Yet his hands, having now lifted my skirt completely over my hips, were currently taking liberties with the bare skin of my torso, my back, and delving into the lace of my underwear.

"I forgive you," I gasped, a hot cascade of chaotic need coursing through me, everywhere he touched igniting my arousal. My movements became jerky and frantic as I pushed away his jacket and coat, and grabbed for his zipper.

"Kaitlyn—"

"Everything is forgiven," I added in a rush, tired of talking. We weren't friends—well, we were friends. But now we would never be *just* friends. There was no reason we couldn't get started being more than friends.

Right. This. Second.

Martin caught my wrists, halting my progress, his breathing labored. "No, no—we're not doing this yet."

"But I need you, I need to feel you," I whined.

"Don't—"

I tried a different approach, lowering my voice and cupping his erection through his pants. "I love you. I want to make love to you. I need you inside me."

Martin groaned inelegantly, a despairing, needy sound. Pressing his lips against mine, he silenced me with the hot slide of his mouth, his invading tongue. Martin brought my hands to his sides and trapped them there.

My heart soared even as my lower belly flip-flopped then twisted with erotic anticipation. He released my wrists and one of his hands moved on my thigh and between my legs, shifting the lace panties to one side so he could touch my center. I inhaled sharply, arching at the contact, my eyes half closing.

"So wet for me...I love how you feel. I've missed you so fucking much." He sounded mesmerized and a little vicious. "Tell me how much you need me."

I couldn't form words because...sex.

"Say it." He paired this demand with a stroke of his finger. I realized he was unbuckling the belt of his pants with his other hand.

I shuddered in response to his skilled fingers, having to hold onto him "I need you, I need you so much," I barely managed to say.

I felt the words.

I felt them to my bones.

I never wanted to be separated from him again.

He was pressing me against the coats and my hands wound around his neck. His pants dropped to the floor, leaving him in boxer briefs. I reached for them frantically and pushed them down, freeing his penis.

I gripped it. Stroked it twice. I felt it, and it felt amazing, and right, and crucial.

He hissed, "You're still on birth control, yes?"

I nodded, rocking my hips into his hand, feeling him there, needing more.

He kissed my lips harshly, then said against them, "I haven't been with anyone but you. Not since the boat. Not for months before that. I haven't wanted anyone but you. I never want to be with anyone but you. You're all I can think about. Just you, only you."

I moaned. The time for coherent thought had officially passed. I understood what he was saying so I nodded my head, giving him permission to do what I'd been fantasizing about since it first happened.

"Please…please." I rubbed against him, wanting to completely give myself over to passion.

"I'm sorry I have to do this," he said. His voice held true regret. He then proceeded to tear my new lace underwear in two.

I didn't have time to react because the next thing he did was grab my bottom, lift me up, and turn my back against the wall. He then brought me down, filling me in one swift stroke. He rocked back then filled me again with another inelegant thrust of his hips, pinning me to the wall, spreading my legs wide, to his satisfaction.

My head fell to his shoulder. I closed my eyes. I felt.

I felt myself adjust to him.

I felt him stretch me.

The beautiful friction his body made with mine.

I felt my love for him, and my desire, asphyxiate and overwhelm me.

I felt our combined passion for each other and the insanity of it, how mad and reckless we were.

"Say it again." He moved in then out, slowly at first, but then increasing the tempo to a punishing pace. "Tell me again."

I knew what he wanted. "I love you."

"I want you in so many ways, so many ways—"

"Then take me."

He growled and my back hit the wall. I was uncomfortable and completely, irrevocably aroused. There was nothing smooth, practiced, or controlled about what we were doing. Only greedy and needful. Essential. It was all passion and no technique.

I was mindless with selfishness. I couldn't think past this moment because I wanted it so badly. So I'd taken it. It was raw, and it was real, and it was true. We both came quickly, hard, loud, and together. And I immediately wanted a repeat. Or a threepeat.

In the aftermath our ragged breaths married, and his mouth sought then mated with mine—slow, sensual, and loving. I whimpered, sore but needing him still. He laughed wickedly, grinding into me.

It's true. We'd just had sex in the front closet of my apartment while my roommate was in the next room, likely laughing her ass off. I didn't care. I had no regrets. Actually, quite the opposite.

When Martin carefully lowered and released me, my feet touched the ground and my legs were wobbly. I leaned heavily against the wall and tried to right my dress with clumsy fingers as he finished buttoning his pants, a devilish and satisfied smile claiming his features.

I opened my mouth to say something—that we should go make love on my bed now—but then he kissed me senseless once more, getting me hot and bothered in the closet all over again. Pulling away after several long, wonderful minutes, he whispered hotly against my ear, "The next time we make love, it will be in our home, in our bed, the one we share with each other."

He leaned away slightly, capturing my gaze, his dazzling gaze telling me he was serious.

"But—"

"Because I can't live without you anymore. I can't spend any more days and nights not knowing when I'll see you, hear you play, touch you. I won't settle for less." His tone was stern, implacable, as though he'd reached the end of his patience.

I exhaled my frustration, because I was already calculating how to get him totally naked tonight. "But you live in New York and I live here."

"Then I'll commute."

My head hit the wall behind me and I glared at him. I couldn't think. "This is not a decision to make right now. We need time, we need to talk—but later. Much later. Not tonight."

"No. Talk now." His eyes were uncompromising and belligerent, sharp and pointed, and I knew it would be nearly impossible to talk him out of this. But I didn't want to talk him out of it, I just wanted him to cede that we had time to discuss living arrangements later. Living arrangements, cities, zip codes, commuting—that could all wait.

But right now, I didn't want to think about being responsible. In fact, I didn't want to think at all. I wanted to focus on feeling and touching, and logic and reason be damned.

Passion for the win!

"Martin, Christmas was…it was good, I think, and last spring we had a beautiful week—"

"Don't you get it yet, Kaitlyn?" He sounded tortured, at his wit's end.

Martin's eyes captured mine and he held me, all of me, hostage with the savagery of his gaze. Martin's hands lifted to my face, his rough calluses against the smooth skin of my cheeks and jaw, his fingers threading slightly into the hair at my temples. When he spoke his voice was raw with months of hope and need and desperation.

"I don't want a beautiful week with you. I want a beautiful lifetime."

***

MUCH TO THE disappointment of my pants, Martin and I did not have the sex again that night.

I started referring to it as "the sex" in my brain while we were still in the closet, because sex with Martin wasn't ever going to be sex. It was THE sex. Everything with him felt like it should have a definite article (the) in front of it, as though all verbs became nouns and took on a special meaning.

The sex.

The cuddling.

The touching.

The whispers.

The laughter.

The words.

The feelings.

The teasing.

The love.

I couldn't wait.

But rather than "the sex," Martin pulled me away from Sam's rainbow of coats, out of the closet, and to my bedroom. While I straightened myself, he waited for me, throwing his coat, jacket, and tie to my desk chair. He watched me in the reflection of my dresser mirror, and I found I couldn't, nor did I want to, feel embarrassment when his gaze was so possessive and predatory.

When I faced him, he stalked to me, walked me backward until my legs met the edge of the mattress, all the while staring at me like *this* was Christmas morning and I was everything he'd ever wanted and hoped for.

I lay down first, he stretched over me, his lithe form above. I reached for him. I touched him. We kissed.

We kissed for a long time and his hands never strayed to the hot zones; though I could feel his want for me, his desire with every shift of his hips. And each time things became a bit frenzied he would retreat, breathing heavily and reining himself by placing whisper-soft kisses over my face, jaw, and neck. Or he'd just hold himself still above me, slowing his heart.

And I cherished him. I poured my desperate longing and care for Martin into my touch. I stroked his back lovingly and held him in a way I hoped communicated the gravity of my affection. I returned his kisses and gave him several of my own. I managed to untuck his shirt and slide my hands along the sides of his torso, memorizing and remembering the feel of his skin.

Eventually the urgency tapered, something in my soul soothed, and he rested beside me. I was tucked tightly against him, my head on his shoulder, my body curved into his side, his hands in my hair, and his lips at my forehead. We both basked in each other's presence along with a deep sense of decisive contentment.

And strangely, my mind was blank. I was truly in the *now*. Likely because the *now* was so very, very good.

But Martin had clearly been thinking, because he asked, "Why didn't you tell me when I came to the coffee shop last week?"

I turned into his shoulder and hid my face. "If you must know," came my muffled response, "I did decide to tell you. I was going to call you and schedule a time to meet. Then you came by my work and asked for girl advice. And tonight, we arrived at the restaurant and I assumed you were taking me there on a reconnaissance mission for your date."

"My date?"

"The girl? The one you like? The one you wanted advice about last week when I narrowly managed to refrain from stabbing you with my butter knife."

He groaned, shaking his head. I lifted my chin so I could see his face. When his eyes opened they were equal parts amused and frustrated.

"Kaitlyn, *you're* the girl. I never gave up, I just figured I needed to take a different approach. I kept fucking things up when you were in New York, even though I was trying to be so careful. I needed your advice because everything I did seemed to push you further away."

I smiled against his starched shirt. He smelled like Martin: expensive sandalwood-scented soap, and even more expensive aftershave.

I knew my smile and voice were dreamy as I said, "When I first saw you, after the show in New York early in December, I didn't know what to think. I hadn't expected to ever see you again. Eventually I thought you were trying to give me closure. But then, when you came to me a few weeks ago and wanted to discuss the terms of our friendship, I figured you wanting friendship meant you were indifferent to me, that you didn't want me anymore."

"No." He communicated so much with the single word, and it was a violent rejection of my assumptions. As well it imparted the depth of his frustration. "How could you possibly think I was indifferent to you?"

"Well, you said—our last night on the island—that you could never be friends with me because you'd never be *indifferent enough*. Drawing the logical conclusion, I assumed you were now indifferent enough to want friendship."

He heaved an exaggerated sigh. "I told you the truth on the island. Like I said in the closet, I never wanted to be just a friend. But, since you offered me nothing else, I was willing to settle for it—for a time—if it ultimately got me what I wanted."

This made me grin.

I felt his answering smile as he continued, "I thought you'd read the interviews. When I first saw you in New York after your show I was waiting for you to either tell me you'd moved on or tell me you felt the same. But then you were quiet. Evasive. So I thought, if I could just..." He shifted on the bed, holding me tighter. "When I found out you hadn't read anything, that you'd actually been avoiding all mentions of me, I realized how badly I'd fucked up. So when you came to New York for the week before Christmas I tried to give you your space."

"So you stayed away that week because you didn't want to push me?"

"Yes. I wanted you to see that I'd changed, that I wasn't...demanding."

"But you are demanding."

"Well, not as demanding."

I slipped my hand under his shirt, wanting to touch him. "So what happened? Why didn't you say something on Christmas?"

"I'd planned to. I thought, you would see the piano Christmas morning and then I'd *gently* explain about the foundation. You would forgive me, see I was right, and then we'd get back together."

I tried not to laugh. "Gently?"

He ignored me. "But you fell asleep in the car. And then took a shower and were sneaking around the apartment."

"I wasn't sneaking. I was trying to put your gifts by the fireplace."

Again, he ignored my statement. "And I couldn't sleep. I needed…to touch you, or have a strong drink. And then we drank and I was an asshole."

"Because I implied you never loved me."

Martin shifted to the side, glanced at me from the corner of his eye, and contradicted, "No. You didn't imply. You flat out said it. And I got so pissed."

He sounded angry now, just remembering it. I decided it was best to move the conversation forward.

"I finally read your interview from Men's Health where you called me The One."

"When?"

"After I got your text on New Year's."

He didn't respond right away, and when he did he said, "Huh."

He looked so handsome, lying in my bed thinking with his big head, so I brushed my lips against his. This of course led to us kissing like mad again.

When we finally pulled apart, Martin was above me once more and his breathing was labored. "Kaitlyn," he started, then stopped.

"What is it?" I reached for him, smoothed my hands over his jaw.

I saw his chest rise with an impressive inhale before he spoke. "I did choose you. You know that, right?"

I waited for him to continue. I wasn't certain what to make of his statement, to what—in specific—he was referring.

He shifted on the bed, turning onto his side and propping his head up, his arm bent at the elbow. His other hand gripped my hip.

"I didn't choose anything at first, after you…left. Like I told you last week, I kept thinking you were going to agree to see me in secret. In my mind, we weren't over, not at all. But when you didn't change your mind, nothing about revenge or seeing my father humiliated meant anything. I saw you were right and I walked away, though I think a part of me will always want to see him suffer."

I was quiet while he had his moment of anger. Martin's father was a bad guy. I knew the best Martin could hope for was indifference toward the man.

Eventually, he shook himself and continued, "I dropped out of university because you asked me to leave you alone, and I couldn't do that if I stayed on campus. But then I couldn't let you go, even when I didn't see you. So almost everything I did—setting up the foundation, the interviews, publicly calling my father a dickhead—was all about earning you back, earning your trust, hoping you would consider taking me back once I'd made everything right."

I felt my chin wobble and was relieved these threatening tears were happy ones.

"Oh, Martin." My voice was shaky, but I didn't mind. "Did you really call your father a dickhead?"

He nodded. "They didn't print that part, but he is a dickhead."

I laughed, wishing the newspaper had printed that Denver Sandeke was a dickhead. But I also wished for so much more.

"I wish I'd read your interview when it was printed. I wish I'd gone back to you after our initial fight and tried to work things out, find another way. I wish I hadn't been hiding in the closet all summer, avoiding all mentions of your name."

"I don't." He shook his head with a remarkable kind of certainty, like he knew all the secrets of the past and the future.

"You don't?"

"No. Because, even without you, I am happier than I've ever been. As soon as I walked away from my father, I started working on projects that interested me. You know those sketches on my drafting table? I'm inventing again. My purpose is now about what I want and not dictated by my hatred for him. If you hadn't called me on my bullshit, then…" He didn't finish the thought. Instead his eyes lost focus, as though he were imagining an unpleasant alternate reality.

I felt myself smile. Martin had been the catalyst for my choice to embrace my music and, as such, passion. He forced me out of my closet of expectations and purposeful obscurity. Even separated from him, I was happier in my life than I'd ever been before.

And, in that moment, I had a thought.

Maybe that's what real love is.

Maybe love, at its essence, is being a mirror for another person—for the good parts and the bad. Perhaps love is simply finding that one person who sees you clearly, cares for you deeply, challenges you and supports you, and subsequently helps you see and be your true self.

Love, I decided, is being a sidekick.

CHAPTER 15
Strengths of Covalent Bonds

"**WHEN WILL YOU** be home?"

He didn't answer right away.

In fact, he was noticeably quiet, as though he were enjoying the question, the moment, and everything it meant.

But I *knew* he was smiling.

I felt my automatic answering smile, the kamikaze leap of my heart, and the igniting Bunsen burner in my pants—a trifecta of happiness and anticipation—at his silence.

The last month had been bliss. BLISS I TELL YOU!

We dated. We went on dates. I saw him almost every day. Although I hated he had such a long commute. During the week when I had classes, Martin stayed with me at my place every night. My weekends were pretty tied up with shows and work. Sometimes we stayed in New Haven and sometimes we crashed at his place in New York. Yet wherever I slept, he slept too.

But notably, we'd only made love three more times since the closet, each time he swore it was the last until we moved in together, and I was frustrated. Pragmatically speaking, it's a crime against humanity to have a boyfriend as hot—body hot, brain hot, heart hot—as Martin Sandeke and *not* have the sex.

He was being stubborn, and though I'd been able to entice him a few times, he wanted to wait until we had our own place. Really, he was blackmailing my pants.

"Soon," he responded from the other end of the phone, his voice so low and lovely, and laced with meaning, the single word a promise.

I heard the urgent *vroooom* of his car and pressed my lips together so he wouldn't hear me laugh, but I was unable to keep the amusement out of my voice. "Really? How soon? Because I was thinking of running some errands."

"Parker, don't tease me."

Oh...sigh.

Tonight he was coming home to our home.

Home was a really, really small one-bedroom just two blocks from the apartment I'd shared with Sam...until yesterday. The timing had been perfect because her friend Kara ended up moving into my room.

Honestly, I didn't know what Sam was more excited about: me and Martin *finally* getting back together—as she put it—or the fact she didn't have to pack up her stuff and move into a three-bedroom. Of course, she also took an alarming amount of pleasure in tearing up my chore chart.

Regardless, today was my first day in our new apartment and tonight would be our first night in the apartment together. I hoped it would be sans underwear.

I leaned against the kitchen counter, my legs feeling a little wobbly, my heart feeling a lot full. "Fine. I'll wait for you. But soon better mean soon."

"Soon means soon." This was accompanied by another *vroooom.*

This time the sound made me frown.

"Don't kill yourself trying to get home."

"I won't."

"Remember, I have my weekly call with my parents in about ten minutes. It shouldn't last longer than a half hour, so you don't need to rush."

"I won't rush." Just as he said this I heard his car *vroooom.* Before I could interrogate him about it, he added, "And I picked up dinner."

"Oh! What did you get?"

"Tacos."

I grinned. Over the last month he'd frequently brought New York takeout for dinner. I suspected he did this in an attempt to win Sam over. It worked. The first time he arrived with lasagna from Little Italy she forgave him for everything.

I further suspected he picked up dinner so often because it was informally exempt from my sharing expenses rule.

Upon my insistence, we'd decided to split everything for our new apartment down the middle—rent, utilities, groceries, everything. Strangely, I didn't have to insist at all. Martin didn't argue. I surmised he recognized how important my financial independence was to me; he understood I needed to prove to myself I could make a living as a musician.

I did mostly lose our argument about furniture though. He didn't mind second-hand furniture, but he didn't like the idea of pressed particle board and plastic. He liked sturdy hardwood antiques—*real* furniture made from *real* materials—Mission or Shaker style and time-period. Most of the items that ended up filling our living space—a turn of the century walnut desk, matching end tables, mirror, and chest, art deco-stained glass lamps, and a black leather loveseat sofa with two matching club chairs—were well outside of my price range.

But he valued genuine and he valued comfort. In the end I relented because we kept my mattress. Honestly, the only items I was attached to were my keyboard, my guitar, and my mattress.

As well, he kept his New York apartment. He owned it outright and it made financial sense as an investment. Plus, it was fun to visit the city (and my piano) on the weekends.

I was about to question Martin further about the tacos when I heard the distinct sound of another *vroooom*.

"You're using your hands free, right?"

"Yes. I'm using the car's Bluetooth."

"Okay…just…just be careful." I worried. I didn't want him rushing through traffic and killing himself.

"I'll be careful. I love you, Kaitlyn."

"I love you, Martin. Bye."

"See you soon," he said instead of goodbye, and then he clicked off.

As I hung up my phone, still in a cotton candy haze of happiness, I realized that Martin never said goodbye. The entire time I'd known him, he'd never said the words to me.

Huh…

Aaaand I was smiling again.

I was still smiling when I opened my laptop and signed into Skype for the weekly call with my parents. I hadn't yet told them about Martin and me, but I did ask George to add an item to the agenda this week entitled, *Kaitlyn's new address*. I figured I'd give them the heads-up once we came to the topic. They would make note of it. We would move on.

That is not what happened.

As soon as the video image of my parents came up on my screen I could see that my mother wasn't smiling. This was atypical now that we did our calls via Skype. Usually she was happy to see me. Today she looked concerned and preoccupied.

Furthermore, she started speaking immediately. I didn't even get a chance to greet my father and George.

"Kaitlyn, some pictures were sent to me today from an associated press photographer of you and Martin Sandeke. And my office received calls from several newspapers asking about the status of your relationship."

My attention drifted to my dad. He looked grim, like he'd just recently argued with my mother. They didn't argue often, so I could tell when they did because he always looked grim afterward.

"Uhhh…" I gathered a steadying breath and said the first thing that came into my head. "Do you want to skip forward on the agenda?"

"The agenda?"

"Item number seven, my new address."

My father's eyes lifted, he was now looking at my image on the computer screen with curiosity. George was taking notes, appearing neutral as usual. My mother was obviously confused and a little stunned.

"What does your new address have to do with…?" I could see she'd answered her own question before she'd finished asking it.

I gave her a moment to absorb reality, my eyes flickering again to my dad. He was giving me a small smile.

"Oh, Kaitlyn." My mother shook her head, bringing my attention back to her. She looked concerned. "You didn't even consult with us about this."

I stared at her for a long moment, unsure how to respond, especially since old Kaitlyn and new Kaitlyn had two completely different instinctual reactions to her statement.

Old Kaitlyn was mortified I'd disappointed my mother.

New Kaitlyn was pissed.

New Kaitlyn won, though, and I felt myself flush with mortification and discomfort. "Mom, why would I consult with you on where I live?"

"Not where you live, it's with whom you live. Your decisions affect more than just yourself."

"That's right. They affect *Martin* and me." I started to sweat.

"Yes. They do affect you. Martin's father isn't likely to let the fact that his son absconded with one hundred twenty million dollars go. Eventually he's going to try to make Martin's life very difficult and you will be caught in the middle."

"Then we'll cross that bridge when we come to it. I have complete faith in Martin that he'll be able to deal with his father."

"But that's not the only factor. Kaitlyn, you must see," she leaned forward in her chair, her voice held a note of pleading, "my opponents will insinuate that you and Martin have been together this whole time. All the denials I made back in the spring will ring false."

"And I'm sure you have a staff that can help you handle these kinds of issues."

My mother sighed. It was not a pleased sigh. "Are you being purposefully obtuse?"

"No. Are you?" I said through clenched teeth.

She stared at me. Or rather, her face on the screen stared at me, and I couldn't tell if she actually saw me or saw a problem to be solved.

After staring for a good while, during which I refused to look away, she shifted in her seat, her eyes narrowing just slightly. "I am curious, how is it that—"

"Nope." I cut her off, feeling a spike of bravery paired with my spike of irritation. "No. You can be curious, but I'm not answering any of your questions. This is not a senate committee meeting and I am not under oath. I am an adult, as you like to remind me, capable of making my own decisions. As such, the identity of my boyfriend is my prerogative, who I live with and who I decide to love is my choice. I love Martin. What you do for a living is your prerogative. If your job has a problem with who I love, then maybe you should stand up and tell your job to mind its own business."

I could see my dad off to the left. He smirked then tried to cover it by rolling his lips between his teeth. When that was ineffective he hid his smile behind his hand.

George, as always, looked bored while taking notes. I could just imagine reading the meeting minutes later...

My mother's calm exterior fractured a little. She appeared to be frustrated, she also appeared to be reluctantly proud. Even so, she surprised the hiccup out of me when she finally said with another sigh. "Okay."

"Okay?"

"Okay."

"Clarify what you mean by *okay*."

"Okay, your points are valid ones. I cede that you are an adult and your decisions are your own. I apologize. I will issue a press release that who my adult daughter dates is no one's business but hers and has no bearing on my career."

"So, you're going to point out the obvious."

My dad chuckled like he couldn't help himself and shook his head.

To my mother's credit, she cracked a smile. "Yes. I'm going to point out the obvious. And I'm also going to redouble my efforts to respect your boundaries. But if Denver Sandeke ever…I mean…I hope you know that I…that—"

I took pity on her. "Mom, it's okay. I promise I'm not going to do anything— on purpose at least—that might cloud or take away from the work you're trying to do. You do good work."

"But again, Kaitlyn, Denver Sandeke is not to be underestimated."

"Yes. I agree. I promise I will let you know if Denver Sandeke ever shows his chinless face. But I have a life to live."

"And I want you to live it." Her eyes were full of uncharacteristic emotion and she appeared to be truly repentant. "We've made progress, you and I. And I don't want anything to jeopardize that progress."

"Me either." I nodded, giving her a warm smile, impressed with myself that I managed to keep my outward cool. I exhaled my relief, feeling like I'd just run a mile.

"Good."

"Good."

And it was. It was good. We were figuring this out, every call and interaction forging a new path, and I was immeasurably thankful she was just as invested as I was in making this work.

George eventually cleared his throat and said in a very George-esque way, "So, back to the agenda."

I was granted a reprieve to calm down. We restarted at the top of the agenda and covered various and sundry topics like where they were vacationing for summer recess, whether I would be home for spring break, and thank-you cards I needed to write to family members for Christmas gifts. My aunt Donna on my dad's side always became a bit twitchy if I didn't write a thank-you note.

Then we arrived at agenda topic number four. I tried not to grimace.

"Have you made a decision about performing in May? At the fundraiser and the benefit concert?" George prompted, rubbing the bridge of his nose where his glasses typically rested.

"No." I shook my head. "How soon do you need to know?"

I hadn't decided. On one hand I was warming to the idea of pushing myself out of my comfort zone. The benefit for Children's Charities in particular sounded like it would be awesome. I liked that there would be kids there and I could compose something specifically for them.

On the other hand…

My mother leaned forward again, her tone was infinitely patient. "I wish you would do it. I think you'd really enjoy yourself."

I glanced at my dad and he spoke up as well. "Katy, you're amazing. It's important to share your talents. I agree with your mom."

"I still need some time." I frowned at them both.

My mother sighed, again frustrated. "You know we just want what's best for you. And I can't believe that you're happy serving coffee and playing weddings every weekend in that little band."

I felt my defenses raise. "Believe it. I'm happy. I'm happier than I've ever been. I don't need to be important—"

"You are important—"

"You know what I mean. I don't need to be notable. I love playing and composing music. And that's enough for me."

My dad placed his hand on my mother's arm and shook his head, then turned his attention back to me. "Just think about it. It's hard as your parents to see you with this remarkable talent, capable of great things, and not sharing it with the world or getting the attention you deserve."

I gave my father a hard look. When I flew home for Thanksgiving I'd played him some of my compositions. He couldn't have been more proud and excited. I figured that was only because he was my dad, he'd always been equivalent levels of proud no matter what I did—whether it be a finger painting or defrosting chicken.

"Just think about it," George chimed in. I was surprised to see him also giving me a pleading look.

"I said I would. I'm thinking about it. I just need some more time."

"We need to know by March first." George refocused his attention back to his notes and I was relieved the conversation moved on to the next topic.

The rest of the call was uneventful and we signed off with sincere *I love yous* and *I'll see you next week*. Although my father threw in at the very end, "I might have a business trip at the end of February in New England. Maybe I can take you and Martin out to dinner? Meet this boy who has captured your heart?"

I only managed to stutter and nod before the screen went blank. My dad was a sneak. Of course he tossed it out there like an afterthought. As far as he was concerned the issue was settled. He would meet Martin at the end of February.

I stared at my monitor and realized I was grinning. I was excited about the prospect. I couldn't wait for them to meet. I also wanted Martin and my mother to get along. They'd started out on the wrong foot and I knew—once they grew accustomed to each other—they'd probably hit it off.

The sound of Martin clearing his throat pulled me out of my thoughts. I glanced over my shoulder and found him standing in the doorway to the bedroom—our bedroom—a small smile lighting his face.

"Your dad is coming at the end of the month?" he asked, looking pleased peppered with petrified.

I jumped up from my place at the desk, but then meandered to him, liking how he looked after a day in his corner office—tie gone, jacket gone, shirt sleeves rolled to his elbows.

"How long were you listening at the door?" I asked as I ogled.

Martin reached for me, wrapped his arm around my waist, his grin growing as he admitted, "Long enough to hear you call me your boyfriend and tell your parents we're living together."

"Oh, so you've been prowling like a creepy lurker the whole time?"

"Yes..." He paused, and his face grew surprisingly solemn. "You should know, you're completely safe. My father isn't going to come after me. He's cut me off, but he won't do anything else."

"Why not? You've told me at least a dozen times how wicked he is. What would keep him from seeking revenge?"

"Because I had ways to collect information while I lived in his house. Bribing senators and corporate corruption aren't the worst of his sins."

My eyes widened as they moved between his. "Do I want to know?"

"No."

"So...you're blackmailing him?"

"Not actively. Let's just say he has incentive to leave us alone."

I tried not to smile. I tried and failed. "And you're not going to use this incentive for revenge?"

"Nope."

I narrowed my eyes on him and gave into the urge to say, "I'm really proud of you."

Martin grinned at me and stood a little taller, like I'd pinned a badge of awesome on his chest. We shared a stare of mutual admiration.

Then his gaze softened and sobered, and he said, "Thank you."

"For what?"

"For choosing me. With your parents just now, thank you for choosing us."

My heart did a funny little dance in my chest—both happy and sad—and I lifted my hands to his face. His was a man's face, his jaw stubbly and rough. I loved my man's face. I lifted to my tiptoes and gave him a soft kiss, and he tasted like coffee and mint gum.

Then I gently rubbed my nose against his before I leaned away. "You know I love you. But it was also the right thing to do. "

He smiled again. "And Kaitlyn Parker always does the right thing."

"Not always. For example, I've fiendishly hidden all of your clothes."

He lifted a single eyebrow in obvious delighted surprise. "Have you?"

"Yes."

"It's not that big of an apartment, I'm sure I could find them."

"Who said they're in this apartment?" I gave him a meaningful look.

The truth was, they were in the apartment. I'd hidden his boxes of clothes in the front closet.

His smile turned into a devilish grin, baring his wonderfully sharp teeth. "What about you?"

"What about me?"

His hands smoothed down my back, into my cotton yoga pants and underwear, gripping my bare bottom. "Should I hide your clothes?"

"No need. I plan to be naked for the next twelve hours."

He groaned. His mouth crashed down on mine, and he walked me backward toward the bathroom, his hands now turning greedy and searching. How we made it successfully into the tiled room was a miracle, especially since we were doing the clumsy de-panting dance on the way. Martin whipped off my top and found I was braless. This elicited a pleased growl as he pressed me against the sink. Meanwhile I worked on the buttons of his shirt.

Stupid business shirt with all the buttons.

We were in a frenzy, our hands covetous as our mouths mated. He slipped his fingers into the front of my underwear, teasing me but not touching where I needed.

I tilted my hips forward, trying to force him to ease my suffering.

"Touch me, Martin. Please."

His head bent and he captured my breast with his mouth, drawing tight circles around the center with his tongue.

I felt his hot breath against the wet spot he'd created when he answered, "First the shower. Then the kitchen table. Maybe the desk."

"What...what are you talking about?" I arched against him, my hands sliding down to his boxer briefs and stroking him through the fabric.

"All the places we're going to make love tonight."

A surprised laugh tumbled from my lips followed by a rough intake of breath as he parted me with his skilled fingers, rubbing my center.

"I thought..." I had to moan before I could continue; he was making me brainless. "I thought you wanted to start with our mattress."

"We've done that, thanks to your trickery," he responded darkly, referencing the three times I'd seduced him over the past month. Martin withdrew his hand just long enough to discard his shorts and reach into the shower to start the hot water. "I want to make memories on *all* the other surfaces."

I smiled, through my haze of love and lust for my Martin, and teased, "Starting with the shower?"

His eyes cut to mine as steam rolled out of the stall, his hands back on my body, peeling away my underwear. His expression and his voice were deadly serious as he said, "Yes. Because I have been thinking about it since Christmas and I need to take you against the wall while your perfect tits and perfect body are slippery and wet, sliding against me."

A flush of feral desire pooled in my belly, making my body feel tender and heavy. His words did that to me; his dirty talk made me feel wanton and bold.

Before I could think better of it I asked, "So you're going to fuck my sweet pussy?"

His mouth fell open with surprise and his eyes widened. Martin blinked at me, like he didn't quite trust his ears. Meanwhile—despite my boldness and arousal—I cringed, feeling silly, and peered at him through one eye.

"Did I say that right?" I asked, still cringing. "Because when you say it, it sounds sexy. But when I say it, it sounds weird and alarming—like a premeditated criminal action."

Then Martin laughed, an uncontrollable, deep rumble of pure happiness. He pulled my naked body against his naked body and hugged me. I could only smile and try not to blush or feel like a dirty talk failure.

"You are so perfect," he said against my neck when his laughter receded; he bit me—hard—like he wanted to devour me, then soothed the area with his tongue. "So fucking perfect."

I tensed, my belly twisting with delight, as his hands were growing amorous again.

"I'm perfectly weird you mean, and I don't like the word *pussy*," I whispered. "It has too many 'S' sounds."

"You're perfect and I love you." One callused hand lifted to my breast and roughly caressed it, pinching me. His other arm, still wrapped around my middle, steered us into the shower and under the spray.

"I'm bad at dirty talk."

He didn't respond. Instead he pressed me against the wall and I was overwhelmed by sensations: the cold tile at my back, the hot water above, his roughened hands rubbing slippery soap over my stomach, thighs, and breasts, his sensational eyes capturing mine and wordlessly telling me he believed I was perfect.

I couldn't keep my hands off his actually perfect body nor did I try. The heat of my earlier embarrassment gave way to a new heat, a building promise between us.

His mouth was everywhere the soap wasn't and when he finished lathering, he held both my wrists in his hands and slid his body against mine, increasing my arousal exponentially until I was brainless.

"Repeat after me." Martin's voice was low, impatient and demanding, his tongue licking water droplets from my jaw as he released my wrists and smoothed his hands down my sides to my hips.

"I, Kaitlyn..."

"I, Kaitlyn..."

He lifted me as though it were the easiest thing in the world. My hands came to his shoulders and enjoyed how they bunched as he flexed his muscles. He spread my legs wide and rubbed his hardness against the yielding slickness of my center.

"Want you, Martin..."

"Want you, Martin—"

I sucked in a sudden breath as he pushed inside me, his face at my neck sucking and biting and licking.

"To take me in the shower..."

"To take...me...in...the shower..."

Everything about this act felt more crucial than I'd remembered, so much more necessary on a base and instinctual level.

"...and make love to me for hours."

"To...to..."

I couldn't finish. I didn't want to talk, I just wanted to feel. I glanced down at him and our bodies where they joined. I enjoyed the sight of our connection—his hard against my soft, my legs spread wide to accommodate his size. I watched my wet breasts moving up and down in time with his rhythm, bouncing in his face; his rigid and sculpted body curved toward mine as I arched away from the wall. It was the sight of us together—of me with him—that made me feel sexy, overwhelmed by how crazy hot we looked.

I wondered if we could install a mirror in the shower.

Aaaaand, with that thought I came—assaulted by water and steam, the slick sliding of his body with mine, and the realization this was the first of many happy—and sexy—memories.

***

WHEN WE CRAWLED into bed it was because we needed sleep. But instead of sleeping, we found ourselves facing each other naked, cuddling and touching, and discussing plans for the future. These plans ranged from the various trips we wanted to take together, to various places we wanted to have the sex—he wanted to christen all the showers in his apartment, meanwhile I wanted to lay claim to his desk at work—to a new gaming store that had opened in Times Square. Martin insisted he'd take me the next time we were in the city. We discussed that my father was visiting at the end of February and where we should take him for dinner.

"Don't worry," Martin squeezed me, "I'll be nice to your dad."

I let my amusement and confusion show on my face. "Well, I should certainly hope so."

He gave me a wry look. "You know what I mean. I've been practicing."

"Being nice?"

"Yes."

I rolled my lips between my teeth because his features held an expression of extreme consternation and I didn't think it would be wise to laugh at him. "How's that going for you?"

"It's been...difficult, but sometimes good."

"Difficult?"

"Yeah, like that annoying girl you work with at the coffee shop."

"You think Chelsea is annoying?" I was surprised. I'd never met anyone—especially a man—who thought she was anything but wonderful.

"She's vain and irritating. In fact, she reminds me of my mother, always expecting strangers to adore her."

I felt my eyebrows jump at his accurate—albeit simplified—description of my co-worker. Perhaps Martin's tendency to value perceived goodness and genuineness stemmed from his disdain for his mother.

After a beat Martin surprised me by changing the subject. "Do you want to perform at the benefit your parents were talking about? Yes or no?"

I hesitated, took a moment to trace my index finger over the line of his collarbone. "Kind of. But I don't want to do it because my parents think I need to be more impressive. I like playing in my *little band.* Just being around music every day is a dream come true. I don't need accolades and attention."

"But you saying no just because your parents think you need to be more impressive is allowing them to dictate what you do. If you're saying no because of what they think, that's just as bad as saying yes because of what they think."

I frowned at him and his sensible words. *Stupid sensible words.*

Meanwhile he smiled at me like he knew what I was thinking, and he knew I knew he was right. His smile turned smug.

"Fine," I admitted finally. "You're right. Is that what you wanted to hear?"

"No. I already knew I was right. I was hoping for something more like, *Oh, Martin, you are a sexy genius. I can't live without you and your big...head.*"

I couldn't help my sudden laugh, though I did smack him on the shoulder. He continued his smugly smiling ways and leaned forward to give me a kiss.

"Seriously though, do it if you want to do it. Or don't. But make the decision based on what you want to do, not to avoid or cater to someone else's expectations."

I nodded, feeling my chest flood with warmth and affection. He really was my mirror. He was on my side. We were a team. We moved in unison, toward a common goal, and it was a beautiful thing.

Martin's hands hadn't quite settled on my body. He'd move them every so often—from my hip to my thigh, from my thigh to my breast—like he was taking full advantage of his all-access pass. It had the byproduct of warming me up.

Apropos of nothing, I pushed, "But getting back to having the sex on your desk at work, what days next week are you free for lunch?"

He gave me a funny look, like he thought I'd been bluffing earlier. "You really want to do that?"

"Yes. Do you have walls or blinds?"

"Walls facing the rest of the office, but windows to the outside."

"Good."

"What's gotten into you?"

"Technically, you have—"

"Ha, ha."

"But, actually…nothing. I just like the sex. I like the sex with you. I like how sexy it makes me feel. I like the making out and the foreplay, and the orgasming. I like thinking about it and planning our next encounter. And, even though I am a girl, I don't think that makes me weird. I think it means I have a healthy sexual appetite, and I'm in love with the man I crave. I refuse to apologize for it."

His mouth hooked to the side. "I'd never ask you to apologize for it."

"Good. Because I won't."

Martin's eyes narrowed on me, like he was in deep thought, but his smile never wavered.

Then he said, "In the closet."

I waited for him to explain. When he just continued to look at me, his eyes heated with meaning, I prompted, "What about the closet?"

"Let's make love in the closet."

"But we've already done that."

"No. I mean all the closets. Every closet we can find."

I grinned. "Every closet?"

"Yes."

I threw my head back and laughed, thinking of all the closets in the world and how I'd struggled to avoid them, to avoid indulging my fears and reclusive inclinations, now that I'd found the courage to follow my heart. Little did I know following my heart would bring me right back to the closet.

But this time I would be with Martin and we would be making love. Or maybe we wouldn't.

Maybe we'd just be sharing a private moment alone.

Maybe we'd be hiding from the world—just a little—but that was okay.

Because the world could be unpleasant and overwhelming. A demanding place full of uncertainties and expectations and fears. I was coming to realize retreating, hiding from the world on occasion, was not a bad thing to do, as long as I didn't do it too often or because I was afraid of living my life.

Sharing a closet with Martin—closed away from everything else but our mutual love, respect, and devotion—might be a very healthy thing. We were a team, a perfectly situated pair of sidekicks.

And sharing a closet with my sidekick sounded like paradise.

~THE END~
☺

Extra Scene: Early Reactions

Meet Martin 6-months before the island

THIS GIRL.

Right now she's reaching into the equipment cabinet and I'm watching her bend over. I crane my neck, tilting my head to the side as she leans further forward. I'm checking out her ass. This might be my only chance.

For the first time since meeting Kaitlyn Parker three weeks ago, she is wearing something that actually allows me to see she has an ass and tits and a waist and legs. I'm certain she has no idea she possesses an ass and tits and a waist and legs. Because if she did know, she'd use them. Especially her tits. Christ almighty, her tits are perfect.

From what I know about this girl, I'm pretty sure she is more intimate with her TI-89 graphing calculator than she is with her body. And that's a fucking travesty.

I'm also positive she has no clue every move she's making is making me crazy. If she did, then she'd use that too. I readjust myself on the stool; my jeans are suddenly too tight.

It's her red pants. Or it's the white tank top. I'm not sure which. Maybe it's the broken air conditioner in the building. The window is open but it's not enough. Whatever the reason, this chick is getting me hot, and all she's doing is looking through a goddamn science cabinet.

"I can't find the graduated cylinders." Kaitlyn straightens, places her hands on her narrow waist, and turns toward the shelves on the far wall. "Do you see the cylinders?"

"You mean the test tubes?" I'm being purposefully stupid. I'm hoping it'll make her look at me, because she never looks at me.

I'm awarded for my pretend ignorance. Her blue-gray eyes cut to mine and I see she's irritated. "Never mind. Forget I asked."

Kaitlyn looks back to the shelves. She's studying them, frowning.

I know where the graduated cylinders are. They're on the bottom shelf, all the way to the right, hidden by two large beakers. Usually I'd tell her where they are. Not today.

Today she's wearing tight red pants and a white tank top. The longer she stands there searching the shelves, the longer I get to watch her twist at the waist and grumble with frustration. I've never seen her look so much like a girl, and I have to be honest, it's like an early Christmas present. Really early, Christmas in September early.

My attention briefly flickers to the safety shower in the corner and I picture her beneath it. I'm not saying I have plans to injure or endanger this girl, but maybe I could switch out the HCl with vinegar and manufacture an emergency rinse off. A medically necessary wet T-shirt contest with one contestant.

I chew on my pen, examining her body as she searches for the cylinders, and I try to picture what she'd look like in just her bra and underwear. I'm guessing they're plain white cotton, or beige, or maybe they have little purple and pink flowers.

I wonder what she'd do if I asked her to take off her clothes and show me. Or maybe take off the bra, too. Better yet, take everything off.

She'd probably punch me in the face. This thought makes me smile because a punch in the face might be worth her outraged expression. Then again, she might not be as much of an anomaly as I'm thinking. Maybe her intelligence and indifference is an act, and she's just like all the others. Maybe, if I asked her to strip she'd do it, want me to buy her something expensive, and then ask how far to bend over.

This thought makes me both frown and grow harder.

I need to know. I need to know if she's the same as everyone else. I lick my bottom lip, the question is on the tip of my tongue, when she speaks.

"This is ridiculous," then adds under her breath, "Absurd, inexplicable, odd, strange, bizarre…"

I stay quiet because she's now lifting her long, brown hair away from her neck and twisting it on the top of her head. She reaches into her pants pocket and takes out a pen. I watch with rapt fascination as she miraculously secures her hair in place with a writing utensil.

Mostly though, I'm staring at the skin of her shoulders, back, and neck. Her pen-hair trick has left an expanse of perfect creamy skin exposed. I devour the unblemished region with my eyes, for some fucking reason, my mouth starts watering. I'm finding it hard to look away from the elegance of her collarbone.

"Without the cylinders we can't do the experiment," she says, a hint of resignation in her voice. "I'll email Ryan and tell him there are no cylinders."

Kaitlyn turns from the shelf, her face scrunched in a frown, and I see she's intent on her bag. She's planning on leaving. The ruse is up.

Mourning the end of my ogling, I point with my pen. "Aren't those the cylinders?"

She follows my line of sight and squints at the oversized beakers. I see the moment she spots the containers because her eyebrows jump on her forehead and she smiles.

She smiles at lab equipment like it makes her happy. She also strokes it sometimes. Last week she kept fingering the test tubes so I took them away, moved them out of her reach. She didn't object, just gave me a dirty look while she punched the buttons of her graphing calculator with more force than necessary.

This girl.

Kaitlyn keeps the table between us as she sets the three cylinders on the black top. I have a suspicion she keeps her distance purposefully because last week every time I walked around to her side, she found a reason to move to the spot I just left.

"In this experiment, you will standardize a solution of base using the analytical technique known as titration. Using this standardized solution, you will determine the acid neutralizing power of a commercially available antacid tablet," she reads aloud from the chem lab handout.

She's assuming correctly that I haven't read the experiment outline, which is irritating. She thinks I'm stupid, I can tell. A big dumb jock. Usually I don't care, and I don't precisely care now…

Actually, inexplicably, I do care.

So I grunt, "I can read, Parker."

"Oh, good. That should come in handy." She's still looking at the handout as she says this.

Her tone, like she's congratulating me on my ability to read, almost makes me laugh. Almost.

"You don't need to read the experiment to me."

"I'm not reading it to you, I'm reading it to me."

"Out loud?"

"Yes. I'm an auditory learner." I watch her attention dart over the chemical formulas on the handout. But then she surprises me by abruptly lifting her eyes to mine and asking, "What kind of learner are you?"

I have her gaze for the first time in three weeks and my mind blanks, so I repeat, "What kind of learner?"

"Yes," her smile is tentative but friendly, again catching me off guard, "how do you learn best?"

I hold her stare—which can only be described as genuinely curious—for a full five seconds and I'm at a loss; I don't know what to do. I get the distinct impression she doesn't want anything from me except to know *how I learn best*. I don't know why, but this question feels too personal.

Therefore, instinct kicks in and I allow a slow, meaningful smile to spread over my face before responding, "I'm more the touchy-feely type."

Her eyes dim and her mouth flattens, like my response is wrong or she's disappointed, and I see I've lost her again even though she says, "That's kinesthetic learning."

"You do much kinesthetic learning?" I'm flirting, or I'm trying to. But all I can think is: *This is stupid*.

Especially when she responds to my question with, "Not since pre-school."

... ahhh fuck.

She's turned her attention back to the handout. A foreign sensation makes my chest uncomfortable, like I've lost something important. I stare at her pretty profile and wonder why I care whether or not this girl thinks I'm an idiot.

However, I'm glad I didn't ask her to strip, because now I'm convinced she wouldn't have punched me in the face. I think she would have just shut down, ignored me, and then asked me to pass her the hydrochloric acid.

"In order to determine when a solution has been exactly neutralized, an acid base indicator is used that changes color in a certain pH range..." her words are softer this time and it's clear she's reading to herself, like I'm not even there.

And so the hour passes. Kaitlyn Parker goes through the motions of the experiment and I try to keep my boner hidden, all the while imagining her reaching into my pants and rubbing me off.

While topless... Fuck it, while *naked*.

These fantasies are sometimes interrupted by her being just too goddamn brilliant for her bra size. Today she quickly works through a difficult equation and solves for an unexpected outcome. The problem is, each time she demonstrates how clever she is, and how ambivalent she is to my presence, the fantasy grows dirtier.

By the end of lab we've already fucked three times, she's had six enthusiastic orgasms, and I've come in her smart mouth twice. Of course, she swallows like it's candy.

In reality, however, I'm sporting an angry hard-on, unable to lift my eyes past her tits, and she's still ambivalent to my presence. I've basically become the idiot she assumes I am.

Welcome to my Friday.

I think back, trying to remember a time when I was half this preoccupied with a girl. I can't. Even after I leave I'll still be thinking about her mouth and what it would look like sucking me off. I close my eyes briefly, indulging, and imaginary Kaitlyn says something about copper chloride solution just before she takes the flat of her tongue and licks me from shaft to head.

Clenching my jaw, I force myself to clear the image from my mind because I need to walk to my next class in less than a half hour. This girl is clearly smart, beautiful, and I'm halfway convinced she either doesn't know who I am or doesn't care, honestly and truly doesn't give two fucks. And I'm close to suffocating in my need to touch her.

"I'll put away the equipment," she says unnecessarily. She always puts away the equipment.

I should offer to help but my throbbing dick protests the idea of walking, or any movement not involving satisfaction and relief. I watch her bend and reach into the science cabinet again; strangely, all I can think about is how I won't see her again for another week.

This thought leads me to say without thinking, "You should give me your number."

Yes, these words are unpremeditated, but I'm not sorry for them. If anything I'm feeling like an idiot for not asking prior to now.

Kaitlyn frowns, like maybe I just asked her for an organ donation, and doesn't look at me. She says nothing, as though if she pretends I didn't speak then she won't have to answer. The only sound in the chem lab is her packing up. This lasts for a full minute.

I know she heard me and I know she has an excellent grasp of the English language. By now it's clear she has no intention of responding.

So I decide to push. "Parker, give me your cell number."

She stiffens, stands straighter, and stares at her bag like it has the answers to our midterm.

But then she waves her hand through the air and says, "Nah."

I feel my eyebrows inch higher on my forehead. "Nah?"

"Nah."

Nah. What the fuck does that mean?

"Does that mean 'no'?"

"Nah means no," she says offhandedly while she moves to grab one of the graduated cylinders and takes it back to the shelf.

I'm not surprised.

I'm astonished.

This has never happened to me before. Never. When I was seventeen I asked the twenty-eight-year-old wife of a diplomat for her phone number. She wrote it on my hand with her lipstick. Usually I don't have to ask at all.

Therefore I can't help but press further. "Why not?"

Kaitlyn loiters in front of the equipment shelf like she's cataloging its contents; still not looking at me, she answers, "I don't give it out."

"You don't give out your cell phone number?" Like a dumbass, I can only repeat her words.

"It's one of my life rules."

"So, no one has your phone number?"

"I didn't say that. I didn't see you record the findings today. Do you need to borrow my notes?"

Her tight tone tells me my pushing is making her uncomfortable. And this makes me grit my teeth. I don't want to make her uncomfortable, I just want her to give me the time of day. Also maybe spend a week with her on a deserted island. Naked. Fucking.

And talking... I blink at this last unbidden thought.

I haven't recovered from the notion that my interest in Kaitlyn Parker might be something more than carnal when she shoves several papers at me.

"Here, these are my notes from today. Just leave them in the lab cabinet when you're done, under the Bunsen burner tray."

"Under the tray?" I repeat... like a dumbass.

"Yes." She hitches her backpack higher and moves around me toward the door, tossing over her shoulder, "If you need to tell me something just use on-campus email or leave a note in the science cabinet."

I turn to watch her go. "Nobody checks their on-campus email."

I see her shoulders shrug but she doesn't answer. Then, like she can't get away from me fast enough, she's gone.

I stare after her, at the empty doorway, for an embarrassingly long time. I'm hoping she forgot something and she'll come back. When she doesn't and I realize what I'm doing, I shake my head, disgusted with myself, and glance at the notes she's given me.

Her handwriting is neat, small, all capital letters, and it looks like she's used a ruler for her graphs. Not knowing why, I flip through all five pages, admiring the faultless logic seemingly intrinsic to her thoughts. But then my attention catches on a faint, errant doodle on the third page, what looks like notes to a song run along the top of the paper.

She didn't use a ruler for the lines and the notes aren't neat. They're messy. And she's tried to erase them.

Fantasies of my hands cupping her perfect tits fade, and I imagine her playing music. I deliberate what instrument she uses. Now I'm imagining asking her about the song. I wonder what she'd do if I asked her to play music for me.

Admitting the frustrating truth to myself, I know she'd ignore me, ignore the question. This thought pisses me off and I don't like that I'm thinking about Kaitlyn Parker in terms other than her perfect tits.

The uneasiness is back, an uncomfortable sense that I've lost something. I fold the notes, stuff them in my backpack, and decide to skip my next class to go on a run instead. A really long run. Followed by ten thousand meters on the erg.

I also decide I'm going to stop torturing myself. I'll just stop fantasizing about this girl—the gap between her front teeth, her eyes that aren't quite blue or grey, how she strums her fingers on the lab table and recites synonyms when she's flustered, her flawless reasoning and impressive intellect, and relentless willingness to be helpful—because this girl isn't interested in me. Why waste my time?

Yeah, I'll stop fantasizing about Kaitlyn Parker.

… just as soon as this semester ends.

About the Author

This is the ninth novel published by **Penny Reid**. Her days are spent writing federal grant proposals for biomedical research; her evenings are either spent playing dress-up and mad-scientist with her two people-children (boy-8, girl-5), or knitting with her knitting group at the local coffee shop. Please feel free to drop her a line. She'd be happy to hijack your thoughts!

Come find Penny-

Mailing list signup: http://reidromance.blogspot.com/p/mailing-list-sign-up.html

Email: pennreid@gmail.com …hey, you! Email me ;-)

Blog: http://reidromance.blogspot.com/

Twitter: https://twitter.com/ReidRomance

Ravelry: http://www.ravelry.com/people/ReidRomance (if you crochet or knit…!)

Goodreads: http://www.goodreads.com/ReidRomance

"The Facebook": http://www.facebook.com/PennyReidWriter

Please, write a review!

If you liked this book (and, more importantly perhaps, if you didn't like it) please take a moment to post a review someplace (Amazon, Goodreads, your blog, on a bathroom stall wall, in a letter to your mother, etc.). This helps society more than you know when you make your voice heard; reviews force us to move towards a true meritocracy.

Other books by Penny Reid

Made in the USA
Charleston, SC
29 May 2015